Rodina

A Novel of Mother Russia

by

Kirsten E.A. Borg

TRAFFORD
USA • Canada • UK • Ireland

Cover Art: Charles H. Mertes
        Stalingrad War Memorial

Note for Librarians: A cataloguing record for this book is available from Library and Archives Canada at www.collectionscanada.ca/amicus/index-e.html

ISBN 1-4120-7876-8

Printed on paper with minimum 30% recycled fibre. Trafford's print shop runs on "green energy" from solar, wind and other environmentally-friendly power sources.

PUBLISHING™

Offices in Canada, USA, Ireland and UK

This book was published *on-demand* in cooperation with Trafford Publishing. On-demand publishing is a unique process and service of making a book available for retail sale to the public taking advantage of on-demand manufacturing and Internet marketing. On-demand publishing includes promotions, retail sales, manufacturing, order fulfilment, accounting and collecting royalties on behalf of the author.

Book sales for North America and international:

Trafford Publishing, 6E–2333 Government St.,

Victoria, BC V8T 4P4 CANADA

phone 250 383 6864 (toll-free 1 888 232 4444)

fax 250 383 6804; email to orders@trafford.com

Book sales in Europe:

Trafford Publishing (UK) Limited, 9 Park End Street, 2nd Floor

Oxford, UK OX1 1HH UNITED KINGDOM

phone 44 (0)1865 722 113 (local rate 0845 230 9601)

facsimile 44 (0)1865 722 868; info.uk@trafford.com

Order online at:

trafford.com/05-2774

10 9 8 7 6 5 4 3 2

To the RUSSIAN PEOPLE,

with admiration
respect
gratitude
… and love

CONTENTS

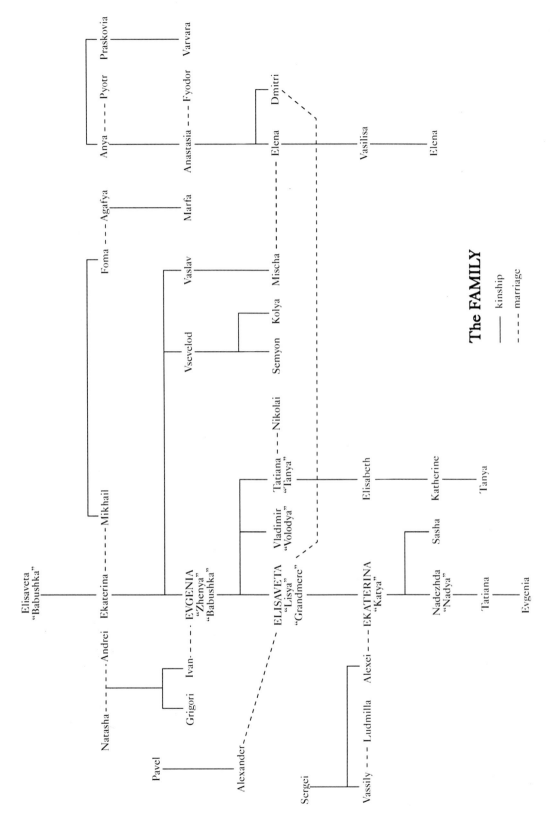

The FAMILY

—— kinship

- - - - marriage

PROLOGUE
Leningrad: June, 1987

As the plane slowly circled for a landing, Katherine peered impatiently out the small window, straining for glimpses of the city below. Shining canals threaded their way among vast blocks of grey and green; the sun glittered off soaring golden spires and gleaming onion domes. Even from the air, Leningrad loomed larger than life, its brilliant edifices set off by intermittent shadows of swirling haze. Abruptly the plane dove for the airport; as the city rushed up to greet her, Katherine held her breath.

When the rattling Aeroflot jet finally bumped to a halt, she stood up and anxiously gathered her baggage. Giant butterflies were galloping through her stomach as she stepped down off the plane and walked to the terminal, unconcerned that she was gawking like a tourist. Not that there was much to see, yet; so far, the airport just looked like an airport – though somehow larger. Not big, like huge, busy O'Hare in Chicago, where she had taken off almost twenty-four hours – and many planes – ago, but immense, in a monumental sort of way.

As she lined up at Customs, Katherine's stomach began to lurch. Apprehensively she watched the variously uniformed officials, surprised that none of them seemed to be armed. When it was her turn, a young Customs officer fixed her with what was supposed to be an intimidating glare. Scowling back and forth several times between her face and her passport, he finally handed it uncertainly to his superior. A lengthy conference in heated Russian followed, joined by a few other officials who seemed to have nothing better to do.

Eavesdropping as unobtrusively as she could, Katherine made out that what had attracted their attention was her Russian name – and that she was an American traveling alone in the Soviet Union, part of no group or delegation, here on no apparent business.

"You are a tourist?" asked the Customs officer, in agreeably accented English.

"No – not exactly." She started to smile – but seeing his glare struggling to reassert itself, thought better of it.

"Then why are you here?" he asked, this time in Russian.

"I promised my *babushka*," Katherine replied, also in Russian, "that someday I would come here and see where she used to dance." It seemed the simplest way to explain what friends and family back home had been unable to understand.

"Your grandmother was a dancer here?" The cold stare abruptly disappeared.

"Yes," Katherine smiled – just a little. "At the Maryinsky."

"Ah!" The young man's face lit up as he stamped her passport and waved her on.

Soon, Katherine was on her way into the city, to the hotel where she had reservations. Unable to restrain her excited curiosity, she continued to stare unabashedly. People with ancient scythes mowed hay on the highway median between speeding trucks; horse-drawn carts trotted next to jumbo jets. Old women sweeping streets with twig brooms toiled in front of subway stations; onion-domed churches nestled beside high-rise apartments. Everywhere were unfinished buildings surrounded by purposeful-looking scaffolding on which no one seemed to be working, and everything – except the public monuments – had the weather-beaten look of a society huffing and puffing to keep up with an overpowering environment. Even the enormous buildings seemed insignificant compared to all the space above and around them. No matter which way she looked, Katherine saw endless vistas which hulked broodingly into the distance.

The people on the bus stared curiously at her. When she smiled at them, they smiled back, but did not stop staring. An old man with one arm and several medals on his chest stood up and offered her his seat. Embarrassed, she tried unsuccessfully to refuse.

"*Amerikanka, da?*" he beamed, insisting.

"*Da, da, spasibo,*" she smiled, and finally sat down.

At last, at the hotel, the burly doorman standing guard was unwilling to believe that she did indeed belong inside. That she attempted to persuade him of this in Russian seemed only to add to his suspicion. Producing her passport, however, quickly resolved the matter, and he allowed her to enter. Inside, Katherine crossed a lobby as big as Wyoming to an official-looking desk, where a rather sullen clerk gave her several forms to fill out. En route to her room, the bellhop offered her black market rubles for blue jeans. Shortly after he left, the chambermaid brought in fresh towels; she wanted to trade caviar for condoms.

Finally bolting the door, Katherine undressed and took a shower – which, to her relief, had plenty of hot water. Wrapped in her bathrobe, she flopped down on the bed and looked around the room. Except for the single beds, she decided, it had the look of a vintage Holiday Inn. It was much better than she expected.

Exhausted as she was, however, sleep would not come. Despite the long flight and numerous plane changes, she was still wound up. Deciding to call her Russian cousin, she picked up the phone. After some confusion and much shouting over stopped-up ears which had popped painfully during take-offs and landings, it was finally arranged that Katherine would meet Cousin Nadya the following day, at the War Memorial across the street.

Suddenly hungry, she dressed hastily and went down to the dining room. After waiting a long time, she was informed by a yawning waiter – item by item – that most of the menu was temporarily unavailable. Katherine persisted and eventually found something to which he did not say *nyet*. Fortunately, the vodka she ordered arrived much sooner than the food. By the time dinner was served, anything would have tasted good.

Returning to her room considerably more relaxed, Katherine opened the window and looked out. For such a large city, there were few vehicles on the no-ticeably quiet streets. Everywhere, however, people were out strolling, enjoying the white nights.

Across the broad avenue under her window, Katherine saw a tall obelisk marking the place where she was to meet Cousin Nadya. Around it were several groups of statues, one of them lowered into a large concrete ring. Soft, sorrowful music drifted gently out of the Ring up to the window ledge where she leaned, and with it a strangely intense presence. Unable to take her eyes off the compelling circle, Katherine thought about the mysterious quest that had brought her halfway around the world.

Her earliest – and most treasured – memories were of her Grandmother Tatiana singing her Russian lullabies and telling her Russian fairy-tales. Her favorite had been about a wonderful city, where a beautiful princess had danced in a glittering palace for the Tsar. It was only as she grew older that Katherine realized that this story was about Babushka herself.

It often seemed to Katherine that she had learned most of what really mattered from her grandmother. Babushka took her to concerts, where she learned to appreciate music that came from the soul; Babushka taught her ballet, which

5

enabled her to move in harmony with it. Best of all, Babushka taught her to speak Russian. Though she of course navigated her American world in English, Katherine always thought about what was most important to her in Russian. English somehow never seemed enough to express what she felt. And the way the Russian phrases curled around and rolled off her tongue was as satisfying as singing.

Katherine had eventually found herself reading whatever she could about the mysterious land her grandmother spoke of so longingly. But what she read in newspapers and heard on radio and TV often confused her. Could the Evil Empire portrayed there really be the same place Babushka still considered home?

Not that Babushka ever called it that. Nor did she and Katherine ever speak Russian in public – or even at home in front of visitors. But Katherine knew Babushka was homesick – by the sadness which never left her eyes, by the indefinable emptiness which she somehow sensed aching within. She would come home from school to find Babushka reading Tolstoy or listening to old records of Russian music. Katherine would sit with her and listen; something about the singing reached down and touched her deeply. Sometimes she, too, would cry, without knowing why.

Babushka died not long after Katherine's daughter, Tanya, was born. "Promise me," she had said, holding Katherine's hand tightly, "that someday you will go back – to see where I danced." And then a beautiful smile lit up the old face, giving Katherine a brief glimpse of the lovely young woman her grandmother had once been.

There was, however, little time to grieve. Katherine's marriage ended, and the demands of being a single parent soon pushed Babushka's memory into a seldom frequented – and less painful – corner. Often, at first, she resolved to pass on to her daughter what she had learned from Babushka, but somehow the Russian words stuck in her throat. Eventually they, too, faded.

Then, suddenly, Tanya was a young woman, off on her own. Not long after, the dreams started. At first, Katherine welcomed them. Several times a week, Babushka would drift through her sleep in a gentle, graceful pavanne, her comforting presence easing the emptiness left by Tanya's growing up. Gradually, however, the dreams grew more insistent. Babushka began to sing mournful Russian songs, inconsolable tears raining from her sad, beautiful eyes. "Take me home," they pleaded. "Take me home."

Finally, Katherine could stand it no more. Up the attic stairs and over years of clutter, she climbed unerringly to where it had been waiting – unopened – since

Babushka's death. Kneeling before the dusty trunk, Katherine slowly unclasped and opened the lid. Inside were several old books, most of them by Tolstoy, and a modest stack of vintage phonograph records with Russian labels. Slowly sounding out the Cyrillic letters, she suddenly recognized the top one: Fyodor Chaliapin singing arias from *Boris Godunov*. How often she had sat with Babushka listening to the great basso bring to life his greatest role. That the tortured, guilt-ridden tsar should sound so beautiful had always amazed – and puzzled – Katherine.

The books, too, were familiar. Gently, she picked up a thick volume bound in worn red leather. *Voyna e Mir – War and Peace*. Katherine smiled as the Russian words leaped out at her, remembering how often she had fallen asleep in Babushka's lap to the sound of Tolstoy's resounding prose. At the end of each reading, Katherine would awaken just as Babushka reverently closed the book and laid her hand on it in graceful homage. Warm tears filled her eyes as Katherine realized that she had grown up before Babushka could finish reading it to her.

Next to the books was a faded shoe-box, elegantly inscribed with the name of a Parisian shop. Katherine knew what was inside; Babushka had always ended her tales of the Maryinsky by showing her the shoes she had last danced in there. Lifting the lid, Katherine saw that though the smooth satin had yellowed, the slippers still lay gracefully in the tissue-lined box.

Tucked in one of the stiffly padded toes was a gold chain with a small carved wooden cross. Babushka had worn it – always – around her neck in a manner which quietly stated that it must only be touched with reverence. It had been made by her father, she had explained with a sad smile. Holding up the chain, Katherine looked intently at the dangling cross, wondering again what had happened to him. But even as a child, she had known better than to ask.

Under the shoe-box was an elaborately embellished frame, surrounding a cheap paper reproduction of an old Russian Orthodox icon. Every night, Katherine remembered with a frown, Babushka had said her prayers before it.

"But why does such a shabby picture," Katherine had once blurted out when very young, "have such a pretty frame?"

"Because it reminds me of a much nicer one that didn't need a frame," Babushka had sighed. "My grandfather painted it for the icon corner of our home by the Volga."

Sometimes Babushka told her stories about the village where she had grown up.

"Someday, will you take me there?" Katherine had begged.

"No, it's too far." Babushka had sighed again. "I can never go back." Seeing the huge tears clouding the clear blue eyes, Katherine knew she must never ask why.

Gently she picked up the shoe-box, the Chaliapin recordings, and the old copy of *War and Peace*. The cheap icon in the ornate frame she avoided touching. Closing the trunk, she returned quickly to her room.

For several days she remained there, listening to Chaliapin on the scratchy old records and reading from the worn old volume of Tolstoy. Syllable by syllable, she sounded out the long unused words. Slowly familiar phrases came floating – then flooding – back. By the time she had finished Tolstoy's epic, she was once more thinking in Russian. She slept soundly that night, untroubled by dreams.

The next morning she returned to the attic and again opened the trunk. Sorting through the books and records, she lifted the tasteless icon to see if she had missed anything. Underneath were two bundles of old letters, each neatly tied with a red silk ribbon.

Surprised to find something unfamiliar in the trunk, Katherine slipped off the ribbon of the first pile and quickly sorted through the letters. All of them were from the same address and in the same hand, addressed to her grandmother in various European capitals. All were postmarked 1914. Opening and scanning the first one, she surmised that it was from Babushka's only sister, Elisaveta, who had always figured prominently in her grandmother's stories. Those in the second bundle had the same handwriting and return address, but were addressed to her grandmother in New York. And all of these were postmarked much later.

Although Babushka tended to be vague about dates and actual events, Katherine had eventually figured out that she had left Russia just before World War I. Though she never dared ask, Katherine assumed that her Russian family had perished during the Revolution. Why else did all of Babushka's stories end around 1914? Why else did Babushka refuse to talk about them in a later context? Why else had she never returned to her Motherland? Yet here were these other letters from her sister in Russia, the first dated 1925, the last 1930. Deeply perplexed, Katherine went back down to her room and began reading them.

Hours later, drying her eyes and blowing her nose, she tried to make sense out of what she had read. From the first group of letters, it was apparent that Babushka had not wanted to leave Russia; from the others, it was equally clear that she had tried to return. Then how had she ended up in America, stranded in a place that could never be home?

And what had happened to her family? The later letters not only indicated that they had been alive, but doing rather well under the new regime. Was it possible that some of them were still there? Might she be able to find them? Was there, after all, someone who could fill the void left by Babushka's death, someone she could be Russian with again? That night she dreamed of Babushka; this time, however, her grandmother was smiling.

With an excitement she had not felt since before Tanya had flown the nest, she began to search. Not surprisingly, mail sent to the return address on the letters came back unopened. Inquiries sent to the Maryinsky Theatre were more successful; eventually she had tracked down the granddaughter of Babushka's only sister. This was Nadya, whom she would meet tomorrow.

Nadya's letters had seemed as excited about reestablishing contact as she herself was; the cousins had eagerly bombarded each other with questions. It became apparent after a while, however, that much of what needed saying could only be done face to face. And many of Katherine's questions were simply unanswerable in words. "Come here, to Russia," Nadya's letters said in a thousand ways, "and I will show you what you are looking for." It had taken many years for family finances and international politics to align favorably, but here she was at last.

"Because I promised my Babushka," she had told the young man at Customs. But why had Babushka been so insistent? Why had she ached so for a place she had forsaken decades ago? And why did Katherine herself feel the sad emptiness which had never left her grandmother's eyes?

"To see where I danced." Yes. And all that Babushka wouldn't speak of – couldn't speak of – about what she had left behind. Exactly what Babushka wanted her to do, exactly what she herself hoped to find here, she did not know. But a compelling force – something reaching deep into the core of her being – had inexplicably pulled her to this vast, mysterious land.

The next morning, Katherine rose early. Down in the dining room, she ignored the menu and simply asked the indifferent waiter to bring her breakfast. After waiting a not unreasonably long time, she ate the plain but nourishing fare with relish and drank several cups of strong tea. Then she left the hotel and crossed the street to the War Memorial. As she approached the tall obelisk, she saw a pair of newly-weds – he in a new suit, she in a long white gown and veil – solemnly lay a bridal bouquet among the fresh flowers which surrounded it. As she waited on the steps for Nadya, several other people brought flowers, too.

Looking at the statues around her, she noticed that instead of the usual heroic equestrians romanticizing war, these were of ordinary soldiers, horror and suffering etched deeply on their faces. "War is Hell!" they said – and meant it.

A group of young soldiers was shepherded past her. As they stopped to look around and listen to their guide, Katherine studied them. Under their Red Army caps were rosy cheeks that had rarely seen a razor, here and there peppered with acne. *They're still just babies!* Katherine thought, suddenly glad for all the honest statues. *At least these boys won't go off to war thinking it's a game.*

As the group disappeared down into the Ring behind the obelisk, Katherine's attention was drawn with them. Once again, she became aware of something strong emanating from it. Up closer, it drew her irresistibly.

Then she felt someone's eyes on her. Looking up, she saw a tall, rather stout – but strangely familiar – woman moving gracefully toward her. Like most of the Soviet women Katherine had seen so far, she was solidly built, plainly dressed, carrying a worn shopping bag, and looked years older than she probably was.

"Katya?" the woman asked, with a tentative smile.

"Nadya?" echoed Katherine.

Katherine felt strong arms wrap firmly around her. After several resounding smacks on both cheeks, she was reluctantly released.

Totally unselfconscious rivers of tears were rushing down the crevices of Nadya's deeply-lined face. Katherine, meanwhile, already had a headache from trying to restrain her own emotion.

"I would have known you anywhere," said Nadya, suddenly smiling like a rainbow, "even if you didn't look so American."

"So would I," laughed Katherine, blowing her nose. "You look a lot like my grandmother."

"You resemble mine, too."

"Maybe that's why they talked to us so much –"

"Especially about things they couldn't talk to others about."

"Yes."

"You speak Russian very well," said Nadya.

"Babushka taught me."

"Good. It will be easier for you to find what you seek. Tomorrow I will take you home to meet the rest of the family. It will be a real Russian feast! They, too, are eager to see you."

Katherine nodded, pleased.

"Have you been inside?" Nadya gestured toward the circular shrine.

"Not yet."

"Then let's go now. Some things you must see – and feel – in order to understand." And Nadya proceeded to explain that this War Memorial had been built by the people of Leningrad to commemorate the 900-day siege of their city by the Germans during World War II.

As they descended quietly into the Ring, a low woman's voice singing a wordless song of unutterable sorrow reached out and wrapped around them, pulling Katherine and Nadya to the group of large statues in the center. These were not of soldiers, however, but of women mourning their dead. One of the mourners was cradling a young soldier, another was holding an old woman. Beside them, a weeping mother lifted her dead baby. Countless offerings of fresh flowers had been lovingly laid around the sculpture's huge base.

Nadya led Katherine away from the statues, into an underground museum dimly lit by 900 torchlights. Amidst large mosaic murals were glass cases displaying small souvenirs of the Siege: a "stove" made of tin can and candle, which Nadya explained was for heat and cooking during the terrible winters; a small piece of bread, half of it sawdust and pine needles, which she said was their daily ration; a battered violin, dropped by a musician dying of hunger on his way to rehearsal. Each of the artifacts carefully identified by Nadya had its own story of quiet heroism. By the time they left the museum, Katherine had stopped trying to restrain her tears.

Sitting down on a bench against the inner wall of the Ring, Katherine finally wiped her eyes.

"I had no idea. About any of this."

"Most Americans don't," shrugged Nadya sadly.

Katherine looked at Nadya's strong face. "You were here," she said wonderingly at the deep lines surrounding her eyes, "during this terrible Siege?"

"Yes," she nodded, "for all of it."

"You must have been only a child."

"At the beginning, yes. But I grew up fast."

"And your family… ?" Katherine hesitated.

Nadya paused. Then she pointed at the statues. "There!" she said, *"There* is my family!"

Katherine looked up at the bronze bodies of the dead child and the slain soldier. Then she looked into the eyes of the grieving mother. Her gaze settled finally on the dying old woman, whose face she had seen before…

"There is my family," Nadya repeated, taking Katherine's hand. "And yours."

11

Part I

Derevnia, 1861

Chapter 1: The VILLAGE

A month before the first guns of the American Civil War fired on Fort Sumter – on the very eve, in fact, of Abraham Lincoln's inauguration as President – Tsar Alexander II issued a manifesto which officially ended serfdom in Russia.

"We all know that the existing order cannot remain unchanged," he said, as he signed the momentous decree. "It is better to abolish serfdom from above than to await the day when it will begin to abolish itself from below."

In the year of the Emancipation, a sturdy baby girl was born to a peasant family who lived in Derevnia, a village on the Volga. Ekaterina, the baby's mother, had been in labor all night; the infant was in no hurry to leave her snug haven. Slowly and carefully, she made her way from the dark warmth into the startling bright beyond. Strong, welcoming hands reached out and soothed her. She relaxed and greeted the glowing rays of the rising sun with a melodious cry.

"This one does not fear life," said the baby's grandmother approvingly.

The old woman gently bathed the infant and wrapped her in a clean lambskin. Mikhail, the baby's father, was then allowed to view his new daughter. Carefully surveying the child's strong body and well-formed limbs, he noted with satisfaction the tiny fists calmly saluting him and the reassuring ring of her uncomplaining cries.

Smiling broadly, he returned the baby to her mother and tenderly kissed them both on the forehead. Then he strode exuberantly to the tavern to celebrate.

Mikhail was an important man in the village. Every Sunday – at the opposite end of the road down which he was now eagerly heading – he chanted the prayers and liturgy in church. His deep bass voice was well-known even beyond Derevnia. Sometimes people from outside came just to hear him sing.

Mikhail's first wife and child had died during a cholera epidemic. His status as chanter had enabled him to remarry quickly – and to one of the most desirable village maidens. Ekaterina was strong and healthy, of an amiable disposition, and pleasant to look at. And as the daughter of the village midwife, she had inherited many useful skills.

Besides Ekaterina and the baby, Mikhail's family included his younger brother, Foma, and his pregnant wife, Agafya. Since Ekaterina's father had also died during the plague, her mother moved in with them as well.

Ekaterina's expanding belly had inspired Mikhail to build a new house for his growing family. Before raising the log walls, he killed a rooster, sprinkled the foundations with its blood, and buried its head under the corner where the icons were to be. When the *izba* was ready, Babushka – which was what everyone in Derevnia respectfully called Ekaterina's mother – put the embers of their stove in a jar and solemnly carried them to the stove of the new house.

"*Domovoi*," the family said, as she put the old embers into the new stove, "the sleigh is ready for you, go with us."

And so was their ancestral house spirit settled into his new home. Not that any of them had ever seen their *domovoi*. But they knew that he was warm and soft and protective – like a sheepskin coat – and occasionally prone to malicious teasing. The small food offering left out at night to propitiate him was always gone in the morning. Mikhail also hung a bear's head in the stable to protect them from the house spirits of their neighbors. That the first baby born to the new household was so healthy was a good omen. They had built well, and the spirits were satisfied.

"Her name is Evgenia," announced Ekaterina, when it was time. "After my grandmother."

In the first months of what was to be a very long and eventful life, little Zhenya saw the world from a cradle suspended from the ceiling of the *izba*. At frequent intervals, various smiling faces picked her up and kissed her affectionately. Eventually she identified the quiet, russet-clad one who fed her as mother, and the noisy, bushy-faced one who sang to her as father. By the time she was weaned, Zhenya had names for all the others whose laps she often climbed into after the evening meal. Rarely did any of them have time to play with her, but they were usually glad to have her toddle along and watch as they went about their tasks. She soon learned not to get in the way.

The log *izba* in which Zhenya grew up was built high off the ground, its timber floor raised over a shallow cellar. A shingled roof sloped sharply above several small windows cut in walls of long logs. Window frames and shutters were decorated with carved animals and birds, flowers and geometric designs. At the ends of the roof ridge was a pair of carved horses' heads facing in opposite directions. In the yard in back was a barn, hayshed, threshing floor, garden, and small storage shed. Sometimes in the summer, Mikhail and Ekaterina – or Foma and Agafya – slept in the shed. Yard, outbuildings, and house were all enclosed by a low wooden fence.

Except for a small, unheated vestibule, the *izba* had only one large room. In one corner was a large brick stove with a flat top high above the floor. It was used for everything – heating, cooking, baking, washing, drying, even sleeping. Just out of the cradle, Zhenya slept on top of the stove with Babushka. As she got older, she moved to the sleeping loft over it, where she was soon joined by cousins and brothers.

Diagonally across from the stove was the Red corner. Here the family icons hung, decorated with vigil lights, colored eggs, dried flowers, and doves made out of dough. Here, too, the family gathered at a large table for all its meals. And every night just before bedtime, Zhenya joined Babushka and Ekaterina, on their knees before an icon of the Virgin. In her prayers, Zhenya spoke familiarly, though respectfully, to the icon. The Virgin, she thought, rather resembled Babushka, only prettier.

In the corner by the entrance was a wide bench with a carved horse's head. As master of the house, Mikhail usually slept there. The rest of the adults slept on the other benches which surrounded the room. Above the benches were shelves on which rows of carefully carved, brightly decorated household utensils were neatly lined up. On one side of the stove was a water barrel and dipper for washing. On the other was a large cupboard, under which a small stairway led to the storage cellar. And in the adjacent corner was a harmoniously proportioned spinning wheel, and a loom that was the envy of every woman in the village. Except for the stove and cooking pots, everything was made of wood.

When Zhenya was about six, she began helping with the housework. Carefully she set out and cleaned up the wooden bowls and spoons for each meal. Conscientiously she shook out and swept up after the straw sleeping pallets. Fondly she helped care for cow, sheep, and poultry.

On weekdays, Ekaterina did all the cooking in the morning, before breakfast. Zhenya brought up sauerkraut, onions, salted cucumbers, and buckwheat groats from the cellar, which her mother made into *shchi* and *kasha* for dinner and supper. She also drew *kvas* from the barrel in the cellar to drink with the dark sourdough rye loaves they usually ate for breakfast. Periodically, the women would spend the day baking bread. Just out of the oven, its aroma almost covered the odor of *kvas* and sheepskin, tallow and leather which usually filled the *izba*.

Theirs was a well-ordered household; Ekaterina insisted on that. In her carefully arranged spinning corner, everything was always in its proper place, uniform as the yarn spun on her continuously turning wheel, lined up straight as the warp on her constantly shifting loom. The spare, efficient movements with which she neatly shuttled the weft and evenly peddled the wheel set the rhythm for household tasks and wove the family together in a firm web of quiet industriousness. Even the cockroaches and bedbugs stayed out of sight. The lice, too, were kept at bay, and fewer flies buzzed in their *izba* than elsewhere in Derevnia. Babushka said it was because they had an outhouse; most of their neighbors simply dumped the night bucket into a hole in the anteroom floor.

It was while learning all these household tasks that Zhenya first began noticing the differences between girls and boys. While she was cooking and sweeping and weeding the garden, her brothers were chopping firewood and helping to sow and plow. While she was feeding the chickens and milking the cow, they were tending the horse. And while she was learning to spin and knit and weave and embroider, they were learning to carve spoons and bowls and make baskets and *lapti*.

There were other differences, too. Zhenya, like all the other girls, never cut her hair, wearing it in a long braid down her back. Like all the other boys, her brothers had theirs trimmed in the shape of an inverted bowl. And she wore a *sarafan*, a long full jumper with narrow shoulder straps, over her shirt, while they wore trousers under theirs. When clothes got dirty, the women washed them – in a long, shallow tub halved and hollowed from a log by the men.

She also noticed that only men had beards, and that sometimes they went out after supper, returning late and laughing loudly. Only women's bellies, however, periodically swelled up – though some did so more often than others. Aunt Agafya's belly got big every year. Usually a baby eventually appeared in the cradle; sometimes, after a while, it vanished. And sometimes Agafya's belly suddenly got small without a baby appearing. Then Babushka would give her some special tea, and hold her hand while she cried. In any case, Agafya was always back at work within the week.

Her own mother's belly got big much less often. She rarely had to drink Babushka's special tea, and the babies didn't usually disappear. And Babushka never let her go back to work for at least a few weeks.

Some things, however, seemed the same for boys and girls, men and women. They all wore felt boots in the winter and linden-bark sandals in the summer.

They all slept under their sheepskin coats at night. And they all worked very hard.

Ж Ж Ж

Zhenya crept softly through the tall grass, carefully making her way toward the place where she had found the nest. Suddenly a large bird ran clumsily into the vast open plain, ponderously flapping its heavy wings. Halfway across, the awkward gait miraculously transformed into strong, graceful flight.

Zhenya sighed. No matter how hard she tried, she was never able to get close enough. How could something so slow on land be so fast in the air?

The strange birds returned every year, just as the steppe was magically changing into brilliantly blooming flowers. Zhenya sat down on the warm earth, marveling that just a short time ago it had slept beneath a thick, dazzling blanket of snow. Already, the spectacular color of the unending expanse before her was turning bright gold.

The wind now rose with the sun, picking up velocity as it reached its zenith, and then, all afternoon, tore across the steppe like a herd of stampeding horses. Zhenya loved the sound of the wind whirling through the tall grass. And the clear brilliant sky was breathtakingly beautiful. Looking up into the bright azure dome, she felt herself grow big inside, part of something infinitely immense.

Seeing that the sun was already high in the sky, she quickly stood and made a few half-hearted attempts to brush the dust off her old *sarafan*, glad that it was last summer's, happy that it was now short enough to run freely in. Absently she smoothed back the thick brown strands forever escaping from her braid, and headed back to the village. Carefully she threaded her way through the patchwork fields of bright green flax and waving grain golden as her own sturdy limbs. Cattle and sheep were grazing placidly in the pasture. Everything was just as it had been last year, and the year before that, every since Zhenya could remember.

Zhenya went quickly past the tavern, onto the narrow road between the double row of fenced-in farmsteads lined up along the river. Warm mud squished up between her bare toes as she walked toward the large group gathered in front of the firehouse. Above all the shouting, Zhenya heard her father's deep voice and soon spotted his stocky body gesturing expansively in the middle of the crowd. Today's meeting was very important; though only heads of households could vote, everyone in Derevnia had turned out, and was very excited.

The fields on which they all depended were divided into strips, each sepa-

19

rated by a narrow band of grass. To make sure everyone got a fair share of the best land, each household received several strips in several different locations. Periodically the land was reapportioned, according to the changing size of village households. Today the new land allotment was to be decided by the village commune. So it had been done for as long as anyone could remember, and so, it was assumed, would it always be done.

Just as the people of Derevnia relied on tradition to apportion the land, so they farmed it much as their ancestors had. The fields were planted on a three-year cycle, rotating between winter grain, spring grain, and pasture. Horses and oxen pulled wheeled wooden ploughs; wind and water power ground the grain. Mowing was done with scythes, reaping with sickles, threshing with flails made of wood. At harvest time, everyone except the very young and very old took tool in hand and labored from dawn to dusk. The grain crop thus gleaned provided food for the family, seed for next year's crop, and feed for livestock.

Most of this, of course, happened without the need to call a meeting. Zhenya herself did not understand what the meetings were for, except that everyone – the men especially – seemed to enjoy them. The gathering that day was especially noisy and almost came to blows when someone brought up the subject of the Emancipation.

Zhenya knew that she had been born in the year of Emancipation. She wasn't entirely sure what that meant, but from listening to the men arguing about it, she gathered that it hadn't quite turned out as expected.

"The only difference," shouted Foma, "is that now we belong to the commune instead of to the landlord. And instead of owing labor, we owe money."

"But at least *we* are the commune," Mikhail yelled back. "And someday the land will belong to our grandchildren."

When the men had finally shouted themselves hoarse, everyone went down to the log bath-house by the river. The large brick stove inside was quickly stoked; soon it was snapping and sizzling whenever someone threw a dipper of water on it. Thick clouds of steam rose to the tiers of linden shelves on which the entire village sweated out a week's worth of grime and toil. Perspiration trickled down Zhenya's hardy little body, making amber trails in the dust which covered it; stray locks from an unevenly plaited braid plastered her face and neck. Finally, when it was almost too hot to breathe, everyone ran outside and jumped in the river.

Splashing happily in the cool water of the Volga, Zhenya joined the laughter.

Ж   Ж   Ж

Leaning against the trunk of a young oak tree, Zhenya sat contentedly, listening to Mother Volga sing.

Not far from Derevnia was a tiny bay where the river cut gently into the shore. A small, sandy beach and a slow, silent current made it ideal for swimming. The northern bank sloped abruptly up to a modest promontory from which an unimpeded view of the mighty Volga was possible. A small grove of trees crowned the lookout point, shielding whomever sat there from sun and wind.

It was Zhenya's favorite place, and she came here as often as she could. Sometimes she watched fishermen catching silvery salmon and large sturgeon in their hoopnets. Sometimes she saw huge rafts of timber floating lazily down the river. And sometimes, too, she saw narrow flat-bottomed barges being hauled up the river by a long line of harnessed men. They trudged and strained slowly and rhythmically, staying in step with a repetitive refrain they chanted endlessly. Sometimes Zhenya sang with them, hoping to lighten their load.

Occasionally a steamboat chugged noisily up the river, puffing out clouds of black smoke. Her father, who sometimes sat with her, said that such vessels carried passengers and cargo between the great cities of the Volga. The great river was thousands of *versts* long, he told her; it was the largest this side of the mountains and the most important in all of Russia. By portage and canal, one could take it almost anywhere.

As a young man, Zhenya's father had explored the Volga, working on barges and boats. She loved to listen as he told her of the wonders he had seen – the dense marshy forests in the North, the vast open plains to the South, the great Caspian Sea at the river's delta. During the winter, when the river froze, he had worked in the cities on its banks. As he described the fortresses and factories and teeming throngs of exotic peoples, Zhenya pictured them in her mind and felt as though she, too, had been there. Best of all were his stories of the fairs held along the Volga, the greatest of them at Nizhny Novgorod. As Zhenya listened, she vowed that one day she would go to the great fair and see for herself.

Babushka, too, told stories about the Volga. Her tales, however, were of endless waves of invaders laying waste to its people. From ferocious Vikings in fleet dragon ships sailing down the flowing river to fearsome Mongols on terrifyingly swift horses galloping up the frozen river, all had left a legacy of terror. Praise be to God that the tsars had since made Russia big enough and strong enough to resist such invasions!

That there were places outside Russia, Zhenya knew vaguely. But in her soul, she never went beyond the immense land that was *Rodina* – the Motherland where she had been born and where her grandmothers had always lived, the place her granddaughters would always call home. She was centered in this vast heartland. What need was there to leave it?

And – other than seeing the fair at Nizhny Novgord – why would she ever want to leave the village where she was so firmly rooted? In Derevnia, she was nurtured by *Rodina*, and connected to all of Russia by Mother Volga. In her flowing waters, Zhenya saw the sparkling light of the sun and the luminous glow of the moon. In the river's everchanging moods, she witnessed the constant cycle of the seasons.

Zhenya smiled, and began to sing with the mysterious music of the eternal Volga, knowing that she was part of something that would go on forever.

Ж   Ж   Ж

"Over there. See them?" Babushka pointed to a deceptively lovely patch of mushrooms growing beguilingly under a slender young tree. "Leave those be! They kill."

Zhenya nodded, and obediently bypassed the delicious-looking mushrooms. Babushka was always right about these things. Besides, her basket was already full of nuts and berries and mushrooms Babushka had told her to pick.

Shafts of sunlight pierced tall trees, crowded together as if in church. Birds twittered overhead, and occasionally there was a rustle as they startled a rabbit or deer.

Sometimes, on their frequent walks, they glimpsed a fox or a lynx. Once they had even encountered a huge elk browsing lazily on the new shoots of a felled oak tree. Raising his massive antlers, he had gazed inquisitively at them. Then, pawing the earth with one of his long legs, he unhurriedly ambled off.

Most Derevnians were afraid of the forest. It was dark and dense; one couldn't see very far. And it was peopled with wild beasts and magical spirits who made strange noises.

Zhenya, however, came here often with Babushka, helping her gather medicinal herbs. The old woman knew which plants were harmful and which helpful. Patiently, she taught Zhenya how to recognize them, and what they were for.

"Lean too close to the river and the water spirits will pull you in," she usually grumbled whenever Zhenya had been off in her little grove by the Volga.

But Babushka was on very friendly terms with the spirits of the forest, and often conversed familiarly with them.

Babushka herself often reminded Zhenya of a tree – a very old tree with very deep roots. Her strong hands were tough as bark, her weathered skin wrinkled like fallen leaves. Snow-covered hair crowned by a moss-colored kerchief framed a face etched deep by long winters and lashing storms. Babushka's cracked voice, rustling like wind-blown branches, often spoke of hardship, but never in anger or with bitterness. Her sturdy trunk firmly planted in the earth, she endured the rigors of her beloved homeland with dignity and compassion. And in the sad, wise old eyes, Zhenya sometimes thought she could see the entire forest looking back.

Zhenya herself loved the beautiful trees almost as much as she did Babushka. The smell of pines was exhilarating, and the green foliage of spruce was stunning against the deep white snow. The massive oaks made her feel safe; the slender birches made her want to dance. Her special friends, however, were the linden trees. Tall and graceful, irregular heart-shaped leaves growing in densely symmetrical outline, Babushka said that many of them had been there when *her* grandmother was a girl. Tough inner bark was used to make rope and sandals; firm but yielding branches were carved into all kinds of utensils. And when the lindens blossomed, bees buzzed happily near the clusters of small cream-and-gold flowers. Zhenya and Babushka gathered and dried bunches of them to make tea for winter maladies.

In a small clearing encircled by linden trees were several beehives. Walking slowly toward them, intending to harvest some honey, they suddenly heard crashing branches and a loud, terrifying growl. And there in the clearing, standing on all fours, was an enormous bear. Zhenya stared at its broad powerful chest, its round laid-back ears, the long brown fur bristling on its neck. Babushka grabbed Zhenya and froze, as the bear continued to bark out short hoarse cries, its sharp white fangs gleaming deep inside its mouth.

And then, just as the bear seemed about to attack, three small but very agile bear cubs shot out of a tree not far from them. As the cubs rushed to their mother, she lost her aggressive stance. Still glaring at the motionless humans, she rose up to her full height – about ten feet, Babushka reckoned later – and proclaimed a final, protective roar. Then she dropped down, turned and ran into a thicket of spruce trees. Her rounded backside, covered in long dark fur that shook with every step, disappeared into the forest along with the three little faun-colored rumps of her cubs.

Slowly Babushka released Zhenya from her surprisingly strong grip. She kissed the little girl's forehead and smiled at her. Zhenya relaxed, knowing that Babushka and the mother bear understood each other very well.

Ж   Ж   Ж

Not long after the first snowfall, Derevnia celebrated St. Philip's Day. Then began the Advent fast, which ended on the Winter Solstice. Zhenya preferred the feasting to the fasting, but Advent really wasn't so bad. It didn't last too long – and there was Christmas to look forward to.

On Christmas Eve, Zhenya watched Babushka make wax candles for the small fir tree Mikhail cut from the forest. Then she helped Ekaterina make *kresty*, crosses of baked dough, and *kutya*, boiled wheat sweetened with honey and sprinkled with poppy seeds. After dinner, everyone threw a spoonful outside for Grandfather Frost and left a little in their bowls for departed ancestors.

On Christmas Day, the whole village dressed up in their finest clothes and went visiting. In every *izba*, tables were spread with nuts and dried fruits, pickled mushrooms and gingerbread cookies. Affectionate kisses and vigorous hugs were exchanged all around. For the next two weeks, Zhenya and her family went to parties, and almost every evening young people came caroling. Singing songs invoking good harvest, wealth and luck, the carolers went from *izba* to *izba*, scattering grain on the listeners.

Yuletide officially ended on Epiphany. Everyone followed a cross-bearing procession from the church to a hole cut in the river's ice. After the priest consecrated the water, Foma joined the hardy souls who took a quick dip.

Although the weather was bitterly cold, January and February were relaxed and pleasant. Besides basic chores, there wasn't much that had to be done. The men hauled hay from the meadow, the women skimmed cream and churned butter. Other than that, they sat inside around a crackling stove smelling of birch and fresh bread, the women spinning and weaving, the men carving. Neighbors often joined them to sing and listen to Babushka's stories about Baba Yaga and the Snow Maiden, Tsarevich Ivan and the Firebird, of braves princes defending the Motherland from fierce dragons and savage centaurs.

The latter tales Babushka told with particular relish, always ending with the same inevitable conclusion: "When the invaders come, hide in the forest." As many times as she had heard it, the back of Zhenya's neck still prickled.

When the sun shone, the men raced their horses on the frozen river. The children built snow forts and played games in the snow. Best of all, Zhenya liked the ice slide. On sleds ornamented with fantastic carvings and colorful designs, people of every age whizzed down the high wooden platform covered with shining ice, steering expertly with their hands. Zhenya's brothers liked to show off, lying flat on their backs, arms crossed over their chests, or going down head first on their stomachs. People tumbled all over each other at the bottom, laughing and shouting good-naturedly.

Then came Zhenya's favorite holiday, *Maslenitsa*. "Butter Week" began on Sunday, eight weeks before Easter. Figures in masks dashed about, dancing bears and Petrushka puppets appeared, itinerant vendors sold nuts and oranges, and everyone ate *blini* – little round pancakes smothered in butter – at every meal. Down by the river, swings of supple young birch branches were erected; flying out over the frozen water, Zhenya could hear balalaikas playing in rhythm. Gaily beribboned sleighs drawn by jingling horses harnessed troika-style drove in circles around Derevnia.

On the last day of *Maslenitsa*, a straw Prince Carnival was seated on a sled and drawn through the streets. "Stay, stay!" shouted everyone. "Stay with us forever!"

But at the end of his triumphal procession, he was ceremoniously enthroned on a pile of dead branches. The onlookers sang bawdy songs, urging winter's departure, as they watched their straw prince burst into flames. And then, finally, the church bells tolled. Everything stopped. Everyone went home to prepare for the Great Fast of Lent.

Zhenya didn't like Lent. No one did, except for some excessively pious old women nobody liked. After the carnival, the street was littered with nutshells and orange peels. The swings were taken down and the ice slides broken up. Everyone was dejected and listless. For the next seven weeks, no one ate any animal products – no meat, poultry, or fish; no milk, eggs, butter, or cheese. And no sugar. And, of course, no vodka. On Wednesdays and Fridays, the exceptionally devout ate nothing at all.

As Lent dragged on, the roof of the *izba* began to leak. Ice on the river broke up, and roads turned to mud. As the sleigh was put away, tiny green shoots of winter wheat appeared in fields and birds began to return from the South.

The last week was almost unbearable. Every day, they went to church; Zhenya got tired standing during the long services, and her stomach rumbled emptily. On Good Friday, the church was dark; a sarcophagus was placed next to the cross in front and draped with cloth embroidered with the body of the Redeemer. Believers filed past to kiss its wounds. No one ate all day Friday and Saturday.

Toward midnight of Easter Eve, the church was filled. People stood crowded inside with unlit candles, as the priest slowly and mournfully read the Mass. The choir sang in a minor key, the music low and subdued. Then, just before midnight, the candles were lit, each person sharing the flame with those around. And finally, at midnight, Easter burst forth in all its glory. Mikhail's deep booming voice, big and beautiful as the Volga, rolled out like thunder. The golden doors of the iconostasis swung open, the tomb and cross removed. The priest led the people out of the church and around it, singing in search of the risen Christ. After the third time, the doors were thrown open.

"*Khristos Voskrese*!" the priest joyously announced three times. "Christ is risen!"

"*Voistinu Voskrese*!" came the ringing response from the crowd. "He is risen indeed!"

All returned to the illuminated church as the choir sang triumphantly and the bells pealed joyfully. All over Russia, Zhenya knew, bells were ringing. And as she stood in the densely-packed church, wedged tightly among her family and neighbors, she felt safe and secure in the bosom of Holy Mother Russia, connected to all Her children everywhere.

Three hours later, the priest passed between a double row of plates winding inside and around the church. Tall loaves of freshly baked *kulich* surrounded by white lilacs, triangular towers of deliciously rich *paskha* decorated with leaves and red eggs, all received the priest's blessing. Despite the long service, Zhenya was not tired. With the entire village, she returned home to feast until dawn.

Friends and neighbors exchanged brightly decorated eggs; children played with them and had egg fights. And everyone drank joyously. The whole village, in fact, was drunk for days.

Easter was a magical time. Everywhere spring gushed forth like a waterfall. Suddenly everything was blooming – violets and bluebells and lilies of the valley and gloriously fragrant lilacs. During the seven weeks until Trinity, Zhenya joined the other young people in joyous singing and dancing.

All of them, of course, also helped their families with the important work of Spring. The men plowed and sowed wheat and oats. The women manured their gardens and planted cabbages and potatoes. On St. Vlasia's Day, all the village cattle were driven to the communal pasture, where they were blessed by the priest. Later, the men sowed buckwheat and barley, and plowed manure into the fallow fields.

After Trinity Sunday, St. Peter's Fast began. And then came St. John's Day, the last celebration before the most grueling work of the year. On Midsummer's Eve, the Derevnians built bonfires and jumped over them. A straw dummy was buried amidst lamentations. And as the sun finally set on the festivities, Zhenya knelt to it with the others and bade farewell to Spring

The next day, the entire village turned out in the common meadow. The men cut hay with their scythes, the women reaped grain with their sickles. As they mowed and reaped, the people of Derevnia sang in rhythm with their slowly swinging bodies. Zhenya heard it in the *izba*, where she tended the babies. She hummed along with the stolid chants, lulling the little ones to sleep.

When autumn arrived, the pace picked up, as everyone labored to be ready for winter. The men cut firewood, repaired *izba*s, and brewed beer; the women harvested gardens, sheared sheep, and slaughtered chickens. Somehow everything got done in time. And as Zhenya watched the first snow fall, she had the warm, snug feeling of being tucked in for the winter.

Ж   Ж   Ж

From her father's stories about the Volga, Zhenya knew – vaguely – that not everyone lived as they did. But like everyone else in Derevnia, she believed that their life would go on in the future just as it had in the past. Rarely, if ever, did it occur to anyone that anything could – or should – change. The way things were was how they always had been – and always would be. And that was that.

When the harvest was good, Zhenya's family was content. When it wasn't, they prayed for a better one next year. Meanwhile, they drew comfort from the ever-changing seasons which marked the never-changing cycle of their lives.

Zhenya and her people told time by the sun and the moon – and by the church bells. The bells called Derevnia to worship and measured its life. They sounded alarms and warned of storms. They told of disasters and funerals, holidays and festivals. Whenever Zhenya heard them ringing out from under the onion-shaped dome, she crossed herself. Everyone was born and then died, each in their own time. But the bells kept ringing.

And as she listened to their music – now joyful, now sorrowful – she knew that as long as the bells endured, so would Derevnia.

Chapter 2: The NARODNIK

The peasants of Derevnia did not welcome the unusual. Heavenly visions out-of-the-ordinary were especially upsetting. Zhenya had heard strange tales about the most recent one. Though the master of the manor had tried to explain it as something called an eclipse, he, too, was afraid when it began to grow dark. People started to wail and many tried to hide. Rumors tore around Derevnia that white wolves would overrun the earth and eat everyone up, that birds of prey would swoop down, and that Trishka himself would soon appear. Trishka was the Antichrist, a wonderfully magical and clever man, who would dazzle and lead Christians astray shortly before the end of the world.

Just as the panic reached its height, someone spotted a strange creature approaching the village. It appeared to have the body of a man with a large, marvelous head.

"Oiy, Oiy, Trishka's coming! Trishka's coming!" some of the more gullible souls began to shout.

On closer inspection, the "Antichrist" turned out to be Kostya the cooper, who was carrying an empty tub on his head.

Fortunately, such happenings were rare. But at the time Zhenya was passing from childhood to girlhood, another event occurred which caused almost as much alarm. Zhenya herself was transfigured by it, and village life was eventually transformed.

Ж   Ж   Ж

Late one hot summer day, a curious stranger appeared in Derevnia. He smiled and waved familiarly as he walked slowly on the dusty road. The villagers stared.

He was dressed in a loose shirt of embroidered Irish linen, baggy trousers of British broadcloth tucked into high boots of French kid, and a sleeveless coat of Italian velour which flowed below his knees. His hair was long and so was his beard. The astonished peasants continued to stare as this outlandish – but vaguely familiar – apparition reached the end of the road and entered the tavern.

Word quickly circulated that the stranger was buying vodka for everyone. Within a remarkably short time, the tavern was full of staring men. The visitor attempted to engage them in jocular conversation, making earthy jests in a stilted accent. The Derevnians drank his vodka, but did not laugh at his jokes. Finally, accompanying himself on the balalaika which usually hung over the bar, he began to sing strange songs. His voice, the listening peasants conceded later, was not bad, but it took several refrains for them to recognize what he was singing. More than one of them felt an urge to show the insolent stranger how *their* songs should be sung; courtesy – and free vodka – restrained them.

The stranger continued to sing at the crowded room of silent, staring peasants. In between, he nervously emptied bottle after bottle of vodka, filling the glasses of his taciturn but politely smiling guests and tossing back frequent shots with an obviously inexperienced hand. After a few hours, he crashed to the floor in total oblivion.

"He'll be out for a long time," observed Mikhail matter-of-factly. "I suppose we shouldn't just leave him here."

"But where does something like him belong?" wondered Foma.

"With clothes like those and the way he talks," shrugged Andrei the icon-maker, "where else?"

And with that, Pyotr the potter effortlessly slung the inert stranger over his shoulder, dumped him good-naturedly into his cart, and drove him out to the manor several *verst*s from town.

Sure enough, Pyotr reported the next day, he turned out to be a distant cousin of her ladyship. The house servants said he was a student at the university in Kazan, and that he talked to them a lot about very peculiar things. With the gentry, however, that was nothing new. Most of the Derevnians dismissed the stranger as an eccentric nobleman.

A few weeks later, he showed up at church on Sunday morning. This time he was dressed in homespun and *lapti*. After the service, he stood outside the church and addressed the departing congregation from the steps. They listened politely, without understanding most of what he said. But certain phrases – "a suffering pilgrim for the cause", "redeeming the Fatherland", "repaying our debt to the poor", "going to the people with the book, the word and with love" – led them to believe that he was a religious pilgrim. As such, they greeted him respectfully and wished him Godspeed.

To their surprise, however, he did not continue his pilgrimage. When he returned the next week, he made a speech in front of the firehouse. He kept repeating puzzling slogans about how they must overthrow the Tsar and transform Russia. Then he passed out some leaflets – which, of course, none of them could read.

The bewildered peasants were angry about what he said about the Tsar. And they weren't sure what to do with the leaflets. Some thought they should destroy what was obviously the work of the devil. Others argued that the words might be holy – like the Bible. Finally, they took the leaflets to the priest.

"It says here," read Father Igor slowly, "that the village commune is a natural form of socialism which guarantees justice and freedom. And that it treats all its members equally – unlike the government and the gentry, who take away the peasants' land and liberty."

A murmur of assent rippled through the listening crowd.

"The commune is also an antidote for the poison of capitalism," the priest continued, "which is destroying the workers in the cities."

Puzzled looks and indifferent shrugs.

"Were the peasants to declare themselves free," Father Igor hesitated, "their might would be felt throughout the land." He paused.

A mild rumble circled the scowling bearded faces.

"The government would disappear," he resumed reluctantly, "replaced by a free federation of communes whose echoes would be felt all over Europe."

For the next week, the stranger and his leaflets were discussed heatedly. Some continued to maintain that he was nothing but a crazy nobleman. Others were now convinced that he was one of God's Holy Fools. Still others feared that he was the Antichrist.

Meanwhile, it was learned that he had moved out of his cousin's mansion into one of the log huts in which her house serfs had once lived. This astounding piece of information added fuel to the fires of all three theories about the mysterious stranger.

What tipped the balance, however, was his next visit to town. This time, he went from *izba* to *izba*, speaking to each family separately. He explained that he was devoting his life to "raising their consciousness." And would they like to send their children to his school? If so, he would teach them to read.

"Well, sir, that's very kind of you, sir – but I need my boys in the fields."

"Well, then, send your daughters."

After that, village opinion quickly became almost unanimous. The men, at

31

first, simply laughed at the silly notion of girls reading. The women, however, were outraged; they soon convinced their men that the stranger must, indeed, be the Antichrist.

"Trishka has come," murmured the old women ominously. "Beware!"

Ж Ж Ж

As she approached the manor, the strange-looking house loomed menacingly before her, like one of the monsters in Babushka's tales. Zhenya was sure she had made a mistake in consenting to come. Only reluctance to break her promise to Anastasia kept her from running back to the village in panic.

Anastasia was her best friend. Her mother, Anya, was the cook at the mansion. It was common knowledge that Anya was the result of the old master's liaison with a serf-woman. He had died years ago, leaving his estate to his only legitimate child, Praskovia. There were rumors that her late husband had been attracted to his wife's unacknowledged half-sister in the kitchen. Agafya's tongue was among those which sometimes wagged maliciously about Anastasia's parentage. But never when Mikhail was around. Anya's husband, Pyotr, was his good friend. Nor did Ekaterina join Agafya's gossip – even when Mikhail wasn't around. Ekaterina and Anya were not close friends, but they got along better than the two sisters-in-law did.

Zhenya didn't like Agafya very much, either. She disliked her cousin, Marfa, even more. Marfa, too, had been born in the year of the Emancipation, not long after Zhenya, but there all similarity ended. Marfa was plain, dull, stubborn, and sullenly unimaginative. And while she was not a mean child, she occasionally displayed flashes of her mother's waspish disposition. Zhenya did her best to be kind and loyal, but she was always glad when Marfa was not around.

Anastasia was not like Marfa. She wasn't like anyone in Derevnia. She walked too gracefully, her manners were too refined, and she wore her plain, peasant clothing with too much style. Agafya and Marfa complained that she put on airs, but Zhenya knew that pretense was not part of Anastasia's character.

Though Zhenya liked being with Anastasia, she was not eager to visit the manor house where her friend spent so much time. But finally, one night, she agreed to help serve a dinner party there. Anya had promised her some of the left-overs, describing them so temptingly she was unable to resist.

Once inside the mansion, Zhenya was too nervous to notice much. Dinner was served in the garden, in a log gazebo vaguely resembling an *izba*. Praskovia Nikolaevna, mistress of the house, was wearing a plain dark-brown dress and a head-scarf like Babushka's. She and her guests ate truffles off crude pottery, and drank champagne out of wooden cups only slightly fancier than those Mikhail made.

"This isn't exactly what I was expecting," said Zhenya later, holding up one of the cups she was washing.

Anya and Anastasia burst out laughing.

"It's not what they're used to, either," said Anya.

"It's the latest fashion, these days, to act like peasants," added Anastasia.

After the kitchen was clean, Anastasia dragged Zhenya – on tiptoe – to the door of the parlor and made her peek in. At first, she was too scared to see anything. But then, just as she was about to withdraw her head and bolt for the relative security of the kitchen, her eyes fastened on a most amazing sight. Praskovia Nikolaevna was holding a *book* in her hands, and she was *reading*!

In Zhenya's world, only priests read, and all they read was the Bible. Her ears strained, and soon made out that Praskovia Nikolaevna was *not* reading the Bible. To her enormous surprise, Zhenya recognized a story similar to those Babushka told. But the words were put together like nothing she had ever heard. They danced and sang, and made her want to laugh and cry. In them she heard the river singing and the wind blowing through the tall grass, she saw the trembling leaves of the lindens and smelled their fragrant blossoms, she felt sleighs flying over moon-soaked snow to the end of the earth.

Zhenya thought of nothing else for days. Finally, she went back to the manor house with Anastasia. When everyone else was busy, she slipped quietly into the empty parlor and looked carefully for the book with the magical words. But it was nowhere to be seen. She went back into the kitchen and burst into tears.

Anastasia had never seen her cry. *She* was usually the one who did that. But between sobs, she was at length able to piece together the cause of Zhenya's despair.

"Come with me!" Anastasia held out her hand with a sudden smile.

Through a veritable labyrinth of rooms and corridors, Anastasia confidently led her trembling friend. Finally they entered a room so strange, Zhenya could not at first even guess what it was. In the middle was a large table, around which were several leather-cushioned chairs. On the walls were floor-to-ceiling shelves. And on the shelves… no, it wasn't possible. Her eyes went from the few books on the table to all those lining the shelves, then back to the table again. Slowly she approached, carefully reached out her hand, and reverently touched one of the books. Looking at the crowded shelves with awe, the realization of what they held slowly dawned.

"Do you suppose," she asked in wonder, "that all these books tell different stories?"

"Of course," Anastasia replied breezily. "The gentry don't like to have things the same. They get bored too easily."

"I wonder where it is – the book she was reading the other night."

"I don't know," shrugged Anastasia. "I guess you'll have to learn to read to find it."

Zhenya had left that marvelous room reluctantly, with Anastasia's words ringing sadly in her ears. Only boys learned to read – and only a few of them, at that. Father Igor would never consent to teach her, even if she could somehow convince her family.

Then she remembered Praskovia Nikolaevna. *She* could read. But how did she learn? Who taught her? True, she was gentry. But she was still a woman. If it was possible for her…

It was in this state of mind that Zhenya heard about the stranger. From Anastasia she learned that his name was Pavel Vladimirich and that, despite his strange behavior, he was a very nice young man. A little crazy maybe, but nothing to be afraid of.

And then Anastasia announced that she was going to the new school. Zhenya was shocked, then elated, and then vowed – somehow – to join her.

Ж　Ж　Ж

Zhenya went first to the ear she expected to listen most sympathetically. Babushka was not an indulgent grandmother, but she was a very devoted one. To Zhenya's surprise, Babushka was aghast at what she was proposing, and set herself firmly against it.

For the next week, Zhenya was bombarded by a barrage of baleful pronouncements by her family – and from a steady stream of Derevnians who stopped by to have their say in the matter.

Ekaterina said less than most, and was visibly irritated when Agafya began preaching self-righteously about what properly brought-up girls should – and shouldn't – do. She got so carried away gloating that one night at supper she began to pick at Anya.

"Be silent, you stupid cow!" Mikhail finally roared, his eyes like thunderclouds. "She who sails in shallow water herself is the one who picks quarrels!"

34

Usually, Mikhail resembled a good-natured bear. When he got angry, however, his stocky body seemed much larger than it really was. And when he asserted his will, he somehow looked huge. At such times, not even Babushka opposed him.

He had been strangely silent throughout the entire controversy. The next day, he followed Zhenya to the Volga and sat down beside her in the little grove.

"When I was exploring the great river," he began after a while, "I spent my first winter in Kazan. At one of the big churches there, they heard me sing and said they'd pay me to join their choir. Just imagine!"

He smiled, remembering, his wide mouth disclosing a remarkably full set of teeth which flashed engagingly.

"At the first practice, the director handed out some strange paper covered with lines. Everyone but me seemed to know what it was for, so I pretended I did, too. But I held mine upside-down, so the director asked me to wait after the others left."

Zhenya looked at her father in surprise. She had heard all his stories – she thought – many times. But this one was new.

"He was a fine man, he was. He said my voice was a God-given talent, and that if I could read music – that's what those strange papers were – I could learn more songs to praise God with."

Mikhail paused, his deep-set eyes gazing pensively at the river.

"I remember how I felt when I realized there were such things as musical notes – and that they were written in special symbols – and that by knowing what they meant, I could just look at this magical paper and instantly make all kinds of wonderful music."

Watching her father intently, Zhenya's astonishingly clear eyes were shining like the summer sun on the Volga.

"And when I finally mastered them, when the notes on the paper turned into the song I was singing –" his voice broke. "Ah, Zhenya, my girl, that was the finest day of my life!"

The next night at supper, his bear-like body looming formidably at the head of the table, Mikhail announced that Zhenya was going to the new school.

Babushka turned pale. Agafya got very red in the face. Ekaterina smiled – just a little.

Ж   Ж   Ж

On the first day of school, Zhenya was terrified. She dressed carefully that morning, in her second-best shift and a new *sarafan* her mother had just made for her. It was dyed deep russet-red, a color only Ekaterina knew how to reproduce. No one could match it, and all the women were envious. For once, Zhenya was grateful for the care with which her mother tried to dress her. She even took time to braid her hair straight.

The schoolhouse turned out to be not so frightening after all. Another of the abandoned huts on the manor had been cleaned up and equipped with a chalkboard and a few crude desks. It was comfortingly plain and, as she and Anastasia were the only pupils, just the right size.

Pavel Vladimirich had, by this time, learned how to dress properly. Sometimes he almost looked like a real peasant. That, too, helped. And Anastasia was right. He *was* a very nice man – gentle and patient and very eager for them to learn.

The first day he taught them the alphabet. On the chalkboard he drew several strange-looking symbols. As he pointed to each, he made a different sound, which he had them repeat. After a few times through the list, they grasped that the symbols represented the sounds. Pavel Vladimirich explained that all words were combinations of these sounds, and that when they had learned them they would be ready to read. Then he wrote all the letters on a piece of paper, which he urged them to study.

Zhenya took the precious paper, hands trembling with excitement, and ran home. She finished her chores with amazing speed, and hurried off to the grove by the Volga. To her satisfaction, she was able to remember most of the sounds. She looked at the magical letters and repeated them over and over, until it was finally too dark to see.

At the next lesson, Pavel Vladimirich wrote a word on the board. First he sounded the letters one by one – slowly, then faster, then all at once. When he repeated the process, they did it with him. He wrote several more words on the board, and they spelled them out together.

Then he wrote a new word, and asked Zhenya to spell it out by herself. Her face flushed and she hesitated. Then, encouraged by his smile, she plunged in.

"Zh–e–n–ya. Zh-e-n-ya. Zh-e-n...Zhen-ya. Zhenya... Zhenya!" she almost screamed with delight. "Zhenya! Zhenya!"

His face beaming, Pavel Vladimirich excitedly led her to the blackboard.

"Here!" he said, giving her the chalk and pointing to her name.

She knew what he wanted her to do, but the chalk felt strange in her hand. When she moved it over the board, it screeched horribly. The smile on Pavel

Vladimirich's face changed to a perplexed frown. She tried again, with even worse results. Suddenly, the smile reappeared; he grabbed her hand and pulled her quickly outside.

Taking up a small stick, he wrote "Zhenya" in the dust. He pointed at each of the letters, and she spelled them out. Then he handed her the stick. She nodded and slowly, awkwardly, carved out a recognizable copy underneath. Then another. And another. And another and another and another, each one followed by increasingly excited exclamations from Pavel Vladimirich. Finally the whole yard was full of scribbled "Zhenya's."

Then Pavel Vladimirich, his face a huge smile, took a broom and swept them all away. In the center of the now blank yard, he inscribed a large "Zh" with the handle of the broom. Taking the broom from him, Zhenya neatly carved "enya" next to it and then underscored it with a flourish.

"Hurrah!" yelled Pavel Vladimirich, as he threw the broom into the air and grabbed her hands. And together they danced around the big letters, laughing and shouting. "Zhenya! Zhenya! Zhenya!"

Ж Ж Ж

Lessons progressed rapidly after that. He would ask them for words which described their world; he would write and they would read them. Then he began to ask them simple questions. "When is the grain planted? How do you make sauerkraut? Why do you like Easter?" He would write and they would read their answers. Then they asked *him* questions. "Where do you come from? Why are you here?" He would write and they would read their own questions.

And then he answered them.

"I am from Kazan, a big city north of here. But just like Derevnia, my home is also on the Volga. And my grandfather was a serf, too. So you see, we are not really so different."

"Does your father live in Kazan, too?" asked Anastasia, wondering how Pavel Vladimirich had gotten to be gentry. "What does he do there?"

"He is the Chief Inspector of the schools in Kazan. He started out a schoolteacher and worked his way up. And so I was born a nobleman – but just barely." He laughed, but not enough to disguise the pride in his voice.

"My father told me there's a university in Kazan," said Zhenya, not exactly sure what a university was. "Do you ever go there?"

"Yes, I'm a student there. I listen to lectures by learned men, and read books about science and history and such."

"What's history?"

"It's about what happened in the past."

"Like Babushka's stories?"

"Well, not exactly… But yes, in a way."

"What's science?"

"Knowing about the laws of nature."

"Like Babushka does? She knows all about trees and birds and animals and everything in the forest."

"So your Babushka is a scientist as well as an historian?" smiled Pavel Vladimirich. "Perhaps we should make her a professor at the University."

"No. She can't read," said Zhenya solemnly. "Besides, she'd never leave Derevnia."

"And what about you?" asked Pavel Vladimirich. "Would you ever leave?"

"No," replied Zhenya firmly.

"Why not?"

"Because Derevnia is my home. I don't want to leave."

"Well, *I* do," Anastasia exclaimed.

"And where would you go?" asked Pavel Vladimirich.

"I don't know," she sighed sadly. "But why," her mood changing abruptly, "do your eyes look different?"

For the most part, Pavel Vladimirich was a remarkably ordinary looking man. His features were regular, his body of average height and weight. Nothing about him was unpleasant, but had it not been for his dark, slanted eyes, he would have been easy to overlook. The exotic eyes usually hid behind his glasses, but when he was enthused, they came to life and transformed his plain face. On such occasions, he was almost handsome – and impossible to ignore.

Blushing slightly, Pavel Vladimirich took off the wire-rimmed glasses. "My eyes are like this because my great-grandfather was a Tartar."

"Did he gallop up the frozen river," gasped Zhenya, "and drink mare's milk from human skulls?"

"I doubt it," smiled Pavel Vladimirich. "We don't do that anymore. Nor do any of the Tartars who still live in Kazan."

"Are there lots of them there?" asked Anastasia.

"Oh, yes. And there are several mosques in Kazan, too."

"What's a mosque?"

"A church for Muslims."

"What's a Muslim?"

"Someone who worships God in a different way."

"Like the Old Believers – or the Jews?"

"Yes, something like that."

"Do they believe in Jesus?" asked Anastasia.

"Only as a prophet."

"Do they believe in the Virgin?" asked Zhenya.

"No."

"Oh." Zhenya changed the subject. "Why did your father become a teacher?"

"Someone taught him to read, and he wanted to repay the debt."

"Is that why you're teaching us?"

"Partly."

"Is being a teacher hard?"

"Not when your students want to learn. Maybe someday *you* will become a teacher."

"Me!? But what could *I* teach anyone?"

"You could teach your people how to read. And you could teach *my* people what your Babushka is teaching you."

Zhenya was silent, pondering that.

"Why did you leave Kazan?" asked Anastasia.

"Because I have a mission. Mother Russia is in danger, and only those of her children still close to the soil can save her. So I am here to learn from you and your people – and to teach you how to lead us all to revolution."

"What's revolution?"

"Changing things so that instead of the Tsar ruling the country, the people would – through their communes. A commune, you see, is like choir. In a choir, no voice is lost, but is heard in the harmony of all the voices. And so in the commune, the individual is not lost, but finds himself in the harmonious accord of its brotherhood."

At this point, eyes flashing with enthusiastic zeal, Pavel Vladimirich would often get carried away into realms of ideology too abstract to follow. But even if she did not always understand them, Zhenya loved to listen to his words. Many of them she had never before heard, and the mystery of their meaning was a sweet siren's song.

When they were ready, he brought a book to read. Zhenya held it nervously, fearful she might somehow ruin the wonderful thing in her hands. It was by someone named Turgenev, and about a hunter who roamed forests and fields, telling stories about what he saw. There were many words that Zhenya had never heard, and even the ones she knew were put together in unfamiliar ways. Pavel Vladimirich patiently explained what the new words meant, and helped her relate the new patterns to what she was used to. Gradually the words began to come alive in Zhenya's mind – much like listening to her father's stories.

Zhenya didn't like the shooting parts in Turgenev's book, but the author's feelings about the land were very much like her own. And although he was gentry, most of the people he described were peasants. Many of them reminded her of people in Derevnia. Pavel Vladimirich said that the Tsar himself had read this book, and that he had liked the serfs in it so much he decided to emancipate them.

Zhenya was impressed. That she and the Tsar could actually read the same words and stories! Amazing! And that a book could actually influence those with power on behalf of those with none! Even more amazing!

By the time they finished Turgenev's book, Zhenya had mastered the mechanics of reading. The next book Pavel Vladimirich brought was by a man named Tolstoy, and was about Napoleon's invasion of Russia. To Zhenya's dismay, it was very thick and very long. She was sure she would never finish it. There were even more new words, and the sentences were much longer, and the people in it often talked for pages and pages about things that didn't exist. Pavel Vladimirich said it was called philosophy, and that she would understand it better when she got older.

Even so, there were other problems. Turgenev's book was about country life and peasants and the land; Tolstoy wrote about cities and rich nobles and powerful rulers. Zhenya found it difficult – and frightening – to relate to these foreign worlds and their people. Turgenev's stories took place in the here and now, and didn't go anywhere – like life in Derevnia. Tolstoy's book happened years ago – and in a world that was constantly changing. The idea of past tense was certainly not new to Zhenya. But the past on which village traditions were founded was one that assumed past, present and future were a seamless, unchanging whole. Just as today was the same as yesterday, so tomorrow would be no different. In Tolstoy's book, today often bore little resemblance to yesterday. Zhenya found that idea unnerving. What was even harder to grasp was that Tolstoy seemed to believe that people influenced their tomorrows by what they did today.

Eventually, however, she found some common ground. There were peasants, too, in the huge book, many of whom Tolstoy obviously held in high regard. And he, too, loved the land. As she read on, she began to see that even the richest nobles had something in common with the people of her village. They all laughed and cried, sang and danced – and were born and died. She found herself admiring some of Tolstoy's characters, and despising others – just like in Derevnia. And by connecting to the ones she liked, she traveled to places and times far away from her village on the Volga – much as she did when listening to Babushka's stories.

Zhenya worked hard at understanding Tolstoy's heavy book. Laboriously she divided the long sentences up into smaller parts, and tried to remember what the big words meant. Eventually, with Pavel Vladimirich's help, she was able to translate enough of it into simpler language to say that she had read it. She still did not understand the philosophical discussions, and she did not like the battle scenes, but she knew that she was much bigger inside for having journeyed with Tolstoy. And she knew that someday she would read it again – and again.

Next, they read poetry.

"The poet is a sublime being," said Pavel Vladimirich, taking off his glasses. His eyes leaped out of hiding and lit up his plain face. "An instrument of God, he is privy to mysteries denied to ordinary mortals."

Zhenya was not so sure about that, but she loved the way the poets made words sing – even though she didn't always understand what they meant. And then one day, eyes aglow, Pavel Vladimirich recited from a book which flew right to her heart. She listened, enthralled, to the effervescent beauty of the lilting lines, shimmering like a butterfly's wings. She marvelled at the music and movement, measure and harmony, and wondered how so few words could say so much.

As Pavel Vladimirich read on, Zhenya felt a tremor of excitement shake her soul. These wonderful singing, dancing words were somehow familiar. She had heard them before – not the exact words, but the strangely thrilling way in which they were put together.

"What is it?" she finally exploded.

Pavel Vladimirich stopped reading, a quizzical look on his face.

"The book you're reading," she pointed impatiently, "who wrote it?"

"See for yourself," he said, handing it to her.

"P-u-sh, Push...k-i-n, kin... Push-kin. Pushkin! Who was he?" she asked, holding the book tightly.

"The greatest of all Russian poets," replied Pavel Vladimirich, eyes blazing. "He gave us an image of ourselves as Russians – full of grace and warmth and generosity of spirit, just as he was."

"Where does he live?" asked Anastasia.

"Alas, he is dead. Pushkin savored life. He lived hard and died young – in a duel."

"What was the duel about?"

"A woman."

"Ah!" said Anastasia, her eyes lighting up. "Was he handsome?"

"No, not really, but he was very charming. They say he made all women feel captivating. Few were able to resist him."

Anastasia smiled, trying to look captivating.

"But Pushkin was much more than that," Pavel Vladimirich continued. "He was a free spirit who dared to spoof even the Tsar – and who believed individual freedom must be preserved if life is to have dignity."

"Individual freedom?" asked Anastasia, suddenly serious. "What do you mean?"

"Doing what *you* think is right, rather than what others say you must."

"But what if everyone thinks you're wrong?"

"That is why individual freedom must be respected – to protect your rights."

"But what if everyone else is right?" interjected Zhenya. "None of us can do as we please. If we didn't obey the rules, what would happen to Derevnia?"

"But what if they're wrong?" asked Pavel Vladimirich. "What happens then?"

When the lesson ended, Zhenya was still clutching the Pushkin book.

"Would you like to borrow it?" asked Pavel Vladimirich, smiling.

"Oh, yes!" Zhenya gasped eagerly. "Thank you, thank you!"

She ran all the way home, did her chores with lightening speed, and tore off to her grove on the Volga.

And there, day after day, whenever she could grab some time to herself, she read Pushkin to the Volga. The soaring words blended with the dark, eternal music of the river into a new and wonderful song. And as Zhenya felt it fill her soul, she knew that tomorrow could never be the same as yesterday.

Ж   Ж   Ж

"I caught the cat eating another egg in the chicken coop today," said Agafya at the supper table. "That's what happens when the eggs aren't gathered every-day."

Zhenya said nothing, knowing that the remark was intended for her.

"But I suppose some people have more important things to do," Agafya continued, "than tend to their chores." She looked pointedly at Zhenya.

"I always do my chores," Zhenya said quietly.

"Then why aren't the eggs being collected everyday?!" demanded Agafya.

"I said I always do *my* chores," retorted Zhenya, her face flushing. "But I don't have time to do Marfa's, too, anymore. I *do* have more important things to do!"

"And what's *that* supposed to mean?"

"Ask Marfa."

"Marfa?" Agafya shifted her angry glance.

Marfa hung her head.

"Well?"

"I don't like chickens," mumbled Marfa. "They scare me."

"So you've been taking her turn, too? How nice of you, Zhenya!" interjected Ekaterina sweetly.

"But now you're too busy for Christian charity, it seems," rejoined Agafya hastily, somewhat abashed. "That's what comes of hanging around with that Trishka from the city."

"Pavel Vladimirich is not the Antichrist!" snapped Zhenya.

"No, of course not," Agafya smiled sarcastically. "He's too stupid."

"He's not stupid!" Zhenya said angrily. "He went to the University, and he knows many wonderful things!"

"Then why is he here?" shot back Agafya.

"I say he's here to make trouble!" Foma burst out. "I think he's one of those people who want to shoot the Tsar!"

"Pavel Vladimirich is not a terrorist!" Zhenya said heatedly. "He's a *narodnik*!"

"What's the difference!?" replied Foma. "They're all trouble-makers, with their talk of revolution!"

"But the *narodniki* want to change things peacefully," Zhenya argued, "by going to the people and teaching them."

"What could the likes of him possibly teach us?" queried Babushka skeptically.

"Well – maybe how to change the Tsar's laws."

"What good would that do?" snorted Babushka. "It's tradition that rules our lives – not the Tsar's laws."

Zhenya had no answer for that. For awhile, everyone ate in silence.

"Marfa has made so many embroidered shirts this year," Agafya started in again. "They should bring a good price at the market in Simbirsk, don't you think, Ekaterina?"

"Yes, I'm sure they will," replied Ekaterina evenly, knowing what was coming.

"And how many will you be sending?" asked Agafya, looking maliciously at Zhenya.

"None," mumbled Zhenya, blushing.

"What a pity you don't have Marfa's skill with a needle," oozed Agafya nastily. "It's so important for a girl, isn't it, Marfa?"

"Yes, indeed," Marfa giggled unpleasantly. "How else can a girl have a suitable trousseau when she marries... *if* she marries. Though I can't imagine anyone wanting to marry a girl who reads."

"Perhaps you could help Zhenya with her trousseau anyway," continued Agafya, dripping sarcasm. "Just in case."

"I'd be glad to teach Zhenya something *useful*." Marfa's tone aped her mother's. "That is, if she can tear herself away from her precious books."

"Words are more useful than your silly embroidery!" flashed Zhenya. "When the Great Poet, Alexander Pushkin, died, the Tsar himself wept and paid all his debts and gave a big pension to his widow and children!"

In spite of herself, even Agafya looked impressed.

"And besides," Zhenya shouted, standing up suddenly, "I can knit better than you can!"

And with that, she ran angrily out of the *izba*.

Zhenya was still crying when Babushka appeared at the grove and sat down quietly beside her.

Zhenya looked up, surprised. Babushka never came to the river. Now, however, she put a comforting arm around Zhenya's shoulders.

"Agafya is a fool," she said finally. "Pay no attention to her."

"But she's not alone in feeling as she does," sniffed Zhenya. "I'm afraid they'll drive him away."

"Is he so important to you?"

"What he's teaching me is."

"More important than what I've taught you?"

"No, of course not." Zhenya was silent, and then looked at Babushka, her clear gaze probing the warm darkness of her grandmother's eyes. "Is that what you think?"

"It's not just the chickens you've been avoiding," sighed Babushka. "When was the last time we went to the forest together?"

"Oh, Babushka," Zhenya squeezed the old woman's hand. "Im sorry. I didn't mean to hurt you."

"I know you didn't, child. That's not what's worrying me. I'm afraid this fascinating stranger is going to lure you away from us."

"But I could *never* leave Derevnia! It's my home."

"Then why must you read his books? What can they tell you about living here?"

"It's hard to explain." Zhenya hugged her knees and gazed out over the Volga. "But it's something like how I feel about the river. Sitting here, listening to Her sing, I feel connected to the whole world – and bigger inside my soul. Reading is like that – only in my mind."

"And someday, will you grow too big and go off on the river – like your father?"

"No. I have no need to go anywhere, not when Mother Volga – and these books – bring the world here. Besides, Father came back."

"True. But he was never the same."

"Is that so terrible?"

Now it was Babushka's turn to be silent.

"You love the river, just as your father does," she began again, slowly. "I respect Mother Volga, but I fear Her, too. She has brought too many invaders who destroy the life we labor so hard to preserve. I fear this stranger may be one of them."

"But Babushka, he's a kind man – a gentle man. He doesn't want to harm us!"

"*He* may not want to hurt us – but what about his ideas? All he talks about is changing things. We live by *Rodina*'s ways, by what we learned from our grandmothers and our grandmothers' grandmothers – what I have tried to teach you. He wants to destroy all that."

"No, Babushka, he doesn't want to destroy our traditions. He respects our ways and wants to learn from us."

"But he thinks *his* ways are better!"

"I don't know. Maybe. But *I* don't think so. I just think that *some* of his ideas could make life here better."

"Tradition is what makes our village work," Babushka shook her head dubiously. "Tinker with it too much and people lose their balance."

"But Babushka, the world out there is changing. And we must change, too, if we are to survive."

"Perhaps you're right," the old woman sighed. "In any case, I fear that the invaders have already landed – and it's too late to hide in the forest."

Ж   Ж   Ж

At the end of the lesson, Pavel Vladimirich cleared his throat self-consciously.

"This will be our last class," he said, his dark brown eyes drooping mournfully behind his glasses. "Tomorrow I must return to Kazan."

Anastasia emitted a small, strangled gasp.

"I want you both to know how much teaching you has meant to me," he continued, clearing his throat again. "You are good students, and I hope you will continue to learn with what I have taught you."

"It's Derevnia, isn't it!" Anastasia burst out angrily. "They're driving you away!"

Pavel Vladimirich looked at her sadly and said nothing.

"I'll never forget you," said Anastasia, her voice choking.

"Nor I, you," he murmured softly.

Anastasia stood up suddenly, kissed his cheek, and then ran sobbing out of the little schoolhouse.

"What she said – it's true?" asked Zhenya, after a short silence.

"More or less," he sighed. "Though I suppose I have been more fortunate here than many of my friends in other villages. Some of them have been arrested – and worse. I have merely been ignored."

"Not really," said Zhenya gently. "They're just pretending not to notice you."

"And their silence," he replied bitterly, "is more cruel than persecution." For the first time, Zhenya saw anger in his beautiful, gentle eyes.

"I'm sorry."

"I came with such high hopes. There was so much I wanted to do here. I could have helped them so much!" He bowed his head. "But they didn't want what I tried to give."

"*I* did," Zhenya said softly.

He raised his head and looked at her.

"Thank you," she said simply. "I know that's not enough, but I don't know how to say more…"

"No, no," he said quickly, "it is I who should be thanking you. Because of you, my time here has not been wasted."

"The others... they're just afraid."

"But why? 'These peasants are people!' That's what I came here thinking. I leave disillusioned. *These people are peasants!* And I don't understand them."

"They have always been like this."

"But they can't stay this way! For their own good – for Russia's sake – they must somehow grow beyond where they are."

"Father says that virgin soil must be worked, not with a shallow plow," Zhenya said thoughtfully, "but with one that raises the depths."

"I wish," smiled Pavel Vladimirich pensively, "that your father and I could have known each other."

"You did," replied Zhenya. "Through me."

"Yes, of course," he said slowly, after looking at her for a long time. "And perhaps you will be that plow which raises the depths."

Zhenya nodded, soberly reflective. "What will you do now?"

"I'm not sure. Some of my friends are turning to terrorism... But I don't think that's for me. I think perhaps I will return to the University and study law."

"So that you can change it?"

"Something like that. Maybe, in Russia, revolution must come from the top down rather than the bottom up."

He stood up and reached into his desk. "Praskovia Nikolaevna promised me you could use her library. But when you can't get there, this is for you."

Zhenya took the book with trembling hands. It was a thick volume, with crisp new pages and bound in sturdy red leather. Opening the cover, she saw that it contained the poetry of Alexander Pushkin. Gently, she pressed it to her heart and looked at him, tears flooding her clear, guileless eyes. A tear slowly trickling down his own cheek, Pavel Vladimirich kissed her gratefully on the forehead.

Ж   Ж   Ж

After Pavel Vladimirich left, Zhenya spent as much time as possible with her book in the Volga grove. Except for Anastasia, she spoke to no one.

At last, not long before Easter, Mikhail appeared there and sat down beside her. Neither spoke, as they watched the river in silence.

"Mother Volga seems eager for Spring," said Mikhail finally, trying to sound nonchalant.

"Yes," replied Zhenya, politely.

Silence.

"It will be good to eat your mother's *paskha* again. She's such a good cook."

"Yes."

More silence.

"In the cities I visited," Mikhail tried again, "it was the custom for the people to read the scriptures on Easter Eve."

Zhenya gave him a quick sidelong glance.

"I've convinced Father Igor that we, too, should start practicing this fine old custom – now that we have some people who can read."

Zhenya turned slowly and looked up at her father. The high rounded cheeks and high broad forehead, the crinkling eyes and wide nose curving cheerfully to a slightly tilted point – it was impossible to resist such an open, generous face.

In her eyes a small smile broke through, like sun on the Volga after a storm. Relieved, Mikhail squeezed her hand.

"And now," he said, standing up, "come help your mother with the *paskha*."

On Easter Eve, about an hour before midnight, Zhenya came forward and stood behind the lectern. Looking out over the crowded church, she felt a fleeting moment of terror. Then, remembering Pavel Vladimirich, she began to read from the large Bible before her. Soon she was lost in the passionate journey of Jesus to his cross. By the time Mary Magdalene had discovered the empty tomb, Zhenya felt that she, too, was there, searching for the risen saviour.

She looked up and saw the rapt faces of her neighbors, many with tears in their eyes. Her family was standing near the choir loft, as always. There was Agafya, trying unsuccessfully to cover her scowl with a look of piety, and Marfa, jealousy and boredom doing battle on her blunt face. Next to them was Foma, impassive as usual. Then Zhenya caught Babushka's eye and saw approval. Ekaterina was smiling with pride. And up in the choir loft was Mikhail, his beaming smile as big as his beard.

As she felt Spring about to burst forth, Zhenya thought of Pavel Vladimirich – and then forgave her people.

Chapter 3: The CHURCH

"In Siberia, even the mosquitos are big as buzzards!" exclaimed Andrei proudly. "And riding along the road at night, little gleams of light seem to come from tiny huts in the forest. But no, it's the wolves, watching and waiting."

Andrei the Icon-maker was Mikhail's best friend. He had grown up in Siberia, and Zhenya loved to listen to him talk about it.

"Sometimes a sound like thunder echoes through the forest!" Zhenya's eyes grew wide, as Andrei roared. "The Siberian tiger, stalking his territory. Biggest cats in the world! Bigger even than me!"

And Andrei was a big man, tall and broad-shouldered, with high cheekbones and enormous fists. His voice matched his physique and the terrain from which he sprang; deep and sonorous, its dark rounded vowels boomed big and open as Siberia itself. In their cups together, Mikhail and Andrei were fond of rumbling about Derevnia in earth-shaking duet – loud enough to raise the dead, said the village proudly.

Andrei was different. He always addressed everyone as an equal, no matter who they were. He never fawned, not even on those regarded by everyone else as superiors. "In Siberia there is plenty of land for all," he explained proudly. "Everyone owns their land, but nobody ever owned anyone else. All is from God and for the people."

Siberia was a wild, untamed frontier. Notorious as a place of penal servitude and exile, it was also a refuge for religious dissidents, a haven for runaway serfs, an opportunity for adventurers. The vast, undeveloped expanse of the Siberian wilderness breathed a spirit of rugged freedom into the sparse settlements which dotted its rigorous landscape. Those stalwart enough to withstand its unyielding climate were a unique breed.

"People come from all over. Every kind you can imagine, all together in one place. But they're too busy trying to stay alive," Andrei laughed, "to fight each other."

In his youth, Andrei had been seized by the urge to go wandering. What started out a relatively brief pilgrimage to the tomb of St. Innocent of Irkutsk was prolonged by tantalizing tales of the wonder-working icons of Moscow. Andrei slowly made his way to the great cathedrals of the Kremlin, and there discovered the magnificent art of Russia's great painters. The glorious icons went straight to his soul, and he vowed that someday he, too, would praise God in such fashion. And so, for several years, Andrei wandered throughout Russia, paying homage to all the great icons and searching out those skilled in painting them.

In his threadbare grey coat and worn felt boots, Andrei joined the ragged stream of pilgrims who were a familiar sight on any Russian road. With their staffs and knapsacks, they were accorded hospitality everywhere as a matter of course. In return for a crust of bread and a dry place to sleep, they edified their hosts with stories about their sojourning. From all rungs of society, pilgrims took to the road for many reasons – to expiate a crime, to fulfill a vow, to render thanks to God. Year after year, they trudged across the country in search of spiritual guidance, waiting endlessly at cells of revered elders and priests. Some pilgrims were quite peculiar, dressing eccentrically and discoursing in garbled, jerky phrases. No one, however, looked askance at even the strangest of them.

Andrei's quest was not altogether unique. Some monasteries and churches kept cells especially for icon-painters. Andrei learned much from the masters who occupied them; often they invited him to share their quarters. His education as an artist took him to Yaroslavl, Vladimir, Pskov, Novgorod – all centers of various icon-painting schools. He also spent much time studying the great masterpieces at the Novodevichy Convent in Moscow, the St. Sergius Monastery in Zagorsk, and the Cathedrals in the Moscow Kremlin.

Early on in his artistic quest, Andrei found a spiritual mentor. Of all the icons encountered, none moved him more deeply than those of Andrei Rublev, famed artist of the 15th century. To contemplate his work was to see the loftiest qualities human beings could attain. And when Andrei himself began to paint, he, too, tried to create introspective icon-images of noble spiritual purity. Painstakingly he attempted to replicate the prominent, pondering brows which rose dome-like over the ascetically sculpted cheeks and the bearded jutting chins. With infinite care, he endeavored to copy the straight, narrow noses which swept unswervingly to a benevolent point, and the long, slender fingers raised in perpetual benediction. With arduous patience, he struggled to portray the compassionate depths of the big, mournful eyes. Into all his efforts, he poured his own intense inner life, so characteristic of the pilgrims who wandered from one end of Russia to the other.

When Andrei could think of no more places to go and learn, he decided to return to Siberia to practice his craft. En route he stopped to visit his uncle, the parish priest in Derevnia. There he met Natasha – and decided to stay. Natasha was of a long line of house-serfs specially trained as dancers for the amusement of the gentry. Watching her dance in the village festivals was something no one ever forgot. Unlike most of the village women, she was slender and supple as a young tree. And from her laughing dark eyes to her magically skipping feet, she was a marvel of moving music. Every man in Derevnia wanted her – but she chose Andrei.

The enmity the others might have felt toward an outsider winning the prize was partially offset by his being the priest's nephew. Mostly, though, his almost immediate acceptance was due to his skill as an icon-maker. Icons were thought to perform miracles. Anyone who could create them was obviously valuable to have around.

Soon after his marriage, Andrei began to paint the iconostasis of the village church. Eventually it came to be rather famous in the region. A double tier of rugged-looking Siberian saints with sensitive Rublev-esque faces and brooding introspective eyes gazed out over the worshipers. The effect was quite startling.

It was while he was painting the iconostasis that Andrei and Mikhail became friends. It did not take them long to discover they had much in common. As he watched Andrei paint, Mikhail recognized a kindred soul; and as he listened to Mikhail sing, Andrei heard what he was painting in his icons.

When he finished the iconostasis, Andrei began painting household icons. Soon every *izba* in Derevnia had at least one in its icon corner. When Mikhail married Ekaterina, Andrei presented them with a copy of the *Virgin of Vladimir*, one of the most famous icons in all of Russia. Always it occupied the place of honour in the icon corner of their *izba*. And always, before she went to bed, Zhenya said her prayers gazing into the sad, knowing eyes of the Virgin.

Ж　Ж　Ж

"No, no, NO! That's not it. Here, listen again." Mikhail sang the brief song slowly and carefully, trying to keep the exasperation out of his voice. Vaslav opened his mouth and began singing enthusiastically. Soon, however, his thin, reedy voice wandered away from the simple melody. Sighing, Mikhail turned to Vsevelod, whose loud, startling voice barked out a rendition not even close to the original. Throwing up his hands in despair, Mikhail stormed out of the house, leaving his sons in tears.

Almost as soon as they could walk, Mikhail had begun singing to them. They had gurgled back agreeably, but eventually it became apparent that neither had inherited his father's voice. Doggedly, Mikhail persevered with the singing lessons. Despite his resolve to be patient, the unpleasant scenes multiplied. Stubbornly, he refused to admit that neither of his sons could carry a tune.

Finally, Ekaterina convinced him that it was hopeless. The boys were relieved; the usually ebullient Mikhail was morose for months. And then one day, he heard Zhenya singing at the butter churn. He listened for awhile, and then abruptly interrupted her. He sang pitches for her to match, phrases for her to imitate, songs for her to repeat. To his growing excitement, she passed all his tests effortlessly.

"Why didn't you sing sooner?" he demanded.

"I've been singing all my life," replied Zhenya.

"Then why have I never heard you?"

"You were too busy listening to the boys."

From that day on, Zhenya went to choir practice with her father. Mikhail was an exacting choirmaster, directing primarily with his remarkably mobile face, whose bushy hooked eyebrows often seemed to have a life of their own. Poor intonation, in particular, was likely to set off especially vehement gyrations. Under the energetic tutelage of those agile brows, Zhenya and the other singers learned to build resonant chords on the impeccably tuned bass notes laid down by Mikhail's infallible ear, and to match the timbre of his ringing voice. Their little choir consequently sounded much larger than it was.

And reading music, Zhenya discovered, was almost as exciting as reading books. How many marvelous ways to pray in song! How wonderful to join the melodious notes to the beautiful liturgy! How much bigger she felt inside singing in harmony with others! And how much deeper the words resounded as her voice grew into a full, rich contralto.

Singing in the choir not only gave Zhenya a different perspective on religion; it also caused her to spend more time in church.

Of the many children born to Andrei and Natasha, two sturdy sons had survived childhood. Both were serious and pious, and early on had stated their intention of entering the priesthood. When they came home on vacation from the seminary, they, too, spent much time in the church. And so it was that Zhenya became friends with these two rather mysterious young men.

It was Grigori who first struck up a conversation. They talked about Tolstoy, whom he, too, had read. Or rather, Grigori made learned-sounding observations and Zhenya nodded. After awhile, she decided that he probably hadn't understood it all, either.

Summoning her courage, she then asked about the seminary. Grigori told her that, in addition to the usual secondary-school subjects, they studied theology and Church history, the Old and New Testament scriptures, Latin and Church Slavonic. And, of course, they were learning all the complexities of Church liturgy firsthand. He complained that they went to church morning and night, keeping all-night vigil on the eve of all the Feasts.

It was at this point that Ivan spoke up. In a gently authoritative voice which did not appear to rebuke his older brother, he made it clear that he, for one, did not object to attending church so much.

"After all," he said solemnly, "that's why we're there."

"True, little brother," Grigori laughed, "but I wish the good Fathers would give us just a little more time to see Kazan." Grigori then launched into an enthusiastic description of the wonders of the city, to which Zhenya listened avidly.

On another occasion, the brothers told her about a pilgrimage the seminary students had just made to the famous Monastery at Zagorsk founded by Saint Sergius. This time it was Ivan who did most of the talking.

"It is the most beautiful place in the world," he said with serious enthusiasm. "White churches with blue and golden domes in the middle of a huge forest! And the singing! And the bells! Surely God must dwell there! You can *feel* what a holy place it is!"

As Ivan spoke, Zhenya began to notice how much he resembled his father's icons. Deep-set compassionate eyes, burning with a quiet inner light, looked out of a sensitive, ascetic face remarkably like those painted on the walls of the church.

Soon, Ivan began to start the conversations, sometimes even without Grigori. One night, after choir practice, he confided his concern that many of the seminarians were lacking in piety. "How will they ever be good pastors?" he worried. "As St. Paul says, we must 'be an example to the believers in word, charity, spirit, faith, and purity!'"

On another occasion, as they were watching Andrei retouch the beard of one of the Siberian-looking saints, Ivan told her that his favorite was St. Serafim of Sarov. "One of the Fathers at the seminary says that he is much like the Catholic St. Francis of Assisi," he said, thoughtfully. "But I think he must be more, because he is Russian."

"'God is like a fire that warms the heart and the belly,'" quoted Zhenya. She, too, was partial to St. Serafim, and had read of him with admiration.

Ivan nodded at her, his beautiful, unassuming smile slowly lighting up his face. "'Stand with your mind in your heart,'" he quoted back, "'to warm knowledge with the warmth of your heart, so that we may arrive at peaceful order and complete unity.'"

Then Zhenya remembered that St. Serafim had become a religious hermit. She felt a small thud in the pit of her stomach.

One afternoon, Zhenya volunteered to clean the baptismal font. Ivan was already there, his long slender fingers gracefully filling the icon-lamps.

"Have you ever met any unbelievers in Kazan?" Zhenya asked, breaking the silence as they worked.

"Alas, yes," he sighed. "Unfortunately, there has been a steady loss of faith in educated circles."

"But why?"

"I think it started when Tsar Peter put the Church under the thumb of the government," he replied, thinking aloud. "And many of his reforms drove wedges between the Church and the rest of Russia."

"How did he do that?"

"Well – take language, for instance. For everyone else, he made the alphabet simpler. But the Church continued using Church Slavonic. Have you ever noticed that Father Igor has a rather peculiar accent? And that he uses a lot of archaic expressions no one else does? Most of the priests at the seminary talk the same way. I even catch myself doing it, sometimes."

Zhenya smiled, thinking Ivan's slightly peculiar mode of speech quite charming.

"I think that, in some ways, the Church has stagnated," Ivan continued earnestly, "and that it needs some changing."

"Maybe you can do something about that when you become a priest?"

"I hope so – though I'm not sure how far the government would let us go. Anyway," he shrugged, "I'd have to be a bishop to make any real change."

"Would you like to be a bishop?"

"Perhaps." Ivan snuffed out a candle. "But you have to become a monk, first."

Zhenya felt a small dark cloud pass over her heart.

The next day, Ivan went back to the seminary. She did not see him again for almost a year.

It was the Feast Day of the Nativity of the Blessed Virgin. From the choir loft, Zhenya looked out over the crowded congregation. Abruptly her scanning eyes stopped and fastened on Ivan, standing near the back of the Church. He had sprouted a beard, and his face was nothing like the sensitive countenance she remembered so fondly. And the way he was staring at her was most definitely *not* how icons looked. Embarrassed, she averted her eyes. A sharp twitch of Mikhail's left eyebrow warned her that her voice was straying from the pitch. Hastily she returned her glance to the music the choir was singing in honor of the Virgin. But her eyes kept wandering back to Ivan, and every time they did, she saw that he was still staring.

She encountered him often during the next few weeks, usually at church. It was like meeting a stranger. Gone was the easy ecclesiastical repartee; gone was the comfortable confiding. Whenever she spoke to him, he mumbled and looked away, blushing. But wherever she went, his dark eyes – blazing with something that made her intensely uncomfortable – seemed always to follow.

Zhenya was furious. Angrily, she swept up billowing clouds with her broom. The chickens ran clucking out of her path. And when she milked the cow, the poor creature mooed painfully.

Ekaterina finally had a talk with her. In tears, Zhenya poured out her frustration. "We used to be such good friends," she wailed. "And now he acts like a stupid lout! What's the matter with him?!"

"Go look at yourself," Ekaterina burst out laughing, "and see!"

Zhenya stopped sobbing and looked at her mother in surprise.

"You've grown up a lot this year," Ekaterina said, gently smoothing back the hair that perennially escaped from her daughter's braid. "You aren't a child anymore."

Wiping her eyes, Zhenya walked slowly to the little grove by the Volga, and stopped by the small pond next to it. There was no wind, and the water was calm as a mirror. She looked thoughtfully at the reflection which gazed up at her, trying to see herself as he did. With a shock, she began to realize what her mother meant.

Who was this tall young woman staring up at her? The sturdy limbs suddenly round beckoned enticingly; the curved hips and ripe breasts swayed urgently, like an unharvested field. The face, too, was different, its well-shaped contours more pronounced and its planes stronger. The high cheekbones were more prominent; so was the wide nose whose swooping outward curve ended in a slightly upward point. The mouth was wider, with full lips that whispered provocatively. And underscoring the broader, higher forehead were gracefully hooked eyebrows that danced beguilingly.

The new face was framed by the same dark brown hair, but the rebellious wisps slipping out of the long thick braid now shone with glints of gold. Only the eyes were still familiar. Translucently clear, the color of the Volga, they looked up at her – as always – with utter honesty and without a trace of guile. But there was something in them that had not been there before.

Her mother was right. She wasn't a child anymore. Slowly, she raised her hand and sadly waved farewell to the child she had been. The strange young woman waved back, excited anticipation mingling with more than a trace of apprehension.

Ж   Ж   Ж

Zhenya held up the linen towel, eyed it critically and decided that the tree she was embroidering needed another leaf. Around her in a large circle sat all the marriageable girls in Derevnia, each diligently stitching brightly-colored birds and lions, flowers and horses, suns and moons and stars. Since Epiphany, they had gathered every night to work on their trousseau. Behind them sat their mothers, supervising the traditional designs and sharing woman's lore handed down to them by their own mothers years before.

Many of the women were sharing their second-best recipes, in hopes that Ekaterina would disclose the secret of the deep russet hue she always wore. Except for the color, Ekaterina's clothes were scrupulously plain, cut exactly as custom dictated, and sewn carefully with evenly spaced stitches of uniform length. A clean, crisply-tied kerchief covered her thick brown hair which, to Zhenya's amazement, always seemed content to stay in place.

Ekaterina was knitting as she listened, her capable hands moving rhythmically with spare, economical motions. In the knitting basket at her feet were three symmetrical balls of yarn of exactly the same size, an extra set of knitting needles, two wooden stitch holders, four yarn bobbins, and a small cutting knife. All were comfortably lined up in precise but effortless order, readily at hand whenever she reached for them.

"Give your man a hot cup of my special tea after dinner," one of the mothers was bragging, "and he'll never go off to the tavern."

"That's because you slip some vodka into it," laughed one of the others.

"Only a fool keeps vodka in her kitchen," said Anya mildly. "Why ask for trouble that comes often enough as it is?"

"Men are men," shrugged Agafya sourly, "with or without vodka."

"Only if you argue with them," said Ekaterina, in a quiet tone which somehow commanded everyone's attention.

"You mean we're supposed to give in to them?" Anastasia was skeptical.

"Of course not," replied Ekaterina matter-of-factly. "Just smile and go about your business without a fuss."

"And let them *think* you've given in," laughed Anya.

"Exactly." Ekaterina loosed one of her remarkable smiles, suffusing her face with a combination of charming righteousness and confident benevolence difficult to resist.

"But that doesn't work," objected a woman sitting across the room, "when they've got something on their mind."

"Something in their pants, you mean!" The woman next to her rolled her eyes.

"The bigger the better!" smirked Agafya.

"But then our bellies get bigger, too," worried Anya.

"What else are women for?" Agafya's voice had a nasty edge.

"Women should sometimes let their fields lie fallow," Ekaterina interjected evenly, "so that they do not exhaust the earth."

"'Be fruitful and multiply!'" retorted Agafya irritably.

"But not on Fastdays," Ekaterina pronounced cheerfully. "How wise the Holy Virgin was, persuading the church fathers to decree so many of them!"

Her mother, Zhenya noted proudly, usually had the last word on these matters.

Next to Zhenya sat Anastasia, embroidering a towel with designs no one had ever seen before. More of these exquisite but decidedly untraditional patterns adorned her immaculately white shift, over which an unusually fashioned sky-blue *sarafan* clung gracefully to her slender body. Anastasia's breasts and hips had also bloomed, and her silver-blond hair crowned a pale, delicately featured face now flushed with excitement. In the room full of women sturdy as trees, Anastasia was a fragile blossom, a high-strung thoroughbred in a herd of draft horses.

Across the room was Marfa, who had unquestionably developed, too – albeit rather lumpishly. *Like an overweight heifer*, grinned Zhenya, knowing she should feel guilty about such unkind thoughts, but glad that she didn't. Somehow it was impossible to be nice to Marfa.

At the sound of loud masculine laughter outside, the girls nervously put away their embroidery. Into the room burst the unmarried young men, carrying firewood or refreshments or a balalaika. Most of them gravitated toward Zhenya and Anastasia.

Leading the pack was Grigori, who had been there almost every night, paying more attention to Zhenya than to anyone else. He, too, looked at her differently – but was at least not rendered speechless. Zhenya was flattered by his obvious interest and enjoyed dancing with him, but often her eyes wandered expectantly to the door, wondering. Finally, tonight, there was Ivan, standing hesitantly behind his brother. All evening, he stuck like glue to Grigori and tried unsuccessfully not to stare at Zhenya. She, in turn, did her best to engage him in conversation; after several rounds of his stammering and flushing, she gave up in exasperation.

As the winter progressed, the young people began to pair off. Certain young men began escorting certain young women home. Even Marfa had a clumsy young clod eagerly paying court. Anastasia, of course, had latched on to the charming visitor all the other girls were fussing over.

Fyodor was the nephew of the coachman at the manor, and from a village far to the South. No one knew much about him except that the party never really started until he arrived. He danced with exuberance, told stories with eloquence, paid compliments with elan. He was exciting, exotic – and evasive. Anastasia was crazy about him, a feeling he appeared to reciprocate. Every night, they left hand-in-hand, gazing endlessly into each other's eyes.

Meanwhile, Zhenya waited impatiently for Ivan to make a move. She tried everything she could think of to encourage him.

She asked questions about the seminary.

Monosyllabic grunts.

She made intelligent observations about relations between Church and State.

Brief, curt replies.

She discussed Natasha's engagement to Prince Andrei in *War and Peace*.

He blushed furiously.

She asked him to dance.

He stepped on her feet.

She ignored him.

Worried stares.

She flirted with Grigori.

Sullen stares.

Finally, she tried the direct approach. "What's wrong with you?" she said, stamping her foot in exasperation. "Why don't you *do* something?!"

Ivan fled. He did not return the next night, or the next.

At home, Zhenya was uncharacteristically foul-tempered. The family was surprised – even Agafya, who couldn't resist gloating about Marfa's suitor. Zhenya snapped at everyone, kicked the chickens out of her way, and even yelled at the cat. Ekaterina wisely excused her from milking the cow.

And then, on the third night, just as everyone was about to leave, Ivan appeared. Walking solemnly up to Zhenya, he made a deep bow. "If you would allow me the honor of escorting you home," he said, in a carefully rehearsed voice, "your carriage awaits." And he made an extravagant flourish toward the door

This time it was Zhenya's turn to stare and blush. At last, taking his arm in stunned silence, she accompanied him outside in utter astonishment. And there, in the snow, stood a gaily painted sleigh, to which was harnessed a troika of horses. The middle one was yoked; the other two were loosely attached, held only by a single rein.

Ivan gallantly helped the still astonished Zhenya into the seat of the sleigh, and tucked a warm wolfskin robe around her. Then he stood up in front and took the reins. Skillfully he trotted the horses out onto the open plain. Then, glancing back at her, he urged them on. The side horses broke into a gallop, their heads lowered and twisted backward; Zhenya could see their wild eyes and steaming nostrils. The night was sparkling with stars as they galloped across the frozen snow. The full moon cast a mysterious silver glow on the winter whiteness all around them. Faster and faster, they glided like pure song into the silent steppe, the counterpoint of the horses' hooves beating compellingly on the sleeping earth.

Zhenya could not tear her eyes from Ivan, standing so strong and proud and beautiful before her. As he confidently guided the horses, she could sense the rhythm of his powerful muscles merging with theirs. For the first time, she became fully aware of him as a man; a wave of dark, sensual excitement swept through her with frightening intensity. Just as the troika seemed to fly into the sky, Ivan turned and gave her a dazzling smile. A radiant light burst forth from Zhenya's heart and surrounded him with gold.

When the troika finally galloped up to her *izba*, Ivan swung her out of the sleigh and kissed her passionately. Then he jumped back in, and galloped off into the night.

Ж   Ж   Ж

Ivan left the next day, without a word. He was gone for several months. From Andrei, Mikhail learned that he had gone on a pilgrimage to the shrine of St. Serafim of Sarov.

Zhenya was depressed. She said little and rarely smiled. Nor was her mood improved by Marfa's constant giggling with her loutish suitor, always underfoot and grinning happily at his intended's ample bosom. Zhenya could not stand the sight – or the sound – of their clumsy courting. Lent was unbearably bleak. Even Easter did not lift her spirits.

Finally it was Midsummer's Eve. Bonfires were lit by the river bank, where everyone gathered. All the unmarried girls wore flower wreaths on their heads. At Ekaterina's urging, Zhenya had listlessly made one, too. Now she stood on the edge of the circle, disconsolately holding it in her hand, the shouts of laughter and the strident beat of the balalaikas jarring her pounding head.

Inside the circle, couples were lining up to leap the fire. Custom had it that whoever made it safely over, still hand-in-hand, was "handfasted" and would be married before the year was up. The air was thick with the smell of burning wood and a sweet, musky scent. The music shifted to a strangely haunting rhythm as the couples began to leap, the firelight flickering across their excited faces. Zhenya watched as Anastasia and Fyodor flew gracefully over the center of the fire, and as Marfa and her grinning lout – his eyes still fastened on her agreeably bouncing bosom – clumped awkwardly around its edges.

A tall, lean figure silently appeared beside Zhenya. Looking up, she saw Ivan's solemn face, its ascetic planes transformed by what burned in his dark, dark blue eyes. Slowly it entered her heart, dispelling the grey restiveness of the past months, then swept through her body, igniting its smouldering desire. Smiling in recognition, she assented to his inquiring gaze. Very carefully, he took the wreath she held and put it on her head, gently smoothing back a fugitive lock from her long braid. Holding out his hand, he led her into the circle. Then, their eyes locked, they leaped through the fire. For a long terrifying moment, Zhenya felt the heat and flames leap up and engulf them. Then, suddenly, they were on the other side, eyes and hands still clasped – and something else, too, for which she had no name. All around them were clapping hands and stamping feet. Ivan bent down and kissed her.

Later that night, they walked silently to the little grove by the Volga. As they stood listening to the rushing water, Ivan took Zhenya's wreath and threw it into the river. Then they sank down to the warm earth and melted into the night.

Ж　Ж　Ж

Officially, they were married after the harvest. The engagement was negotiated by their families, with the help of the local matchmaker. Not that there was any question the marriage would take place – both families were delighted by the match. But certain rituals had to be observed, and the amount of the dowry, as well as of the groom's contributions to wedding expenses, had to be discussed. Once everything was settled, Zhenya was excused from all chores to work on her trousseau, which was an important part of the dowry.

During the months that followed, Zhenya spun and wove and stitched diligently. Often she sang as she worked, enormously pleased with the snug web she was weaving. Often, too, she thought of that night in the grove by the Volga, surges of dark sensuality sometimes causing stitches to wander from the intricate patterns she was embroidering.

Though they had tacitly agreed not to return to the grove until after their marriage, the betrothed couple spent most of their evenings together. Side by side, they prepared for their future home, Ivan's sensitive fingers busily carving to the accompaniment of Zhenya's singing wheel. Though they spoke little, the silence was not uncomfortable, both absorbed in anticipation of what was to come. As the wedding day approached, Zhenya's shuttle danced faster and faster, while the chips flew from Ivan's flashing axe.

Suddenly it was time. The night before the wedding, bride and groom were carried off to the bathhouse. Ivan was swept into one side by a group of guffawing young men, Zhenya was taken to the other by several giggling young women. As she lay, naked and sweating, on the warm linden shelves, she noticed that it had suddenly grown quiet beyond the partition. Grinning, Anastasia pointed at its peepholes, then stood up and wiggled her hips in mock provocation. Two other girls tiptoed up to the thin wall and threw a big bucket of water at it. A good-natured roar erupted from the other side.

Leaving the bathhouse, Zhenya caught a glimpse of Ivan, surrounded by Grigori and his friends, all noisily heading toward the tavern. Most of the men of Derevnia had already gathered there for a long night of loud singing and bawdy jokes.

Zhenya, meanwhile, went home to an *izba* full of women singing sad songs about "she who was free is now to become a slave." Zhenya knew she was supposed to go weep in the corner, but since she didn't feel like weeping, some of those who had been married awhile did it for her. While Anya unpacked a basket of pastries "borrowed" from the manor kitchen, Anastasia rebraided Zhenya's wet hair. As the colorful ribbons and fragrant flowers were woven among the thick strands, Zhenya suddenly realized that it was the last time her hair would be in a single braid, that she was saying goodbye to her life as it had been. Under all the nervous excitement, she felt a pang of nostalgic sadness.

When Mikhail stumbled home late that night, the women went home for a few hours of sleep. Zhenya herself slept fitfully, barraged by a jumble of strange, erotic dreams.

The next morning, she was up with the sun. Soon, the younger women returned to help her dress. Amid a babble of admiring exclamation, a long white linen skirt, intricately embroidered with elaborate red flowers, was carefully lowered over her head. Then she was squeezed into a bodice of gold cloth bordered with pearl embroidery. Both Babushka and Ekaterina, somewhat smaller in their youth than Zhenya, had worn it at their weddings. The sleeves were fortunately loose and full, tied up with red ribbons and edged in lace. Trying not to breathe too deeply, Zhenya was then ceremoniously adorned with all the family jewelry, borrowed for the occasion from relatives near and far. Gold hoops were hung on her ears, a string of river pearls fastened around her neck, and several rings twisted onto her fingers. When she was ready, everyone oohed and aahed. Ekaterina blew her nose noisily.

Then they waited. At first, delighted with her unaccustomed finery, Zhenya swished about the *izba*, enjoying the swing of the full skirt and the sweep of the flowing sleeves. Eventually, however, she grew bored with the admiring glances of her friends, and tired of holding her breath against the straining bodice. Fidgeting with the ribbons on her sleeves and nervously twisting the rings on her fingers, Zhenya began to think about the sad songs of the night before. Suddenly she felt like weeping.

Just as she was about to rip off the unbearably tight dress and bolt for the Volga, Zhenya heard a distant hum of cheerful male voices and gaily jingling bells.

"He's coming! He's coming!" shouted Anastasia excitedly, flinging open the door.

Zhenya rushed over and stood beside her, anxiously looking down the road. Driving a troika decorated with ribbons and bells and red handkerchiefs, Ivan was standing proudly. He was wearing a dark blue caftan which flared out just above the tops of his high leather boots. The color matched his eyes and the tight fit emphasized his lean, muscular body, but the closely buttoned collar looked almost as uncomfortable as her dress.

Behind Ivan trouped all his friends and his entire clan, marshaled by Grigori. At the gate of the *izba*, the parade halted and Ivan eagerly dismounted. Seeing her standing in the doorway, he stopped abruptly and stared out of eyes Zhenya was relieved to see were only slightly bloodshot. His dazzled gaze, she decided, made the excruciatingly tight bodice worth it.

After some refreshments, which everyone but the bride ate enthusiastically, Mikhail solemnly blessed the young couple. Then Ekaterina unbraided her daughter's hair. Zhenya's long, lustrous tresses blew joyously in the wind; inhaling deeply of this delicious freedom, she felt the dress begin to rip. All the way to the church, Ivan could not take his eyes off the shimmering, rustling curtain which cascaded to her knees – and conveniently covered the small, threatening hole in the back of her elegant dress.

The wedding procession – which by now had swelled to include all Zhenya's family and friends – circled the church three times before entering. Before them marched Grigori, shooting his gun into the air and cracking his whip to ward off evil spirits. Still worrying about her dress, Zhenya noted that his eyes were considerably more bloodshot than Ivan's. Ivan himself continued to gaze at her with an intensity that was almost frightening. By the second time around the church, she had forgotten about the ripped dress. When they finally entered the church, Ivan smiled his wonderfully heart-melting smile and took her hand. Zhenya knew then that what they were pledging this day was a bond which would never be broken.

Standing beneath golden crowns held by Anastasia and Grigori, Zhenya held on to Ivan's hand. Surrounded by Andrei's glowing icons and Mikhail's deep chanting, she felt that Father Igor was blessing their marriage in the name of everyone who had ever lived in Derevnia. And when she kissed their wedding icon – a copy of the *Virgin of Vladimir* given to them by Andrei – it seemed that all of creation rejoiced in their union.

After the long ceremony, Anastasia plaited Zhenya's flowing hair into two braids and crowned them with a crescent-shaped *kokoshnik* of red velvet, heavily embroidered in gold thread. A pearl net descended over her forehead and a long gauze veil covered her braids – as well as the growing rip in her golden bodice.

Everyone then went to Andrei's *izba* for the first day of feasting. On a white tablecloth festooned with flowers and brightly colored ribbons, Natasha set a tall wedding cake of flour and honey with almonds on top. Around it were several artfully arranged dishes of sweetmeats and preserves and dried fruits. Ivan and Zhenya sat down in the icon corner and accepted the congratulations and good wishes of family and friends. Soon everyone but Zhenya was consuming great quantities of food and drink.

As day became evening and the wedding guests began to celebrate in earnest, Mikhail sat down beside her. Smiling, he gently tucked a loose strand of hair back under her *kokoshnik*. "This is for you," he said softly, handing her a wooden distaff on which he had obviously lavished much time and effort, "and for those to come." Carefully carved and intricately decorated with bright red designs, it was painstakingly inscribed in his unschooled hand, "Spin, preserve the distaff, and pray God for thy father."

Gratefully Zhenya accepted the gift, letting its familiar warmth nestle reassuringly in her cold hands.

By this time, Zhenya's stomach was rumbling noisily. In deference to her precariously snug wedding dress, she had eaten nothing all day. But no matter how often she demurred, the unending toasts were inescapable. Someone was always at her elbow, urging her to drink, then instantly refilling her never empty glass. As the festivities wore on, she began to feel strangely light-headed; the music sounded louder, the colors looked brighter, and everything everyone said was inexplicably hilarious.

As evening became night, the wedding guests began to dance. "Gorko! Gorko!" they called out in between each progressively more boisterous dance. "Bitter! Bitter!"

At each shout, the newlyweds kissed – to sweeten the meal, it was said. At first, Zhenya was embarrassed; Ivan, she knew, was too. But as the vodka flowed more freely, they both entered ever more enthusiastically into the game, their kisses resounding like minor explosions. In between, they giggled foolishly. With each kiss, the rip in the dress grew.

When Grigori finally led them to their marriage bed in the small storage shed outside Andrei's *izba*, they were both laughing hysterically. Alone, inside, they collapsed on the sheepskin robes just as the beleaguered bodice burst asunder. Zhenya screamed with laughter. Ivan, gasping for breath in between huge, uncontrollable guffaws, vainly endeavored to unravel the unfortunate garment from her tangled wedding veil. Finally pulling off her *kokoshnik*, Zhenya dropped her head on Ivan's sturdy shoulder and put her arm across his lean, muscled chest. Wearily he wrapped his strong arms around her, and gently stroked her hair.

All around them, the entire village was dancing and singing bawdy songs. But within minutes, the two were sound asleep.

Ж   Ж   Ж

Zhenya was sitting on the bed, slowly – very slowly – brushing her hair. Ivan was lying down, watching her. She could feel his questioning gaze, but carefully avoided meeting his eyes.

Now that it was too cold to sleep in the storage shed, they had moved in with Father Igor. Having long since lost his wife and children to a cholera plague, he regarded his grand-nephew as a surrogate son and was grooming him as heir to his parish. The parsonage was no bigger than Mikhail's *izba*, but had the added luxury of a small bedroom. The old priest slept over the stove, where it was warmest, and let the young couple have the bedroom to themselves.

Ivan sat up and, taking the brush from her hand, began gently running it through her thick gleaming hair. Stubbornly, the rich brown tresses refused to stay where he put them. "Your hair is like the earth," he laughed quietly, "beautiful and abundant, but difficult to subdue."

Carefully putting down the brush, he slowly ran his fingers through her rustling locks. Parting them in half, he draped one handful over her right shoulder and softly kissed the smooth golden skin underneath.

Zhenya's back tightened.

Ivan draped the rest of her hair over her left shoulder. "What is it, dear Zhenya?" he murmured into the nape of her neck.

"My name is Evgenia!" Straightening her shoulders, she tried to look prim.

"Mmm… yes… of course," Ivan lifted her onto his lap and kissed her nose.

"After all, I'm the priest's wife now!" Zhenya – Evgenia – tried to sound dignified.

"Mmm… you certainly are," Ivan's sensitive fingers stroked the hair cascading down her soft, warm bosom.

Zhenya stiffened. Ivan's hand hesitated, then lightly touched her cheek and turned her head so that her reluctant eyes were facing his.

"Zhenya – Evgenia?" Ivan's usually serious eyes were smiling. "You weren't like this when we were sleeping in the shed."

Zhenya looked nervously at the wall which separated their bedroom from the

65

stove over which Father Igor slept. "It just doesn't seem right..." she hesitated, "... to do it with the priest in the house."

Ivan roared with laughter. "And what," he gasped, "do you think you were doing 'it' with in the shed?!"

"Oh, but that's different!" Zhenya started to laugh, too, as they fell back on the bed.

"Aha," he said, rolling playfully on top of her, "so it's all right to do it with a priest in bed – but not with one in the house? " He gave her a loud smacking kiss.

"Shhhh," she giggled in alarm, "he'll hear you."

"I doubt it," he murmured in her ear, "He's quite deaf, you know."

For the next few weeks, Zhenya observed Father Igor closely. Finally she, too, was convinced that the old man could barely hear across the dinner table, let alone into their bedroom. Gradually, she relaxed into her new home.

Being married, Zhenya decided, was a very different life. Even though the *izba* in which she had grown up was just down the road, even though the people in the village were as they had always been, even though Derevnia itself plodded along its usual cycles – she herself felt like a very different person. Was it because she was now in charge of her own household, making decisions that affected others? Or was it being the priest's wife and sharing in Ivan's dreams for the spiritual growth of the village? Maybe it was all the grown-up activities she enjoyed with Ivan at night? All Zhenya knew for certain was that her name no longer fit her. *Zhenya is a girl's name. I'm a woman now. I should have a woman's name.* And so, eventually Zhenya became Evgenia.

Evgenia had never had so much space to herself. Compared to Mikhail's full house, the parsonage seemed almost empty. During the day, she was often the only one there. At first, she was lonely. It was good to be away from Agafya and Marfa, but she missed her parents and Babushka. She knew she was fortunate in having no mother-in-law bossing her around, but as the only woman of the house, there was also more work to do. Evgenia, however, was a hard worker and had been well taught in the skills of village housewifery. By the first anniversary of their marriage, she had their *izba* well enough organized to relish being mistress of her own household. The chickens were laying, the cow was giving plenty of milk, and her garden was growing. She was well pleased with herself, as were her men. Ivan smiled almost constantly, and Father Igor often shouted what a dear girl she was, taking such good care of a lonely old man.

Evgenia soon grew quite fond of husband's great-uncle. Though not overly intelligent, Father Igor was shrewd and observant, with considerable common sense and not a little humour. Unlike Ivan, he was not much interested in abstract theology; but he was sincere in his religious belief, and took the world – in which he felt thoroughly at home – as he found it, enjoying its good things when they came to him.

The old priest was obviously glad to have a younger man helping him with the parish, and spent much time instructing Ivan in the duties he would one day assume. Ivan listened carefully – but somewhat impatiently. For though he respected and loved his uncle, and was in no hurry for him to die, he was also eager to run the church *his* way.

"In the words of Saint Basil the Great," Ivan preached enthusiastically at Evgenia, "a priest must be 'an adornment of the Church, a support of the Motherland, a pillar and ground of truth, a stronghold of faith in Christ, a strong defender of his own, an invincible force against the enemy, a guardian of the Holy Church's decrees.'"

Evgenia enjoyed Ivan's private sermons; his dark eyes always flashed their most appealing shade of blue when he was being zealous.

Although Father Igor was a good priest, he did not measure up to Ivan's ideal. But Ivan, himself, intended to. Moreover, he believed that a pastor must not stand apart from the earthly life of his flock. He had numerous plans for the betterment of Derevnia, which he often discussed with his wife.

"The livestock here is too inbred," he said earnestly. "We need some new bulls and stallions."

Eyeing appreciatively Ivan's lean body, Evgenia smiled rather smugly, giving thanks that their *izba* certainly had no such problem – not in the bedroom anyway.

"And we should plant better seeds in the fields," he continued with utter seriousness.

Evgenia smiled again, resisting the temptation to stroke his long muscular torso. After all, it was Lent.

"And we should fix up the bathhouse!" Ivan was not easily distracted from pastoral discourse.

"And how about a real schoolhouse?" said Evgenia, finally joining in.

"Yes, of course! I'm sure I could get some of the men to help me build one. You could teach people to read, and I could lead Bible-study groups!"

"And if the *priest* said it was all right, maybe some of the girls could come, too!"

67

"And we must do something about all the drunkenness."

And so they would talk into the night, full of faith and hope for the future.

Meanwhile, their days were busy making a living. For although Ivan was technically a state official, he received no salary from the government. Neither did Father Igor. Both were dependent on the land, just as the peasants were, and on whatever fees parishioners gave them for performing various religious ceremonies. Although some of the peasants chose to pay these fees by helping the priest till his land, Ivan spent almost as much time plowing and mowing as everyone else.

He also rang the church bells several times a day, a task which required someone considerably less decrepit than Father Igor. Ringing the bells, however, was Ivan's favorite job. He took great pride in "his" bells, and was often up in the belfry fussing over them. Evgenia soon learned to read his moods by the sound of the bells. These days, they clanged enthusiastically, and Ivan would often run home afterward, sweating and laughing, to share his enthusiasm. Lifting her in his strong arms, he would rain happy kisses on her face and ears and neck. Sometimes he would unbraid her hair and bury his face in it. And sometimes, he did not immediately return to the church.

When Father Igor finally died, the village mourned. But they knew he was leaving them in good hands. With simple devotion and plain integrity, Ivan won their trust and respect. He prayed with unaffected sincerity and conducted services with unostentatious dignity. He comforted them in sorrow and heard their confessions with compassion. He worked beside them in the fields, and had as many callouses on his hands – and as much manure on his boots – as they did. And because he understood and was part of their world, they listened to his words. As the years went by, their devotion to him deepened and strengthened. No matter how poor the harvest or how hard the times, they always saw to it that he had as much as they did.

And Father Ivan always made sure that he never had more.

Ж   Ж   Ж

Ivan was sitting at the table, enjoying a quiet cup of tea, gathering energy for the evening chores. Watching Evgenia clean up after dinner, he smiled. She was a good woman, and he thanked God for giving her to him. A gentle wave of well-being peacefully embraced him as he sipped his tea. How good life was! How fortunate he was to have such a worthy calling! How pleased he was to serve!

Later that night, after the chores were done, he prostrated himself in lengthy prayer. In the icon corner were several of his father's creations. Among Ivan's favorites was a remarkably good copy of Rublev's *The Archangel Michael*. Next to it was a rather crude original of St. Serafim praying in the forest to an icon tucked in a tree branch. One of Andrei's first endeavors, Ivan like it for its breath of Siberia. The focus of his prayers, however, was an especially compelling face of the Saviour, framed by the arms of a cross and surrounded by a golden halo. Andrei had copied it from a cathedral in the Moscow Kremlin. The eyes – dark and intense and contemplative – looked deep into one's soul.

As Ivan knelt before the icon, he felt comforted by this penetrating gaze. For it was not the Orthodox way to be tormented by puritanical notions of ir-redeemable guilt. The Fall in Eden had not been cataclysmic; Adam was rather a child who had misbehaved. Paradise, of course, was off limits to such naughty children, but humans were not viewed as creatures contaminated by original sin and perverse lust. This belief in a benevolent, non-punishing God was a source of great strength to Ivan. And just as God was tolerant of human weakness, so did he strive to be.

The Christ to whom Ivan prayed was not the Christ who would come to judge the world. Rather, it was the Christ of the Beatitudes – a reviled, humili-ated, human Christ who staggered under his Cross. His example of voluntary suffering enabled Ivan to accept all that life had to offer. And if it often seemed that his people got more than their share of sorrow, Ivan accepted that, too, in imitation of Christ. Meanwhile, God loved His people and wanted them to be happy whenever possible. Feasting and dancing and even drinking – on occasion – were good. After all, it was Christ Himself who kept the festivities going at the wedding in Cana.

After a special prayer that all his labors be fruitful, Ivan crossed himself de-voutly. Then he went into the bedroom and waited for his wife to finish her devotions.

Kneeling in the icon corner, it was to the Virgin that Evgenia addressed her prayers. Actually, She was not really a virgin but a mother – the Mother of God and, thereby, the Mother of all. Andrei had also made several icons of the Virgin for their corner. In the middle was the *Virgin of Vladimir*, Patroness of the Land. Under the protection of this icon, the Russian people had turned back the Mon-gols time after time. On the most famous of these occasions, Saint Sergius him-self had carried the miracle-working icon before Dmitri Donskoi's army. It was said that in Her halo had been emeralds as large as walnuts, and on Her shoulder an enormous diamond.

Whenever Evgenia gazed into the sad, tender eyes of the Virgin, she knew that the Mother of God understood the woes and weaknesses of womanhood – and that She felt compassion and gave comfort. All Her beloved icons were painted in dark browns and ochers and reds, bathed in deep tones of gold and amber. The colors of the earth, symbols of fertility, Evgenia saw them in forest and field, and heard them in the wind and the river. Whether beseeching the Virgin Mother or singing with Mother Volga, it was all one and the same. Mother Earth and Queen of heaven, both revered the natural processes bestowing fertility.

Earnestly, Evgenia prayed that she be blessed by this fruitfulness. It had been more than a year since her wedding, but still she had not conceived. That Marfa was now flaunting her pregnant belly – for the second time – added to Evgenia's concern.

Remembering her mother's reassurance that she, too, had been slow to conceive, Evgenia crossed herself devoutly. Then she went into the bedroom and climbed into bed beside her husband. Since it was not a Fast day, they embraced tenderly, then passionately, "knowing" each other in the Biblical sense – as always, with joyful zest. And, as always, they slept untroubled by pangs of conscience.

Ж   Ж   Ж

Ivan awoke before dawn, as he always did on Sunday. Quietly he got out of bed, carefully tucking the warm sheepskin around his still sleeping wife. Quickly donning his best cassock, he smiled, remembering that today was St. Vladimir's Day.

In the year 987, according to the Chronicles, Prince Vladimir of Kiev sent out ten good and wise men to seek a better religion for his realm. When the emissaries returned, Vladimir listened carefully to their reports of the many ceremonies and places of worship they had visited. Of all these churches, none compared to the glory of the huge Cathedral in Constantinople.

"We knew not whether we were in heaven or on earth," they reported, describing its beauty. "We only know that God dwells there among His people."

Shortly after, Prince Vladimir was baptized into the Eastern Orthodox religion. His first act of faith was to decree a mass baptism for his people in the Dnieper River. And so it was that in the Russian Orthodox Church, Beauty formed a trinity with Truth and Goodness. And so it was, too, that the Feast of St. Vladimir came to be Father Ivan's favorite Holy Day.

70

Eagerly Ivan strode out of the parsonage, and walked up the small hill on which the little church stood. Like most Russian Orthodox churches, it was built in squares of humanity and circles of God. The square foundation opened into the semicircular altar apse in front and was crowned by the semicircular dome above. Thus, architecturally, did the divine and human merge. Ivan found the symbolism most satisfying. Especially this morning.

Entering the church, he was gently confronted by the iconostasis, a lofty screen concealing the inner sanctuary. The iconostasis was completely decorated with brilliant-colored icons. The walls, too, were covered with them. From every direction, Christ and the Virgin, the Archangel and the Apostles and all the saints looked out at worshipers with compassionate, tender eyes.

Ivan loved the icons Andrei had painted in the church. They sang to him of the divine core within all living things, and exhorted him to open himself to the likeness of God. Standing in the dim silence, he felt surrounded by holiness.

Like his father, Ivan believed that art was a divine gift intended to serve God and uplift humanity. The liturgy of the Church was Ivan's artform, and in this he had a rich vehicle for expression; with his baptism, Prince Vladimir had accepted all the profound poetry and dramatic magnificence of the Eastern Orthodox liturgy. While Ivan's poor church could not afford the gold and precious stones which adorned cathedrals in the cities, it had its share of traditional ornaments and vestments. They provided adequate setting for ceremonies which appealed strongly to senses and imagination, embracing and enveloping worshipers with awe and warmth. The rustic beauty of his little church also underscored the ancient Slavic traditions of community and compassionate peace on which the luxury of the Byzantine Church had been grafted.

Crossing himself devoutly, Father Ivan opened the door of the iconostasis and entered the small sanctuary. Kneeling before the altar only he was allowed to approach, he said a special prayer of thanks for the blessing God had bestowed upon his household.

Then he began to prepare for the day's worship. Services were long and frequent, complicated and full of symbolism. The liturgy for each Holy Day varied; several large volumes prescribed proper rituals for each cycle of the church calendar. Early in the morning or late at night, people stood for hours on the cold stone floor. Yet going to church was not simply what everyone did – it was something most did gladly. Sunday – *Voskresenye* – truly meant "Resurrection." Especially to Father Ivan.

Back in the parsonage, Evgenia stirred and reached for Ivan. Finding herself alone under the sheepskin, she reluctantly left the warm bed and sleepily put on her Sunday clothes. Her stomach growling noisily, she went outside and walked toward the church. Surrounded by the churchyard, it was at right angles to the *izba*s lining the road which ended at its gates. At the head of the column and nearest the church, the parsonage, too, faced the road.

Over the front door of the church was a large icon of the Virgin; as guardian of the gates, the Mother of God opened the path to salvation. Evgenia smiled; she found the symbolism most satisfying. Especially this morning.

Relative to cottages in the village, the church was tall; but by itself, it was not really very large. Its intricate wood shingles – built without a single nail – harmonized reassuringly with the wood dwellings of its people. While striving to reach on high, the church remained firmly on the ground. For Evgenia, the church was a familiar place. There she approached God respectfully and lovingly – but never on tiptoe.

Nodding to her father, Evgenia took her place in the choir loft. "Let us pray unto the Lord." Occasionally Mikhail fished an ancient tuning fork out of his pocket; mostly he relied on his own remarkable sense of pitch to keep his small choir in tune.

Surrounded by the soaring chant of the choir, the congregation moved rhythmically with the waving censers, bowing and crossing themselves. The smell of burning candles and wafting clouds of incense was strong and sweet. And all around the worshipers, close and intimate, were the neighbors they were enjoined to love as themselves.

Ivan celebrated Mass with the grace of dancer. The vestments he wore were embroidered with gold and silver threads, trimmed with river pearls and shimmering sequins of fish scales, lovingly crafted and carefully handed down over generations. Most beautiful of all was the aura which surrounded him at the altar. Evgenia felt the same healing light in his father's icons – and in her father's singing. Its mysterious power cast a deep glow over the crude church with its rustic icons and poor peasants, transforming it into a place of rare beauty. When Evgenia joined her voice in harmony to this song, she felt that she, too, was full of its quietly radiant warmth.

Gently she placed her hand over the small, new life growing within her. How pleased Ivan had been when she told him. And how joyfully he now gave thanks.

Glory to God in Heaven,
Glory!

May the right throughout Russia,
Glory!
Be fairer than the bright Sun,
Glory!
May the great rivers,
Glory!
Bear their renown to the sea,
Glory!

As Evgenia sang, she felt enveloped by the community into which her child would be born. She was connected not only to the people of Derevnia, but to all who prayed in Holy Mother Russia. The bond went deep, reaching back into time and ahead into the future. And she knew that no matter what, as long as this prayerful song continued, the best part of her village – and *Rodina* – would endure.

Chapter 4: The SCHOOL

Evgenia had never really looked at the beams of the bathhouse before. Now she lay on one of its wide shelves staring up at them, panting between spasms of pain. It was, she thought weakly, the very place she had lain the night before her wedding.

The memory fled abruptly, drowned in the pain which once again swept her. Babushka and Ekaterina hovered over her, holding her hands and mopping her forehead. Anya and Anastasia and Natasha were there, too, keeping the fire going and sharing her ordeal.

Something was wrong. That she knew, even without looking at the worried faces of her mother and grandmother. It was taking too long, and no one was telling her to push. Inside, everything felt upside down.

Ekaterina rubbed her back; Babushka led her in an endless litany of brief prayers to the Virgin, interspersed by long, deep breaths.

"Mother of God, protect me."

Breathe in... Breathe out...

"Mother of God, comfort me."

In... Out...

"Mother of God, help me!"

In... Out... In... Out...

Suddenly something small and strong fought free. Anya and Natasha raised her to a half-sitting position. Looking down between her legs, she saw a little foot protruding from her body. The tiny toes were wiggling triumphantly.

Babushka's gentle hands reached within and expertly guided the other foot. The baby slid out smoothly, its minute fists crossed over its chest. Last to emerge was the head, emitting a long wail of relief once it had cleared passage. The baby's cry was taken up by all the women clustered round. And relief became joy as Ekaterina cut the umbilical cord with the distaff Mikhail had given Evgenia at her wedding.

"Her name is Elisaveta," Evgenia announced a few days later. "After my grandmother."

On the eighth day after her birth, young Elisaveta was formally received into the community. The entire village crowded into the cold church to watch the naked baby be dunked three times in a large basin of cold water.

About all this, Evgenia was exceedingly nervous.

"Couldn't we do it at home, in front of the stove?"

"But I'm the Priest," replied Ivan. "People expect my child to be baptized in church."

"But it's winter. What if she catches cold?"

"The Lord will keep her warm." And Ivan proceeded to deliver an enthusiastic sermonette on the sacrament of baptism. "What joy it will be when she becomes a member of the Church! Her entire being will be renewed."

"But she's only a week old," grumbled Evgenia. "She doesn't need renewing."

In the end, they compromised. Just before the ceremony, Babushka brought heated water from their stove, and filled the baptismal font only partially full, enough for a dip but not a dunk. As Ivan raised his daughter aloft for the blessing, he felt his wife's anxious stare drilling threateningly. The prayer was a short one, and the ceremony completed in record time. The baby nevertheless shrieked indignantly, and subsided only when she was snugly rewrapped by her godmother, Anastasia. She did not object, however, when around her chubby neck her father gently hung a small wooden cross he had carved himself.

After the ceremony, Evgenia sat holding her baby in the icon corner, imploring the Mother of God to protect her child from the perils of infancy. To the red cord on which the baby's cross hung, she added a small medallion of the Virgin.

Little Lisya was a good girl. Everyone said so. She was healthy and even-tempered, pretty and affectionate. She rarely cried, learned quickly, and usually did as she was told. Evgenia enjoyed her company and sang to her as she did her chores.

Yet even as she delighted in her baby, Evgenia perceived that there was something different about Lisya. As the little girl grew up, Evgenia became increasingly aware that some things about her daughter she would never understand. So much of what was important to everyone else didn't seem to matter to Lisya. And what appeared to be important to Lisya often seemed to have no place in Derevnia. Though she did her chores cheerfully and with impeccable care, she frequently had to be reminded. And except for daily tasks, Evgenia had to show her again and again how to do them.

Ekaterina noticed it, too, especially when she endeavored to instruct her granddaughter in the ways of the forest. Lisya enjoyed these long walks in the woods and looked forward to them. So did Ekaterina – who nonetheless always returned perplexed. "She loves the forest," she worried to Evgenia, "but she remembers nothing about it."

Lisya would proudly place on the table the birch-bark baskets brimming with colorful berries and mushrooms. "But don't ever send her alone," sighed Ekaterina to Evgenia. "She still can't tell the good ones from the poison."

It was only in the little grove by the Volga that Evgenia recognized the key in which Lisya's temperament was pitched. Mother and daughter were clearly as one in their love for the river. Lisya soon began repeating back lines of Pushkin Evgenia read to her. And in the singing words of the great poet and the flowing songs of Mother Volga, they forged a bond deep enough to withstand all that was to come.

Ж   Ж   Ж

On her next visit to the bathhouse, Evgenia had no time to stare at the ceiling. Within a few hours of the first labor pains, the baby shot out straight as an arrow and filled the room with enthusiastic, melodious cries. Unlike Lisya, he came out headfirst. They cut his cord with Ivan's axe.

Ivan himself was ecstatic. The church bells rang louder and longer than since the first months of their marriage. "His name is Vladimir," he announced, when it was time.

Like his sister, young Vladimir was strong and healthy, intelligent and obedient. Unlike her, he had a formidable set of lungs which he frequently exercised in bouts with his decidedly uneven temper. And as he grew up, it soon became apparent that whereas Lisya seemed incapable of marching in step to anything in Derevnia, Vladimir was always out in front leading the parade.

Almost immediately, Ivan began grooming his son to follow in his footsteps. Nor was this tutelage a difficult one, for seldom had father and son been so alike. From the moment of his first steps, young Vladimir trotted after his father like a little shadow. Ivan even showed him how to ring the bells; the two spent many happy hours puttering around up in the belfry. Though physically they resembled each other little, Evgenia sometimes had trouble telling them apart. For even as a very young boy, Vladimir exhibited the same earnestness which so marked his father. And he inherited his way with wood. During the winter, the two would sit side by side carving, the movement of the small hands an identical miniature of the large ones. Watching them often brought tears to Evgenia's eyes.

Ivan was fond of carving bas-relief plaques with religious themes. One of his subjects was Christ sitting in prison. Vladimir was especially fascinated by this image, and would sit for hours watching his father create it. But try as he might, he could never successfully reproduce it himself.

Though spiritually Vladimir was like his father, physically he took after his mother's family. His resemblance to his grandfather was, in fact, quite striking – the more so as he seemed to have also inherited his voice. Mikhail needed no urging to take the boy under his musical wing.

Like everyone else, Lisya loved Volodya – as he soon came to be called. Eagerly she helped her mother take care of him; when he toddled outside, she hovered nearby to keep him out of danger. She was unfailingly patient and kind, and fiercely protective of her baby brother. This, too, often brought tears to Evgenia's eyes.

It did not take Lisya long to figure out that her younger brother somehow had the mysterious gift of being able to please. But no matter how hard she tried, she was unable to figure out just what *he* was doing that *she* wasn't.

As they grew older, they began to fight. As with virtually everyone else in Derevnia, Volodya could not open his mouth without making Lisya want to contradict him. Though she had learned that it was usually safer to pretend agreement with others, her tongue sometimes refused to obey her. But with Volodya, she didn't have to pretend. They almost never agreed, either, but it was such a relief to say what she really thought without worrying! With him she could be herself. With him she could speak freely, knowing that she would never see that look in his eyes, the one that said there was something not right about her. And so, paradoxically, the louder their arguments, the deeper grew the bond between them.

The next time Evgenia hastened to the bathhouse in labor, she brought forth someone with whom Lisya could be herself without fighting. Like her sister and brother, Tatiana was healthy and intelligent. She was even prettier than Lisya and more likeable than Volodya. And unlike either of them, she had an unusually flexible character. The ways of the village appealed to her down-to-earth practicality, just as Lisya's stubborn nonconformity and Volodya's passionate zeal appealed to the part of her that had its head in the clouds. Unlike her sister, very little was unacceptable to Tatiana; unlike her brother, she considered very little worth fighting about. And she somehow managed to see something likeable in everyone and everything.

Even as a baby, it was apparent that Tatiana preferred to communicate with her body rather than her voice. Rarely did she have quiet gurgling conversations with herself as Lisya had, and never did she emit the loud good-natured exclamations with which Volodya had tested the limits of his world. But Tatiana's cradle was constantly in motion, as she happily waved and wiggled and kicked and bounced from the moment her bright blue eyes opened wide in the morning until they abruptly closed in utter exhaustion at night. Her first steps were precise and confident, with none of the uncertain wobbles of other toddlers, and whenever Evgenia sang to her, Tatiana rocked smilingly in her lap in time to the song. When Tatiana wanted something, she usually asked for it with one of the charmingly eloquent gestures which rarely failed to yield the desired result.

As Tatiana grew older, she began spending more time with Ivan's mother, to whom she obviously bore much more than a striking physical resemblance. Natasha understood her granddaughter's language better than anyone, and conversed with her in her own idiom. Gradually she helped Tatiana enlarge her vocabulary of movement, and showed her how to turn it into dance.

What a miracle that such different beings could all emerge from the same womb, Evgenia wondered for at least the thousandth time as, kneading bread by the window beside the stove, she watched her children do chores outside. Volodya was cleaning the barn, periodically bursting out with huge forkfuls of manure, which he enthusiastically flung into a pile near the door. Lisya and Tatiana were feeding the chickens.

Every morning Lisya carefully braided her own hair, and then Tatiana's. The resulting long brown plaits were impeccably symmetrical and, to Evgenia's amazement, remained so all day. No rebellious strands dared escape from either of the emphatically neat braids under Lisya's supervision. Absently Evgenia pushed back a stray wisp of her own undisciplined hair dangling before her eyes, leaving a small smudge of flour on her nose.

Lisya and Tatiana were both wearing *sarafan*s made by Ekaterina. Dyed brown so as not to show the soil of weekday chores, the rich hue somehow suggested a ripe field of grain – unlike the mud-colored sacks in which Marfa's innumerable children plodded about. Evgenia was suddenly glad that Ekaterina had never shared her dye recipes with Agafya.

As Lisya threw carefully measured handfuls of grain to the chickens, Tatiana ran after them, imitating their clucking excitement with such exaggerated silliness that Lisya burst out laughing. Evgenia smiled, partly at Tatiana's droll caricature, partly in response to Lisya's all too rare laughter. Only Tatiana, it seemed, was able to coax a smile from her usually serious elder sister.

After carefully closing the chicken coup, Lisya began weeding the garden. Warily she scrutinized the plants, trying to remember which was which; reluctantly she pulled up those designated weeds, as though not entirely convinced that they were of lesser value than those left standing. Tatiana, meanwhile, flitted up and down the rows of vegetables pretending to be a butterfly.

Finally Lisya reached the cucumbers, her special nemesis. Sitting down behind the low trellis, she frowned intently at the bristly vines. At that moment, Volodya exploded out of the barn with an especially large, particularly juicy forkful of manure. As he energetically heaved it into the growing pile of fertilizer outside, a moist brown ball fragmented loose and flew over the cucumbers, right into Lisya's lap.

Leaping to her feet, Lisya began yelling at Volodya. Big for his age, already taller than she was, he retreated even so before her angry tirade, trying not to laugh at the gooey specks now splattering the face his sister always seemed to have just scrubbed.

Attracted by all the commotion, the new calf trotted out to investigate and started jumping playfully around the noisily arguing children. Tatiana soon began chasing him, each of her attempts to mimic his frolicking leaps more ludicrous than the last. Alarmed by this strange pursuer, the calf bolted for the open gate.

The argument ended as abruptly as it had started, as Volodya made a dash for the gate, trying to head off the calf, and Lisya ran along the edge of the garden, herding him away from the ripening vegetables. Volodya made it to the gate a split second before the calf did and, with a great flying leap, slammed it shut just in time. Lisya, meanwhile, grabbed the last of the chicken feed and held out enticing handfuls to the calf. Scrambling to his feet, Volodya slipped his already strong arms around the young animal's neck. Tatiana grabbed his tail. Together they persuaded him to return to his mother.

The calf finally penned up, the three children sat outside the barn, breathing hard. Grinning, Volodya wiped the specks of manure off Lisya's face with his sleeve. Carefully she tied her kerchief around the knee he had skinned diving for the gate. Then, Tatiana tucked comfortably between, they all leaned back peacefully against the wall of the barn.

"...And we thank Thee for the bounty of Thy fields, of which we are about to partake. Amen."

Ivan unfolded his long slender hands and the children shifted in their seats as Evgenia regretfully ladled out the *shchi* and *kasha* she served her family almost every night. Despite experiments with various herbs, which sometimes succeeded in making what everyone ate taste like something else, even so – it was still just *shchi* and *kasha*. How wonderful it would be, she thought guiltily, to have access to the well-stocked kitchen at the manor where Anastasia now did most of the cooking. With an effort, Evgenia tried to erase the image of that copious larder – and the marvelous meals she could serve her family from it – and focused on the conversation around the dinner table.

"We'll be using the special liturgy for St. Vladimir's Day on Sunday," Ivan was saying to Volodya, "so be sure to wear the good cassock."

"In the procession, shall I carry the cross in front or behind the icon?" asked Volodya, between enormous mouthfuls of dark rye bread.

"Since it's St. Vladimir, the icon, I think, should come first," replied Ivan, considering carefully. "And maybe you should carry it."

"Oh, could I?" the boy's animated face beamed with pride.

"On the Virgin's Feast Days, the cross always comes first," objected Lisya. "Why should St. Vladimir be treated better?"

"Because he started the Holy Church," said Volodya knowingly, "Of course he's more important."

"Just because he told his people to jump in the river and get baptized?" Lisya took a small bite of bread and chewed it skeptically. "What choice did they have? He was the Tsar, after all."

"So what?" answered Volodya, irritated at having to explain the obvious. "They all wanted to be Christians anyway."

"Why? So they could get up early and stand for hours in a cold church?" Lisya took a larger bite of the bread she was holding and chewed more rapidly.

"But Lisya, *everyone* goes to church!" Incredulity ignited Volodya's fervent blue eyes. "It's where they belong!"

"*You* can say that," Lisya dropped the bread on her plate, "because you're always up there at the altar."

"Where else should an altar boy be? Someone has to help father."

"And why aren't there any altar *girls?*"

81

"Because girls don't have beards."

"So?"

"To be in a holy place, you have to have a beard – like God does."

"You don't have a beard!"

"Not yet!" Volodya's face was almost as red as his hair. "But I will some-day!"

Lifting the hem of her *sarafan*, Tatiana held it around her chin like a beard and frowned solemnly. Everyone laughed. Hastily, Evgenia passed the bread.

For awhile, everyone concentrated on their food.

Then Ivan cleared his throat. "Lisya, maybe you could join your mother in the choir."

"But no one would hear me," Lisya replied sadly. "I can't even sing as well as Volodya."

"God has given each of us different gifts," said Ivan, in his comforting-priest voice.

"Up at the manor house they have something called a piano that makes won-derful music!" Lisya looked at her father hopefully. "Maybe the church could get one, too, and people who can't sing could play it."

"Only the voice of His own creation is suitable to praise God." Ivan tried not to sound sanctimonious.

"But maybe God would like other music, too," Lisya pressed eagerly, "if he had a chance to hear it."

"The Devil uses that kind of music to lead people astray," Ivan reproved, trying not to sound irritated.

"But why should something so beautiful belong to the Devil?"

"Because the Holy Church says so."

"But why?"

"Because it has always been so." Ivan's answer dissatisfied him almost as much as it did Lisya. Both subsided into frustrated silence.

Evgenia passed the bread again. No one wanted any.

Finally, Tatiana slid over and leaned her head against her older sister's shoul-der. "You can stand by me in church, Lisya," she said in the clear voice she used so seldom. "Then you won't be lonely."

Everyone looked at Tatiana in surprise. Gratefully Ivan reached over and ca-ressed her cheek. Lisya slipped an arm around her sister. Evgenia, about to pass the bread again, relaxed.

Ж Ж Ж

Evgenia's last maternity visit to the bathhouse ended less happily than her previous ones. This time, she knew, something was *really* wrong. The pain was even worse than when Lisya had kicked her way out. What she felt now was not a rebellious spirit breaking free, but something sick her body was trying to expel. When it was all over, Ekaterina wrapped the something up and buried it somewhere. Inside, where the pain had been, Evgenia felt only dark numbness, cold as death.

Carefully they brought her home, and for several weeks she lay inert in the bedroom, drifting in and out of consciousness. Babushka moved in to take care of her and the household. Lisya took charge of the other children.

Finally, Babushka informed her it was time to get up. Evgenia didn't believe her, but no one ever argued with Babushka. Listlessly, she dragged herself out of bed and made an effort to get back to work. Inside, however, she still felt dead. Even when she looked at her family, she saw only the grey fog of despair.

As the weeks passed, she became dimly aware that something was going on outside. The men in her family – and several others from the village – were hammering and sawing and doing all the other things men do when they are building something. Evgenia wondered weakly what they were making, but was too fatigued to look out and see. Nor could she find the energy to ask. These days, she spoke to no one. It took too much effort.

Then, one day, all the noise stopped. Ivan, Mikhail and Andrei, Vaslav and Vsevelod appeared in the doorway, hopeful grins on their faces. Ivan took Evgenia's hand and gently led her out of the parsonage. A wave of panic swept over her; she would have run back inside but for Ivan's firm grip on her hand and Mikhail's reassuring arm around her shoulder.

Past the church they led her to the site of all the recent noise. And there, on the other side, was a sturdy little building unlike any in Derevnia. It was bigger than an *izba*, but smaller than the church. On top was a small belfry with one modest bell, light enough for any woman – or child – to ring. Inside was a big enough stove to keep the entire room warm.

Evgenia let go of Ivan's hand and slowly walked up the aisle between the rows of small desks. In front was a large desk. She stared at it through a hole in the despairing fog. Tentatively she reached out and touched it. Finally, she walked around and stood looking out over the empty classroom. The hole in the fog got bigger as she gazed at the eager smiles of the waiting men.

Then Ivan walked over to the rope dangling from the belfry. Smiling he held it out to her. As she took the rope and pulled on it, a friendly bell began pealing out a gentle message of welcome.

The small hole in the fog suddenly turned golden, and lit up the edges of the vast grey mist still surrounding it. Evgenia pulled the bell harder and, for the first time in months, smiled.

Ж   Ж   Ж

Evgenia was sitting on the edge of her desk, waiting for her class to finish reading the paragraph she had written on the board. In the front row, her nephews sat clustered around Tatiana. Behind them sat Lisya and Volodya, flanked by Anastasia's children.

Anastasia and Fyodor had been married shortly after Ivan and Evgenia. They had two children, Dmitri and Elena. A sturdy boy about Lisya's age, Dmitri had inherited his father's good looks. Unlike Fyodor, however, he was quiet and sensitive. Still studying the board, Dmitri leaned over and whispered briefly in Lisya's ear; after a moment, she nodded briskly. Watching them, Evgenia smiled. Dmitri was almost the only person Lisya never argued with.

Next to Volodya sat Elena, a few months younger, who was unable to control the sidelong glances she frequently cast in his direction. Like most of the girls in Derevnia, she was smitten with him. Though always kind to the crowd of young females who dogged his footsteps, Volodya was largely oblivious to his own charm and gently ignored the possibilities inherent in such an entourage. But Elena was thrilled to be sharing a desk with him. She was as pretty as her mother, but inside as strong and steady as a rock.

Evgenia stood up and quietly walked over to the stove. How she loved sharing what she knew! And how exciting it was to learn along with her students! Not surprisingly, her small class learned quickly – and seemed to enjoy school almost as much as she did. Feeding a piece of wood to the stove, she remembered that a few new students – mostly boys – had trickled in last winter. She was expecting them back soon, maybe with some of their friends.

Evgenia walked over to the window and glanced out at the snow just beginning to fall. One of Marfa's boys was trudging sullenly down the road. Marfa had married her lout shortly before Evgenia had wed Ivan; by now, she had an enormous family. None of them, however, were ever allowed to set foot inside the school. Evgenia was not really sorry. They were a dull brood, with perpetually runny noses wiped noisily on perennially dirty sleeves; Evgenia was never able to tell them apart. Marfa herself had become more ill-tempered. Her once bouncing bosom now sagged pendulously; her cloddish spouse no longer grinned.

As Evgenia turned back from the window, her glance fell on her nephew, Mischa. Reminding herself, as she always did on those rare occasions when he caught her eye, that she really should pay more attention to him, she called on Mischa to read the paragraph on the board. He obligingly did as he was told, very carefully, very accurately – and very slowly.

In between words, Evgenia wondered again why Mischa was so easy to ignore. He was a good boy, and certainly not stupid. The other children always let him join their games; but watching them in the schoolyard, Evgenia noticed that they forgot about him even more than she did. Except for Elena, after whom Mischa trotted like a loyal dog.

Having conscientiously finished reading the paragraph in his customary monotone, Mischa returned his gaze to where it unfailingly went between assignments. His large, thoroughly reliable eyes stared steadfastly at Elena – who was looking just as adoringly at Volodya.

Evgenia's sympathetic sigh evaporated abruptly as Volodya – as oblivious to the triangle itself as he was to its romantic dynamics – excitedly identified, chapter and verse, the passage from the Bible Mischa had just read.

Father Ivan regularly read to the class from Holy Scripture. Sometimes, too, he told them stories. His favorite was about a Holy City, concealed by the Virgin at the bottom of the Volga to protect it from invading Tartars. Invisible to the eye of the sinful, the city could only be entered by a chosen few – the pure of heart – who would never return. It was usually Dmitri who requested this story. Occasionally Evgenia saw him walking slowly on the riverbank, looking intently into the dark waters of the Volga.

After everyone in the class had read the paragraph aloud, Evgenia sat down on top of her desk and began to tell one of Babushka's stories. It was about an orphan girl named Maryushka, who could make magically beautiful things with her needle. Though she used only simple materials found in forest, river and field, none could match her skill. Merchants came from far and wide to see her marvelous work, promising her riches and glory if she would come away with them.

"Riches I do not need," Maryushka replied to all these offers. "I shall never leave the village where I was born."

Eventually, Maryushka's fame reached the ear of the sorcerer, Kostchei the Immortal, who raged to learn that there existed beauty he did not possess. So

85

he took the form of a handsome youth and flew over the deep oceans and tall mountains and impassable forests until he came to Maryushka's cottage. When Kostchei saw her work, he was envious that a simple country girl could fashion things finer than he, the great Kostchei, could.

"Come with me," he said in cunning tones, "and I will make you Queen. You will live in a palace of precious jewels. You will eat off gold and sleep on eiderdown. You will walk in an orchard where birds of paradise sing sweet songs, and golden apples grow."

"I need neither your riches nor your strange marvels," answered Maryushka, "for there is nothing sweeter than the fields and woods and rivers where one was born. Never shall I leave *Rodina*, where my grandmothers lie buried and where live those to whom my work brings joy."

"Because you are so loath to leave your homeland," said Kostchei, his face dark with fury, "a bird you shall be, and no more a maiden fair."

And there, flapping its wings where Maryushka had stood, was a beautiful Firebird. Kostchei himself became a great black falcon and swooped down on the Firebird, grasping her tight in his talons and carrying her high above the clouds. Maryushka, however, resolved to leave a memory of herself behind. So she shed her brilliant plumage, which covered the meadow and forest with glowing rainbow colors. As the feathers fell, Maryushka's strength ebbed. Though she died in the talons of the Falcon, her feathers continued to live; but only those who loved beauty – and who sought to make beauty for others – could see them.

Evgenia paused, letting her students think about the story.

"I think Maryushka did right," said Elena finally. "I would rather die than leave Derevnia."

"I think she should have struggled with the falcon," said Volodya firmly "Or at least tried to persuade him to stay, too. Evil can't always be allowed to have its own way."

"Who says Kostchei was evil?" shot back Lisya. "Just because he wanted to take her away? She was stupid not to go!"

"Because she didn't want to be rich?" asked Elena, incredulously.

"No," replied Lisya, "because she didn't want to try somewhere else."

"I wonder where Kostchei came from?" interposed Dmitri. "Maybe Maryushka would have been happier there."

"But to leave her roots?" Elena shook her head. "How awful!"

"And how could she leave the land!" said Mischa, with immovably planted certitude.

Everyone stared at him, reminding themselves with difficulty of his presence, mildly shocked that he had joined the discussion. Mischa spoke less than everyone – except for Tatiana. But no one ever ignored her. When Tatiana got excited – which was often, especially about stories like the Firebird – it was hard fo her to sit still.

"But maybe it was Maryushka's duty to go with Kostchei," said Volodya fervently. "Maybe his people needed her more than her village did."

"And maybe they would have been more like her than the people in her own village," said Lisya sadly.

"And maybe someday she could have come back," added Dmitri hopefully.

"But Maryushka was a truly noble soul," insisted Elena, "to give her beauty to her people."

"But what if none of them could see her beautiful feathers?" Lisya's voice had an edge of despair.

Ж   Ж   Ж

The big house was half-hidden amidst a large grove. Approaching it through an avenue of linden trees, Lisya was pretending that its large veranda and massive white columns belonged to her. It had two storeys and – by her count – at least twenty-one rooms. Furtively, she slipped into the wide entrance hall; peering carefully into the large dining room and even larger parlor on either side, she scurried up the staircase. Upstairs were an amazing number of bedrooms, all filled with massive mahogany furniture and austere family portraits. Quietly, Lisya hurried to the end of the corridor and quickly let herself into an unoccupied room. Slowly, she sat down on the bed and closed her eyes, letting the snug, soothing sense of leisure pervade her. How remote she felt here from the daily bruising of village life.

After a few restrained bounces on the bed, she walked over to the dresser and looked into the huge mirror hanging over it. "I'll bet I know this house better than any of *them*!" she said to the grey-blue eyes staring solemnly back at her.

Throwing a defiant glance at the portraits on the wall, she walked over to the window and looked out. Behind the mansion was a large orchard of apple, pear, and cherry trees; in the center was a building made of glass in which grew small orange trees and other exotic plants. Planted flowers grew obediently around an artificial pond, beside which stood a small theatre. Further away were stables, coach house, barns, mills, workshops for shoemakers and tailors, and a small infirmary. Lisya knew that some of these buildings were no longer used, but the barns were still full of cows and chickens, as well as sheep and hogs and even turkeys. Several fine horses lived in a stable bigger than her family's *izba*, and a large kennel housed a pack of Russian *borzoi*. On the outer edge of the estate were rows of crude cabins intended for domestic serfs. Since Emancipation, most had fallen into disuse, as the hired servants usually preferred to live in Derevnia.

Sighing, Lisya walked back to the mirror and stared at her reflection. "I don't understand why they want so much," she frowned, "when everyone else has so little." The girl in the mirror shook her head.

"And why don't they do things like everyone else?" The frown disappeared. "Why do they wear fox and sable? And use saddles on horseback."

The men of Derevnia all rode bareback, and scoffed at saddles as fancy toys which gave sore behinds.

"And why do they use forks and napkins?"

The men of Derevnia scoffed at that, too. What need of napkins had a man with a beard?

"But I don't have a beard. Maybe I should use a napkin, too."

Remembering suddenly the question that had brought her here, Lisya waved hastily to herself in the mirror and ran silently down the back stairs into the kitchen.

Anastasia was slicing cucumbers and greeted her without surprise, a smile momentarily lighting up her usually sad eyes.

"Why don't the gentry talk like we do?" Lisya asked, sitting down next to her.

"They have more things, so they probably need more words."

"No, that's not what I mean." Lisya carefully arranged the cucumber slices on a china platter. "Lots of their words don't even sound Russian."

"That's because they're speaking French."

"What's French?"

"What people who live in France speak."

"Where's France?"

"Somewhere outside Russia."

Lisya pondered that for days. The idea of a foreign country, where people spoke – and maybe even thought and acted – differently was an exciting concept. The next time she was sent to the manor library, she found a book on France and sneaked it in with the ones for the school.

As usual, she stopped in the kitchen.

Anastasia turned away when Lisya walked in. But not quickly enough to hide the ugly bruise on her cheek. It was not the first one Lisya had seen there. Anastasia began to cry soundlessly.

In her youth, Anastasia had hoped that Fyodor might somehow still the restlessness in her soul. But after a brief, blissful honeymoon, she discovered that he had merely deepened her discontent. As the romantic glow faded, she recognized his charm as vanity and extravagance. Worse yet, she realized he was lazy.

Fyodor's only useful skill was that he knew all there was to know about horses. They responded to him instinctively, at first touch. And he cared about them passionately – more so, Anastasia was sure, than he did about her.

Fyodor's second passion was vodka. If there was carousing or brawling going on anywhere in Derevnia, he was sure to be in the middle of it. "In Russia you can't live without drinking and fighting," he often said by way of excuse. Not that this convinced Anastasia. They argued often and sometimes disastrously.

"I thought he was better than the other men around here," Anastasia said tearfully, suddenly facing Lisya, "but he turned out to be even worse."

"Then why don't you leave?" asked Lisya, trying not to stare at the bruise.

"Where would I go? I'm just a peasant, too. Sometimes men can move up the ladder – but women can only marry up. And I'm too old for that now."

As Anastasia wiped her eyes, Lisya patted her hand.

"But you, Lisya – you have a chance!" Anastasia said fervently. "You're a priest's daughter. That could get you places I could never go."

Lisya thought long and hard about this revelation. She finally concluded, however, that it wasn't enough to leave Derevnia. To part from her family – whom she did, after all, love deeply – there had to be somewhere to go.

In many of Babushka's stories, magical beings often appeared to ordinary folk, offering to grant them any wish. Lisya was always exasperated by the stupidity with which these lucky people usually squandered their wishes. Given the chance, she knew exactly what *she* would wish for. What she wanted, more than anything, was to be able to sing.

Lisya was not, by nature, a jealous person. But she truly envied her brother – and her mother and her grandfather – their glorious voices. Seeing them up in the choir loft, she longed to join them. Walking in the forest or sitting by the river, music churned constantly within her, desperately seeking expression. But whenever she opened her mouth, only a pale whisper of what was singing in her soul emerged.

And then, one night, there was a big party at the manor house. Lisya was helping Anastasia in the kitchen, as she often did on such occasions – not so much for the left-overs, as for the chance to observe the gentry at closer range. They interested her, not because they were aristocrats, but because they were different from people in the village.

As Lisya brought another tray of hors-d'oeuvres into the parlor, she heard an achingly beautiful sound, unlike any she had heard before. Searching out its source, she discovered that the strange music was coming from an exotic-looking man standing in the corner. Under his chin was an oddly shaped wooden box, across which he was drawing a long stick with horsehair attached. As he moved it, a cascade of exquisite notes poured out, rivaling any singing Lisya had ever heard. Going closer to the mysterious music-maker, she saw that the box had strings, much like a balalaika. Unlike its crude cousin, however, this marvelous instrument sang instead of twanging.

Later, in the kitchen, Lisya breathlessly approached the stranger – who turned out to be a gypsy hired for the evening. The music box, he told her, was called a violin. Seeing the look in her eyes, he let her try it. After several squawks and scratches, a long true note miraculously sounded. More scratching – and then another. And another. Only with difficulty was the gypsy able to leave with his violin. Lisya walked slowly home that night, stunned with happiness.

As the days passed, the joy of having at last found her voice gradually evolved into wondering how she could repeat the experience. It was Anastasia who found the solution.

"Here," she said, smiling and holding out a dusty old violin case.

"Where did you get it?" gasped Lisya, carefully lifting out the violin. The strings were broken and horsehair was flying from the bow, but the mellow wooden body was still intact.

"In the little theatre building," replied Anastasia, excitedly. "In the old days, they used to have a whole orchestra of serfs playing here on the estate. The mistress said if you can fix it and learn to play it, you can have it."

Lisya ran all the way to the village and went straight to her grandfather. "Well?" she puffed, holding out the old violin with shining eyes.

Mikhail examined it carefully, and then looked intently at the eager face of his granddaughter. "You look just like your mother did when she was your age," he said softly, gently touching her cheek. "Yes," he nodded, "I think I can fix it."

Ж   Ж   Ж

Every moment Lisya could snatch from school and chores, she spent in the grove by the Volga, making friends with the violin Mikhail had rehabilitated. It was slow – and painful – going getting a feel for how much speed and pressure to apply to the bow. Gradually, however, the excruciating squawks diminished. After that, the rest was relatively easy. Fingering different pitches, she surmised correctly, was based on the same principle as playing a balalaika. With appropriate adjustments, she was soon picking out tunes her mother sang around the house. After several months, she was "singing" them just as well.

For awhile, she was content to sing to the Volga. Expressing what had been so long dammed up was almost unbearably sweet relief. Eventually, however, playing folk music on her violin began to strike her as unaccountably inadequate. Vaguely she sensed that this wonderful new voice was meant to sing a different kind of song.

Her nameless problem was unexpectedly resolved by Praskovia Nikolaevna.

"Well, has she learned to play it yet?" the mistress abruptly asked Anastasia one day.

When Anastasia nodded, Praskovia Nikolaevna summoned Lisya to the manor for a command performance.

Lisya was scared. For all her prowling about the manor and observing the gentry, she had never actually spoken to any of them. Nor did she particularly want to. They fascinated her, but she did not really like them.

When Lisya walked quietly into the parlor, her hands were sweating – but her head was up. Praskovia Nikolaevna was sitting in a massive throne-like chair. Next to her, in a somewhat smaller chair, was a younger woman whose resemblance was pronounced, though milder. Praskovia Nikolaevna fixed Lisya with a stern gaze which missed very little. Lisya longed to drop her eyes, but did not. The old woman looked her slowly up and down.

"Play!" she commanded, with an imperious wave of her cane.

Lisya put her violin under her chin. As her trembling hand drew the bow across the strings, she closed her eyes and began to play a song about the Volga. Soon she was away from the big dark room with its big dark furniture, standing on the banks of the river. Happily she sang with the rippling waves, as the sunlight reflecting on the shining water swirled gently around her. And when, at last, she returned, she was startled to see a tear in the dour old eyes which no longer stared quite so fearsomely.

"Play some Beethoven, child," Praskovia Nikolaevna said abruptly. "My daughter will accompany you." This time she waved at the younger woman next to her, who dutifully walked over to the piano and sat down on the bench. Lisya hesitated, and then followed.

"Shall we try this?" The daughter held up some music.

Lisya's face turned scarlet. She could not read music. No one had ever thought to teach her.

The woman at the piano began to play a dark, brooding melody embroidered with refined, elegant sounds. Lisya listened, embarrassed but intrigued. This was new music, of a kind she did not know, but under all the embellishment was a basic melody not unlike those she heard around her every day. Hesitantly, she began to play along, moving over and around the melody, singing with it as she did the Volga. As the music unfolded and developed, her violin played with the excitement of encountering an old friend. And as it danced, simply and slowly, in and out of the piano's elaborate chords, Lisya knew that making this music – all of it – was what she *had* to do. Somehow she must learn to build the complex structure of what she was hearing upon the solid foundation of what she already knew. The last refrain was over before she wanted it to be.

"Bravo!" shouted Praskovia Nikolaevna, waving her cane. "Varvara, see to it!" And she clumped noisily out of the room.

Varvara Petrovna looked up at Lisya and smiled. "You did that very well."

"Thank you," mumbled Lisya, uncertain what to do with the compliment.

"Especially since you don't read music," Varvara Petrovna added, rather condescendingly.

"But I can read books," Lisya retorted quickly.

"My mother thinks you have talent," Varvara Petrovna began again, more carefully. "She wants me to help you develop it."

"Why?"

"She remembers the old days when they had a whole orchestra of serfs. She misses the music."

"I'm not a serf."

"And *I* am not a teacher. But in return for music lessons, Mother hopes you will occasionally entertain her."

"That music we were playing," Lisya asked, after a pause, "is there more like it?"

"You mean the Beethoven?" Varvara Petrovna laughed. "Oh my, yes. Beethoven was very prolific."

"And do other people write music like this – Beethoven – does?" Lisya persisted.

"Well, not exactly." A trace of condescension crept back into her voice. "But there are many other composers who wrote this kind of music in their own style."

"If I could read music, could I play it?"

"Yes, I think probably you could – though some of it is very difficult."

"Where could I find it?"

"We have some here." Varvara Petrovna stood up, opened a tall cabinet next to the piano, and began taking out stacks of music, all with different titles. "Let's see – Mozart… Bach… Haydn… Schumann… Brahms… and here's some more Beethoven."

"If I perform for the mistress," Lisya asked eagerly, "can I use all this?"

"Yes, of course. This is her favorite music. How else will you learn to play it?"

Lisya walked slowly home, thinking hard. It would not be easy getting permission to accept the unexpected and exciting proposition she had just been offered. Her father would disapprove of her wasting energy on something of no use to the church. Her mother would worry about her spending too much time at a place she considered dangerous. Her grandfathers – especially Andrei – would resent her being patronized by the people who lived there.

And Lisya herself had reservations, too. The thought of performing again for Praskovia Nikolaevna terrified her, and she was none too keen about the prospect of being with Varvara Petrovna on a regular basis. True, the daughter was less formidable than the mother, but Lisya did not relish being treated as an inferior by someone so spoiled and insubstantial. Years of gentry-watching had persuaded her that though different in some respects, rich people were no better – or any more like her – than peasants.

Still, they knew things that she didn't and had things she wanted. And, remembering how her violin had felt as she played the Beethoven, she knew that she would do anything to learn the music her soul yearned to make.

She found an unexpected ally in Babushka. "The child was born upside down," the old woman said firmly, in a voice which silenced all opposition. "Of course she must do this contrary thing." And that was that.

Before the lessons began, however, Mikhail taught her to read music. "No sense taking what we don't need," he grumbled quietly.

Lisya was grateful, and consequently approached her first lesson with somewhat less trepidation.

Varvara Petrovna turned out to be kinder than expected. As Lisya's talent became increasingly evident, she even began to take a personal interest in her protegee's progress. To be sure, Lisya taught herself more than her teacher did. But playing with accompaniment was a new and valuable experience, from which she learned that her violin sang better *ensemble* than alone.

As Lisya worked her way through the stack in the music cabinet, she became more and more fascinated by the large and complex instrument that amplified her violin so beautifully. She began coming early so she could tinker with it herself. Making chords on the piano, she discovered, was exciting. To sing with her violin was indeed wonderful, but the piano enabled her to be the whole choir – all alone.

Varvara Petrovna was easily prevailed upon for piano lessons. She was a skilled – though unremarkable – pianist and was able to teach Lisya the necessary rudiments. The more Lisya learned, the quicker she progressed, and the more immersed she became in the new world opening up within her. It was not long before pupil surpassed teacher.

Ж Ж Ж

"Sit down," ordered Varvara Petrovna one day, as Lisya was about to disappear into the kitchen. "Over there." She pointed at a table covered with white lace cloth and set with delicate china and ornate silverware.

Carefully Lisya perched on the fragile-looking chair across from Varvara Petrovna and looked apprehensively at the table between them. All of these elegant objects she had seen before – in the kitchen. Helping Anastasia wash them was one thing; but was Varvara Petrovna actually expecting her to eat with these complicated utensils?!

Anastasia glided in with a tray of artfully arranged food. Lisya tried not to stare. In the village such variety was available only at wedding feasts. And no one ever had so much meat.

Anastasia noiselessly placed the tray on the table and, with a quick smile only Lisya could see, gracefully flowed out of the room. Varvara Petrovna's eyes followed, a small frown wrinkling her pale forehead.

"Now then, Lisya dear, pick up your fork," she said, in the same voice with which she addressed the small spaniel usually trotting at her heels. "No, no, don't clutch it. Let it balance between your fingers – like this."

Awkwardly, Lisya tried to copy Varvara Petrovna's light grasp. The strange implement felt nothing like the wooden spoons at home.

"Put the knife in your other hand. No – don't hold it like an axe. Pretend it's your violin bow... There – that's better." Varvara Petrovna deftly transferred a piece of roast pork onto her plate and cut it into tiny pieces, each of which she lifted into her barely open mouth.

Lisya watched, amazed that the small morsels stayed on the fork, and that Varvara Petrovna did not seem to chew.

"Now, you try."

Nervously Lisya tried to lift the smallest piece of pork on the platter. Midway to her plate, it slipped off her fork and plopped juicily onto the white lace tablecloth. Her cheeks burning, she quickly speared the wayward pork and completed the transfer. Taking a deep breath, she began sawing at the meat. When, at last, the silver knife screeched raucously against the porcelain plate, Lisya saw with dismay that the nearly severed piece was still attached to the main slice. Rather than risk another screech, she tried to pull the meat apart. When the stubborn string finally snapped, the piece on which she had labored so long flew onto the floor, where it was promptly gobbled up by Varvara Petrovna's dog.

The little beast looked greedily up at her, licking his lips. Resolving that such a fat, spoiled creature should get no more of what her family rarely tasted, Lisya concentrated on what was left of the meat.

By the time she laid down her knife, beads of sweat dotted her forehead. The pork, however, was neatly sliced into pieces even smaller than Varvara Petrovna's. Several of the tiny cubes fell off her fork while traversing the unaccustomed distance between her plate and her mouth, but every time she lowered her head, Varvara Petrovna slapped her chin with a rolled-up napkin. And even after the succulent tidbits had reached their proper destination, Varvara Petrovna admonished her – with no little disgust – to close her mouth and stop smacking her lips. By the time Lisya was finally allowed to leave, she had decided that fancy food was wasted on people who did not allow themselves to enjoy it

After that, the music lessons frequently ended with an "invitation" to tea or – occasionally – lunch. Lisya learned quickly – partly to spare herself from the way Varvara Petrovna's voice sounded whenever she spilled something, partly to irritate the fat little dog, whose greedy eyes followed every morsel from plate to mouth.

When Lisya had learned to eat without making a great deal of noise, Varvara Petrovna moved on to other matters of etiquette.

"This was my daughter's," she said, holding up a not particularly attractive grey silk dress covered with ruffles. "Anastasia can fix it for you."

During the next week, Anastasia proceeded to rip off the ruffles, pouf the sleeves, and edge the neckline with lace from an old tablecloth. From the hem of draperies in a guestroom no one ever used, she snipped enough velvet for a sash; its rich dark blue brought the dull grey silk to life.

"Now it matches your eyes," said Anastasia, as Lisya tried on the dress.

Lisya's pleasure in her new dress, however, was dampened by the complicated undergarments Varvara Petrovna said she must wear with it.

"I can hardly move with all this stuff on," she grumbled to Anastasia.

"A lady doesn't have to move," replied Anastasia.

"I'm not a lady."

"But you look like one in that dress."

And at her next lesson, Varvara Petrovna began teaching her how to act like one. Some of the new manners Lisya took to quickly. Dropping into a graceful curtsey and sitting with her ankles neatly crossed harmonized well with the music she was learning; sipping from the delicate tea-cups seemed more appropriate than slurping. And listening to her mother read Pushkin had already made her speech closer to Varvara Petrovna's pronunciation than to the village accent. Even so, she was always relieved to leave the constricted etiquette of the manor, and to exchange the tight shoes which matched the new dress for her comfortable *lapti*.

"Mother is having a soiree next Thursday," announced Varvara Petrovna. "The Beethoven Sonata you've been working on will be just fine. And some of these Mozart etudes will be nice, too."

Aghast, Lisya realized that it was pay-back time. To her enormous relief, she had rarely encountered Praskovia Nikolaevna since that first terrifying day she had played for her. But now, she would not only have to perform again for the fearsome old woman, but for her aristocratic friends as well. Out of sight of the mansion, Lisya vomited behind one of the linden trees lining the driveway.

On Thursday night, she waited nervously in the kitchen.

"You look as beautiful as your music, Lisya," said Anastasia proudly. "Don't be afraid."

Despite her nervousness, Lisya knew Anastasia was right. The dress was uncomfortable and the shoes were too tight, but at least she didn't look like a peasant.

Only with difficulty did Lisya walk through the crowded room without fainting from sheer terror. Standing by the piano, she barely noticed Varvara Petrovna's encouraging glance. Somehow she made it through the etudes they had rehearsed. And then she was sitting all alone before the piano, her sweating palms poised over the keys. Looking out at the blur of faces, her nervous glance suddenly focused on the encouraging smile of a man sitting near the back of the room. His kind face was filled with compassion – and admiration. Meeting his eyes, she smiled back – and then plunged into the Beethoven Sonata. After an eternity of feeling her heavy fingers marching woodenly over the sticky keys, it was finally over. A sharp glance from Varvara Petrovna reminded her to bow to the polite applause. The stranger, she noticed, was clapping with genuine enthusiasm.

Praskovia Nikolaevna rewarded her with a gruff pat on the head, and allowed her to stay for refreshments.

"You did very well tonight," said the stranger, offering her a piece of cake. The delicate plate balanced reassuringly on his adept fingers.

"You think so?" Lisya looked up at him, wondering who he was. All the others she had seen before, peeking out of the kitchen door.

"You have a remarkable gift," he replied earnestly, his slightly slanted eyes lighting up behind his wire-rim glasses. "It is wonderful to hear you using it. And exciting to think how much more music you have in your soul."

"I love the music, but…" She motioned with dismay at the rows of now empty chairs.

"That will get easier," his voice was gently confident, "the more you do it."

"That you were here…" she hesitated "… it made the fear not so big."

"Then I will be here, at all your concerts."

Walking back to the village, she realized she didn't even know his name. No matter. He would keep his promise. They would meet again. The thought soothed her, as did the quiet pleasure evoked by remembering his reaction to her music. Ah, if only her family understood as this stranger did!

The onion dome of the bell tower was silhouetted against the rising moon by the time she returned home. Pausing before the gate, Lisya looked longingly at the graceful little church. If only it had a place for her, too; if only she, too, could belong there. Hugging her violin, she turned wearily toward her family's *izba*.

Ж   Ж   Ж

Babushka was dying. Everyone in Derevnia knew it. All day, people of all ages came to say goodbye, and to thank her for soothing their pains and easing their ills for so many years.

Babushka had moved into the parsonage after Evgenia's last pregnancy; she had stayed to help with the household when the school started. Lately, however, her strength had ebbed markedly.

"No, there's nothing wrong with me," she protested, when Evgenia expressed concern. "I'm just getting old."

One night at supper, Babushka passed her bowl of *kasha* to Tatiana and set down her spoon with an air of finality. In a hollow but still firm voice, she announced that she had lived long enough. She climbed on top of the stove, and ate no more. No one argued with her.

Many of those who came to see Babushka had been helped into the world by her strong, gentle hands. She remembered all of "her" children, and smiled with pride as each of them kissed her farewell. When everyone else had paid their respects, Babushka's clan crowded into the *izba*. To each of them she distributed her personal possessions and a last word of parting.

To her daughter, she gave her special herbs and healing tools. "Now *you* must be the Babushka," she said proudly. Ekaterina nodded and smiled tearfully.

To Evgenia she gave the brightly flowered shawl she had always worn on Feast Days. "You will be midwife to much change in Derevnia," she said quietly, squeezing her granddaughter's hand. "You were right to prepare for it."

And to her namesake, Lisya, she gave her distaff. "Your daughter won't be born in Derevnia," she said sadly, patting her great-granddaughter's cheek. "But cut her cord with this, so that we can be with you."

Then Babushka asked Evgenia to sing her favorite song. To everyone's surprise, she also asked Lisya to play. Astonished, Lisya fetched her violin. She was nervous, more so even than when she performed at Praskovia Nikolaevna's. Cheeks blazing, she tucked it under her chin. No one in her family had ever heard her play.

Evgenia began to sing a song about the forest. After the first verse, Lisya joined in harmony. As the dark throbbing sound of the violin matched and melded with the deep richness of her mother's voice, Lisya felt connected to her family as never before. In her mother's singing, she heard understanding; on her father's face, she saw no disapproval. Her grandmothers were smiling, her grandfathers beaming with pride.

And when, at last, the sadly joyous song was ended, Babushka's sightless eyes looked up at them all in utterly fearless peace.

Chapter 5: The PLAGUE

Evgenia sat despondently at her desk, looking out the window at the dreary snow. It had been on just such a day, last year, that the Little Father had been assassinated.

After countless bungled attempts, the Terrorists had finally succeeded. The bomb went off right at the Tsar's feet, ripping open his abdomen, tearing off one leg and shattering the other. He died in a pool of blood, with an unpublished constitution for Russia in his pocket.

And then, not long after Easter, her brother Vsevolod's eldest had been drafted into the army. Evgenia had wept; the boy was not only her nephew but one of her best students. Conditions in the army were hard and the length of service long. Chances of returning alive were not good, even in peacetime.

In keeping with custom, young Semyon and his friends had gone on a drunken debauch which lasted until the day of his departure. After a huge funeral feast, at which the entire village mourned his loss, they all escorted him to the edge of the village. Evgenia embraced him tearfully, and waved until he disappeared into the forest. She knew she would never see him again.

Semyon's empty desk stared reproachfully at her. Perhaps what she had taught him might somehow increase his chances of survival? Probably not. Ever since his departure, the inevitability of his fate – and her powerlessness to change it – had cast a pall over her teaching. What was the point of trying to educate cannon fodder – or workhorses or brood mares? What good did it do to teach children about a world that could never be theirs? And what hope was there for reform if even the Tsar was butchered for his efforts?

"Excuse me." A politely authoritative voice startled her out of her gloomy reverie. Standing at the door was an urbanely-dressed young man who looked remarkably familiar.

The stranger introduced himself as the son of her teacher, Pavel Vladimirich… Yes, of course. She could see it now. He was taller and more self-assured, but the resemblance was quite strong. The black hair was just as straight, the plain features almost as ordinary. And though the slanted brown eyes were not as exotic, in them burned the same gentle zeal.

Pavel Vladimirich, young Alexander Pavlovich informed her, had become a successful lawyer in Kazan. He had several wealthy clients, but spent much of his time defending the poor and championing good causes.

"I'm glad to hear he decided not to become a terrorist," smiled Evgenia.

"Yes," Alexander Pavlovich smiled back, "he said you would be."

"What else did he say about me?"

"That you were his best student – and that you would help me."

Alexander Pavlovich was a doctor, and had recently been assigned by the government to the rural area which included Derevnia.

"And just how did your father say I would help?" asked Evgenia.

"He said you would teach me," Alexander Pavlovich smiled again, remarkably like his father.

"And what can the wife of a village priest teach a learned young doctor from the city?"

"Maybe how to teach the people of her village."

"About what?"

"About how to prevent plague – and keep the babies from dying."

"You can do that?" Evgenia looked at him skeptically.

"Modern medicine can," he replied enthusiastically, "but not without people's cooperation."

"And that's where I come in?"

"Yes. Will you help?"

"First you'd better teach me something about this marvelous modern medicine of yours."

Alexander Pavlovich had fortunately arrived during the relatively inactive months of winter. Evgenia was therefore able to find time for what turned out to be an increasingly absorbing subject of study.

At their first lesson, he drew several strange-looking symbols on the chalkboard. Some were small rods, some looked like tangled strings of tiny beads, others were comma-shaped with a single whip-like hair at one end.

"These are bacteria – or germs," he announced, pointing to the board.

"What are they?" asked Evgenia, wondering if this was some sort of scientific alphabet.

"Tiny organisms which cause disease," he replied. "This one causes tuberculosis... and this, scarlet fever... and this nasty one with the whip – cholera."

Involuntarily, Evgenia crossed herself.

"Many people here have died of such illnesses," she said, puzzled, "but none of these – germs – have ever been in Derevnia."

"Yes, they have. You just can't see them"

"You mean they're invisible – like evil spirits?"

"No, they're just too small to see – without a microscope."

And with that, he took a complicated-looking device out of his leather medical bag. On a small piece of glass he dabbed a drop from the bucket of water near the schoolhouse door.

"Here," he said, putting it under the microscope. "Look at this."

"Ugh!" exclaimed Evgenia at the teeming jungle she beheld. Some of the strange wriggling creatures were grossly ugly, others were bizarrely beautiful, still others oddly humorous and vaguely frightening. "Is all that in there?"

"Unfortunately, yes." Alexander Pavlovich looked carefully at the slide under the lens. "Look again... See there, up in the corner?"

Evgenia peered into the microscope again, and nodded.

"Now look at the board – see the similarity?" he asked.

She looked at the drawings, then back in the microscope, and once again at the board. Suddenly, she drew back in alarm.

"Yes, that's right . Cholera!"

"But how can something so small," Evgenia looked dubious, "cause so much trouble?"

"Germs get inside the body and then multiply, causing infections."

"Like being possessed by a demon?"

"Well... yes, I suppose you could call it that."

"But we've been drinking from that bucket for several days. No one has cholera – yet." Evgenia shuddered.

"And probably you needn't worry – yet. I doubt that there are enough cholera bacteria in this water to beat down your body's immune system. But in summer, germs of all kinds multiply more rapidly – especially in babies, and people who don't have enough to eat. They're too weak to resist disease."

"Is that why so many babies die every summer?"

"In general, yes."

"These germs – they're alive?"

"The ones that make you sick are."

"That cholera germ there," she motioned nervously toward the microscope, "is it still alive?'

"I'm not sure. It's hard to tell."

"Can we kill the germs?"

"Certainly, though some are harder to do away with than others."

"How could we kill this cholera germ?"

Alexander Pavlovich rinsed the slide in the bucket of water and put it on the stove. When it had boiled for awhile, he put it back near the door to cool.

"Is it dead?" Evgenia asked anxiously.

"Yes."

"Are you sure?"

Without a word he walked to the bucket and drank deeply from the dipper. Evgenia gasped. Smiling, he held out the dipper. She hesitated, thinking about all the mysterious creatures she had seen swimming around under the microscope.

"Are they all dead?"

"All those that will harm you."

She closed her eyes, drank a quick mouthful, and sat down to ponder this startling demonstration.

"So then, cholera…" she paused, struggling with the realization," is not punishment for our sins?"

"No – just poor sanitation."

Ж　Ж　Ж

And so, science was introduced into the curriculum of Evgenia's school. Alexander Pavlovich came often to instruct them all in its wonders. Meanwhile, Evgenia read the rural health pamphlets he gave her.

A group of concerned doctors had written and published the pamphlets, which contained much enlightening and useful information about how to prevent epidemics. But as Evgenia worked her way through the stack, she became increasingly irritated.

"They assume that peasant mothers are too ignorant and lazy to care about their children!" she finally burst out angrily to Alexander Pavlovich.

"Well… but… of course, there are exceptions," he stammered, somewhat taken aback.

"None of the women around here can afford to be lazy!" she went on, indignantly. "They have too much work to do!"

"But surely that does not preclude their taking precautions of simple hygiene."

"Simple hygiene is only simple for people who can afford servants or indoor plumbing – and who don't live in a crowded *izba*!"

Alexander Pavlovich subsided into embarrassed silence.

"And another thing," Evgenia continued, "your pamphlets say only modern medicine can cure illness. My mother, and her mother before her, have been healing people for longer than your modern medicine has existed!"

A few days later, Alexander Pavlovich returned with a peace offering – a samovar. It needed only a bit of charcoal to boil and provide safe drinking water.

"My father was right," he smiled apologetically. "I have much to learn from you."

"And I'm sure I will learn from you, as I did from him," Evgenia smiled back, delighted with the samovar. Soon, many of the more prosperous *izba*s had one, too.

And so began the long and arduous task of educating the people of Derevnia in the practice of preventive medicine. She began with her students.

"Before we start today's reading lesson, I want to see the handkerchiefs I gave you on Friday."

Lisya quickly took three neat folds of cloth from the pocket of her remarkably unwrinkled *sarafan* and lined them up on her desk. Elena proudly spread out an elaborately embroidered piece of cloth whose corners had been rounded and laboriously edged. Tatiana put hers on her head like a hat.

Noticing Dmitri rummaging frantically in his pockets, Lisya quietly slipped him one of her immaculate squares. Mischa's was around his neck, already covered with the dust and sweat of the fields. Triumphantly fishing his out of his lunch basket, Volodya sneezed noisily into its rumpled folds.

"Good!" laughed Evgenia. "That's what it's for. Remember that, girls."

Lisya wrinkled her nose in distaste. Elena frowned at the elaborate swirls her mother had spent so much time on. Tatiana plucked off her improvised hat and waved it.

"And Volodya, don't forget to bring a clean one tomorrow."

Turning to the blackboard, Evgenia suddenly noticed a fly buzzing overhead. Slowly raising the fly-swatter hanging from her belt, she stalked the fly to Semyon's old desk and unerringly smacked it. Just on the verge of dozing off, Kolya, Semyon's younger brother, sat up, startled. Evgenia arched an eyebrow at him and walked to the blackboard.

During the course of the reading lesson, Evgenia's fly-swatter was ever vigilant, zealously hastening the demise of any flying insect foolish enough to come near.

"Seven!" giggled Tatiana softly, as Evgenia righteously demolished a tiny typhoid carrier brazenly resting on the woodpile.

"Eight!" whispered Volodya, as she deftly flicked another from the rim of the water bucket.

"Nine!" exclaimed Dmitri aloud, as Evgenia reached high for a huge droning pest and struck it down in mid-flight.

During recess, Kolya and Volodya practiced fly-swatting near the outhouse. With Elena watching attentively, Kolya demonstrated his new backhand technique, to which Volodya responded with an overhand smash. The contest escalated rapidly as the boys tried increasingly daring postures, swatting under kicking legs and behind turned backs and over upside-down heads. Finally Volodya made a great flying leap, slashing his swatter like a sabre. Missing the targeted fly, he crashed sprawling to the ground.

"Volodya! Are you hurt?" Elena rushed to his side.

Volodya lay still, his eyes closed. After a few moments, his lips began to twitch and he burst out laughing. Relieved, Elena and Kolya laughed, too, and helped him up. The contest continued less athletically – but with greater accuracy.

On the steps of the schoolhouse sat Lisya and Dmitri, decorating a new fly-swatter for his mother. Tomorrow was Anastasia's birthday. Nearby, Tatiana whirled happily, inscribing graceful circles with her swatter, and gaily waving her fluttering handkerchief.

In the open door, Evgenia stood smiling. Her campaign was off to good start.

The rest of Derevnia, however, was not so easily persuaded.

With Ivan's help, she convinced several of the men that draining the swamp south of the village would drive away the "fever maidens" of malaria. When her children got scarlet fever, she sternly quarantined them. And both Evgenia and Ivan allowed themselves to be publicly inoculated against smallpox, discrediting those who murmured that the vaccination left the mark of the Antichrist. Surely it could not be so if their undeniably pious priest wore it.

Mostly, though, Evgenia's germ warfare hammered away at the twin problems of sewage and water supply. Convincing the women that they needed an outhouse and nagging their men to build it far enough away from the well was slow and uphill going.

"Germs breed in human waste," said Evgenia for the hundredth time, trying to ignore the sharp stench inside Marfa's doorway. "You should have an outhouse in the yard, in the far corner."

"And carry the slop buckets all that way?" Marfa, as usual, was pregnant. "No thanks. Too heavy, too far."

"But if you all used the outhouse instead," Evgenia wiped her watering eyes, "you wouldn't have to carry any buckets." One of Marfa's naked brood urinated into the dumping place in the entry hall. His aim was poor and splattered the feces surrounding the reeking hole.

"Too cold in winter," Marfa shrugged, and gave the grimy child an affectionate cuff. Grinning, he licked a trickle of snot from his upper lip

"But the hole is too close to the well." Evgenia quickly stepped aside as the boy darted out the door. "It poisons the water."

"Been drinking that water for years." Marfa hoisted her swollen belly out the door and waddled over to the well. Dipping into the bucket perched next to it, she drank noisily. "See! I'm not dead."

"Where are these germs you keep talking about?" piped up Agafya from the small crowd of women who had followed Evgenia to Marfa's gate. At each *izba*, the group had grown larger. "I don't see anything."

"Evil spirits know how to hide," said Anya, who stood opposite Agafya.

"But surely they can be chased off by something smaller than an outhouse," retorted Agafya.

"Maybe something we could make ourselves," said Anya hopefully, "instead of trying to get our men to do it."

Heads nodded, as a murmur of assent passed around the women at the gate.

"Germs can't be scared away," said Evgenia, turning to the women. "Only good hygiene can prevent them from spreading disease."

"Plagues are God's punishment for our sins," said Agafya sanctimoniously.

"Maybe for *your* sins," snapped Ekaterina, who had been listening quietly at the edge of the crowd, "but not for our children's!"

Everyone stared at the uncharacteristic outburst.

"My *izba* would certainly smell better without that awful hole in the entrance," said Anya wistfully. "If only I could talk Pyotr into building one…"

"Humph!" snorted Agafya. "My Foma has more important things to do!"

"Maybe that's why my Mikhail encouraged him to build his own *izba*," said Ekaterina icily. To everyone's relief, Agafya and Foma and their large family had finally moved out.

"With an outhouse, there won't be so many bugs in your homes," interjected Evgenia hastily, trying to keep the debate from degenerating into a personal feud.

"There were always bugs in my grandmother's *izba*, there are bugs in mine," grunted Marfa, defiantly sticking out her huge belly. "It's how things are."

"When tradition makes people sick," said Evgenia, trying not to lose her temper, "it's stupid to hang on to it!"

"So!" bristled Agafya, "You think you're too good for the old ways!"

"Old or new, who cares!" interrupted Anya. "I just want an *izba* that doesn't stink!"

"I'll ask Mikhail to help Pyotr build you an outhouse," said Ekaterina, glaring at Agafya.

"And I'll ask Father Ivan to bless it when it's finished," added Evgenia, glaring at Marfa.

Though Ekaterina actively supported the sanitation campaign, she kept her distance from Alexander Pavlovich. He, too, seemed to go out of his way to avoid her. Evgenia, however, began spending more time at the manor's old infirmary, which the young doctor had remodelled into a surprisingly well-equipped clinic. As she helped him with the occasional patients who trickled in – many of them at her urging – she began to see that he knew ways of healing unknown even to Babushka.

But the more Evgenia watched him, the more she also began to see that there was much about healing that Alexander Pavlovich did not know – things that she had learned from Babushka. And she observed, too, that the old and new medicine had more in common than just the dedication of their respective practitioners. Not a few things were the same – though called by different names. Gradually, Evgenia combined the best of both. And in so doing, built a bridge between Ekaterina and Alexander Pavlovich. It was to be many years, however, before either deigned to cross it

Ж   Ж   Ж

Moonlight streamed in through the open shutters of the loft. Lisya and Tatiana lay side by side on the bed they shared, not wanting to let go of the magic of Midsummer's Eve.

"Everything looks so beautiful," sighed Lisya, gazing out the window at the shimmering night.

"Like when you played the piano tonight." Tatiana raised an arm and slowly waved it in the silver glow. "That's how it sounded."

"I'm glad you liked it." At Praskovia Nikolaevna's Midsummer soiree, Lisya had – as usual – performed. For the first time, Tatiana was there, too, watching from the kitchen with Anastasia.

"The music – it's so *different*!" Tatiana jumped up and struck an oddly elegant pose.

"You look like Praskovia Nikolaevna without her cane," giggled Lisya, sitting up. "Though it's hard to imagine her with a braid."

"Your new music," Tatiana began rotating her head, swinging her long braid in wide, sweeping arcs, "it makes me want to dance in new ways."

"Yes, I know," smiled Lisya, dodging her sister's flying braid. "I feel different when I'm playing it, too... Like I'm somewhere else."

"Some place with no one like Marfa's children?"

"Well... yes. I know they're cousins, but..."

"The oldest one has a crush on Elena. You should have seen him chasing after her tonight, trying to get her to jump the fire with him." Tatiana dropped to all fours, grunting like pig, and hopped clumsily over her sister's knees.

"Poor Elena!" Lisya giggled again. "What did she do?"

"She flew away –" Tatiana stopped grunting and started flapping her arms gracefully "– after Volodya."

"Who probably didn't even notice." Lisya smiled and shook her head.

"But he noticed that you weren't there. So did I."

"I stayed at the mansion to help Anastasia clean up." Lisya's smile faded. "She doesn't belong here, either."

"Don't worry, Lisya." Tatiana was suddenly still. "Someday you'll find a place that is home." Lying down next to her, Tatiana leaned her head reassuringly against her sister's shoulder.

Resting her cheek on Tatiana's tousled hair, Lisya drifted off to sleep, grateful that she was not alone.

In her dream, a beautiful bird with Tatiana's face was flying through the silver sky. Suddenly a large, menacing shape blotted out the light and swooped down on the bird, who screamed with Tatiana's voice.

Lisya awoke suddenly in the dark room. The moonlight was gone and Tatiana was moaning feverishly.

"Tanya? Tanya, what is it?!"

Tatiana clutched the right side of her stomach. "It's like a knife – there," she cried out in pain.

Bounding out of bed, Lisya slid down the loft ladder and ran into her parents' small bedroom. "Mother! Mother, wake up!"

Evgenia's eyes opened and, after a few seconds, focused enquiringly on Lisya.

"It's Tanya. She hurts bad!"

Evgenia was out of bed and up the ladder almost as quickly as Lisya had come down.

"You'd better get your grandmother," she said, frowning, after examining Tatiana.

Lisya tore down the road to Ekaterina's *izba*.

The old woman moved with surprising speed as she followed Lisya back up the road, questioning her carefully about Tatiana's condition.

After carefully probing Tatiana's lower abdomen, Ekaterina's face blanched. Climbing laboriously back down to the kitchen, she began to brew one of her herbal remedies.

"Is it what I think?" asked Evgenia, who had followed her down the ladder.

"Yes." Ekaterina's brow was wrinkled with concern too great to hide.

"What can we do?" Evgenia's face was even paler than her mother's.

"This will ease the pain," Ekaterina said quietly, nodding at the pot on the stove.

"But it won't heal her?"

"No."

"Does anyone –" Evgenia hesitated "– recover from this?"

Ekaterina, too, hesitated. "Not that I've ever seen." Tears welled up in her eyes. "But we can pray."

Evgenia stared at the icon corner. Then, resolutely, she returned to the bedroom to rouse her husband. A few minutes later, Ivan ran out the door and rode off on the horse. Evgenia climbed back up to the loft.

"Is she going to die?" whispered Lisya anxiously. She had never seen her mother so worried.

"I don't know," replied Evgenia, unable to mask her concern. "I sent your father to get Alexander Pavlovich. Maybe there's something he can do." She slipped her arm under Tatiana's shoulders. "Here, help me get her down by the stove. We can make her more comfortable there."

Ekaterina's medicine dulled Tatiana's pain. She dozed fitfully and was frighteningly still. Lisya sat at her side, clasping her hand and desperately willing her sister's inert body to *move*.

At last, Ivan returned with the doctor, who strode quickly to the bench nearest the stove, on which Tatiana now lay. While gently probing her stomach, he carefully questioned Evgenia about her symptoms.

"Her appendix is inflamed," he finally announced quietly. "I'll have to operate immediately, before it bursts and spreads the infection."

"Can you save her?" burst out Lisya, still holding Tatiana's hand.

"I think so," replied Alexander Pavlovich, regarding her solemnly. "We can perform the operation on the kitchen table. Help your mother scrub it while I prepare my instruments."

Grateful to have something helpful to do, Lisya scrubbed as though twenty demons were chasing her. By the time Ivan carried Tatiana to the table, Lisya's arms and shoulders were aching with fatigue.

Ivan made the sign of the cross, kissed Tatiana tenderly on the forehead, and then sank to his knees in the icon corner. Still yawning, Volodya knelt beside his father, having been finally awakened by all the commotion; once asleep, it was almost impossible to rouse him. Beside him, Ekaterina, too, was praying – though with one eye on Alexander Pavlovich. Evgenia stood next to the doctor, ready to assist him.

"Please, may I stay here?" asked Lisya.

"There will be a lot of blood," cautioned Alexander Pavlovich, "and other unpleasant things."

"I know," replied Lisya, averting her eyes from all the sharp instruments laid out before him. "But she won't be so scared if I hold her hand."

Tatiana looked up at her gratefully, and then closed her eyes.

Once the anesthetic had taken effect, Alexander Pavlovich went to work. After the first incision – which made her queasy – Lisya tried not to watch what he was doing. Eventually, however, she could not resist the sight of his quick, deft hands moving so authoritatively in the wriggling mass of her sister's intestines. Just as he had warned, it was all very unpleasant. Yet despite the blood, she could not help but admire the skill with which he manipulated the shiny tools lined up so precisely on the table. And by the time his small, strong fingers had neatly sewn up the incision, Lisya could almost understand why someone as dignified as Alexander Pavlovich had chosen such a messy profession.

No one slept that night. Except for Lisya – who refused to leave Tatiana's side – the entire family knelt praying in the icon corner. In between prayers,

Evgenia hovered anxiously over her sick child, murmuring quietly to Alexander Pavlovich. On her knees before the icons, Ekaterina – keeping a watchful eye on her granddaughter – continued to eye the doctor suspiciously.

Holding one of Tatiana's pitifully limp hands, Lisya, too, prayed fervently. That her buoyant little sister could be forever still – no, that was unthinkable. And that she might lose the only person who accepted her without reservation – that was unbearable.

Alexander Pavlovich kept vigil at Tatiana's other side. The same strong hands which had so surely cut away her diseased flesh, now took her pulse and touched her brow with infinite gentleness. He did not pray, but Lisya could tell that he, too, was worried.

Finally, as the sun climbed reluctantly into the sky, Tatiana opened her eyes. Confused and a little frightened, she looked inquiringly about the room.

"It's all right, Tanya," said Lisya, comfortingly. "You had a pain in your stomach, but Alexander Pavlovich cut it out."

"It still hurts," Tatiana smiled wanly. "But different."

"That will go away soon," said Alexander Pavlovich reassuringly, "and then you'll be good as new."

The family gathered hopefully around Tatiana, kissing her alarmingly pale face as if she might break.

"Will she really be all right?" asked Evgenia after Tatiana had gone back to sleep.

"I think so. The operation went well, without complications. But she's not out of danger yet," cautioned Alexander Pavlovich. "We'll know for sure in a few days."

And for the next three days, Ivan and Volodya prayed, Evgenia and Ekaterina hovered; Lisya sat steadfastly at Tatiana's side, coaxing her to eat during her short waking intervals, and holding her hand during the long hours of sleep.

"You must get some rest, Lisya," said Alexander Pavlovich on one of his frequent visits. "One patient in this household is enough."

"No," Lisya shook her head stubbornly. "Not until I know she's going to be all right."

Finally, on the morning of the third day, Tatiana sat up. On her pale face was a real smile. "Go to bed, Lisya. I'll keep an eye on the doctor." She narrowed her eyes and pursed her lips in a subdued, but remarkably accurate imitation of Ekaterina.

Lisya burst into tears and hugged her sister. Tatiana was back! All was well.

"Yes, yes! She will be fine," announced Alexander Pavlovich triumphantly, when he visited later that day. "Yes indeed, my dear, you'll be dancing again in no time!" A huge smile lit up his plain but regular features and, for a moment, Lisya thought the dignified doctor might himself start to dance.

Word of the miracle quickly spread. Everyone in the village stopped by to see for themselves. As Tatiana was much beloved, the people of Derevnia were overjoyed at her recovery. There was, however, much discussion about how she had survived a malady which killed everyone else.

"It's because we all prayed for her," said Anya.

"And because her father is a priest," added Natasha proudly.

"Or maybe it was witchcraft," hinted Agafya darkly.

"Nonsense!" retorted Ekaterina. "The doctor saved her life." She did not, however, say this when Alexander Pavlovich himself was in earshot.

As for Lisya, she had no doubt that Alexander Pavlovich had saved her sister.

"Thank you," she said simply, stopping at the clinic one day after her music lesson. "If anything had happened to Tanya…"

"Tatiana is a very special girl," said Alexander Pavlovich gently. "I would have missed her, too."

"How can I ever repay you?"

"You already have – with your music."

True to his promise, Alexander Pavlovich had, ever since that first evening, attended all of her performances at the manor. Knowing he was there had eased what never ceased being a difficult ordeal. Praskovia Nikolaevna certainly enjoyed the music, but barely recognized Lisya herself as human, let alone a person worthy of respect. Alexander Pavlovich, however, genuinely loved music, and held her in high regard as a musician. Each time she played, he never failed to pay her discerning compliments. Lacking active encouragement from her family, she valued his appreciation all the more.

"Will you be there next week – at Praskovia Nikolaevna's," asked Lisya. "I've learned a new Beethoven Sonata."

"I look forward to hearing it – as I do everything that you play."

"In Kazan, do you hear much music?"

"Oh yes," replied Alexander Pavlovich, enthusiastically. "There are many fine musicians, and I go to their concerts as often as possible."

"Next to them, my music must seem…" Lisya hesitated, not sure how to finish her question.

"I enjoy your music as much as anything I've heard there," he assured her sincerely.

"But surely, there in the city, the people who make music are more... more..." Again, she was unsure just what she was asking.

"Are they better musicians? In terms of talent, no. In terms of knowledge and experience – yes. But there is about your music a passion most of them lack. When you play, it is obvious how deeply you care about what you are doing – even at Praskovia Nikolaevna's." Alexander Pavlovich smiled. "And as for the other, that can be learned."

"How?"

This time, it was Alexander Pavlovich who hesitated. "Well, some of my friends are musicians. Maybe they could send some books or magazine articles, or perhaps some new music."

"Thank you, but..."

"What you need to know can't be learned from a book?"

Lisya nodded, relieved that someone understood so well what was so important to her. "I don't need new music. I need to know how to play better what I already have."

"Much of that must come from within. The more you grow inside, the bigger and better your music will be."

"And when that's not enough?"

"Then you must go where there are people who can teach you what you need to know."

Lisya again nodded, frowning. "I'll have to leave Derevnia."

"Perhaps," replied Alexander Pavlovich, gently patting her long, slender fingers. "But not for awhile."

Lisya gave him one of her rare smiles. What a remarkable man the doctor was! He knew so much about so many things, and had been to so many places. He had saved her sister's life. *And* he understood about her music.

For the first time in her life, Lisya had a hero.

Ж   Ж   Ж

Sunlight shone through the door and reflected off the white walls of the clinic. Alexander Pavlovich had worked hard cleaning up the old infirmary – though at Evgenia's suggestion, he had not fixed it up *too* much. Modern equipment mingled incongruously with traditional implements, and the well-scrubbed interior still retained a familiar *izba*-like atmosphere. That Russian peasants were not easily moved to change – even if in their best interests – he had learned from his father's mistakes. Earnestly he resolved not to repeat them.

"Your peasant is still a mystery to me, a man of many contradictions," he pondered, stacking the old sheets donated by Praskovia Nikolaevna on the examining table. "On the one hand, I see – and often admire – his piety, his closeness to the earth, his devotion to Mother Russia. But on the other, I also see behavior motivated by the crassest materialism. Remarkable kindness is interrupted by outbursts of unbelievably cruel fury; impetuous sentimentality lives side by side with immovable stubbornness."

"We are what the land has made us," Evgenia shrugged, ripping one of the sheets.

"Yes, I know," he sighed, deftly rolling a strip of the sheet into a neat bandage. "Who but the Russian peasant could tolerate such despotism and exploitation for so long – or explode in such sudden and violent rebellion!"

"No one can escape their destiny," mused Evgenia.

"If I believed that, I wouldn't be a physician. And I doubt you would be a teacher. But most people here seem to accept everything as God's Will. 'The Lord God knows better than I do what I need. He has sent me a cross to show that He loves me.' How can there be progress with such an attitude!"

"But for people with little control over their lives," objected Evgenia, "isn't this simply being wise enough to accept what they can't change?"

"A tragic by-product of our autocratic tradition," he conceded. "Like their notion of freedom being a man's right to do as he pleases. 'If I want to, I can; there's nothing to stop me.' That's how they think whenever the whip is removed."

"'As ye sow, so shall ye reap,'" murmured Evgenia.

"And the bragging that goes on! Well beyond the usual Russian penchant for hyperbole. And people seem to believe the most outrageous lies."

"Oh, you mean *vranye*," laughed Evgenia. "A harmless enough tradition. If you haven't anything to show off, you make something up. It's simply a way of saying you're here."

"But surely everyone knows it's a lie?"

"That's not the point," Evgenia shook her head. "The idea is to make yourself more interesting and exciting. If you do it well, you'll get respect for being a good liar. Besides, all good *vranye* has some truth in it."

"So clever lying is considered good entertainment?" laughed Alexander Pavlovich.

"A good story is a good story."

113

"Only people used to trouble would see it that way."

"If we didn't, we would die of despair."

When all the bandages were rolled, Evgenia walked back to the village, reflecting with satisfaction on Alexander Pavlovich's progress. He was beginning to understand more – and criticize less. Though in fairness, many of his criticisms of her people were just. For alongside the forgiving kindness, there was also a darker, violent side. And because she knew it more intimately, her concern at what it might do was even greater than his irritation at what it was preventing.

As she approached the tavern, she shuddered. Marfa's husband was lolling in front, scraping the wax off the top of a vodka bottle. After a skillful knock on its bottom to shoot out the cork, he threw his head back and poured the pure liquid straight down his skinny throat. As she passed the bench on which he was sitting, he grinned blearily, waving his penis from his open fly. Shaking her head, Evgenia looked away and walked up the road. Marfa's husband wasn't the only one who sought the brutal oblivion of vodka. Violent fighting sometimes broke out among those who overindulged. Stupid accidents happened, too. Few in Derevnia, fortunately, could afford to drink all the time. But many of them – especially in the winter – did so periodically. It was the easiest way to escape the long gloomy nights.

A few days later, she stopped at Marfa's house to drop off some of Ekaterina's herbal remedies. Marfa's husband was sitting dully at the table, his face swollen and bloated. His hair and beard were tangled and encrusted, but his fly was buttoned and he wore a repentant look.

Marfa's left eye was nearly swollen shut, and a large purple ring radiated out and around it. Defiantly she took the herbs, and did not offer tea. Relieved, Evgenia left the dank *izba* and continued on her way out to see Anastasia, who also had need of the herbs.

"My man never touches vodka," Evgenia had often heard her mother boast. Any woman whose husband avoided vodka was envied. For all too often, in between the vertical and horizontal stages of its obliterating intoxication, violent rage would possess those under its influence. The usual target was the man's wife. Beating one's wife, in fact, was considered by many a mark of manhood. And many of the women wore their bruises as badges of their husband's honor.

Like Marfa, Evgenia thought. Pity turned to anger as she remembered all Marfa's snide remarks about Ivan's manhood because he never beat her. Even more annoying were her taunts about Evgenia not being constantly pregnant. Marfa, of course, was – and wore her fertility as her own badge of honor. In vain did Evgenia – and Ekaterina and Babushka, before her – urge women like Marfa to periodically let their wombs lie fallow, and tell them there were ways to sometimes avoid pregnancy. In most cases she was no more successful than Ivan, who exhorted the men not to drink so much.

As Evgenia left the village and headed out to the manor, angry pity for Marfa was chased out by concern for Anastasia. That a dull sow like Marfa should be beaten by her even duller husband was too bad. But beautiful, spirited Anastasia? No! That was tragic. And Evgenia was worried.

Anastasia's husband had a wild, expansive temperament which, by nature, tended to excess. No one cursed more colorfully or danced with more energetic abandon than Fyodor. And when, bottle in hand, he harnessed his horses and rode whooping through Derevnia, many who heard him shrugged in covert pride. Because of the exuberance with which he indulged his appetites, Fyodor somehow transcended mere coarseness. Drunk or sober, he was undeniably charming.

Fyodor was usually able to convince himself that whatever he did was right, and resolved any resulting problems which arose by simply ignoring them. When confronted with his misdeeds, he seldom even bothered to deny them.

"Half the tales are lies, of course," was his standard response, "but as for the rest, we are all human, after all."

What Fyodor wanted from life was simply to do exactly as he pleased. Morality troubled him not at all; truth was whatever he could get away with. His only fear was that someday he would no longer get away with doing as he pleased.

Only Anastasia ever tried to put a bridle on Fyodor. Usually he managed to evade her. But when cornered, he would strike back. The occasional bruises which resulted came as close as anything ever did to eliciting remorse. In his way, he loved Anastasia – and depended on her to enable his doing what he pleased. After a fight, he would exert himself to be attentive. In the end, his charm would wear her down; after the brief pleasure of making up, he would return to his wild ways.

Evgenia was not among those charmed by Fyodor. Even so, she knew that he was not entirely to blame for Anastasia's unhappiness. Fyodor was what he was. But sometimes it seemed to Evgenia that Anastasia needlessly riled him. Certainly, there was much of which he could justifiably be accused. Anastasia, however, rarely confronted him with his real faults. Instead, she picked at him for not being what she wanted him to be.

While Fyodor was undoubtedly lazy, his skill with horses was truly remarkable – and exceedingly valuable in a society which depended so heavily on them. Everyone in Derevnia consulted him in matters of horseflesh. Fyodor was proud of this, his only real virtue. But Anastasia never seemed to notice.

The visit was not pleasant. Anastasia cried; Evgenia tried to comfort her.

"Maybe if you just took him as he is," she suggested kindly, "he wouldn't get so angry."

"He's a peasant!"

"But he's so good with horses."

"But he's so lazy!"

"Well… yes."

"Easy for *you* to say. Not everyone's a saint like your husband," snapped Anastasia, flaring up. "But at least Fyodor's a real man!"

Walking home, Evgenia's anger cooled quickly. Anastasia knew better; it was her pain which had lashed out. Sadness swept through Evgenia; her friend's situation could only get worse.

A few nights later, Fyodor finally drank too much and drove his horses too fast. There was an accident. Alexander Pavlovich was able to save his life. But while he was up and around in a remarkably short time, seemingly back to normal, he often suffered bouts of excruciating pain. He tried desperately to hide his agony – especially from Anastasia – but gradually, everyone in Derevnia became aware that Fyodor had changed.

Before, he had gotten drunk to indulge. Now, he looked to alcohol as a pain reliever, with vodka the quickest route to oblivion. He began to drink steadily and single-mindedly, and was often found intoxicated early in the day. He became subject to prolonged and morose fits of depression, and drank even more to drown his despair. Gone was his charm. Gone was his exuberance. He even neglected his horses. And Anastasia was seldom without bruises.

And then, one terrible night, Evgenia was awakened by frantic knocking. Elena burst in, sobbing, and begged Evgenia to come at once.

She threw a shawl around her nightgown and ran after the distraught girl. Entering the dimly-lit *izba*, Evgenia's eyes searched for what she dreaded to find. And there, on the floor in the icon corner, was Anastasia. Her clothes had been savagely ripped and there were bloody welts and hideous bruises all over her body. Her swollen eyes were closed, and she was frighteningly still. Dmitri was sitting on the floor next to her, sobbing desperately, holding her hand and begging her to wake up. There was no sign of Fyodor.

After finding a weak pulse, Evgenia sent Elena for Alexander Pavlovich.

Gently, she began to bathe her friend's wounds. When the doctor arrived, he stitched up a long, gaping gash on Anastasia's cheek and bound up her cracked ribs. Together they reset her dislocated shoulder. And then, covering her with warm, clean blankets, they sat down to wait. Dmitri had long since cried himself to sleep, his head in his sister's lap. Evgenia sat down and put her arm around Elena. The girl's frightened eyes looked up at her, and then slowly closed.

Anastasia finally regained consciousness the next day. A few days later, they fished Fyodor's body out of the Volga. Most of the wounds he had inflicted on his wife's body eventually healed – though the gash on her cheek left an ugly scar. But Evgenia knew that something inside had broken – and that it would never mend.

Ж   Ж   Ж

It had been a long while since Evgenia had visited the grove by the Volga. It was difficult to find time, these days. Today, however, was Sunday; the unseasonably warm spring weather beckoned irresistibly.

Evgenia leaned against her favorite tree and greeted the river. As she basked in the unfamiliar leisure, she reflected with satisfaction on what she had accomplished since the arrival of Alexander Pavlovich. Several village households now boasted samovars and outhouses. Fly-swatters with beautifully carved, painted handles had become popular gifts. Most of the women now considered it impolite not to use a handkerchief. The wells were deeper, and many an *izba* smelled cleaner. The incidence of typhoid and malaria had dropped noticeably, and a small but growing number of people were submitting to smallpox vaccination. With Ivan, she rejoiced that there were fewer funerals.

She was pleased with all this progress, and proud of her labor in bringing it forth. But somewhere, in the back of her mind, something ominous distracted. The snow had stopped too soon, it nagged, and the rain had not yet come. The clear, sunny days were very pleasant now, but what if they continued into the summer? With a shudder, Evgenia remembered that wolves had been seen around the village last All-Souls' Day. A sure sign, Ekaterina had muttered, of approaching famine.

By St. Peter's Day, there was still no rain. The men mowed the hay in an alarmingly short time. Everyone could see that the meager haystacks scratched together out of the parched grass would never last the winter. And the straggly winter wheat reaped by the women was just as sparse. By St. Elijah's Day, the only clouds appearing were those of swarming insects, which swooped hungrily on anything hardy enough to grow out of the sun-scorched earth. From dawn until dusk, women and children carried buckets of water from the river, vainly attempting to nourish their gardens. In the fields, the men fought a losing battle with the bugs. By harvest time, there was little to reap. Old people said it was the worst crop failure they could remember.

For lack of fodder and feed, the cows dried up and the hens quit laying. When the slaughtered animals had been consumed, people reluctantly ate their seed grain. And when that was gone, they weakened and grew anemic. With heavy heart, Evgenia watched helplessly as children's bellies grew swollen with hunger.

The wolves howled, that winter; many in Derevnia died. Evgenia and her family survived because her garden was bigger, and because devout religious fasting had accustomed them to eating less. What little they had, they shared. Miraculously, more lived than died. But Evgenia knew that worse would follow. For in the wake of famine always came pestilence.

It struck first in Astrakhan at the mouth of the Volga. As the weather warmed, cholera spread with ghastly rapidity and killed thousands. A wave of terror followed, as mass hysteria swept the terrified population. Fear of "*ona*" – "she", they called the disease – turned into blind destruction as frenzied mobs invaded quarantine barracks, attacked medical personnel, "rescued" patients, and burned down buildings. Meanwhile, the government imposed a rigid naval quarantine in the harbor, halting hundreds of ships with thousands of passengers. Food and water became scarce as the woefully understaffed medical team took days to examine them all. At last a government vessel steamed into sight, raising hopes of relief. But instead of supplies, the ship brought – coffins.

Fleeing the disease and riots and troops sent to enforce quarantine and quell disorder, crowds of migrant workers hurried north along the Volga, spreading panic – and the disease itself. As the cholera worked its way up the river, the news grew ever more alarming. Not only was the scourge growing more virulent, but casualties among those trying to cope with it were increasing. Several doctors had already fallen victim to mob violence. When it reached the city of Saratov, Alexander Pavlovich was ordered there by the government. Evgenia saw him off with no little trepidation. Several weeks later, he returned to Derevnia, visibly shaken by what he had witnessed.

"There I was, trying to get people to wash their hands and boil their water," he complained bitterly to Evgenia, "while the local priest was telling them that

God was punishing them for their sins – and warning them not to listen to those of us arrogant enough to try to flout God's Will."

"Ivan would never do such a thing!" exclaimed Evgenia indignantly.

"I know. But unfortunately many priests are not so enlightened." Alexander Pavlovich shook his head in disgust. "The ones in Saratov organized large religious processions to avert God's wrath. Prayers from seven in the morning until four in the afternoon – and here was this huge crowd parading all over the city – hot and sweating and drinking water right from the river!"

The government had responded by banning such gatherings and rigidly regulating funerals and burials. Ritual bathing of dead bodies was forbidden, as were services inside churches. Victims were buried undressed, covered with lime-soaked sheets, often without last rites from priests unable – or unwilling – to travel to distant cholera cemeteries. Meanwhile, compulsory hospitalization in the dreaded quarantine barracks continued.

"Then the religious processions became ugly mobs." Fear and frustration mingled in Alexander Pavlovich's voice. "With my own eyes, I saw them beat our chief physician to death. They dragged him out of his house, grabbed his feet and beat his head on the ground. When they had trampled and butchered him beyond recognition, they jeered and spat on him, rejoicing that he had received proper retribution."

"For what?!"

"For allegedly poisoning the wells with 'ona', and forcing healthy people into the barracks to contaminate them. That's what they think doctors do. And supposedly we cart off wagons full of writhing bodies to be buried alive."

"How could anyone think such a thing?!"

"Cholera is a particularly ghastly disease," he shrugged wearily. "What it does to its victims is really horrible to behold. And post-mortem muscle spasms often occur. To see such ghoulish-looking corpses move is unnerving – terrifying to the uneducated."

"What did the authorities do?"

"What they usually do in situations of mass disorder – mass arrests and mass floggings. And of course, death sentences and punishment at hard labor. None of which has had much effect on the cholera."

"Will it be here soon?" asked Evgenia quietly, after a long pause.

"Yes."

"Then we must prepare."

It came even sooner than they expected. While making his rounds of the nu-

119

merous villages under his jurisdiction, Alexander Pavlovich came upon a tragic scene at an outlying *izba*. Inside was the mother, dead of cholera, still holding the warm body of a tiny infant who had died of hunger. Outside lay the father, dying of cholera, and two frightened, starving small children. There was no one else around.

And so began a long nightmare of continuous diarrhea, interspersed by sudden bouts of violent vomiting, followed by severe cramps and massive dehydration. Sunken eyes looked up out of drawn cheeks, weak voices croaked hoarsely from between blue lips, cold clammy hands with withered skin clenched in hopeless misery.

Evgenia organized her students into squads to pass out the disinfectants Alexander Pavlovich begged from one of the cities upriver. The women of many households gratefully followed her instructions. Others – like Agafya – scornfully refused; anything which smelled so bad, they said, must be the work of the devil.

Everyday, Evgenia visited every *izba* in Derevnia, reminding people to drink only boiled water and urging them to send their sick ones to the clinic for quarantine. But everyone was reluctant to go to what seemed a house of death. Patiently, Evgenia explained – over and over – the purpose of quarantine. In their fear, many refused to understand. Marfa, she knew, was hiding at least one sick child in the *izba* she stubbornly refused to let Evgenia enter.

Some of the peasants, however, relented when she offered to take their sick to the clinic herself. And when they saw that she stayed to care for them – and that Father Ivan was there, too – more began to disgorge their pathetically ill relatives. Most of the time, those afflicted arrived too late. Evgenia did what she could to comfort the wasted bodies which lined the infirmary – and to keep the awful stench from overpowering them all. In this, she was aided by Ekaterina, who came – for the first time – to the clinic. Together, mother and daughter scrubbed ceaselessly and worked tirelessly to ease the pain and discomfort of their doomed neighbors. And, when it was time, Father Ivan helped them die in peace, with as much dignity as the ghastly scourge allowed.

For the most part, Alexander Pavlovich left the clinic in Evgenia's charge. He himself traveled endlessly throughout his too large district, teaching peasants to boil water and disinfect their houses, detecting and caring for those already stricken, organizing quarantine barracks and attending to dozens of exhausting but necessary details. He received little assistance outside of Derevnia – but neither was he attacked.

As winter approached, the plague grew less virulent. As the clinic began to empty – and stay that way – Evgenia allowed herself a few tentative sighs of relief. Not long before Christmas, the last cholera victim was brought in.

Elena brought her at the first sign of the illness. As they carried her into the infirmary, Anastasia looked up apologetically out of still lovely eyes. Seeing her stricken so, a spasm of fear gripped Evgenia's heart. After a long night of tannin enemas and injections of saline solution, she appeared better. Then, abruptly, she entered the second stage of the disease. Alexander Pavlovich said it was kidney failure; Evgenia knew it was because her spirit was broken.

Evgenia and Elena stayed at her side throughout her long, painful delirium. And when, at last, Anastasia's suffering was mercifully over, Elena wept for her sad, beautiful mother, and Evgenia mourned the treasured companion of her youth.

Gently, she crossed the withered arms on the motionless chest of her once lovely and spirited friend. And as she stared at the clenched, peeling hands, blue-black like octopus spawn, she remembered the legend of the Firebird.

Where had Anastasia shed her shining plumage, Evgenia wondered mournfully. Then she looked at Elena – still weeping – and smiled sadly.

Ж   Ж   Ж

Christmas that year was celebrated with quiet relief. The clinic was finally empty. Alexander Pavlovich reported that there were no new cases of cholera anywhere in his district.

Except for Anastasia, the plague took none of Evgenia's loved ones. Of this the village took note. And while some were disposed to attribute this rare good fortune to God's protection – or witchcraft – others remembered that these were also the people who had practiced Evgenia's preventive measures most rigorously. Others – like Agafya and Foma – had perished.

Among those favorably impressed was Ekaterina. One day she appeared unexpectedly at the door of Alexander Pavlovich's tiny office at the clinic.

"Could you use some help here?" she asked quietly.

He looked up at her in surprise. They stared at each other for a long time. Then a small, reluctant smile grew slowly in his eyes and twitched at the corners of his mouth.

"Yes," he replied evenly, trying not to sound too pleased. "Yes, of course."

Ekaterina shrugged back with a half-smile. Within a remarkably short time, she was running the clinic.

The last of the cholera funerals was Anastasia's. After gently washing the ravaged body, Evgenia and Elena dressed Anastasia in the clothes she had worn for her wedding. Beside her, they laid her distaff, a loaf of bread and a lump of salt. Then Pyotr and Mikhail, Andrei and Alexander Pavlovich, hoisted the coffin on their shoulders and carried it slowly to the church. In front walked Father Ivan, Volodya beside him carrying a large cross. Behind walked Evgenia and Elena, Dmitri and Lisya, followed by the rest of the village – all weeping profusely and wailing loudly.

Anastasia's coffin mercifully remained unopened in the church. Far better, thought Evgenia, to remember her like the flowers – from Praskovia Nikolaevna's greenhouse – which lay gracefully and fragrantly on the closed lid. Amidst the candles and incense, Evgenia joined the choir in hymns of consolation. In prayer and song, the mourners asked God to grant the deceased peace of soul in the habitations of the just.

"Verily, verily, I say unto you, the dead shall hear the voice of the Son of God," read Father Ivan from the Book of John, "and they that hear shall live." Then he solemnly intoned the prayer for the remission of sins. The bells tolled sorrowfully.

They buried her just before sunset, so the sun could light her soul to the other world. The heartbreaking laments ended in a lively feast, at which Anastasia's memory was fondly toasted. Life was noisily celebrated and homage paid to Death, the greatest of all blessings. The place of honor was left vacant – for Anastasia's spirit.

Later that night, alone in front of her icons, Evgenia entreated the Virgin to guide her friend in this, her long awaited journey. All night she kept vigil and when, at last, the moon set and the first rays of dawn mingled with the flickering candle, she felt a light and buoyant presence beside her. And she knew that lovely, graceful Anastasia had finally found a place where she belonged.

Chapter 6: The BEAR

"Have you ever touched bottom in the middle of the Volga?" asked Dmitri, as he slowly washed the chalkboard.

"No, I haven't," answered Evgenia. "I usually stay close to the bank."

Silently Dmitri finished the board, and then went outside to chop firewood. After bringing in several armloads, he carefully stacked the wood next to the stove.

"If fish could sing, I think their songs would be sad," he said abruptly.

Evgenia nodded and smiled at Anastasia's son.

Between them was a continuous conversation. Dmitri's terse observations were interspersed with long periods of solitary meditation. Evgenia was used to his singular statements and could always connect them, no matter how much time intervened.

Dmitri and Elena had moved in with Anastasia's parents. In return, the children helped the old couple with household chores and in the fields. Both worked hard, but still came to school. Dmitri often stayed after class, quietly doing odd jobs. Evgenia appreciated the help, and found his unobtrusive presence soothing.

Of all her students, Dmitri came closest to sharing her love of Pushkin. The others enjoyed the stories, but only Dmitri truly understood – and thrilled to – the magical beauty of the words.Whenever Evgenia read Pushkin to her class, the look on Dmitri's face mirrored her own soul. And when she asked him to read the poems aloud, he somehow endowed them with rich new harmony. He borrowed her treasured volume of Pushkin as often as she would let him. Sometimes she would see him sitting on the riverbank, silently reading to the Volga.

Not long after his mother's death, Dmitri began to write. Shyly he brought his poems to Evgenia, his eyes begging her not to laugh at them – or to scold him for his effrontery. Clumsy and self-conscious, his verses were full of pain and passion and raw beauty. Evgenia encouraged him as much as she could.

At first, Dmitri's poems were about the river. Little by little, Mother Volga began to resemble his own mother; his paeans to her beauty turned slowly into weeping laments. Sorrow then became dark, brooding anger, which circled around – but never dared touch – the terrible night his father had gone away. And then, just as Evgenia was beginning to fear that Dmitri's rage might consume him, the darkness perceptibly lightened. Once again, he began writing about the river. But now, instead of a tragically beautiful woman, the Volga became a lovely young girl.

Meanwhile, Dmitri was spending less time after school. And as his poems grew lighter and more lyrical, he also gave Evgenia fewer of them to read. It was not difficult for her to guess why.

On a particularly balmy day in early Spring, she stole a rare hour for herself. As she approached the little grove by the Volga, she heard a husky young male voice reciting verses full of shy admiration and budding passion. Between squeaks of the tentatively deepening voice were hints of cautious devotion. After a pause, the tender poem was answered by a poignant song mirroring its sentiments. There was, however, nothing tentative in the clear voice of the violin which sang it. And there were no squeaks. Smiling, Evgenia walked quietly away.

Ж   Ж   Ж

"I wonder if fish know their fathers," said Dmitri, lying on his side gazing at the river.

"Maybe they don't need to," replied Lisya, leaning against the tree giving the best view of the Volga.

"Do some fish behave better than others? Like people, I mean."

"Probably. When they're fighting for food, some seem hungrier than others."

"Or maybe they're just born meaner." Dmitri sat up and looked at her.

"Like some people are born nicer?"

"Like your father."

"Yes," agreed Lisya, "but sometimes it's hard to be the priest's daughter."

"Because more is expected of you?"

"No. Because I'm expected to fit in."

"Not everyone wants you to be like everyone else," said Dmitri fervently. "I like you just the way you are."

"So did your mother."

"She didn't fit in, either."

"I miss her," said Lisya after a long silence, tears filling her eyes.

"So do I," said Dmitri, his voice catching. "But I don't miss her so much when I'm with you."

"It's the same for me. I can be myself with you," replied Lisya, putting her hand tentatively in his, "just as I could with your mother."

"I wonder what she would think of my writing?"

"Probably the same as she did about my music. She was the only one who encouraged me, at first."

"It really matters to you – your music, I mean."

"I never really felt alive until I found it. Now I can't imagine my life without it. Is that how you feel about your poetry?"

"Not exactly. Mostly, writing takes away things I'd rather not feel. But sometimes I write about what makes me happy." He squeezed her hand.

"Are you happy now?"

"Yes." Dmitri shyly kissed her cheek, then leaned against the tree beside her. "Oh yes."

Lisya leaned her head against his strong shoulder. "So am I," she said happily. "So am I."

And together they smiled at the singing river.

As time passed, Lisya and Dmitri spent more and more time together by the Volga. His poems became less tentative and her songs grew more intimate. As his uncertain voice evened out and her body began to blossom, a gentle aura gradually surrounded them which lighted his sad eyes and quieted the discord in her soul. And as the awkward boy grew up into a tall, sensitive man, the solemnly charming woman Lisya was ripening into ignited the quiet glow between them into blazing passion. His poems burned with ardor; her violin pulsed with urgent intensity.

Evgenia rejoiced. Soon, she was sure, they would leap the Midsummer's fire together.

Ж   Ж   Ж

As the *S.S.Alexander Nevsky* steamed up to the floating landing pier, Evgenia could barely contain her excitement. Uncharacteristically, she chirped and nagged at her children, who grinned and ignored it. They, too, were excited.

The harvest had been exceptionally bountiful that year, and the commune council had voted to purchase a new bull. As the breed desired was to be found at some distance upriver, it was decided that shopping for the collective stud could best be done at the Great Fair in Nizhny Novgorod. It was also decided that village handicrafts were likely to bring a higher price there than at the local fair just down the river.

The delegation selected to arrange these matters included Derevnia's most educated citizens, Ivan and Evgenia. The council also allowed Evgenia to persuade them that her children would be of invaluable assistance to the projected trade mission. Extra hands were needed, and the additional cost was small.

After boarding and settling in, the young people explored the wonders of the ship – which included a throne-like toilet to which one ascended via four steps. Numerous visits were paid to this awesome commode, most of them unnecessary. Though they had brought their own food, the family also had lunch one day in the ship's restaurant.

None of them had ever been in such a place before. Only Lisya did not feel uncomfortable sitting at the linen-covered table. The tablecloth was not as fine as those at the manor, nor were there as many kinds of silverware as Varvara Petrovna had shown her how to use. When the food was served, she confidently picked up the proper implements and neatly negotiated the contents of bowl and plate. When the rest of the family – with evident relief – awkwardly copied the procedure, Lisya felt a rare surge of pride. It was not often that her family allowed her to teach them something they wanted to know.

"We should have some of these at home," grinned Volodya, enthusiastically spearing a piece of beef with his fork.

"Only people who eat meat regularly need such utensils," said Ivan, though without disapproval. He was manipulating the unfamiliar cutlery more dextrously than the rest of the family, but even he kept a close eye on Lisya's precise movements.

"We'd have to kill Korova's children to have beef," said Evgenia, giving her small portion of meat to Volodya.

"Moooo!" said Tatiana with mock mournfulness, twirling her fork in graceful circles.

As usual, everyone burst out laughing. Awkwardness dissolving, the family relaxed and enjoyed the adventure of doing something new together. Even Lisya's usually solemn face was covered with a smile that lasted longer than any Evgenia could remember.

During the rest of the voyage, Evgenia spent most of her time on deck. Watching water-drenched meadows and sunlit white churches pass by, she felt as though she were part of the Volga, seeing the land through Her eyes. The boat whistled brazenly – a strange sound, halfway between exotic harp and donkey's bray. At night it was joined by balalaikas along the banks. Passengers and sailors sang with them, accompanied by the soft splashing of water against the sides of the steamer.

As they neared Nizhny Novgorod, everyone's excitement mounted. The city was situated at the Volga's junction with the Oka river, which flowed from Moscow in the west. The Fair's position at such an important crossroads made it the largest in all of Russia. And goods from all over Asia made their way here every year.

Evgenia was suddenly afraid. So many strange people doing so many strange things in so many strange places. It was almost overwhelming to one used to the smallness of Derevnia and its reliably slow pace. Frantically, she made sure her children were all within grabbing distance.

All of them, however, were avidly watching the approaching conglomeration of new sights and sounds, their heads twisting and turning in a vain attempt not to miss anything.

Tatiana, as usual, was spinning around and waving her arms, though faster than usual. Squealing with delight, her eyes were a blur of blue and her braid was slapping Volodya's shoulder.

He, however, was too intent to notice. "Look there, Lisya, at those big buildings! Why, at least ten of father's church could fit in there! And see all the horses! How beautiful they are, and what different kinds of carts they're pulling! And what's that over there those men are holding, and what are they doing with it?!?"

Lisya, however, was staring excitedly at all the people. Of all shapes and sizes and hues, they were dressed in a vast array of enchanting styles and vivid colors. Never had she seen such a huge gathering of so many different kinds of people. Her heart beat so joyfully, she could barely speak.

As Nizhny Novgorod loomed up before them, Evgenia stared in amazement at the profusion of strange-looking buildings and structures. Wharves were piled high with bales and stacks of all kinds, and countless boats swarmed near them. As they landed, her ears were assaulted by a jumble of unfamiliar sounds. Somehow, Ivan guided them to the bridge which led to the fairgrounds. As far as the eye could see, the river was alive with steamboats and barges, tugboats and rowboats. The bridge itself floated on pontoons, over which speeded carriages and drays and carts of every description. In between thronged a bewildering array of people. Evgenia stared at the long blue robes and brilliant sashes of Persians and Armenians, and gaped at their huge turbans, conical fezzes, and high Astrakhan hats. Tartar workmen in rust-colored jackets jostled with Georgians and Turks in baggy pants. Mounted Cossacks, with flashing eyes and fiery horses, rode back and forth trying to police the vast, noisy crowd.

The Fair itself was a separate city, surrounded on three sides by canals. It was dominated by a huge building, brightly ornamented with colorful flags waving from pyramid-shaped cupolas and lavishly carved arches surmounting countless large windows. It looked, Evgenia decided, like a palace from one of Babushka's tales.

Their destination was the humbler section of the fairgrounds. Slowly, they made their way along a broad avenue crisscrossed by numerous streets. Strolling jugglers and itinerant musicians entertained the crowds; vendors of pies and cakes wove in and out hawking their wares. Men, women and children gathered about tubs of pickles or sat on benches munching sunflower seeds and eating dried fish washed down by *kvas*. Steam from samovars curled in the air, barbers shaved heads under the open sky, flocks of pigeons fluttered and cooed on roof-tops.

Finally they stopped at one of the inexpensive inns lining the streets, where Ivan negotiated a small room for the entire delegation. After depositing their numerous bundles, they went back into the street. Evgenia bought one of the huge watermelons lying in heaps everywhere. Finding an empty bench, they all happily slurped and spit seeds.

On one end, Ivan and the other men from Derevnia were debating the next step in the strategy of the village trade mission, trying not to be distracted by all the unfamiliar activity. Evgenia and her children, however, gave themselves up to all the exotic sights and sounds swirling about them. Now that they had a home base, albeit crowded, Evgenia had relaxed enough to start enjoying the excitement.

"What shall we do first?"

"Let's find the opera house!" exclaimed Lisya, uncharacteristically ignoring the few drops of watermelon juice on her chin. "Alexander Pavlovich said they have quite a good one here, and that the seats up in the balcony don't cost much!"

"I want to go to the circus!" exclaimed Volodya, his large hands sticky with remains of watermelon.

"I want to see – all this!" exclaimed Tatiana, clutching two watermelon rinds and throwing wide her arms to embrace everything going on around them.

"So do I," laughed Evgenia.

Lisya hugged Tatiana. Volodya gave her braid an affectionate tug.

And so, while Ivan and the other men went off to find a booth from which to sell the village crafts, Evgenia and her children went shopping. An overwhelming array of treasures stretched unendingly before their delighted eyes. Piles of silk and satin, broadcloth and muslin, chintz and velvet were laid out next to cashmere shawls and gold embroidery thread. Amethyst, aquamarine, amber and topaz sparkled beside malachite, jasper, turquoise and lapis. Boots of felt and Siberian wool rugs lined up near wolf-skins and tiger-skins and fine glossy sable. One shop was stacked with wooden trunks strapped in brass and iron, painted scarlet and green and blue, ornamented with fruits and flowers and strange Arabic patterns. Another sold candles, embellished by gilding and garnished with glistening pieces of red and blue glass; some were thick as a man and tall as a pillar, others were spun out to the fineness of yarn. Booths were filled with copper samovars, kegs of caviar, and elegant leather goods. Above them hung portraits of the Tsar, long festoons of dried mushrooms, small cages of nightingales and larks. And at every street corner were tables of money changers, piled high with the coin of every conceivable realm.

Through the streets strode men with huge loads on their heads – pyramids of oranges, whole shelves of eggs, even troughs of water full of live fish. Evgenia marveled that nothing ever seemed to spill. And all around her was a bustling kaleidoscope of singing vendors.

"Milk! Fresh milk!" caroled the milkwomen.

"It boils! It boils!" the tea vendors sang back."Will anybody drink?"

"Honey *kvas*! Raspberry *kvas*!"

"Rolls! Rolls! Whole wheat and crusty!"

"Beautiful violets, carnations, geraniums!"

"*Pirogi, pirogi* with carp! With peas! With mushrooms!"

The delicious chorus swirling about made Evgenia feel hungry – and, after awhile, at home. People back in the village sang, too – to their horses and cattle, at their spinning or carving, in the fields or simply standing about. Here, however, the continuous song was laced with whooping coachmen, ringing church bells, and the call of the muezzin from the mosque next to the fairgrounds. And often she heard snatches of accordions and barrel organs, military bands and balalaikas chase each other up and down the streets.

They all took turns at the stall in the open-air market where peasant handicrafts were sold. Several of Andrei's icons were lined up next to Ivan's religious carvings. Mikhail's small sleds, decorated with bears and whimsical birds, flanked the other side of the booth. Study *lapti* and smooth wooden bowls stood on wooden cartons serving as a counter; embroidered shirts and shawls hung from the low awning overhead. Those dyed with Ekaterina's distinctive russet hue sold especially quickly.

In between, they attended the numerous entertainments to be found at the Fair. There were several sideshows with magicians and fortune-tellers, strongmen and midgets. There were singers and dancers and musicians of every kind. Actors performed plays on outdoor stages, and everyone cheered for beloved, unhappy Petrushka the puppet.

In one of the squares was a high, greased pole with a basket on top filled with prizes. The crowd laughed good-naturedly as those trying to climb it slid back down the slippery pole. Volodya tried, too. As he wriggled to the top, the crowd cheered. Triumphantly he grabbed a mug decorated with the Tsar's portrait, and then shot back down the pole. Flushed with excitement and covered with grease, he bowed happily to the laughing applause.

Everyone went to the Circus, drawn by the flags and streamers, booming drums and brass bands. Evgenia was as fascinated as her children by the fierce-looking tribe of Indians from South America, and as delighted by the various acts with trained animals. Their favorite sent a piglet up in the small gondola of a balloon. When it had floated as high as it could, the small pig was ejected and parachuted gracefully back down into the ring. Volodya went back the next day just to see the parachuting pig again. But this time, the parachute failed to open and the poor creature crashed. The clown to whom the deceased piglet belonged wept broken-heartedly, while the angry crowd nearly attacked him, shouting that he was a monster for torturing animals. Volodya came home with red eyes, and cried himself to sleep that night.

Tatiana, too, went back to the circus to see the ballet, a grandiose production complete with ships sinking in the ocean, cataracts spouting from high cliffs, wild animals and forest fires. But it was the dancing itself that she found most stirring. The performers moved with a studied grace and precise elegance that was somehow more exciting than the unrestrained enthusiasm of village folk dances. Sometimes the women even went up on their toes, gliding effortlessly across the stage. Almost immediately, Tatiana began to mimic the elegant dancing, clad in her own improvised versions of the exotic costumes.

For Lisya, the main attraction of the Fair was the opera; night after night, she sat on wooden benches high up in the balcony. One evening, the singers got so carried away by their stage fighting that the director of the orchestra had to break up the ensuing brawl with a fire hose hung near the curtain. Despite this unrestrained excitability – or maybe because of it – many of the performances were truly thrilling. For Lisya, it was as though the very heavens had opened.

During the day, she took more than her share of turns at the handicraft booth. Most of the customers were not peasants, and she enjoyed the continuous stream of human diversity which flowed by her snug vantage point. Her village's crafts were, she knew, of high quality; the admiring comments of the well-dressed customers made her feel proud.

"I like it when you smile a lot," said Tatiana, who often kept her company.

"I like it, too," replied Lisya, putting her arm around Tatiana. "It feels good."

"Then you should do it more often." Tatiana leaned affectionately against Lisya.

"It's easier to smile here than at home."

"Because there's more music?"

"Mostly, yes." Lisya frowned, thinking about it. "And because not everyone is the same here."

"Not everyone is the same at home, either."

"Well – yes, that's true. But it's a lot harder to be different there."

"And make different music?"

"Especially the kind of music I need to make," agreed Lisya.

"And no one to make the music with?"

"Exactly!" exclaimed Lisya, startled by the understanding Tatiana manifested during her rare bouts of stillness.

"I like the dancing here better, too," said Tatiana, who rose on tiptoes and struck an elegant pose. "Especially when they glide on those pointy shoes. I want to do that, too."

"And dance with other people?"

"Oh, yes!" Tatiana wrapped one of Ekaterina's russet shawls around her and made several small pirouettes.

"Enough to leave home?"

Tatiana stopped, mid-pirouette, and stood motionless for longer than anyone had ever seen, "Home is bigger than Derevnia," she said finally. "Home is anywhere the Volga goes – anywhere people know Babushka's stories."

"Home is Russia?"

"Yes, that's it."

"And beyond Russia?" asked Lisya softly. "Beyond the Motherland, beyond *Rodina*?"

"Beyond?" A dark shadow passed over Tatiana's usually sunny face. "No, no, beyond Russia could never be home."

"But home could be here?"

"Oh, yes." The shadow passed and Tatiana resumed her pirouettes. "Or in Derevnia. It's easy to smile in both places."

Lisya sighed, wishing things were as easy for her as for Tatiana.

"But we're not in Derevnia now," grinned Tatiana, "so you should smile again."

Lisya kissed Tatiana's cheek and complied.

The night before they returned to Derevnia, Evgenia and Ivan went walking along the river. The village crafts had sold even better than hoped and, after much spirited haggling, the men had purchased a fine young bull. Colored lanterns reflected in the water; music and the hum of voices filled the air. In momentary lulls, they could hear the croaking of frogs.

"Do you hear him?" Evgenia stopped and listened. "That big booming bull-frog who seems to be leading the choir?"

"He sounds like your father!" Ivan laughed, pulling a package out of his pocket. "A souvenir of the Fair – and of this beautiful night." Giving it to her, his wonderful smile spread slowly over his face, illuminating his icon-like features in a way that never failed to stir her soul – and rouse her body.

Wrapped in a small piece of red silk was the copy of Tolstoy's *War and Peace* she had been eyeing so longingly in a second-hand bookstore. Evgenia caressed the binding gratefully and held it to her heart. The look in her eyes matched his – less dazzling than on that Midsummer's Eve when they had first declared their love, but deeper and more radiant, full of trust and loyalty and faith.

But their kiss still burned like the bonfire, as together they leaped over it once more.

Ж   Ж   Ж

Sitting down in her enormous chair, Praskovia Nikolaevna thumped her cane imperiously. Varvara Petrovna, who had been flirting idly with Alexander Pavlovich, hurriedly sat down next to her. Most of the other guests soon lined up on either side. Lisya was waiting in the hall, clad in last year's fashion from Moscow. The dress was a hand-me-down from Varvara Petrovna and made Lisya feel very grown up. Glancing in the mirror, she knew she looked better in it than Varvara Petrovna had.

Staring straight ahead, Lisya walked quickly to the Piano, sat down and began to play a new Beethoven Sonata she had just learned. Afterward she stood, blushing at the polite applause, wondering how soon she could make her escape.

"Bravo!" a loud voice shouted from behind Praskovia Nikolaevna's throne.

Looking up in surprise, Lisya saw Alexander Pavlovich applauding vigorously. She smiled.

Alexander Pavlovich had just returned from a year in Petersburg, where he had been summoned to teach other rural doctors his techniques. Lisya was glad he was back. He had been her most enthusiastic fan, rarely missing an opportunity to hear her perform, often encouraging and complimenting the gift which he – more than anyone in Derevnia – admired and appreciated. His presence at Praskovia Nikolaevna's receptions had made performing there less intimidating.

And she had always found her occasional visits to his clinic interesting. Usually she had stopped there on her way home from piano practice, looking for her mother. But it had been pleasant to find him there alone sometimes, despite the awe which he had inspired since Tatiana's miraculous cure. But he was a very down-to-earth hero, who shared his knowledge without flaunting it. Lisya admired that almost as much as his medical skill, and appreciated how seriously he took her and her music.

As her mother's friend and colleague, Alexander Pavlovich had always treated her with grave, avuncular familiarity. Now, however, he addressed her formally and with some confusion. "Well done, Elisaveta Ivanovna," he said with a slight blush, approaching her in the hallway after the recital. "You play Beethoven with exceptional – ah – passion – ahem – that is, for one so young." Then he hurriedly excused himself.

After a brief moment of surprise at this lapse in the doctor's customary dignity, Lisya shrugged. Her mind was on more exciting things – and people – than her mother's old friend. She thought no more about it.

Alexander Pavlovich, however, found himself unable to think of anything else, and began manufacturing excuses to be in her company.

He began appearing at the manor during her piano practices, supposedly looking for Varvara Petrovna, whom he couldn't stand. He made house calls to the *izba*, claiming concern for Tatiana's post-operative scar, which had long since

133

healed. He even started going to church, something he had never done before. On all these occasions, his eyes were only for Lisya, and he gravitated to her side like a bee to linden blossoms.

"Good morning, Lisya – er – that is, Elisaveta Ivanovna," he would say, with considerably less than his usual dignity. "Your father's sermon today was – ah – interesting – ahem – don't you think?"

"If you'd heard as many of them as I have," grinned Lisya, momentarily surprised by his formal address, "you might not think so."

"Well – ah – perhaps we need to listen more –" Alexander Pavlovich's face reddened slightly. "That is – I mean – maybe Father Ivan was – er – speaking in religious – ah – metaphor."

"Father never speaks in metaphor," replied Lisya, wondering at the doctor's flustered embarrassment. "He knows people here wouldn't understand it."

"Yes, well – ah – he certainly is – ahem – a wise man," Alexander Pavlovich said lamely. And then he would stand speechless for awhile, murmur a few words of departure, and reluctantly make his exit.

The old women were soon gossiping good-naturedly. After a while, even Lisya noticed Alexander Pavlovich was spending more time with her than her mother. She did not, however, attach any significance to this fact, preoccupied as she was with other matters.

Ever since returning from Nizhny Novgorod, she had been obsessed with going back – permanently. In the city, for the first time in her life, she had felt she belonged. The music she heard there stirred her deeply. She wanted to be part of it.

In her enthusiasm, she naturally turned first to Dmitri. "The music was so wonderful! All these musicians playing *together* – oh, the sound was unimaginably beautiful – it was beyond words!" said Lisya ecstatically, for at least the hundredth time. "And there were so many different kinds of people! For the first time in my life *I* didn't feel different!"

Dmitri, as usual, looked at his feet and grunted.

"I want to play that music, too! I have to! I know I could find people there like me – people who wouldn't think there was something wrong with me – people who would appreciate who I am!"

Dmitri, however, said nothing and shuffled uncomfortably.

"You could find other poets there, too – I'm sure of it! Think of the life we could have there together, among all those writers and artists and musicians!" she urged, again and again, desperately seeking response. "Come with me! Please!

Dmitri finally looked at her. He was terrified.

Crushed and confused, Lisya found herself confiding more and more in Alexander Pavlovich – who somehow always seemed to be around when she needed him.

"It wasn't just the music itself," she said, sitting on the piano bench at the manor. "I've already learned a lot of that here." She nodded toward the music cabinet in the corner.

"But now you need to be around other musicians of your calibre?" asked Alexander Pavlovich, sympathetically.

"Yes, exactly. And I need to make music with someone besides Varvara Petrovna."

"Someone more – um – harmonious?" grinned the doctor. In the face of Lisya's dilemma, his embarrassment had fled.

"Someone who doesn't look down her nose at me!"

"You'd find plenty of people who would welcome your music – and respect you for it – in any Russian city. Even in Kazan. You wouldn't have to go all the way to Nizhny Novgorod."

Elated, Lisya renewed her campaign to extract Dmitri from Derevnia.

"Kazan's not so far away," she enthused rapturously. "We could come home and visit a lot. Alexander Pavlovich knows lots of poets and musicians there. He said he'd introduce us, and get me some auditions. Maybe he could even find you a job! Oh, please! Come with me! It's where we belong!"

"Maybe it's where you belong," Dmitri finally responded, "but for me…"

With dismay, Lisya saw only terror in his eyes.

"Those orchestras I heard in Nizhny Novgorod," said Lisya later, continuing what was by now a long and frequently resumed conversation with Alexander Pavlovich, "sounded much bigger than they looked."

"That's because the sum of creative people interacting is greater than its individual members," he replied, nodding.

"So if I make music with others, we amplify each other." Lisya also nodded. "And we create much more together than we could just by ourselves."

"That happens in my work, too," he added. "When I was in Petersburg last year, I learned much more about medicine by sharing my ideas with other doctors than I could by just reading and writing about them. It was very exciting!" His usually unremarkable face glowed with enthusiasm.

"You feel about medicine as I do about music," observed Lisya, also noticing what a nice-looking man he was.

"Which is why I am returning to Petersburg," said Alexander Pavlovich, his voice faltering just a little. "The Medical School there has offered me a permanent teaching position. It's a wonderful opportunity, and I've decided to accept."

Lisya was stunned. "But how can you leave us?" she finally blurted out with dismay. "We need you here!"

"Not anymore. What is of real use to Derevnia I've already taught your mother and grandmother. It's time for me to take what I've learned from them back to the city. And I can help people here more by going to the capital than by staying."

"I don't understand," Lisya shook her head.

"The main obstacle to decent rural healthcare is no longer peasant ignorance – at least not here, it isn't. No, the main problem now is the stupidity and ineptness of the government's health regulations." He began to warm to his subject. "Take famine relief, for instance. Any fool knows that malnutrition is the root cause of most illness. Yet the government obstinately refuses to let doctors do anything about it. 'You can treat the sick,' they tell us, 'but you can't feed the hungry as a preventive measure.'"

As he spoke, his eyes glowed with conviction and lit up the well-proportioned features of his customarily impassive face. Lisya again noticed that Alexander Pavlovich was really quite attractive – for someone so old, anyway.

"In Petersburg, do you think you can change that?" she asked, catching his enthusiasm.

"I certainly intend to try!" he replied, pleased at her response.

"When will you leave?" she asked, her face suddenly falling.

"That depends on you," he replied, a slight tremor in his voice.

"Me?! I don't understand." Lisya looked at him in surprise.

"Petersburg is a wonderful place, with many opportunities for a talented musician." He paused and cleared his throat. "Come with me, Lisya! It's where you belong!"

"Come with you!?" Lisya stared at him, shocked. "But how – ?"

"As my wife." Blushing furiously, he plunged ahead. "Yes, I know, I'm older. And you don't love me. But I know you're fond of me. And you know you can trust me… And how else are you going to get out of here?"

Lisya continued to stare – and suddenly noticed that behind the wire rims of his glasses, his eyes were blazing in a most uncharacteristic manner.

"And besides," he added quietly, "*I* love *you*." Gently he kissed her hand and was gone.

For the next week, Lisya avoided both Dmitri and Alexander Pavlovich. At home, her chores were left half-finished and she was unusually silent, not even arguing with Volodya. She did not go near the piano at the manor, nor did she touch her violin. Finally she went to the grove by the river, and flopped down on its small jutting promontory. Staring moodily across the Volga to its distant shore, she trailed her slim graceful hand through the rippling water, absently flexing her strong agile fingers against its leisurely current.

Recognizing the brisk tempo of firm footsteps, Lisya sat up and saw her mother approaching on the narrow path from the village. Evgenia sat down next to her, silently greeting the Volga. Finally she turned to Lisya and scrutinized her with the astonishingly clear, light eyes which concealed – and flinched at – nothing.

"You look so very much like me – when I was your age," she said finally. "Though you have your father's stubborn chin."

Lisya smiled. "I have his hands, too," she said, waggling her long slender fingers.

Evgenia looked at her own strong, capable hands and smiled. "They certainly aren't like mine. But the rest of you… though somehow I don't remember being so beautiful," said Evgenia wonderingly, putting her arm around her daughter's shoulders.

"Am I really beautiful?" Lisya rested her head against her mother's shoulder.

"Alexander Pavlovich certainly thinks so."

"He's asked me to marry him," Lisya said, after a long pause.

"Yes, I know. He talked to me about it first."

"I don't know what to do," Lisya drew up her knees and crossed her arms on top. "At first, I thought it was ridiculous. But the more I think about it…"

"Have you talked to Dmitri?"

"No." She rested her chin on her arms and stared at the river. "I don't think he would understand why I'm even considering Alexander Pavlovich's offer."

"And why are you?"

"Because I *have* to get out of here! And now, at last, there's some place to go – and a way to get there."

"Maybe you could leave with Dmitri?"

"Dmitri is afraid to go." Lisya shook her head sadly.

"How do you feel about Alexander Pavlovich?"

"Not the way I do about Dmitri," answered Lisya, her brow furrowed in concentration. "But I'm very fond of him – and he's easier to talk to – and to be with."

"Alexander Pavlovich is a good man. He would make a kind husband."

"And Dmitri?"

"I love Dmitri, too, but I don't know…

They stared silently at the river, begging Mother Volga for guidance.

"I can't bear the thought of leaving Dmitri," Lisya said finally, in despair, "but if I don't go, I'll die inside."

"I have never understood *why* you must go," said Evgenia slowly, "and *I* can't bear the thought of you going away. But I know you must."

She put her arms around her daughter, and they wept together, staying there for a long time.

A few days later, it was Dmitri sitting next to Lisya in the grove. After staring at the Volga for an impossibly long time, Lisya finally broke the silence which hung heavily between them.

"I'm going to Petersburg," she said flatly, more clumsily than she had intended. "With Alexander Pavlovich."

Dmitri winced, then turned wounded eyes to her.

"He's asked me to marry him." Lisya could not meet his stricken gaze. "And I'm going to say yes."

"But why?" Dmitri could barely utter the words.

"You know why!" exclaimed Lisya angrily.

"But I love you!" His voice, too, was angry.

"And I love you," she replied sadly. "But it's not enough. I *have* to leave."

"And I can't," he said softly, after a very long time.

"I know," she replied, tears raining from eyes that were grey with sorrow.

Dmitri took her hand, and they sat together in silence until the sun was setting. Then Dmitri stood suddenly and fled noiselessly.

The next day, Lisya gave Alexander Pavlovich her answer. He was so overjoyed he forgot to be dignified. "You won't be sorry!" he said jubilantly. "I promise you! No one could love and treasure you as I will!" Tenderly he kissed her hand. "And someday, my beautiful Lisya, you may even love me. But you will never have cause to regret this day."

With a sore heart still full of misgivings, Lisya silently hoped he was right.

Ivan married them in the little church, in the presence of most of the village. Dmitri, of course, was not there – nor did Lisya expect – or want – him to be. As she stood under the golden crown just barely held aloft by Tatiana, Lisya resolved to lock away his memory and pledge herself to a new life with the man who was now pledging his love to her. Seeing the tears in his eyes, she knew he would keep his vow, and cherish her with all the steadfastness which so defined his character. And someday, maybe the deep affection and admiration she had for him would grow into something more. She vowed to try. Surely it could not be hard to love such a kind, gentle man!

Volodya, meanwhile, had been holding the groom's wedding crown above Alexander Pavlovich. As he already towered over most of the villagers, he had no difficulty reaching over the doctor's head – but he held the crown with somewhat less enthusiasm than Tatiana's tiptoed reach. Like the rest of Lisya's family, he had mixed feelings about the marriage. All of them, of course, held Alexander Pavlovich in high esteem. But he was taking Lisya so far away. And then, there was Dmitri…

As Evgenia watched her husband performing the marriage ceremony, she could sense his ambivalence even in his graceful gestures. Though she knew his respect for the doctor was genuine, she also knew that he was worried about sending off the child he had never understood to a place he had never been with a man he suspected was an atheist. As for Evgenia, she did not worry about Lisya's well-being. She knew Alexander Pavlovich would take better care of her daughter than even she herself could. But the thought of her first-born being so far away cast a pall over the pleasure of seeing her beautiful daughter dressed in the same finery she had worn at her own wedding. Lisya's well-proportioned curves fit comfortably into the garment. Evgenia smiled, remembering her own battle with its tight bodice.

Afterwards there was a very proper – but not particularly enjoyable – wedding feast at Praskovia Nikolaevna's. Everyone agreed that the food was good, but that there wasn't enough vodka. Ill at ease in such an elegant setting, most of the guests lacked their usual exuberance on such occasions.

Lisya tasted her first champagne that day – and decided that it would not be her last. Waltzing with her new husband, feeling his joy surround her like warm fur, she felt some of her misgivings melt.

The entire family saw them off the next day, at the new railway station several miles from Derevnia. Evgenia clung to her daughter, even after she felt her pulling away. As the newly-weds boarded their carriage, the excitement in Lisya's eyes was reassuring. But as the train moved slowly out of sight, Evgenia felt a great gaping hole wrench open inside. She continued to wave long after the train had disappeared over the horizon.

Ж   Ж   Ж

Ekaterina's capable hands moved briskly, calmly preparing tea from carefully-marked packets of herbs in her medicine box. Setting the fresh brew down in front of Evgenia, she gently patted her daughter's hand and smiled sympathetically. Evgenia was grateful for her mother's soothing company; only in her presence did the emptiness seem bearable.

The first winter after Lisya married and moved away was grey and bleak. Evgenia's energy waned and her menstrual cycle became a nearly continuous hemorrhage. She performed her household duties listlessly, and was cold and distant with Ivan. Tatiana's perpetual motion irritated her; Volodya's loud voice gave her a headache. In school, she snapped at her pupils.

"All of this will pass," said Ekaterina reassuringly. "Eventually."

"Why should un-becoming a woman be so difficult?" grumbled Evgenia.

"Becoming a woman is also hard," replied Ekaterina. "Why should going out the back door be any easier?"

"But at least going into womanhood, we have something to look forward to."

"The discomforts of pregnancy? The pain and danger of childbirth? Be glad you're free of that," said Ekaterina, not unkindly. "Now that your body is becoming less burdened, your mind will see things more clearly."

"Was it this painful for you?" wept Evgenia.

"My body bled for a long time, too," began Ekaterina, then hesitated ".... but my heart never ached so."

"Because I stayed in Derevnia?"

"Yes." Ekaterina put her arms around her daughter. "Thank you."

Just as her mother promised, eventually Evgenia's body ceased to bleed – but the void inside continued to ache.

Ж   Ж   Ж

Had it only been a year, wondered Evgenia, since she had last stood on this platform, gazing anxiously at the empty railroad tracks. It seemed like so much more! Time had dragged so slowly, refusing to heal her aching heart. But now, at last, the waiting was over. Lisya was coming home! That it was only for a visit, she pushed out of her mind as she stared at the horizon, willing the train to appear.

At first, she barely recognized the elegant young woman who confidently stepped off the train with Alexander Pavlovich. Her daughter's subdued, well-tailored city clothes were somehow more sophisticated than any of the gaudy Moscow imports worn by Praskovia Nikolaevna and Varvara Petrovna, and she wore them with an assurance that was almost intimidating. Lisya's hair, no longer in braids, was styled in a softly twisted knot whose clean lines matched the rest of her. Unlike the married women in Derevnia, she did not wear a kerchief; her impeccably neat coiffure was crowned instead with a quietly becoming hat whose upturned brim curved intriguingly to a point over the center of her forehead.

Evgenia cautiously approached this rather daunting new person – who suddenly smiled with marvelous familiarity. Evgenia saw her own full-lipped mouth beaming broadly and Mikhail's deep-set eyes sparkling out from under the brim of the hat, as Lisya's long slender hands – so like Ivan's – reached out to embrace her.

The first days of the visit flooded Evgenia with animation. Mother and daughter talked nonstop, continuing the conversation as together they did chores. Gone was the bleakness, as Lisya excitedly described the wonders of her new life in Petersburg.

"I'm taking piano lessons at the Conservatory," said Lisya, her face glowing, "and my teacher thinks I have talent. And I've made friends with some of the other students – they actually like me!"

"Of course they do!" said Evgenia, mother hen feathers bristling. "Why shouldn't they!?!"

"You know what I mean." Lisya smiled, setting down the wooden bowl she was washing, and looked at her mother.

"There was never anything wrong with you, Lisya. You just weren't like everyone else," replied Evgenia, tenderly touching her cheek.

"Which is why I had to leave."

"Yes," admitted Evgenia, "I see that now." How wonderful it was to see her daughter so happy! Even if it meant being so far away.

"I'm also playing in the orchestra at the Maryinsky Opera House," Lisya went on excitedly. "It's the best in all of Russia – sometimes the Tsar even comes to the performances. And I actually get paid for playing all this wonderful music with all these wonderful musicians! I'm saving up to buy a real piano!"

"And what does Alexander Pavlovich think of all this?"

"I think he's almost as excited about it as I am! He comes to all the operas! And sometimes we go to other concerts together! And he bought me a piano so he can listen to me practice! It's just an old upright, but it will do until I can afford a grand piano like my teacher has in her studio!"

"And is he a good husband," asked Evgenia carefully, "in other ways, too?"

Lisya paused. "In most ways, yes." She hesitated again. "Yes. Yes, he is. He is kind and gentle and loving. And a good friend. I am fortunate to be married to such a fine man."

"And do you care for him as much as he deserves?"

Lisya again paused. "It's not hard to care for someone who appreciates me so much. I return his admiration, and am grateful for the life he has given me. We are very comfortable together. And yes, I think he is happy with me."

"And are you happy with him?"

"Yes." This time, Lisya did not hesitate. "Yes, I am. I know I can depend on him. And he wears well."

Evgenia rejoiced in her daughter's happiness, and was relieved by the contentment which permeated Alexander Pavlovich. Both were obviously pleased with the bargain they had struck, and were conscientiously fulfilling its terms with honor and affection.

Tatiana and Lisya also had long talks – especially about the Maryinsky.

"The ballets are just wonderful – I can see them all from my seat in the orchestra pit! The dancing is marvelously elegant – the costumes, too! And the dancers are so good, even the Tsar comes to watch! Especially when we do Tchaikovsky – you remember how much you liked it when I played his music –" Lisya paused to catch her breath.

"I've never seen you so excited, Lisya," said Tatiana, her bright blue eyes reflecting her sister's happiness. "Petersburg must be a wonderful place."

"It is! It's filled with big, beautiful buildings, all kinds of interesting people, and lots of interesting things to see and do!"

"Like Nizhny Novgorod?"

"Yes – but bigger – and better!"

"What's your favorite place in Petersburg?"

"The Maryinsky, of course! I love being part of the magic that happens there every night! So many talented people, singing and dancing and making music, doing what they love, and when it all comes together – Oh, Tanya! Such joy! You must come and see for yourself!"

"Father would never allow it," replied Tatiana, her face suddenly solemn.

"Just for a visit?"

"It wouldn't just be a visit. Once I'd seen them dancing at the Maryinsky, I could never go back to what I do here. Just hearing you talk about it makes me hungry to move that way."

"Then come to Petersburg and learn how!" urged Lisya. "There's a ballet school there that trains talented young people to dance at the Maryinsky. You learn other things, too, and the Tsar pays for it all."

"But could someone from Derevnia go there?"

"*Anyone* can audition. Just like I did at the Conservatory and the Maryinsky!"

"But you already knew the music. What do I know about ballet?! And I'm so young!"

"They start the ballet students younger. And they're not looking for skill, but talent. Oh, Tanya, I know you have it. And I know you want this as much as I need my music!"

"Here, I can only dance by myself – because no one can keep up." Tatiana sat very still, concentrating on her words. "I want to dance with other people. I want to be part of that coming together you do at the Maryinsky. I don't want to be like the Firebird and make beautiful feathers all alone."

"Yes, I know. Some of my friends at the Conservatory want to be soloists. Not me!" Lisya shook her head. "I had enough of that at Praskovia Nikolaevna's soirees! I just want to be adding my music to something bigger and more beautiful. I don't know what to call it, but I think maybe it's what Mother feels when she sings in the choir."

"And what Father feels when he says Mass?"

"I don't think he'd like to hear that – especially from me."

"He worries that you don't believe in God," said Tatiana earnestly, "and that Alexander Pavlovich is turning you into an a-thist."

"You mean an atheist," laughed Lisya.

"Well, is he right? Do you believe in God?"

"I'm not sure I know what God is."

"I do!" exclaimed Tatiana, jumping up and twirling around, hands reaching upward.

"Then maybe that's how we can persuade Father to let you come to Petersburg."

"What about Mother?" Tatiana stopped spinning.

"Hmmm, yes. She let me go because she knew I was never happy in Derevnia – but that's not true for you."

"Maybe she'll let me go to Petersburg because she knows you need me there."

Tears suddenly came to her eyes as Lisya looked at her sister, wondering how one so young could be so wise. "Yes. You're right. I do. Here, I needed you because I was different. There, I need you because you're part of home."

"Yes, I know."

"But Tanya, won't you be homesick in Petersburg?"

Tatiana bowed her head and was silent. "No, I don't think so," she said finally. "Derevnia is *Rodina* – and so is Petersburg. Anywhere in Russia I can feel close to the people I love."

Ж Ж Ж

As the day of departure approached, Evgenia felt quiet dread invading the void Lisya's visit had temporarily filled.

"But why must you take Tatiana away, too?" she pleaded. "She's happy here."

"But she'll be happier in Petersburg, where she can *really* dance." Lisya returned her mother's pleading look. "And I need her there."

"Yes," Evgenia finally said, in a low voice, "I understand – but I don't think your father will."

"NO!" Ivan was outraged when Evgenia told him. "Absolutely not! It's out of the question!"

Evgenia said nothing and waited.

"One daughter in Petersburg is bad enough. But *both* of them gone? So far away? No, no, Tatiana's too young!"

"But Father, it's where I belong," said Tatiana firmly, when Ivan told her no. "You belong here."

"Yes. But I have to dance, too – just like you have to be a priest."

Ivan went to see his mother. "I've taught her all I can," said Natasha, when he told her. "You really must let her go."

Ivan said nothing and wept.

"Thank you," said Lisya, when it was finally all decided. Tears welled up in her eyes. "I'll take good care of her."

"I know you will," Evgenia's voice choked. Ivan bowed his head.

And then, they were all at the train station again. This time, it was even harder. Lisya had left home almost a woman; Tatiana was still a girl. After a blur of tearful goodbyes, the train pulled away. All Evgenia could remember were Tatiana's eyes, shining like the sun in a clear Spring sky.

Back in Derevnia, Evgenia walked slowly to the grove by the Volga. Sadly leaning against her favorite tree – now much bigger than when she had first befriended it – she wondered how it could hurt so much to be as empty as she felt. But then the river began to sing to her of memories past – and of a future yet to come. The benediction of quiet resignation slowly descended upon her. Her daughters were going where they needed to be. They would take care of each other. That was what counted. And though they were far away, she knew that part of them would always be with her, here by the Volga.

The emptiness within stopped aching. Loving – and letting go of – her daughters had made her bigger inside. Now there was room for her soul to grow.

Ж　Ж　Ж

The steamboat blew its braying, harp-like whistle. Quickly, Volodya bent down and kissed his mother, his nervous smile faltering as he saw the tears in her eyes. Then he turned to his father; though still a boy, already he was as tall.

"It seems like just yesterday that I baptized you and dedicated you to God," said Ivan, loving pride glowing in his eyes, as always, when he regarded his son.

"Mother says I bellowed louder than Grandfather when you dunked me in the baptismal font," replied Volodya, his face breaking into a characteristically engaging grin.

"A good priest can always use a loud voice," Ivan smiled back. "When you finish the seminary, you'll be able to give me *and* your grandfather a rest."

"I'll make you proud, Father," said Volodya, filial love written all over his earnest face.

"You already have," replied Ivan, thanking God – as he did every day – for giving him such a wonderful son.

Devotion never questioned and harmonious excitement mingled in the look father and son exchanged. Lovingly they embraced. Volodya picked up his suitcase and loped up the gangway.

After he left for the seminary, the *izba* seemed unnaturally quiet. But Kazan was not so far away, and Volodya's absence, after all, was temporary. Ivan busied himself with excited plans for the day when his son returned a priest. He even picked out a proper wife; when it was time, Elena would be perfect. Evgenia concurred – nor did Elena object. It was assumed that Volodya himself wouldn't, either.

At first, his letters were enthusiastic, full of new friends and experiences. Gradually, however, they became guarded and perfunctory. Finally, they stopped altogether.

Ivan refused to be worried. "The boy is too busy studying to write. Anyway, he'll be home soon for vacation."

The young man who subsequently disembarked from the steamboat was not the same person they had earlier sent off. It wasn't just that he had grown taller. Evgenia knew something was wrong when Vladimir – as he now insisted on being called – went out of his way to announce that he was a vegetarian.

Such an announcement, of course, was bound to invite ridicule from people who regarded all food as a none too certain blessing from God. Why make a fuss about denying something most of them rarely tasted anyway? If he didn't want to eat meat, he should simply fast more – like other holy men.

Vladimir, however, emphatically insisted that he had "given up" meat because he was now a Tolstoyan. "How can I live in truthfulness and with a clear conscience if I am eating other living beings?!"

Nor did it stop there.

"The government is merely a conspiracy for dragooning the people," Vladimir thundered at the dinner table. "Its pretext for existence is a fraud designed to deceive the masses and preserve itself."

"That may be," replied Ivan calmly, "but it is necessary to protect us from invasion."

"Huge armies are a sham!" Vladimir's big voice filled the room. "All wars are instigated by governments, not people. We derive no benefit from them. On the contrary!"

"I, too, dislike war," responded Ivan evenly, "but surely some government is necessary to protect property."

"Armed police protect the property of the rich," boomed Vladimir zealously. "The modest property of humble men is only threatened by rich men and government officials."

"But someone must keep order!" said Ivan quietly, with a trace of exasperation.

"There is no legitimate justification for a government whose real reason for being is the conquest of its own people!" Vladimir pounded the table with his fist. "And there is every reason for the abolition of an institution whose true role is no more than that of a robber levying blackmail on his neighbors!"

"And what would you have us do about it?" asked Ivan, controlling his temper with difficulty. "Shoot the Tsar again?"

"No," Vladimir shook his head sadly, his voice suddenly quiet. "Fire cannot be quenched by fire. No more can evil be destroyed by evil."

And on that, father and son agreed.

To Evgenia's surprise, Vladimir began to hang around the schoolhouse. Watching him stack wood next to the stove, she noted that his resemblance to Mikhail had become even more marked. The planes of his broad, open face had grown more pronounced; the curve of his nose swept into a longer point and the high cheekbones had lost their baby fat. The hooked eyebrows, too, were bushier. But though his genial mouth had grown wider, the bear-like grin which usually hovered there was noticeably absent.

While cleaning the blackboard one day, he finally confided that the seminary had precipitated much confusion in his soul. As he spoke, his voice almost as deep as Mikhail's, his arms reached out with the same expansive gesture.

"Before I went away, I thought I understood the world, and my place in it." Vladimir's dark blue eyes, so like Ivan's, filled with pain. "But now I see that things are not so simple. I'm not sure what to believe anymore."

Evgenia's heart ached for her troubled son. Sadly she reflected that whereas Lisya, in going away, had found her place, Volodya seemed to be losing his way.

"The boy's just testing his faith," Ivan assured her when she confided her fears. "Kazan has always been crawling with radicals. He'll work his way through them to the truth. It's just part of his education."

Nonetheless, Ivan wrote a letter to the seminary, inquiring as to his son's progress. The reply was not reassuring. Though starting out an exemplary student, he had since turned away form his schoolwork. Even worse, the young man who had at first displayed so much zeal in prayer and fasting was now challenging authority at every turn.

When Vladimir next returned home, Ivan confronted him with the letter from the seminary.

"Of course I'm challenging their authority! What else can I do?" Vladimir burst out in angry frustration. "In the name of Jesus, who taught that we should not resist our enemies, Orthodox Metropolitans bless the allegedly 'Holy' armies of the Tsar. The Church has become the brocaded arm of a violent, tyrannical regime. The clergy are ignorant and corrupt, the bishops are little more than pawns of the state!"

"I agree that the Church is not always what it should be, and that some priests are lacking in faith," Ivan replied sadly, "but it is, after all, made up of humans, who are bound to err. All the more reason why we need the Church as a guide."

"But the Church itself is the problem! Its very exclusiveness makes it a force for division, not brotherhood. And its theology and ritual obscure man's personal relationship to God."

"But surely," pleaded Ivan, "you would not have us condone heresy!?"

"He who begins by loving Christianity more than truth, will end by loving his own church more than Christianity, and then in loving himself more than all."

"Is that you – or Tolstoy?"

"Both!" Vladimir retorted emphatically.

"But religion as Tolstoy proposes it is ultimately a thing of Law rather than Grace," argued Ivan earnestly. "A scheme for human betterment rather than a vision of God penetrating a fallen world."

"Everyone, each in his own way," said Vladimir, "is called upon to cultivate his own soul."

And on that, father and son once again agreed.

But to his mother, Vladimir confided that he hated the seminary. "They police us like criminals. They answer our questions with punishment. They humiliate us – and the Church – with their hypocrisy. It's a dark, oppressive, joyless place."

When Vladimir returned to school, Evgenia saw him off with a troubled heart. She was not surprised when another letter from the seminary arrived a few months later. They were regretfully informed that Vladimir's inappropriate behavior had necessitated disciplinary action. They were further enjoined to pray for their son and exhort him to mend his ways. Ivan was furious.

Predictably, the storm erupted when Vladimir next returned home. Taller now than Ivan, and even broader than Mikhail, his gangling body was still burgeoning.

"What is the meaning of this?!" demanded Ivan, waving the letter in his face.

"They put me in a punishment cell and then took away my library privileges! And do you know what for?" Vladimir was indignant. "For reading Tolstoy!"

"But the Tolstoy you were reading has been censored by the government!"

"For telling the truth about our corrupt government!"

"But the Church has excommunicated Tolstoy for writing this book he so blasphemously calls *Resurrection*."

"Because he told the truth about the Church's hypocrisy!"

"But surely the Holy Church knows better than we do." Ivan's voice was troubled. "Surely we must bow to their wisdom."

"At the expense of Truth?"

And for that, Ivan had no answer.

To Evgenia, however, Vladimir confided that he was no longer a Toystoyan. "I have met people tortured and exiled for their political ideals." The deep sensitive eyes, so like his father's, burned with righteous indignation. "What good is Tolstoy's nonviolence in the face of such oppression?!"

The day before he returned to the seminary, Vladimir shaved off his beard. Though it had been a rather scraggly one, the gesture was not lost on his parents. Shaving, said the Church, was blasphemy. God had a beard, and had created man in His image; men were therefore to pride themselves on theirs – and priests were expected to set an example.

With difficulty, Ivan heeded Evgenia's advice to contain his wrath – and said nothing. But neither he nor his wife were surprised when another letter from the seminary arrived soon after. This time, Vladimir was in real trouble.

Finally, Vladimir himself wrote.

Dear Father,

I regret that I must write this letter, but I have no choice. My best friend has been expelled from the seminary for the heinous offense of reading *Das Kapital*. Those of us who oppose this arbitrary action have banded together to protest. The seminary has threatened to expel us, too, unless we recant. I have no intention of doing so. And if they don't expel me, I shall resign anyway.

God has forsaken this place. Truth can no longer be found here. I, too, must leave – to find Truth and seek God.

My one regret is disappointing you. I am truly sorry for that. Try to forgive me.

Your loving son,
Vladimir

Ivan took the first steamboat to Kazan. Vladimir, however, was no longer at the seminary, nor could anyone say where he had gone. In the course of the next year, rumors began drifting down the river – of revolutionary circles meeting in student flats and open fields and backrooms of stores, at which Vladimir had been sighted. Some even said he had joined the terrorists. To all these stories, Ivan responded with outraged disbelief.

And then, one day, Ivan got a letter from his brother. Grigori was priest in a small town not far from Kazan. Gently he informed Ivan that Vladimir had been arrested for handing out revolutionary leaflets printed by terrorists. Grigori had interceded with the local police and obtained his nephew's release. But after a long talk, Vladimir had disappeared again. "The boy is quite sincere about his belief in his new cause," Grigori had ended his letter, "and I doubt that anyone – save himself – can dissuade him from it. I certainly tried. He has always tended towards extremes – he is, after all, very Russian – so be patient with him. His is a beautiful soul; someday he will find his way."

Ivan crumpled Grigori's letter, flung it at the icon corner, and stomped out of the *izba*. Soon the bells began ringing in furious rage. Peasants came running in alarm, wondering what catastrophe had befallen. Evgenia reassured them and sent them home. Then she knelt in the icon corner and implored the Virgin to help Ivan. The wrathful pealing went on and on. And then, suddenly, the bells were silent.

Ivan stayed in the church all night. Evgenia kept vigil at home, in front of the icons. Finally, with the dawn, the bells began again. This time they tolled with profound, infinite sadness; slowly and sorrowfully, they wept with limitless grief.

When Ivan returned home, at last, he was an old man.

Part II

Petersburg, 1904

Chapter 7: The MARYINSKY

It was almost curtain time. Anticipation was mounting in the elegantly dressed audience. Lavish jewels, looking as if they had been ignited by the huge crystal chandelier suspended from a golden white dome, flashed and danced in its light.

As many times as she had witnessed the opening of the great gold and blue curtains of the stately Maryinsky Theatre, Lisya still felt the excitement. Looking up at the tiers of cream and blue rococo boxes, emblazoned with gilt bas-reliefs and upholstered in icy blue velvet, she wondered what it would be like to watch a performance from such an exalted perch. Not that she was unhappy with her seat in the orchestra pit; hers was the outermost chair in the last row of the First Violin section – far enough from the pit's back wall for a good view of the stage, far enough from the conductor to make use of it.

Premiere among Petersburg's many theatres, the Maryinsky was where the best performed. Lisya was proud to be part of the grand operas; her violin never tired of singing with the world's most beautiful voices – like that of the great Chaliapin, who would be appearing next month. The first time she had heard him sing – as Mephistopheles in Gounod's *Faust* – his richly beautiful basso voice had thoroughly captivated her. One night she had even dreamed of her grandfather, Mikhail, chanting the liturgy in church, suddenly being transformed into a glorious devil.

Next month, however, Chaliapin was to sing Moussorgsky's *Boris Godunov*. As guilt-ridden Tsar, surrounded by churches and icons and bells, priests and boyars and holy fools, he was somehow more comfortingly Russian. And the opera itself was one of her favorites – though as to that, it was hard to choose. All of them – whether they offered the brooding arias of Tchaikovsky or the comic antics of the Italians – were wonderful. She begrudged none of the long hours spent rehearsing and performing at matinees and evening performances.

Tonight was Sunday. That meant ballet. Glancing at the audience, Lisya noted that the balletomanes were out in force, as they were every Wednesday

153

and Sunday evening at the Maryinsky. Armed with binoculars, venerable civil servants and heavily decorated army generals had, as usual, occupied the best seats in the stalls.

Lisya enjoyed the ballets as much as the operas. Tonight, however, she was uncharacteristically on edge, nervously wiping her sweating palms with her handkerchief. Tatiana was dancing for the first time at the Maryinsky. How proud she was of her little sister!

Before going to the orchestra pit, Lisya had stopped backstage to see Tatiana. Up to the very top floor, she had climbed to the dressing room of the corps de ballet, where rows of excited young women were busily transforming themselves into the elegant figures who would soon grace the stage. A jumble of tulle and satin and artificial flowers mingled agreeably with the scent of face cream and powder and burned hair. Back in the farthest corner, she found Tatiana in front of a mirror, fussing with her makeup. Its sharp planes dramatically highlighted, her face bore an incongruously striking resemblance to Ivan's icon-like visage.

"I remember my first night at the Maryinsky," said Lisya to Tatiana's reflection.

Tatiana turned around and looked nervously at her.

"This is from Alexander Pavlovich." Lisya handed her a small nosegay of fresh flowers. "He had to deliver a baby, or he would be here himself. But he said to tell you that he is sure that this is the first of many bouquets."

Smiling gratefully, Tatiana took the flowers and grasped her sister's hand. "What if I fall?!"

"You won't," replied Lisya, confidently. "You've been dancing all your life."

"But not for people like those out there." Tatiana gestured in the general direction of the theatre boxes, her arm uncharacteristically stiff and tense.

"Who have paid to see *you* dance, because *they* can't."

"Someone said the Tsar is coming tonight!" Tatiana's face was almost as white as her powder.

"The Tsar appreciates a good performance," replied Lisya, recalling how intimidating the Tsar's presence had felt during her earlier years with the Maryinsky Orchestra. "Just dance for yourself – and everyone out there will see how much you love it."

Tatiana nodded, releasing her grip on her sister's hand. "How do I look?" Her usual smile suddenly played around the edges of her carefully painted mouth.

"You'll outshine everyone else on stage," said Lisya quite sincerely, marveling that the beautiful woman before her was actually her little sister.

"I'd better not!" laughed Tatiana, her voice a lovely cascade of sparkling light. "Kschessinskaya doesn't like to share the spotlight."

Lisya grinned. Then, after an approving glance at her sister's costume, she patted Tatiana's shoulder reassuringly. "I have to tune up," she said, and threaded her way through the other dancers back to the door.

Down in the pit, the end of her violin resting on her knee, Lisya glanced up at the Imperial Box. Sure enough, there was the Tsar with one of his daughters, the eldest of the little Grand Duchesses. The Empress was conspicuously absent – tonight the celebrated Matilda Kschessinskaya was dancing. The Tsar's affair with the prima ballerina of the Maryinsky had ended before his marriage, but she still wielded immense influence at Court – and at the Theatre. No one crossed Kschessinskaya and got away with it.

The audience hushed into a ripple of applause as the conductor entered and bowed, turned and raised his baton. Lisya tucked violin under chin, put bow to strings and waited. And then the downbeat, and once again it all started. As the overture played and the curtains opened, a wondrous blur of color and movement and rhythm and sound swirled through her.

Tonight was Tchaikovsky's *Sleeping Beauty*. Kschessinskaya burst on stage, dashing and vivid and sparkling with real diamonds, whirling like a fiery ball shooting out tongues of flame. But this time, Lisya barely saw her. Remembering Tatiana's face, white with tension even under her make-up, excitement and apprehension chased her bow as it flew over the violin strings. Her stomach began to knot up.

And then, at last, it was time. Among the gorgeously costumed couples, the swaying garlands and baskets of flowers, Lisya finally saw her. In the back row, Tatiana was bowing and pirouetting gracefully. Lisya craned her neck, trying to see more, forgetting her violin. After what seemed an interminable interlude, the rows opened into two columns, each couple coming forward and then wheeling about to the back of the stage. Tatiana moved downstage, her slim body swaying proudly, head held high. As she reached the front of the line, her dancer's composure faltered for just an instant. For a split second, Lisya glimpsed the little girl Tatiana had once been, dancing happily to the innocence of Tchaikovsky's waltz. And then the grown-up ballerina swept triumphantly around and moved on, a joyous swirl of blue tulle and pink flowers.

Her violin in her lap, tears stung Lisya's eyes. She didn't even notice the conductor glaring at her.

Walking through the corridors of the Conservatory was a challenge. From behind every door came sounds of musicians practicing – sweet notes suddenly going sour, virtuoso runs abruptly crashing, lush harmony turning into discord. To stop and tune it up – or to flee from the noise? But as always, Lisya just kept walking, marveling that so much music eventually emerged from this busy kaleidoscope of sound.

Reaching the closed door of Madame's studio, Lisya could hear the student inside still playing. She sat down on the chair next to the door and put her music portfolio in her lap. As she waited, she thought briefly about how much time she had spent sitting in this particular chair. In all the years she had studied piano with Madame, never once had her lesson started on time. When Madame was on the trail of a musical habit to be mended, clocks were irrelevant. Once inside the door, she gave each student her total attention until the lesson was over – whenever that happened to be.

Like everyone else on the Conservatory's faculty, Madame prescribed heavy doses of Mozart and Chopin, and coached her students in the concertos of Beethoven and Tchaikovsky. The avant garde grumbled, but Lisya was grateful for what she had learned from musicians like Madame.

Still, the new music was interesting, too. Just last week she had heard some of the more adventurous members of the Conservatory orchestra trying out Igor Stravinsky's latest composition. Despite her loyalty to Madame, she had been tempted to join in; under the jarring chords and unnerving changes in tempo, the new forms had paid tribute to the old classics in a surprisingly lyrical way. And even Sergei Prokofiev – who couldn't seem to put two notes together without creating dissonance – knew how important musical tradition was or he wouldn't be here.

The door of the studio abruptly burst open. Lisya was suddenly enveloped by the forceful personality flooding the corridor.

"*Bonjour, ma chere,*" Madame beamed. Madame frequently spoke French. No truly cultivated person, she often stated firmly, spoke *only* in Russian.

"*Bonjour*, Madame," Lisya replied. She had learned quickly.

Madame swept her into the studio and shut the door on the rest of the world.

Reverently, Lisya sat down at Madame's gleaming mahogany piano. The huge concert grand endowed everything played on it with a melancholy majesty nearly as overwhelming as Madame herself. To be worthy of this magnificent instrument was one of the reasons Lisya practiced so hard for her lessons. Madame herself fussed over it like a cherished child.

The lesson began. First, the Scriabin. Lisya had been surprised when Madame assigned it – and not just because Scriabin was from Moscow. But Madame had attended one of his concerts and been charmed by his charismatic personality. Scriabin claimed to travel to lofty spiritual realms, and had grand mystical schemes of bringing the world to nirvana through music. Lisya was more skeptical about that than Madame appeared to be, but they were both intrigued by his shimmering overloaded harmony.

And then, at last, the Rachmaninov. Lisya had been working on his new Piano Concerto for months. Today she was to perform the entire work for Madame. In preparation, she had checked out the orchestra accompaniment from the Conservatory Library and studied the score carefully. And so, from the first dramatic opening chords until the stunning excitement of the finale, Lisya was not only playing the piano but the whole orchestra, reacting to the slightest nuance of her fingers on the keyboard. Together they wept through Rachmaninov's abundant melodies and soared through his lyrical Romanticism. And when at last the final chords were ringing triumphantly, Lisya heard thunderous applause in Madame's proud smile.

Ж Ж Ж

Teatralnaya Ulitza was quiet today. Walking between the identical yellow buildings, white pillars stretched out on either side, was like entering an enormous ballroom, shining like the sun even in gloomy weather. Lisya turned into one of the buildings and walked up a wide staircase, under a large awning and through big doors, remembering how full of carriages the street had been that first day when she had brought Tatiana to audition for the Imperial Ballet School. They had both been intimidated by the doorman with the long grey beard and gold Imperial eagles on his uniform.

Today, however, he smiled and nodded as she entered and went up another wide staircase. At the top was a large rehearsal hall, with high semicircular windows overlooking the street. One wall was covered by a huge mirror; along the others were barres for dancing exercises. The floor was gently slanted, at the same degree as the stage of the Maryinsky. Around the hall, in wide gold frames, were portraits of Nicholas II and other Tsars. Lisya walked over to the grand piano in the corner, sat down on its bench, took out her music and waited for the ballet students.

On days when she had no rehearsals or lessons, Lisya played piano for the girls' ballet class. She had started doing so shortly after Tatiana had been acepted as a student. At first, she had taken the job to keep an eye on her little sister. Eventually, however, she had come to love being part of the place which created such magically beautiful movement. And so, even after Tatiana graduated, Lisya kept playing.

At around ten o'clock, the girls filed into the studio. Lisya knew they had already washed and dressed and stood inspection, and prayed and breakfasted and studied for their afternoon classes. They now wore gray practice dresses and gray linen dancing shoes with hard soles and box toes. They lined up at the barre and, as Lisya started to play, began their exercises.

Two hours later, they changed back into uniforms of long blue wool skirts, thick stockings and flat laced shoes. After lunch they would walk – in pairs and in a line – around the inner courtyard of the School for exactly twenty minutes. Then they would march to regular school classes until dinner at five, followed by music lessons, homework, needlework for the girls and military drill for the boys. Everyone would be back in long rows of dormitory beds by nine o'clock.

Still, children were children – even in the regimented discipline of the Imperial Ballet School. In her early years at the School, Tatiana had gone through a gymnastic phase. Her favorite stunt had been to "walk" up the walls of the narrow corridor between the washroom and the dormitory by pressing hands on one wall and feet on the other. Until one night when the governess appeared, just as Tatiana was about to "walk" back down the wall. She froze near the ceiling, while the woman walked under without noticing her. The stares and giggles of the other girls, however, drew her eyes to the body hovering strangely overhead. The startled governess turned white, as Tatiana tried to decide the proper thing to say. Lisya only heard about this much later.

As Tatiana passed into the Upper Division, the routine changed somewhat. Academic classes were smaller and taught by specialists with appropriate degrees. Art was taught by artists from the Academy of Art, music by musicians from the Conservatory. Older students could stay up an hour later, and moved out of the long narrow dormitory of fifty into a smaller room of six. But the girls were still not allowed to leave the School unaccompanied. Even when Lisya came to take her out on Sunday afternoons, Tatiana had to stop by the desk to pick up a pass card.

The girls, of course, were rigorously segregated from the boys, only occasionally catching glimpses of them, marching to and from class in handsome light blue uniforms with silver lyres. Even during rehearsals they were not allowed to speak. The girls stood along one wall, the boys lined up opposite. When they danced together, they were silent.

As Lisya put her music away, she glanced at the Tsar's portrait, remembering the long table placed beneath it the previous May. Behind had sat the Director of the Imperial Theatres, the faculty, and other dignitaries When her name was called, Tatiana walked proudly forward, the hated uniform exchanged for an elegant rose lace dress. She received her diploma, the New Testament, the complete works of Tolstoy, and one hundred rubles. The next day she became a member of the Maryinsky corps de ballet.

Lisya closed the keyboard, stood up and slowly crossed the room to the door. Suddenly, the shadow of a young girl in practice dress flitted across her mind's eye and danced around the corners of the studio. And Lisya knew that, no matter what, she would always find her little sister here.

Ж　Ж　Ж

Lisya fumbled in her purse and fished out five kopeks. Paying the vendor at the fruit stall, she took a bag of red currants. Opening it, she offered some to Tatiana. Together they strolled along the Nevsky Prospekt, enjoying the sunshine, occasionally popping currants into their mouths.

They did not really look like sisters. Lisya took after their mother, and tended toward the full-bodied beauty which characterized women on that side of the family. Tatiana favored their father's people, and had the slender small-bosomed build of their grandmother, Natasha. While not as tall as Lisya, Tatiana's lean body and long slim legs gave her the appearance of being so. And while her theatrical features were not as pretty as Lisya's rounded contours, her sharply sculpted cheekbones and gracefully pointed chin and nose were strikingly attractive. Both young women had inherited their mother's dark, abundant hair. Tatiana wore hers pulled straight back in a large bun; Lisya's draped softly around her ears and was pinned gently at the nape of the neck in a generous knot. Tatiana's large blue eyes were the color of the sky in Spring, and matched her lovely rippling laugh which delighted in everything. Lisya's grey-blue eyes were usually serious; only occasionally did they light up with a smile. Tatiana walked like a dancer – dramatically, and with feet turned out. Lisya walked no less gracefully, but to a more determined beat.

Yet for all the differences, it was obvious that they were sisters. Everyone commented on the resemblance – though no one could quite explain it. Lisya herself often wondered that looking at Tatiana was like looking in a mirror – and yet not.

As they walked along the Nevsky in comfortable silence, Lisya was again grateful for the sister who was also her best friend. Between them was complete trust; there was nothing they could not tell each other. And that they both worked at the Maryinsky, each doing what she loved best, deepened an already close bond.

When Tatiana had been at the Ballet School, except on visiting days and at dancing class, the sisters had not seen much of each other during the school year. But during the long summer days, they had explored Petersburg thoroughly. And now that Tatiana was at the Maryinsky, they had more time together.

Sometimes they went to bicycle races or horse shows. On hot days, they went bathing in the Neva. Often they attended an operetta at the Theatre Bouffe, or a play at the Drama Theatre. Occasionally, too, they explored the palaces around Petersburg: Peterhof, endless and enormous and colossal and overwhelming – like its builder, Peter the Great; and Pavlovsk, unimposing – like Tsar Pavel, for whom it was built – but more comfortable. Military bands there gave outdoor concerts in gardens filled with gazebos and bronze statues and natural-looking landscaping.

Only once did they visit Tsarkoe Selo, where the Imperial Family usually resided. Walking in the areas open to the public, they had admired the elegant palace, hoping to catch sight of the Tsar and his family. But though its graceful proportions were less intimidating than huge Peterhof, Tsarkoe Selo made them uneasy.

"It's like playing Mozart on a piano just slightly out of tune," Lisya remarked, on the way home.

"Or like dancing on a broken toe shoe," nodded Tatiana.

Best of all was Petersburg itself. Walking along its straight, broad avenues, they gazed at its grand, exquisitely proportioned buildings. Across large open piazzas and along wide meandering canals were Italian-style palaces the color of sunlight. Fancy carriages drawn by beautifully accoutered horses flew up and down the streets like arrows, their coachmen shouting "Watch out!" to those on foot. Iron-hooped wheels of droshkies crackled on the cobblestones, and horse-drawn streetcars scraped their rails as they whipped up speed to cross canal bridges. Men in colorful uniforms strode briskly by, the ring and rattle of their trailing sabres punctuated by church bells.

Surrounded by this symphony of urban life, Lisya and Tatiana made their way slowly up the Nevsky Prospekt, pausing to drink in the beauty of the Anichkov Palace, to admire the semicircular colonnade of the Kazansky Cathedral, to window-shop in the arcades of the Gostiny Dvor. A rather small man pulled by a very large dog passed them on the sidewalk. The sight of the master puffing to keep up with his pet made both sisters giggle. Turning off the Nevsky and heading toward their favorite bench on the Neva Embankment, Tatiana did a subdued imitation of both man and dog. Lisya hummed an appropriate accompaniment. The sisters laughed and sat down on the bench.

As she watched the sunlight glittering on wavelets in the river, Lisya thought of how often she and Tatiana had shared their hopes and dreams in this place. With the grandeur of the Winter Palace in the background and the golden spire of the Petropavlovsk Fortress a gleaming beacon before them, anything seemed possible.

"Do you think life will always be this good?" Tatiana threw her head back and embraced the world with her smile. "I'm dancing with the best dancers in the best theatre, and living in the most beautiful city in the world! What could be better?!"

"Being Prima Ballerina?"

"Maybe for some," mused Tatiana, "but not for me. I love dancing with others, being part of the whole. It makes me feel like I'm more than when I'm just doing it by myself. No, I have never wanted to be a soloist."

"Neither have I," agreed Lisya. "It's the harmony of making music with others that uplifts me. I feel like I belong."

"If only it could go on forever."

"Why can't it?" Lisya frowned, and felt a small moment of darkness flit across the bright waves of the Neva.

"For you, maybe it can," replied Tatiana, "but dancers can't dance forever."

"Kschessinskaya probably will," laughed Lisya.

"No doubt." Tatiana, too, laughed. "But someday I would like to have a child."

"So would I," agreed Lisya, "but not yet."

"Alexander Pavlovich will be a good father."

"Yes. Yes, he will. But…"

"Have you ever been sorry?" asked Tatiana, after a long pause.

"No. No, not really." Lisya hesitated. Only around Tatiana did she ever allow herself to think of Dmitri – though sometimes there were dreams she could not control. But even with Tatiana, she would never speak of him. "Without Alexander Pavlovich, I would not have this wonderful life. I belong here, and when I look in his eyes, I see myself as I was meant to be."

"He adores you," smiled Tatiana.

"Yes, I'm grateful for that, too." A glow of genuine contentment suffused Lisya's face. "And I love him, too. But more quietly."

"*Too* quietly?"

"Well, maybe sometimes..." Lisya again paused. "But I, too, value the person *he* is. I admire his devotion to his work – and I know I can count on his loyalty. He is a good man, a kind man, and I feel safe with him."

"So great friendship is preferable to grand passion?" grinned Tatiana.

"In the long run, yes. It's certainly easier to live with." Smiling, Lisya offered Tatiana the last of the currants. "Keep that in mind, little sister, when it's your turn."

"I think perhaps Mother and Father have both." Tatiana chewed meditatively. "But most people probably aren't so lucky."

The fanfare of trumpets interrupted. From the gates of the Winter Palace, several rows of Horse Guards trotted out and lined up. A band played "God Save the Tsar" as the Emperor, in a dark uniform with blue sash, rode beside the Empress's carriage, through ranks of hussars in colorful uniforms astride spirited thoroughbreds. Behind him came the generals and aides-de-camp, their uniforms in varying degrees of rank. The regiment cheered as the Imperial procession passed by; in the crowd which had gathered, however, many stood in sullen silence.

Lisya and Tatiana slowly followed the parade to the Summer Gardens. By the time they entered the tall wrought-iron gates, the Emperor and his suite had already returned to the Palace. Quietly, the sisters walked along broad paths which stretched on and on, lined by towering old linden trees. In spring, their blossoming fragrance sweetened the air; in autumn, their changing leaves painted the sky. And now, their branches gave cooling shade to the two young women sitting on the benches beneath. The venerable trees reminding them of the forests around Derevnia, they sat serenely in the place where home – past and present – seemed to merge.

"Remember when Babushka used to take us into the forest?" Tatiana gazed affectionately at the huge trees. "I miss that."

"I don't. I could never remember what things were."

"And Babushka used to sigh and groan under her breath," giggled Tatiana.

"Until you started taking the bad mushrooms out of my basket, and putting in good ones from yours."

"Do you think she knew?"

"Probably," chuckled Lisya. "I doubt that anything fooled Babushka."

"Someday I want to be a babushka. I think that would be wonderful, don't you?"

"I don't think I'd be very good at it," replied Lisya ruefully.

"Maybe not in Derevnia, but here in Petersburg – of course, you would," protested Tatiana earnestly. "City people need a babushka, too."

"Well, maybe. But only if I don't have to wear a kerchief."

They both laughed, then leaned companionably against each other, enjoying the music of the rustling linden leaves.

Then the sun set and a strangely beautiful light appeared, as if shining through translucent glass. Rousing herself from the hypnotic spell of the white nights, Lisya stood up resolutely and insisted that it was time to go. Reluctantly, Tatiana agreed and they walked rapidly to the gates, knowing that it was much later than it seemed. The eerie glow drew them to the foot of the Liteiny Bridge, now bathed in what was neither darkness nor light. Across the bridge was the Vyborg district, a part of Petersburg the sisters never visited.

Vaguely, Lisya knew that the factories over there were not like the beautiful palaces she and Tatiana chose to stroll past, and that the workers who lived there were not like the people at the Maryinsky. Beyond that, she never ventured. Nor did she ever cross the bridge. And only once a year – during the running of the ice – did either of the sisters even set foot on it.

Every Spring, people crowded bridges and quays, watching this awesome rite. As the sun warmed, the ice on the river darkened, swelling and cracking and splitting, then suddenly moving in one great relentless mass. Huge pieces of ice drifted slowly forward, pushing against each other and smashing into the banks, crashing and reverberating for miles.

At such times, Lisya and Tatiana were drawn to the river by an elemental force of frightening power. As the roaring ice crashed under the Liteiny Bridge, they were enveloped in the primitive beauty of its wild music, listening in fascination to its sudden changes in tempo, from dark and brooding and sensuous and mysterious to wild and powerful and brutal and frenzied.

Remembering the violence of those strange melodies and chaotic churning chords, Lisya reached for Tatiana's hand. As she grasped it – just as she did every Spring on the Bridge – the pulse of the now quiet river flowed reassuringly through them both.

Shaking off the moment, the sisters turned away from the bridge and walked home.

Ж　Ж　Ж

A tall footman, in a grey tailcoat with yellow braid and brass buttons, escorted Lisya to the ballroom. She walked slowly through the huge elegant room, trying not to stare too obviously. The glittering crystal chandeliers, the blazing gilt candle sconces, the intricate wooden parquet floor, the jade damask of curtains and upholstery, the ornate bas-reliefs on the walls, the classical figures painted on the ceiling – all swam together in an opulent blur.

The prima ballerina, Matilda Kschessinskaya, was having a housewarming party in her new palace on Kronversky Prospekt. Members of the Maryinsky orchestra were providing the music. Like everyone else, Lisya had heard about Kschessinskaya's country house in Strelna, with its own electric power station and special trains and lavish fetes. She, of course, did not move in sufficiently exalted circles to be on the prima ballerina's guest list. But when the orchestra conductor asked for volunteers to play at what promised to be the soiree of the season, Lisya could not resist signing up. The new palace was said to be even grander than the one at Strelna.

Most of the other musicians were already seated and warming up. Finding an unoccupied chair among the violins, she sat down and took out her instrument. After tuning the strings and playing some scales and arpeggios, she check the music on the stand. As expected, several Strauss-like confections were lined up. Playing such insubstantial fare would be tedious, but tonight she didn't mind. Not having to concentrate on the music would free her attention for what she had come to see.

After making sure there were no difficult passages to practice, she scanned the room more slowly. Eventually her eyes were drawn to the grandiloquent mural which busily romped across the ceiling; especially fascinating was the muscular Greek god chasing a scantily-clad nymph directly overhead. Only when the concertmaster signaled – for the third time – that it was time to begin did Lisya's gaze return to her music stand.

As the fluffy music rolled automatically off her strings, Lisya watched the guests congregating in the ballroom. Some of the ladies wore court dresses, cut

164

very low, with bare shoulders and long trains. One of these *grandes dames* was chatting amiably not far from the orchestra. Her chestnut hair was decorated with a diadem set with two rows of diamonds; a delicate chain with a single huge diamond crossed her forehead. A complicated diamond necklace clasped her neck and two cascades of diamonds hung from her ears. Her dress appeared to be of bright blue satin, but was encrusted with still more diamonds. Around the neckline was a thick border of diamonds, and on the back, a large flower of diamonds. From it two diamond chains led, like enormous threads of fire, to the front of the bodice and then to the diamond buckle at the waist.

After staring at this blazing apparition for several minutes, Lisya's aching eyes shifted to the lady's companions. Like many of the other male guests, they were wearing uniforms. One young man wore a trim scarlet jacket with metallic eagles on front and back, and very tight elk-skin breeches. *However did he get those on?* wondered Lisya. *He can't possibly be wearing underwear.*

Blushing slightly, she shifted her glance to the next cluster of guests. Less dazzlingly attired, Lisya guessed they were members of the city's artistic elite. Here and there, she recognized stars from the Maryinsky and other well-known Petersburg musicians.

When the room was finally filled with brilliantly clad people, the concert-master, directing from his seat, struck up a stately ballet march. The room suddenly hushed, as Matilda Kschessinskaya made her imperious entrance. Like Moses parting the Red Sea, a path in the crowd opened before her impeccably choreographed series of flowing, significant gestures and mobile, noble poses. Every conceivable part of her body was adorned with rings, brooches, pendants, and diadems of rubies, diamonds, amethysts and emeralds – all of which were said to be gifts from various grand dukes. Next to Kschessinskaya, everyone in the room seemed drab.

After the Hostess had passed through the room, the orchestra took a break. Though they had entered at the rear, the musicians were allowed to eat freely at the numerous buffets, all laden with exotic hors d'oeuvres on heavy gold plate. For they, too, were Artists of the Imperial Theatre, albeit of lower status than those on stage.

Lisya and her friend, Olga, stood together in a corner near the food, munching caviar and marinated mushrooms. Olga was a cellist, and had joined the Maryinsky orchestra just before Lisya. Tall and big-boned, cheerfully skeptical and good-naturedly outspoken, she had no time for artifice – and usually no qualms about saying so. But she, too, was curious about Kschessinskaya's glittering lifestyle, and had come tonight for the same reason as Lisya.

Cloaked by the invisibility of their plain black gowns, the two young women stared unabashedly at the luxurious dining room. Paneled in dark oak, all around it were shelves of gold and silver platters, goblets and vases, and precious china services. The huge oval table was covered with a fine lace tablecloth, and the fireplace was so large the footman adding logs to the fire was able to stand inside it.

"Well," said Olga, when her curiosity had subsided sufficiently to speak, "the awesome Matilda has certainly done well for herself."

"Yes, indeed," agreed Lisya, helping herself to more caviar.

"What a pity," sighed Olga, "that grand dukes never seem to find cellists attractive."

"It's the costume," grinned Lisya, "and the position of the legs."

Olga laughed, her large plain face crinkling up with good humour. "It's probably just as well. I prefer to be judged on the merits of my musicianship."

"Mmmm, yes," assented Lisya, "but Kschessinskaya really *is* a good dancer, too. Tatiana genuinely admires her. And as much as the other ballerinas resent having to dance her left-overs, they all respect her talent."

"Well," replied Olga, "I'm not really into ballet – opera's more to my liking – but I admire Kschessinskaya's independence. She's smart and strong and knows how to use her influence. She gets what she wants and doesn't let anyone walk on her. Not many women have that kind of control over their lives."

During a later break, Olga and Lisya tried the champagne being served by swarms of servants in black tailcoats and white gloves. Emboldened by the bubbles, they wandered off to explore the rest of the house.

"Just pretend you're one of the servants," giggled Olga, "and they'll never notice us."

Kschessinskaya's palace was a veritable labyrinth of brocade and gold and crystal and velvet, of canopied beds and blue tiled stoves and elaborate furniture and ornately framed paintings. In one room were oriental lanterns and red ceiling tiles and aggressive-looking golden dragons. In another was a huge billiard table standing on a very thick carpet. Still another was dominated by an enormous organ, pipes reaching up to the ceiling and filling the entire wall. Lisya's favorite was filled with tropical plants and illuminated with fantastic green lights. A fountain spouted from the center of a round pool, sparkling with swimming goldfish.

Olga and Lisya were about to settle down around the pool with another glass

166

of champagne, when they heard distant strains of a rather saccharine mazurka. Olga muttered something Lisya pretended not to hear, and both walked hastily in the direction of the ballroom. No one in the orchestra really seemed to notice – or to care – as they slipped quietly into their chairs and picked up their bows. From the vague nod of the concertmaster, Lisya surmised that she and Olga were not the only musicians who had been sampling the champagne.

The evening wore on into the early hours of the morning. The sticky-sweet music began to grate on Lisya's nerves; its cloying fluffiness mixed unpleasasantly with the caviar and champagne. The heavy opulence gorging the palace grew stifling; dazzling jewelry and blazing chandeliers gave her a throbbing headache. The lavishly attired guests began to resemble garish wind-up dolls whose springs were wearing out. During the last waltz they whirled with frantic surrealism, while the orchestra seemed to wind slowly and relentlessly down, down... and then to stop... forever.

When it was all over, Lisya ran into the water-closet off the cloakroom and was sick.

Chapter 8: The DOCTORS

Lisya was making dinner in the kitchen of their modest fifth floor apartment. Cooking had never fired her imagination, and – even if they could have afforded it – she was not an adventurous cook. Her repertoire of dishes was small but tasty, prepared without enthusiasm but with the quiet pride which accompanied all the tasks necessary to her well-ordered household. As she prepared the food, her fingers moved quickly and efficiently, wasting nothing, the spare motions soothing in their repetitive familiarity.

Despite her indifference to cooking, Lisya enjoyed being in her kitchen. L-shaped around the large closet recently turned bathroom, it somehow suggested the possibility of more space than it actually enclosed. A large window facing onto the courtyard let in as much light as Petersburg's sky permitted. Rows of well-scrubbed pots, neatly-stacked dishes, and gleaming cutlery lined up reassuringly on adjacent shelves. That each object had its place, and that all was where it should be, added to the room's tranquil harmony.

Flanking the kitchen were her husband's study and Tatiana's room. Across the short hall, windows facing the street, were the dining room and living room, and the bedroom she shared with Alexander Pavlovich. Though none of the rooms were large, the apartment was pervaded by a comfortable sense of security.

The district in which they resided was not fashionable, but very respectable. In addition to his medical practice, Alexander Pavlovich taught at the Medical School. This extra stipend enabled them to live more securely than most doctors' families, even to have a few luxuries – like the wardrobe with the mirrored door in their bedroom, the well-stocked bookcases in the living room, and the upright piano trimmed with ornate carving. Someday, when she had saved up enough from her earnings at the Maryinsky, she would have a concert grand – like Madame's.

Slicing cucumbers, Lisya looked down into the courtyard. It was surrounded on three sides by the apartment house in which they lived, and on the fourth by

169

the large windowless wall of the building next door. The courtyard was painted yellow, and had wooden walks over the cobblestones from the building's entrances to the arched oval gateway, stretching like a tunnel through the front wing of the house to the heavy outside gates. At night, these strong oak doors were guarded by a stern custodian who slept on a bench nearby.

In a separate building in the courtyard, hired laundresses did the wash. Lisya could see billows of steam escaping from its open vents and heard the women singing mournfully. She paid one of them extra to help with cleaning, shopping and cooking, especially on evenings when she performed at the Maryinsky.

Next to the laundry shed were stables and a coach-house. An old Countess lived on the second floor, and a retired general on the third. Both could afford their own coachmen and grooms. Alexander Pavlovich had an arrangement with one of them, who cared for their mare and harnessed her up to their small open carriage and sleigh. He also carried up their firewood from the deep cellar where it was stored.

Tonight the Maryinsky was silent; Tatiana had gone to the opening of an Art Exhibit with friends. As she always did on such occasions, Lisya was preparing her husband's favorite dishes. She enjoyed fixing the undemanding recipes he preferred, just as he appreciated her reliable cooking. He would, she knew, be home early tonight. As always, the thought pleased her.

She had just put the cabbage-beef *pirogi* into the oven when she heard Alexander Pavlovich enter the front door. Coming back into the kitchen, he greeted her cheerfully and kissed her affectionately on the forehead. Under his arm was the bottle of good wine – one of the few luxuries he permitted himself – customarily brought home for these occasions. One of his patients had an excellent wine cellar, and sometimes paid his bill in kind.

Alexander Pavlovich's modest appetites matched his unassuming demeanor. Of average build and medium height, he was only a little taller than his wife. Short, very straight black hair combed neatly back and a carefully trimmed goatee had just a few streaks of grey. Behind scholarly-looking glasses, slightly slanted brown eyes were crowned with sharply arched eyebrows. A quiet smile now overlaid his customary look of judicious compassion.

As she returned her husband's greeting, a gentle wave of well-being softly enveloped Lisya. While she brought out a small platter of *zakuski*, Alexander Pavlovich's skillful fingers carefully opened the wine bottle and held the cork to his nose. Pouring a little into a wineglass, he tasted it thoughtfully and sighed with satisfaction. When Lisya sat down at the table, he filled both their glasses.

"An exceptionally fine bouquet, Alexander Pavlovich," said Lisya, as she sipped the wine.

"Yes indeed, Lisya, my dear," responded her husband genially. "Courtesy of Fyodor Petrovich's gout. He seems to have taken my temperance admonitions quite literally. Let us hope he continues to evacuate his wine cellar in our direction."

Lisya laughed appreciatively, and offered him the *zakuski*. "And how did your classes go today?"

"Rather well, considering. Sometimes it's difficult to get students to concentrate on medicine, what with all the unrest." Alexander Pavlovich contemplated his wineglass. "Still, it's always exciting to see students from such diverse backgrounds getting along and working together. There's no better leveler than dissecting cadavers. Perhaps I should invite members of the government to attend my anatomy labs."

"I'm sure the radical students would give them a warm welcome," smiled Lisya.

"Indeed, yes," he chuckled. "In my day, the rabble-rousers were mostly the seminarians. But now, all of the students are upset about one thing or another."

Uncomfortable with the turn the conversation was taking, Lisya went into the kitchen to get the lemon soup. She did not want to hear about the turbulence outside her own peaceful little world.

After dinner – and compliments on the *pirogi* – Alexander Pavlovich slowly poured himself a cup of tea from the samovar. Lisya brought in some *pirozhki* filled with apricot sauce.

"And how," he inquired, "was your lesson with Madame?"

"It went well, I think. She seemed pleased with the Rachmaninov."

"Did she like your interpretation of the last movement?"

"She seemed to," replied Lisya, also pouring herself a cup of tea. "She said the dynamics and tempo variations were especially effective."

"Good, good!" beamed Alexander Pavlovich, helping himself to more *pirozhki*. "And now, would Madame's star pupil honor her greatest fan with a command performance?"

After she had cleared the table, Lisya sat down at her old piano and ran through a few warm-up etudes. The upright had good tone, but was never quite in tune. After adjusting the bench and placing her feet on the pedals, she glanced at Alexander Pavlovich, waiting expectantly in his favorite chair.

Her husband, she knew, worked very hard at maintaining the controlled demeanor he considered appropriate for a man of science. Rarely did he express anger – or, for that matter, any other strong emotions. Only in the presence of good music did he allow himself to wholeheartedly disclose what he was feeling. And so now, his usually inexpressive face was alight with anticipation. For just an instant, he looked like someone else.

Quickly Lisya closed her eyes and began to play, reminding herself that she would never have a more attentive, appreciative audience than the utterly loyal man sitting across the room. As her fingers caressed the worn keys, the forbidden memory faded and she began to hear her music through her husband's ears. By the end of the Concerto, the old upright had been transformed into a concert grand.

"Brave, bravo!" Alexander Pavlovich applauded enthusiastically, tears in his eyes. "Encore, encore!"

Lisya obliged with a Chopin nocturne. Then she closed the keyboard and sat down in her chair with her mending basket. Alexander Pavlovich opened a book and began reading aloud. It was Turgenev's *Fathers and Children*, and they were about halfway through.

Alexander Pavlovich read with the same understanding and compassion he brought to his work. Lisya respected that, as she did much else about her husband. And she knew how fortunate she was to be married to a man so supportive of her music career. When she joined the Maryinsky orchestra, he had taken her to one of Petersburg's best dressmakers for her black concert gown. And for the rare evenings when they went out together to concerts, he made sure she had a fine dress to wear. Its saffron velvet and cream lace were no match for those glittering in the Boxes, but up in the Gallery she cut an elegant figure. Though Alexander Pavlovich pretended not to notice the admiring glances in her direction, the arm he offered to lead her to their seats always lifted a few notches.

Other than concerts, their social life together consisted primarily of informal gatherings with friends. Regardless of whose home, all these soirees were virtually identical. Mostly the guests were doctors and their wives, and mostly the conversation revolved around the glowing future of modern medicine – and how unappreciated doctors were. Lisya did not find these evenings very exciting, but they were predictably pleasant. The doctors were earnest and dedicated – like Alexander Pavlovich – and their wives were maternal and middle-aged – unlike herself. But they were reliable, unpretentious people with whom she felt comfortable. And sometimes talking about medical causes roused her husband to periodic bouts of eloquence; in his good suit, graying temples framing eyes flashing with righteous indignation, he looked quite distinguished.

Lately, though, these gatherings had been less comfortable. All the doctors seemed to talk about was politics. She told herself she was bored, because it had nothing to do with music. But the truth was that she was afraid. All this dangerous talk sounded a disturbing chord, out of tune with the harmonious, secure world she had carefully created for herself.

Lisya brought her attention back to the socks she was darning and Alexander Pavlovich's gentle voice. She liked when he read to her, even if she didn't always concentrate on the words. The sound of his voice soothed her, and made her feel safe.

Finishing the chapter, he put the book back on the shelf and walked across the room to her chair. "I'll be going to bed soon," he said quietly, "as soon as I finish writing a very short letter."

Lisya smiled and nodded, then listened to her husband walk down the hall and into his study. Quickly putting away her darning, she went into their bedroom, changed into her only lace-trimmed nightgown, and climbed between the freshly laundered sheets of their comfortable bed.

A few minutes later, Alexander Pavlovich silently joined her. Affectionately returning his long sweet kiss, Lisya relaxed into his gentle embrace. As his hands tenderly caressed her, Lisya felt her body quietly respond. And when, at last, he entered her, she opened herself gladly.

Later, her husband snoring softly beside her, she lovingly smoothed his tousled hair. He stirred, sighed contentedly, and rolled over on his side. Lisya nestled against him and kissed his back, happy that she had given so much pleasure to the man who made her feel so loved. Then she drifted off into peaceful, dreamless sleep.

Ж   Ж   Ж

Far off in the distance, Alexander Pavlovich heard someone knocking. Reluctantly he climbed out of the warm, soft cocoon enfolding him and slipped into his old wool robe. Stumbling into the hall, he heard Tatiana's voice outside the front door.

"I'm so sorry," she said quietly as he let her in, "but I forgot my key." As she glided down the hall to her room, she gave him one of her dazzling smiles.

Alexander Pavlovich's annoyance abruptly dissipated. Returning to the bedroom, he gazed lovingly at his sleeping wife. Carefully tucking the blankets around her, he lightly kissed the top of her head. Then he crossed the hall and closed the door of his study behind him.

Sitting down on the small couch in his study, he slipped his feet into an ancient pair of felt slippers and wrapped the warm old robe more tightly about him. Sighing deeply, he leaned back and contemplated his life.

How fortunate he was to have that beautiful woman across the hall as his wife! What joy her wonderful music had brought him! What happiness her presence in his home gave him! And how much he wanted to go back to their bed and take her in his arms and… But no. That was not the nature of their love. Nor was he that kind of man. Though sometimes he wondered what it would feel like to be someone whose wife called him Sasha instead of Alexander Pavlovich.

Shaking his head, he smiled ruefully. Even *he* couldn't call himself anything but Alexander Pavlovich. That was who he was. And who his wife trusted him to be. And who he *would* be to protect her from the dangerous world lurking outside. And from the despair which sometimes washed over him.

Unlike his wife, he had crossed the Liteiny Bridge – many times– and knew the Vyborg District well. And so, while he, too, loved the beautiful buildings and culture of Petersburg, primarily he was conscious of it as a big noisy city teeming with the drunk and destitute. Away from the splendor, it sprawled – dirty and decrepit and unattended – with old wooden buildings and evil flats. Whether winter, the air thick with heavy brownish smoke, or summer, the still evenings overlaid with a blue grey pall and rotting sewage, he felt oppressed by the overpowering sky and at the mercy of the miserable climate.

But what else could one expect of a city built on a swamp, whose every foundation stone represented a worker's life, whose monumental beauty and grace rested on massive human suffering! It was still just as Pushkin had written in *The Bronze Horseman* – the bog gods of the swamp struggling to take back what had once belonged to them. Only now, too, factory chimneys blackened the grey mists of the Neva. But even so, Alexander Pavlovich loved Petersburg as much as Pushkin did. And he knew he would fight beside the Bronze Horseman against bog gods, smokestacks or anything else menacing his city.

All these dark ruminations he was careful to keep from his wife. He made no effort to discourage her one-sided view of Petersburg; he never talked to her of the working-class slums where his medical practice often took him. The sheltered world in which she moved was beautiful and respectable and safe – and he had every intention of keeping it so. In her innocence and her wonderful gift of music, he found respite from a violent world.

He himself, however, could not afford the luxury of seeing the world through such naive spectacles. No doctor could. A good physician depended on making correct diagnoses, upon his ability to recognize symptoms and name disease. *We are not necessarily more dedicated to truth than anyone else*, reflected Alexander Pavlovich wryly, *but our profession requires that we bear it more closely in mind.*

Not that any of them got much thanks for carrying this extra burden – or, for that matter, any of their other responsibilities. Being a physician was not merely a thankless, low-paying, low-status job; it was also genuinely hazardous. Death at an early age was common among physicians, leaving their families in often dire straits.

Above his desk was a framed copy of the oath he had taken at his graduation from Medical School. Not that he needed it to remember the duties and responsibilities he had sworn to uphold. Closing his eyes, he could see a younger, more idealistic version of himself repeating the words which still guided so much of his life. "I vow to aid those who suffer and request my assistance, and not to abuse the trust shown in me."

Like most members of the Russian intelligentsia, Alexander Pavlovich had hailed with enthusiasm the industrialization his country was belatedly copying from Europe. As a physician, however, he also knew the adverse effects of factories on public health. He knew, too, how quickly contagious disease raced along the improved waterways and railroad lines, claiming hundreds of thousands of victims – including many of the medical personnel obligated to serve in such emergencies. Sensitized by their medical practice to their nation's needs, Alexander Pavlovich and his colleagues worked hard to improve conditions in factories and tenements, orphanages and schools, in malaria infested regions and along routes of migrant workers.

And as their responsibility for public health increased, so, too, did their zeal as reformers; both fueled their resentment of their low status and their frustration at the government's intransigent inefficiency. Many physicians, including Alexander Pavlovich, had joined the Opposition.

He sat down at his desk and pulled out the article he was writing about the recent Pirogov Congress. Leafing through the thick stack of paper covered with closely-spaced lines of his small neat hand, he paused occasionally to add or delete a word. Originally intended as a brief report for a medical journal, the project had proliferated. Somehow, the more he wrote, the better he felt.

The Pirogov Society of Russian Physicians, founded in memory of the famous physician, Nikolas Pirogov, had fostered many reform efforts and done much to stimulate the consciousness of Russian doctors. Alexander Pavlovich had been an active member for years. But never had he seen the members of his profession so agitated as at the last Pirogov Congress. The auditorium bulged with hundreds standing, while milling crowds outside tried to get in. Often it was impossible to hear over the hissing and whistling and stamping and applauding. And when, midway through the congress, the city prefect locked the doctors out of the hall where they were meeting, they angrily reconvened at the Medical School. Alexander Pavlovich remembered coming home from that meeting so enraged that Lisya had feared for his health.

He had, however, felt marvelously elated, surging adrenalin pumping years of frustration out of his soul, as what started out a medical convention rapidly turned into a political rally. Out of all the controversy came 100 resolutions, in which the doctors demanded economic and social reform, representative government and basic civil liberties.

Alexander Pavlovich knew he would never forget that last meeting. After two speeches on scientific subjects, the chairman announced that due to "special circumstances," the resolutions could not be read. He pronounced the congress closed. A stunned silence swept the hall. Angry muttering and outraged hissing were drowned out by the spirited playing of a military band. The crowd began to shout and whistle. Finally, in an attempt to silence the band, the doctors smashed their chairs and threw the pieces at the musicians. The crowd sang the *Marseillaise* and shouted "Down with Autocracy!" And so it went, until the police finally dispersed the rioting doctors.

Alexander Pavlovich had thrown his chair, too. But even now, he felt no shame. He wondered about that. True, he had not aimed at the musicians, nor had he hit anyone else.

Still… he had not told Lisya.

Ж   Ж   Ж

It was late – very late – but Lisya could not sleep. Finally she shivered out of her bed and went into the living room, where she lit a candle and resolutely picked up her knitting.

The winter darkness of Petersburg was heavier than usual. Even Christmas had done little to lighten it. Lisya knew it was not just the weather. Something ominous – something too frightening to name – was prowling the streets of her city.

She knew it had something to do with the War.

When the Japanese had launched their surprise attack on the Russian fleet in Port Arthur, the nation had – at first – rallied patriotically to the cause. The war, however, was a disaster. Even Lisya – who worked harder than most to ignore these things – could see what a toothless dinosaur the Russian military had become. Unrest and agitation, temporarily diverted by the war, broke out anew and with increased fervor.

Despite her best efforts not to understand what was happening, the prowling beast forced its way into Lisya's world. Many physicians were now in uniform. Alexander Pavlovich was, fortunately, not yet one of them, but he got letters from friends who were. They testified to the massive inefficiency with which the war was being waged, and were full of the incompetence and graft and needless suffering on the Far Eastern Front. After reading each letter, Alexander Pavlovich would turn purple, run into his study, and slam the door.

So here she was, knitting socks for the soldiers in the middle of the night, wondering why the darkness would not let her sleep. Suddenly she was startled by a frantic knock at the door. Running to the door on cold feet, she opened it cautiously and was shocked to see her brother leaning weakly against the wall. She barely recognized him.

"Volodya, what on earth – ?"

"Lisya," he interrupted, his face white, "I must see Alexander Pavlovich."

"He's not here," began Lisya – and then saw the blood on his sleeve.

Taking him by his other arm, she helped him into Alexander Pavlovich's study – the room nearest the door – and sat him down on the couch. With a pair of scissors, she gently cut away the bloody sleeve and helped him remove the rest of his dirty coat. Going quickly to the kitchen for a basin of hot water, she carefully washed the wound and applied compresses to staunch the bleeding.

Vladimir began to tremble and lay down on the couch. Lisya ran into the bedroom, took all the extra blankets from the trunk at the foot of the bed, and bundled them around her brother's shaking body.

"How could they?... How could they?" he gasped between clenched teeth. "We just wanted to give the Tsar our petition... We just wanted to tell him how bad things are... to ask him to do something..."

"Shhh-shhh," Lisya tried to calm him.

"All we had in our hands were icons and banners... not even a stone in our pockets... We were singing... religious songs... the Tsar's hymn... 'God Save Thy People'..."

His voice broke and he was silent for awhile.

177

"When we got to the Palace, the Cossacks were there, waiting, all lined up... They charged... galloping, slashing at people on both sides of their horses... Men, women, children dropped like logs of wood... moaning, cursing, shouting... But we kept going, Lisya!" He grabbed her hand. "We kept marching!"

Lisya held his hand between both of hers, hoping Alexander Pavlovich would be home soon.

"And then they opened fire. The man next to me was carrying the Tsar's picture. 'How dare you fire on the portrait of the Tsar!?!' That's what he roared just before they shot him dead in his tracks... And after... blood all over the snow... and all over the Tsar's picture..."

Lisya held his hand until she heard Alexander Pavlovich unlock the front door.

Seeing the light in his study, he rushed in, the question in his eyes answered by the scene on the couch. Without a word, he readied his medical instruments, gave Vladimir some anesthetic, and removed the bullet from his arm. Lisya bandaged the wound and cleaned up the blood. After Vladimir fell safely asleep, they went to the kitchen for a cup of tea.

Sitting across from her at the little table, Alexander Pavlovich looked at his wife quizzically. "You were very good – in there."

"You're surprised?" she returned his gaze levelly.

He dropped his eyes and was silent. "It's just that... you reminded me of... you were so like your mother."

Lisya sipped her tea slowly. "What did you expect?"

He raised his eyes and smiled.

Ж   Ж   Ж

Alexander Pavlovich was back at the hospital when they started bringing in the other victims, and worked even later than usual treating the wounded and identifying the dead. Eventually, he was able to piece together what had happened.

What had started out a strike at the Putilov arms factory soon spread. Led by a priest named Georgi Gapon, a vast crowd converged on the Winter Palace. The Tsar was not there, but at his usual residence in Tsarkoe Selo. When the procession reached Palace Square, it was ordered to disperse. The demonstrators refused, and the troops – after one blank volley – fired straight into the crowd.

The Russian people were outraged. Riots and demonstrations flared up, universities closed in protest, strikes spread throughout the country, acts of terrorism multiplied. When the war finally ended, with a humiliating treaty ceding to the Japanese part of the Trans-Siberian Railroad, the railroad workers joined the other strikers in protest. A wave of noisy demonstrations soon swept Petersburg. Windows were smashed and police patrolled the streets.

The Conservatory, too, caught the fever. After the bloody Sunday in January, professors spent more time on politics than music. Classes were held sporadically, performances became raucous political events, students polarized into factions. Lisya tried, unsuccessfully, to stay out of it, but conflicting loyalties buffetted her about. Even Madame sometimes cancelled lessons.

Finally, the music students, too, went on strike, presenting a long list of noisy demands. When their director, Rimsky-Korsakov, was fired, most of the students threatened to quit in protest. Eventually police on horseback surrounded the chaotic Conservatory. Meanwhile, some of the students staged a private performance of Rimsky-Korsakov's censored opera, *Kostchei the Immortal*. The police intervened and stopped the concert. But not without a struggle.

Agitation also erupted among the Maryinsky dancers. A stormy meeting in the rehearsal hall led to an equally stormy confrontation with the company's director. After six long hours, the director left the hall to whistles and shouts. The angry dancers called a strike for the next day's matinee of *The Queen of Spades*.

That afternoon, Tatiana resolutely stayed home. It was the first time she and Lisya ever really argued.

"But why?!" demanded Lisya.

"Because no one else is going," replied Tatiana calmly.

"What kind of reason is that?!"

"What would you have me do? Go and dance by myself? If the whole orchestra stayed home, would you sit all alone in the orchestra pit?!"

"The orchestra would never do that," said Lisya, somewhat taken aback. "Musicians have more sense than dancers."

"Judging by what's been going on at the Conservatory, I doubt that!" Tatiana was almost angry.

"But we're artists!" protested Lisya. "What we do has nothing to do with all this political squabbling."

"If that's true, then we're not very good artists!"

"But all this rebellion is dangerous!"

"It's what people are rebelling against – and why – that's dangerous!"

"But what will happen to us if it all doesn't stop?"

"I don't know." Tatiana's anger suddenly evaporated. "But I'm afraid, too."

At the opera, all the ballet scenes had to be cut, forcing the singers to improvise – none too gracefully – during the ballroom act. In retaliation, the director barred the striking dancers from the theatre. Some gave in, Tatiana among them. The troupe polarized and feelings were strained.

The violence penetrated even the Maryinsky, abruptly terminating a performance of *Lohengrin*. At the end of the first act, someone shouted "Down with the Autocrats!" The audience jumped up, officers pulled out swords, chairs were thrown from loges. Lisya ran out of the orchestra pit, shielding her violin from flying objects, wondering what, indeed, her world was coming to.

Finally, after much hesitation and reflection, Tsar Nicholas was prevailed upon to grant a constitution. "We call on all faithful sons of Russia," the manifesto ended, "to remember their duty to their Fatherland, to assist in putting an end to these unprecedented disturbances, and to make with Us every effort to restore peace and quiet to Our native land."

The next day, Alexander Pavlovich stood with cheering thousands in front of the University. Vladimir was there, too, farther back in the crowd. From one of the balconies, a fiery orator warned them all not to trust an incomplete victory. He tore the Tsar's manifesto to pieces and scattered them to the winds. The crowd ignored him. Vladimir, however, thought he recognized the man on the balcony as the one they called Trotsky.

Ж   Ж   Ж

Lisya waited until Vladimir was up and around before she cornered him. Unable to resist his older sister's stern questioning, he soon confessed.

Vladimir had arrived in Petersburg several months before he showed up, bleeding, on her doorstep. He had made no effort to contact her, because no one was supposed to know he was there.

Some time before, after much prayer and hesitation, Vladimir had quit the seminary and committed his fervent and passionate nature to the "People's Will" – the terrorist branch of the Socialist Revolutionaries. He was subsequently sent to infiltrate Father Gapon's movement in the capitol.

"But why, Volodya?" Lisya demanded angrily. "What good can come of shooting people?"

"In a highly centralized state like Russia," he replied defensively, "assassination of the right people can send a strong message."

"Oh yes! Yes, indeed! And just see how they have answered you," she snorted, waving at his bandaged arm.

Vladimir towered over her, as he did most people. Broad shoulders and strong arms seemed to strain at whatever clothing he wore. A bushy beard and dark reddish hair that never stayed combed added to his powerful presence, as did a deep booming voice. Eyes so dark the blue was scarcely noticeable burned with unanswered questions.

Enormous as he was, he was still her little brother; she felt obliged to scold him. Vladimir hung his head and did not argue, wondering whether he believed it anymore himself. For in the process of trying to push Father Gapon's movement in the direction of the "People's Will," he had instead been taken over himself. Unable to resist the young priest's fervor and obvious willingness to lay down his life, Vladimir had marched beside Father Gapon, that bloody Sunday, a true believer.

Despite his terrorist affiliation, the blood and fallen banners had shocked him. But as his arm healed, so also emerged a clearer path amidst his tangled beliefs. The priest's basic strategy – organizing the workers to demand reform – that, decided Vladimir, made sense. But there were better ways to go about it than turning the other cheek to the swords of the Cossacks.

As soon as he was able, Vladimir found a job at the Putilov Iron Works. Despite his youth and strength, the work was hard and the hours long. He nonetheless moved out of Alexander Pavlovich's study into appropriately wretched quarters in the working-class district. Soon he became a leader of the Metal Workers Union.

One of Vladimir's assignments was organizing self-education clubs for the workers. Societies of concerned professionals also gave them free lectures. Alexander Pavlovich was among the founders of these "People's Universities," and tended to look down his nose at Vladimir's proletarian clubs. Vladimir, in turn, resented his brother-in-law's patronizing attitude. After all, what could these hopelessly bourgeois liberals possibly know about the class struggle?

To Lisya's consternation, Vladimir and Alexander Pavlovich argued continually. Attempting to change the subject was as futile as trying to stop the running of the ice.

"The workers must liberate themselves!" exclaimed Vladimir passionately, his voice filling the dining room. "Then Russia will be free!"

"The masses are too ignorant to know what they need!" exclaimed Alexander Pavlovich, raising his voice with nearly equal ardor and volume. "We must educate them!"

"Their hungry bellies tell them what they need!" Vladimir slammed his fist on the table, rattling the dishes. "They don't need the fat bourgeoisie telling them that!"

"Hunger is not a sufficient teacher for effective social change!" Alexander Pavlovich's eyes blazed behind his glasses. "The intelligentsia must guide the downtrodden toward constructive reform!"

"But surely the need is such that the masses could use all the help they can get?" interjected Lisya nervously, worried by the constant wrangling. "Wouldn't both your efforts be more effective if you worked together toward what is obviously a common goal?"

Both men paused, mid-rhetoric and mid-gesture, and stared at her as if she were an imbecile.

"Go and play the piano, Lisya," Alexander Pavlovich said, in a condescending tone that was beginning to irritate her.

One of the concessions granted by the Manifesto was the convening of a national representative assembly.

"The new Duma will be the dawn of constitutional monarchy in Russia!" proclaimed Alexander Pavlovich jubilantly.

"It's an opportunity for the liberation of the masses!" agreed Vladimir with almost as much jubilation.

"I think I can make a worthy contribution to this marvelous political experiment!" Alexander Pavlovich glowed with pride at having been elected a member of the Duma.

Vladimir, too, was delighted by the possibilities. "The Union Deputies can forward the agenda of the workers!"

Lisya smiled, relieved that for once Alexander Pavlovich and Vladimir did not argue when he came to dinner.

Unfortunately, the Tsar was not so enthusiastic. Nonetheless, he dutifully agreed to receive members of the Duma. The reception was held in the Imperial Palace at Tsarkoe Selo. Like many of the other deputies, Alexander Pavlovich was in formal attire; it had taken him all morning to get dressed in the borrowed suit. Even so, the liveried palace servants made him feel drab and provincial.

The deputies entered a large room, lined up in a semi-circle, and waited. At exactly two o'clock – just as the invitation had stated – an elegant uniform appeared in the hall and announced in pontifical tones, "His Majesty, the Emperor."

The room grew hushed. In walked a middle-aged man wearing a raspberry-colored silk shirt, the uniform of the Sharpshooters Regiment. He was followed by a tall woman in a large hat, all dressed in white. She was leading a charming little boy in a short white shirt and a high sheepskin hat. Alexander Pavlovich watched nervously out of the corner of his eye as the Imperial trio worked their way down the line, pausing to speak to each deputy. Finally they stopped before him.

The Emperor greeted him in a quiet but assured voice. And for a brief moment, Alexander Pavlovich looked into the eyes of his sovereign, Nicholas II, Supreme Autocrat, Tsar of all the Russia's. Pleasant and good-natured, the emperor's gaze was punctuated by a slight jerking of his shoulders. Alexander Pavlovich tried not to notice the mildly annoying gesture, as he tried also not to notice how cold the Empress's fingers were when she ceremoniously – and very nervously – extended her hand. Looking down, he saw the little Crown Prince staring at the medical insignia on his hat. Without thinking, he bent down and showed it to him.

"What is it?" asked the Tsarevich, completely at ease in the roomful of adults.

"It's my doctor's badge," replied Alexander Pavlovich, noticing that the boy was pale and looked unwell.

"If you're a doctor, why are you here?"

"Because I want Mother Russia and all her children to be strong and healthy."

"That's father's job."

"Yes, I know. But Russia is so big. Maybe he needs help."

The Tsarevich frowned. "When I am Tsar," he asked, pondering, "will you help me, too?"

"Of course, Your Highness," Alexander Pavlovich smiled, inclining his head. "I shall be pleased to be at your service."

The Tsarevich's smile was dazzling, reminding everyone what a beautiful child he was.

As he straightened up, Alexander Pavlovich again looked at the Empress. Her strained expression gone, she smiled at him and beamed at her son.

Moving on down the line, her stiffness returned. And then one of the priests, muttering tearfully, went down on his knees before the approaching Tsar. Embarrassed, Nicholas helped the weeping priest to his feet, received his blessing and kissed his hand.

When he reached the end of the line, the Tsar made a short speech. Alexander Pavlovich noticed that he had just the trace of a foreign accent. The deputies shouted, "Long live the Emperor!" Excusing himself with a very polite nod, he left the hall with his family. Only the Tsarevich seemed reluctant to leave.

Ж   Ж   Ж

Not all gatherings of the Duma were as orderly as the reception at Tsarkoe Selo. At most sessions, the chairman was forever ringing his bell and begging deputies to wait their turn. After a few weeks, someone had the good sense to nail down the lids of desks at which deputies were sitting. Too many had developed the habit of banging them in disapproval. Which – considering the many divergent factions represented – was virtually all the time.

Still, as Alexander Pavlovich frequently pointed out, it would take time to get used to representative government. "Even the British didn't learn it overnight," he said sagely at dinner. "We must be patient."

He was obviously enjoying the Duma. It was all he talked about. And though Lisya still labored mightily to avoid all the political controversy, she began to realize that her husband's political involvement was affecting their marriage in some unexpected ways.

The most noticeable was that safe, comfortable Alexander Pavlovich was – sometimes – yes – exciting. When he talked about the Duma and his hopes for Russia, his face blazed with passionate idealism, his arched eyebrows crackled like thunderbolts, his plain persona was suddenly – and remarkably – attractive. The cozy domestic dinners *a deux* began adjourning more quickly to the bedroom and ending in all kinds of unpredictable and unprecedented ways. Lisya no longer merely accepted her husband's body with quiet affection, but began to initiate activities that made her blush later. Sometimes she didn't even call him Alexander Pavlovich.

About all of this, he was enormously pleased. Lisya herself was ambivalent. And frightened. What would all this emotional turmoil do to her secure little world? Was she losing her reliable, dependable husband? If she understood what was changing him, could she prevent it from changing her life?

Lisya decided to see for herself.

On the appointed day, she arrived early at the Tauride Palace, a sprawling peaceful-looking building with columns in front and a dome perched like a hat on top. Inside, swirling crowds of deputies milled noisily around the large rotunda. Lisya slowly made her way through the excited throng to the door of the assembly chamber. She was shown to the gallery which overlooked the amphitheater on three sides, and found a seat in the center. Directly in front of her, on the fourth side, was the rostrum. Carved of heavy oak, above it hung a full-length portrait of the Tsar painted by Repin.

The deputies began to file in. Alexander Pavlovich took his seat with great dignity, and then – somewhat surreptitiously – glanced up at the gallery to make sure she was there.

The session opened with a prayer – which was as quiet as the room ever got. For the rest of the day, the noise never went below a dull roar. During the opening preliminaries, Lisya tried to figure out who was who. Those on the right were outspoken and excitable and fond of shouting "Long live His Majesty the Emperor! Hurrah!" Which usually evoked a strenuous response from those on the left, who yelled back something about revolution. Those in the middle expressed themselves with more restraint; Alexander Pavlovich sat with them. In between, there seemed to be numerous other factions, but Lisya was unable to determine how they differed from the three main groups. All over the hall, deputies were constantly jumping up and sitting down again, like big *vanka-vstanka* dolls.

The debate itself got off to a rousing start with an eloquent speech exhorting the Duma to abolish capital punishment.

"Gentlemen, members of the State Duma," the speaker began. "The death penalty does not deter anyone. On the contrary!"

Lisya leaned forward, straining to hear him over the noisy crowd.

"The Russian press right now is filled with articles that treat the death penalty as if it were holy."

Alexander Pavlovich had read her some of those articles; she had not liked them.

"But gentlemen," the speaker went on, "you don't need to be theologians to deal with this question. You only need to know this: 'Love your neighbor as yourself.'"

Lisya applauded vigorously as he sat down. A short man with a pince-nez then mounted the rostrum and attacked the speech and the man who had given it. Lisya gathered that his principal objection to the previous speaker was that he was a union leader. After Pince-Nez's long speech, a motion was made to suspend debate on the issue.

From his seat, the union leader shouted, "I wish to personally object to the motion."

"Excuse me," the Chairman said, and then, after a whispered consultation

185

with two men sitting behind him, "Before we vote, Duma member Union-Leader may have the floor."

"Duma member Pince-Nez," said Union-Leader, obviously incensed, "said that the proposal to abolish capital punishment is insincere. He characterized –

He was interrupted by clamour from the right. The Chairman rang the bell for silence.

"In order for Mr. Pince-Nez to talk about sincerity or insincerity," continued Union-Leader, undaunted, "he must have proof, otherwise it is nothing but a deliberate lie. But Deputy Pince-Nez is always excused –"

Noise from the right. "And you aren't?!"

"– because he has so little understanding –"

Laughter from the right. "Ass!" yelled a tall man with a big moustache.

"– of what is sincere and what is not, that he has trouble discriminating between the two."

"Idiot!" yelled Big-Moustache from his seat.

"I would ask you, Mr. Chairman," said Union-Leader, addressing the rostrum, "to protect me from such outbursts."

"Allow me to ask you not to interrupt," obliged the Chairman, "but if you must, then do it so the Chairman can hear you."

"I told him that he is an idiot!" shouted Big-Moustache, amidst laughter from the right.

"Throw him out!" yelled the left.

"Duma member Big-Moustache," said the Chairman, irritated, "not only makes remarks that are inappropriate in a properly conducted session, but also repeats them. I move that he be expelled until the end of the session."

"Allow me to explain," demanded Big-Moustache, indignantly.

"Deputy Big-Moustache has the right to express himself on this issue," conceded the Chairman.

"Pince-Nez will speak for me," shouted Big Moustache.

"He can do that," said voices from the right, in response to rumbling from the left.

"Duma member Pince-Nez has the floor," said the Chairman, throwing up his hands.

"I cannot totally justify my colleague's remark," began Pince-Nez, standing near his seat, "but I must say that it was brought on by the words of Duma member Union-Leader. It is not my habit to respond to such comments, but Big-Moustache, who has a quicker temper, said what I should have said myself."

Pince-nez sat down to loud applause from the right.

"The debate," said the Chairman with irritation, "is now over –"

"But I have not finished," protested Union-Leader.

"And what about Big-Moustache?" exclaimed several indignant voices from the left.

"Gentlemen, members of the State Duma, please take your seats," exhorted the Chairman over the din, "Duma member Union-Leader, I ask that you not use this forum for wrangling."

Glancing down at the deputies seated in the center, Lisya saw Alexander Pavlovich nodding and applauding.

"Pardon me, gentlemen, but lack of self-control is unacceptable." The Chairman, by now, was thoroughly exasperated. "I implore you to have some regard for the dignity of this assembly."

As loud applause broke out on all sides, Alexander Pavlovich's head nodded more vigorously.

"On the one hand, the speaker is told, 'You are a striker.' The response is, 'You are brainless, you are an idiot.'"

"I did not say that," Union-Leader protested

"Gentlemen, it is up to you. The Chairman cannot do everything. If you have any pity, spare me!"

And so, on into the night, the cradle of Russian democracy marched, squabbling and bickering like a roomful of undisciplined children. Finally, Lisya could stand it no longer. With a pitying glance at the Chairman, she fled the noisy hall. By the time she got home, she had a pounding headache.

Ж   Ж   Ж

Alexander Pavlovich sat quietly in the audience, waiting for the Conservatory Orchestra to finish warming up, its cacophony not unlike that of the Duma. He smiled sadly, once again wondering that something so disorderly could have so absorbed him.

The year following the Manifesto had been an exciting one. Vladimir's unions had won benefits for the workers; his own Duma had discussed – albeit noisily – the nation's problems. Both he and his brother-in-law had put in long hours at their respective political endeavors; both had felt their efforts leading to constructive change.

Toward the end of the year, however, the light in their eyes began to dim. On the labor front, union gains had frightened employers into forming associations of their own and launching a counter-offensive, circulating blacklists and organizing lock-outs. The unions began to lose support.

And then, on a particularly grey day in late winter, the ceiling of the Duma's assembly hall collapsed. Heavy pieces of stucco molding lay everywhere, the chandeliers were mangled. The deputies' seats were filled with plaster. Had the session not opened late, several representatives would undoubtedly have been killed.

The next day, the Duma was called to order in the rotunda. The discussion was even more disorderly than usual. Standing on chairs, deputies expressed their indignation. Some saw the cave-in as criminal negligence; others saw it as an attempt on the lives of the people's representatives. Alexander Pavlovich had blamed it on old loose nails. Nonetheless, it was a gloomy omen.

Finally, just a week ago, in violation of the constitution granted by the Tsar himself, Prime Minister Stolypin had dissolved the Duma. There were to be new elections for a new Duma – but according to a new electoral franchise, also in violation of the constitution. Vast geographical areas were disenfranchised completely, while an indirect system of voting rigged elections to ensure deputies more amenable to the government. His days in the Duma over, Alexander Pavlovich was still wrapped in the sadness which had swept over him.

The main work on the program tonight was Tchaikovsky's Sixth Symphony. Supposedly the great composer's requiem, its performance so soon after the demise of the Duma was no coincidence. As the conductor strode on stage, Alexander Pavlovich applauded absently. From long habit, his eyes fastened on his wife, sitting among the First Violins.

On stage, Lisya sensed the somber mood of the audience, a fitting accompaniment to the music – especially the First Movement of the Symphony. Its theme, the Orthodox burial hymn, conjured up striking images – a funeral bier standing in church with coffin lid open, everyone kneeling around and weeping; the priest intoning prayers, the choir chanting in response.

The world – so incredibly beautiful. Life – so full of sweetness and joy. And yet, so much sorrow and struggle. Somehow the ancient hymn combined the pain and the beauty. And underscored belief that in overcoming suffering, the soul triumphed – even in death.

Had Tchaikovsky left it there, the symphony would indeed have been a requiem. But it went on for three more movements as if to say, "What now? After death, what then?" And in each of them, several possibilities were posed. Lisya found none of them comforting.

As she played the familiar music, thoughts of the Duma added a new dimension. Vladimir and Alexander Pavlovich were both mourning its dissolution. Even Lisya sensed that something important had died. But exactly what, she could not say. As she played the rest of the symphony, she looked for answers to a question she could not even ask.

The Second Movement danced by, oddly playful in a strange 5/4 time, like a cripple waltzing. And then the Third, a peculiar combination of martial triumph and scurrying mice. And, at last, the monumentally despairing Finale. Intense anguish, building and mounting, then falling and breaking, until it slowly died away…

Her bow poised soundlessly on the strings of her violin, Lisya listened to the cellos decrescendo into nothing. In the silence which followed, she was slowly flooded by nameless dread and inexplicable sorrow.

Chapter 9: The WOMEN

It had happened before the end of the Duma. Of that Lisya was absolutely certain. And now, months later, this tiny mysterious creature was in her arms. The baby yawned, its mouth taking over its entire face, and then subsided into exhausted grogginess.

Lisya herself felt strangely exhilarated. It had been a long hard labor – though fortunately without complication. Alexander Pavlovich said that – for a first baby – she had gotten off lightly. As if from a distance, she remembered the final intense pains which had swept her body, penetrating even the remotest corners, over and over and over – until she had thought she would burst apart. On the other side of all that, she allowed herself an affectionate snort of indignation. Men! What did they know!

Throughout the long hours, Tatiana had been with her. And, at first, so had Alexander Pavlovich. Everytime she cried out, he had looked at her with guilty anguish, murmuring anxiously, "Now, now, Lisya dear, it's really not so bad." But it *was* that bad – and worse. No mere man could ever have withstood it. Finally, she had ordered him out of the room. After that, she had screamed as loud as she needed to.

As the edges of consciousness had blurred, she held on desperately to Tatiana's reassuringly strong hand. Just as she thought she could stand no more, she looked up at her sister. Deep furrows seemed to etch themselves into the smooth skin, the dark brown hair turned grey, a faded flowered scarf somehow wrapped itself around her head. And for just an instant which stretched far back into time, she saw her mother and grandmother – and *their* grandmothers – all smiling down at her from her sister's face. Relief and happiness and security flooded through Lisya, as tears of joy rolled down the beautiful wrinkled face and washed over her like a benediction.

During the final stages, Alexander Pavlovich had come back to help. With something to do, his professional manner reasserted itself. Lisya was glad he was there, as together they brought their child into the world. When it was all over,

Tatiana – minus the wrinkles and grey hair – bathed the baby and gently laid her in Lisya's arms. As she beheld the wonder of her new daughter, she could still sense that other presence, hovering joyfully.

After making sure all was well, Tatiana and Alexander Pavlovich went off to get some sleep. It had been a long night for everyone.

Alone with her newborn child, Lisya stared, in awe of her tiny wholeness. Then a sudden wave of alarm, as she quickly undid the wrappings in which the baby was swaddled. Carefully, she surveyed the infant's body, checking the arms and legs, counting all the fingers and toes. When she was finally satisfied that everything was as it should be, she bundled the baby back up and tucked her in the crook of her arm. Leaning back against the pillows, she tried to relax.

When, at last, Lisya settled down into a light sleep, she dreamed of her grandmother teaching her to spin. Round and round the spinning wheel turned, humming quietly and soothingly, as her grandmother's fingers skillfully worked the wool into yarn. Then it was Lisya's turn. The yarn became hopelessly tangled and the wheel started to screech. She awoke to the baby crying, her tiny voice squalling urgently and her minute fists waving angrily. Lisya felt a stabbing sensation inside, and for a horrible moment felt utterly helpless. Then she held the baby to her breast; after a few minutes of frantic fumbling, she stopped crying. After awhile, the sucking noise stopped; the baby sighed contentedly, emitted a loud burp, and went back to sleep. Lisya felt something warm and wet dampen the bottom of the bundled blanket.

And so it went, round the clock – eat, sleep, wet; eat, sleep, wet; eat, sleep, wet…

Try as she might, Lisya could not connect this constantly hungry little creature with the being who had shared her body for nine months. She did not seem to feel what mothers were supposed to feel for their babies. All she could manage was pity for the pathetically helpless – and rather ugly – red bundle which now dominated her life.

And then, a few days after she had given birth, it happened. The baby stopped squinting and opened her eyes – wide. They were large and soft and brown. As Lisya stared in surprise, the incredibly beautiful eyes looked into hers, reached down deep into her heart, and grabbed hold with a tenacity which would never be dislodged. At that moment, she could almost feel the earth shake. A radiant golden light suffused the baby's little face, as Lisya suddenly beheld the most beautiful creation that had ever graced the planet. A symphony of unimaginable joy burst forth within. *And I made you,* she realized in awe. Everything else paled by comparison.

"Her name is Ekaterina," she told Alexander Pavlovich, when he returned home from his classes. "After my grandmother."

Ж   Ж   Ж

Lisya sighed, as her fingers stumbled over an etude she could usually rattle off flawlessly. Taking a deep breath, she tried again – and again – and got no further.

"Why can't you ever be in tune?!" she exclaimed irritably – but not too loudly – at the old upright piano where she now did all her practicing. Sighing again, she slumped over the keyboard, leaning her head on arms folded against the music rack, fighting back tears of frustration.

Little Katya had certainly changed her life! Every corner of it, inside and out. There never seemed to be enough time anymore. Regretfully she had taken a leave of absence from the Ballet School. She had even proposed quitting the Maryinsky orchestra; Alexander Pavlovich, however, would not hear of it. And so, not long after Katya's birth, she and her violin resumed their usual place in the pit. Fortunately, rehearsal schedules were usually different for dancers and musicians, so Tatiana was often able to mind Katya. On evenings when they both performed, Alexander Pavlovich stayed home with the baby. Lisya was grateful for his support; she knew that not many husbands were so helpful.

He had also insisted that she continue her lessons with Madame. About that, too, she was grateful, but it was so much harder to keep up! Because she was unable to get to the Conservatory except for lessons, all of her practicing had to be done at home. And oh, how she missed the well-tuned pianos in the practice rooms! Nor would there be a new piano of her own anywhere in the foreseeable future; the money saved up had already been eaten away by baby paraphernalia.

Turning her head, Lisya looked at the elegant pram parked next to the old piano. A small modest one would have done as well, but when she had seen all those baby buggies lined up in the store – like a caste system on wheels – she behaved most uncharacteristically. Instead of choosing sensibly and within her means, she picked one of the most expensive. The thought of her magnificent baby riding in anything but the best was intolerable, and that was that. Smiling, she remembered how amazed – and dismayed – Alexander Pavlovich had been when she brought it home. Seeing the look on her face, however, he had wisely said nothing.

Lisya did not regret the pram. Not many sunny days passed without a promenade to the Summer Gardens. With or without Tatiana, Lisya walked briskly along Sadovaya Ulitza, pushing the pram as proudly as Matilda Kschessinskaya making an entrance.

Lisya sat up straight and shook her head. No matter what she did, half of her was always with Katya. And how could she make music with only part of herself! Sighing yet again, she knew that tomorrow's lesson would be as unprepared as all the others since Katya's birth.

About all this, Madame had been surprisingly understanding. She, too, was a mother – a discovery which amazed Lisya, who had never pictured Madame anywhere but at the piano – and had not forgotten the strains imposed by caring for a young child.

"Don't worry, *ma chere*," she would say when Lisya got discouraged, "what you lose now, you will get back many times over. There is more to being a musician than just playing the notes. Your child will make you bigger inside. And someday that will make your music better, too."

A small sound from the next room, and Lisya's sagging spirits were instantly alert. Quickly she stood up and walked into the bedroom. And there was Katya, all smiling and sweet and begging to be held. As Lisya's arms wrapped themselves around her baby's warm, soft little body, she knew that Madame was right.

Ж   Ж   Ж

"… And then, when the evil germs crept silently inside, the big bear became very sick." Katya was sitting in Alexander Pavlovich's lap, looking up at him with wide eyes. "But the *murzilki* were on guard, and sailed after them into the bear's belly."

Katya giggled as he gently tickled her stomach.

"It took them a long time to catch up with the germs, because it was a very big bear. Finally they found them in an old palace, having a big party. The *murzilki* talked it over and voted to send the king of the germs a petition, asking him to help make the bear better."

Katya began to tickle her father's belly.

"But the king refused to leave his palace. A big fat old general came out instead to shoo the *murzilki* away."

Katya kept tickling; Alexander Pavlovich began to smile.

"And then Babushka Murzilka walked up to the fat general and smacked his bottom with her twig broom."

Katya laughed, inadvertently emitting a small but very distinct fart.

"And out came the germs," said Alexander Pavlovich, laughing too.

"Poop, plop," said Katya, squealing with laughter. Alexander Pavlovich laughed even harder.

"And so the bear was purged," he finally gasped, wiping his eyes.

Sitting in the dining room, Lisya laughed, too. She was polishing the samovar – not because it needed cleaning, but because it provided a good excuse to eavesdrop. The *murzilki* were tiny creatures no bigger than a pin, who could get in anywhere and see everything. Their ongoing saga always started out a vehicle for lessons in anatomy or politics – but somehow usually ended up an excuse to be silly. Sitting on her father's lap, Katya would find something to giggle at; the more she laughed the sillier he got, and the sillier he got the more she laughed. Usually, they both ended up laughing uproariously at nothing.

The samovar gleamed back at her, but she continued to polish the warmly glowing copper. Tatiana was cooking the Christmas feast. On such occasions, Lisya stayed out of the kitchen as much as possible. Tatiana was a temperamental culinary artist and – in the throes of inspiration – a very messy cook. Better to view the shambles of the carefully organized kitchen on a full stomach of Tatiana's delectably prepared cuisine.

Christmas was Lisya's favorite holiday – especially now that Katya was old enough to enjoy it, too. Yesterday afternoon, Alexander Pavlovich had taken her to the Maryinsky for the first time, for a special children's performance of *The Nutcracker*. Katya was enthralled; she barely moved a muscle during the entire performance – except to cry when the King of the Mice was slain. She was in awe of the elegant lady playing the violin who looked so much like Mama. And she stared in disbelief at the beautiful woman dancing on stage who so resembled Aunt Tanya. Afterwards, Alexander Pavlovich took her to the orchestra pit and backstage. Up close she could see that the violin lady was, indeed, her mother; besides, she recognized the black dress. But Tatiana – in her make-up and flower costume and strange shoes – was another matter. Not knowing how to react to this magical being who was her aunt – and yet somehow not – she curtsied politely and smiled shyly.

Lisya looked at the clock, and then got up to light the candles on the enormous Christmas tree Alexander Pavlovich had brought home last night. Sparkling with golden stars and silver tinsel, it reached all the way to the ceiling. When all the candles were lit, Vladimir burst into the room, dressed as Father Frost. All in red, he had powdered his hair and beard and sparkled with snow. "Ho-ho-ho!" he boomed, as he distributed gifts from the bag of presents on his shoulder.

Katya stared for a moment, perplexed, then ran to her uncle, who gently lifted her to his other shoulder. Her small fingers poked and prodded carefully at his hair and beard, looking for the familiar reddish color. Laughing, Vladimir carried her to the tree, showing her a golden squirrel just like those who jumped on silver branches in Father Frost's forest. Then he swung her down and they became shaggy bear cubs dancing around Father Frost's big silver Christmas tree. Soon Tatiana emerged from the kitchen and joined in; even Alexander Pavlovich got down on all fours.

Meanwhile, plunging into the disarray of her kitchen, Lisya rescued the platters bearing Tatiana's creations and placed them on the carefully set dining room table. A host of tempting aromas wafted up and mingled with the smell of the tree and the scent of the candles. The rest of the family soon appeared and sat down eagerly to the feast. Tatiana's masterpieces looked as good as they smelled – and tasted even better. Almost worth the mess in the kitchen, Lisya decided. Even Katya stuffed herself. Afterward, hands and face still sticky, she climbed into Tatiana's lap.

At last, they all leaned back in groggy silence, staring dazedly at the remains of Tatiana's triumph. Even Lisya was too full to restrain the resounding belch which rumbled up from her satiated stomach. Tatiana grinned and beamed with satisfaction.

Finally, Lisya roused herself, sat down at the piano and began to play Christmas songs. Vladimir sang along, his beautiful voice a deep flowing wellspring. Softly the others joined in, letting the music wash through them. Soon Katya was sound asleep on Tatiana's lap.

After Lisya had carried the sleeping child to bed, she sank down on the sofa and leaned comfortably against Alexander Pavlovich.

"Well," Tatiana cleared her throat purposefully, "I think there's still time to make it to the midnight mass."

Lisya felt Alexander Pavlovich stiffen. "I'll stay with Katya," he said quickly, before she could open her mouth.

Her one sure escape cut off, Lisya tried another. "I have to clean up the kitchen," she said feebly.

"That can wait until tomorrow," replied Tatiana firmly, knowing full well that it would anyway.

Vladimir shuffled his feet uncomfortably, and then shrugged. Tatiana so rarely made demands, it was impossible to say no when she did – especially on a full stomach of her succulent food.

Meekly, Lisya and Vladimir allowed Tatiana to herd them – belching and burping – down the street to the Cathedral of the Protector. As they entered the densely packed church, there was a solemn stillness. And then, as the candles were blown out, a long moment of dark mystery. Standing between her sister and brother, Lisya felt their warmth. Tatiana was praying fervently.

And then a radiant light, as the choir came in, singing like the heavenly host. Behind them marched priests, velvet *kamilavki* on their heads, and deacons and altar boys in brocade vestments. And finally, chasuble glittering, the Metropolitan himself. Without thinking, Lisya crossed herself and joined in the prayers. After a while, she noticed that Vladimir was praying, too. As Tatiana's hand grasped hers and squeezed tightly, Lisya's other hand found Vladimir's. And for awhile they stood, close and connected, locked in memories of shared childhood.

Ж   Ж   Ж

By the time Katya was walking and chattering, Lisya realized that far more than her way of life was changing.

It started slowly.

Her love for Petersburg had previously made her oblivious to its wretched climate. The fact that so many spent so much time coughing and sneezing had not concerned her. But now, when Katya caught cold, Lisya suffered a thousand agonies listening to her labored breathing and congested wheezing. At the slightest mention of illness anywhere, she pricked up her ears and feared the worst. At the medical soirees, she began paying attention to the endless discussions about sanitation and public health. Before, epidemics had not concerned her; they happened to other people, in other places. But now, any epidemic, anywhere, was a threat to her child.

Nor did her growing awareness of how hazardous the world was end with how it affected Katya. She began to wonder what the laundresses in the courtyard did with their children while they worked. She began to notice pale ragged urchins hanging around the city's alleys. She began to hear drunken shouting and children screaming from its basements.

One evening, not long after Katya had taken her first steps, Alexander Pavlovich invited some friends over. Most of them were the usual crowd of doctors and their wives. Since the Duma, however, his circle had widened; sometimes there was a new face. Tonight's novelty was Dr. Mariya Ivanova Pokrovskaya.

Once upon a time, Mariya Ivanovna had probably been a handsome woman, decided Lisya, trying not to stare too obtrusively. But never had she met anyone so carefully dressed *not* to call attention to herself. Dr. Pokrovskaya's apparel retained only those feminine encumbrances absolutely necessary, without which plain and nondescript would have crossed the line into shocking and scandalous. On any other woman, the costume would have been merely frumpy; on Mariya Ivanovna, it almost neutralized the fact that she was female.

Unlike the other women, Mariya Ivanovna joined in the medical talk. When she spoke, her face lit up in a way that reminded Lisya of Alexander Pavlovich. The other doctors listened to what she said – though with varying degrees of condescension. Most of their wives were polite – but suspicious.

Eventually Lisya found herself sitting next to her. The conversation they struck up lasted all evening. When she said goodnight, Mariya Ivanovna invited Lisya to visit her clinic.

When Lisya later informed Alexander Pavlovich that she had accepted the invitation, he was upset. So was she, when he informed her that the clinic was located over in the Vyborg District. Clearly he expected her to back out – which was perhaps why she didn't. But she gratefully accepted his insistent offer to take her there himself.

On the appointed day, as they approached the Liteiny Bridge, her stomach began to lurch. Alexander Pavlovich stopped and looked at her, regret mingled with a strange yearning in his questioning gaze. As she met his eyes, Lisya suddenly remembered how much they were like Katya's. Summoning her courage, she nodded. Clutching her husband's arm, she closed her eyes and listened to the mare trot staunchly across the Bridge.

The clinic was in the heart of the working-class district. Mariya Ivanovna met her cordially at the door and invited her into a room filled with gaunt exhausted women and pale hungry children. She was a vigorous women of about Alexander Pavlovich's age, and effortlessly enlisted Lisya as her assistant for the afternoon.

As the pathetic procession filed through the examining room, Lisya was appalled. Famine and plague she had witnessed in Derevnia, but this was something else. No medical expertise was needed to recognize that much of what ailed these women and their children was preventable. By the end of the day, she felt like bursting into tears – or losing her temper.

Instead, she simply looked at Mariya Ivanovna, her question all over her face.

"They work in factories," the doctor replied, as if that said it all.

Lisya was too embarrassed to admit that, for her, it was not enough of an answer. When Alexander Pavlovich picked her up later, she rode home wrapped in silence, deeply disturbed. Unable to forget what she had seen, the bleak faces at the clinic haunted her.

A few weeks later, Vladimir came to dinner. Alexander Pavlovich had an important meeting at the Medical School, and excused himself soon after they had finished eating. After Lisya put Katya to bed, she sat down at the table again with Vladimir.

Over their tea, they conversed idly about various topics which, over the years, they had discovered were safe. After a while, there was a pause. And then Lisya heard herself timidly asking Vladimir what it was like to work in a factory. He stared at her for several minutes, and then a strange smile spread over his face.

"If you really want to know," he said finally, "come see for yourself."

And so, once again, Lisya crossed the Liteiny Bridge. This time, Alexander Pavlovich had been even more upset, but he did not try to talk her out of it. And as she clutched Vladimir's arm, Lisya again closed her eyes, listening to the tramcar screeching raucously across the Bridge.

In Derevnia, everyone had worked hard, but this was worse than she could ever have imagined. That human beings could work so long and so hard in such stinking, unsanitary, unsafe places shocked her. That the work done was dehumanizing dismayed her; that the workers themselves were constantly humiliated angered her.

Worse yet was where they lived – far worse, even, than the most miserable *izba* in Derevnia. At first she could not comprehend why anyone would choose to exist in such circumstances. But when Vladimir told her how little most workers were paid, she was too shocked to be embarrassed by her stupidity. *I couldn't even feed my family on that*, she realized. And then she remembered the gaunt pale faces at Mariya Ivanovna's clinic.

Vladimir's tour deepened her distress. There was something about this whole business that was still foggy around the edges. A very important piece of the tragic puzzle was eluding her. She decided to invite Mariya Ivanovna to tea.

"Well?" the doctor asked abruptly, as soon as Lisya had poured the tea. Mariya Ivanovna didn't believe in wasting time on unnecessary etiquette. Lisya told her what she had seen with Vladimir.

"And?"

"It seemed like..." Lisya hesitated, trying to finger the buzzing noise in her head, "Is it true... that there are more women in some of those factories than men?"

Mariya Ivanovna nodded her head. "Especially the ones that make textiles."

"All of them – the workers, I mean – seemed badly treated," Lisya continued, "but the women looked worse than the men – hungrier, more tired."

Mariya Ivanovna nodded again, sadly. "They are. They work just as hard as the men all day – and then go home to tend their families."

"In the textile factories, I saw pregnant women operating looms."

"All too common, I'm afraid," Mariya Ivanovna sighed. "Most of them work up to the last possible moment, and come back almost immediately after giving birth. They're afraid of being fired if they don't."

"And what happens to their babies?"

"If they're lucky, they stay home with a grandmother or an older child. Or are farmed out to old women in the country who earn their living caring for as many children as possible." Mariya Ivanovna's eyes clouded over. "They don't get much attention, though, and sometimes not enough to eat. And they're the lucky ones."

"When I was at your clinic... Many of the women – and even the children – had horrible bruises and broken bones..." Lisya struggled to unlock what she had always known. "They didn't get all of those... at the factory... ?"

"No," said Mariya Ivanovna quietly, the lines around her eyes deepening.

Lisya looked down, as one of the tangles in her head came undone. Mariya Ivanovna squeezed her hand.

Alexander Pavlovich was working late that night, for which Lisya was profoundly grateful. After Katya was asleep, she poured herself some tea, sat down in the darkened living room, and lit a small candle. Staring at it, she reminded herself of how much her present way of life depended on Alexander Pavlovich's good will. He could, if he wished, forbid her to play at the Maryinsky or to study at the Conservatory. He could also wear her out with constant childbearing – as even many of his doctor friends did to their wives. And even though the law now forbade it, he could beat her and probably get away with it. Old customs die hard, she reflected bitterly. *And if I didn't like it, what could I do? I do not even have the right to live alone – even if I could afford it!*

Ridiculous! She told herself firmly. Alexander Pavlovich is a decent man. He would never do any of those things.

But *what if...* said a small voice from a dusty corner of her mind. And the last tangle came undone.

What would happen to Katya when *she* married? And what would happen if she did *not* marry?

Yes, the world in which she lived was dangerous for all children - but especially so for *girl* children. Boys grew up to be men, who could hope to have some control over their lives. But girls grew up to be women, who were totally at the mercy of men.

The injustice of it all swept over her with hot fury. What she had always accepted unquestioningly for herself, she would not accept for her daughter. She deserved better. And somehow, Lisya vowed, she would make it better.

Ж Ж Ж

Once again, Lisya crossed the Liteiny Bridge – this time alone, and with her eyes wide open.

"I want things to be better for my daughter," she said to Mariya Ivanovna, sitting in her tiny office at the clinic. "What can I do?"

"A lot," Mariya Ivanovna smiled, obviously pleased. "But first you must understand what is going on." And she gave Lisya several issues of a journal she edited called *The Women's Herald*.

That very evening, after Katya was tucked in and asleep, Lisya began.

Zhenskii Vestnik was like nothing she had ever read. In it were facts and figures documenting the appalling lives of factory women, lamenting the degradation of women and how damaging it was to family life. What emerged over and over was that ending this oppression depended on women gaining the right to vote.

After Lisya read through the whole stack of *Zhenskii Vestnik*, she joined the League for Women's Equality and threw herself into the campaign for women's suffrage. She also attended a Congress of Women's Organizations. The importance of their common goal gave the meetings an urgency which was exhilarating; she began to understand why Alexander Pavlovich had been so caught up in the Duma. She also began to understand why there had been so much arguing.

As the Congress progressed, she began to see that though there was general agreement on the basic objective of women's rights, there was nothing even approaching consensus on how to get them – or on how many were needed. And she was embarrassed by the contrast in dress between relatively affluent delegates like herself and the poverty-stricken working women who eventually walked out of the Congress.

Later, she asked Vladimir about them. He looked at her, blankly. And when she began to question him about the role of women in his trade unions, it was clear that he had never given the matter much thought.

The following week, he brought her some pamphlets. They were about the "woman question," written by women who were Marxists – including someone name Krupskaya, who was married to the leader of one of the Marxist factions. Lisya did not ask which one. She did, however, read the pamphlets. Cutting through the rhetoric, she gathered that they disapproved of "bourgeois feminists" like herself. The main fight, they believed, was not men vs. women but class vs. class. By the time she had finished reading, she was convinced that the Marxists had put off the "woman question" until the day after the Revolution.

When Lisya challenged Vladimir about this, he quoted Marx at her. "Capitalism has transformed all human relations into marketable commodities. Women have thus become instruments of production, reproduction and gratification. Marriage is legalized prostitution! Capitalist society is a giant whorehouse!"

Lisya was shocked. For once, she had no ready answer.

"Don't you see, Lisya?" he pressed on, pursuing the rare moment. "The oppression of women is the result of the class struggle. Abolish private property, and women will be liberated, too."

"But Volodya, what's wrong with Feminism?" asked Lisya, recovering her composure somewhat.

"Feminism is hopelessly bourgeois. It addresses only the special needs of educated and wealthy women. It serves their need to participate in the system's exploitation and partake of the privileges of the ruling class." A dogmatic gleam flashed in his eyes."Their alleged struggle for sexual liberation is totally frivolous."

"But I'm a Feminist!" exploded Lisya. "And I'm not frivolous!"

"No," retorted Vladimir, face red and voice trembling, "you aren't – but you *are* bourgeois! Why else would anyone be silly enough to want to vote in an autocracy!?!"

They did not speak for days. Then, as usual, they tacitly forgave each other. But Lisya could not let go of her conviction that to the Marxists, the "woman question" was an unwanted side issue of distinctly marginal importance. She resented that. She was not marginal. And neither, certainly, was Katya.

The Marxists, of course, were not the only ones who deprecated the women's movement. The Conservatives referred to Feminist meetings as assemblages of prostitutes. The Moderates opposed women suffrage as unprecedented or unnatural or – worst of all – said there was no need for it. Even Alexander Pavlovich did not whole-heartedly support her cause. "Of course I favor it," he said, when pressed for his stance, "but the time is not ripe. Women don't even have the vote in Europe yet."

But more discouraging was how the women themselves reacted. Members of the conservative Union of Russian Women were downright hostile. So were many career women, who saw no need for change. They had made it on their own; why couldn't everyone? Tatiana said that some of the prima ballerinas took this attitude. And even Madame, to Lisya's dismay, sometimes echoed such sentiments. Worse yet were the apathetic ones, and the naive society ladies who periodically did good deeds for the poor. The women who worked in factories, of course, could not afford to be naive. But they were not much more politically aware than the others. They listened politely when she talked to them about the suffrage movement, but her words evoked no enthusiasm.

"What do you expect?" asked Mariya Ivanovna. "Between their jobs and taking care of their families and being pregnant or miscarrying or aborting – they're too exhausted to get into anything as abstract as the right to vote! Now if you were advocating Temperance – that's something they can relate to. Almost all their husbands drink too much – and too nastily – on too little money. Meanwhile, none of these women ever get enough to eat. And their children are always hungry."

Lisya blushed at her own naivete. Perhaps Vladimir was right about her being "bourgeois."

"But why," she persisted, "are the women not more active in the trade unions? Don't the men want them?"

"Mmmm, yes and no," replied Mariya Ivanovna. "The men welcome their support in the demonstrations, but when it comes to the unions themselves – that's pretty much a men's club. Besides, the women just don't have time."

Then, too, Lisya discovered after further investigation, most of the women felt intimidated at the union meetings.

"Well, I do want to express myself," admitted a faded but intelligent-looking woman Lisya met at the clinic. "But then I think it over. So many people – they will all be looking at me. And what if someone laughs at what I say?" She shook her head sadly. "I grow cold with these thoughts. My heart is inflamed, but I sit silently."

Weeks later, the woman's words still rang in Lisya's mind. How often she, too, had sat silently – heart inflamed – in the presence of men! Must it be so for Katya?

Ж   Ж   Ж

The problem, Lisya finally decided, was that people had a lot of strange ideas about what women were – and weren't – supposed to be. Some thought them inferior to men, others considered them better. But no one seemed to believe that women were equal, capable of exercising the same rights and responsibilities. Lisya wasn't even sure that she did.

But just what was woman? In the operas and ballets she accompanied from the orchestra pit, she began to see much that alarmed her.

The European operas were loaded with ethereal heroines on pedestals and innocent creatures nobly sacrificing themselves – or wicked enchantresses seducing men. True, Wagnerian women had more meat on their bones and were more athletic, but they, too, usually ended up controlled – or reviled – by the heroes. And while much of the best music was *about* women, it was usually sung by men. Tchaikovsky's operas were more encouraging. Many of his heroines were rather noble, but they were never on a pedestal.

"That's because chivalry has never existed in Russia," said Olga the cellist, with whom Lisya often discussed these matters. "Russian women never get rescued by knights on horseback. We're too busy being the horses."

"A pity," sighed Lisya.

"Not entirely," Olga disagreed. "All that chivalrous adoration is just another form of control. And besides, only the pretty ones get rescued."

Ballet, too, was full of mixed messages. The typical female role was usually innocent maiden and vulnerable victim – or dangerous enchantress and tempting fraud. And the good women always seemed to give their lives – or their sanity – for their men.

"That's because the librettists and choreographers are men," explained Tatiana, with whom Lisya also discussed these things.

"But yet, it's the ballerina who is the center of the ballet," puzzled Lisya. "The danseur's role is primarily a supporting one."

"Yes, that's true," agreed Tatiana. "Except for lifting ballerinas, we do everything the men do – and more – and we do it on our toes."

"But why do you work so hard to look…" Lisya searched for the right word, "… fragile?"

"I prefer," said Tatiana with a rueful smile, "to think of it as being graceful."

"But all that frail vulnerability the balletomanes find so appealing – doesn't that just perpetuate a dangerous stereotype?"

"Well, I suppose that's one way to look at it. But surely there's nothing fragile about Kschessinskaya." Tatiana laughed. "She'll probably dance until she's a hundred. I can just see her, quavering out orders: 'Help me get up *en pointe*; after that I know what to do!'"

They both laughed, picturing the redoubtable Matilda, still awesome as a centenarian, still dripping with diamonds.

"But what about Pavlova?" Lisya persisted

"Ah yes, Pavlova. Now Anna is another matter. She *is* rather frail – physically. Next to Kschessinskaya, she looks like a delicate giraffe. And she lacks Matilda's superb technique – which is why she concentrates on all those lyrical poses and ethereal arabesques. But there is tremendous inner strength in her dancing."

"So Kschessinskaya dances with the force of her personality, and Pavlova dances with her soul?"

"Yes, exactly," agreed Tatiana. "And there's nothing weak about either one of them, no matter what the balletomanes like to think."

A few weeks later, they did *Swan Lake* at the Maryinsky. As far as Lisya was concerned, it had never been a very satisfying story. But this time, playing Tchaikovsky's familiar overture from her accustomed chair in the pit, she became uneasily aware that there was more to it than that.

Her uneasiness grew in Scene II. The music began – intense, poignant, dramatic – as the curtain opened on a darkly mysterious lake suffused by moonlight. Into its lunar magic danced the enchanted swans, moving together with grace and precision. Among them, Lisya spotted Tatiana. Even on point, her smile never faltered. *How can they look so beautiful when their feet are killing them?* wondered Lisya for at least the thousandth time. From Tatiana she knew that gliding around in toe shoes was painful.

Into the midst of the swans burst the hero. Each spectacular leap was more flamboyant than the last, full of grandiose fanfare which seemed to say, "Look how strong I am." And then he was gone. The women, meanwhile, continued to dance on – but with more restraint. Lisya knew that what they were doing took just as much strength – Tatiana's leg muscles were like steel – but somehow they didn't make such a fuss about it. *The men appear in bursts of energy, like beautiful comets blazing across the sky. The women just keep on spinning and turning – like the Earth.*

What had never seemed fair to Lisya was that the Swan Queen had to pay for the hero's betrayal. Granted that this fate all too often mirrored reality. The orthodox moral of the story, after all, was that her tragic death redeemed his soul. And that in so dying, she transcended herself. A wave of blind fury suddenly swept over Lisya, as she contemplated the true significance of this apotheosis of female suffering.

As the Swan Queen died to Tchaikovsky's tragically transcendent finale, Lisya knew that she wanted no part of such a futile death. There had to be a better way to *live*. There had to be more choices. Women were more than what they were allowed to be. Much more.

As the curtain closed, she was already rewriting the script.

Chapter 10: The ROOTS

Evgenia was sitting next to her grandmother's grave in the cemetery back of the church. Before eating the small lunch she had brought, she placed a piece of bread on the grave and poured some *kvas* over it.

She came here whenever the *izba* felt unbearably empty. These days Ivan rarely spoke, and often went through the motions of his life like an absent-minded ghost. And he never went near his bells.

Across a narrow path, just opposite, was Anastasia's grave. Sometimes Evgenia brought lunch for her, too. Today, however, Elena was coming.

Seeing Elena walking lightly up the path, Evgenia smiled. Even in the plain clothes she always wore, she looked more like her mother now than ever – except that Anastasia's ethereal beauty had somehow made contact in Elena with the earth. She had ripened into a beautiful young woman as golden as a wheatfield, and in her lovely eyes – instead of restless despair – was strength far beyond her years. Elena had the courage to see things as they were – and the wisdom not to yearn for more.

Elena greeted Evgenia warmly, sat down next to her mother's grave, and laid an egg on it. "From Praskovia Nikolaevna's henhouse," she said, with a grin. "For services rendered." Elena now helped her grandmother, Anya, cook at the mansion.

Reaching again into her basket, she pulled out a piece of elaborately decorated cake and handed it to Evgenia. "I used to bring Volodya left-overs from the kitchen, too." A sad smile clouded Elena's kind face. "He really liked the fancy pastry."

"Probably he got his sweet tooth from me." Evgenia, too, smiled sadly.

Elena leaned back against her mother's tombstone, munching carefully on brown bread and sliced cucumbers. "Why did they all leave?" she wondered quietly, after awhile.

"I don't know," replied Evgenia, slowly savoring the piece of cake Elena had given her, "but I know that they had to."

"Just as some of us must stay here to tend our roots."

"Everyone needs some place to call home – even those who never come back."

"They'll *all* come home – someday, somehow."

"I hope so." Gratefully Evgenia relaxed against Babushka's gravestone. Elena, she knew, would never leave Derevnia.

Ж   Ж   Ж

Ivan was standing at the lectern, practicing next Sunday's liturgy in his empty church. The familiar phrases rolled soothingly off his tongue and echoed back comfortingly.

"The Church Fathers were great poets," said Dmitri, emerging from behind a pillar near the door.

Ivan smiled. Dmitri's sudden appearances were always welcome. Somehow the church seemed less lonely.

"Pushkin himself never wrote anything more beautiful." Dmitri sat down on the steps near the lectern.

"Beauty exists to praise the Lord." Ivan sat down next to him.

"Only in church?"

"God is in all of Creation."

"Even in the poetry of Pushkin?"

"Well… in most of it, anyway." Why, Ivan wondered, could he discuss anything with Dmitri – whereas with Lisya, everything inevitably led to an argument.

"She's coming home next month," said Ivan quietly.

Dmitri looked at him in surprise, hope flashing through his sad eyes.

"But only for the summer," Ivan added quickly.

"Oh." Dmitri looked away. "Is she coming alone?"

"No," answered Ivan gently, "She's bringing Katya with her."

"I should have gone away with her, when she wanted me to," said Dmitri, his voice constricted with pain.

"But you didn't."

"Because I was afraid." Dmitri buried his face in his hands. "People who go away never come back."

Ivan laid his hand comfortingly on Dmitri's shoulder. Frowning thoughtfully at the icon of St. Serafim of Sarov, he watched the candle glimmering before it burn low.

Finally he cleared his throat. "Maybe you should go away, too," he said kindly, "just for awhile."

"Where?"

"To Kazan. It's not far – and it's still on the Volga."

"But what would I do there?"

"Work in a factory. There are plenty of jobs. My brother, Grigori, could help you find one. You should be with other young men like yourself – and talk about whatever it is young poets need to talk about!"

Why, Ivan wondered, was he advising Dmitri to leave? Maybe he, too, would never return.

"If I go," said Dmitri firmly, "I'll come back."

Fervently Ivan prayed that Dmitri would be able to keep his promise.

Ж   Ж   Ж

As their train slowed up at the small station, Lisya saw her family standing on the platform, waiting impatiently. After lifting Katya off the train, she watched her daughter toddle eagerly toward the faces beaming joyfully in welcome.

Tears sprang to Lisya's eyes as her mother scooped up Katya and enfolded her in arms that would not willingly let go. Carefully Evgenia examined the little face before her, while Katya curiously regarded the woman who was so obviously thrilled to see her. Both were enormously pleased with what they found, and smiled hugely.

Finally, a russet-clad woman whose wrinkled face was smiling just as ecstatically, tugged on Evgenia's sleeve. "She's *my* granddaughter, too," Ekaterina said with uncharacteristic insistence, as she firmly appropriated her namesake.

Riding back to Derevnia in Mikhail's cart, Katya jumped happily from lap to lap, delighted at all the indulgent attention being lavished upon her. Finally, much later that night, she fell asleep in Evgenia's arms.

The next morning, bright and early, Old Ekaterina showed up with a small russet-colored *sarafan*. Dressed as a peasant girl, Katya romped barefoot in the forest and by the river, flourishing in the unending song which surrounded her. Only letting her out of their sight while she slept, the grandmothers tried to pack all of her childhood into one brief summer.

Lisya willingly relinquished her daughter, smiling often at her mother's zealous instruction and her grandmother's determined hovering. A few months of such concentrated loving would not hurt any child. But by the end of the first week, Lisya herself was bored.

Hoping to use the piano, she visited the manor. Praskovia Nikolaevna and Varvara Petrovna were delighted to see her. Even more bored than she was, they peppered her with questions about Petersburg – and then sent out invitations to a soiree at which, of course, she would entertain.

Lisya arrived that night expecting to be treated as a guest. Instead, after her performance, she was sent to the kitchen for refreshments.

"Some things never change," she sighed to Elena.

"Yes, they do," replied Elena, patting her shoulder. "Some people just don't notice."

Lisya smiled, thinking how much Elena reminded her of Anastasia. Carefully, she avoided asking about Dmitri. Just as carefully, Elena avoided asking about Vladimir.

After that, Lisya stayed away from the manor. And only once did she go to the little grove by the Volga. Putting her violin under her chin, she began playing the songs she had sung to the river so long ago. Imperceptibly the music changed key as, in spite of herself, she wondered about Dmitri.

Evgenia had tactfully informed her, the day after her arrival, that he was in Kazan. Relieved and disappointed, Lisya tried not to see him in all their familiar growing-up places. But it was impossible, especially here by the Volga. Sobbing, she packed up her violin and fled the grove. She did not return there, either.

Finally, she began hanging around the church. Though she had never been comfortable there as a child, she was drawn to its rustic beauty – and by something else she could not name. Frequently, of course, she encountered her father. Pleased to see her there, he nonetheless felt as awkward in her company as she did in his. And despite both their best efforts, it was not long before the running argument between them erupted.

Though he appreciated its contribution to Church liturgy, Ivan himself was not musically inclined. And since the Church did not allow musical instruments in its service, he had little use for his daughter's talent. Her violin evoked distaste; he had never heard her play the piano.

"But composers like Tchaikovsky have written beautiful music for the church as well as for the concert hall," Lisya argued, vainly trying to counter her father's intolerance.

"Yes, and then they blaspheme the holy liturgy by performing it outside of church," Ivan replied self-righteously.

"But maybe in the concert hall it can reach people who don't go to church," Lisya suggested hopefully.

"Concert halls merely divert people from going to church," said Ivan stubbornly.

"No!" said Lisya, just as stubbornly. "For some people, going to concerts is better than going to church. Music can enlighten the soul."

"That is the purpose of prayer."

"But making music is my way of praying! It makes my life worth living."

"How can life be worth living without the Church?"

"It is to me."

"You don't go to church?"

"No."

"Not ever?"

"Sometimes on Easter or Christmas – if Tatiana insists."

"Alexander Pavlovich doesn't go to church?"

"No. Never."

"Why?"

"Because he's an agnostic."

"And that's why you stopped going!" Anger and pain mingled in Ivan's voice.

"No! That's not why," insisted Lisya, pleadingly. "I don't go to church because I can't believe in it! I know you do – and I respect that, even envy you for it. But I've tried and tried, and I can't find God in your Church!"

"But you do in your music?"

"Yes."

Father and daughter subsided into silence, both wondering why the other was unable to understand that which was most important.

"You hurt Dmitri very much," Ivan began again.

"I know. And I'm sorry. Truly. But I had no choice."

"But why?"

"Eagles can swoop lower than chickens," replied Lisya, flaring up, "but chickens will never reach the clouds."

More uncomfortable silence.

"Vladimir lives in Petersburg now, too," Lisya tried again. "I see him often."

"And was it you who persuaded him to leave the seminary and go to Sodom and Gomorrah?" This time it was Ivan who flared up.

"Of course not! I don't particularly like the company he keeps now, either, but at least it's *his* choice!"

"And the seminary wasn't?"

"That was *your* idea!"

"And *his*, too!"

"Maybe. But you didn't give him enough room to choose it as his own. You were always with him... And *never* with me!" Lisya ran sobbing out of the church.

In the end, they declared a truce.

"I want you to baptize Katya," Lisya informed her father a few days before returning to Petersburg.

Ivan worked late into the night carving a small cross, which he gently hung around his granddaughter's neck at the ceremony. Katya smiled as her great-grandfather's big voice embraced her and the pretty pictures on the walls – painted, she knew, by her other great-grandfather – blessed her.

The little wooden church glowed with rare beauty that day. Soft beams of light joined with warm notes of love in an exquisite chorus Lisya knew she would never forget. And she hoped that Katya, too, would always remember.

Ж   Ж   Ж

Parting with Katya, Evgenia decided morosely, was even worse than saying goodbye to Lisya. Her own children's leaving had wrenched a hole in her present; this one opened a gaping void in her future – and her past.

Later she went walking in the forest, along all the old trails she had taken so long ago with Babushka – and just yesterday with Katya. And she wept that she would not be able to pass on to her granddaughter all that she had learned from her grandmother.

As she leaned disconsolately against a big linden tree in a small clearing, she suddenly heard rustling leaves and gruff snorting. A huge bear walked into the clearing. It stopped, startled, and then calmly looked her up and down. Evgenia's eyes met those of the somehow familiar bear and locked in a long, fathomless gaze. She remembered the three bear cubs she had encountered with Babushka in this very spot, and how ferociously protective their mother had been. Afterwards, Babushka had told her that bears were the best of mothers.

"They protect their young fiercely, and teach them how to take care of themselves," she had said approvingly. "And then, when it's time, they push them out of the den."

For just an instant, the bear seemed to nod. Then, obviously at peace with herself and the world, she grunted amiably and ambled slowly off into the forest.

Ж   Ж   Ж

Ever since she had graduated from the Ballet School, Tatiana had come home every summer. Her annual visits were brief but harmonious. Both Ivan and Evgenia looked forward to them.

Evgenia was standing by the window next to the stove, watching Tatiana feed the chickens. Having shed her citified travel clothes, she was dressed in a chestnut brown *sarafan* she had made for herself – with Ekaterina's help – last summer. Her arm scattered the grain with grand, sweeping gestures, while her shuffling feet mimicked the excitement of the silly birds. As always, Evgenia laughed. It was hard to believe Tatiana had ever left.

But, of course, there were changes, too. Tatiana had grown up. She was a woman now – which took some getting used to – and she no longer talked only with her body. Every evening, as the sun was setting, they would sit together – spinning and weaving – talking late into the night.

"Petersburg is my home," said Tatiana, her body inscribing small circles in rhythm with the spinning wheel, "but so is Derevnia."

"Petersburg is Lisya's home, too," said Evgenia, smiling at Tatiana's unconscious *pas de deux* with the evenly turning wheel, "but I doubt Derevnia ever was."

"Not like it is for me – or for you. But here is where her roots are."

"But does *she* know that?"

"I do my best to remind her."

Evgenia peered quizzically over her loom on which was strung yarn – dyed by Ekaterina – the color of fallen leaves.

"When Katya was born," Tatiana raised her distaff, "I cut the cord with the one Babushka gave Lisya – you remember, the night she died."

"Lisya didn't object?"

"She was grateful. She always is, even when she doesn't admit it."

Tatiana stopped the wheel and carefully wrapped more wool around the distaff.

"Don't you ever get homesick?" Evgenia's shuttle moved steadily back and forth through the reddish-brown yarn. "For Derevnia, I mean."

"No, not really," Tatiana's body began swaying in rhythm to Evgenia's shuttle. "Of course I miss you – and this – and other things, too. But Petersburg is

213

Mother Russia's daughter just as Derevnia is, so they're really not so different. As long as we all live here in the Motherland – in *Rodina* – we're still connected."

"If only it didn't take so long to get from place to place," sighed Evgenia. "Russia is such a big village."

Every morning, just after sunrise, Tatiana went to the church.

Ivan was already there, on his knees before the iconostasis. Tatiana knelt silently beside him and crossed herself reverently.

Finally, when both had finished their private matins, they sat down together on the steps by the baptismal font.

"You were the only one who didn't cry when I baptized you," Ivan smiled. "Lisya shrieked indignantly – even then she was arguing – and Volodya let out a howl that drowned out the whole choir."

"But I'll bet I wiggled a lot," laughed Tatiana, leaning comfortably against her father.

"Your little feet were kicking so hard, they splashed water all over me," Ivan laughed too.

"They aren't so little now," smiled Tatiana, stretching out her feet and wiggling her toes, "but they're still kicking."

"You're happy there?" asked Ivan, suddenly serious, "Dancing in Petersburg?"

"The ballets at the Maryinsky are wonderful," replied Tatiana, considering carefully, "but dancing itself is often very painful."

"So is being a priest – but I could never be anything else."

"That's how dancing is for me."

Ivan nodded, relieved that he understood at least one of this children.

"And it's how Lisya feels about her music," added Tatiana softly.

Ivan sighed. "Why is it so hard for me to accept that?"

"Perhaps because she can't understand your church."

"And Volodya?"

"Someday he'll come back." Tatiana intertwined her slender fingers in his. "But in his own way, in his own time."

Ivan sighed again, and gently squeezed the warm hand so like his own. "You, at least, will never leave the Church."

"How could I? The Holy Church is home. It's Russia. It's where I belong."

Later, at the train station, Ivan gave her his blessing, the sweepingly graceful gesture so much like Tatiana it brought tears to Evgenia's eyes. She herself clung to her daughter, unwilling to let her go.

As always, she watched the train disappear over the horizon. But this time, just as it slipped from sight, she felt a heart-breaking wrench.

"No, no!" she shouted into the emptiness. "Come back, come back!"

Ж   Ж   Ж

Candlelight glowed warmly around the golden crown. Under it stood Elena, calm and beautiful as a field of grain. Next to her was Mischa, so happy he could barely stand still, an enormous smile nearly consuming his inconspicuous face.

Unlike her brother, Elena had not wasted time pining for a lost love. Though saddened and disappointed by Vladimir's disappearance, she had matter-of-factly turned her attention to finding a more willing suitor. It was not difficult. Her amiable blond beauty attracted the young men; her practical common sense endeared her to their families. She therefore had her pick of Derevnia's eligible bachelors. After careful consideration, Elena chose Mischa, eldest son of Evgenia's brother, Vaslav.

Even as a child, Mischa had trailed faithfully after Elena, one of the few people who ever paid attention to him. Not that anyone disliked him. But so perfectly did he blend with his surroundings that he was hard to notice. No one ever told Mischa to stay or go away, because he rarely made anyone aware of his presence. Elena had always been fond of him – when she remembered he was there. But after Vladimir vanished, there was Mischa, still waiting patiently. Elena took a good look, and saw a sturdy reliable man whose plain face said he adored her – and would never leave.

It was a good match. Mischa had grown up into a strong practical-minded young man, dedicated to the land and deeply rooted in the village. He also possessed a passably good bass voice. Mikhail began training him as his successor – though with less enthusiasm than he had groomed the more gifted Vladimir. The new chanter-apparent did his best to live up to his grandfather's standards, but Mikhail often complained that Mischa sang as if he had manure in his throat.

No one in Derevnia loved the land more than Mischa, and no one put more effort into making things grow. From before dawn until after dusk, he thought of little else. A born farmer, he sensed even as a boy that there were better ways of going about it. As soon as he learned to read, he had approached Alexander Pavlovich for information about agriculture. Mischa devoured the publications and periodicals – which continued to arrive even after the obliging doctor moved to Petersburg – and eventually became the village expert on modern farming techniques. Though he learned slowly, Mischa was very thorough. By the time he took charge of his family's land allotments, he knew that what ailed Derevnia was part of a much bigger problem, one that went far beyond agriculture itself.

The entire village had turned out for the wedding. Back in the shadows stood Dmitri, a sadly ironic smile on his face. Mischa, he knew, would take good care of his sister. And she, he also knew, would be content. If only it were that simple for him.

Dmitri had returned home for only a few days; tomorrow he was taking the boat back to Kazan. His first embarkation, he remembered, had been terrifying. Father Grigori, however, had helped him find a job. True, he hated being cooped up in a factory, but he was used to hard work. And Kazan, too, was on the Volga. That made it bearable.

Not a day passed, however, that he did not yearn for the familiar ways of Derevnia. Every night he poured out his homesickness in increasingly eloquent poems, which Father Grigori encouraged him to read to the young men's group at his church. Like Dmitri, they had migrated from villages up and down the river.

After the meeting, a few of the seasoned hands, also poets of sorts, invited Dmitri to a café frequented by the local literati. The place reeked of sweaty proletarian odes and verse which conjured up manure. Dmitri's shy readings were greeted with noisy enthusiasm. Soon he became one of the regulars; gradually he absorbed some of their skeptical self-confidence.

As Father Ivan pronounced them man and wife, Mischa looked at Elena, his smile nearly devouring his entire body. Dmitri's sadness suddenly disappeared; it was impossible not to be happy for someone like Mischa. And as the melancholy momentarily lifted, he realized how much he missed his new friends in Kazan.

After the ceremony, Dmitri approached Father Ivan.

"I came back," he grinned.

"So I see," smiled Ivan, obviously relieved and happy to see him. "How was Kazan?"

"Crowded and dirty," shrugged Dmitri, "but exciting, too."

"Cities usually are – especially for the young." Ivan searched his face. "No one who goes there remains unchanged."

"I'm going back tomorrow," said Dmitri proudly.

"I thought you might," nodded Ivan.

"But I'll be back for the harvest." Dmitri's sad eyes were the color of the earth. "Derevnia will always be home."

"Yes, I know." Gratefully, Father Ivan gave Dmitri his blessing.

Shortly after Dmitri's return to Kazan, news came of Lev Nikolaevich Tolstoy, who – at age eighty-two – had finally found the courage to leave his life of ease for one more consonant with his ascetic beliefs. The great writer had been found gravely ill on a train. All over Russia, people prayed for him, dying in the backroom of an isolated railway station. In the cities, throngs stood in the snow, waiting for extra editions of newspapers, which followed the progress of his illness. Dmitri and his friends kept vigil for a week, until finally Tolstoy died.

It was the end of an era – and soon, much else.

Part III

Revolution, 1914

Chapter 11: REBELLION

Alexander Pavlovich carefully steered his carriage through the narrow streets. Feeling anxious, he urged his horse to go faster. The old mare, however, was accustomed to one speed, and refused to hurry her pace. As she trotted placidly through the Vyborg District of Petersburg, he tried to focus on the familiar rhythm of her clopping hooves. These days, however, it was impossible to relax – especially at night, when the dark restlessness stalking the city seemed most intense.

It had started after the Duma dissolved. Terrorists had assassinated thousands, and even blown up Prime Minister Stolypin's palace. The prime minister himself had escaped – that time. But there were several more attempts on his life, despite the elaborate system of agents and informers with which he attempted to infiltrate the revolutionary movement. The espionage provoked counter-espionage and remarkable double agents, who simultaneously led the revolutionaries – and then informed on their own activities to the police. From the rumors Alexander Pavlovich heard of these complex plots, it was difficult to tell whose side anyone was on. And from what Vladimir said, many of the double agents themselves weren't sure. It had, in fact, been one of these underground policemen who had finally shot Stolypin.

After crossing the Liteiny Bridge, the mare stopped where Sadovaya Ulitza intersected with the Nevsky Prospekt. Alexander Pavlovich looked up and down the brightly lit avenue. It was late, but noisy nightclubs were full of carousing citizens drinking too much and gambling too extravagantly. Prostitutes in garish makeup strolled provocatively along the Nevsky, openly soliciting customers. Elaborately dressed society ladies entered restaurants, which – until a few years ago – had been frequented only by men and "professional" women. Carriages filled with boisterous revelers galloped up and down the boulevard.

The mare trotted across the Nevsky and continued on Sadovaya Ulitza, until she stopped in front of their apartment building. Alexander Pavlovich rang the bell and, after a few minutes, the sleepy gatekeeper let them in. Driving through the courtyard to the coach house, he relinquished the reins to a yawning groom. Climbing the stairs to his apartment, he quietly let himself in.

Late as it was, he was too tense to sleep. Stopping first in his study to pour himself a small glass of brandy, he went into the living room and sank down gratefully in his favorite chair. On the table next to it was his newspaper and the lamp Lisya had left lighted.

After a slow sip of brandy, Alexander Pavlovich opened the newspaper. Scanning the ads, he noted the usual ones advertising cures for syphilis and gonorrhea – all of them "guaranteed to stop the most stubborn discharge in no time." If only, he sighed, it were that simple. He thought of the woman whose difficult labor he had been called to assist tonight. She had almost died. Nor was this the first time. Alexander Pavlovich had long since lost count of how many children she already had, and the woman herself probably wasn't sure how many miscarriages there had been. Just last month, he had treated her husband for venereal disease; despite his best efforts, he knew it was only a matter of time until that, too, became her burden.

Sighing again, he returned to the newspaper. A bookseller was advertising the latest bestseller by a mediocre writer Alexander Pavlovich found especially offensive. He had borrowed the book from a friend, and it had disgusted him. Even worse than all the explicit sex was how the book's characters used it as an antidote to nihilistic boredom. And it was not well written – an insult, in fact, to Russian literature. That so many were buying this pornography was yet another disturbing sign of the times.

Ever since the dissolution of the Duma, this nameless cancer had been growing. Slowly at first and then, lately, in great ballooning tumors. An epidemic of suicides – especially among the young – was growing into alarming proportions. Cynical indifference plagued the rest of society, its one driving force a feverish urge to get rich as quickly as possible. "It is a kind of frenzy that has seized people on every hand," warned an editorial, "to get the most they can out of a state of affairs that cannot last much longer."

On the next page was an article about the celebration of the Tercentenary of the Imperial House. The Romanovs had occupied the throne of Russia for three hundred years. Alexander Pavlovich doubted if they would last much longer. From his medical colleagues, he had picked up some alarming – but carefully guarded – information about the young Tsarevich's poor health. A wave of sadness swept through him for the beautiful child who had so briefly charmed him at the Imperial reception.

And then, his radiantly healthy little Katya filled his heart, and he thanked the God he hoped existed for the wondrous gift of his daughter. As he did countless times every day. But along with the joy of beholding his beautiful wife and child also came dread that he would not be able to protect them from the darkness threatening Petersburg. His doctor's mind told him that the sickness invading Russia was serious – possibly even fatal. His soul convulsed with fear that perhaps he could do nothing to cure it.

Hastily he returned his attention to the newspaper. Earlier that year, Repin had exhibited a huge and terrifying painting of Ivan the Terrible. Alexander Pavlovich had seen it – and found it frighteningly good: Tsar Ivan holding his son, whom he has just killed, both bathed in blood, and in the Tsar's eyes a look of monumental horror. Just last week, the paper reported, the painting had been slashed by vandals.

And on the back page, the paper also reported that the Tsar and his family had recently attended a performance of His Majesty's favorite opera – Wagner's *Gotterdammerung*. Alexander Pavlovich shuddered, and quickly downed the rest of his brandy.

Ж   Ж   Ж

They met on the Liteiny Bridge to watch the running of the ice. Lisya and Tatiana were huddled close to the embankment; Vladimir was standing at the apex of the bridge, halfway between the Vyborg and the Palace side of the Neva. Leaning on the railing, he stared moodily into the churning river. How like the chaos in his soul!

Ever since he could remember, Vladimir had been searching. At first he had not known what to call this indefinable something which had no name. His father taught him to call it God, and for awhile, in the security of his church, Vladimir thought he had found it. An exceptionally pious altar boy, he had solemnly vowed to become a priest like his father and, at the appointed time, had gone off to the seminary, just as it had always been agreed he should.

Away from the shelter of his father's unwavering faith, however, Vladimir was beset by doubts and confusion. At the seminary, he encountered others who believed that they, too, had found *IT* – but they called it things like the "People's Will" or the "Dialectic of History." Worse yet, he discovered that the Orthodox Church was not like his father. In his disillusion, Vladimir became easy prey for those who claimed that *IT* was not God but something else. Not to have something to believe in, heart and soul, was unthinkable.

223

Gradually he worked his way through the myriad of revolutionary doctrines. Some were more satisfying than others. Many of the leaders of these various creeds, however, were avowed – and zealous – atheists. While Vladimir could understand – even applaud – their attacks on the Church, he could not muster much enthusiasm for an *IT* that was essentially a not-*IT*. And so, while the left hand was organizing unions and reading Marx, the right hand continued to be fascinated by the mystical sects and charismatic cults which dotted the Russian landscape.

Nor was he alone. Everywhere there was a sense of impending doom and loss of faith in the official Church. The search for *IT* became more frantic, as people worshiped strange gods and cultivated strange saints. Rumors were persistent that the AntiChrist had been born, and that the world was about to end. Reports of miracles regularly appeared in the newspapers. *Startsy* – holy elders thought to be blessed with God's wisdom – wandered throughout Russia and abounded even in the cities. *Yurodivye* – Christ-like simpletons – also proliferated.

The "holy fool" was an ancient – and respected – institution in Holy Russia, a survival of the notion that God endowed the mad with a peculiar kind of sanctity. While Vladimir was somewhat skeptical of these holy fools, his revolutionary side wryly acknowledged their usefulness. Thus had Vassily the Blessed been endowed with awesome spiritual authority. In his iron cap, hair shirt and penitential chains, he had made even Ivan the Terrible tremble.

Most of the holy men existed on the fringe of the Church, but some were more respectable than others. Father John of Kronstadt, for instance, was a priest at the Andreevsky Cathedral. Reputed to be a healer and miracle worker, he was considered by many a likely candidate for sainthood. Vladimir, too, made more than one pilgrimage to Kronstadt.

Less appealing was a deformed mute named Mitya Kolyaba who howled and roared during epileptic seizures. Some saw this as speaking in tongues and acclaimed him a prophet. Introduced to various God-seeking members of the aristocracy, he was even received at Court. So was the pilgrim Vassily, whom Vladimir occasionally encountered on the Nevsky Prospekt. In his cassock and thick beard, he always went barefoot – regardless of the weather – and carried a heavy staff with large silver cross on top. It was said that he had advised Tsar Nicholas during the turmoil in 1905.

Now there was a new favorite – a monk from Siberia named Rasputin. Enthusiasts could not agree on whether he was a holy elder or a holy fool – but all agreed that he was a potential saint. After a few visits to the sickly young Tsarevich, he also became known as a healer.

Vladimir had seen Rasputin only once. A broad-shouldered greasy-haired peasant in loose blouse and baggy trousers tucked into high boots, he ate with his fingers and used his beard as a napkin. But his eyes! Small, tiny eyes that burned right through you! Still, Vladimir was inclined to dismiss Rasputin as an opportunistic charlatan.

Rasputin's effect on women, however, was extraordinary. Rumor had it he was an insatiable satyr, irresistible to half the women in Petersburg. Nor did he ever make the slightest effort to hide either his lust or his unbridled indulgence of it. For Rasputin had somehow convinced his female followers that they could achieve grace only through orgasm, and that the holy spirit descended to them via his genitalia. Repentance is pleasing unto God, taught Rasputin. In order to repent, you must first sin.

As Rasputin's influence grew, so did his excesses. His drinking and debauchery reached epic proportions. Gossip and scandal grew apace. Not that Vladimir believed the rumors about Rasputin and the Empress. A woman like that? No, it was impossible. Besides, everyone knew the Tsar was a model husband. Most likely it was through the Tsarevich that Rasputin derived his privileged position. And doubtless he presented a much different face at court than the one he wore at his drunken revels. Still, that such a man was received by their august sovereign and his family!

Vladimir the revolutionary perceived with satisfaction that such a state of affairs could only hasten the Revolution. Vladimir the true believer, however, continued to regret that all of them – the Church and the Tsar, *startsy* and *yurodivye*, even Rasputin – were not what everyone wanted them to be.

Looking down at the frozen spars passing noisily under the bridge, Vladimir was suddenly afraid. As cold dampness swept over him, his heart began beating rapidly. Bruised by the crashing ice, his soul struggled to breathe amid the swirling mists. Abruptly he walked down to where his sisters were standing, and wrapped his strong arms around their reassuringly warm bodies. As they looked up, he saw his own fear reflected in their eyes. Yet they stood there together until long after dark, enthralled by the enigma of the spectacle, fascinated by its awesome power.

Ж Ж Ж

Tatiana talked of nothing else, and all her free time was spent rehearsing Stravinsky's ballet the Maryinsky wouldn't touch.

The *Firebird* was Igor Stravinsky's first ballet. It was no coincidence that he was using the same legend that had gotten his teacher, Rimsky-Korsakov, into so much trouble. Which was why the Imperial Theatre would have nothing to do with it – officially. Unofficially, several of the Maryinsky dancers joined the new troupe.

Some of them did so as an act of rebellion. Not so, Tatiana. "I love *Swan Lake* and *Sleeping Beauty* and all the rest," she reassured Lisya, "but I think that this, too, will be wonderful."

And so it was, but in a different way. At first, Tatiana came home from rehearsals frustrated. "It's the new rhythms," she complained. "None of us have ever danced to anything like this before. It's hard to get used to."

Lisya knew what she meant. Earlier – before word had gotten around – Stravinsky had tried out his new score on the Conservatory orchestra. The musicians had fumbled its strange time signatures and abrupt changes of tempo, and griped about its odd harmonic structure.

The *Ballet Russe* – organized by the controversial impressario, Sergei Diaghilev – attracted much attention. Most of the dancers performed at the Maryinsky during the regular season, and then toured Europe with Diaghilev in summer. Factions soon formed around the "Diaghilevtsy" And the "Imperialisty." Tension finally came to a head when the phenomenal danseur, Vaslav Nijinsky, was dismissed from the Imperial Ballet. In a performance of *Giselle*, he had shocked the Dowager Empress by refusing to wear the customary short trunks over his yellow tights.

Rumor had it that Kschessinskaya's admirers at court were somehow involved in the affair. Some of the other *Ballet Russe* dancers resigned from the Imperial Company in protest. Tatiana, however, was not among them.

"These new ballets – they're very exciting – and I love being part of them," she explained reassuringly. But my soul is at the Maryinsky."

"As is mine!" replied Lisya, unable to keep the anxiety out of her voice.

"Where else could it be?!"

Despite growing apprehension, Lisya helped Tatiana prepare for her first tour of Europe. And when, finally, she saw her off with the *Ballet Russe* corps de ballet, Lisya was almost as excited as her sister.

Ж   Ж   Ж

For the first summer in years, Tatiana was not there to share the beauty of Petersburg's long White Nights. Lisya missed her sorely. Even on her promenades

226

with Katya, part of her felt empty. She watched the papers for news of *Ballet Russe* performances, and eagerly kept track of their progress.

Stravinsky had written two more ballets for the *Ballet Russe*; Lisya was pleased to read that *Petrushka* was being acclaimed, dismayed that the *Rite of Spring* had caused a riot in Paris. The sophisticated Parisians had shouted insults, howled and whistled, slapped and punched each other. So great was the tumult, the dancers could not hear the music. Tatiana's next letter described how Nijinsky, who had choreographed the ballet, stood on a chair backstage, yelling numbers at the dancers and clapping out rhythms.

Tatiana wrote often, her enthusiastic letters full of new experiences and the wonders of Europe. Between the lines, however, Lisya sensed an undercurrent of homesickness, stronger even than her own longing for her sister's presence. At the end of the summer, she was at the station long before Tatiana's train was due, nervously pacing the platform.

Tatiana jumped off the train – which chuffed into the depot right on schedule – laden with exotic looking bundles, which she proceeded to distribute as soon as they were home. The biggest ones were for Lisya.

Tatiana watched impatiently as her sister slowly opened them. Inside the first was an elegant street suit of dark copper-colored wool, cut and tailored in the latest Parisian style. In another box was a matching hat, trimmed with pheasant feathers – and very chic. Delighted, Lisya caressed the soft fabric and smoothed the silky feathers. Then she picked up the whole ensemble and ran into her bedroom. After a long appraisal before the wardrobe mirror, she made an entrance.

"Ooh, Lisya," giggled Tatiana appreciatively, as Lisya struck a pose worthy of Kschessinskaya, "What an actress you would make!"

Later, after Katya was asleep and Alexander Pavlovich had gone to his study, they sat down with their tea for a long talk. At dinner, Tatiana had shared her European adventures. Now the conversation turned to the new ballets.

"I hear that Stravinsky's score for *Rite of Spring* is even more difficult than *Firebird*," said Lisya.

"Yes, definitely," replied Tatiana, nodding her head vigorously. "All these odd chords and strange rhythmic patterns, none of them happening at the same time, like everyone playing a different piece all at once! Even Diaghilev was shocked."

"Some of the critics say it isn't music – just noise."

"No, no," Tatiana disagreed. "That's not fair. When I first heard it – well, yes, I might have agreed. But after a while… there's a mesmerizing effect that reaches deep into forgotten corners…"

"What did it feel like to dance to it?"

"At first, awful," Tatiana frowned, remembering. "My feet, especially, hated it. After years of perfecting my turnout – and then to dance for hours with my feet turned in! And all those clumsy, uncouth movements. Lisya, it was impossible to be graceful!" She got up and stomped around the room, feet turned in and knees bent, shoulders hunched and fists clenched.

"Well," Lisya laughed appreciatively, "at least you don't look fragile."

"And no toe shoes, either." Tatiana continued to lumber around the room, making short sporadic hops and pawing the earth. "And no ballerinas being carried around by danseurs – or *pas de deux* – or symmetrical lines – or great soaring leaps." As Tatiana stopped the awkward grunting and stood thoughtfully, her torso unconsciously assumed a classical pose, feet turned out. "But yet... amidst all the primitive growling and howling, and the bones and fur and skins... there was something terribly compelling. Dancing it was like being back in the Stone Age. And deep down, a part of me – a part I never knew existed – wanted to be there. It felt like..." she searched for the right words. "It felt like... the running of the ice!"

Lisya shuddered, remembering the savage music of the ice crashing under the Liteiny bridge. Tatiana sat down quickly beside her. They were quiet for awhile.

"In the ballet," Lisya broke the silence, "a sacrificial maiden is chosen – and she dances herself to death."

"Yes, I was wondering when you'd get around to that. But Lisya, there's nothing at all ethereal or vulnerable about the way she does it. Her dance is very earthy – and very strong."

"But she still dies," persisted Lisya.

"Yes, but not because of some silly man. She dances – and dies – to save the Earth."

"But she is still a victim," argued Lisya.

"Not really. Her death is an expression of faith – a belief that what we humans do can make a difference. To choose to die for something bigger than yourself – that is an act of ultimate freedom, even if the choice is forced upon you. No, the Chosen Maiden is not a victim. Now, Petrushka – there's a victim!"

"Ah yes, the puppet in Stravinsky's other ballet.

"Nijinsky was absolutely brilliant! His Petrushka was so piteous. Oh Lisya, I weep even thinking about him. Just looking at him, you could tell poor Petrushka was not much valued by the Magician pulling his strings. Such a pathetically blank face! And when he danced… "

Tatiana stood up and began to imitate Nijinsky's puppet-like movements. Her head became a heavy wood block, hanging forward, rolling from side to side, then propped unnaturally on her shoulder. Her hands and feet turned into stiff wooden paddles, dangling loosely from her arms and legs. Her knees bent suddenly under the weight of her body, the knock-kneed legs swaying. She began to dance around the room as if using only the heavy wooden parts of her body. Swinging, mechanical , empty motions jerked her arms and legs upward in extravagant movements of joy and despair.

Moved by Tatiana's portrayal of the poor trapped soul, struggling to escape his fate, Lisya felt tears in her eyes.

"When the show is over," Tatiana stopped dancing, "the Magician throws Petrushka into a dirty corner of an old box. In the center of the wall of his box-room is a portrait of the Magician. Its eyes follow his every move. There is no place to hide." Tatiana pounded wooden paddle-like hands against the wall, pouring out anger and resentment at the portrait. Finally, the puppet collapsed in despair on the floor.

"I wonder," mused Lisya, as Tatiana got to her feet and sat down beside her again, "if Petrushka was better off without someone pulling his strings."

"He became human."

"And got himself killed."

"But he was free."

"Only to die."

"There are worse fates." For once, Tatiana's eyes were not smiling.

Silently, they sipped their tea.

"Stravinsky's music for *Petrushka* is wonderful," Tatiana continued after a while. "Under all the strange chords and rhythms, it's still so Russian. One moment you're sobbing in despair with a poor tragic puppet, the next – galloping joyously in a troika out onto the open steppes."

"You missed home, didn't you," Lisya said quietly. "Even in all the glamour of Europe."

Tatiana nodded. "Not just you – or Petersburg – but all of *Rodina*." She threw out her arms in a large sweeping gesture. "Russia is Home. Away from her, I feel like an uprooted tree."

Lisya gently squeezed Tatiana's hand. The candle fluttered out. The sisters sat silently, the bond between them a beacon in the darkness.

Chapter 12: WAR

Lisya walked carefully along the busy platform, conscious of the stylish suit she was wearing, concerned that people streaming by might somehow mar its elegance. Next to her, Tatiana also wore a fashionable ensemble, purchased – like Lisya's – the previous year in Paris. Tatiana's outfit was vivid blue, matching her eyes, now particularly bright with excitement.

Lisya's eyes, however, were unusually grey, which was why she was focusing so hard on her clothes. Tatiana was again off to join the *Ballet Russe* tour of Europe. Lisya's heart felt like a stone; she was trying hard not to let it spoil her sister's anticipation.

An unsettling restlessness hovered over Petersburg. People seemed to be waiting for something, but no one knew what it was. The uneasiness filled Lisya with vague foreboding. Whatever was coming – somehow it threatened everyone she loved. To reassure herself, Lisya reached out and took Tatiana's arm.

Behind them walked Vladimir, carrying Tatiana's new suitcases. Halfway down the platform, they found the neat little compartment she was sharing with other members of the corps de ballet. Effortlessly Vladimir stacked the heavy luggage in the rack above Tatiana's comfortably upholstered seat. Then he stood for a moment, awkwardly trying to reduce his formidable bulk to the size of the small compartment. Tatiana grasped his calloused hands and smiled. His awkwardness immediately replaced by furtive tears, he gazed lovingly at his little sister. Carefully he wrapped his arms around her, trying not to lift her off her feet. After kissing her soundly on both cheeks, he abruptly left the train.

Tatiana quickly sat down, Lisya on the empty seat next to her.

"Do you have your ticket?" asked Lisya nervously.

"Yes, right here in my purse."

"Did you pack plenty of clean handkerchiefs?" She plucked at non-existent pieces of lint on Tatiana's traveling suit.

"Enough for the entire corps de ballet." Seeing her sister's agitation, Tatiana smiled, trying to lighten the mood.

231

"Watch out for those Frenchmen!" warned Lisya solemnly.

"I doubt I'll have time for anything like that." Seeing that Lisya was not to be coaxed out of her worrying, Tatiana grasped her fluttering hand and squeezed it reassuringly.

"All aboard!" sang out the conductor.

Lisya stood up quickly, then bent down and kissed Tatiana's forehead.

"Hold on to your purse. And wash your stockings every night. And don't forget to write…"

Gently she reached down and smoothed back a stray hair which had escaped from Tatiana's tightly-coiffed bun. Then she turned quickly and left the train.

Outside, standing next to Vladimir, she watched Tatiana, all beautiful and bright blue, waving excitedly through the window. A wave of dizziness swept over Lisya; her pounding heart echoed deafeningly with what suddenly felt like an empty cave. Tatiana lowered the window and leaned out, reaching for her.

As they grasped each other's hand, the train began to pull away. Lisya walked alongside, until their hands wrenched apart. She walked faster, and then ran, their eyes still locked, blurred by streaming tears. At the end of the platform she stopped and watched until Tatiana's clouded face disappeared, and then waved at the train until it, too, disappeared.

The empty tracks stretched out endlessly before her.

Ж　Ж　Ж

No matter how often Alexander Pavlovich explained it to her, Lisya still didn't understand.

"But what does the assassination of an Austrian archduke have to do with Russia?"

"Well, you see," answered Alexander Pavlovich patiently, "the assassin was a Serbian nationalist."

"But he's a terrorist!" exclaimed Lisya. "Surely the Tsar should not be supporting the likes of him!"

"Well – ah – yes, but – well, we have a treaty of alliance with Serbia."

"So?"

"Austria has demanded that Serbia hand over the assassin," replied Alexander Pavlovich, "or else."

"So?"

"The Treaty promises that Russia will aid Serbia, if attacked."

"Even over something like this?" demanded Lisya incredulously.

"Well," said Alexander Pavlovich, trying to sound convincing, "a nation should keep its word."

Lisya, however, remained unconvinced. During the tense summer of 1914, she watched with dismay as the crisis mounted. Ultimatums flew back and forth between capitals; armies began mobilizing. And then, suddenly – to everyone's surprise – all of Europe was at war.

Petersburg – now Petrograd – was transformed. Petersburg, it was argued, was too German – a symbol of Slavic subjection to the abominable Hun. At the Maryinsky, every performance was preceded by the national anthems of all the allies. In the squares, policemen with heavy ledgers lined up large groups of conscripts, most of whom marched off to war – sober. The government had banned the sale of liquor; drunks virtually disappeared from the streets – for awhile.

Most remarkable was that patriotism was suddenly in vogue. People who only a few weeks before had been heaping abuse on the government, were now enlisting in the army and volunteering to be nurses. And when the Tsar addressed the new Duma at the Winter Palace, the deputies exploded with enthusiastic chauvinism. Alexander Pavlovich, attending with a friend who was still a member, returned home glowing with the excitement of the event.

"It was incredible, Lisya! A huge crowd, all milling around the Tsar in an emotional frenzy, shouting 'Lead us, Sire!' And this from a group dedicated to being a thorn in the Imperial side!"

Lisya knew that her husband had joined the countless hurrahs for the Tsar. She, too, would have yielded to the patriotic orgy had it not been for her growing apprehension.

At the first sign of trouble, Lisya had written to Tatiana, urging her to come home at once. Her sister's reply had dismissed the brewing crisis, sure that it would soon blow over. Most of the letter was filled with glowing accounts of activities shared with someone named Nikolai. "He manages the sets for all our ballets. And he's such a wonderful artist! And feels about his art the way I do about dancing! And sometimes we stay up half the night just talking and talking about everything!" Tatiana ecstatically rambled on and on, in praise of the young man who seemed to be occupying her attention to the exclusion of all else.

Her protectiveness instantly aroused, Lisya's worried reaction to Tatiana's obvious infatuation was nonetheless secondary to her fear that Tatiana seemed blind to the danger around her. "This is no time for her to be falling in love!" she grumbled to Alexander Pavlovich, who shared her concern.

After war was declared, there were no more letters. Anxiously, Lisya scanned the newspapers. "GERMANS DESECRATE ORTHODOX ICONS... The Germans have been killing wounded men... The Germans are severing arm tendons of Russian soldiers taken prisoner. After this, they will never again hold rifles... Arise, Great Nation of Russia!... God Strike the Aggressor!... Hands off Holy Russia!... We are ready to make any sacrifice to defend the honor and dignity of the Russian state..."

Yes, yes, yes, thought Lisya irritably, as she searched frantically for news of the Ballet Russe. *But let not one of these sacrifices be my sister!*

At last, a letter from Tatiana finally found its way to Petrograd. In between interminable rhapsodizing about Nikolai, she assured Lisya that she was quite safe. The ballet company was staying in France for the duration of the war. "Everyone here says that of course it can't last more than a few months. So I should be home in time to dance *The Nutcracker.*" Relieved as to Tatiana's safety – and wondering when she would meet this Nikolai person – Lisya stopped reading the newspapers. But a cold gray whisper of foreboding crouched in a corner of her mind.

A few weeks later, she found herself at the train station again, this time with Vladimir. Ever since the declaration of war, she had known that her brother's fervent soul could not long resist the tide of patriotic mysticism engulfing Russia. And so, when Vladimir announced his enlistment at dinner one night, she was not surprised. The passionate glitter in his eyes, however, made her sigh. She had seen that look before.

The station was jammed with excited men in uniform and weeping women. As Vladimir paused before the crowded troop train, Lisya threw her arms around her brother and kissed him. He stepped aboard the densely packed train; after a shrill whistle from the engine, he reached out the window to her. As she grasped his hand, she saw the radiant smile on his face. Then, after many false starts, the overloaded train crawled slowly out of the station. The soldiers began to sing; Lisya watched as Vladimir's glowing song disappeared into the twilight.

Ж   Ж   Ж

Lisya was standing in front of the mirror in their bedroom, trying to focus on how well the saffron velvet dress still enhanced her image. Behind her was Alexander Pavlovich, wearing his new uniform for the first time. Not unexpectedly, he had been called up for service in the Medical Corps. He had received his commission a few weeks ago, and would soon be leaving for the Front.

Lisya stepped aside so that he could see his reflection. Her intended compliment stuck in her throat. The uniform fit well enough, and even made him look rather distinguished. But Lisya hated it.

Alexander Pavlovich himself was surprised at the almost commanding figure which gazed back at him from the mirror. Even so, he was obviously uncomfortable in the uniform. Though he had sometimes allowed himself to be caught up in the patriotism, Lisya knew her husband had at least as many reservations about the war as she did.

"I fear that we have learned nothing from the fiasco with Japan," he had confessed one night, shortly after his commission arrived. "And many will suffer and die needlessly!"

"Perhaps your skill can save some of them," replied Lisya, trying to comfort him.

"Yes," he sighed, "Perhaps so. In any case, I took an oath. I've always tried to live by it – and I'm too old to change now... But..." he took her hand and squeezed it tightly, "leaving you and Katya... I don't know if I can bear it."

Remembering, Lisya stepped in front of him, blocking out the unwelcome image.

Relieved, Alexander Pavlovich fumbled in his pockets and pulled out a beautiful amber necklace. Relaxing in her surprised smile, he carefully clasped it around her neck. "Whenever you look at this," he said, blushing slightly, "remember me – and my feelings for you." As Lisya looked in the mirror, the warm golden amber quietly glowed back at her.

Later, as their hired carriage approached the palace on Kronversky Prospekt, Lisya saw a long line of horse drawn conveyances, all shapes and sizes, waiting to unload their occupants at the entrance. She remembered the other time – long ago, it seemed – she had attended one of Kschessinskaya's soirees. Then she had entered at the rear, with the rest of the hired help. This time she would be at the front door, with the guests.

As their carriage pulled up at the entrance, Alexander Pavlovich carefully climbed out, trying not to wrinkle his new uniform. He held out his hand to Lisya, and helped her down with just a trace of awkwardness. The carriage drove off, leaving the two of them standing alone at the bottom of the huge staircase. For a long intimidating moment, they hesitated. Then Alexander Pavlovich offered Lisya his arm, and slowly they ascended the stairs.

Were it not for the war, Lisya mused wryly, *we would be using the back door.* The ball was in honor of all the officers leaving for the Front. Lisya glanced at her husband, as he stiffly led her toward the receiving line. His hair and beard were

235

grayer now than when they had married, but Alexander Pavlovich still carried himself with the quiet dignity which had won her respect years ago.

To Lisya's surprise, Kschessinskaya actually knew who they were. In the spirit of wartime camaraderie, she politely inquired about Tatiana and mentioned friends who were patients of Alexander Pavlovich. Then they were ushered into the huge ballroom.

Together they surveyed the glittering throng, anxiously looking for some other drab spots toward which to gravitate. Instinctively, Lisya started toward the orchestra. En route they encountered some other doctor-officers and their nervous wives, all of them trying unsuccessfully not to gawk. After exchanging pleasantries, Lisya led them to the refreshments. As she passed the orchestra, Olga waved gaily with her bow. As before, Lisya helped herself liberally to caviar and numerous other delicacies piled on the tables. All the doctors and their wives did, too, their attempts at nonchalance only slightly more successful than their efforts not to stare. Though she was careful not to overdo this time, Lisya also had some champagne. Glass in hand, she turned her attention to the crowd in the ballroom. She recognized several prominent aristocrats from their boxes at the Maryinsky, and of course the ubiquitous grand dukes always following after Kschessinskaya. As usual, the men were covered with medals and the women dripped with diamonds. While the presence of less exalted guests like themselves added some democratic overtones, the scene was not much different from what she had seen years ago.

Except for the swords. Men in full dress uniform always wore ornate swords. Before, they had simply been part of the costume. But now, their real purpose leaped out at her. Few of these elaborate blades, she knew, would be carried to the Front, but the realization of what they symbolized suddenly conjured up bloody images of Vladimir skewered on a German sabre. She shuddered and looked for Alexander Pavlovich.

Two glasses of champagne later, she reflected with wry satisfaction that she was no longer intimidated by all this brilliant plumage. *When it's time*, she thought sadly, *we'll all shed the same blood and the same tears.*

Just then, the orchestra struck up a waltz. Alexander Pavlovich was bowing gallantly before her, asking her to dance. Steering her carefully out onto the floor, at first they stayed in a corner, inscribing small tight circles with self-conscious feet. Slowly, slowly, the circles grew larger, as memories of their life together rose up fondly and swirled gently around them. Imperceptibly, they softly spiraled to the center of the ballroom. All around them, other couples blazed and sparkled.

But looking at her husband's face, Lisya knew that for him she was the only woman in the room. The deep quiet glow in his eyes matched the beads of her necklace, and she relaxed into the warm amber which seemed to envelop her. As they danced on and on, caressed by golden spheres of loving trust, the glitter of the crowd faded. Lisya knew she had no regrets. She would not trade her amber for all of Kschessinskaya's diamonds.

Ж Ж Ж

Vladimir's song lasted all the way into East Prussia. Everywhere the train stopped, the troops were met with bands and flags. And when at last they disembarked and lined up, Vladimir could hardly contain his excitement. Finally, the endless ranks of soldiers in long-skirted greatcoats marched forward. At the head of his regiment, Vladimir marched with the choir, singing the regimental marching song like a long-caged falcon soaring into flight. And when, after they had made camp for the night, he looked out on campfires burning like icon lamps in front of the tents, he felt an inner harmony he had not known since leaving his father's church.

Before long, however, the troops were afflicted with the inevitable muddle of a huge army on the march. For several days, they marched along the railroad tracks. As empty trains rattled mockingly by, Vladimir felt heavy packstraps cutting into his shoulders and stiff boots carving up his feet.

Many of his comrades began dragging their rifles like useless sticks and took off their hot boots. Slung around their necks on pieces of twine, they reeked of unwashed feet. Resolutely, Vladimir kept his rifle at his shoulder and his boots on.

By the third day, most of the regiments were straggling badly, their officers fruitlessly trying to sort out strays. Wagon trains and herds of cattle driven along by the supply corps became entangled in the ragged column of men. Steadfastly Vladimir exhorted his battalion to maintain discipline, his formidable bulk and awesome voice keeping many of them in line.

But on the seventh day, after covering ten miles, the profusely sweating column stopped on a path in the middle of a forest. The men threw themselves down to rest in the shade. Worried- looking officers galloped back and forth. Finally, amidst much creaking and shouting and lashing of horses, the entire column turned around.

Stomachs were rumbling and the sun was setting, well past the time when they should have bivouacked for the night. But back they marched over the same road and through the same stretch of forest. Vladimir's comrades began muttering that the officers were Germans in disguise, intent on driving them to exhaustion before they had even started fighting. But obediently they retraced their steps and finally made camp in the same place as the night before. It was almost morning by the time anyone got to sleep.

A few hours later, they gulped down breakfast and marched back onto the same road. After an hour or so, the column halted. For the rest of the morning, they stood at attention under the blazing sun. Finally, at high noon, the whole brigade turned around again and set off on another road heading back in the same direction. Except that this road was narrower and in much worse shape. All the bridges had been blown up, causing lengthy detours as the troops hauled themselves and their equipment up and down steep embankments. Dripping with sweat, they also discovered that the Germans had filled all the wells near the road with refuse.

All of these trials Vladimir endured with religious stoicism. Vaguely he reasoned that it was some sort of test. And when, finally, they approached the Front, he felt that his Great Moment was at last near. All around them, artillery droned. Shells flew high above their heads, hitting unknown targets. To Vladimir it sounded oddly familiar, and to this strangely compelling music he marched to the altar of war.

Suddenly the nervous stutter of machine gun fire erupted. Bullets began piercing the treetops, whistling loudly. Some ricocheted off hard birch trunks, twisting and turning and shrieking unbearably. And then the earth was disemboweled by a massive explosion. As the shells started screaming straight at them, Vladimir and his comrades dived into the nearest trench. Shaken, deafened, showered with earth and whining splinters, they were nearly overcome by the clinging reek of imminent death. A black, smoking, pounding night suddenly obliterated the sun and descended them all into Hell. On and on the bombardment raged. Huddled in the trench, Vladimir felt surrounded by terror. But like rocks carved by glaciers, all the peasants in uniform sat it out.

Abruptly, the firing stopped. And then, slowly, up the hill marched the enemy in ugly spiked helmets. Vladimir's shoulder itched for his rifle butt, and he stood up in line with his comrades, emptying his magazine, reloading, aiming, firing, picking a new target, cheering as the attackers fell.

The Germans began to falter. Slowly they retreated under the fury of Russian fire. And then, finally, the shooting stopped. In the silence which followed, Vladimir felt a bursting exaltation unlike anything he had ever experienced. Stepping

238

over corpses and bumping into wounded, he walked to the end of the trench and climbed out. The ground was littered with bloody bandages and shrapnel balls. A man was crawling in front of him, another was clutching his bandaged head, still another was sitting down, pulling off his boot and pouring the blood out of it like water from a jug. A young soldier lay staring up with lifeless eyes. None of this registered in Vladimir's mind. All around him the earth was bathed in a peculiarly lucid beauty. Never had life seemed so precious and wonderful. As he walked slowly over to a battered tree and sat down under it, Vladimir felt that he had found what he sought.

Ж   Ж   Ж

As the ecstasy of victory faded, Vladimir longed for another chance to rediscover the altered consciousness of that first battle. He was soon to get his wish – again and again. But all he found was the despair of defeat…

He remembered charging out of a trench with nothing but a bare bayonet, and being knocked down by a giant blinding pain. Emerging from the heavy blackness which engulfed him, he saw birds circling in the sky, swooping down and crying excitedly in a dozen different voices. Turning his head to the sound of a nearby movement, he looked into the gentle helpless-looking muzzle of a bay horse. It was still in harness, dragging the traces of the cart from which it had broken free. Exhausted and hungry, it was wandering hopelessly, head hanging down. Reaching feebly at the horse, Vladimir cried out in pain. The horse shied and ran off, nervously skirting the corpses of other horses lying with legs pointed stiffly into the air, bellies disemboweled. Insects buzzed greedily over the rotting entrails.

Gradually, Vladimir perceived that, on the field in front of him, hundreds of other horses were wandering about in painful confusion. Some were wounded. A pair with a broken draft bar between them stumbled aimlessly. On one side of the field, German soldiers were rounding up captured horses; on the other side, they were lining up a column of Russian prisoners. Those too badly wounded were being shot. Wounded prisoners who could walk were leaning on comrades. The unwounded were harnessed to captured artillery.

Along the road rattled a crude tumbril pulled by a team of draft horses. On it rode several Russian generals, sitting dejectedly on a bench. A German general stopped the cart and motioned toward four automobiles parked nearby. With shamefaced relief, the Russian generals acknowledged the gesture of their German colleague, and climbed down from the humiliating hay cart into the comfort of the cars. As they drove off, the other prisoners were fenced into a makeshift cage of barbed wire.

Vladimir's anger was temporarily submerged by the more urgent need to avoid being shot or penned up. Ignoring the pain in his shoulder, he crawled slowly through an avenue of bloated horses and buzzing flies to the shelter of the nearby forest. Breathing heavily, he stood up against a gnarled old tree, hesitated uncertainly, and then plunged shakily off in what he hoped was the direction of Russia.

After walking slowly for several hours, he heard a strange roaring sound. Climbing with difficulty up a long hill, he at last looked down on a scene of massive chaos. At the entrance to a small bridge across a narrow but swift river, two roads converged. On each of these roads were large remnants of the Russian army, all intent on retreating from the Germans. The bridge had become a bottleneck of heavy artillery, ammunition wagons, men on horseback and troops on foot, all trying to cross at once. Horses which had collapsed, exhausted in their shafts, were being unharnessed and shot. Wagons entangled, one of them ramming into the team in front, killing a horse. Over the frightened neighing, men screamed at each other and waved their bayonets.

Steadying himself, Vladimir looked across the river to the top of the bank on the far side. It had a familiar, battered look. Suddenly he recognized it as the site of an earlier battle. Then, thousands of Russians had been spent pushing the Germans a few miles west. Now, thousands more were crowding and threatening their way across a tiny bridge so that the Germans could push the Russians back east.

Vladimir sighted comrades from his regiment and hurried to catch up. Eventually they fought their way across the bridge and back into the forest. Gradually, however, it became clear that the Russian army had been outflanked by carefully planned German pincers. To break out of the encirclement, they would have to leave the forest. But this the Germans would not allow; each time the retreating Russians emerged into open country, they were met with enfilading fire of devastating artillery. In defense, they had little more than their bayonets. At each bitterly contested roadblock Russian ranks grew thinner. Finally, in the desperate hope of slipping through a crack somewhere, Vladimir and what was left of his battalion took off across the forest on their own. On an improvised stretcher of overcoat and rifles, they took turns carrying a soldier too wounded to walk. Next to him lay the furled colors of their regiment. On and on they struggled,

240

until they reached the heart of the forest. When they stopped to rest, they noticed that the man on the stretcher was dead.

Slowly, the survivors dug a shallow grave and laid their comrade in it. One arm in an improvised sling, Vladimir silently picked up the tattered flag, held it over the grave, and then laid it beside the sturdy peasant body. The slain soldier had been one of many sent to the front unarmed, told by commanding officers to scrounge among the dead for weapons. And yet, like the others, he had fought with extraordinary bravery, often meeting machine-gun fire with bayonet and little else.

The war had not penetrated this far into the forest. The trees were unscarred and it was marvelously quiet. As the men gathered around the grave, Vladimir turned to the setting sun and, in the strong deep voice of his grandfather, intoned to the high pine tops: "In peace let us pray to the Lord!"

"*Gospodi pomilui.*" The others crossed themselves and bowed to the east. "Lord, have mercy."

On and on, Vladimir chanted the familiar, still beloved liturgy of his boyhood. And as he did, he knew that he was burying his faith in what he had been brought up to respect.

"That the Lord our God may take him into the place of light and plenteousness and peace, where all the righteous repose, let us pray to the Lord."

As he heard his own voice echo back, Vladimir despaired of ever finding such a place.

Later, plodding gloomily behind the stolid backs of his comrades, Vladimir brooded on how like Russia they were – inexhaustibly strong, but governed by a pack of fools. And he resolved that he would not rest until his people had the government they deserved.

Ж   Ж   Ж

When he finally reported to his assigned medical unit, Alexander Pavlovich was shocked. Entering the filthy field hospital, he was almost overcome by the thick stench of blood and putrefaction. The commandeered manor house was overflowing with sick and wounded men, lying hungry on dirty straw, amidst snow drifts blowing in broken windows. Discovering some cholera victims, he immediately galvanized what staff he had into isolating the contagious cases and cleaning up the wards. He then sent his orderly – a resourceful peasant of indeterminate age – to the local village, and two of the nurses to a nearby convent. Within a few days, the windows were fixed and the hungry patients fed. He himself did what he could to ease the pain of those he examined on his interminable rounds.

Late one freezing night, just as he thought his hospital under control, there was a knock at the door. In walked a frozen soldier with a bandaged arm. After some hot tea by a warm stove, the exhausted man answered the doctor's questions.

"Where did you come from?"

"The Front."

"How far is it?"

"About thirty kilometers."

"How long have you been walking?"

"About ten hours – I'm not sure." The soldier winced as Alexander Pavlovich examined his wound. The dressing was soaked with blood, and a bullet had broken the bone.

"When was this put on?"

"Back there, near the trenches, a medic put it on."

"And you didn't get a fresh dressing anywhere else?"

"No. I didn't see a light anywhere until the lantern in your window."

The wounded man made no sound as Alexander Pavlovich attempted to splint his shattered arm. He smiled gratefully at the nurse who brought him more tea, this time laced with wine. Soon other freezing soldiers began trickling in and huddling by the stove. Like the first arrival, they were all able to walk. And like their comrade, they, too, did not cry out as Alexander Pavlovich tried to fix what was left of their arms. Trying hard to detach himself from the mangled flesh, he knew with sickening sureness that there would be many more – and much worse – before the night was over. And that many of the wounded would never make it this far.

Almost two days later, he finally emerged from the operating room, numb from the violent parade of overwhelming human agony and bodies shattered too horrendously to mend. Men with guts hanging out, brains spilling out of skulls, arms and legs smashed and amputated – what demon had created weapons which could wreak so much destruction!

Exhausted though he was, Alexander Pavlovich could not sleep. Waiting for the accumulated tension to subside, he walked into one of the wards and sat down next to the nurse on duty. She wore a white kerchief which, by kerosene lamplight, seemed to resemble a veil. At the end of the ward, a priest was administering extreme unction to a dying man whose face he had covered with his stole.

"I believe, O Lord, and I confess…" Alexander Pavlovich knew the priest had intoned those words at least as many times in the last few days as he had wielded his scalpel. When he finally fell into exhausted sleep, Alexander Pavlovich dreamed of his wedding. Lisya was wearing a nurse's kerchief and her father was giving him last rites.

Ж　Ж　Ж

Alexander Pavlovich sat in a medical van, trying unsuccessfully to catch up on sleep. His unit, en route to another station, was trapped in a traffic jam. Vehicles before and behind had not moved for hours. There was no way around except on foot; impassable mud lined both sides of the narrow road. There was nothing to be done but wait, as hours dragged and the infantry slogged by through the muck.

How typical this was of the whole war! Nothing ever seemed to get where it was needed. And no one ever had enough of what was necessary to do what had to be done. While German artillery rained torrents of huge shells, Russian guns were rationed to a few rounds per day. No gas masks were distributed. Instead, troops were told to urinate on their handkerchiefs and knot them around their heads during poison gas attacks. Many regiments had bayonets but no rifles; some were even worse off. Even so, millions of peasants charged enemy trenches, ordered into battle with little purpose. "We don't want to die with sticks in our hands!" cried an army of men dying in vain. Wounded German prisoners complained of having to burrow through mounds of Russian corpses in order to get a clear field of fire against still more assaulting waves.

Whenever he had a few hours to himself, Alexander Pavlovich wrote long despairing letters to Lisya about the spectacular disorganization, the horrendous losses, the disastrous retreats. Only then did he allow himself to shed bitter tears for the barefoot soldiers fighting without guns.

"We belong to the Kutuzov tradition," he wrote one cold night, when the war had dragged on far longer than anyone had dreamed possible. "Patient as donkeys, a bit slow maybe, but we win in the end by sheer tenacity and imperturbable acceptance of everything. But I wonder if, this time, they have pushed the Russian people too far. This, I think, is how the war will finally end: Our peasants will thrust their bayonets into the ground and leave."

The marooned column finally lurched slowly forward, into the thunder of artillery not far off. Alexander Pavlovich knew it was only a matter of time – and not much – until they would all be heading in the opposite direction in retreat. And not long after reaching the field hospital to which he had been reassigned, he was told to organize its evacuation.

Somehow, they found transport for the most serious cases. Everyone else, including the staff, walked. Except for one motorcar, the motley procession of carts, vans, and wagons was pulled by tired hungry looking horses; the wounded groaned in delirium as they jolted along the rutted road. Around them flooded rapidly retreating troops – first the artillery, then the infantry. Coming upon a railway track, Alexander Pavlovich turned his group off the road and followed the railroad. Eventually they found an abandoned station, in which more than a hundred wounded had been left. Miraculously, the station switchboard was still operational and one of the walking wounded was a telephone operator.

"Call the station master up the line," ordered Alexander Pavlovich. "Tell him we have seriously wounded men and need a train to move them. Understand?"

"Yes, sir. We need a train for the wounded."

After organizing his staff to tend to the new patients, Alexander Pavlovich returned to the switchboard.

"They promised to send a train, sir."

"Good."

"Glad to be of service, sir!"

Alexander Pavlovich nodded and went back to work. When he later returned to the switchboard, the operator was frowning.

"Sir, they said there aren't any closed cars, just open flatcars. And they would have to find them. And the locomotive is gone, but it will return, they said."

"Well, we'll wait –"

They waited a long time, but no train came. The operator kept calling, but no one answered. Finally Alexander Pavlovich sent his most persuasive paramedic in the car. After several hours, the telephone operator motioned excitedly.

"Sir, they want to talk to you."

Alexander Pavlovich picked up the receiver. It was his envoy. "The train is leaving now," the voice crackled over the line.

Just as he was announcing the good news, two more wounded soldiers came stumbling wearily up the road. Breathlessly, they begged for a wagon to go back for comrades who could not walk. Two of the orderlies volunteered to go instead. As Alexander Pavlovich dressed their wounds, he questioned the new arrivals about the condition of those left behind. From what they said, he guessed that several would need immediate surgery. Moreover, he calculated that the distance back to the stranded soldiers was farther than the distance to the railroad station from which the train was due to arrive. And the sound of artillery fire was coming steadily closer.

As they all awaited the train, Alexander Pavlovich paced the platform, pausing periodically to gaze thoughtfully at the stars. Finally, he went into the station master's deserted little office and closed the door. Taking out the last sheet of paper from his medical bag, he began to write.

A few hours later, the train arrived with ten open flatcars. They loaded the wounded, doing what was possible to keep them warm. Just as the train was about to leave, Alexander Pavlovich stepped back onto the platform.

"Ask them to send another train back for the rest of us," he said to his next-in-command. The younger doctor looked at him with dismay. "And please get this to my wife – somehow," he added quickly, handing him a letter.

As the train pulled slowly away, Alexander Pavlovich saluted once, and then watched it disappear up the track. He was all alone on the platform. As he looked up at the stars again, he heard himself repeating the oath he had sworn as a young doctor. He smiled sadly, and sat down calmly to wait.

Ж   Ж   Ж

"Don't take your boots off on the train," Elena said to Mischa, embracing him firmly. "Someone might steal them."

Mischa nodded, smiling bravely, and kissed his wife and children. Then he disappeared into the mass of uniformed peasants herded aboard the crowded troop train.

Father Ivan had read the declaration of war in church, and then posted it in the churchyard. Though the announcement proclaimed Russia's mission to liberate Slavic Christians in the Balkans from Turkish oppression, no one in Derevnia could understand why it was necessary to fight Germany and Austria, too.

There was no cheering. Nor did they discuss the war. Like famine and plague, of course, no one welcomed it. But the people of Derevnia accepted the war – and the conscription orders issued by the district commandant – as they did everything else. It was not for them to question the Will of God.

On the other hand, no one volunteered. One of Marfa's boys even shot off the big toe on his right foot to avoid the draft. The commandant, alas, was not persuaded. A few weeks later, the unfortunate lad was still among those marched off to do their duty. The other peasants thought him foolish for wasting his toe, but no one called him a coward.

Mischa was not happy about leaving his farm and family, but he was determined to fight the war through to the finish. With the bearded and badly outfitted army of the Tsar, he moved westward across Russia into Poland. The motley horde dug few latrines and often drank water fouled by troops further upstream. They left dead animals rotting in their wake, and carried malaria, typhoid and typhus with them.

Finally, Mischa's regiment reached the front lines. Not far from the booming guns, they began to dig trenches. After digging all night in freezing drizzle, they were ordered into battle. Mischa's platoon put down their tools, clambered out of the trench, and fell into line – most of them without weapons.

"Are you wearing crosses?" shouted the officer.

"Exactly so, Sir!" they shouted back.

"Well, then – pray!" he roared.

A brief moment of silence, and they charged wildly forward. Soon they passed sprawling bodies of other bearded soldiers. Mischa saw those running ahead stoop down and grab guns from those fallen. Seeing a still armed corpse under a nearby tree, he dodged over and bent down quickly. As he loosened the rifle and ammunition pouch, the dead soldier stared up through him. Looking away quickly, Mischa ran forward again, catching up with his platoon.

After it was all over, and the Kaiser's troops had temporarily retreated, they scoured the battlefield for weapons and boots, blankets and tents and warm clothing. But the spiked German helmets they scorned.

"We don't need helmets," growled one of Mischa's comrades. "Our caps will do. Russians have thick skulls."

How many times this sequence was repeated, Mischa soon lost count. All he knew was that they were always cold and hungry. But they fought on, fording freezing rivers and shivering under their wet dirty overcoats. Most of them knew nothing about European politics or why the war was being fought, still less about what battle the army was fighting or even the objectives of their battalion. Yet they did not waver or run away.

Finally, they were ordered to cover the army's retreat. Doggedly they withstood the pounding German artillery. And then, when their meager supply of scavenged ammunition had been exhausted, they stood up and walked into enemy fire with silent deadly bayonets – not just once but three times. The Germans finally halted. Russian casualties were staggering; Mischa was among ten survivors who carried away their colors and the body of their colonel.

Like most of his comrades, Mischa suspected that his generals were fools – and was sure that his supply officers were thieves. He knew very well that boots which fell to pieces and biscuits filled with weevils were not supposed to be standard issue.

"Ah, if the Tsar only knew!" For surely the best friend of soldiers would correct these problems, if he learned of them. But the Tsar couldn't know everything; Mischa expected no relief. So he went on doing his duty, hoping that some day things might get better.

Mischa never forgot the day the Tsar reviewed the troops. He saw his own excitement reflected on the faces around him, as they greeted their "Little Father" with a long, enthusiastic shout which rolled out unendingly. Mischa truly envied those on whom the Tsar personally bestowed medals. Long after, that shining moment he glimpsed his sovereign's face glowed before him.

Even so, Mischa knew that the war was not going well. Sometimes he overheard recruits from the city complaining that it was somehow the peasants' fault – that the "big children" would not grow up, and so were poor candidates for the technical reforms required of modern armies. Mischa suspected they were right, but angry tears stung his eyes whenever he heard such talk. Whose fault was it that the peasants knew nothing of this modernization? And who was to blame that all they knew how to do was endure and die?

The war stalemated; the wanton bloodletting continued. Agitators began to infiltrate the troops. "They make fools of us, and even call us cattle," they murmured in gradually more willing ears. "Now, brothers, it's time for us to open our eyes and see who we are killing and for what."

Mischa tried not to listen, but the continual humiliation of the very men whose blood and courage were keeping the army going fanned the flames of his resentment. He began to bristle at having to shout "Glad to try, Sir!" when given orders they all knew were stupid. But more than anything, he resented the officers using the regimental singers for entertainment.

At first, Mischa had been proud to march at the head of the column, singing the cadence and encouraging the troops. And he had been flattered when their chorus had been asked to perform at the officers' club. The banquets, however, had long since degenerated into brawls, at which the singers were treated worse than trained bears.

And then, one night, they were ordered to march in on their hands and knees.

Mischa's face was blazing with shame as he entered, on all fours, with his still lustily singing chorus. The officers cheered raucously, throwing things and poking at them as if they were animals. Mischa's head pounded with humiliated rage, until finally they were allowed to leave.

Silently, Mischa walked to the forest at the edge of the camp, and sat down under a tree. He remembered all he had endured – the cold and hunger and privation, the wounds he had suffered, the countless times he had risked his life with comrades falling around him. And all without adequate weapons and equipment – without even simple thanks!

"What an incorrigibly resilient people we Russians are!" one of the agitators had sighed. "No disaster, no amount of bloodshed is ever enough to galvanize us out of our passive endurance."

Until now, Mischa thought suddenly.

He had done his duty, risked his life, given his all – and for what?

For the Tsar?

No. The Tsar could never approve of the humiliating behavior his loyal soldiers had just been subjected to.

Nor could he want to continue such a terrible, stupid, wasteful war!

Mischa looked up at the stars for a long time. Then he slowly stood, threw his bayonet into the earth, and started walking toward the Volga.

Ж   Ж   Ж

One step at a time, Alexander Pavlovich wearily extracted himself from the cold mud sucking at his boots. The guardhouse was not far, but every day the distance seemed greater and the urge to devour the bread in his pocket grew stronger. Relieved that he had resisted temptation for one more day, he stepped quickly inside the tattered tent which served as the hospital. Like the prison itself, it was improvised and inadequate. Even so, he was glad for the shelter it provided from the rain – which never seemed to stop. And his mission to the camp commandant had been successful. In return for treating the guards – many of whom weren't much better off than the prisoners – he had been given extra rations for the wounded. And even some clean bandages.

How long had he been here? It seemed an eternity since that night he had sent off the train and waited on the railway platform. After several hours, the wagon had returned with more wounded. As he had expected, many of them had required immediate surgery. As he worked to repair what he could of the carnage to which he would never grow accustomed, the sound of artillery grew louder – and closer. *Too many shells to be ours*, he thought, amputating yet another shattered limb.

Hours later, he emerged from the railway station to discover that he and his patients were surrounded by Germans. The commanding officer was not pleased with the human obstacles so inconveniently placed in the path of his advancing battalion. Young and inexperienced at giving orders, he was obviously uncertain what to do about this unexpected dilemma.

"These men are too injured to be moved," said Alexander Pavlovich, in as authoritative a voice as he could muster.

The young officer hesitated.

"And as you can see," continued Alexander Pavlovich boldly, "none of them are able to fight."

"But I can't just leave you here," protested the officer. "I have to take you prisoner."

"Yes, of course," agreed the doctor. "Just post a few guards, and we'll wait for you here."

"Well, no," Again the officer hesitated. "No, I don't think we can do that. You'll have to go to the prisoners' camp."

"And how far might that be?" asked Alexander Pavlovich.

"I don't know," snapped the officer, increasingly irritated at the situation.

"Perhaps you could send a few scouts to find out," suggested Alexander Pavlovich. "And have them bring back some wagons, too, for those unable to walk."

The young officer scowled, then grunted at a subordinate, who rode back to the waiting troops. After a brief conversation, two German soldiers walked briskly back down the road, obviously relieved to be heading away from the sound of exploding artillery shells.

Leaving a small detachment to guard the prisoners, the young commander reluctantly marched the rest of his squadron in the direction of what appeared to be the Front.

As Alexander Pavlovich had hoped, the scouts did not return until the next day. Somehow, they had even found a wagon and bony horse to pull it. As slowly as he dared, the doctor began to prepare for evacuation. Only one of the Germans stood guard; the others clustered about the stove inside the station. Though they were just as fatigued and almost as dirty as the retreating Russians, they were well armed with new rifles and plenty of ammunition. And all of them had gas masks, the doctor noted with envy, remembering all the soldier peasants he had seen with insides as ravaged as their outsides.

Not eager to leave the warmth of the stove, the guards allowed Alexander Pavlovich to stall the evacuation for as long as they dared. But when the artillery barrage again crescendoed in their direction, the corporal in charge reluctantly ordered the doctor to start moving his patients.

"If the commander finds us still here," he said, frowning, "he will order us to shoot all who can't walk."

And so began yet another retreat. It made little difference, Alexander Pavlovich reflected ruefully, that they were now prisoners. His silently suffering patients were in no more pain and died no more quickly. And he felt no more – or less – frustrated at not being able to save them.

But by the time they arrived at where the scouts had last seen the POW camp, it had moved. And when the new site was finally located the following day, Alexander Pavlovich realized that hell, indeed, was relative. Even the worst field hospital now seemed almost tolerable by comparison. For whereas before, he had been appallingly under-equipped and woefully under-supplied, he had still been able to salvage some of the shattered bodies which passed unendingly before him. But here, there was nothing. Nothing at all.

And so, Alexander Pavlovich had finally resolved that he would at least do what he could to enable the men in his care to die as well as was possible in such circumstances. But the inevitability of this decision did not lessen the pain of reaching it. Reversing what was, after years of medical practice, a virtually automatic habit of trying to heal was hard enough. But recognizing – even welcoming – death as an ally confronted him with an acute spiritual dilemma. How could one befriend Death without also meeting God? But if Death was the Enemy, how could one make peace with its Author?

Standing at the entrance to the "hospital," Alexander Pavlovich braced himself for the seemingly interminable walk between the rows of cold hungry men lying on nothing but straw. At the end of the aisle was a small alcove, set apart by a curtain of remnants cut from ragged overcoats issued when the war had commenced so long ago.

Behind the curtain was a crude wooden platform, on which a man could lay down out of the mud. From a post at the foot of the bed hung a small icon of The Virgin. Nodding to the peasant stretched out on the plank, Alexander Pavlovich sat down on a rickety box next to him. Carefully he removed a filthy bandage from the man's festering hand and replaced it with one of the clean ones the commandant had given him. The man smiled gratefully, then gazed at the icon and feebly crossed himself. When the doctor offered him a large piece of bread – part of the extra rations negotiated from the commandant – the man's other hand involuntarily darted out to grab it. But after one ravenous bite, he stopped. Chewing very slowly, he looked longingly at the bread held very gently in his clean bandaged hand.

"Thank you," he said, his voice almost too weak to hear, "but no – give it to the others."

As the dying soldier slipped in and out of consciousness throughout the night, Alexander Pavlovich sat at his side, determined that even if he could not save him, he would at least not let him die alone. *He fears Death as much as I do,* pondered Alexander Pavlovich, as he always did on these vigils. *But he does not regard it as the Enemy.* And, once again, he was amazed – and deeply moved – by how unconditionally all these dying peasants accepted death as part of life. *They need a priest now – not a doctor.* And for just a moment, Lisya's father seemed to be sitting there, too, keeping vigil with him.

As Alexander Pavlovich's head fell forward on his chest, he jerked awake and rubbed his eyes. Checking the dying man's pulse, he knew it would not be much longer. Settling back on his makeshift stool, he reflected that lately Father Ivan's image was much in his mind, especially on nights such as this. He had always envied the priest's unwavering faith, so clearly the motive force of who he was. How comforting it would be to believe that God exists! And how much simpler everything would be if he knew what God was!

Just before dawn, the man died peacefully. In the pale light his body was briefly illumined, a gentle presence hovered momentarily. And suddenly Alexander Pavlovich *knew* that Death was no longer an obstacle to God.

All day long, he felt unaccountably tranquil, the turmoil in his soul gone. As he made his usual rounds, his heart swelled with gratitude for how much his dying patients had taught him. That he could not translate what it was into words – and did not even care to try – was as it should be.

That night he slept on the wooden plank in the alcove, and dreamed of Lisya and Katya. Joyful dreams of their happy life together, untroubled by the worry which had previously overwhelmed his images of them. How blessed his life had been! How marvelous the chance to love and be loved! How fortunate the opportunity to use his talents! And to have all this amid so much glorious music!

As dawn slipped into the alcove, Alexander Pavlovich saw his beloved Lisya sitting at the magnificent grand piano he had always wanted to give her. As her slender fingers caressed the keys, golden waves of melodic beauty enveloped him. And as her smile met his, the steadfastness of their love became pure harmony which completely filled his soul.

Ж   Ж   Ж

It was Sunday. They were strolling along the Neva. The sky was grey and threatening; Lisya clasped Katya's warm little hand in her own, trying to keep the clouds at bay.

Even with concert halls turned into hospitals and refugees pouring in, Petrograd's artistic life glittered. In the orchestra pit of the Maryinsky, Lisya's violin accompanied the still lavish operas and ballets; lessons with Madame were as demanding as ever. And, now that Katya was older, there was almost enough time to practice. Sometimes it was hard to remember the war.

Except, of course, for the absence of so many she loved. Besieged by a jumble of fears, only Katya kept Lisya from yielding to constant anxiety. Today she was determined to enjoy the outing, and smiled at her daughter, chattering brightly along with the river.

Suddenly Katya exclaimed with delight. Standing near the embankment was an organ grinder with a bizarrely painted hurdy-gurdy, smiling – as always – from under his hat of shabby but jaunty plumes. On his shoulder perched an exotic bird, who – for a kopek – would pull out a card with a fortune written on it. Katya held out her hand for the coin Lisya usually gave her. This time, however, there was a strange look on the face of her mother, who suddenly started walking rapidly in the opposite direction.

When they got home, there was a letter waiting. Katya watched her mother pick it up with trembling hands, walk into her father's study, and close the door. She stayed in there for a very long time.

My Dearest Wife,

I write to you from the eye of the hurricane, in a world gone mad. All around me, our troops are retreating in disorder. This time, I think, many of them will not stop. Nor can I condemn them. They have fought heroically and suffered magnificently – as our people always do – but for what? The government of the Tsar has betrayed them by its corruption and colossal mismanagement of this tragically pointless war. Mother Russia has sacrificed her children in vain. And yet so many still fight on – bleeding, dying, refusing to desert their duty. And so must I. Not for the Tsar, not even for Russia. But because I took an oath. As long as there are those who need my help, then here I must stay.

Though I have never been able to share it, I have always admired your father's faith. A man needs something bigger than himself to believe in. But I hoped that being a doctor would be prayer enough. And now, in the midst of all this suffering, I know that it is. The greater good I serve is as big as I need.

To look back on one's life and say "I did my duty, I made a noble vow and I kept my word" – ah yes, that is a fine thing. So do not weep for me.

My only regret, my beloved Lisya, is that I may have to leave you and Katya. Such joy and beauty you have graced me with – forgive me for never being able to tell you how much. But know that I have always loved you to the depth of my soul.

Do not let Katya forget me. If I do not return, tell her what her father lived – and died – for.

　　　　　Your loving husband,
　　　　　Alexander

Chapter 13: PETROGRAD

Petersburg – Petrograd – no longer glowed. As she walked glumly home from rehearsal, Lisya passed the equestrian statue of Peter the Great; street urchins were swarming all over the Bronze Horseman, hanging on the horse's tail, smoking under its belly.

Shivering, she focused on the orchestra's next performance, trying to push away the cold greyness which so often enveloped her these days. Only at the Maryinsky did she still find the brilliance which had once pervaded her city. Only its sparkling ballets and operas could make her forget.

Later that night, after Katya was asleep, Lisya paced restlessly in the dark living room, trying not to wonder why someone so tired could never sleep. As the darkness of the night deepened, she was startled by a quiet knock on the door. With an effort, she steadied her hands and lit a candle. Walking down the hall, she carefully averted her eyes from the forlorn door of the abandoned study.

"Who's there?" she asked tensely.

"Volodya," a familiar voice replied quietly.

"Volodya?" her fingers fumbled at the lock. Vladimir slipped through the door and quickly closed it behind him.

"Volodya?" Lisya's voice trembled as she stared at her brother. "Oh, Volodya!" She threw herself into his arms and wept. For a long, long time.

At last, they went into the kitchen. Vladimir sat down, Lisya brewed tea. When dawn broke, they were still sitting at the kitchen table talking.

After finally breaking out of the German encirclement, Vladimir told her, he had simply kept on walking. En route to Petrograd, he had persuaded others to follow his example.

"They didn't need much encouragement," he said sadly, "to stop being cannon fodder."

"How many have stopped fighting?" asked Lisya hopefully.

"More and more every day," replied Vladimir, "but not enough to end the war."

"And the ones who stay at the Front," asked Lisya, an edge in her voice, "Are they fools?"

"No," said Vladimir quietly. "No. Victims of misguided loyalty, yes. But no, not fools. Brave men who do their duty are never fools, no matter how foolish their cause."

"But what good can possibly come from so much unnecessary suffering!" exclaimed Lisya bitterly. "And why must so many good men be wasted!"

"Sometimes suffering brings out the best in people."

"Now you sound like Father!"

"He was right about some things," said Vladimir carefully. "Especially about knowing how to die."

Lisya gave her brother a searching look.

"Some of the soldiers I talked to, on my way to Petrograd, had escaped from a German POW camp." He paused, then continued gently. "They told me about a doctor there who saved their lives. And who helped those he couldn't save die in peace. And whose compassion – even in such a terrible place – enabled them to hold on to their humanity."

"And what..." Lisya struggled with the question. "And what happened... to this... doctor?"

"He, too, died in peace," replied Vladimir, taking her hand. "Everyone in the camp thought he was a saint. Even the German commandant."

"But he – the doctor – was an atheist!"

"Apparently not at the end."

Lisya was silent. "He wasn't a fool," she said finally.

"No," agreed Vladimir. "He died with courage and honor."

"But he didn't need to be a hero – or a saint!"

"True," Vladimir once again agreed, "but he needed to die well."

"And he certainly did," said Lisya at last.

"Yes," sighed Vladimir. "I hope I can do as well."

"I don't want *you* to be a saint, either!" exclaimed Lisya. "Just stay alive!"

A few days later, Lisya entered Alexander Pavlovich's study for the first time since his letter. The agonizing uncertainty was over. Somehow, she had known that Vladimir would return, just as she knew deep within that Alexander Pavlovich never would.

Once again, she took his last letter out of its worn envelope, noticing that one corner was smudged with blood. This time, however, she allowed the words on the wrinkled paper to enter her heart. Slowly she felt her husband's quiet, steadfast love embrace her as his earnest, utterly dependable image rose before her. How safe she had always felt with him!

But now...

Carefully she started sorting through his books and papers. As her husband's life as a physician unfolded before her, she began to understand that he had chosen to die as he had lived. And as her regret at his passing mounted, so did her respect for his life – and his death. Lovingly, she held each object, warmed by the memory of his touch and by gentle tears which bathed her, knowing that his spirit would never desert her.

Finally, she packed away the most important of his things in a large box. She marked it "For Katya," and put it under the desk. Then she put fresh bedding and blankets on the couch. That night Vladimir moved in.

As he unpacked his battered duffle bag, Katya stood at the door, watching with quiet concern.

"This is my father's room," she said finally, in a polite but nonetheless challenging voice.

"Yes, I know," said Vladimir, thinking how much the slant of her eyes and the arch of her eyebrows reminded him of Alexander Pavlovich. "I'm just using it for awhile."

"Why did he go away?" Katya had a way of asking questions that were as insistently straight as her thick, dark hair.

"Sometimes men have to," Vladimir replied uncomfortably, wondering how such a little girl could ask such difficult questions. "There's something they have to find."

"What is Father looking for?" Katya stepped inside the door and sat down on the couch.

"Your father is lucky. He's already found it." Vladimir sat down next to her. "He went away to make sure he didn't lose it."

"He's not coming back, is he?" Katya's eyes, big and dark, filled with tears.

"No," said Vladimir very quietly, gently putting his arm around her small shoulders.

"Now, who will tell me stories?" Katya's voice was forlorn.

"I will," answered Vladimir, his big voice suddenly husky. "Yes... I will."

Gratefully, the little girl leaned against his huge chest and relaxed in the haven of the strong arms shielding her.

Ж   Ж   Ж

257

"You need to talk to Katya," said Vladimir the next morning, "about her father."

"She's too young to understand," replied Lisya, startled by her brother's vehemence.

"No, she's not. She knows he's not coming back. And she needs to know why."

Stunned by the obvious truth of what he was saying – and by the realization that she had not considered Katya's feelings – Lisya retreated to her bedroom.

How could she have neglected something so important? How could she have ignored what was Katya's loss, too? How could she have been so distracted from her daughter's needs!

That afternoon she showed Katya the box.

"This is for you – from your father."

"Why isn't he coming back?"

"Because he had to go to the War."

"But he's not a soldier!" objected Katya.

"Doctors have to go, too."

"But doctors aren't supposed to hurt anyone!" argued Katya. "Father told me he had to promise never to hurt anyone before they let him be a doctor."

"And he kept that promise," assured Lisya. "Doctors don't fight. They take care of the soldiers when they get hurt fighting each other."

"Well, that's good!" Katya was obviously relieved. "The soldiers need someone to make them better."

"Yes, they do. And your father was a very good doctor."

Katya was silent for awhile, pondering.

"In a War, soldiers sometimes kill each other?" she finally asked. "Do they kill the doctors, too?"

"Not on purpose. But War is dangerous for everyone."

"Did Father get killed?"

"No. But he died trying to help some wounded soldiers."

"That was a brave thing to do."

"Yes, it was," agreed Lisya. "Your father was a brave man. And a very good man."

"I miss him." Two large tears spilled out of eyes so like her father's.

"So do I," replied Lisya, putting her arm around Katya.

"Does he miss us?"

"Yes, I'm sure he does. He loved us very much."

"But not as much as the soldiers he helped?"

"Well," began Lisya, hesitating as she considered how best to answer such a complex question. "He didn't help the soldiers because he loved them, but because it was his duty. And if he hadn't tried so hard to do his duty as a doctor, he wouldn't have been able to love us as much as he did."

"Why not?" asked Katya, perplexed.

"Because –" Lisya again hesitated, considering the question. "Because to be a good doctor, you have to believe in something bigger than yourself. And that makes you bigger inside."

"And there's room for more love?"

"Yes, that's exactly it."

"Did loving us help father do his duty?"

"Oh yes. Yes, of course."

"So we all helped the wounded soldiers," said Katya slowly, considering what that meant. "And did that make us bigger inside, too?"

"Certainly," Lisya nodded. "It's why we love each other so much. And why we miss him so much."

"Sometimes, it hurts to love."

"Yes, I know. But that makes us bigger, too."

"Sometimes I wish I could just be a little girl," sighed Katya.

"So do I," sighed Lisya, putting her other arm around her daughter.

Ж   Ж   Ж

That autumn, the thirteenth million were called to the colors. It was cold and wet. Winter came early, the worst Lisya could remember. Outside all the food shops were long lines. The black market flourished and prices soared. Yet even as Petrograd grew colder and hungrier, racing continued at the hippodrome and Kschessinskaya continued to blaze across the stage of the Maryinsky. Watching her from the orchestra pit, Lisya guessed that she was not suffering unduly from wartime shortages. Probably the rumors about her speculating on the black market were true.

As winter wore on, the incongruities mounted: The glittering boxes at the Maryinsky, the cloak-and-dagger doings of the revolutionaries, the millions dying heroically at the Front, the tens of millions going hungry at home. The always extreme conditions of life in Russia were surfacing and straining; the tsarist regime was creaking and groaning and foundering aimlessly.

Both Lisya and Vladimir knew that something momentous was coming. Exactly what it was, neither of them could say. That it would change their lives drastically and irrevocably – that, too, they knew. And so they waited, united for once in their uncertainty and fear and hope.

Ж   Ж   Ж

As news of Rasputin's death swept Petrograd, the streets became virtually impassable. Everywhere hordes of strangers were kissing each other and yelling that Russia had been saved from the AntiChrist. Crowds lined up outside the cathedrals to light candles in thanksgiving.

Rasputin had been assassinated. And, judging by the condition of his body, his assassins had not had an easy time of it. Massive doses of cyanide – enough to kill a whole regiment of *startsy* – had been followed by several bullets, one right through the heart. Rasputin had then been beaten and drowned in the Neva. Stories were already circulating that he had refused to stay dead, rising again and again to torment his terrified assassins. Rumor also had it that Rasputin's penis had mysteriously disappeared, and that several of his female disciples – including a few close to the Empress – had already enshrined it as a holy relic.

At the Maryinsky that night, the audience demanded to sing "God Save the Tsar." As her violin played along with the stirring anthem, Lisya wondered how long it would be so.

It soon became known that the assassins were aristocrats. Rasputin's power over the Empress had grown enormously. For many, it was easier to blame the fiasco of the war on his evil influence than to accept the incompetence of the Tsar's regime.

"The fools think they have saved the Tsar," Vladimir said sadly to Lisya, "that now Holy Russia will be victorious. But Rasputin was only one small worm in a rotten apple. Killing him has merely exposed the rest of a much bigger canker. And now they have no scapegoat."

Lisya handed him another cup of tea, wondering that her brother the revolutionary wasn't more jubilant about this blow to the enemy's camp.

"Rasputin wasn't what he claimed to be – or what others claimed he was," Vladimir mused thoughtfully, "but he was no fool. 'If they destroy me, Russia is finished.' That's what he said. 'They'll bury us together.'"

Lisya shuddered.

"I wonder…" Vladimir stared into his tea. "Perhaps he was right…"

Ж   Ж   Ж

As the darkness of the bitterly cold winter deepened, so did the hunger and misery. Lisya was hard pressed to find food and fuel; sometimes her family went to bed cold and hungry. And from Mariya Ivanovna she knew that things were much worse among workers in the Vyborg district.

Finally, the long lines of tired women waiting in front of empty food stores could stand no more. They erupted in a riotous demand for bread which spilled over the Liteiny Bridge and swept the city, refusing to be silenced. Soon factory workers carrying red banners were striking. When police attempted to restore order, army veterans in the crowd fought back.

Lisya kept Katya home from school. One day, dodging and ducking her way home from a partially successful food foray, she collided with a bread riot being dispersed by a troop of Cossacks. Running back into the alley from which she had just emerged, she watched in horror as a mounted Cossack charged by and plunged his sabre into a boy about Katya's age. The child crumpled into a bloody heap. Lisya ran back down the alley, made a wide detour and finally dashed into her apartment.

"Katya!" she called breathlessly, as she slammed the door behind her. "Katya! Katya!"

Alarmed, the little girl came running. Lisya threw her arms around Katya and held her close.

Neither of them went out again that day.

The bread riots went on. The business of the city came to a standstill; even the tramcars stopped running. The Tsar dissolved the Duma, and then left Petrograd.

The city was seething. Demonstrators surged into the center of the city and swelled throngs on the Nevsky Prospekt. Gesturing crowds in heavy winter coats and thick scarves streamed along the grey streets, exhorted by speakers shouting "Down with the War! Down with the War!"

Meanwhile, fighting broke out in the Vyborg district. That, too, swept across the Liteiny Bridge. Troops finally opened fire, leaving corpses strewn everywhere. As mounted police began firing at a crowd gathered along the Catherine Canal, a detachment of the Pavlovsky Regiment wandered into the zone of fire. Seeing the wounded falling around them, the Pavlovskys opened fire on the police. And so began the first of the mutinies. Soon the Volhynsky, Preobrazhensky, and Izmailovsky Regiments followed suit. By the next day, disorderly groups of soldiers were fraternizing openly with the working class crowd. Armed men dashed about the streets, finally going off with a roaring crowd to burn the prisons. The liberated political prisoners then led the swelling throng to the Tauride Palace.

Vladimir soon joined them. All around him rushed cars and trucks full of soldiers and workers and students. Everyone was extremely excited, shouting and waving. Near the entrance to the Palace, he saw motorcars being loaded with supplies. Men and women armed with machine guns were getting into them, amidst much shouting and confusion.

Vladimir pushed his way into the main entrance and elbowed his way toward the hall on the left where the first session of the Soviet of Workers' Deputies was trying to elect a presiding committee. Over two hundred were already present, and new groups kept pouring in. Several soldiers suddenly interrupted and demanded the floor. Standing on stools, rifles in hands, they told of what was happening in their regiments.

"We're from the Volhynsky Regiment... the Pavlovsky... the Lithuanian... the Keksholm... the Preobrazhensky... the Chasseurs... the Izmailovsky... the Finnish... the Grenadiers..."

The name of each regiment roused a storm of applause.

"We had a meeting... We refuse to serve against the people anymore... We're going to join with our brothers to defend the people's cause... We would lay down our lives for that... Long live the Revolution!" Each delegate's voice was extinguished by the throbbing roar of the assembly.

Then news arrived that the Petropavlovsk Fortress had surrendered without a shot. And then, that the naval base at Kronstadt had joined the Revolution. Vladimir cheered and cheered until his voice was gone.

At 4 AM, the Soviet recessed until noon. Vladimir wandered back to the Catherine Hall, where he found large groups of soldiers sitting on the floor. Their arms stacked next to them, they were eating bread and drinking tea that someone had somehow provided. Others were asleep, stretched out on the floor, huddled together for warmth. The floors were slippery with mud and snow, a cold draft chased mercilessly up and down the corridors. Everywhere was chaos and the reek of soldiers' boots. Outside, the square in front looked like a camp. Soldiers stood in groups around campfires; armored cars hung with red flags sputtered among cannon and machine guns.

Wearily, Vladimir went back to the hall where the Soviet had been meeting; tired workers and soldiers were now dozing in empty deputies' chairs. Finally finding an unoccupied corner in the gallery, he stretched out on the floor under his coat and fur hat. For the first time in months, he slept soundly.

He awoke, hours later, to a strange sound. Over the chairman's rostrum was Repin's portrait of Nicholas II. Two soldiers had their bayonets hooked into the canvas and were ripping it down.

People were already crowding back into the Palace. Deputies were sitting on chairs and benches, at the tables and along the walls. In the aisles and at each end of the hall, people of every description were standing. As afternoon became evening, the crowds became so dense it was difficult to push through. Those who had chairs stood up to see over those in front. A few hours later the chairs vanished and everyone, pouring with sweat, was standing tightly squeezed together.

Like in church on Easter, thought Vladimir. His eyes were drawn to the empty frame over the rostrum. With the crown still above, it gaped at him in silent reproach.

A few nights later, another crowd advanced on the Tauride Palace. Several thousand men in full formation were marching along the street, keeping ranks in spite of obvious exhaustion. They all had rifles and cartridge belts slung over their shoulders. There were no officers in sight.

Falling in step next to them, Vladimir learned that they were troops sent to put down revolution. They had, however, stayed loyal only as far as the railway station in Petrograd. Now they were joining the Revolution. Their commanders had vanished.

When the Soviet was not in session, Vladimir usually hung around the room where the Executive Committee was headquartered. Sometimes he answered the constantly ringing phone.

"Tsarkoe Selo Railway Station speaking – Commissar of the Committee of railwaymen," he heard, as he picked up the receiver one morning. "Grand Duke Michael Alexandrovich in Gatchina is asking for a train to go to Petersburg."

"Tell *Citizen* Romanov," Vladimir replied, "that he can buy a ticket and take a public train to *Petrograd* like everyone else."

He hung up the phone with a deeply satisfied smile.

That same afternoon, he overheard a conversation between one of the Executive Committee members and an elegant lady who looked familiar. She was accompanied by a resplendently dressed gentleman with magnificent moustaches and a bland face. The lady, complaining irately, was obviously distressed. The official finally looked questioningly at her companion.

"This is Madame Kschessinskaya," he said, bowing, "*Artiste* of the Imperial Theatres. I am her agent."

Kschessinskaya, it turned out, had come to protest about her house. It was, she insisted tearfully, being plundered by a vast mob who had taken residence there.

"Where is your house?" the official asked, obviously uncomfortable.

"On the Embankment," she replied, offended and incredulous. "You can see it from Trinity Bridge, you know."

"Come now!" added the agent. "The house is very well known in Petersburg."

The official, obviously not a ballet fan, looked embarrassed and tried to pretend that he, too, was familiar with it. "And who has occupied it?"

"It has been occupied by the –" Kschessinskaya paused, as though what she was about to utter would defile her – "by the Socialist Revolutionary Bolsheviks."

Vladimir was nearly overcome by a huge laugh rumbling up and threatening to erupt. He walked quickly away; Lisya had told him too many stories about the awesome Matilda. Out of range of her wrath, he exploded in uproarious laughter.

Two weeks later, the trams started running again; the streetcars came out decorated with red banners. On his way home at last, Vladimir waved at them and cheered.

Ж   Ж   Ж

Eventually, someone got around to the business of what to do about the Tsar. The new Provisional Government sent a few emissaries to Nicholas II, who quietly abdicated in favor of his brother Michael. The next day, Grand Duke Michael abdicated – period. The news created much excitement in the Tauride Palace and all over the city.

After that, the closest the Provisional Government ever came to a leader was Alexander Kerensky, a socialist lawyer who burst in and out of rooms like a tornado. Vladimir had heard that Kerensky's nickname among the Secret Police was "Speedy." Before the Revolution, he had been fond of rushing conspiratorially through the streets, leaping in and out of moving tramcars. Police spies were unable to keep up with him

None of this had prepared Kerensky – or anyone else –to make order out of the chaos which now reigned in the Tauride Palace. In addition to thousands engaged in clamorous mass meetings, the Regiments also began lobbying in force. First the Volhynsky Regiment, bands playing and flags flying, marched in to greet the Provisional Government. The next day the Pavlovskys appeared in similar array. And then the Semyonovskys and the Preobrazhenskys and the Ismailovskys and the Lithuanians and the Third Rifles and Petrogradskys and on and on. The *Marseillaise* rolled out continuously, punctuated by mighty choruses of "hurrah!"

Even more compelling was the testimony of simple soldiers. One day, a tired peasant climbed on the platform dragging a dirty sack. "We decided to bring you the most precious things we had," he said with weary dignity. "In this sack are all the medals we won with our blood. I've been sent to give them to you, together with our sacred, unbreakable vow to lay down our lives for the freedom that has been won, and to serve the Revolution." The Tsar was gone, but clearly the peasants would still fight for Holy Mother Russia.

Another day, a good natured lad cajoled his way onto the platform and described how the trenches had greeted the Revolution. "We began yelling 'Hurrah!' and singing – what's it again? – 'Arise, you prisoners...' Well! The Germans were only about as far away as that. They heard us and yelled over 'Hey, what have you got over there?' We yelled back 'We've got a revolu-u-ution! No more Tsar!' They began singing and yelling 'Hurrah!' Then we yelled over 'Hey – what about you? Now you can get rid of that – what's his name?'"

As the crowd laughed and cheered, Vladimir began grappling with the dilemma which faced them all – that revolution born out of war weary disillusionment might need to keep on fighting to defend itself. But against whom and what, he was not sure.

A frenzy of chauvinism swept the city – and beyond – as Kerensky proclaimed a new offensive against the Germans."In the name of the salvation of free Russia," read his order to the army," you will go where your Government sends you. On your bayonets you will bear peace, truth, and justice. You will go forward, kept firm by supreme love for country and the Revolution."

Vladimir was in anguish. Of course he would fight for the Revolution. Of course he would give his life to defend Russia. But was continuing the same war which had seemed so pointless under the Tsar any more noble now? True, the Provisional Government had declared its aims to be "without annexations or indemnities." Supposedly that meant Russia was simply defending herself – and the Revolution – against the imperialistic designs of other nations. But was Germany any more of a threat than France or Britain? Surely the German soldiers were as sick of the trenches as the Russians were! Wouldn't it make more sense for them to get rid of the Kaiser? Then everyone could go home.

And yet, Vladimir knew that he must fight for something, that the Revolution – and the Motherland –must be defended. But somehow he sensed that Kerensky had fingered the wrong enemy.

One night, as Vladimir was walking home, a lanky figure staggered toward him out of the darkness. A strange looking man was waving his arms and singing drunkenly. "Let us pra-a-y to the Lord," he chanted in the basso profundo of an archdeacon, "for pea-a-a-ce for the wo-o-rld, without annexations or inde-e-emnities…"

Ж   Ж   Ж

The throng in front of the Finland Station blocked the whole square. Even the trams could hardly get through. Innumerable red flags surrounded a huge banner embroidered in gold: "The Central Committee of the Revolutionary Socialist-Democratic Workers' Party." Troops were in formation near the entrance. From one of the side streets, a mounted searchlight cut through the crowd, abruptly projecting stark strips of the city.

Through the crush of tightly packed people, Vladimir slowly pushed his way inside the station. In the room where the Tsar used to wait for the Imperial train, he saw representatives of the Soviet waiting behind heavily bolted glass doors. Soldiers ready to present arms were lined up along the platform. Banners and triumphal arches were everywhere, adorned in red and gold revolutionary slogans. At the end of the platform, where the railway car was expected to stop, stood a band and a group of Bolsheviks holding flowers.

The train was very late. When it finally arrived, a thunderous *Marseillaise* boomed forth amid ringing shouts of welcome.

"Please, Comrades, please! Make way there! Comrades, make way!" several Bolshevik heralds shouted. And then, marching along the platform to the *Internationale*, under the arches and between the troops, Lenin came at last. Between a round cap and an enormous bouquet of flowers, Vladimir glimpsed a guarded but alert face with a short clipped beard. Suddenly the momentum of the crowd propelled the honored one into the waiting room of the Tsar, where he nearly collided with the welcoming committee from the Soviet.

"Comrade Lenin," intoned its representative, "in the name of the Petrograd Soviet and the whole Revolution, we welcome you back to Russia."

Lenin shifted the incongruous bouquet to his other arm.

"Dear Comrades, soldiers, sailors, and workers!" he said in a loud voice, as he turned toward the crowd. "I am happy to greet the victorious Russian Revolution, and greet you as the vanguard of the worldwide proletarian army."

Vladimir listened intently, noticing the roll of Lenin's guttural r's.

"The piratical imperialist war is the beginning of civil war throughout Europe," Lenin continued. "The hour is not far distant when the people will turn their arms against their own capitalist exploiters. The worldwide Socialist Revolution has already dawned. Germany is seething. Any day now the whole of European capitalism may crash. The Russian Revolution has prepared the way and opened a new epoch. Long live the worldwide Socialist Revolution!"

To another *Marseillaise* and the shouts of thousands, among red and gold banners illuminated by searchlight, Lenin was carried out of the station. Before he got into the waiting car, he climbed onto its hood and made another speech. Then, surrounded by bands and flags and workers' detachments and army units and the enormous crowd, Lenin's armored car crossed the Sampson Bridge and moved slowly on to Bolshevik headquarters. At every street corner, the triumphant procession stopped for impromptu rallies.

Vladimir flowed with the noisy crowd all the way down Kronversky Prospekt, where it finally halted in front of Kschessinskaya's Palace, recently appropriated by the Bolsheviks. It, too, was decked out in red flags and all the lights were burning. Soon Lenin appeared on the second floor balcony to make another speech. By now hoarse, only remnants of his words drifted down to Vladimir: "shameless imperialist slaughter... extirpation of the nations of Europe for the sake of profits of exploiters... Defense of one set of capitalists against another..."

"Ought to stick our bayonets into a fellow like that!" a soldier standing near Vladimir suddenly shouted.

Vladimir said nothing, but began pushing his way to the front entrance of Kschessinskaya's Palace. As he shoved into the huge doors and climbed the imposing staircase, a draft of miraculously warm air greeted him. *No one in Petrograd,* he thought wonderingly, *has been this warm in months.* And then he remembered the rumors about Kschessinskaya and the black market. In spite of himself, he had to admire the Bolsheviks' practical foresight.

Inside, amid ornate walls and exquisite ceilings, a few primitive tables and unpretentious chairs were scattered about. Kschessinskaya's movable property had apparently been put away somewhere. The ballroom was full of workers and professional revolutionaries, half of them standing or sitting on the tables. Someone had been elected chairman, and various people were making speeches. Finally, Lenin came in off the balcony and made still another speech. This one lasted two hours.

Lenin was a very powerful orator, Vladimir decided as he listened. Not because of fine sounding phrases or wit or appealing to people's emotions, but because he broke down what was complicated into its simplest parts – and then hammered them into the heads of his audience until he took them captive.

"We don't need a parliamentary republic," hammered Lenin, "we don't need bourgeois democracy, we don't need any government except the Soviet of Workers', Soldiers' and Farm Laborers' deputies!"

By the time Vladimir left Kschessinskaya's Palace, Lenin's ideas were firmly entrenched in his mind. But still, he hesitated.

And then Trotsky returned to Petrograd. Vladimir went to a mass meeting to hear him speak. Almost as soon as Trotsky strode on stage, the hall heated up. Piercing eyes and unruly hair underscored powerfully vivid pictures drawn by the fiery leader's ringingly eloquent words. Vladimir wept as Trotsky described the suffering in the trenches, and thrilled to his resounding call for change. As Trotsky's fervor mounted, so did Vladimir's excitement. Only with difficulty did he resist the urge to cross himself.

"Let this be your vow – with all your strength and at any sacrifice, to conclude the victory of the Revolution, and to give peace, land, and bread to Russia!"

Listening to Trotsky echoing Lenin's words sounded almost like a hymn. The passion of his oratory seemed to fill a huge void within. And when Trotsky finally joined the Bolsheviks, so did Vladimir.

Ж   Ж   Ж

As the war dragged on, "Peace Land Bread" attracted more and more attention. Factories shut down, food supplies dwindled, the ruble plummeted. Soldiers deserted en masse. Even so, the Provisional Government stubbornly refused to end the hopeless war.

Vladimir joined the Red Guards. Led by Trotsky, they laid plans to overthrow the Provisional Government. *Then*, thought Vladimir, *we can end the war and get on with the real Revolution.* And he threw himself zealously into preparing for the coup, relieved to at last have a cause for which to fight.

Finally, late in October, they were ready.

With the other Red Guards, Vladimir led the motley troops to the Winter Palace. They marched quietly up the street to Palace Square and halted. Then voices began to give commands, and in the thick gloom the shuffling feet and clinking arms moved forward. Like a black river, they poured through the Arch and into the vast Square. Then they were running, stooping low and bunching together, their pounding feet echoing in the silent darkness. In the light streaming out of the Palace windows, Vladimir suddenly saw a barricade. He clambered over, giving a triumphant shout as he leaped down inside. On both sides of the main gateway, the doors stood wide open. As Vladimir ran toward them, he stumbled on a heap of rifles thrown down by those defending the barricade.

Carried along by the eager wave of attackers, Vladimir was swept into a huge vaulted room in the cellar, from which issued a maze of corridors and staircases. Pausing to decide where to go, the attackers noticed large packing crates standing about. Battering them open with the butts of their rifles, they began pulling out carpets, curtains, linens, porcelain, glassware. One man strutted around with a bronze clock on his shoulder; another stuck an ostrich plume in his hat.

"Comrades! Don't touch anything!" Vladimir suddenly heard himself shouting. "Don't take anything! This is the property of the People now!"

The looters stopped, surprised.

"Stop! Put everything back! Don't take anything! Property of the People!"

Members of the Red Guard snatched away the damask and tapestry and feathers and crammed them roughly back into the crates. Vladimir posted sentries, and then continued through the corridors shouting, "Revolutionary discipline! Property of the People..."

Hours later, when the last of the Provisional Government's defenders had been rounded up, Vladimir walked through the empty rooms of the Winter Palace. The paintings and statues and tapestries were unharmed. Beds, however, had been stripped of their covering and wardrobes ransacked. Leather upholstery had been ripped from chairs. Vladimir shrugged. It was, after all, likely to be a very cold winter.

In front of a not especially imposing door, a few old Palace servants, still dressed in blue and red and gold uniforms, stood nervously. "You can't go in there," they repeated from force of habit, as Vladimir headed toward the door. "It is forbidden!"

Vladimir ignored them, and entered a gold and malachite chamber with crimson brocade hangings. In the middle was a long table covered with green baize. Before each empty seat was pen and ink and paper. The papers were scribbled with rough drafts of proclamations and manifestos. Vladimir picked up one of them and read "The Provisional Government appeals to all classes to support the Provisional Government..." Someone had scratched a line through it; the rest of the paper was covered with absent minded doodles.

Vladimir sat down heavily in one of the chairs. Slowly, he looked around the small room where the Provisional Government had surrendered without a fight.

"Revolutionary discipline," he murmured wearily, crumpling up the paper. "Revolutionary discipline. Property of the People..."

Ж   Ж   Ж

Lisya and Olga were walking home from the Maryinsky, at a rapid pace which taxed even Olga's long legs. Lisya, however, was thankful not to be alone. To pool resources, Olga and her sister had moved into Tatiana's room. Only temporarily, of course. Or so Lisya tried to reassure herself.

As they hurried along the dark street, Lisya tried not to think of how the Maryinsky had changed. Soldiers and sailors now filled the balconies, smoking and eating sunflower seeds, tapping their heavy boots in time to the music and cheering noisily. They sat on the railings, legs dangling, always applauding at the wrong time. The singers, meanwhile, were swathed in heavy coats and the dancers wore long underwear under their costumes. Dressed in layers of clothing, Lisya and Olga shivered in the orchestra pit, playing their instruments in gloves with tips cut off.

Suddenly Lisya felt a clutch of fear in the pit of her stomach. Olga's stride became even more determined, as a gang of ragged figures emerged from the gloom. Lisya struggled to keep up. The pack moved in closer, growling menacingly. Then some of them grabbed at Olga's cello, while a few others reached for Lisya's violin. Into her mind flashed the image of a bonfire fueled by their beloved instruments, the thieves warming themselves around it. Hot fury suddenly swept through her. She swung her purse as hard as she could; someone groaned. Olga kicked strategically, yelling amazingly colorful obscenities. Lisya was too angry to blush and, as the adrenalin surged, found herself swearing at the attackers with surprisingly authoritative profanity.

The pack ran off yelping, disappearing as abruptly as they had appeared. Lisya and Olga ran home as fast as the cello would allow. Not until they were safely inside did Lisya allow herself to feel pity for their would-be muggers. Many of them, she realized with a shock, were no older than Katya.

"Why don't you take Katya home to the Volga," Vladimir urged a few nights later, after an unusually lean dinner. "You would both be safer there."

270

"No," Lisya shook her head stubbornly. "Petersburg is my home. I will not leave it."

And then Katya became ill. As she grew bonier and paler, she began to cough. She became listless and ceased her usual questioning. Her nose ran constantly and her gums were often bleeding. And every time Lisya combed her hair, the braids were thinner.

That Katya's malady –and its remedy –were easily diagnosed only added to Lisya's frustration. Malnutrition was a totally preventable disease which – until now – only happened to other people's children.

Frantically, she scoured the city for vegetables; one day, all she could find were two carrots. Full of anxiety, she watched her beautiful child fade.

Meanwhile, true to his promise, Lenin made peace – but on German terms. The price was giving up huge chunks of Russia. At first, Vladimir – like Trotsky, who was now Commissar for Foreign Affairs – refused to accept this humiliating treaty. Eventually, however, he realized – like Lenin –that there was no choice. But the loss of so much western territory left Petrograd virtually on the border of what was left of Russia, facing the German puppet states set up in the newly separated areas of Poland, Finland, Lithuania, Estonia, Latvia, and the Ukraine.

And then, one day, Vladimir came home with the news. "The capitol is moving to Moscow. It's further from the Germans and will be easier to defend."

Lisya dropped one of the dishes she was washing.

"I have to go, too, Lisya. You know I do," he looked at her imploringly. "Please come with me. I couldn't bear to leave you and Katya here alone. Not now."

Lisya sat down and slowly shook her head. "No," she said firmly, "I could not bear Moscow. And besides, there are no more carrots there than here."

"No," she repeated, standing up resolutely. "I will take Katya home to the Volga."

Chapter 14: CHAOS

The capital of the tsars was being evacuated. Trains laden with museum treasures and gold reserves and metal stores from factories passed endlessly out of Petrograd's railway terminals. Other trains were crowded with refugees. Lisya and Katya soon joined the exodus.

Vladimir used his connections at Smolny headquarters to get them tickets. Even so, finding a place on the increasingly unavailable trains was largely a matter of luck. But after waiting all night and most of the day, their train finally arrived. In his Red Guards uniform, Vladimir fought through the huge crowd and commandeered a corner for them on a top bunk in one of the hurriedly adapted freight cars. There he deposited several large bundles filled with things to barter for food along the way.

Gently, he lifted Katya and looked lovingly at her.

"Don't worry," said Katya, tenderly patting his bearded cheek, "we'll come back."

"Yes," Vladimir smiled, "I know."

"Will you be here when we do?" Katya's voice quavered uncertainly.

"Yes. I will." He gently kissed her forehead. "I promise."

Effortlessly, he swung her up on the bunk and then, turning to Lisya, searched his sister's eyes. Without a word, they embraced quickly, her arms as fiercely protective as his. Vladimir turned abruptly and fought his way out of the freight car.

Lisya was glad there was no window near their bunk; it would be easier to pretend that this wasn't a railroad station, that she wasn't saying goodbye to someone she loved, someone she might never see again. Arranging their baggage as comfortably as she could, she curled up, Katya in her arms, and fell into wary, fitful sleep.

Hours later, she sat up and looked around. Every available inch of the large freight car was crowded with people of every imaginable age and status. All of them were bundled up in several layers of clothing, and were sitting and leaning on as much baggage as they could carry. The huddled bodies provided what warmth there was; a few windows let in small drafts of fresh cold air. Other than a couple of uncloseted buckets on either end, there were no amenities. With dismay, Lisya realized that this was to be their home for she knew not how long.

Gradually, her grey mood was distracted by a much more elemental urge. Just as she was almost desperate enough to head for the buckets, the train mercifully slowed down. Someone opened the door to a forest running by. As the train stopped, she saw several bunches of peasant women holding baskets with delicious- looking contents. Grabbing a small bundle of soap and cigarettes wrapped in a fine linen towel, she jumped down and ran for the nearest tree. Then she sauntered over as casually as she could to the waiting peasant women. After examining their wares with benevolent hauteur her rumbling stomach belied, she finally traded her bundle for some cottage cheese, boiled beef, rye pancakes and – best of all – carrots.

Back up in their corner, Lisya and Katya ate as they had not for months. Then, after putting away the carrots and giving the rest of the pancakes to the family next to them, Lisya looked closely at her sleeping child. Wan and pale, Katya smelled of kerosene, rubbed on her neck and wrists to keep lice away. But cuddled up with her doll, she had a small smile on her face. It was the first Lisya had seen there for many weeks. Sighing in relief, she lay down beside her.

Gradually, life on the train became almost tolerable. Cramped though they were, long delays at every station enabled prolonged airing and stretching, as well as profitable bartering with the inevitable peasant women. With every stop, Katya's cheeks gained a bit more color. Had it not been for the lack of water to bathe in, Lisya might almost have been content. But rubbing her hands and face with snow merely tantalized her creeping flesh; gradually her unwashed body fused with her unchanged clothes into gross reeking scales.

Sometimes the train stopped out in the middle of nowhere, waiting for hours while they all listened nervously to distant shooting. Sometimes, too, the train was snowbound. Once, it took three days for the passengers to dig it out.

Eventually, however, the days melted together. Rocked by the freight car jolting over the tracks, Lisya finally fell into a drowsing haze which shut out the itching of her filthy body – and the smell of everyone else's. As the train erratically crawled through the dense, towering forests and over the vast, unending plains, waking dreams of what –and whom – she would find in Derevnia began filling the void of the long, monotonous days.

At first, when Dmitri's face began insistently rising before her, Lisya guiltily pushed the memory back into where she always stuffed it, and firmly slammed the door. But as the Volga drew ever nearer, she began to realize that his image no longer had to be locked up. As she slowly relaxed years of vigilance, remembrances of Dmitri suffused the emptiness left by Alexander Pavlovich's death.

She saw Dmitri's sadly beautiful eyes, and his serious face which had to strain so hard to smile. She heard his soft voice wrap around her like thick warm sheepskin. She felt his strong hands gently stroking her hair, and her own fingers running through the short curls which softened his angular contours. She remembered how, leaning against his tall body, she had felt the dark peace of the forest – and how, when they embraced, the woods had suddenly been ablaze. But most of all, she remembered the poems he had read only to her. They had burned through him with intensity almost too searing to behold. At such times, she had wept – with joy at his beauty, and with sorrow at the deep pain she knew was its wellspring.

All of that, of course, she had resolutely packed away when she married Alexander Pavlovich. Sometimes, she had even been able to forget – almost. But now, thoughts of Dmitri began wafting unbidden from dusty crypts, like ghosts reclaiming a house that had always been theirs.

Like the chaos and violence all around her, the wind and snow battered the rattling freight car. Lisya huddled in her tiny corner, clutching her daughter, yearning to run into her mother's arms.

Ж Ж Ж

The candles in the church flickered bravely, wearily beating back the cold bleakness. Gaunt haggard women prayed silently around listless little boys and exhausted old men. By the door was Dmitri, returned from the War, his arm in a sling. Up in front stood Mischa, who had limped home just in time to sing at the funeral. Elena was close by, gazing at him like Lazarus risen from the dead.

It had taken Mischa more than two months to travel the thousand miles between the Front and the Volga. At first, he had avoided main roads and railways. Later, as the stream of deserters became a flood, he was occasionally able to find space on crowded erratically running trains. Mostly, though, he walked. When his boots wore out, he tore up part of his ragged overcoat and wrapped it around his feet.

Like the countless other frozen villages he made his way through, the war had taken its toll on Derevnia. As the horses and younger men had disappeared into the trenches, the women and older men took up the slack. Mikhail, who had long since passed his prime, took charge and threw himself into the task of feeding his people with the energy of a man half his age. Planting his feet far apart and squaring his broad shoulders, he exhorted them in the fields as in church, reaching out with the deep rounded tones of his huge soul. From dawn until dark, he plowed and sowed, chopped and hauled, mowed and stacked, refusing to bend under a load far too heavy. Seeing his determination, the others followed his example. And no one in Derevnia starved.

Finally, Mikhail's great heart burst, and his mighty voice boomed forth no more. The sorrowful village was now gathered to say farewell.

"Repose the soul of your deceased servant with the saints." How many times they had heard Mikhail chant those words! Mischa reached down into the roots of his soul to be worthy. Deep tones welled up, soft and strong as the earth itself, filling the little church with the comforting balm of continuity.

Father Ivan's expressive hands inscribed the final blessing. And then he led the weeping procession out of the church to the cemetery, where they buried Mikhail not far from his wife's mother. And close to his old friend, Andrei the Icon-Maker.

Mischa soon stepped into his grandfather's shoes. And while no one – least of all Mischa himself – considered him more than a worthy echo in church, everyone agreed that he surpassed Mikhail in the fields. Gradually his quiet resolution permeated Derevnia, as once again they began to rebuild.

Meanwhile, Revolution spread like wildfire. Local Soviets sprang up everywhere, amidst much clamorous discussion. And across the land erupted violent terrible hatred, kindling for centuries. Not a few landlords suffered ugly retribution at the hands of their tenants. In Derevnia, dark glances were cast at the mansion, as muttering groups of peasants congregated in angry knots. Thanks primarily to Father Ivan, Praskovia Nikolaevna and Varvara Petrovna got off relatively lightly.

Both were widows, whose universally despised spouses had often made the peasants victims of their excesses. Fortunately, the errant husbands had long since drunk and dissipated their way to early graves. Praskovia Nikolaevna – though eccentric and snobbish – had always dealt fairly, if not particularly cordially, with the peasants. Although many felt cheated of a target for revenge, Ivan was able to persuade his parish that neither justice nor vengeance would be served by attacking the women of the manor. Most of their livestock appeared in various farmyards in Derevnia, and some of the village women suddenly began wearing fancy dresses and elaborate hats to church, but there was no violence. Everyone, of course, stopped paying rent for the land leased from the manor.

As the summer heated up, the strains of a vast country cut loose from its moorings began to tell. And the dark beast bred by centuries of oppression broke loose.

In a neighboring village, after confiscating the local aristocrat's land, the peasants immediately began quarreling over how to divide it. As the argument proceeded, they broke into the landlord's warehouse, in which was an ample supply of liquor. Nearly drowning in the alcoholic deluge, the inebriated peasants accidentally set fire to the place. Four of them burned to death. The rest fell into a violent brawl, in which thirteen were killed and fifteen carried off seriously wounded.

In another nearby village, several men seized the grain reserves of their richer neighbors. A meeting called to resolve the matter erupted into a violent fight, killing three and badly wounding five.

While cooler heads usually prevailed in Derevnia, Father Ivan and Mischa worried about the growing discontent expressed by many of their neighbors.

"There is not enough seed corn and I have only one horse. The other died last month."

"There is no hope for us till the landlords and capitalists go!"

"What's the use of a Revolution, if it only means that somebody else sits in the palace of Nicholas Romanov?"

"If I thought praying would save us from famine this winter, I'd be on my knees all day."

"But you attend meetings of the Soviet. Do you think that will work any better?!"

Meanwhile, the Provisional Government had floundered, refusing to deal with land reform. Worst of all, the war which had toppled the Romanovs dragged on.

When the Provisional Government fell in October, the village shrugged and hoped the Bolsheviks would do better. Lenin quickly issued the land decree so long awaited. In theory, it abolished private ownership and nationalized the land; in practice, it legitimized the peasants' confiscation of land.

Mischa welcomed the decree. By day, he labored tirelessly to reorder and recultivate the land of Derevnia. By night, however, he was often visited by disquieting dreams of the Tsar, and he began to brood about what had been prophesied long ago.

The first Tsar Nicholas, so it was said, had asked a venerable holy man about who would succeed his son, Alexander, as tsar.

"Alexander," he had replied. Nicholas was astonished and dismayed, as his eldest grandson was also named Nicholas. Alas, this promising young man did indeed die before he reached the throne. His younger brother, Alexander, instead became tsar.

"And after him?" the Tsar had persisted.

"Another Nicholas."

"And then?"

The holy man fell silent. The Tsar urged him to speak.

"And then will come a peasant with an axe in his hand!"

Ж   Ж   Ж

Ivan stood alone in the center of his church, staring meditatively up at the dome. It was where he always came when troubled. His lips moved silently, beseeching the Infinite to enlighten the finite church he loved and served so faithfully.

Guide us, O Lord, into paths of righteousness, and give our leaders wisdom.

Yes. Especially the leaders.

Since even before his ordination, the Church hierarchy had dismayed Ivan. Obsessed with canonical trivia, they seemed more concerned about protecting their territory than in propagating the faith. But he had always tried to rationalize this impious preoccupation with politics by blaming it on the government's control of Church affairs. Even so, that the bishops so enjoyed their brocaded cage shocked him.

How often he had argued about this with Vladimir! But somehow, the closer his son came to the mark, the more Ivan himself had felt obliged to defend the Church. Within the privacy of his own soul, however, Vladimir's attacks had all too often resonated with his own doubts. Perhaps that was why he had usually lost his temper.

Ivan sighed, and shifted his gaze to the iconostasis. A warm smile passed over him as he thought of his father. Above the altar, next to the Saviour and the Virgin, was St. Vladimir, patron saint of Russia. Andrei had lavished particular care on this icon; it bore a striking resemblance to Old Mikhail. And to Vladimir.

The familiar pain stabbed him. No matter where he started, somehow things always came back to Vladimir. With an effort, Ivan resumed his train of thought.

When the Revolution removed the heavy hand of the Tsar, Ivan had looked forward to a purified Church, free of the state's corrupting control; he had rejoiced when the Provisional Government allowed the meeting of a national Church Council. Almost immediately, however, this long-awaited *sobor* polarized. Thereafter followed a bewildering series of coups and counter-coups among Church leaders, as religious schism erupted like boils all over the Russian Orthodox Church. Patriarchs followed one another in rapid succession, deposed by rival groups of believers or arrested by the new Bolshevik government – as confused as anyone else about who stood for what.

After a mighty effort to keep track of the complicated meanderings of all these groups, Ivan finally lost count. Disgusted with their interminable bickering and disastrous power games, he gave up hope of any of them providing guidance through the crisis at hand. He grieved for Holy Mother Russia, so desperately in need of moorings in the midst of so much upheaval, and was ashamed of his Church for abdicating its responsibility.

Ivan sank to his knees before the iconostasis, entreating the Saviour and the Virgin and all the saints to help him find a way through all the chaos.

Ж   Ж   Ж

Shortly after they left Nizhny Novgorod, Lisya began to feel apprehension and anticipation chasing each other around in her stomach. By the time the train reached Kazan, she was so excited she could hardly sit still.

Early the next morning, she and Katya were standing alone on the platform of the isolated railway station nearest to Derevnia. After looking in vain for some means of local conveyance, they began walking down the road that led to the village. The large bundles Vladimir had carried aboard in Petrograd had long since been bartered for food. Their luggage now consisted of only two small suitcases, several layers of clothing, and some cucumbers wrapped in a towel.

Although Derevnia was only seven miles from the station, it took them all day to get there. Katya was still weak, and they had to stop often and rest. Finally, late in the afternoon, a passing cart gave them a ride. Just as day was fading into dusk, they plodded up the familiar village road. Spring was only hinting its arrival, but already the road was muddy. Passing through the rows of small wooden houses, the cart stopped in front of the church. Its shingled walls and onion-shaped dome rose gracefully against the endless open sky.

On the porch of the parsonage stood Ivan, dressed in a long cassock. On his head was a tall round hat, around his neck a large gold cross. Lisya walked slowly up the steps, shocked at how grey his long beard was.

"Hello, Father," she said quietly, kneeling and kissing his hands.

Silently he gave her his blessing.

She stood up again, looking inquiringly into the deep blue eyes under the mournfully sloping grey brows. Behind his carefully guarded gaze, she saw relief.

"You're just in time for Evening Vespers," he said in his benevolent priest voice, which quavered only a little. And then he walked down to meet Katya, his radiant smile slowly suffusing the silver in his beard.

Sighing, Lisya walked into the *izba*.

Evgenia was standing by the stove, fixing supper. Looking up, her face flooded with relief as she saw Lisya at the door. "I knew you'd come home" she said softly, her smile glowing like dark amber.

Lisya ran to her with a sob, and felt her mother's strong arms gently close around her.

She was home.

Ж   Ж   Ж

She had known he would come.

A week after her return, Lisya began to go there every evening after supper. The secluded little grove on the banks of the Volga was just as she remembered it. Watching the river flow endlessly by, memories which had crept in during the long journey now flooded over her.

And then, one night, Dmitri was sitting beside her. Silently he took her hand and they sat quietly, listening to the rippling water. Softly he began to recite a poem, blending its lush cadences with the familiar rhythm of the Volga. It was about his love of the river, about a young girl loved and lost, about a women who would someday return.

With every stanza, she felt the years slipping away, as time seemed to stand still and then turn back. Once again she was an ardent young girl with a long thick braid down her back, thrilling to the sound of his voice and the touch of his hand. His verses soared and plunged, wept and exalted. Her face was wet with tears when he finished.

She turned and looked at him. His thick hair, now streaked with grey, still curved about his head. Lines were etched around the sad eyes, which still reached within and melted her heart. The passion which permeated him still burned, dark and deep and compelling. And, at last, she let it surround her.

The summer passed in a blaze of earthy ardor. Years of pent-up lust exploded

280

and mingled poignantly with nostalgic love. Every night they met at dusk, and did not part until dawn. Looking up at the stars, she felt the soft summer wind caressing her bare flesh as she yielded joyously to his strong gentle hands and lean, hard body. Within the sheltering branches of their grove, the music of the Volga flowed ecstatically around them.

Of the past they spoke little, and of the future, not at all. And when, at last, the leaves began to turn, Lisya knew that the fire of that summer would sustain her for a long time.

Ж　Ж　Ж

Evgenia set the heated samovar on the table in the icon corner, and carefully placed a small plate of *sukhariki* next to it. Carefully Lisya fixed a cup of tea – just the way he liked it – and passed it to Ivan. He smiled, pleased. Evgenia held out the plate to Katya, who quickly appropriated two of the sweet biscuits. One in each small hand, she leaned comfortably against her grandfather, alternately nibbling each of the *sukhariki*. Smiling again, Ivan put his arm around her.

Lisya spooned a bit of jam into her own teacup and sipped it, grateful to be sitting down. Her legs still ached from standing through Sunday Mass. Every week, it seemed, they felt worse.

When all the *sukhariki* were gone, Katya slid over next to her grandmother. Evgenia kissed the top of her head. Quickly finishing her tea, she took Katya's hand and disappeared happily out the door. They would be gone all afternoon, Lisya knew, walking in the woods and singing to the Volga.

"She reminds me of Tatiana," said Ivan, refilling his teacup, "when she was that age."

"Yes," agreed Lisya, "I know what you mean." She, too, refilled her cup.

"I wonder if she's still in France," said Ivan after a long pause, his voice carefully controlled.

"I hope so," answered Lisya, unsuccessfully trying to match his tone.

"Then you haven't heard from her, either?"

"No. Not since before the war."

Ivan stared at his tea. "If only she'd never left Derevnia." This time he could not keep the anger out of his voice.

"She's safer out of Russia!"

"But what if she never comes back!?!"

Lisya, too, stared at her tea, trying hard not to think the unthinkable. The silence between them was heavy.

Finally Ivan patted her hand awkwardly. "Wherever she is," he said as convincingly as he could, "I'm sure she's dancing."

Lisya nodded, willing herself to keep back the tears which somehow seemed to threaten Tatiana's return.

"At least we know Volodya is still in Russia." Ivan's voice was filled with pain.

Lisya looked up and saw the unshed tears in his eyes.

"How is he?" asked Ivan quietly.

"He's still Vladimir," replied Lisya gently. "He worships other gods these days, but he's still searching."

"I pray that he will find his way."

"I think he will – someday." Tentatively she reached out and laid her hand on his.

Just before sunset, Evgenia and Katya returned; the little girl's cheeks were rosy and she was chattering happily. Just after sunset, they all went to Vespers. Katya skipped blithely ahead, eager to see great-grandfather's pretty pictures. All during the service, she stared at the icons so fixedly she forgot to wiggle.

Lisya held Katya's hand, envying her concentration, hoping her own aching legs would outlast her father's lengthy prayers.

"… and have mercy on your departed servant, Nicholas Alexandrovich, Tsar of all the Russias…"

From the soothing drone of her father's voice, the words jumped out at Lisya. For the past month, fearsome bloody rumors had been floating down the Volga. And then, yesterday, a letter had arrived from Uncle Grigori in Kazan, confirming that the Tsar and his family had been killed.

"… Repose the soul of our late Tsar and of his Empress…"

The Imperial Box at the Maryinsky flashed before her. From the orchestra pit, its occupants had always looked like elaborately dressed dolls. No matter what the music, the slightly uncomfortable expression on the blandly pleasant bearded face never seemed to change. Nor did the stiffness ever leave the tensely attractive woman next to him. Still, they had been part of the Maryinsky. Lisya regretted their passing as she did that of the great theatre's other handsome trappings.

"… Gather in Your Arms the spirit of the little Tsarevich and guard the souls of his sisters…"

They, too, had sometimes been up there, tucked away in that isolated box. Poor sick little boy! Poor lonely little girls!

Ivan began to read from the Book of Revelations.

"And I saw the dead stand before God; and the books were opened; and the dead were judged according to their works.

"And the sea gave up the dead; and death and hell delivered up the dead; and they were judged every man according to their works.

"And whosoever was not found written in the book of life was cast into the lake of fire."

Would the Tsar be cast into the lake of fire? Or would all of Russia end up there for rejecting God's anointed ruler? With an effort, Lisya reminded herself that she didn't really believe in the Bible. Still, she had heard her father read it so much, it was hard not to wonder.

"And I saw a new heaven and a new earth; for the first heaven and the first earth were passed away; and there was no more sea."

Vladimir thinks he is building a new heaven and earth with the Bolsheviks. Maybe he is right. Lisya looked at the icon of St. Vladimir, before which a candle always burned. *Or is the apocalypse still to come?*

The candle flickered as a cold wave of fear assailed her.

ж ж ж

The locomotive loomed dark against the night sky, its blunt snout glowering silently at the forest that stood between it and the Dnieper. On a flatcar in the rear, the muzzle of a heavy caliber gun pointed straight at the city. In between were several cars whose doors constantly opened and slammed shut. Beside the train, Vladimir strode methodically up and down the track. Clad in a long great-coat, torn felt boots, and a sharp pointed hood, his shadow marched over the snow beside him. Most of the officers and commissars no longer did guard duty – especially not on such a savagely cold night. Vladimir, however, considered it imperative to set a good example of revolutionary discipline.

Right from the beginning, of course, he had been in the thick of the ugly civil war which flared up everywhere. First he had been sent to the Ukraine, where a bewildering array of conflicting factions defied any attempt to understand who was doing what to whom. Reds and Whites, Germans and Allies, independent Ukrainian nationalists and German supported Ukrainian nationalists – all did battle against a backdrop of ubiquitous peasant uprisings and pillaging brigands.

Vladimir had fought with a poorly equipped Ukrainian army, hastily impro-vised from various socialist partisan units. Eventually they were forced to retreat through the territory of the Don Cossacks, who had overthrown the Soviets and come to terms with the Germans. For three months, Vladimir's group fought their way through, rebuilding bridges and shoring up dykes as they went. Tens of thousands of exhausted, ragged refugees came with them. Finally, they joined other Red forces at Tsaritsyn on the Volga. Under siege by several Cossack regiments, the city's defense had been organized by a Bolshevik called Stalin. Despite heavy and bitter fighting, Tsaritsyn held out against the White forces.

News eventually filtered down the Volga that the entire Imperial family had been shot – at whose orders, no one was quite sure. Vladimir said nothing, and tried not to think about it. Abdication and exile to Siberia – yes, that was fitting. Maybe even a firing squad for Nicholas – and probably Alexandra, too. But to hack the children to pieces...

Meanwhile, another rebellion had risen east of the Volga. Thousands of Czech POWs, who had previously surrendered to the Russians rather than fight for Austria, now decided to fight against the Bolsheviks. The Czech legion took Kazan and prepared to cross the river, threatening the road to Moscow.

Until then, scattered uprisings had been put down by semi-guerilla Red Guards and loosely organized Red Army units. Now, however, the creation of a regular army seemed vitally necessary. The Central Committee declared the republic in danger; Trotsky was appointed People's Commissar of War. He promptly commissioned thousands of ex-tsarist officers previously blacklisted. To keep an eye on them, he also appointed politically reliable commissars to share all command decisions. The commissars were to be Communist "samurai," dedicated warriors who knew how to die – and who would teach others how to fight for the cause of the Revolution. Vladimir soon became one of the new commissars, and threw himself into his new vocation with the relieved energy of one who had finally found his calling.

With Trotsky in command, Kazan was retaken. And then they were sent back to the Ukraine to pacify the nationalists. This time, Vladimir and his comrades speeded across the heart of Russia in an armored train. They had stopped several miles outside Kiev, and were now waiting for orders.

The Ukrainians, Vladimir knew, would not be easily discouraged. They, too, had learned how to fight in the war with Germany; they had also brought back – and hidden – weapons and ammunition. And, now that the Germans had finally left, they were dreaming of a Ukraine free from outside domination. Polish troops, however, had meanwhile invaded and were now marching on Kiev. The

Ukrainians hated the Poles even more than the Russians; the Bolsheviks were banking on that.

Vladimir hurriedly saluted as one of his men relieved him, and jumped quickly back onto the train. As he huddled near the stove, trying to warm his frozen body, he listened hopefully for the Polish guns.

The Poles did, indeed, take Kiev. Like the Germans, they set up a puppet government. Unlike the Germans, they regarded themselves as liberators. The Ukrainians, however, wanted no part of them, either. The Ukrainian people rose up in defense of their homeland, and with the Red Army, drove Polish forces out of Kiev and back to Poland. Vladimir's armored train thundered after in pursuit.

"Red armies, forward!" ordered Trotsky. "On to Warsaw!"

Warsaw, however, did not want to be "liberated" anymore than did the Ukraine. On the banks of the Vistula, the Red Army was forced to retreat. Soon, the armored train was speeding south to the Crimea to fight the last of the White armies. Finally, Vladimir watched what was left of them board ship and sail unto exile.

And then, suddenly, they were sent back to Petrograd. The Kronstadt sailors had mutinied. Vladimir's unit was ordered to suppress the uprising. As he charged across the ice toward the fortress, Vladimir tried not to remember the heroic role of the Kronstadt sailors in the Revolution, tried not to think about how history seemed to be doing a headstand, tried not to notice his leaden feet.

Trotsky said the sailors had been misled by a White general, and that the mutiny was inspired by counter-revolutionaries and foreign agents. Was there no end to those who would attack the Motherland! Must *Rodina*'s loyal sons constantly fight the enemies who encircled her borders! Babushka's stories of fearsome invaders ravishing Mother Russia rang in his ears. Only now, the enemy was within as well as without. The sailors, after all, had attacked the Party! And without the Party, what was there?

"Revolutionary discipline," he murmured sadly, after it was all over, pouring himself another glass of vodka. "Revolutionary discipline..."

Ж   Ж   Ж

By the time Lisya and Evgenia got the class down to the river, the whole village had gathered to wait for the propaganda boat.

Lisya was helping her mother with the school. At first, she had volunteered to avoid certain chores she had always disliked. Hard work had never bothered her, but digging her hands in the ubiquitous muck and manure of rural life did.

Worse yet were tasks that required understanding of plants and animals, forest and field. Such things were not unpleasant, but nowhere in Lisya's mind was there any place to attach them. Forgetting how to do such mundane work was both embarrassing and exasperating.

And there was a void where her music had been. To bring her violin on the crowded train from Petrograd was, of course, unthinkable; but she had expected to at least use the piano at the manor – even if it meant giving command performances. Both the manor and its occupants, however, were in a lamentable state of disrepair. Praskovia Nikolaevna thumped feebly about, imperiously waving her cane at no one; Varvara Petrovna sat in a chair which stank of urine, babbling pathetically about the old days. And the piano was hideously out of tune. Lisya did not return.

At the school, however, she felt genuinely useful. Helping the children learn was satisfying, and she enjoyed relating to her mother as a colleague. Katya, of course, was now one of the students. To Lisya's relief, she had effortlessly made friends with the rest of the class, most of whom were cousins of varying degree. She was especially close to Vasilisa, eldest daughter of Elena and Mischa. Vasilisa was a few years older than Katya, already on the threshold of puberty and her mother's golden beauty. Watching them together on the dock, Lisya smiled and thought of Tatiana.

Meanwhile, everyone in Derevnia was watching curiously as a boat decorated with red flags chugged up to the small pier. Out on deck came a man in uniform, carrying a large victrola with a huge shell speaker. Martial music blared forth, and then a recorded speech by Lenin. The words were simple but eloquent, easily understood by those listening. Afterwards, a few asked cautious questions, to which the uniformed man gave forthright friendly answers. Others joined the discussion, and by the time he was packing up his victrola, many were nodding in agreement. As the steamer moved upriver, everyone smiled and waved.

Eventually, however, the stranger was followed by numerous other visitors with less friendly means of persuasion. Soon various factions of Reds and Whites and other unknown groups were chasing each other up and down river, back and forth across country. The Whites engaged in traditional looting and trampling of fields and requisitioning of food and livestock. The Reds confiscated whatever the peasants grew, under what they called the "surplus food appropriation system." On territory occupied by Whites, land was returned to the large landowners. On Red territory, the government tried to form state farms – "food factories to emancipate the socialist system from dependence on the small proprietor." Either way, the peasants considered themselves robbed.

Caught in the squeeze of an increasingly vicious civil war, people in Derevnia grew more and more bewildered. They knew that the Tsar was no more, and that the land was theirs, and that they were free – whatever that meant. But they also felt that some huge trick had been played on them. Soldiers of every kind and armed men without uniforms kept swooping down on the village, taxing and confiscating and pillaging. One by one their men were drafted – often not knowing into what army – and then the boys began to be taken. Generals and commissars kept coming and carrying everything away. And then all the horses and cattle were gone, and they had to pull the plows themselves.

Desperately, Lisya tried to keep the chaos at bay. But finally it exploded into her life.

One afternoon, she was visiting Elena, as she often did when there was no school. Sometimes Katya came along to be with Vasilisa. Today, however, Old Ekaterina was teaching Katya the secret of how to dye yarn the special shade of russet so envied by the other village women.

"Dmitri is happier than I've seen him in years," smiled Elena over the perennial cup of hospitality tea. "Though happiness is perhaps not the appropriate word for someone like Dmitri."

"Or for me?"

"No, you're just different," replied Elena in her usual forthright manner. "Dmitri is – well, more than different."

"Dmitri is – Dmitri."

"And much too sensitive – about everything." There were small furrows in Elena's usually smooth forehead. "I worry about him."

Suddenly there was loud, angry shrieking from the yard out in back.

"It's Vasilisa!" Elena was immediately on her feet and out the door.

Lisya followed.

Two armed men in uniforms too worn to recognize were dragging Vasilisa off to the forest. The front of her dress was ripped, and she was kicking and screaming. Elena came running out of the barn after them, yelling and waving a scythe.

Lisya froze, then noticed that in the stump used for slaughtering chickens was a hatchet; she grabbed it and ran after Elena. She caught up just as Elena swung the scythe in a wide, practiced swath which very nearly sliced off the head of one of the men. The other man turned and swore angrily. Lisya raised the hatchet, its blade still sticky with blood and chicken feathers, and let it fall on him with the force of her sudden anger. A mouth full of decayed yellow teeth and gold fillings gaped in surprise at her. Then something exploded and Lisya lost consciousness.

When she came to, Dmitri was hovering anxiously. Neither of the brigands, he told her, had been mortally wounded. But they had been injured seriously enough to leave Vasilisa and run back into the forest – and angered enough to fire at all of them. Fortunately they had been drunk, so only Lisya had been wounded.

Relieved, she went back to sleep. When she awakened the following morning, Evgenia assured her that the bullet had passed cleanly through her flesh. Her physical recovery, she knew, would be rapid. But the rest of her was still badly shaken. Vasilisa was not much older than Katya. The bile of outrage and fear rose within her and left a bitter taste.

The next day, Mischa began organizing a band of guerrillas. A week later, Dmitri told Lisya that he was joining them. "I have no wish to kill anyone," he said sadly, wringing his large calloused hands. "But I would rather kill to protect my own, than for the Reds or Whites."

Cold fear clutched her stomach. But when Lisya opened her mouth to protest, she could think of nothing to say. He was right. They both knew that.

"Before I leave," continued Dmitri, "I want us to be married."

"Why?" The question was out before she could think to stop it.

"Isn't that obvious?" Dmitri looked wounded. "We belong together."

"Yes, of course. But – married? Now?"

"After all these years – isn't it time?"

Everyone else seems to think so, thought Lisya. *Why don't I?*

It was Ivan who helped her decide.

"Dmitri doesn't understand why you don't want to marry."

"I know," said Lisya, surprised that her father – not her mother – was approaching her about the matter. "But I've *been* married – and see what happened!"

"What *did* happen?" asked Ivan gently.

"He was just supposed to be a doctor – but he turned into a saint instead of coming home!"

"I doubt that Dmitri has the makings of a saint."

"So do I," replied Lisya, "but he'll think he has to be a hero!"

"Maybe so. But he'll do that, married or not."

288

"Why does everyone expect us to get married?"

"Because they want you to be part of Derevnia," replied Ivan quietly.

"Even you?"

"Especially me."

"Because Tatiana isn't here?"

"Partly, yes."

"I miss her so much!" Tears too long denied suddenly burst forth.

"As do I." Ivan put his arm around her. "But not as much as I've missed you all these years."

Lisya looked up at him, surprised.

"I've never been able to enter your world," Ivan said sadly. "And you left mine. Come back – just for awhile."

"But if I marry Dmitri, will I ever be able to leave?"

"Will either of our worlds even exist anymore?" Ivan shook his head. "What is coming will be different for all of us. We must make the most of whatever good endures."

And so, before Dmitri left, there was a wedding in the little wooden church. Echoes of Old Mikhail's deep voice boomed reassuringly from the shadows. Andrei's rustic icons glowed down at them. And as he blessed the long awaited union, Father Ivan's beatific smile embraced them both.

Lisya took Dmitri's arm, and leaned toward him. Out there, the world was tearing itself apart. But in here was peace, beauty and love – if only for today.

Ж   Ж   Ж

Lying on her stomach beside the road, Lisya crept forward to get a better view. Her baggy trousers snagged on the bush under which she was hiding. Reaching down quickly, she broke off the sharp twig and then readjusted the butt of the ancient shotgun against her shoulder. The old homespun shirt she was wearing itched against her skin. Nervously she glanced at Dmitri, lying watchfully beside her. Silently he shifted his weight; feeling his reassuring warmth against her, Lisya exhaled slowly.

The day after their wedding, Dmitri had vanished into a great mass of peasants, all desperately fighting to protect themselves from all comers on all fronts. Back in Derevnia, Lisya had been consumed with anxiety. Every night, she paced restlessly.

Finally, her mother had handed her a bundle filled with bandages and medicinal herbs and various makeshift medical supplies. "They need a nurse," she said quietly. "I'll take care of Katya."

A few days later, Dmitri and Mischa had slipped back into the village for supplies. When they left this time, Lisya went with them.

At first, Dmitri had insisted she stay in the camp. But waiting for him to return was almost as bad as being back in Derevnia.

"Next time I'm coming with you," she said firmly, after treating a minor wound which had festered evilly on the long trek back.

Dmitri didn't argue with her, but consternation was all over his face.

"I could have fixed *that* more easily," she continued vehemently, pointing at the sweating grimacing wounded man, "if I had been closer to where it happened."

Despite Dmitri's unspoken qualms, Lisya went along with the raiding parties after that. Her first engagement was with a squadron of Red Army troops who had just requisitioned all the seed grain of a nearby village. Watching from the tree behind which Dmitri had sternly admonished her to stay, armed with a stout club he had given her for protection, she saw a wounded soldier crawl out from under one of the wagons and take aim in Dmitri's direction. Rushing up behind him, she smashed the club down as hard as she could; his body went limp over his firearm.

Later, Dmitri handed her the shotgun. "Next time, use this," he said gruffly, showing her how to hold it. There was no spare ammunition with which to practice firing. Even Dmitri had only a few extra rounds. And most of the men had guns not much better than the vintage weapon he had given her.

Catching up with a large detachment of White troops who had looted and burned the stables of another village, Mischa's little band managed to stampede the livestock. From behind a tree where Dmitri had again exhorted her to wait, Lisya watched for her opportunity. At the end of the temporarily confused column, two White soldiers lay motionless, each felled by a single expertly placed bullet. Darting over to the nearest body, Lisya pulled off the full cartridge belts crossing his chest. Slinging them over her shoulder, she started toward the other fallen soldier, suddenly aware that he was feebly reaching for his gun. With what she hoped was a menacing gesture, she pointed her own shotgun at him. Undeterred, he raise his weapon and aimed it straight at her. Lisya froze, staring down the barrel of a foreign made rifle into eyes as terrified as her own. Seeing how young he was, she lowered her gun. Suddenly the face at the other end turned cold, as with an ominous click, he cocked his shiny new weapon. Raw fear swept over Lisya. Clutching the rickety shotgun to her shoulder, she pulled the trigger.

The thing in her hands exploded, striking her shoulder and stunning her ears. The staring face disappeared before her horrified eyes; blood spurted from what was left of the body. Quickly Lisya reached down and jerked the gun from its still determined grasp; warm blood splashed her hands. Running back behind the tree, she tried unsuccessfully not to be sick.

Remembering, Lisya leaned closer to Dmitri. Down the road rumbled several wagons, guarded by a small, ragged battalion. Who were they? Reds? Whites? Political opportunists? Hungry brigands? What did it matter. They were all Russians.

Carefully Dmitri pointed his new gun at one of the wagons. He had been so pleased when she gave it to him; she herself could barely stand to look at it.

Dmitri, she knew, was aiming at the driver. Dutifully she lined up her sights on the man riding next to him. Waiting for the signal, she broke out in a sweat. To kill in the heat of the moment – in defense of someone she loved, to protect her own life – that was one thing. But this? Cold, calculated, premeditated – could she do it?

Maybe the wagon contained guns and ammunition. Maybe even some medical supplies. Thinking how pitifully armed her brave, desperate comrades were, she tightened her grip on the unwieldy shotgun. Recalling how many had been wounded fighting in such an uneven struggle, she cocked the clumsy weapon. Remembering those she might have saved with better medical equipment, she closed her eyes and fired.

After the bruising blast, she opened her eyes – and saw with relief that she had missed. Later, she traded the old shotgun to one of the new recruits for a pistol of even earlier vintage

As Mischa's band grew, the radius of its activities expanded to include several other villages near Derevnia. Carefully they tried to limit armed confrontation only to those who inflicted harm on the land and people within this perimeter. Gradually, however, conditions grew so chaotic that the appearance of *any* armed strangers had to be regarded as a threat.

On the grounds of poor marksmanship, Lisya was excused from the front line of attackers. But she soon became expert in scavenging weapons and ammunition, checking first to make sure their previous owners were indeed dead. Always the pistol was tucked carefully in her belt; only occasionally did she have to use it.

Gradually, too, she improvised methods for treating wounds without even rudimentary medical supplies. In so doing, she relied heavily on advice from Old Ekaterina, who was gratified that some of her lore was at last finding a useful mooring in her perplexing granddaughter.

Lisya, in turn, was struck by how much her grandmother now resembled Babushka. The same ancient eyes looked out from a face now carved deep by rivers of centuries old tears. And often, when Lisya slipped in to visit Katya, she found her leaning against Old Ekaterina, listening wide-eyed to tales of flying dragons and savage centaurs roaring up and down the Volga.

As the months turned into a year, and then another, Lisya's life became a blur of running and hiding, attacking and retreating, fighting and bleeding and dying. Fading in and out of forest and farm, it began to seem as if she had always worn *lapti* and Dmitri's old clothes and a kerchief tied around her hair. And she was sure that never again would her hands be clean.

In the razor sharp perils of guerrilla life, her bond with Dmitri – always beside her – intensified. As the violence magnified, so, too, did the darkness in his soul. Sometimes, during the endless bouts of fighting and killing, it erupted with terrifying ferocity. Afterward they would find an empty barn or burrow into a haystack, stealing a few hours of intimacy from the hideous chaos which raged around them. The darkness would again explode, this time with searing passion, the flame between them burning ever deeper, scorching them with its ecstasy.

One by one the factions of the Civil War killed each other off, or were defeated by the Red Army. Finally, only the peasants were still fighting. Moscow sent the armored trains to put out the revolts. Hostages were taken from villages, automatically shot if any rebel units appeared. Families of known rebels were deported to no one knew where. Meanwhile, after three bitter winters of unbridled civil war, a devastating famine swept the land.

"It's hopeless, isn't it," Lisya said wearily to Mischa.

He nodded his head sadly.

"Then why are we still fighting?" she asked.

Persuading his comrades that going home was the best way to protect their land, Mischa disbanded his guerrillas.

"You must get Katya out of here," Evgenia said, when they returned to the village. "It will soon get even worse. In the cities are the people with power. Whatever food there is will end up there."

Lisya nodded her head sadly.

The next week she was standing with Katya on the same isolated railway platform on which they had landed eons ago. This time, however, they were not alone.

As the train crawled toward them across the vast plain, Katya flung herself into her grandmother's arms. "Goodbye, Babushka," she sobbed. Lisya and her mother silently embraced. The train stopped. Dmitri swung Katya up into the freight car; Lisya loaded their baggage. Then they both climbed aboard. As the train pulled away, all of them waved until the indomitable old woman on the platform finally disappeared over the horizon.

Ж   Ж   Ж

This time, when the train at last slipped from sight, Evgenia felt relieved. *Let it speed them to wherever they will be safe!* What was coming, she knew, would be far worse than anything she had yet known. If there was sanctuary to be found anywhere in Russia, it would be in a place like Petrograd. And if not, at least it was close to the border.

Not that she had ever voiced such thoughts around Ivan, who worried continually about Tatiana's uncertain whereabouts. Evgenia, too, was concerned about Tatiana being in a strange land; but surely she would be safer if she delayed her return until the Motherland was not so hungry.

No one in Derevnia was surprised when the famine came. Up and down the river it stalked, as Mother Volga wept for her starving children. The new government, almost as exhausted as those defeated in the war, unsuccessfully tried to muster aid. From church, school and clinic, Ivan and Evgenia endeavored to organize what resources the village had as efficiently as possible.

When Evgenia heard the church bells ringing the alarm, she knew that it was not like those sounded so often during the Civil War. Running up to the small hill on which the church was built, she anxiously scanned the horizon. Off in the distance, like a swarm of giant insects, a ragged mob was crawling relentlessly toward the village. Mischa, who had sounded the alarm, ran up next to her.

"What is it?" she asked anxiously.

"Hungry people looking for food," he answered tersely, clutching his rifle.

"But surely we can spare some," she said, eyeing the gun apprehensively.

"You know we can't," he said flatly. "But even if we could, it wouldn't matter. They've gone crazy with hunger, and are slaughtering everyone in their path. What they did to the forester and his family… it was terrible."

Several other armed men joined Mischa; together they went out to meet the starving horde. Evgenia watched from the hill, as Mischa held up his hand and shouted a warning. The snarling mass continued to spill up the road toward the village. Mischa and his men raised their guns menacingly. Still the droning throng came on. A volley of gunshots fired over their heads. The hungry pack hesitated, then pressed on, howling angrily. Another round of shots, this time into the mob. Screams punctuated the moaning, but still they came, climbing over the bodies of those who had fallen. The ghastly chorus of shooting and screaming seemed to go on forever. Finally the rest of the pitiful skeletons hobbled away.

Later, Mischa and his men buried the victims, many of whom were women and young children. As Ivan said prayers over the grave, Evgenia felt sick with horror. Mischa stood next to her, head bowed, his face covered with shame.

Thereafter, they posted a guard. Even so, Evgenia lived in fear of that desperate moaning coming at them again over the horizon. And then, a few weeks later, she heard a different kind of assault bearing down. Running up to the church, she looked out over the devastated fields. Mischa joined her, took one look, and ran off to ring the alarm. The fields were alive, teeming with undulating waves of small furry bodies. With a shock, Evgenia realized that another hungry horde was invading – this time rats and mice, desperately on the move in search of food. Grabbing her broom, she ran down to beat the frenzied rodents off, the sound of their tiny stampeding paws pounding in her ears.

This time, they ate the victims. And when that was gone, became emaciated beyond recognition, creeping about the village like mummies. Ivan began to notice that some of the corpses he buried no longer had arms and legs – and that sometimes dead children were never buried at all. People began to keep to themselves, not sitting together at table, not daring to look at one another.

Ivan and Evgenia did not yield to these desperate measures – nor did they condemn those who did. No one, of course, talked about it, but Evgenia's empty stomach sometimes tempted her to wonder...

"It tastes quite good," a dying old peasant confessed, "and doesn't need much salt."

And then, when even Ivan and Evgenia were almost too weak to leave their bed, the Americans came. On boats filled with food and medicine, they steamed down the Volga, stopping at every village to distribute their lifesaving relief. A protective squad of government troops surrounded the frightened volunteers passing out food; elsewhere they had nearly been trampled by starving recipients. The benefactors called themselves the Society of Friends, and told Evgenia that they opposed war but rendered aid to its victims. Derevnia received the American Quakers and their miraculous gifts with feeble – but heartfelt – blessings. When the survivors were strong enough, Ivan led them in a special service of thanksgiving.

They were, Evgenia knew, among the fortunate. Many villages had not been able to survive long enough to benefit from the American aid. Others had exploded in futile protest. Thanks primarily to Mischa, her village did not join this pointless uprising – and was thus spared the further suffering of government reprisals.

When it was finally all over, millions of Russians had joined the millions already killed in the war with Germany – and the still more millions who had perished during the long agony of the Civil War.

One of the victims was Old Ekaterina.

After Mikhail's death, she had moved in with Elena and Mischa. As soon as the famine struck, she stopped eating and gave her share to her grandchildren. When it was time, Evgenia sat by the dying old woman's side.

Old Ekaterina had never been fond of unnecessary words, and she had often seemed to disappear in the noisy shadow of her husband. But over the years, particularly since Lisya and Tatiana had left home, Evgenia had grown closer to her mother. Often she had found solace in the wise old soul of this small silent woman. And now, she, too, was leaving.

"You won't be alone when I'm gone," Old Ekaterina said quietly to her weeping daughter. "There's another Ekaterina now."

The wrinkled old hand gave a final reassuring squeeze, and then grew cold.

Now I am the Babushka, thought Evgenia. Wiping away her tears, she crossed herself.

Part IV

Utopia, 1921

Chapter 15: The REDS

It took even longer to get back to Petrograd than it had to leave it. All along the route was the carnage and wreckage of the long Civil War. Lisya did not dare think how many must have perished, nor did she allow herself to contemplate the enormity of the devastation. As it was, they were lucky to reach Petrograd alive. Only Dmitri's ingenuity and resourcefulness kept them from starving. Lisya soon learned not to question what he brought back from his forays during train stops – or where he had gotten it.

At long last, they arrived. Despite all that she had seen along the way, Lisya was shocked at how Petrograd had changed. The magnificent buildings had been subdivided into tiny apartments and offices; iron pipes attached to crude home-made stoves protruded through windows. The Winter Palace was run down, the Summer Gardens overgrown. Streets were full of holes where drains had choked and water mains burst. Even on the Nevsky Prospekt were hungry-looking people in ragged clothing.

Walking through the streets of her city, Lisya wept at its fallen state. Each familiar place seemed shabbier than the last. Finally, she sat down despondently on a ledge of the Embankment; all the benches had long since disappeared. Dejectedly she looked into the river, flowing along as imperturbably as ever.

The Neva, at least, had not changed. It looked the same as on her first day in Petersburg. And in its rippling reflection, the grandeur of the city could still be glimpsed. Somewhat heartened, she returned home.

Olga had remained in Petrograd throughout the Civil War. From the little she would tell – and from what remained unspoken in her eyes – life had been grim. Her sister had not survived the especially horrible winter after Lisya had taken Katya to the Volga. Olga herself had nearly died of typhus; her once lovely long hair had been cropped. She was now sharing the apartment Lisya had left in her care with several other people. True to her promise, she had zealously watched over the piano and carefully tended Lisya's violin, and had somehow managed to keep the living room unoccupied. In this cramped space, Lisya began to make a home for Katya and Dmitri.

Lisya was relieved to see her violin again. She had left it in Petrograd reluctantly, deciding that it would be safer with Olga's cello than on a crowded freight car rattling uncertainly to the Volga. And after years away from a piano, even the cranky old upright was a welcome sight. Lisya traced the rather pretentious pattern carved on the front panel of the modest instrument, comforted by its enduring sameness, touched even by its changeless lack of taste.

Sitting down on the floor, she opened the worn trunk next to the piano. On top was the velvet dress she had waltzed in at Kschessinskaya's palace. Lightly she stroked the soft fabric with her calloused fingertips, wondering if she would ever get the dirt out from under the nails. Sighing, she closed the lid and dropped her hands in her lap. How well they matched the rough homespun of the dress she now wore!

A few days later, Olga quietly handed her a rumpled, much traveled letter. Lisya recognized the handwriting immediately and opened it anxiously. Judging by the date, it had taken a long time to get to Petrograd.

November 11, 1918
Dear Lisya,

The war is finally over, and I want to come home! But the stories we hear about Russia are so ghastly. All the emigres say we'd be fools to return.

"We" is Nikolai and I. He's the artist who designs sets for Diaghilev; I know I told you about him in my other letters. Anyway, he wants us to get married and go to America. I want to marry him, too, but I want to go home.

Oh Lisya, tell me what to do! I love Nikolai, but I'm so homesick sometimes I think my soul will drown in tears. I tell Nikolai maybe the rumors are exaggerated. He tells me it's foolish to hope, that I must choose between him and Russia. But what worries me is that maybe I have no choice – maybe Russia is no more.

Please help me, Lisya. Please tell me the truth.
                    Your loving sister,
                    Tatiana

Lisya sat staring at the letter for a long time. Tatiana had written it over two years ago. Where was she now? Had she married Nikolai? Were they in America? She tried to picture Tatiana, but the image refused to come.

The truth! Tatiana had begged her for it. Had Lisya received the letter in time, what would she have replied?

Carefully, she folded the letter and put it in her pocket. Slowly, she went down the stairs and out into the street. Sadly, she followed the familiar route to Tealtralnaya Ulitza. The Ballet School, like everywhere else, looked weather-beaten and shabby. No doorman in elegant livery greeted her at the entrance; the rooms were bare and cold.

She climbed the wide staircase to the rehearsal hall and looked in the door. The portraits of the tsars were gone and the mirrors were cracked, but there in the corner was the piano she had played so many years ago. And at the barre was a small group of thin ragged-looking ballet students, doing their exercises as diligently as ever. She walked over to the piano, lifted the lid from the keyboard, and began to play some simple practice etudes. Her calloused fingers clicked uncertainly on the smooth ivory keys, hesitantly finding their way to familiar places. The students looked up, startled, and then adjusted their rhythm to her music. Afterward, they smiled gratefully and left her alone with her memories.

Lisya sat silently until the sun went down. Gently she took Tatiana's letter from her pocket and tenderly kissed it. As she slowly stood up to leave, the glow of the sunset filtered through the dirty windows. And there, in the shadows of the fading light, flickered the image of a young girl in practice dress and dancing shoes. For just a moment it danced joyously – and then was gone.

Ж Ж Ж

The kitchen seemed much smaller with all of them crowded around the table. At either end sat Vladimir and his old friend, Sergei. For years, the two men had organized unions and plotted revolution together. After Lisya had gone to the Volga, Vladimir had invited Sergei to share the apartment – and to keep an eye on things while he was off fighting. Sergei and his younger son, Alexei, now lived in the bedroom; his elder son, Vassily, was in the dining room with his wife, Ludmilla. Vladimir had eventually returned to the small study. Olga and her cello remained in Tatiana's little room.

And, of course, there were the ghosts. Besides Olga's sister, Sergei's wife had died during the famine, as had Ludmilla's baby. But no one ever talked about any of them.

It had taken Lisya less time than expected to get used to the crowded apartment. As she looked around the table at the now familiar faces, she conceded that the arrangement could have been worse.

Sergei, as usual, was dominating the conversation. He was a bluff hearty man with big calloused hands and crude manners. Beside him was Vassily, a smaller but better educated version of his father. Next to Vassily crouched Ludmilla, plain and kind, still wrapped in grief for their only child. Only occasionally did she emerge, usually in response to the energetic boy at her elbow. Young Alexei was making faces and winking conspiratorially at Katya, giggling at him across the table. Lisya, too, grinned; like the other women, she adored and mothered Alexei.

For the most part, they lived together in relative harmony. Sharing the kitchen resulted in sharing the cooking, which Lisya decided was an improvement. Sharing the bathroom, however, was not. There was always a line, and the facilities were constantly breaking down. Fortunately, Vassily and Sergei were good at fixing things. And not only the plumbing. Sergei was a commissar at the Putilov steelworks, and soon found Dmitri a job. Vassily was rising quickly in the Party, and saw to it that they were never hungry. Vladimir, now a high ranking military commissar, had more clout than anyone, but steadfastly refused to use it for his own gain. He did not, however, object to Sergei and Vassily pulling strings for the family's benefit. And everyone knew that Vladimir's presence cast a protective shield over them all.

As stark privation began yielding to mere shortage, anarchy began evolving into something truly exciting. No one had very many possessions, but everyone seemed to have an abundance of new ideas. Everywhere was excitement about possibilities, difficult to resist. It was, Lisya decided, almost worth the communal bathroom.

And so, at the end of their first year together, they decided to celebrate the holidays. Christmas, of course, had been theoretically erased from the calendar; in practice, its celebration and accompanying traditions were simply moved to New Year's.

Everyone had participated in the preparations with childlike enthusiasm. Axe in hand, Vladimir had exuberantly descended upon the surrounding countryside and returned with a New Year's tree; Katya had excitedly made ornaments to decorate it. And now they were all eagerly inhaling the tantalizing aroma of a roast goose Vassily had managed to procure. Ludmilla had been in the kitchen all day, basting and stuffing it with sugared apples. As they sat around the table, savoring the succulent meat, sighing and grunting with almost anguished appreciation, Ludmilla's sad eyes lit up with tentative pleasure.

"Ludmilla, my dear, your goose is a triumph!" said Vassily, kissing his wife's cheek.

"Indeed, yes!" agreed Sergei heartily. "I can't remember goose ever tasting so good."

"I can't remember ever eating goose," grinned Alexei.

Everyone laughed and, as usual, smiled at Alexei.

"I remember eating something that looked like goose at one of Kschessinskaya's soirees," said Olga between mouthfuls.

"The table was huge and loaded with all kinds of food I never even knew existed," added Lisya. "We really stuffed ourselves."

"Like a goose?" giggled Katya, glancing at Alexei.

Everyone laughed, including Alexei. Katya beamed.

"More like ten geese!" replied Lisya, hugging her daughter and kissing the top of her head.

"Someday, there will be a goose in every pot," stated Vladimir, "instead of the bourgeoisie having more than they can eat."

"When their goose is cooked!" quipped Alexei.

Vladimir laughed, his big hand affectionately rumpling Alexei's irrepressible hair.

When their bellies were stuffed for the first time in years, Sergei brought out several bottles of vodka and some real French champagne.

"To the Victorious Proletariat!" Sergei raised his glass. "And to higher production by the workers!"

"To the People's Revolution!" Vladimir refilled his glass and raised it again. "And to the Triumph of Socialism!"

"To the Party of the People!" said Vassily after everyone's glass had been refilled. "And to their Glorious Leadership of the People's Government!"

"To Peace, Land, and Bread!" added Dmitri quietly. "Especially for the People who are peasants!"

"To a goose in every pot!" chimed in Alexei, raising the one glass of champagne he was being allowed. "And to no one's goose getting cooked!"

"And to young poets," rejoined Dmitri, giving Alexei one of his rare smiles, "who need to find new metaphors."

"To our family, old and new!" Vladimir's eyes filled with tears. "May we always protect it!"

"To good comrades, old and new!" Sergei blew his nose. "May we always be loyal!"

With each refilling of their glasses, the men grew more verbosely sentimental. Finally, when the bottles were almost empty, Lisya and Olga played a duet. Dmitri recited a few poems he had written for the occasion, and then encouraged Alexei to try out some of his fledgling verses.

At midnight they popped the last of the champagne corks and toasted the New Year. Then they moved into the room with the piano. Lisya struck up some lively folk tunes, joined by Olga on a balalaika. Everyone else began to sing enthusiastically. As night turned into morning, friends and neighbors poured in and emptied out, singing and dancing and enveloping each other in great bear-hugs and exuberant smacking kisses

Finally, when all the bottles were empty, Dmitri read his poems about the Volga. Lisya took his hand, remembering the little grove near their village. Katya and Alexei were curled up together in a corner, sleeping like overgrown kittens. Lisya smiled, and leaned her head on Dmitri's strong shoulder. As the first dim radiance of dawn softly lit the room, she sank into peaceful sleep, full of hope for the future.

Ж   Ж   Ж

The piano at "The Bright Reel" was even worse than the old upright at home. Beneath giant images flickering on the screen, Lisya tried to avoid the keys which were especially out of tune. As she began clinking away for the second feature, she tried to imagine that she was playing Madame's concert grand.

Shortly after returning to Petrograd, Lisya had gone back to the Conservatory. Madame was still there, having taken up residence in her studio.

"How better to take care of my beautiful piano," she had shrugged matter-of-factly, "*n'est-ce pas, ma chere?*" Lisya had nodded, as Madame tenderly stroked the painstakingly polished mahogany.

Pleased as she was to see Lisya again, Madame had refused to resume her lessons. "I have nothing more to teach you," she said simply. Instead, she proposed that Lisya give lessons to the younger students.

"Too many of our musicians have left Russia," Madame shook her head sadly. "We need you here."

After some initial misgivings, Lisya began to take pride in her new role. An added benefit was that, as Madame's colleague, she was occasionally allowed to practice on her piano. Those rare hours were like sparkling diamonds, glittering in the sun of high noon.

Giving piano lessons unfortunately paid very little. So here she was, playing piano for the movies in a drafty theater which reeked of unwashed clothes. The new cinema, however, was often excitingly innovative – more creative, in fact, than some of the musical experiments she was witnessing from the orchestra pit of the Maryinsky. Glinka's *A Life for the Tsar* had become *Hammer and Sickle*, Puccini's *Tosca* had been renamed *The Battle for the Commune* – and so it went, as the old classics became political updates. The music itself was as wonderful as ever, but sometimes the rest of it seemed a bit clumsy. And Chaliapin was unfortunately not there to sing it. Like many other performers, he had fled the Motherland.

During the short break before the late show, Lisya went to the back door of the theater and quickly opened it. Dmitri slipped quietly in, squeezing her hand and sitting down in his usual seat behind her. Sometimes, if there was a Charlie Chaplin film, he brought Katya and Alexei with him.

Stretching her shoulders wearily, Lisya sat down again on the stool as the lights dimmed. Playing piano for movies was tiring work, she reflected, but not really so different from playing for ballet students. The Ballet School, like everything else, was now a much leaner version of its former elegance. Fewer students, on obviously smaller rations, lived and practiced in its colder rooms. Funding for the school was irregular and uncertain, as was Lisya's salary. But when large parcels of food and clothing arrived from emigres – Pavlova was especially generous – she was given a fair share.

Despite the shabby trappings, the excitement was still there. Students still graduated into the Maryinsky ballet troupe, where – even without the lavish accoutrements – they still performed magic. Young dancers like Balanchine and Danilova danced the classics minus the spectacle, but with energy and vitality that made the classical forms reverberate with new power.

And the dancers were also creating new forms. In the studio and on stage, Lisya watched as they became more athletic and dynamic. Some of the new ballets, to be sure, bordered on the ludicrous, with suffering slaves writhing under the lash of capitalism or heroically breaking their chains. But some of the experiments were truly brilliant, ingeniously creating the visual equivalent of the music. The daring choreography somehow combined the best of the old with the new.

It was well after midnight when the screen was finally still and the lights came up. Lisya closed the rickety keyboard and took Dmitri's arm as they walked out the backdoor.

"Tired?" Dmitri gently stroked her hand.

"Exhausted," sighed Lisya. "If only it were a decent piano."

"Like writing without paper?"

"Or painting without canvas and paints."

Silently they walked through the dark streets. "But isn't it strange," said Lisya, as they approached their apartment building. "Even without decent instruments – and paint and paper – it's still such an exciting time to be an artist!"

"We are like a garden of nightingales," said Dmitri. "Poets are springing up everywhere. People barely have the strength to live, but we are all singing."

Ж   Ж   Ж

Crammed with extravagantly gesturing people in the throes of exuberant conversation, the small apartment was thick with smoke, enthusiastically belching forth from a myriad of vigorously puffing cigarettes.

"We live in an epoch of unparalleled heroism," Dmitri was declaiming passionately, "ushered in by the noblest, greatest upheaval in human history!"

"Now is the time for greatness, for grandiose artistic structures," fervently agreed the tall, extremely thin man standing next to him, "not for the delicate sensibilities of personal poetry."

"Lyric bards have twittered away about their private sensations long enough," added a short bushy haired man vehemently. "They are due to go out of production."

Not long after his arrival in Petrograd, Dmitri had found a niche for himself in one of its numerous literary circles. He was no stranger to such groups. Often, in earlier years, he had wintered in various cities along the Volga, from Nizhny Novgorod to Tsaritsyn. He therefore knew how to seek out other poets – and how to behave in their company. Now, at last, he was near the hub of Russian literature. He had thrown himself into the literary battles of the day, and soon established a modest reputation for himself as the "Volga Poet."

From one corner of the obfuscated room came Boris Pasternak's booming Muscovite accent, mooing musically in homage to eternal woman. Across the room paced Vladimir Mayakovsky, mumbling sharp, staccato verses.

"Comrades!" Mayakovsky suddenly shouted in his deep, powerful voice. "Throw the old greats overboard from the ship of contemporaneity!"

Mayakovsky was the leader of those who wanted to burn the old museum masterpieces to make way for the new art of the People

"Citizens!" Maxim Gorky roared back through the smoke. "The old rulers have departed, leaving behind them a great inheritance which now belongs to the entire people. Citizens, protect that inheritance!"

Then Mayakovsky began reciting his poetry. As he read, he became more and more agitated, his beautiful voice rushing over the phrases, his body swaying rhythmically. Finally he was so overcome with emotion that he broke down, unable to finish.

Only occasionally were they invited to mingle with such elite literati; Dmitri's usual circle was less exalted. Though not particularly fond of poets in general – why couldn't they ever say what they meant! – Lisya was never bored at these bohemian soirees. Mostly she enjoyed watching her husband revel in his element, relieved to see the dark sadness almost leave his eyes. Sometimes, too, the behavior of the others was so outrageous, she laughed in spite of herself. Mayakovsky, in particular, despite his noisy attacks on the classics she revered, was difficult to resist.

And so, on their anniversary, Dmitri took her to see Mayakovsky's play celebrating the Revolution. *Mystery-Bouffe*, he had quite aptly named it, for it was an allegorical farce parodying the old religious mystery plays. Sitting in the theatre, holding hands, they watched the proletarian heroes on stage sail their Communist Ark through the revolutionary flood, propelled by the clever verse of Mayakovsky's relentless satire. They laughed at whining devils and the silly horrors of their Hell – pleasantly warm compared to Petrograd. They booed at lazy angels in Heaven, eating cloud bread which didn't fill their bellies. They cheered when the workers stole God's thunderbolts to electrify the countryside. And they cried when workers and machines finally made common cause and realized Utopia.

Afterward, Lisya and Dmitri walked slowly home along the Neva. They stopped for awhile, sitting on the embankment. The warm summer breeze caressed them; the rippling Neva made sensuous music. Leaning close to him, Lisya closed her eyes and was once again in the little grove on the Volga. Dmitri touched her cheek tenderly.

"Here, by the river," he murmured, "it almost seems like home."

"Being by the Volga – especially with you," Lisya smiled up at him, "was where I felt most at home. Back there, I mean."

"And here?"

"Petersburg is my home," replied Lisya. "It's where I belong."

"Even now?"

"Especially now."

"I'm not sure I do." Dmitri looked away. "There are so many buildings. I can't see the land. And I have to walk so far to see the river – which isn't the Volga."

"But there's so much being created in these buildings!" said Lisya, wondering. Dmitri didn't usually talk so much. "The poets – and the theatre – you like all that, don't you?"

"Yes, of course I do." He smiled. "And being with you. That's the best of all. I would go anywhere to be with you."

Dmitri gently put his strong arms around her. Lisya relaxed in the haven of his sturdy tree-like body. Silently they held each other, drawing strength from the deep bond between them.

Finally, he handed her a small package. In it was a golden brooch, shaped like a blazing sun. Wrapped around the beautifully wrought ornament was a poem. Its luminous verses sang of their love, and of their joy in rekindling the passion which burned between them. His words flamed across the page, into the shining sun in her hand, and radiated around them.

Looking into the intense darkness of his eyes, she wondered again at the fire of his poetry. Beneath the steady love which gazed out at her was pain that never left. Lisya put her arms around him, trying to comfort him, knowing that she could not.

Ж   Ж   Ж

Katya and Alexei also went to see *Mystery Bouffe*. They talked of nothing else for weeks. Especially the City of the Future, where Mayakovsky's proletarian heroes finally landed. When the gates flew open in the final scene, their young eyes had seen translucent factories and shimmering apartment buildings towering grandly up to the sky, trains and streetcars and automobiles wrapped in rainbows, a garden of stars and moons and the radiant crown of the sun.

"What Mayakovsky is saying," said Alexei fervently, "is that the new society can transform the world by direct action, through work toward a common goal."

"Immense suns will light our future lives," agreed Katya, with equal fervor. "Artists will turn the grey dust of our cities into rainbows."

"We must abandon self-expression," asserted Alexei, "and construct a new culture for our new society!"

"Every object of art must be an example of the new order," echoed Katya, "and show the way to the new society!"

"We must concentrate on the concrete, down-to-earth world of today," declared Alexei, "and someday we will achieve Utopia."

When Katya and Alexei began attending the University, they joined a group of students similarly intent. Together, they flexed their burgeoning idealism by copying Mayakovsky's window propaganda. Alexei wrote stirring verses, exhorting citizens to rally to the cause of Communism; Katya illustrated them with charcoal sketches. They hung their posters, colored in bold red and yellow and black, in the windows of various university haunts. Paper being in short supply, they pasted bits and scraps together. For several months, buckets of glue bubbled sluggishly on the stove.

Then – again, like Mayakovsky – Alexei decided they should do advertising. For awhile they turned out jingles and cartoons, urging people to buy their new galoshes and baby pacifiers from government outlets rather than on the black market.

"Poetry should be closer to everyday life," said Alexei to Lisya's raised eyebrow, "where its power can be a vitalizing force."

Fortunately, government advertising was shortly superceded by public art; Alexei and Katya were soon engrossed in the movement to bring art out of the galleries and into the streets.

"Artists and writers," Mayakovsky exhorted, "have the immediate duty to paint all the sides, foreheads and chests of cities, railway stations and the ever galloping herds of railway carriages."

To the best of their limited resources, Alexei and Katya answered the call. The corridors of the apartment building were soon adorned with heroic figures proclaiming heroic slogans. With thousands of others, they sang in mass spectacles staged on the monuments of Petrograd.

By this time, Katya had decided that she was an Artist. At first, she called herself a Supremacist and did paintings in the style of Malevich. Those in the first batch were collages of odd shapes and symbols, focused around a copy of some famous painting by one of the old masters. The Rembrandt – or Leonardo da Vinci or Botticelli or whatever – was always ostentatiously crossed out.

"In his day, yes, of course, Rembrandt was a great artist," Katya explained patiently to her mother's frowning face. "But his way of painting gets in the way of what artists should be doing today. Why look to the past with so much of the future before us. That's what Malevich meant when he crossed out the *Mona Lisa*."

Lisya had seen the painting her daughter was so enthusiastically trying to emulate. She liked it even less than Katya's chaotic efforts.

"But Katya," she persisted, "you've crossed out the best part of your painting!"

"Oh, Mother!" sighed Katya, with the exasperation of self-righteous youth.

The next phase was even worse. The walls of their room were soon covered with large geometric shapes, often in black.

"But don't you see, art must paint out the past and begin again," Katya tried to explain to her mother's puzzled face. "These paintings are the still silence before the new beginning. When we can no longer hear the past, we will be able to build anew. That's what Malevich proclaims in *Black Square*."

Lisya had seen that painting, too. It didn't offend – it was just silly.

"Then why not," she grumbled, "just stop painting for awhile."

"Oh, Mother."

Katya soon got bored painting only black squares and circles, and began to call herself a Constructivist. The apartment filled up with oddly shaped models of various heroic structures; geometrically shaped mobiles dangled from the ceiling. Lisya rather liked the mobiles, and only protested when the models took up all the available floor space. She even went with Katya to a Constructivist exhibition entitled *5 X 5 = 25*. At the end of the gallery was a painting by Rodchenko which astonished Lisya even more than Malevich's *Black Square*. The entire canvas was covered with nothing but red paint, and was called *The Last Painting*.

"Well," said Katya, tentatively, "I think this is a protest against the illusion of painting. Malevich is opposed to the art of the past. Rodchenko is just anti-art. Period."

Lisya said nothing, but shuddered at the thought of what was going to happen on their apartment walls.

Sure enough, within the month, all the walls were covered with bright mono-colored paint, fortunately of various hues and shades. Lisya held her tongue and waited. Eventually, Katya put away her paints and brushes and took up photography. With Alexei, she became an ardent devotee of the cinema; for the next year, student talk around the kitchen table focused on the films of Eisenstein. Lisya was relieved that her daughter was finally involved in something she could understand.

Though – occasionally – she did miss the mobiles.

Ж   Ж   Ж

Lisya took her usual chair in the orchestra pit of the Maryinsky. How often she had participated in the strange, cacophonous ritual of tuning up! And how marvelous that out of the chaos of so much discord could come – at the flash of a baton – the wonderful order of music!

Out of long habit, her eyes systematically surveyed the balconies, still surprised that they no longer glittered – then relieved that loud muddy boots no longer dangled over the railings. In the old Imperial Box sat someone Lisya had not seen for years – Sergei Prokofiev. He had left Russia shortly after the Revolution, and had only now returned. In his honor, the Maryinsky was performing his opera, *Love for Three Oranges*.

As the curtain rose, she eagerly turned her attention to the quirky music. Absurd touches of concrete reality rubbed shoulders with the fantastic, as the hero – a prince with incurable hypochondria – was finally cured by laughter. The audience, too, roared with laughter – and then cheered and applauded, long and loud, after the final curtain fell.

After the concert was a reception in Prokofiev's honor. Several years abroad had done nothing to improve his manners. Impeccably dressed in the latest Parisian chic, his condescending abruptness grated on those who had come to welcome him back. As Lisya looked around the shabbily-dressed gathering, she knew she was not the only one who resented Prokofiev's demeanor.

"A grown man," Vladimir had said at dinner the night before, "must clench his teeth and share his country's fate."

Dmitri had nodded in agreement; he, too, had refused to attend the reception.

Lisya herself had no desire to renew her acquaintance with Prokofiev. But she went to the reception anyway, hoping that he might have news of Tatiana. And, after a good deal of prodding, she finally found out what had happened to Tatiana since her last letter.

Tatiana was in New York, dancing with Balanchine's new company, just organized after his recent emigration. And – oh yes – there was a letter for Lisya. Perhaps his wife could find it for her; he had forgotten where it was.

Lisya called at their hotel early the next morning, barely able to restrain her excitement, and waited impatiently while Prokofiev's beautiful foreign wife rummaged sleepily through their luggage. At the bottom of one of the suitcases was a bundle of letters, all in different hands. Yawning, she sorted through them. When one in Tatiana's writing leaped out at her, Lisya nearly snatched it from the other woman's indifferent grasp. Hurriedly, she thanked her – and ran down the hotel stairs, out to the place beside the Neva where she and Tatiana had shared so many confidences.

With trembling hands, she carefully opened the letter.

My dear sister,

When you did not answer my letters, I assumed the worst. So I married Nikolai and we went to America to start a new life – and a new family. From Balanchine, however, I hear that you are still among the living. God be praised! Prokofiev is returning to Russia; Balanchine said he would ask him to give you this. I hope that it will be more successful in reaching you than the other letters I sent.

The most exciting news, my dearest friend, is that I, too, have a daughter. She is beautiful and wonderful and I named her after you. It is only with her – and sometimes when I am dancing – that the pain in my soul is eased. Nikolai is a good man, but he is so intent on becoming American that he cannot understand that I will always be Russian.

The emigres tell such terrible stories! Are they true? Is it any better now? Or has all that we treasure been destroyed? Oh Lisya, sometimes I am so homesick I think that even if it were all gone, I would still give my life to feel Russian soil beneath my feet!

Balanchine let us do *The Firebird* last month. I thought, as I often do, about Babushka's stories – about Maryushka dying when she had to leave home, about the bright feathers she left behind for *Rodina*. I danced with tears in my eyes.

I want to come home! Please tell me how it is in Petersburg. Please help me convince Nikolai that there is something for him to return to. Please give me hope that I will not end my days in exile!

Your loving sister,
Tatiana

When Lisya had reread the letter several times, she put it carefully in her pocket. As she gazed into the Neva, grateful tears mingled with the flowing river. Closing her eyes, she could almost sense Tatiana sitting beside her, her laughter rippling on the water.

Finally, she stood up and walked rapidly home.

My dearest Tatiana,

My soul is singing now that we have found each other again. Yes! Come home! Petrograd is much shabbier than Petersburg. But inside she is as beautiful as ever, and the Neva still flows. We all do without much that we had before. But we are not hungry – and we are full of hope. There is such excitement here!

Like the birth of a child after a long and difficult labor! I would not – could not – live anywhere else.

Come back where you belong!

Your loving sister,

Lisya

Ж   Ж   Ж

Vladimir was worried. Alarming rumors were seeping out of the Kremlin about Lenin's health. He decided to go to Moscow to see for himself.

Permission to visit Lenin took several weeks to arrange. Finally, on the day of the appointed audience, he presented himself at the Spassky Tower of the Kremlin. The guards at the gate wore brown uniforms and flat caps emblazoned with a red star. Wool pants were tucked into knee-high boots; long carbines were strapped over left shoulders. Vladimir gave his name to the guard who carried a pistol. He nodded, and then motioned Vladimir to line up with a small group of other men.

After a few minutes, a man in civilian clothes came out of the entrance. Hearing their names read from a small card fished out of his pocket, Vladimir and the other men followed him back through the gate. Walking silently up several flights of steps and down numerous dimly lit hallways, they approached a lighted doorway. There they were greeted by a small dark-haired woman with a soft but forceful voice. Vladimir assumed that this was Nadezhda Krupskaya, Lenin's wife.

Krupskaya led them into a small room. By the window was a desk covered with blue broadcloth; a few books were on it and a wooden armchair stood in front. To the right was an iron bed; a photograph of Lenin and Krupskaya hung over it and a plaid blanket was folded on top. To the left stood a crowded bookcase with a small sofa in front of it.

They walked through the bedroom into an even smaller room. In the center was an oak table with a white tablecloth, circled by wicker chairs. A large clock was on one wall; some pots of flowers were in a corner.

Without stopping, they entered the living room; Vladimir noticed that it was more dimly lit than the other two rooms. Two sofas faced each other, flanked by a few tables and lamps. All the furniture surrounded a large brightly-colored oriental rug. Along one wall was a spinet piano of dark wood.

At first, Vladimir's eyes were attracted to the rug. Gradually, however, he became aware of two green eyes staring at him from the shadows of the far cor-

313

ner. Focusing, he saw a cat sitting on a man's lap. Shifting his gaze upward, he saw Lenin's face, scrutinizing each of the visitors. Meeting his penetrating eyes, Vladimir had no doubt that they belonged to a formidable mind, fully alert.

Some of the visitors were foreigners. Lenin addressed each in his own language. His voice was soft and the words were slow. When he saw Vladimir's gaze resting on the piano, Lenin explained that his sister often played Beethoven for him.

"I never tire of listening to the 'Moonlight' Sonata," he said, stroking his cat. "It is hard to believe that such fascinating music was written by a human being. I always think with pride what wonders men can do."

The conversation continued in a nonpolitical vein. Then Krupskaya led them back out into the hall. Vladimir took away with him the image of a small thin frail man sitting in a rocking chair – but with dark eyes that drilled holes.

Vladimir returned to Petrograd only partially reassured. Rumors escalated until it was common knowledge among party officials that Lenin was no longer in the Kremlin, that he was recuperating from a stroke that had left him speechless and partially paralyzed. Those who saw him from afar said that he often wept tears of impotence and outrage. Finally, on a cold night in January, it was over. Lenin was dead.

People were shocked. Men, women, and children wept openly, pouring out genuine grief. Vladimir, too, wept. Lenin had been a great leader, a true believer in the cause of Revolution. And he would be almost impossible to replace.

A splendid funeral ceremony was held in Moscow. Red banners floated everywhere and deafening cheers reverberated around Red Square. Stalin delivered the eulogy. In spite of himself, Vladimir was caught up in its liturgical rhetoric. For Stalin, too, had begun his career in a seminary.

"Leaving us, Comrade Lenin ordered us to hold high and keep pure our great calling as members of the Party. We vow to thee, Comrade Lenin, that we will honor this, thy commandment.

"Leaving us, Comrade Lenin enjoined us to keep and strengthen the Dictatorship of the Proletariat. We vow to thee, Comrade Lenin, that we will not spare our strength in fulfilling with honor this, thy commandment.

"Leaving us, Comrade Lenin enjoined us to strengthen and extend the Union of Republics. We vow to thee, Comrade Lenin, that we will fulfill with honor this, thy commandment"

Lenin's widow had requested that her husband not be mourned by such public worship. "If you wish to honor his memory," she pleaded, "build child-care centers, kindergartens, houses and schools."

Instead, Lenin's body was embalmed and placed on permanent display in a glass coffin in the middle of Red Square. Vladimir was among the first of millions to stand in long freezing lines before the mausoleum, rendering homage to the relics of the Revolution's first saint. Statues were erected all over the USSR to Russia's latest icon. Even Mayakovsky wrote a hymn in memoriam.

And Petrograd was once again renamed.

"No! Never!" said Lisya, when she heard that her city was now to be called Leningrad. "This city will always belong to the Bronze Horseman!"

Ж   Ж   Ж

Lisya was standing on the Liteiny Bridge, staring down into the dark river. In her hands she clutched a letter.

Sadly she remembered the one delivered so casually by Prokofiev's wife, and how overjoyed she had been. That earlier letter had sparked a lively exchange of correspondence. Somehow, Tatiana had even persuaded Nikolai to return to Russia. While they made arrangements to come home, Lisya awaited their arrival with an excitement she had not felt in years.

And then, instead, came shattering news. The Soviet government had denied their visa. Enraged, Lisya waved the letter in Vladimir's face, demanding that he do something.

Vladimir tried. For the first time, he used his connections in the Party. He pulled every string possible – and failed.

"They're not giving any more visas to anyone," he finally told Lisya sadly. "All emigres are now considered traitors. The Party says that those who have deserted the Motherland will never be allowed to return."

"But Tatiana is not a traitor!"

"I know," said Vladimir quietly.

"Russia is her home!"

"I know."

"What will she do, so far from home!" Angry despair flooded the place in her heart she had always saved for her sister. "What will *we* do without *her*?!?"

"I don't know," Vladimir had replied, his voice choking "I don't know."

Lisya shivered and shifted her dark gaze from the river to the Vyborg side of the Neva. The old fear swept over her again, this time red with rage. *It's all their fault*, she thought bitterly, as she pictured the torrent of Revolution boiling and flooding across the bridge. It had ravaged her life on the other side – and carried off her sister forever.

Slowly she tore up Tatiana's last letter. There would, she knew, be no more of them. The small fragments of paper drifted down like snow – and then were swallowed up by the current.

Numbly, Lisya walked back to the Palace Embankment. She turned and looked at the Bridge, which seemed to stretch out endlessly into the fog – like the tracks at the station when she had seen Tatiana off so long ago. She closed her eyes and tried to picture her sister's face, tried to imagine her safe in her new home on the other side of the world.

As she looked again at the Bridge, she felt something inside snap and recoil painfully, as though all the strings of her violin had suddenly given way. It was no use. America was too far away.

Ж   Ж   Ж

Lisya was worried.

Dmitri was growing increasingly morose. He was, she knew, homesick. A peasant at heart, he had never really been transformed into a true proletarian.

"I hate having to go to that factory!" snapped Dmitri, when she tried to draw him out of his dark mood.

"But surely it's better now than before the Revolution," said Lisya uncertainly, stunned by his anger.

"Because we're the heroes of the new order?" he retorted sarcastically. "Being a worker still means being cooped up all day with noisy ugly machines!"

"But afterward," persisted Lisya, still stinging from the hostility in his voice, "there is the beauty of Petersburg!"

"Petrograd is a maze of crumbling buildings!"

"But there's the Neva."

"The Neva is too confined, too cluttered, too civilized!" shouted Dmitri. "And it isn't the Volga!"

He strode out of the apartment, slamming doors behind him. He returned much later that night. Climbing into bed beside her, he said nothing. The next day, he acted as though the whole incident had not occurred. But after that, he spent more and more time walking moodily along the river's embankments; each time, he returned gloomier and more irritable.

Part of the problem, Lisya knew, was that the intellectual climate of Petrograd was changing. Dmitri's homesickness had, at first, been overshadowed by his excitement at being, at last, a real writer. Like Lisya, he had been caught up in the creative fervor which swept the city. Lately, however, the government was becoming less tolerant of those writers not exhibiting proper class consciousness. Even Mayakovsky was being publicly criticized.

Nevertheless, Dmitri and Lisya went to the opening of his new play. That *The Bathhouse* was a violent, undisguised attack on Soviet bureaucracy was apparent almost immediately. Important government figures were mercilessly lampooned, party members held up for bitter ridicule.

"All of you – what are you trying to say?" asked the last line of the play. "That people like me are of no use to Communism?"

No one laughed. No one applauded. The audience sat in stony silence.

A few months later, Mayakovsky shot himself.

Dmitri, meanwhile, stopped writing; there were no more poems. After Mayakovsky's suicide, he grew taciturn, retreating farther and farther into the recesses of what Lisya feared was an ever darkening soul.

Desperately, she tried to reach him.

"There's a new Charlie Chaplin movie at *The Bright Reel* tonight," she said, trying to sound cheerful. "Why don't you come to the late show?"

"Watching a stupid American in baggy pants is as stupid as the music you play!" exclaimed Dmitri, his voice dripping with sarcasm.

Speechless, Lisya turned and walked slowly out of the apartment.

By the end of the late show, she had recovered from her shock. Returning home, she slipped quietly into bed with Dmitri, who was still awake.

"The movie tonight was really funny," she began tentatively.

Without a word, he turned on his side, his back to her.

"Have you read Alexei's new poem?" she tried again, after a long silence. "I think he'd really like you to look at it."

More silence.

Cautiously, she reached out to rub his back, gently scratching in the places he liked.

Immediately she felt his body stiffen.

Hesitantly she continued, trying to loosen the tightness in his muscles.

The cold silence continued until she, too, finally turned away. Her back to him, she could not restrain the tears which slid quietly to the pillow.

After that, he often came home late, reeking of alcohol.

One night, she confronted him.

"Dmitri, what's wrong?!"

"Leave me alone!" he snarled.

"Please!" Lisya begged. "Please, let me help you!"

His bloodshot eyes flashed with pain. She reached out, trying to comfort him. The pain changed to anger; he raised his arm to strike her. Her look of shocked disbelief stopped his hand just short of her face. They both stood staring – forever, it seemed – at his poised fist. Finally, he slowly lowered it and walked abruptly out.

A week later, in the long dark night of the cold deadly winter, he threw himself off the Liteiny Bridge.

They never found his body. But Lisya knew that in the river, his soul would more easily find its way back to the Volga.

Which was where he had always belonged.

Chapter 16: The PLAN

The long oval kitchen table had never been so full. Every available space on it was covered with food and drink people sitting around it had not seen in years. Smoked sturgeon was surrounded by thin wafers of smoked salmon; slender rolls of roast chicken accompanied smoked eel layered with lemon slices; salami and sausage flanked pickled beets and freshly boiled potatoes tossed with dill. Baskets of rye bread, sourdough white bread, and Russian black bread stood among several kinds of hard cheese and mounds of unsalted butter molded into fancy shapes. Big bowls of sauerkraut, cranberry-horseradish relish, cucumbers and mushrooms in sour cream alternated with large platters of stuffed eggplant and cabbage leaves. And in the center stood several carafes of vodka flavored with anise, basil, lemon, garlic and various other herbs.

The food had been procured – after much shrewd bargaining – by Sergei and Vassily. It had been prepared – late into the night – by Ludmilla and Olga and Lisya. Even Vladimir had made an exception to his usual rule and negotiated the vodka. And now, watching Alexei and Katya beaming and blushing at the head of the table, they all thought their efforts well worth the result.

The years had passed – too slowly for the bearing of burdens, too quickly for the growing-up of children. Life in the outside world had changed for all of them. And not always for the better. Progress there was, but somehow not so much hope. On this day, however, all that was pushed aside, as everyone focused on the two young people whose nurturing had sustained the adults who loved them through many dark days. Here, in this place, for this brief day, happiness would be seized and life would be enjoyed to its fullness.

Earlier in the day, they had all gone to the new Marriage Palace, where Vladimir had given away the bride and an official had solemnly exhorted the young couple to work together for the Glory of the State. As Lisya watched the starkly simple ceremony, memories flickered unbidden. For just an instant, she saw golden crowns over the bride and groom. Then she looked at the icon above

319

them; instead of the Virgin, it was Lenin. Phantom traces of incense and almost-heard chanting vanished at once. Sadness swept over her.

Standing there, in the made-over saffron velvet dress, Katya was suddenly a woman. Her now contoured body moved with strangely familiar gestures; looking at her lovely face was rather like peering into a mirror. *It's me*, Lisya thought with wonder, *and yet it's not.*

Under arched eyebrows almost as dark as her thick straight hair, Katya's slightly slanted eyes glowed. Around her neck were the amber beads. *Ah yes*, Lisya remembered fondly, *it's him, too.* A warm presence caressed her.

And for awhile, the comforting memory of Alexander Pavlovich obscured the haunting image of Dmitri's tortured face, fist poised to strike her. An image which never left her, day and night, despite her resolution never to talk about it.

Throughout the short ceremony, Katya's eyes never left Alexei's. The look on her face, Lisya decided with satisfaction, made the golden crowns unnecessary.

Alexei's eyes were rather bloodshot. The night before, his friends had assisted him in an old ritual – spelling out the name of his bride in glasses of vodka. *He'd be in better shape today*, Lisya grinned, *if he were marrying someone named Anna instead of Ekaterina.*

At the end of the ceremony bride and groom had kissed, signed the register, and returned home to celebrate. Around the table, students and workers and commissars squeezed next to artists and writers and musicians. More and more guests kept crowding into the already packed kitchen. Eventually they spilled over into the room with the piano, where music began, and into the other rooms, where dancing alternated with lively – if somewhat inebriated – discussions about poetry and art and music and politics. Finally, much later, Alexei and Katya went off to one of the city's better hotels for a brief overnight honeymoon.

As Lisya kissed Katya goodbye, she was suddenly overwhelmed by the bittersweetness of the moment. *After tonight, we will never be the same.* Mother and daughter clung to each other – and then let go.

"Be happy," Lisya said, gently smoothing her daughter's hair.

Katya looked at Alexei. And as her tears became a smile, so did Lisya's.

Ж   Ж   Ж

It was almost dawn. Most of the guests had departed. Lisya and Olga were sitting in the kitchen, finishing off the last of the vodka. Sergei and Vladimir were at opposite ends of the table, snoring loudly at each other. Vassily was on the floor,

320

leaning against the stove, Ludmilla's head in his lap. They, too, were asleep. Occasional balalaika chords drifted in from another room.

"Katya looked so beautiful tonight. And Alexei, so grown up and handsome... I wonder..." Lisya gazed morosely at the remains of the stuffed eggplant, "I wonder how long they'll stay so happy."

"Longer, I would guess, than most couples," Olga replied, nibbling slowly on a piece of salami.

"But marriage can be such a... problem." Lisya poked at the eggplant with a fork.

"Mmm, yes. But not to them. Not now, at least." Olga took another bite of salami. "You've heard them talking about it with their friends... 'In a comradely marital union, neither partner is the property of the other. Each is free to experience life as fully as possible.' And so forth."

"And at least now, the law says women are equal." Lisya popped a piece of eggplant into her mouth and poured herself a shot of basil-flavored vodka. "Katya won't ever *have* to live with Alexei, if he doesn't behave. She can divorce him any time she feels like it."

"And go home to Mother," said Olga, reaching for the vodka.

They both giggled, and swallowed the contents of their glasses with a single gulp.

"The new law also says weak little women like us – hah! – must be protected by all the big strong men." Olga waved a sausage wrathfully. "No thank you, we've had enough of that!"

Lisya poured two shots of garlic-and-dill vodka, and they drank to the strength of Russian women.

"But the law protects us *from* men, too." Lisya smeared some pickled beets on a crust of black bread. "Men actually get punished now for raping and beating their wives and spreading venereal disease. And pimps are jailed instead of prostitutes!"

"And then Comrade Lenin said: 'Let there be athletic competitions and intellectual pursuits' – to sublimate all those troublesome urges!" Olga grinned derisively and tossed back a shot of anise vodka. "My God! There aren't enough libraries in all of Russia to do that. And it would certainly take more than a perpetual track-meet!"

"Maybe that's why they argue so much." Lisya fished a cucumber slice out of an almost empty bowl of sour cream. "I wonder..." she pondered between bites, "when they talk, they always act like they know so much… Do you think they really do?"

"Of course not!" Olga reached again for the anise vodka. "Which is why they will never let the family wither away – no matter what they say now. They need us."

"Then why can't they just admit it?" Lisya's voice trembled. "And let us help them?"

"Because," Olga replied quickly, raising her glass resolutely, "men are fools."

Lisya poured herself a double shot and tossed it back effortlessly.

The two women now earnestly applied themselves to finishing off the remains of the marriage feast. They were especially assiduous in emptying the vodka carafes. And as they progressed in this latter task, they also began an odd litany of pronouncements on the perfidy of the male sex. Slowly, it built in momentum and intensity, as the flashing glasses emptied with increasing frequency. As each age-old complaint of woman against man rolled with eloquent profanity off Olga's tongue, a torrent of anger exploded from Lisya in response. On and on, the dialogue continued, its invective mounting into white-hot fury. Lisya was amazed that such rage – in such words – could be coming from her, but she was past the point of caring. Her anger took on a life of its own, possessing her completely.

At last, after almost all the vodka was gone, the outburst abated. Yelling turned into laughter, as curses called down on the feckless male sex became increasingly ludicrous. Finally they swore a mock solemn oath to continue the Revolution by castrating all men.

"The Socialist does not bow to the laws of nature," proclaimed Olga, brandishing a knife over the snoring Sergei, "but seeks instead to alter them!"

"The dictatorship of the proletariat will never be achieved," gasped Lisya, between spasms of laughter, "until the dictatorship of the penis has been destroyed!"

"And when all the petit-bourgeois balls have withered away," squealed Olga, "then will dawn the golden age of Communism."

Then they screamed with laughter until their sides ached. Emptying the last carafe of vodka, they stood up unsteadily and proposed a last toast.

"Women of the world, unite!" Both of them belched resoundingly. "You have *nothing* to lose."

They drained their glasses and threw them out the window. Hearing them shatter on the pavement below, they slid back down into their chairs and laid their heads on the table.

Lisya's last gasps of laughter caught in her throat, becoming sobs so imperceptibly she hardly noticed. Before she could stop herself, cries of anguish too long restrained burst forth. The grieving went on and on, tears coming from a reservoir of pain too long buried At last, when everything had been exhausted, her weeping subsided

As dawn shone through the window, Lisya reached out and grasped Olga's hand gratefully. Soon, their snores were drowning out those of Sergei and Vladimir.

Ж   Ж   Ж

The Party had changed – drastically. Of that Vladimir had no doubt. But exactly how – of that he was less sure.

Although never one of Lenin's disciples, Vladimir had nonetheless mourned the great leader's death. He had assumed, however, that the mantle of leadership would fall to Trotsky, and that the Revolution would march on to much the same cadence. Instead, dynamic Trotsky was edged out by unspectacular Stalin.

Vladimir was dumbfounded.

"It must be because Trotsky is Jewish," he said to Sergei, scratching his head.

"Maybe," replied Sergei, unperturbed. "Or maybe he couldn't cope with the in-fighting of Party politics."

Stalin, it soon became apparent, was no idealist. Nor was he at all squeamish about dictating his will to everyone. By the time he had firmly entrenched himself in power, it was clear to Vladimir what had changed. The Party no longer ran the country – Stalin did.

Vladimir's first indignation eventually subsided, as the ghost of an unthinkable idea nibbled away at his consciousness. What has happening now was not new. In fact, it was all too familiar. It was not, however, until Stalin announced The Plan that Vladimir allowed himself to think such a thing consciously.

The Five-Year-Plan was to be the final phase of the Great Revolution. It was to finish what had been started in 1917. What had taken Europe hundreds of years was to be accomplished in Russia in just a few decades. In one gigantic leap, the Soviet Union was to be transformed from a backward agrarian economy, at the mercy of just about everyone, into an industrialized socialist society able to withstand capitalist encirclement. At last, the Revolution was back on track!

As The Plan was launched, ever more grandiose schemes were announced. The half-formed idea in the back of Vladimir's mind germinated. And as great dams were built across the Dnieper and new towns mushroomed overnight in Siberia, it insinuated itself fully-grown and fully-conscious. Something like this had happened before, centuries ago, when Peter the Great had assaulted the sleeping Russian bear with Western technology, and then dragged it into the world a great power

"We would have been eaten alive, otherwise," said Vladimir to Sergei, in one of their unending kitchen table debates. "And how much greater the threat is now!"

Sergei, however, needed no convincing. As one of the new managers of the Putilov Steelworks, he was trying to master the new management style preached by the Party. "When the director walks around the plant," they were told, "the earth should tremble."

The new bosses dutifully learned to roar – and to work round the clock, as the staggering complexity of what they were attempting dawned on them. The Plan's success depended on breaking in and adapting an illiterate, predominantly rural labor force to the industrial world. And on teaching them – simultaneously – to operate machines, learn to read, punch a time-clock, and use a spittoon.

Not surprisingly, the whole system lurched ahead in constant jolts and nerve-wracking tilts of changing norms, forced overtime, and rapid labor turnover. Everywhere there was a sense of urgency, as immensity became the guiding principle and over-fulfilled targets the essential goal. Just one more big effort, one more factory built, one more dam constructed – and prosperity and happiness and, above all, security would be theirs. Mother Russia would, at last, be strong enough to resist those who surrounded her. For what was the alternative? Stalin himself had said it many times: "If in ten years we do not cover the distance other countries took 100 years to traverse, we will be crushed."

And so, just as masses of Russian soldiers had been thrown into battle to defend the Motherland, so now millions of Russian peasants were mobilized to complete The Plan. Vladimir himself was ready to give his life, if necessary, to protect the Revolution from those who worked ceaselessly to undermine it. But somehow that didn't seem enough for the immense task at hand.

If only he lived in Moscow. For there they were working miracles – like the Moscow Metro. The massive subway network was being built in record time, to prove that the first communist state could catch up with – and surpass – the capitalists. Then the world would know that Soviet Russia was a formidable power, capable of repelling those who threatened her borders.

Eagerly Vladimir attended the opening ceremonies for the first completed line. He had heard rumors about the grand stations. Even so, he was astonished by the main terminal in Revolution Square. Ornate ceilings rested on massive columns. The floors were marble mosaics, the lights were crystal chandeliers. Everywhere were classical busts and stained-glass windows. And everything was absolutely immense. Never had Vladimir seen anything like it. Not even in church. And, he noted with the professional satisfaction of a military man, the subway was 200 feet below ground. The stations and tunnels would be very useful in outlasting invaders.

There was a huge parade in Red Square to celebrate. Vladimir joined thousands of others cheering the new monument to Soviet Communism. If the new order could accomplish this, surely it could keep the Motherland safe from the enemies who lurked everywhere. And when Stalin himself pinned the new Order of Lenin on the chief builder, Vladimir yearned to be standing in his place.

Ж   Ж   Ж

"It'll do you good," insisted Olga. "All you do is work, and sit in this room brooding."

After the wedding, Sergei had simply taken over her space; so Olga had moved in with Lisya. Katya, of course, now shared the bedroom with Alexei. Olga was a good roommate, but seeing Sergei in the room she still considered Tatiana's irritated Lisya.

At the moment, however, she was more irritated by Olga's announcement that they were going out. Olga never took no for an answer.

"But the theatre now is so... so..."

"So what!" grinned Olga wickedly. "It's still entertaining – in its own way."

"Like the last one you dragged me to? With that horrid actor playing Lenin – twinkling about patting children on the head and giving advice to the lovelorn, and engaging in Socratic dialogue with the proletarian masses? Oh yes, that's real theatre!"

"You laughed, didn't you?" Olga continued to grin.

"But I wasn't supposed to." In the play, Lenin had hired someone to fix the broken clock of the Spassky Tower. During the final scene, as the Great Leader was giving an inspiring speech, the mended clock began chiming. As the curtain

325

rang down on the Kremlin chimes pealing out the *Internationale*, Lisya had been nearly overwhelmed by an overpowering urge to laugh.

"Not to worry," chuckled Olga. "Everyone thought the play had moved you to tears."

"And so it did," laughed Lisya, remembering.

"See? I rest my case."

The new play Olga took Lisya to that evening started out rather badly. It was about a lone woman commissar who, during the Civil War, converted the all-male crew of a naval ship to Communism. As expected, the play was unabashedly overt propaganda. In its appallingly unsubtle musical introduction, overdone crescendoes and heart-searing cries of exaltation burst annoyingly from a gigantic chorus in shining white uniform.

The climactic battle scene was even worse. The outnumbered Communists fought valiantly with whatever they could lay hands on, inspired by the exhortations of the female commissar and the music of the hero, playing the *Internationale* on his accordion. Finally he, too, went down, flailing his sweat-soaked shirt and flinging his accordion in the face of the enemy.

Throughout the play, the commissar was inhumanly calm and indomitably courageous. "Get this into your head," she would scold squeamish crew members. "I will do whatever the Party requires, and you will, too – including destruction of the rotten part to preserve what's healthy. Understand?"

But there was one scene in the play which made the rest of it worth enduring. When some of the non-communists tried to rape her, the commissar's reaction was electrifying. She whipped out her gun, and expertly drilled a bullet through the balls of the leader.

"Anyone else?" she demanded, waving her smoking pistol at the now cowering sailors.

Never had Lisya experienced anything as elementally and vicariously satisfying. She felt a huge primal cheer welling up from deep within, reaching back – far back – into time. At the end of the scene, every woman in the theater was on her feet, applauding wildly.

Ж   Ж   Ж

Shostakovich's new symphony was scored for large orchestra; the Leningrad Philharmonic had borrowed some musicians from the Maryinsky for its premiere. Lisya could feel the tension and excitement, even in the back row of the 2nd

Violins. The audience was packed with Leningrad's artistic and political elite, all waiting to see if Shostakovich could pull it off.

The Arts, too, had been enlisted in The Plan. Henceforth, proclaimed Comrade Stalin and the Party, Soviet Art was to reflect reality. Not as it was, but as it *should* be – and someday *would* be. The new doctrine was called Socialist Realism. Tolstoy and Beethoven were held up as examples.

Musicians soon fell in line as Soviet composers endeavored to produce big music with new simplicity. The ideal was to provide suitable accompaniment to The Plan, creating a musical backdrop that was edifying and accessible, robust and cheerful. Classical composers began writing film music and popular songs for the masses.

New operas and ballets were performed at the Maryinsky, all with folksy settings and perpetually positive heroes, all liberally sprinkled with nasty enemies of Communism. Some were old pieces reworked; others were more original – like Prokofiev's new opera about a virtuous peasant who, surviving the vicissitudes of War and Revolution, emerged triumphant as the manager of an aluminum plant. Listening to an aria sung by the chairman of the Village Soviet, Lisya decided, definitely took some getting used to – as did hearing the recitative of a commissar making telephone calls. And the fate of the hero's sister – who became the director of a model pig farm – was not exactly enviable. Still, it was better than *Swan Lake*.

And then had come Shostakovich's opera, *Lady Macbeth of the Mtensk District*. Anything but cheerful and edifying, the savagely sarcastic music was extraordinarily gloomy, the explicit sexuality shocking.

Stalin was offended. Shortly after he saw the opera, *Lady Macbeth* was withdrawn from the Soviet stage. Shostakovich was publicly denounced as an "enemy of the people."

And so, he had written a new symphony, which he hoped would be heroic enough to prove his loyalty. And which advocates of Socialist Realism hoped would prove that the new Party line could produce real Art.

The excited audience applauded nervously as the conductor strode out on stage and stepped onto the podium. He raised his baton and stood, poised and waiting, as the orchestra took a deep, gigantic breath. And then the downbeat plunged them all into a harsh but noble struggle. Upper and lower strings flung the angular theme back and forth, antiphony slowly building into urgent and purposeful angst, discordant harmonies underscoring the immense conflict. A brash, quirky scherzo full of rollicking bassoons interrupted. An exuberant dance, a good joke, a raucous celebration tucked in between crises – like a burst of fireworks, it was over too soon. A long heartfelt largo of rhapsodic melancholy began to unfold. Sorrowful and introspective and intense, its poignant strains wept on and on. At last, a burst of amazing energy unleashed the creative will of an indomitable people. A whirlwind of woodwinds and hammering percussion lashed the storming assembly lines, as factories and dams and towns leaped up with lightning speed. And then, all doubts resolved, the nation squared its shoulders and marched off to industrial battle. As mighty brass chords and pounding tympani built up to a monumental and massively heroic climax, the grandiose vistas of Mayakovsky's City of the Future rose before them.

Lisya reluctantly pulled her violin out from under her chin. There was a moment of silence as the entire hall exhaled as one. And then, thunderous applause and rapturous cheering. The ovations went on and on and on.

A new Beethoven had been born.

Ж　Ж　Ж

When The Plan had first been announced, Vladimir had immediately thrown himself into building up the Red army with his usual zeal. But he soon discovered that this task was less a question of revolutionary elan than of technology and weaponry. He soon became disenchanted, and began looking for a more heroic way to serve The Plan.

"The socialist city must lead the petit-bourgeois peasantry," proclaimed Comrade Stalin, "by planting collective farms in the countryside and turning it onto a new socialist path."

Of course! That was it! He would go back to his roots and proclaim the Gospel of Socialism! He would uplift his ignorant people and lead them to salvation on collective farms! His fundamentally populist soul quivered with righteous fervor.

Vladimir was among the first contingent sent off to convert the rural masses. On the day he left, all flags flying and chanting heroic poems, Lisya was there to see him off.

How she hated railroad stations! Even so, she could not help smiling as Vladimir waxed eloquent about his latest crusade. He was always so sure that this time he would finally be able to save the world!

"How long will you be gone?" asked Lisya.

"For as long as it takes," boomed Vladimir, his eyes glowing with excitement.

She remembered the last time they had parted like this. Then, she had been the one going to the Volga.

"Be careful!" she shouted over the hissing locomotive, thinking what a foolishly inadequate thing it was to say.

Grinning, Vladimir slung his duffle bag over his shoulder and leaped aboard the train.

"And come back!" Lisya's voice was lost in a blast of steam.

Vladimir smiled and waved, then faced eagerly forward.

As the train puffed slowly ahead, Lisya felt a rush of raw fear. Suddenly breaking into a sweat, she abruptly turned and began walking back down the platform – faster and faster, until she was almost running. *I must get out of here before the train does*! Glancing back, she collided with an old man. The bundles he was carrying went flying. Barely noticing, she did not stop to help him pick them up.

Finally, outside the station, away from all the people saying goodbye, away from the trains going places too far to imagine, away from the sad empty tracks, her panic subsided.

As she walked slowly home, she wondered if, this time, Vladimir would find what he was searching for.

Chapter 17: The KOLKHOZ

Mischa read about it in *Pravda*.

"The Party calls it the Five-Year-Plan," he reported to Evgenia, his sturdy face unusually animated. "The Motherland is to make a great leap forward and become a modern industrial nation."

"Nothing will come of it without the peasants," replied Evgenia.

"But we're to be part of it, too!"

Evgenia had not seen Mischa so elated since Elena had consented to marry him.

"We're supposed to combine all our farms into a *kolkhoz*. It'll be owned by all of us. We'll till the fields collectively, and divide the produce according to how much work we do."

"Isn't that what we're already doing?"

"Well, yes, but in the *kolkhoz* the land won't be divided up so inefficiently. The strips in my allotment now are too small. And they're scattered all around the village. I waste too much energy going from one to another. We all do."

"So the village commune will stay, but the land won't be split up?"

"More or less. But the best part is that the government's to give us tractors and modern tools!"

"And what do we give them?"

"Some of the grain."

"How much?"

"Whatever's fair – how else could it work?" Mischa's usually sober, thoughtful eyes were almost dancing with joy. "At last! I can give my horses a rest, and throw away my wooden hoe."

"I think I'll keep mine," said Evgenia quietly.

Most of the village did not share Mischa's enthusiasm. They were not ready for a great leap forward. Nor were those sent out to lead them any better prepared. Their orders were to be Leninists – but since Lenin had never worked on a farm, no one was sure what that meant. And so they called meetings – and more meetings – and still more meetings. Everyone talked at once. Agendas evaporated, as discussion digressed from farm issues to airing personal grievances or settling old scores. Shouting matches sometimes erupted into bloody brawls.

Finally, most of the peasants put their X on the *kolkhoz* charter. Classes were then started to turn them into tractor drivers, account keepers, and *kolkhoz* chairmen. Mischa was the first to sign up. Conscientiously, he attempted to learn about tractors without a tractor, and about how to manage a collective farm from sometime who had never been a farmer. He cooperated wholeheartedly in the experiments of his *kolkhoz*, and urged his neighbors to do likewise. He even joined the Party. But by the time he was appointed Chairman of his collective farm, even he could see that the Collectivization Crusade was a disaster.

"The problem is that the government doesn't understand what grain means to us!" complained Mischa to Evgenia, in an uncharacteristically wrathful tone of voice. "To them, it's just food for the cities. To us, it's what fuels our whole farming cycle. Upset the balance of grain and you risk the crop itself. But they hand down quotas with no regard for what any fool knows!"

"People living in cities worry about other things," replied Evgenia. "It's easier for them to forget what's real."

Despite the difficulties, the harvest of 1930 was a gift from heaven, the biggest crop since 1913. Mischa and his *kolkhoz* were jubilant. Surely now, things would get better. But in their zeal to satisfy their superiors, local officials exaggerated an already bountiful crop still more, leaving the peasants with less grain and higher quotas.

The lesson was not lost on them. Energy expended on making their *kolkhoz* productive they now turned to devising means of easing an impossible burden. Every ounce of peasant shrewdness was utilized in an all-out effort to survive. With a heart heavy with growing disillusion, Mischa looked the other way.

Even so, they were stripped of their grain reserves. Despite fulfilled quotas, OGPU squads kept coming back, demanding more. Finally they were bled dry of both seed and fodder. When the horses grew too thin to draw even an empty cart, the hungry peasants ate them.

Had it not been for the women, they would all surely have starved.

"No!" said Evgenia resolutely, when the order came to collectivize their cow. Korova was not just a piece of livestock; she was a member of the family. Her ancestors had faithfully served Evgenia's mother and grandmother – and their grandmothers. Evgenia herself had received a daughter of this long and illustrious line when she had begun her moon cycle. Since then, she had lovingly raised several descendants from calfhood, including Korova. She could no more surrender her to someone else's care than one of her own children. Besides, Korova's contributions to the household were vital.

When the next *kolkhoz* meeting was called, Evgenia marched purposefully to the firehouse, Elena at her side. As she strode angrily down the road, the village women fell in behind her. As the men watched, astonished, Evgenia walked up to the brash young government agent and fixed him with a stare into which all her years of motherhood and teaching were concentrated.

"What do you think you're doing?!" she demanded, in a quiet but firm voice which brooked no argument.

He ceased his harangue and looked guiltily at his feet.

"Don't you know how stupid this is?" she continued disdainfully.

"But the government has decreed that the cows be collectivized," he replied, somewhat subdued.

"Why?!"

"So that the quota of the cows' production will be fulfilled," he said, unsuccessfully trying to inject a note of bravado.

"And where does the government plan to put the cows?" asked Evgenia, her cohorts murmuring angrily behind her.

"Well, uh – I suppose in the collective barn."

"And just where is this collective barn?!"

"Well, uh – I suppose you're supposed to build one."

Grumbling from the men.

"And meanwhile?!" Evgenia's eyes continued to drill into the now thoroughly disconcerted young man.

"Well, uh – I suppose we could let you take care of the cows until the collective barn is built."

The women nodded, somewhat mollified. The men looked at them with new eyes.

"But the cows are now the property of the *kolkhoz*," the young socialist said weakly at the women marching back down the road.

Not deigning to answer, Evgenia turned and followed.

The men took careful note of all this and, a few days later, invited the women to join the assembly on a regular basis. Soon, the women were doing most of the talking. If the agent tried to interrupt them, they made such a din that he had to call off the meeting. Meanwhile, the men stood around, leaning menacingly on their pitchforks.

When the men were approached to make their women stay home, they shrugged resignedly. "The women are equal now. As they decide, so we must agree…" This tactic was also useful as an excuse for not following unwanted decrees. "My wife does not want to socialize our chickens," the suddenly henpecked husband would sigh, rolling his eyes helplessly, "so I cannot do it."

Eventually, of course, the agent brought reinforcements to silence the women. The men soon began swinging their pitchforks and chased the agent and his squad out of the village. When order was finally restored, and the men were hauled before the district court, they claimed to have merely been defending their women. The judge let them go with a stern warning not to repeat such bourgeois chivalry.

But when they heard that the kulaks were to be exiled, the women became more militant. Evgenia herself was outraged.

"The Party says the kulaks are in league with the agents of international imperialism," Mischa explained, none too certainly. "If we are to resist capitalist encirclement, we must industrialize and be strong. The kulaks are sabotaging the Plan with a grain strike."

"But what is a kulak? Yes, I know what it means." Evgenia made a fist. "Greedy men who get rich off others by money-lending and trading rather than honest work. There have always been a few like that around here. But there can't be enough of them to constitute a class – let alone a menace to the nation!"

It did not take long for the village to ascertain that what the government meant by "kulak" was simply anyone who was recognizably better off than his neighbors. Often an extra horse or cow could turn a peasant into a kulak, both in the eyes of the paranoid government and his envious neighbors. Not a few "kulaks" thus slaughtered their offending livestock rather than risk the dangerous label. Though most of the village protected their own, some denounced "kulaks" to settle old scores.

Local officials, in turn, decided that "dekulakization" was the simplest way to get rid of anyone appearing to oppose collectivization. Stripped of their land – and often, quite literally, everything else – the kulaks and their families had no place to go. Some fled to cities, where they starved without ration cards; others were herded into cattle trucks and dumped in the middle of nowhere. Many simply disappeared.

In Derevnia, however, the women planted themselves in a firm phalanx before the *izba*s of their unfortunate neighbors.

"Throw your bourgeois humanitarianism out the window and behave like

Bolsheviks worthy of Comrade Stalin," exhorted the leader of OGPU troops sent to disperse them. "Beat down the kulak agent wherever he raises his head. The last decayed remnant of capitalist farming must be wiped out at any cost. It's war – them or us!"

The women were unconvinced, and did not move. Eventually another pitchfork battle erupted, which the superior weaponry of the OGPU troops was finally able to quell.

After that, the women tended their gardens. And when the chaos in the menfolk's fields resulted in famine, the womenfolk's tiny plots fed their families. Frustrated that something so small – cultivated with wooden hoes – was outproducing the giant fields strewn with broken tractors, the government's anger grew.

"The Party says your gardens are survivals of petit bourgeois mentality," said Mischa.

"We must keep our cows alive and make our gardens grow," Evgenia shrugged, "whatever the Party calls it."

"The Party says you must be re-educated out of your greed."

"Is that what you think?"

"No. I just wish I could get people to work as hard in the fields as on their family plots."

"'As ye sow'…"

"Yes, I know," sighed Mischa. "The government is reaping a bitter harvest of its own short-sightedness."

"For which *we* are paying the price – as usual."

"Yes, I know," Mischa sighed again. "The Revolution was supposed to make us all equal. And the Plan was supposed to make life better for everyone. But somehow, we are serfs again!"

"The more things change," replied Evgenia quietly, "the more they stay the same."

Ж   Ж   Ж

Father Ivan was not surprised when the government declared war on the Church.

Ever since the Bolsheviks had seized power, the Orthodox Church had been the target of persecution. But even in religious circles, this was not an altogether unpopular policy. Those previously persecuted by the Church were not sorry to see the once privileged Orthodox singled out for especially harsh treatment. For many of these other religious groups, it was a time of greater religious freedom than they had ever known. They needed no urging to support the new order which had liberated them from the oppressive hand of the Orthodox Church.

Ivan could not really blame them.

"As ye sow," he had sighed, "so shall ye reap."

Nor could he entirely blame the Bolsheviks.

The Patriarch had retaliated with a number of extremely unwise encyclicals, all calculated to raise the hackles of the still insecure new regime. And when the Bolsheviks nationalized Church property, the Patriarch pronounced anathema on the entire government and excommunicated all who supported it.

"Fools!" Ivan had crumpled up the Patriarch's Proclamation and thrown it into the stove.

During the Civil War, the Church had continued to be a thorn in the already beleaguered government's side. Thousands of priests, monks, and nuns were imprisoned. Finally, the Patriarch himself was placed under house arrest. He was released only when he promised to stop opposing the government. The Bolsheviks then switched from open persecution to legal harassment.

"If Lenin thinks he can strangle the Church with red tape," said Ivan, shaking his head, "he's a bigger fool than the Patriarch for thinking the Bolsheviks wouldn't last."

A propaganda campaign was also launched by the League of Militant Atheists. A new publishing house began printing a weekly newspaper entitled *Atheist* and a monthly magazine named *The godless at the Workplace*.

"Fools!" Ivan laughed in disbelief. "Don't they know they're in Russia!?!"

And now, Stalin was trying to liquidate God. "The very notion of God," proclaimed the decree, "will be expunged as an instrument for holding down the working masses."

"Fools," sighed Ivan sadly.

"We must turn our villages into godless collective farms," screamed *Pravda*. "The new *kolkhoz* does not need a church – or a priest."

"People can't live without something to believe in. Even the Party knows that!" said Ivan with disdain. "They're trying to substitute a cult of their own – complete with new icons and liturgy and saints – even pilgrimages to the shrine of an embalmed atheist!"

But Father Ivan did not weep for the Church's lost power. Its privileged position, he knew, had been a bigger threat to its spiritual strength than any government – regardless of ideology – could ever be. The Bolsheviks were a cross the

Church must bear, an instrument of God's Will. The Heavenly Father had sent this suffering because He loved His Church; it was an opportunity for the faithful to transcend the stagnation into which Holy Mother Russia had fallen.

Meanwhile, Ivan was determined to protect the real Church. Wealth and power it did not need, but its churches and bells, its icons and liturgy were a living manifestation of the collective Soul of the Russian People. Father Ivan vowed to preserve the Truth manifested in this Beauty.

And when we become what we say we are, he prayed fervently, *perhaps then even the godless will find God.*

"Father, forgive them..." he murmured softly. "Forgive us all..."

Ж   Ж   Ж

In general, Mischa's *kolkhoz* fared better than most. Partly this was due to his enthusiastic leadership and genuine effort to make the new collective farm work. But it was also because he found a powerful ally at district headquarters.

Mischa had first encountered him at a meeting in a neighboring village.

"Comrades!" the familiar voice boomed out. "I have been sent by our Communist Party to help you organize a collective farm!"

After the meeting, Mischa found himself face to face with a much larger version of Old Mikhail. The man in the commissar's uniform embraced him heartily; throwing an arm over Mischa's shoulder, he led him eagerly back to his makeshift office.

As Vladimir talked excitedly, Mischa noted with satisfaction that his cousin had not really changed very much. He was bigger and looked older and the words were different, but the same ardent soul blazed out undimmed. Clearly, Vladimir had thrown himself into the Collectivization Crusade with his usual fervor.

"Collectivization is a war on backwardness," he exclaimed, with a passion which resounded in Mischa's stolid but no less committed soul. "We must create a population of literate, politically active, loyal Soviet citizens in the countryside. To defend the Motherland, the Red Army needs food and good solid soldiers."

"And we must build a better life for our children, so that they will not suffer as our fathers and grandfathers did." added Mischa.

"And we cannot let anyone stand in our way," continued Vladimir. "The enemies of the Revolution are all around us, waiting for us to fail, ready to take advantage of any weakness. We *must* be strong."

And with that, Vladimir reached into a box under the board serving as his desk and pulled out a half-empty bottle of vodka. Several enthusiastic toasts to their mutual goal followed, which eventually erupted into exuberant singing. Many of the peasants Vladimir had previously been haranguing reappeared; someone had a balalaika, others began dancing energetically. When Mischa finally staggered home, it was very late.

Several days later, Vladimir showed up at his parents' *izba*. Mischa, of course, had forewarned them; nervously, they had tried to prepare for their son's long-awaited homecoming.

The visit was not a success.

Nor was it exactly a failure.

"Welcome home, Volodya," said Evgenia, shocked that the gangling young man whose image she had cherished all these years was suddenly a huge middle-aged man.

"Come in, Vladimir," said Ivan, dismayed by what he saw in the no longer innocent eyes of his prodigal son.

"Thank you," said Vladimir, filled with remorse at how much his parents had aged.

Not knowing how to embrace the big man on her doorstep, Evgenia instead took his hand and led him to the icon corner. Ivan followed awkwardly, and the two men sat down uneasily to the feast she had prepared.

"Mischa says you've been very helpful," began Ivan, clearing his throat in what he hoped was a neutral manner.

"Mischa, too, has been very helpful," replied Vladimir carefully.

"Have some *blini*?" asked Evgenia, on guard for the slightest sign of disagreement. "I made them just the way you always liked them."

"*Maslenitsa* was always your favorite feast-day." Ivan smiled tentatively.

"I always ate more *blini* than anyone." Vladimir smiled back, equally tentative.

"So that you could make it through Lent?"

"Well, maybe. But mostly because I like them."

"But Lent is probably something you don't do anymore?"

"More tea?" asked Evgenia, poised to extinguish the smallest spark of unpleasantness.

"Yes, thank you." Ivan looked up at his wife, then backed away from potentially dangerous territory. "Will you be here for *Maslenitsa* this year?"

"That depends on the progress of the collectivization crusade," replied Vladimir.

"More tea?" asked Evgenia.

"Yes, thank you." Vladimir looked up at his mother, then backed away from the possibly controversial topic. "I'm hoping to get some new parts for the tractor in time for the spring planting."

"Mischa says the tractor breaks down all the time."

"That's because the peasants won't learn how to drive it."

This time, both of them backed away before Evgenia could offer more tea.

And so it went, with father and son tiptoeing so carefully around the powerful emotions they were feeling that neither was able to find the other. And so worried was each about saying something which would offend, they could find little to talk about. The conversation limped painfully. Vladimir excused himself as soon as etiquette allowed.

As she said goodbye, Evgenia searched her son's eyes. There was much there that she did not want to know, but back in a corner she finally found her little boy. She smiled at him; the smile he returned was years younger than the rest of him.

Vladimir rarely came back to the village after that. Sometimes, though, he stopped by the schoolhouse to see Evgenia. Mostly they talked about how the school could be used for the cause of Collectivization. Occasionally he vented his frustration.

"Why do they resist change so stubbornly!?!" he burst out. "Can't they see that their lives would be better?"

"Just to stay alive, they already take too many risks," Evgenia replied. "To change means taking even more. To go on doing things as before seems safer."

"But things *can't* go on as before."

"People here live by a different clock," shrugged Evgenia sadly. "Their life has always been a long question mark between crops."

"But using the land more efficiently would remove the question mark."

"Can your collective farms control the weather?"

"No, but having tractors would make it easier to live with."

"On the outside, perhaps. But inside?" Evgenia began erasing the chalkboard. "The Motherland is strong and beautiful – but she can also be violent and explosive. *Rodina*'s children often take after her."

"Children don't always turn out like their parents."

"But the influence of a mother – or a father," Evgenia erased the remains of the day's writing lesson, "cannot be wiped out so easily as this." She looked imploringly at her son.

During all their discussions, Vladimir would often look expectantly at the door. Ivan, however, was always sure to be in the church. Evgenia knew that he, too, was looking just as hopefully at a door which stubbornly refused to open.

Ж   Ж   Ж

Father Ivan entered the church just as dawn was breaking. Opening the doors to let the rosy sunlight in, he walked reverently to the altar, lit a candle next to the double-armed cross, and sank gratefully to his knees.

The Church was his home. It was where he belonged, where his soul found its path to God. How he loved the richly complex liturgy he performed so joyously here! How he loved this beautifully adorned sanctuary! Truly, his humble little church was heaven on earth.

To his flock, Father Ivan was a true pastor; saying Mass celebrated the profound connection he felt with his congregation. Forged in the mystically sensual worship they shared, this communal bond extended out into the whole life of the village. How fortunate he was to be in a place where he could manifest his faith so completely! Thanks be to God!

In tribute to his calling, Father Ivan solemnly made the sign of the cross. Then, humbly prostrating himself before the altar, he earnestly prayed for forgiveness for his Church. In the past, too many priests had been lazy hypocrites; too many bishops had been seduced by power. The Holy Orthodox Church had been corrupted by privilege. And too many of the faithful had fallen away.

He thought sadly of his daughter's first husband. Alexander Pavlovich had been a fine upright man – yet the Church had failed him. Its hypocrisy had driven him to worship other gods. Perhaps his way had been a true path – Ivan hoped so – but surely it must have been a lonely one.

And then there was Vladimir…

Nor was it just among the intelligentsia that faith in the Church had eroded. In the villages, too, the peasants had often strayed. Some had joined the Old Believers, others had fallen prey to cults. And many had simply reverted to the old pagan ways, overcast with a thin veneer of Orthodoxy.

Father Ivan had lost few members of his own congregation. His people trusted him, and he was grateful. But what would happen when he died? In whom would they believe then? The image of Jesus weeping over Jerusalem had come often to his mind in those days. Often he, too, had wept over the sinful Jerusalem the Orthodox Church had become.

Slowly Ivan rose to his knees. Reaching up to the altar, he pulled himself to

340

his feet, his joints creaking painfully. *Thanks be to God that I have lived long enough to see the New Jerusalem!*

The eyes of the saints on the iconostasis emerged from shadows, as tiny haloes of light gradually illuminated the sanctuary. The women of the parish were arriving for Mass, lighting candles in front of icons on the walls. They were the ones, Ivan knew, that always brought the babies to be baptized and loved ones to be buried. At home altars in icon corners all over Mother Russia, the women worshiped faithfully, their patient steadfastness the bedrock of the Church. And should the day come – as well it might – when no churches at all were permitted, they would remain in their icon corners and keep the faith.

Respectfully shuffling feet now filled the church; bodies clad in homespun bowed and crossed themselves. Joyfully, Father Ivan turned and faced the miracle of his new congregation. No longer was he lonely, frustrated at his inability to share the source of his own intense faith. No more did he grieve when perfunctory observance of sacred ritual distracted from the depth of his own religious experience. No more did he worry about the fervor of his flock being misdirected, in ways he did not understand toward things he did not want to know.

"*Gospodi pomilui.* Lord, have mercy."

The people in his church now worshiped wholeheartedly, prayers rising up from the depths of their souls, resounding in a mighty chorus of religious solidarity. Ivan felt his soul amplified and fortified a thousandfold; never had the church in his village felt so truly like heaven. Thanks be to God for allowing him to share in this marvelous communion of saints!

"*Gospodi pomilui.* Lord, have mercy."

And now that the Church was becoming what it was meant to be, religious differences were melting away, too. As more and more churches were closed, people began paying less and less attention to what divided them. How one worshiped became less important than the fact that one worshiped at all. What one believed became submerged in the all-encompassing reality that one was a believer. Gradually, the faithful of whatever stamp ceased identifying themselves primarily as Orthodox or Old Believers – or Baptists or Catholics, or even Jews or Muslims. Most simply called themselves Believers.

"*Gospodi pomilui.* Lord, have mercy."

Over the centuries, the Russian Orthodox church had survived the abominable Tartar Yoke, the *oprichnina* of Ivan the Terrible, the despotic power of Peter the Great. It had endured countless religious schisms, numerous peasant uprisings, and an almost uninterrupted series of wars. And now the Church was being persecuted by the Soviet Government. This, too, Ivan knew, would pass. For at every turn, even the most inscrutable events were blessed by Divine Providence. And even if the Church was forced underground, in the shadows of the catacombs the flame of the true faith would glow brighter. In its suffering, the Church would transcend.

Slowly Father Ivan mounted the steps of his pulpit.

"It is not the earthly house of God that has strengthened Our Faith through the ages, but rather the Church's inner struggle, its suffering and torment, and its voluntary sacrifice in the image of Christ." Looking out over a sea of rapt upturned faces, he saw his own fervor reflected and magnified in their eyes

"The people of Russia have lived – and will continue to live – through the immutable joys of the Spirit." As sunlight streamed through the church doors, his soul filled with healing love. "And we will continue to follow the Apostolic commandment: 'Rejoice evermore. Pray without ceasing. In everything give thanks; for this is the Will of God.'"

And finally, for the first time in years, Father Ivan rang the bells. Slowly and deeply, they pealed in solemn thanksgiving, throbbing with the miracle of the glowing, grounded Light which radiated from the old wooden church.

Ж Ж Ж

When he found one of the young proletarians urinating on the iconostasis, Father Ivan knew he had to do something. Famine and Persecution were one thing, instruments of God's Will to be endured. But wanton desecration? No! It could not be allowed!

At first, the church had been designated to house the new tractors; the only one to arrive, however, stalled shortly after in the fields. Then the church was declared a social club for the new *kolkhoz*. That, too, was usually no problem, most of the villagers choosing to socialize there only in a religious fashion. But when it was announced that the bells were to be confiscated, Father Ivan decided to act.

He knew very well that taking the bells was more than an anti-religious gesture. For the church bells were also the village tocsin; they not only summoned the faithful to worship – but to resistance and rebellion.

But they were *his* bells! And he would not let them go without a fight.

And so, the night before they came to take the bells, Father Ivan packed a small bundle and set it beside the door of his *izba*.

After dinner, he sat quietly at the table with Evgenia. Both were sipping their tea very slowly, reluctant to acknowledge that the meal was over.

Ivan looked at the icon of St. Serafim of Sarov, hanging just behind his wife's right shoulder, and smiled, remembering. "I wonder if he realizes that he is the patron saint of our marriage."

Evgenia turned and looked at the icon. "Talking about a saint *is* a rather strange way to court a girl." She, too, smiled.

"I didn't know what else to say."

"Yes, I noticed." Evgenia's clear blue eyes gleamed softly. "But I'm glad St. Serafim gave you permission to marry me."

"So am I." Smiling in the same radiantly unselfconscious way that had won her heart so long ago, Ivan gently tucked a stray lock of his wife's silver hair back under her kerchief.

Putting his hand over hers, they sat in silence until the candles in the icon corner had almost burned out.

Finally Ivan stood up and walked to the door. Carefully he picked up the bundle and slung it over his shoulder.

"I have to do this," he said quietly.

"I know," she answered, trying to keep her voice steady.

Leaning down, he kissed her, and felt the steadfast glow of their love surround him.

Then, without looking back, he walked slowly to the church, climbed up to the belfry, and barricaded the door behind him.

Ж   Ж   Ж

When a truck full of burly workers arrived the next morning, they were confronted by an awesome-visaged old man in full clerical garb, clutching an icon of the Virgin and holding a cross aloft. As he thundered down at them to cease their desecration of God's holy house, most of them scuttled guiltily back into the truck. The driver, however, was not so easily put off.

"Come down from there, Old Man," he shouted, with not very convincing bravado, "and let us do our job."

"No!" roared Father Ivan in a Jove-like voice, his long silver beard waving authoritatively.

The driver winced, and scratched his head.

By this time, most of the village had gathered. Mischa came running from the fields and breathlessly pushed his way through the crowd.

Recognizing him as someone with authority, the driver turned to him anxiously. "You there! Make him come down!"

"Father Ivan! Come down!"shouted Mischa, with genuine concern. "You'll get hurt!"

"NO!" roared Father Ivan, waving the cross impressively.

Mischa turned to the driver and shrugged helplessly. "He's very stubborn. You'll just have to go without the bells."

"Well, no, we can't do that. We were ordered to take them and we can't go back without them." The driver and his henchmen had a long conference, and finally agreed that since their orders contained nothing about dealing with a stubborn old priest, they would simply wait until they got some that did. And with that, they settled in for a long nap.

Meanwhile, Mischa raced to district headquarters to get Vladimir.

"Father!" Vladimir shouted up, out of breath and with no little annoyance, "Come down!"

"No!" Ivan shouted down, "You come up!"

After a long hesitant pause, Vladimir walked nervously into the church. Slowly, he climbed the ladder into the belfry, each strong rung feeling smoothly familiar in his hands. As he emerged into the light of the open tower, he was struck by the unexpected beauty of its sudden panorama.

"I never stop being surprised by how wonderful it looks from up here," he said, gazing all around and forgetting, for a moment, why he had come.

Ivan nodded.

"But it always looks like mud – and manure – down there." Vladimir sat down next to his father.

"Mud is beautiful, too – in its own way," said Ivan quietly. "And manure is useful."

"Yes, I know. But I prefer the view from up here," sighed Vladimir.

"You always did," smiled Ivan, "but down there is where people must live."

"And those people down there are all too ready to explode into senseless violence."

"They have been grievously provoked."

"I know. But someone has to keep order."

"By starving them?"

"No one intended that. The government just wants to change things for the better."

"For whom?"

"For everyone."

"*I* believe that," said Ivan thoughtfully, "but those people down there don't."

"Because they are ignorant superstitious peasants!"

"No," Ivan shook his head. "They just want the government – any government – to leave them alone."

"But how can they be hostile to the government of a classless society?"

"A good horse means more to them than your marxist jargon," Ivan smiled wryly, "though they do like the part about the state withering away. They're hoping it will happen before they do."

"And some of them intend to help the process along."

"Probably."

"Which is why we have to take the bells."

"I know."

"Then why are you up here?"

"'Verily, verily, I say unto you,'" quoted Father Ivan, "'Except a grain of wheat fall into the ground and die, it abideth alone; but if it die, it bringeth forth much fruit.'"

Vladimir climbed down the ladder and went back to his office, hoping his father would soon get tired.

The next day, another truck drove up to the church, looking for the first one. Having accomplished their mission, its occupants stood around uncertainly, wondering what to do. After a long noisy conference with the occupants of the first truck, some of the second group piled back into their own and rattled off. The rest stayed to make sure that their quota of lost bell collectors did not disappear.

The day after that, a small contingent of OGPU troops arrived. Their orders were to get the priest out of the bell-tower.

"Old Man, get out of there!" ordered their commander, striding peremptorily up to the church.

"No!" roared Father Ivan, brandishing his cross and icon.

The officer was not impressed, and motioned to one of his men.

"Wait!" shouted Mischa, running forward as the man raised his rifle and took aim.

The officer signaled, and the rifleman paused.

"The old priest is much beloved," said Mischa meaningfully, looking around at the large ring of peasants with pitchforks standing menacingly near.

Seeing that they were outnumbered, the officer nodded quickly. The rifle was lowered. One of the OGPU trucks then raced off, followed shortly by Mischa, who once again went for Vladimir.

This time, Vladimir appeared in his Red Army uniform. The remaining OGPU troops and bell-removers were duly impressed by the awesome commissar, his chest covered with medals. The officer in charge was more than willing to yield to his authority.

"But, you see, it's just that we have orders –" the officer tried to explain, obviously perturbed. "We're supposed to get the priest down."

"If I get him down, will you go away and leave him alone?"

"Of course. Our orders are only to get him out of the bell-tower."

Once again, Vladimir ascended into the belfry, where he found his father calmly carving a piece of wood.

"So that's your new uniform," said Ivan, looking him up and down. "I can tell by the way you wear it that you believe in what it stands for."

"Yes."

"This is *my* uniform," he said, indicating his cassock.

"Yes, I know."

"Then you understand why I must stay here."

"Even if it means your life?"

"*This* is my life." Ivan's sweeping gesture embraced his little church.

"They might destroy the church, too, if you don't come down."

"They already have! They spit on my father's beautiful icons!" Ivan burst out angrily. "How can you let them do that?! And how can you let them bawl drunkenly where your grandfather sang so magnificently?! How can you let them defile your heritage?!... And how could you desert the faith of your fathers –" Ivan stood up and turned away, trembling.

Vladimir bowed his head wearily. "The *Church* destroyed my heritage – and my faith," he said sadly, "but I never deserted you – or this." He stood up and caressed one of the bells, looking lovingly at the onion-shaped dome above them.

"What you rebelled against was not really the Church," said Ivan, after a long silence. "Even *this* is not the Church, beautiful as it is. No, the real Church is in *here*." He tapped his chest reverently.

Then Ivan picked up the carving he was working on and held it out to his son. It was an icon of Christ in his prison cell.

Vladimir smiled, remembering. "When I was a boy, I wanted more than anything to make one like it."

"And have you?"

"No… Not yet."

Ivan looked deeply into his son's eyes. "Maybe you should try again."

Vladimir returned his father's intent gaze. "I have never stopped trying."

And as they stood thus, each probing the other's soul, the tension between them melted – and with it, years of pent-up anger and guilt.

As father and son embraced, tears rained down into their beards, splashing over the uniforms which marked them as enemies in a tragic war.

But at that moment, both Ivan and Vladimir were at peace.

Ж   Ж   Ж

"I think if we all go away, he'll come down – eventually," said Vladimir to the OGPU officer, after descending from the bell-tower.

"Umm… yes, that could save everyone a lot of unpleasantness," he replied, eyeing all the pitchforks nervously. "But what about my orders?"

"Just say they were countermanded by a superior officer."

"Well… but, uh… begging your pardon, sir… what if *my* superiors don't believe that?"

"What would it take to convince them?"

"Maybe you could talk to them – and get them to change the orders – and put it in writing?"

Vladimir hurried back to district headquarters, where he spent hours on the telephone trying to find someone who would take responsibility for *not* removing a stubborn old priest and his ancient bells from a small church on the Volga. Despite pulling rank and every string he could think of, no one would risk it. Finally, in desperation, he himself drafted an official-looking paper, absolving all concerned. As he was about to sign it in a large impressive hand, he hesitated for just an instant. He knew that many had lost their Party cards – and more – for less than having a father who was not only a priest, but sitting up in a belfry publicly giving the finger to the Soviet government.

The moment of fear passed quickly into grudging admiration, as he signed the improvised document with a flourish.

Meanwhile, the second truck had returned with new orders – to help the first truck get the bells down. A few hours later, OGPU reinforcements showed up, with no new orders – but with a truckload of vodka requisitioned from somewhere. Soon, everyone was roaring drunk. And as they were all milling about trying to decide what to do, the problem suddenly resolved itself when the church burst into flames. The peasants tried to extinguish the blaze, but the dry wooden church seemed determined to burn. Vladimir returned just in time to see flames licking hungrily up toward the bell-tower.

Ж   Ж   Ж

After Ivan had locked himself in the church, Evgenia had returned to the icon corner. Kneeling, she contemplated the *Virgin of Vladimir* for a long time.

It had always been her favorite icon. Ever since she could remember, she had been saying her prayers to the Virgin – first in her parents' *izba*, then before the special one Andrei had painted for their wedding day. Something in the Virgin's eyes reminded her of Babushka.

Thinking of Ivan, alone in his bell-tower, Evgenia suddenly felt unbearably empty. She knew why he was up there; she also knew better than to try to stop him. Prostrating herself before the icon, she implored the Virgin to spare her beloved husband.

When, at last, grey dawn slipped into the small windows, Evgenia kissed the icon and crossed herself. Whatever happened, Ivan was being true to his soul. He had spent his whole life trying to do so; it was what made him the man – and the true priest – she loved. She had always respected his calling; she would honor it now, no matter what.

From the small trunk in which she kept her most treasured belongings, she took out the shawl Babushka had given her. Its once bright flowers were faded, but it was still beautiful. Tying it securely under her chin, she picked up the *Virgin of Vladimir* and walked across the road to the school. Hanging the icon on the door, she knelt down before it and silently began to pray.

All day and all night, she quietly kept vigil with Ivan. Elena soon joined her and, by sundown of the first day, Vasilisa was kneeling next to her mother. By the second day, nearly all the women of Derevnia had gathered at the schoolhouse, praying silently to the Virgin.

Finally, at twilight on the third day, Evgenia led them to the church. Around the trucks parked in front milled several dozen strange men in ill-fitting uniforms. None of them seemed to know what to do; all of them were guzzling vodka. Ivan was standing in the bell-tower, dressed in festive regalia reserved for the holiest Feast-days. Looking up at him standing under the wooden dome, Evgenia once again saw the beautiful young man she had married. Clad in robes lovingly embroidered by generations of village women, he blessed the watch-

348

ing crowd with the grace of a consecrated dancer. Evgenia's heart swelled with love.

When the smoke began billowing out the door of the church, and while Mischa's bucket brigade dashed about trying to put out the inextinguishable flames, Evgenia gazed steadfastly at the joyous priest in the tower. And as the fire started consuming the church, she saw not only the man who had shared her life, but Father Ivan celebrating his last Mass. Sorrowfully her voice raised up a hymn of farewell.

Lord, now lettest Thou Thy servant depart,
According to Thy word, in peace.
For mine eyes have seen
Thy salvation.
Thou has prepared
before the face of all people,
A light to illuminate the Gentiles
and the glory of Thy people.

Behind her, she heard Mischa join in. And from trees singing in the wind came echoes of Old Mikhail's voice, booming in welcome.

The flames leaped higher into the night. Through the open door of the church she saw the fire creep closer to Andrei's iconostasis. Tears stung her eyes as she watched its rustic beauty consumed in a savagely glorious blaze. As her father's choir loft was engulfed, she began to sob.

When the fire finally reached the belfry, Ivan began to ring the bells. Loudly and exuberantly they pealed, as in the days when they had been young and full of hope. And joyfully – like the day Vladimir was born.

Mesmerized, Evgenia watched her husband's spirit give itself once more to his people, as he reached for something only he could see. And then, as the platform of the bell-tower collapsed beneath him, he plunged with his beloved bells into the heart of the golden flames.

At that moment, she saw Vladimir gazing in horror at the fire. A terrible cry of agony wrenched from his throat and joined in fearful harmony with the final clang of the bells. The echoes reverberated throughout the village and finally wrapped themselves around Evgenia.

And then everything was silent.

Chapter 18: The UPROOTED

Wrapped in gnarled roots which curled reassuringly around her, Evgenia huddled under the shielding branches of her tree. Numbly she looked at the Volga; though the sun was shining, the river looked as grey as everything else. As from a great distance, she could hear it singing, but there was no answering song within her.

Evgenia now spent most of her time here. Every evening, Elena would come get her, leading her carefully in a wide circle around the charred skeleton of the church. After coaxing a little food into her, Elena would gently tuck her in the warm place over the stove.

One night, as Evgenia lay staring listlessly up at the ceiling, she heard voices.

"I don't think she's getting any better," Elena was saying, "and I don't think she will – not around here. Everything is too painful."

"What should I do?" asked Vladimir, in a constricted voice.

"Get her out of here – away from the pain. It's too heavy for her to bear, this close."

"But where?"

"To Lisya – and to Katya. They need her."

"But she's never wanted to leave here," Vladimir protested. "The village has always been her whole life."

"I know," replied Elena sadly, "but too much of her village is gone. Maybe somewhere else she could at least have her memories."

Evgenia heard their words through a long dark tunnel. She understood, but felt nothing.

"Elena?" Vladimir asked, after a long silence. "Did I hurt you very much?"

"Yes," she said softly, "but I got over it."

"I'm sorry."

"I know. But Mischa's a good man."

A ghost of a smile hovered briefly on Evgenia's face – and then quickly flitted away.

And then they were all at the railway station again. She felt Elena's tears and pressed her close in alarm, fearing that yet another daughter was going away. But this time, she watched Elena and the station disappear over the horizon instead of the train. It was only after several hundred miles of rocking and clacking had lulled her into a different shade of grey that she realized she herself was on the train.

Though they did not speak a great deal through the long journey, Vladimir's stalwart body sitting next to her was reassuring. And in its monotony, the train itself was strangely soothing. And so, her first journey by rail – and her second outside Derevnia – passed without undue trauma. Arriving in Leningrad, however, was another matter.

The journey from the station to the strange stacked-up house was a nightmare. Terrifying sounds assaulted her from all sides. Nothing looked familiar. She was utterly lost in a completely alien forest of huge buildings and noisy machines.

Even her daughter and granddaughter looked unfamiliar. Lisya was no longer a young woman; Katya was not a child. And there were a lot of unknown people around who seemed to live with them, too.

Finally, they took her to one of the rooms and showed her a bed. Hastily she burrowed under the covers and turned her eyes toward the wall. And when, at last, she heard the hovering footsteps tiptoe out of the room and close the door, she relaxed. Her body began to tremble and was suddenly covered with cold sweat. And then, mercifully, everything was silent again.

When Evgenia finally awoke, the trembling was gone. The grey mist, however, hovered familiarly, enshrouding the strange room. Cautiously, she peeked out from under the blankets and slowly looked around. Finally finding her trunk in the corner, she sighed with relief and went back to sleep.

The next time she awoke, Lisya was sitting beside her. At first, Evgenia refused the soup her daughter held out; but then, seeing her anxious look, she relented and took a few swallows. Leaning back, she explored Lisya's face. Older and lined with pain, it was still handsome – different than she remembered, but at least familiar. As she closed her eyes again, Evgenia clung to this new image of her daughter as if to a small rock in the midst of a turbulent sea.

Later, it was Katya beside her with the soup. Her granddaughter looked beautiful – and, under her obvious concern, happy. Not wanting to mar such a pleasant sight, Evgenia took most of the soup without protest. Noticing that Katya looked well fed, she also ate a little of the bread on the plate next to it. Katya's lively face was a beacon in the fog. Evgenia stared desperately at it, and somehow found the courage to get out of bed.

After that, she spent her time sitting by the window. At first, the streets below terrified her. But then, in a small space between the buildings across the street, she glimpsed something that looked like a river. Fastening her eyes on the tiny patch of shimmering water, she gradually overcame some of her terror. Katya often sat with her, reading Pushkin; Lisya, too, kept her company with her music.

While Evgenia had sometimes heard her daughter's violin back in Derevnia, she had rarely had occasion to hear her play the piano. But now, as Lisya performed just for her, the lovely music reached into corners which ached, and soothed them. Though the music itself was unfamiliar, the hands that created it had a familiar touch; and in them, Evgenia heard sorrow that echoed her own.

And then, one night, she had a dream. Lisya was again the rosy chubby child she had once been, crying in her mother's arms with all the earnestness of her serious little soul. Rocking her gently, Evgenia eagerly inhaled her special fragrance and made soft comforting sounds. Almost imperceptibly, the dream faded into waking reality. Across the room, she could hear her daughter sobbing in her sleep. Each choking cry burned in the perpetually hovering fog like a tiny torch. Slowly, Evgenia stood up and walked painfully to Lisya's bed. The room was not large, but this journey of a few steps seemed to take forever; as she battled her way back through the shadows, it was as though she were fighting her way up the Volga in full spate.

Finally, sitting down beside her daughter, Evgenia put her hand on Lisya's shoulder. Her mouth creaked slowly open as she at last broke her long silence. Softly, she sang an old lullaby, her rusty voice cracking uncertainly. Lisya's sobs subsided as she lay awake, listening. Suddenly Evgenia felt her arms around her daughter. This time, it was no dream. As her child's need reached within, she felt a surge of her former strength. And for the first time in months, she did not feel cold.

Ж   Ж   Ж

"It's always the same." Lisya covered her face with shaking hands. "I'm running after Dmitri, but my feet are like huge stones. He's walking away, sinking farther and farther into this dark awful pool. I beg him to stop, I hold out my hands. But he doesn't hear. The closer I get to the pool, the more it disgusts me and the heavier my feet feel. But I keep calling to him. Finally my voice chokes, and I'm standing at the edge, paralyzed, watching Dmitri disappear into this horrible oozing pit..."

Evgenia lit a candle and set it by her daughter's bed.

"... and then I start screaming," Lisya looked at the small flickering light, "... and then I wake up..."

Evgenia nodded and stared into the solitary flame. "Mine always has lots of fire. At first, I'm afraid... Then, unbearably sad... But the fire is warm – and strangely comforting..."

"Why did they leave us?" Lisya suddenly looked intently into her mother's eyes.

"I don't know." Evgenia frowned thoughtfully. "Maybe other things matter more to them than life."

"Like staying faithful to what they believe?"

"It's what marks out a good man from the ones that aren't."

"Like Father?"

"Yes. And Alexander Pavlovich."

"... Dmitri... ?"

"Dmitri was wounded long ago – by what happened to his mother – and his father," sighed Evgenia, "and never really believed he was worth healing."

"But Elena..."

"Elena is a woman," shrugged Evgenia. "Women *have to* endure."

"Why?"

"Because men don't know how."

Lisya nodded sadly and sighed.

"Why do we love them so much?"

"I don't know," pondered Evgenia. "Maybe because we bear sons, as well as daughters..."

"And because we see beauty inside, trying to get out..."

"And because they bring us joy..."

"And sorrow..."

"Which makes us strong enough to live..."

"Yes..."

Both women sighed, lost in memories of happier times.

Ж   Ж   Ж

Evgenia clutched her daughter's arm nervously. It was the first time she had been out since her arrival in Leningrad. The trams and trucks, milling crowds and huge buildings were still overwhelming, but the thought of where she was going gave her courage.

What she had been staring at so hopefully all these weeks turned out to be a canal.

"Well... it's not the Volga," she said, thinking what a paltry thing the Neva was by comparison, "but at least it's water."

"This isn't the Neva," laughed Lisya. "Just wait."

The two women walked slowly along the Fontanka until they reached the Summer Gardens. As they entered an avenue of giant linden trees, Evgenia gasped in recognition. Walking up to the trunk of the nearest one, she reached out and caressed it gently. Looking up at its familiar shielding branches, she felt reassured.

And then, at the end of the avenue, she saw the Neva. Grand palaces lined its concrete embankments and numerous bridges spanned its seemingly civilized waters, but it was a real *river!* Sitting down on a bench under a linden tree, Evgenia breathed deeply and sighed with relief. Hours later, Lisya finally coaxed her to leave.

"It's not the Volga," said Evgenia, smiling for the first time in months, "but it's a grand river!"

After that, she came back to the trees and the river as often as someone could bring her. After a few weeks, she was spending whole afternoons there alone, while her family went about their business. And then, finally, she summoned the courage to walk there by herself. The strange bustle of the city still intimidated her, but the river and the trees were her friends.

One day, she saw a small steamboat pull a big barge from the Neva into the Fontanka canal. Lean muscled men with lined weathered faces pushed long boat hooks against the bottom of the river as they walked along the edge of the barge. A dog ran along the deck barking. Evgenia smiled and waved, wondering if the barge had come from the Volga.

When winter came, Katya took her to the huge palace on the banks of the now frozen Neva. Despite assurances that it was now the People's Art Museum, Evgenia was uncomfortable in the awesome halls where the Tsar had once walked. And compared to Andrei's icons, most of the artwork looked strange. Katya, however, chattered enthusiastically about all of it; not wanting to seem unappreciative, Evgenia tried to listen. Finally, they reached a gallery of paintings that seemed less foreign. One, in particular, jumped out at her.

It was a large canvas – about as tall as she was and extending several yards across the wall. In the background stretched a mighty river she recognized instantly as Mother Volga. In the foreground was a ragged group of men harnessed to a barge, their eyes haunted by centuries of suffering. Evgenia was astonished that something as unreal as a painting could look so real. She could actually see the barge-haulers swaying rhythmically along the bank, and hear them chanting their mournfully beautiful song. Tears stung her eyes as she remembered.

"That's one of Repin's most famous works," volunteered Katya, pleased at her grandmother's obvious interest. "He lived with the boat haulers for a whole summer, making sketches for this painting."

"No wonder it's so real!"

"I think he painted this around 1870."

"I was nine years old then! Maybe this – Repin – was on one of the barges that floated past my village…" Sitting down on the bench opposite, she was soon lost in her memories.

After that, Evgenia often accompanied Katya to the museum. She would sit for hours across from her beloved Volga and the long-suffering boatmen while Katya went off to do research. But as much as she loved the painting, she was never able to muster enough courage to enter alone what she still thought of as the Tsar's Palace.

Katya also took her to the Maryinsky. That, too, was frightening, especially when what had formerly been the Tsar's box was pointed out to her.

"And did he actually sit there while you were playing your violin – right under his nose?" she asked Lisya afterwards.

"Oh, yes. And the Empress and the Grand Duchesses, too."

"And you actually saw him!?"

"Many times. When Alexander Pavlovich was in the Duma, he met the Tsar once – and even talked to the Tsarevich."

Evgenia was impressed – and enthralled by the wonderful singing she heard at the Maryinsky. Sometimes, she pretended that Tatiana was among the dancers on the stage; always, she was aware of Lisya in the orchestra pit. And as she watched her daughter making music in a place she obviously belonged, she finally understood the enigma of her firstborn child. Seeing Lisya so in harmony with her world reminded Evgenia poignantly of the loss of her own. As the pain of not belonging swept over her, she realized how her daughter must have felt in Derevnia.

And listening to her daughter's music began to fill the void of her now muted voice, cracked beyond recognition. The hymn at Ivan's immolation had been her last; the part of her soul from which she sang had gone with him. That Lisya could sing for both of them was comforting.

But the best thing about Leningrad was the Public Library. When Lisya had first taken her there, Evgenia had almost fainted with excitement at the sight of so many books.

"And I can come here, whenever I want," she asked in disbelief, "and just sit and read any of these?"

Carefully, she noted the way home. The next morning she arose early, walked back to the library alone, and was waiting on the steps when the doors opened. Reverently she entered the main reading room and hesitantly looked around. Taking a deep breath, she humbly approached the imposing oak desk in the center of the far wall.

"Excuse me, please," she said, clearing her throat nervously, "I would like to read some Pushkin."

The librarian looked up irritably, then – seeing the look on her face – smiled briefly and helped Evgenia find what she wanted. Finding an empty table in a corner, she sat down and opened the book to her favorite poem. With relief, she saw that the words were exactly as in her own book – and that they sang here just as beautifully as they did at home. As she read, she was transported back to her little grove by the Volga.

Shortly after noon, the librarian asked Evgenia to share her lunch. The two women sat on a bench in a small nearby square.

"I didn't think to bring lunch," said Evgenia, gratefully accepting a cucumber and some black bread. "I didn't expect to stay so long, but when I read, sometimes I lose track of time."

"I could tell. You looked so engrossed," nodded the librarian, "like you were somewhere else."

"I was," Evgenia smiled sadly.

"You haven't been here long?"

"No…"

"My mother moved here from the country, too, a few years ago," said the librarian. "You remind me of her."

"She is no longer with you?" Evgenia asked softly, after a pause.

357

"No," sighed the librarian. "The homesickness became too heavy."

"It's difficult for the old to uproot – especially to such a crowded place."

The library, however, never felt crowded – even though the reading room was always full. It was a quiet oasis in the midst of the city's tumultuous rush. Just sitting among all the books, inhaling the aroma of their venerable bindings and the musty wisdom of their pages, reminded Evgenia of what a huge universe could be found between their covers. It was like watching the Volga.

She came to the Library as often as she could – usually on days when her new friend was on duty. And as she read her way through the shelves of Pushkin and Turgenev and Tolstoy, she found respite from the aching void where her roots had been.

Ж   Ж   Ж

Though Leningrad never felt like home, Evgenia eventually overcame the worst of her fears. And she had to admit that despite the claustrophobia and the crowds, the city had its advantages. Not least of which was being with her children again.

With her daughter, she discovered a whole new dimension of friendship.

"Do you ever miss the Volga as much as I do?" asked Evgenia, as they sat together on a bench by the Neva.

"Only when I think about the little grove," answered Lisya. "Some of my best memories from Derevnia happened there."

"Mine, too. Though it's painful to think too much about some of them."

"True, but it's hard to separate what's beautiful from what hurts."

"I don't think we're supposed to," replied Evgenia, giving the matter some thought. "The most beautiful music is usually full of sadness."

"In Russia anyway," sighed Lisya. "Maybe that's why music is so important to us."

"And when the music isn't like what everybody else sings –" Evgenia's voice caught, "– that must have been so lonely!"

"Yes," agreed Lisya, tears in her eyes, "it was. It's why I had to leave."

"I know that now." Evgenia put her hand over Lisya's, thankful that she finally understood her daughter, grateful that it meant so much to both of them.

As for her granddaughter, Evgenia was thrilled to be sharing her life after so many years apart.

"Do you remember when we used to take walks in the forest?" asked Ev-

358

genia, as they sat together under one of the big linden trees in the Summer Gardens.

"Of course, I do!" answered Katya brightly. "You used to show me which mushrooms were good – and which ones weren't."

"You were very good at telling them apart."

"Because you were always so pleased whenever I did," smiled Katya.

"Your mother could never see the difference," laughed Evgenia.

"No – really?"

"Yes – but don't tell her I told you."

"It'll be our secret," grinned Katya, linking arms with her grandmother.

"I like it here," said Evgenia, looking up at the lindens. "It reminds me of home."

"Mother used to bring me here a lot when I was a little girl. Aunt Tanya usually came along. I think the trees reminded her of home, too"

"I wish she was with us today," sighed Evgenia.

"So do I," said Katya softly. "But I think there must be linden trees in America, too.

"You're a good girl, Katya." Evgenia patted her hand. "Your mother brought you up well."

And she smiled, remembering the mother bear in the forest.

Katya, of course, was busy with her studies – and with Alexei. Her little granddaughter, all grown up and married, was hard to reconcile with her memories. But it did not take long for Evgenia to be almost as charmed with Alexei as Katya obviously was. To Evgenia's delight, Alexei, too, was soon calling her Babushka.

Of Alexei's family, she was less fond – though she gradually negotiated an acceptable modus vivendi. Sergei and Vassily were too urban, too genuinely proletarian for her to have much in common with. Lacking immediate roots in the countryside, they, in turn, found her peasant ways backward, foreign – even somewhat frightening. Eventually, however, they had cause to value her ability as a healer, just as she came to appreciate their urban survival skills. As for Ludmilla, after some territorial skirmishing in the kitchen, the two women gradually evolved an effective working partnership. Ludmilla educated Evgenia in the intricacies of buying food in the city; Evgenia, in turn, showed her how to make better use of what they bought. They shared recipes and sometimes created new ones. Ludmilla soon came to appreciate Evgenia's help in the time-consuming task of feeding their "family," just as Evgenia was glad to feel useful again.

As for Olga, Evgenia was relieved to discover that, at heart, she was still a country girl. Despite her years in Leningrad, Olga's approach to life was efficaciously plain and unfailingly direct; Evgenia appreciated that – and loved the deep earthy music of her cello. Olga was big and noisy, with a heart to match, and could sometimes make her laugh. Occasionally Evgenia even let herself think of Olga as a daughter; it helped fill the empty place where Tatiana should have been.

In Derevnia, she had long since accustomed herself to her younger daughter's absence. But she had always pictured her in Leningrad with Lisya. Now, she would often catch herself expecting Tatiana to come home from the Maryinsky, too. Evgenia knew, of course, that she was living in America. Remembering the Americans who had saved her village during the famine gave her comfort; surely such generous people would make good neighbors. Even so, she yearned for Tatiana's child, the granddaughter she knew she would never see.

"I was very young when Aunt Tanya went away," said Katya sadly, "but I still miss her."

"So do I." Evgenia's voice was hollow.

"I think Mother misses her more than anyone. She can't even bear to speak of her." Katya's look was meaningful. "So no one does."

Evgenia nodded. "They were always so close," she murmured, "even as children."

"I wonder…" Katya hesitated. "Her daughter – growing up so far away – it's hard to imagine. But maybe someday…"

"Children of the Motherland always return," said Evgenia firmly, "one way or another."

Ж   Ж   Ж

Evgenia knocked tentatively on the door of Vladimir's little room. Hearing no response, she gently pushed it ajar and peered in. Vladimir was lying on his cot, staring up at the ceiling.

"I washed your underwear," she said awkwardly.

"Thank you."

Quickly, she stepped into the room and began folding and putting away his laundry with far more attention to detail than the task demanded.

Vladimir continued to stare at the ceiling.

The bareness of his room was chilling, its spartan simplicity relieved only by two incongruous decorations. Hanging on a hook in the wall was Vladimir's

Red Army uniform, carefully brushed and pressed, covered with medals in neat proud rows. On the small bureau next to it stood an unfinished wood carving.

Evgenia smiled, recognizing it. Lovingly, her hand reached out to touch it. "He stopped making these years ago... after you left..."

Vladimir's eyes shifted from the ceiling to the half-carved icon. "He gave it to me... up there..."

Sitting down next to him, she took his hand. "It wasn't your fault."

"How can you believe that!" he burst out in a strangled voice. "I don't."

"He chose to die for what he believed – in a way that gave his life meaning. There are worse fates."

"Yes..." Vladimir's tormented eyes looked away, "like not being sure what you believe... or believing in two opposites which can never come together."

"Night and day are opposite, but there is no conflict. Both are necessary, so they work together in harmony."

"Some things are not so easily reconciled."

"Perhaps because we mistake for a straight line what is really a very large circle."

Mother and son sat together in silence, both wishing that she could soothe away his pain as she had when he was a child, both knowing that he was too old for that.

"I wonder," he said finally, looking at the carving, "if I will ever be able to finish it."

"I think you will... someday... in your own way," replied Evgenia, gently kissing his hand. "You are your father's son."

Ж   Ж   Ж

Evgenia held her breath and flushed the toilet. Watching the water sheet the sides of the bowl, she remembered her battle for outhouses in Derevnia. How much easier that would have been with indoor plumbing! The toilet belched resoundingly. Evgenia relaxed, glad that she would not have to rouse Sergei to fix it.

Standing in front of the sink, she turned on the faucet, marveling once again at the suddenly appearing water. Even so, she was careful not to waste any as she slowly washed her hands and face.

Evgenia always got up before everyone else – partly so that she could enjoy the bathroom without worrying about those lined up outside. Squinting slightly at her reflection in the mirror, she was again startled by the face looking back at her. *I look more like Babushka now than me.*

Suddenly the door burst open. Katya flung herself at the toilet and vomited noisily into the bowl. Afterward she leaned weakly against the wall, small beads of perspiration dotting her pale face.

"How long has it been?" Evgenia asked quietly when Katya's color had returned.

"Long enough to be sure."

"Does Alexei know?"

"No…" Katya hesitated. "Not yet." Abruptly she stood up and began to vigorously brush her hair.

Evgenia sat down on a chair by the bathtub and watched her granddaughter irritably try to discipline her uncooperative mane. Katya's hair was thick and dark and abundant, but did not take orders gracefully. All attempts to confine the resolutely unbending locks were stubbornly resisted, all efforts to impose any configuration but a straight line obstinately rejected. No matter how Katya braided and coiled and curled, the uncompromising strands always triumphantly sprang loose.

"I don't think Alexei is ready for children." Katya put down her brush and faced her grandmother. "He's always saying that the family is an embodiment of counter-revolutionary values."

"And is what starts a family also counter-revolutionary?" Evgenia raised an eyebrow and nodded toward the bedroom across the hall where – judging from what came through the not very thick walls at night – Katya and Alexei were not just reading Marx and Lenin.

Katya blushed. "Alexei says that in a Communist state, children should be raised communally, in state nurseries and day-care centers."

"Humph! And what do you think?"

"I don't want strangers taking care of my baby." Katya stared at a large chip in the bathtub's enamel. "But I don't think *I'm* ready for this, either. I want to graduate first. And all of us, of course, *must* work to build the Motherland."

"Being a mother is never easy," smiled Evgenia, patting Katya's shoulder reassuringly, "no matter what the politics."

When she returned to her own room, Evgenia told Lisya and Olga about Katya's condition.

"Alexei will probably write poems about Katya's impending motherhood," grinned Olga, "but I doubt he'll change any diapers."

362

"They never do." Lisya shook her head. "That's woman's work – or so they say."

"But they never seem to mind when women do men's work," Olga snorted. "Provided, of course, it's boring and unpleasant – or there aren't enough men around to do it. Just look at the Plan – it would be impossible without all the women in the workforce."

"But at least now women aren't unemployed," argued Lisya.

"True," conceded Olga, "but women digging tunnels for subways and hauling concrete for dams is not exactly my idea of liberation."

"Women have always done heavy labor in the country," interjected Evgenia quietly. "Why should it be any different in the city?"

"Well, at least Katya doesn't have to worry about that," said Lisya gratefully. "We have more choices now – and more opportunities."

"But we still shoulder all the burdens at home." Olga waved her hand impatiently. "The government makes a lot of promises, but I don't see it doing anything. There's nothing in the Plan about household appliances or childcare facilities."

"Which brings us back to Katya's situation," sighed Lisya.

"And we will deal with it as women always have," said Evgenia firmly. "*We* will take care of the baby."

Contrary to Katya's fears, Alexei was delighted. Marxist ideology was forgotten in the pride and excitement of impending fatherhood. As Olga had predicted, he waxed eloquent about Katya's pregnancy and was forever scribbling verses and reading them to everyone. To matters of practical preparation, however, he was oblivious. The baby paraphernalia collecting in their room puzzled and perplexed him.

In a forgotten corner of the attic, Lisya unearthed some of Katya's baby things. Somehow, even the pram had been overlooked; behind a wall of clutter, there it stood – proud and elegant as ever. Like all of them, of course, it had aged, but after some tinkering, Sergei restored it to its former grandeur. Ludmilla, meanwhile, patched the old baby clothes, Vassily maneuvered extra food for the expectant mother, Olga converted empty flour sacks into diapers.

Even Vladimir emerged from behind his closed door. Though his usual exuberance was gone, Katya's presence lighted his big sad eyes. He began to linger around the kitchen table after dinner, his large hands silently carving a whole regiment of whimsical wooden animals.

As Katya's belly swelled, so did the household's anticipation. By the ninth

363

month, everyone's nerves were taut with impatience. Katya waddled around like a huge turtle, and seemed always to be in the bathroom. Night after night, she tossed and turned, trying to find a comfortable sleeping position. She snapped constantly at Alexei, whose solicitous platitudes irritated her all the more.

"I can't bear the thought of Katya having to endure the agony of labor," shuddered Lisya, pacing between the beds of the room she shared with Evgenia and Olga.

"I lived through it. So did you," Evgenia said calmly. "And so will Katya."

"But what if something happens to the baby?" Lisya worried. "Worse yet, what if something happens to Katya?"

Lisya, too, began to snap at Alexei.

As for Evgenia, the prospect of a great-granddaughter moved her deeply – especially since it was clear that much of the caretaking would be up to her. It was as though she was being given again all the years she had missed of Katya's childhood. And that the child would be a girl – an heir worthy of the traditions of her grandmothers – of that, Evgenia had no doubt.

Finally, it was time.

At first, Alexei insisted on staying at Katya's side, tenderly holding her hand. Every ten minutes, Sergei excitedly stuck his head in, checking on his grandchild's progress. Vladimir paced silently up and down the corridor outside the door.

As the pains intensified, Katya began to moan – and occasionally scream – and then to shriek. Somewhere between the moaning and the screaming, Alexei blanched and broke out in a sweat. Finally, Olga led him out of the room and into the kitchen, where she poured him a shot of vodka. Sergei joined them, and soon father and son were noisily toasting the new generation. Vladimir, however, continued to pace before Katya's door, a loyal sentinel keeping vigil.

All afternoon and through the night, Katya labored. Flanked by her mother and grandmother, she struggled to carry on the chain of life which bound her to generations past and future. Lisya and Evgenia sat beside her, chanting words of encouragement and grasping her hands as if to infuse her with their strength. Every spasm cut through them like a knife, as they silently begged the powers of procreation to spare her and let them bear the pain instead.

Finally, toward dawn, a mighty scream welled up from Katya's exhausted body. She gripped Lisya's hands, her fingernails drawing blood. And then, as in the village far away on the Volga, Evgenia deftly assisted the birthing of a new soul.

As the baby continued her mother's scream, her grandmother and great-grandmother greeted her with cries of joy and hope. The pain and struggle of the past hours – and the past years – were forgotten as four generations of womankind bonded in a mysterious moment of triumph. Back through the ages and ahead into the future, they all lived in this one girl-child. And so life would endure. And so would they.

Ж   Ж   Ж

"Mother thinks I should name her Evgenia," said Katya, when it was time, "after you."

"And what do you think?" asked Evgenia, pleased.

"I think I should name her whatever you say."

Evgenia went for a long walk along the Neva, comforted as she always was by its ever-changing, yet somehow constant, song. The Neva sang in a different key than the Volga, but a city like Leningrad needed a different kind of river. Staring across to the awesome Petropavlovsk Fortress, Evgenia wondered if her great-granddaughter would ever see the village to which she had given most of her life. With an ache reaching all the way to the core of her being, she realized that her village did not exist anymore – except in the souls of those who remembered it. With sad resignation, she resolved to share the best of those memories with the precious infant who would one day pass the legacy on. Meanwhile, the child's future lay in the city, in the new world called Leningrad.

Evgenia walked quickly home and went directly to her trunk. Taking out an old, carefully carved distaff, she returned to Katya's bedside.

"This is for you," she said, handing it to Katya. "And for the baby – someday."

"It's beautiful!" Katya appraised the intricate carvings with a practiced eye.

"My father made this for my wedding day. When your mother was born, *my* mother cut the cord with it. And I used it when *your* daughter was born."

Katya smiled and gently outlined the carved flowers with her fingertips.

"Old things like this help us remember the past, but this child has been born into a new age," said Evgenia, taking the baby in her arms. "A new way of life needs new traditions – and new names. So call her *nadezhda*, a symbol of hope for the new world she will help build."

"Nadezhda," Katya tried it out. "Hope... Yes, I like it. And what about you, my little Hope? Shall I call you Nadezhda?"

The baby made a tiny fist around Katya's finger and emitted a loud, agreeable burp.

"Very well, then," Katya laughed, "Her name is Nadezhda, after the *spirit* of my grandmother."

Later, Evgenia heard her singing to the baby. The voice sounded remarkably like her own, in her younger years. And the song itself was a lullaby she had often sung to Lisya as a child. Evgenia smiled, once again remembering the mother bear.

The next day, Evgenia sat down and wrote her first letter from Leningrad.

Dear Elena,

I'm sorry I haven't written sooner. But it's been too hard for me to think about home. Some things still hurt too much to remember. But I miss everyone, especially you – as much my daughter as Lisya and Tanya.

Leningrad will never be home, but it is not so bad as I feared. And my family here needs a Babushka. Especially now that I have a great-granddaughter! We decided to name her Nadezhda, instead of Evgenia, as a symbol of hope for better days.

You should see the Library here! It's much bigger than the Manor House, and has more books than anyone could count. I go there every week.

You were right to send me here. It's where I am needed. You are the Babushka in Derevnia now. May the Virgin give us both strength and courage!

Remember me to all those I love,
    Evgenia

Several weeks later, she received a reply.

Dear Aunt Evgenia,

I was so happy to get your letter. I wanted to write before, but I was afraid it would make things harder for you. So I decided that you would write when you were ready – and that I should wait. I'm glad you are getting used to Leningrad. It was hard for me to send you away, but I think you would have died otherwise

Thanks to Mischa, the famine is receding here. The kolkhoz is not what he dreamed of, but he has figured out how to use the system well enough so that we do not starve. He works harder than ever, making deals and arguing with people, and there is always a big stack of papers on his desk. I think he would be happier spending more time in the fields, but we would be lost without him as chairman.

And maybe someday, the kolkhoz will became what it was supposed to be. We do not give up hope.

I think it will please you to know that the clinic sometimes receives supplies from the government, and that most of the children now come to school – most of the time. Where the church used to be, we planted a circle of oak trees. On Sundays and Feastdays, we gather there to sing and pray. Someday, the trees will be as tall and strong as the man whose memory we honor there.

No one here has forgotten you, and not a day goes by that I don't thank the Virgin for all you have given me. I do my best to pass it on.

Embrace Lisya and Katya for me – and give little Nadya a big kiss.

With much love from all of us,

Elena

Ж   Ж   Ж

Evgenia finally found the church. Even though her family pretended it did not exist. Shrouded in an obscure corner, the shabby little church was surrounded by a small forest. Stepping inside this wooded oasis transported her back to the Volga, and she found herself listening for the singing river. Instead, she heard the faint strains of a familiar chant.

Entering the church, the chanting was louder – though still with the hushed quality of someone trying to sing in a whisper. The iconostasis gleamed with gold leaf, sacramental vessels were polished to a rich sheen, candelabras blazed with a thousand slim tapers. Overcome by the familiar beauty, Evgenia prostrated herself and wept in gratitude.

On subsequent visits, she began noticing that underneath the comforting familiarity, there were also some differences. The choir was composed entirely of women and so, usually, was the congregation. Most of them were at least as old as she was, and – like her – sang in voices cracked by grief. Priests with eyes old beyond their years came and went mysteriously; all but the most sacerdotal duties were performed by the women. Though she missed Ivan's graceful Mass, Evgenia eventually came to feel as much at home in this isolated spiritual outpost as in her husband's church. And though she longed for her father's glorious voice, the whispered chanting somehow spoke to her soul more intimately than his booming bass.

One day, when she was home alone with the baby, she opened her trunk and carefully took out Babushka's old shawl. Wrapping it snugly around her head, she bundled up Nadya and took her to the church. Several other old women were

367

there, all with small children of various ages. The priest baptized them in a mass ceremony, and hung small crosses around their necks.

That night, when Katya was putting Nadya to bed, she discovered the cross. She said nothing, but did not take it off. As she lay down next to her already sleeping husband, she gently caressed her own cross, still hanging where her grandfather had fastened it. Smiling, she fell asleep to Alexei's gentle snores.

In the room nextdoor, Evgenia once more opened her trunk, this time taking out the icon Ivan's father had given them on their wedding day. Placing it on top of the trunk, in the corner opposite the door, she knelt and prayed. The *Virgin of Vladimir* gazed compassionately at her, just as She had from that other icon corner beside the Volga.

Tonight Evgenia prayed – as she always did - for her son's soul, fervently entreating the Virgin to protect him while he sought deliverance from his spiritual torment. She added a special prayer that Nadya would someday understand what had happened to her today, and she prayed for her family, that someday they would be able to pray for themselves. *Rodina*'s children were wandering in the wilderness, but someday they would find their way. Meanwhile, the grandmothers would keep the faith.

As she crossed herself and kissed the icon, Evgenia felt a benediction of profound peace descend upon her soul. As the Babushka of her family, she would keep open the doors to the Church – not the brocaded institution in which men were corrupted by power, but the real Church within, the one Ivan had died for. Her grandmothers had served it faithfully for generations, and, when it was time, she knew her granddaughters – wherever they were – would not let the candle go out.

"Mother of God, protect and heal us. Make us strong so that the soul of Mother Russia will endure."

Amen.

368

Chapter 19: The PURGE

Nadya's eyes grew wide as the big bad wolf came snarling out of the forest. Sitting on the edge of her seat, she watched breathlessly as brave little Pioneer Peter captured it. Cheering his triumph, her little feet tapped and her small body swayed in time to the music. Lisya smiled. Coming to the Pioneer Palace had been a good idea; *Peter and the Wolf* – Prokofiev's new musical tale – was a wonderful way for both of them to celebrate Nadya's birthday.

After the concert, they walked slowly home, Nadya chattering excitedly about the performance. As always, they ended up on their favorite bench by the embankment, where they played a guessing game about the musical themes Prokofiev had given the animals in his story. Lisya hummed and Nadya guessed; then they switched parts. As they were about to leave, the little girl smiled up at her grandmother. For just an instant, Lisya heard the sunshine of Tatiana's laughter.

The kitchen smelled wonderful when they returned home; Evgenia had been baking all day. Except for the silver wisps always peeking out from her kerchief, the resemblance to Old Ekaterina – and to the Babushka of Lisya's childhood, after whom she herself had been named – was now too striking to ignore. So when Nadya started talking, she called her great-grandmother "Babushka." Lisya, in turn, encouraged the little girl to call *her* "Grandmere."

When everyone had gathered, Evgenia proudly placed a large pretzel-shaped *krendel*, glazed with sugar and stuffed with almonds and raisins, in the center of the table. Then she brought out a big plate piled high with *khvorost*. The thin deep-fried cookie twists were sprinkled with powdered sugar and looked like twigs covered with snow. Nadya made her way around the table, at home on all the welcoming laps which surrounded it. She finally ended up snuggled cozily against Vladimir's huge chest.

Katya excused herself early, as usual, to study in her room. Olga went to practice her cello. Ludmilla and Evgenia started cleaning up the kitchen. Lisya sat down at the table and began darning socks. At the other end, Alexei and Vassily were playing chess. Sergei was supervising.

Sergei and his sons had prospered, Lisya thought, as she stuffed her darning egg into one of Vladimir's old socks. Alexei had a good position at *Leningradskaya Pravda*, and was a stalwart member of the Writers' Union. Although he always wrote as he was told, Alexei stayed as aloof from practical politics as he could, preferring the heady idealism of abstract patriotism. The intricacies of the Party were left to Vassily, who was rising rapidly at Smolny headquarters. Sergei, meanwhile, had mastered Stalin's recommended style of management and now roared effortlessly at his subordinates. Sometimes, at home, he forgot he wasn't at the factory.

Looking at Vladimir sitting in the corner, Lisya sighed. His bushy beard and reddish hair were streaked with grey. The corners of his wide mouth sagged mournfully, the genial grin which had formerly hovered there gone. His hooked eyebrows drooped despairingly over the dark, sensitive eyes so like his father's – except that in Ivan's gaze, the brooding sorrow had been infused with something Vladimir lacked.

He was smiling now at the little girl in his lap, but only with Nadya did the dark burden usually enveloping him ever lift. With everyone else he was grim and fanatically humorless. Most days he worked late into the night, and then drank until dawn – always alone and behind a closed door.

Once, when Vladimir was in Moscow on Party business, Lisya had gone into his room to put away his mended socks. Stripped of everything but the barest essentials, an aura of self-mortification pervaded the room, heavily overlaid with grey despair. It made her think of a monk's cell. Or a prison cell. A cold shudder swept through her.

That night, she had begun having the nightmare again. Dmitri was sinking into the dark pit, from which she was unable to save him. Only now, the face was Vladimir's.

Ж   Ж   Ж

After dinner, Alexei went to a Writers' Union meeting; he would not be home until late. When Katya went to her room, she asked her mother to come with her.

Lisya knew it must be serious. Katya was working on her doctorate; she rarely let anything interfere with her study schedule.

370

Katya closed the door behind them, paced nervously back and forth in front of it, and finally sat down on the bed.

"Some of the Hermitage paintings are missing!" she said abruptly.

"What?!" Lisya was dumbfounded. "How do you know?"

"Quite by accident, really. I spend so much time there doing research – I've gotten to know some of the staff. A few months ago, I found one of the curators crying in the bathroom. I tried to comfort her – and somehow this strange story slipped out." Katya hesitated , looking over her shoulder. "One night she was ordered to stay late, after closing, and take down Van Eyck's *Annunciation*. After delivering it to someone from the Commissariat for Foreign Affairs, she was told to rearrange the other paintings to look like nothing was missing. And she was to ask no questions. She's been upset ever since."

Lisya murmured sympathetically.

"Anyway," continued Katya, "I checked the records. Around that time, several other masterpieces were transferred from the Hermitage to Moscow, supposedly for cleaning and restoration."

"Is that unusual?" asked Lisya.

"Mmm, yes – but not totally improbable. So I did some more checking, and guess what I found? None of the paintings ever returned!"

"Maybe they're still in Moscow?"

"No, not likely. When I asked around, everyone said they were destroyed by a fire at the Hermitage a few years back."

"You doubt that?"

"I remember where many of the missing paintings used to hang. And those galleries were virtually undamaged by the fire."

Katya stood up and began to pace again, her quick clever fingers pushing her thick straight hair away from her face.

"It's common knowledge around the Hermitage that the government has been selling off the contents of the Romanov palaces. You know – jewelry and antiques and all that Faberge stuff. Apparently there's a big market for it with wealthy American women fascinated by European royalty."

"And you think that –"

"Yes! I do!" Katya exploded. "But how could they! It's one thing to peddle jeweled hippopotamuses and gold umbrella handles and all those stupid eggs. But paintings by Rembrandt – and Raphael and Van Dyck and Velasquez, Botticelli, Titian, Rubens! At least 73 of them that I know of – and who knows how many more!"

"Have you talked to Alexei about this?"

"Yes," Katya snorted. "He said I must have made a mistake."

"But you don't think so."

"Of course not." Katya deferred to Alexei in many matters, but when it came to her work, she was hard as nails – and much too competent to make such a huge mistake.

"Have you considered speaking to Vassily?"

"I already have," nodded Katya.

"And?"

"He neither confirmed nor denied it. But he gave me a long lecture about the realities of modern economics."

"Not exactly my favorite topic." Lisya inexplicably felt a sudden urge to yawn.

"Nor mine – but it was most enlightening. The gist of it was that the only way *not* to be dominated by foreign capitalists is to industrialize ourselves."

"Hence the Plan?"

"Right. But the Plan requires imported machinery and technology, most of which we're buying from the Americans."

"So what's the problem?"

"The problem is that we need American trucks and tractors and turbines more than they need Russian fur and hides and badger bristles. So we pay in hard cash."

"Which rich Americans will pay for famous paintings?"

"Exactly. Vassily says that turning 'Rubens into rubles' – as he put it – will improve relations with the United States. And that it's better than what the tsars did when they sold Alaska."

"Have you discussed any of this with anyone at the Hermitage?"

"Vassily said I should drop it, but I can't. So I went to see Orbeli, the Director of the Hermitage."

"What did he say?"

"He confessed that he had opposed selling the paintings – which he nonetheless continued to deny – but had been overruled by the Politburo. He then assured me that there would be no more of these sales – which, of course, never happened – even if he had to guard the rest of the Hermitage collection with his own body. And then he cried. I took pity on the poor man and asked no more questions."

As Katya blew her nose, Lisya was reminded of how much it resembled Evgenia's – and her own.

"Were all the missing paintings by Western artists?"

"I wondered about that, too," sniffed Katya. "The collections at both the Russian Museum and the Tretyakov Gallery still seem intact. Apparently the government's stance is that if the capitalist West wants its own bourgeois art back, it can have it – along with the debris of the Romanovs and the Russian Orthodox Church. But the Rublevs and Repins and Surikovs are another matter. So are the Kremlin crown jewels."

"Can you live with that?"

"As long as they don't sell the Russian art – I guess I'll have to. What choice do we have?" Katya got up and walked over to the window. She paused, frowning.

"There's something else?"

"Vassily dropped a comment – just in passing…" Katya stared silently out the window. "He said it was better to export paintings than grain." She turned around suddenly and looked at her mother. "But we're exporting grain, too! I've seen them loading it onto foreign ships! But why, when there are hungry people here?"

Neither of them dared answer the question.

Ж   Ж   Ж

Vladimir didn't usually go to the movies. But tonight Eisenstein's new epic, *Alexander Nevsky*, was playing. St. Alexander Nevsky had been Prince of Norgorod in the 13th century, and had beaten off an invasion by the Teutonic Knights. Now he was being re-canonized in the Soviet cinema.

Watching Eisenstein's dramatic images and listening to Prokofiev's stirring score, Vladimir was enthralled. The noble prince was a great statesman and brave warrior, who governed his people with a firm hand and defended them heroically from the monstrous Germans. No wonder Comrade Stalin had given Eisenstein – and the actor who played the title role – the Order of Lenin.

After the movie, Vladimir left the theater in a blaze of nationalistic fervor. In times of crisis, the Motherland had never lacked a supreme warlord to protect her – like Alexander Nevsky, and yes, Stalin. For certainly Stalin was a man of iron, a warrior of steel, a colossus towering over his people. One could see that in the stern statues and smiling icons everywhere. The children at Nadya's kindergarten even mumbled ritual thanks to Stalin as they left the lunch table. Though when Nadya had started doing it at home, Evgenia firmly put a stop to it.

Not that Vladimir believed everything he read. In his opinion, there were far too many articles entitled "Under the Wise Direction of Our Great Genius Leader and Teacher Stalin," in which some scholar would breathlessly declare that "certain prognostications of Aristotle have been incarnated and explained in all their amplitude by Stalin, who, together with Socrates, represents the peak of human intelligence." Such adulation embarrassed Vladimir. "I want to howl, roar, shriek, bawl with rapture at the thought that we are living in the days of the most glorious, one and only, incomparable Stalin!" a prominent writer had proclaimed. "Our breath, our blood, our life – here, take it, O great Stalin!" Surely this embarrassed Stalin, too.

For Stalin was a simple man, a modest pipe-smoking embodiment of common sense, the father of his people, who did not allow his importance to go to his head, who still had time for the common folk. Not that very many of them ever saw him. Stalin rarely left the Kremlin and seldom made public appearances But this was as it should be. Russian rulers were supposed to be mysterious.

It was, therefore, with no little excitement that Vladimir received a summons to visit Stalin in the Kremlin. True, he had been with the Great Comrade at Tsaritsyn during the Civil War. Direct dealings between them, however, had been few and brief and distant; Vladimir's memories were disconcertingly vague. But of course Stalin must have done a brilliant job defending the city; why else would they have renamed it Stalingrad?

And so, as he stood at the Spassky Gate once again, he chose to remember the other time, years ago, he had waited there to see Lenin. The group now was cheerful, good-naturedly teasing the only woman, who worked for the Commissariat of Agriculture. Someone quipped that the increase in watermelon production must have been inspired by her breasts. Vladimir looked away, blushing, but not before noting that they were, indeed, enormous.

Finally, the group was ushered into a large spartan-looking office. Stalin was standing behind an enormous desk. Behind him were portraits of Marx, Lenin – and Stalin. On the other walls were Alexander Nevsky, and Suvorov and Kutuzov and other tsarist field marshals. Stalin was wearing a brown long-sleeved military tunic bare of decoration. His hair and mustache were bushy, and he cupped the bowl of a lit pipe in his hands.

The great leader was surprisingly short. His face was pockmarked and his small yellowish eyes were unfriendly and devoid of humor. He spoke haltingly with a Georgian accent, but unlike most Georgians, seemed cold and unemotional. It was clear, however, that this was not a man to be trifled with. Vladimir could feel the power he exuded. Here was someone who wanted control – and had it.

During the audience, Stalin himself said little, preferring to ask each of his visitors a few questions. Vladimir noticed that all of them were shrewdly put, and that he listened carefully to the answers.

Vladimir never saw Stalin again, except on the reviewing stand at a distance. But as he was promoted upward, he began having occasional dealings with the leader's chief lieutenants. All of them – like Stalin – were workaholics who worked late into the night, seven days a week. They were also a remarkably unfriendly lot, who fought constantly with each other. And judging by the invective which resounded throughout the offices at the Kremlin, Vladimir guessed that Stalin's informal speech was decidedly earthy. *Gavno* and *pizduk* and *svoloch* were standard parlance, and more than once Vladimir was advised to go swing on an elephant's balls.

Well, and what of it! Peter the Great was no gentleman either, Vladimir was reminded as he sat watching the new movie about another of Stalin's predecessors. Tsar Peter was crude and cruel – and so were those around him – but he got the job done.

"I was very harsh with you, my children," he said, in the scene where he lay dying. "Not for my own sake, but because Russia was so dear to me."

Hard times and hard circumstances demanded hard men – men of steel. Like Tsar Peter. Stalin understood that a backward Russia was vulnerable to attack and invasion. He knew that the Motherland was encircled by enemies waiting to pounce at the slightest sign of weakness. But this time, Russia would be strong. Stalin would see to that – just as Tsar Peter had.

On his next visit to the Kremlin, Vladimir learned that a new portrait had gone up on the wall of Stalin's office. Next to recently added Peter the Great now hung Ivan the Terrible. To Stalin, Ivan was a model ruler – great and wise, despotic but respected by the masses – who unified the unruly Russians while guarding them from contamination by foreigners.

Eagerly Vladimir attended Eisenstein's latest movie, *Ivan the Terrible*. As the stunning images crossed the screen – each one more powerful than the last – Vladimir saw the soul of his people unfold before him. Ivan's stern presence was irresistible, as his iron hand mercilessly dealt with Russia's overwhelming problems and manifold enemies. Traitors within and invaders from without fell before his implacable dedication to protecting the Motherland. It was inspiring – and alarming. For as his reign wore on, Ivan began to change. The golden young man in the coronation scene slowly grew darker and more stooped. Glimmerings of paranoia hovered ominously.

Eisenstein's movie was to have a sequel, about the end of Ivan's reign. As Vladimir left the theater, his elation at the past faded into a flurry of small nagging doubts about the present – and then into cold foreboding for the future. He knew how Ivan's reign ended. But what about Stalin's?

Ж　Ж　Ж

A restrained burst of applause distracted Lisya from tuning her violin. Automatically she looked up from her place in the Maryinsky's orchestra pit to what had once been the Imperial box. A short man with bushy hair and large moustache had just entered. With a shock, she realized who it must be. It seemed strange – and yet somehow not – to see Comrade Stalin sitting where Tsar Nicholas had.

Suddenly the polite ovation burst into enthusiastic shouts as another man entered the box. Smiling, Lisya recognized Comrade Kirov, charming and charismatic Party Chief of Leningrad. Sergei and Vassily, she knew, regarded Kirov as their real leader. To Alexei and Katya, he was a hero. Vladimir was less enthusiastic. "Well, at least Kirov is a real Russian," he acknowledged grudgingly.

On a dark winter afternoon, not long after Lisya saw him at the Maryinsky, Kirov was assassinated. Leningrad was numb. A strange sense of doom hung over the city. People waited, not knowing for what. Meanwhile, Kirov was buried in style. Stalin himself took the night train to Leningrad to attend the funeral.

At first, the assassination was ascribed to a conspiracy of White Guards, who had infiltrated the country from Poland and Rumania. Members of this group were quickly rounded up and shot; but soon it was given out that they had been only the tip of the iceberg.

A decree went out from Comrade Stalin ordering cases against terrorists speeded up. All death sentences were carried out immediately, without appeal. Meanwhile, Leningrad Party members – especially those close to Kirov – began disappearing. Sergei became noticeably nervous, roaring more than usual.

Finally, it was announced that the real culprits had been found. Two members of Stalin's inner circle were arrested and given long prison sentences. Shortly after, arrests in Leningrad multiplied. Sergei started to sweat.

Nor did it stop when Kirov's murder had been solved and avenged. For the assassination turned out to be but a tiny part of an infinitely larger, more heinous

376

conspiracy. The target of this plot was not a mere man, but the Party, the People, the Nation itself! And the strategy of attack was not simple terrorism, but sabotage of The Plan! Worst of all, the conspirators were everywhere – in factories and schools, army and police, even in the Party itself!

Although The Plan had yielded impressive results, it was also clear that the economy itself was a huge mess. Heavy industry had indeed made a great leap forward, the army was indeed stronger and more modern, the gap between backward Russia and the capitalist West was indeed smaller – but life was no easier for the people

What had gone wrong? It *could not* be Comrade Stalin's fault. Nor could the Party or the Plan be blamed. Nor could it even be admitted that the task itself was simply too overwhelming to accomplish in such a short time. And to claim bad luck for the chosen people of the marxist dialectic was out of the question. No. Someone had to be blamed.

"Assembly lines do not stop by themselves, machines do not break down by themselves, boilers do not burst by themselves," blared the media. "Somebody's hand is behind every such action." The saboteurs had to be found. The evil spirits had to be exorcised. Scapegoats had to be punished. The more the better.

And so a gigantic witch hunt was launched to root out the wreckers and liquidate the conspiracy. Heads began to roll from the top down, as high Party officials were arrested for treason and found guilty in carefully staged, highly publicized trials. The culprits confessed to everything. Their alleged chief, the exiled Trotsky, was sentenced to death in absentia. Soon he became the devil incarnate as numerous leaders of the government, army, police, and every other major institution were discovered to be Trotskyite-Fascist-wreckers. The Terror moved downward and outward in ever larger circles, as each arrested leader was followed by his surrounding entourage, and then by their friends and acquaintances.

Men sought to save themselves – and their families – by denouncing others. Some informed on those with whom they had old scores to settle. Others were afraid that if they didn't talk, someone else would –and that they would then be arrested for failing to inform. It was rumored that the secret police, too, had quotas.

No one was exempt. No one was above suspicion. No one was safe. Not a few died by their own hand, rather than wait in nerve-wracking suspense for the knock on the door.

One night, Vladimir went to a local Party meeting. There was a standing ovation in honor of Comrade Stalin. Like everyone else, Vladimir stood and applauded until his hands ached. The applause went on and on. No one dared be the first to stop. Finally, a factory director sat down. Vladimir and everyone else stopped applauding, gratefully falling back into their seats.

The next morning, the factory director was arrested.

Ж   Ж   Ж

The discussions around the kitchen table stopped.

At mealtime everyone ate in tense silence, punctuated only by polite requests to pass this or that. Afterward, they scuttled off to their rooms and closed the doors. No friends came to laugh and drink and argue.

Finally, late one night, it happened.

The arrogant pounding on the door awakened Lisya from fitful dreams she was glad to leave. By the time she stumbled sleepily into the hall to investigate, Vladimir had already unlocked the door.

"What is it, comrades?" he asked, alarmed. "Has something happened?"

"We've tracked another traitor, that's what!" growled a man who seemed to blend into the shadows of the dark hall.

"Do you need my help in apprehending him?" asked Vladimir earnestly.

"We've already found him!" snorted another man in nondescript clothes.

"Where?" asked Vladimir innocently.

"Right here, you filthy saboteur!" snarled a third man nervously. "You're to come with us!"

"Now?" Vladimir was dumbfounded. "Where?"

"Where do you think?!" chortled the first man uncomfortably.

"Surely there's been some mistake – " began Vladimir.

"We don't make mistakes!" interrupted the grey-clad man brusquely.

"But I'm a member of the Party!" protested Vladimir indignantly.

"Loyal members of the Party aren't saboteurs!" barked the third man, his eyes shifting uneasily.

"I'm not a saboteur!" protested Vladimir in disbelief.

"That's what all traitors say!" sneered the man who appeared to be in charge.

"I'm not a traitor!" protested Vladimir, stunned.

"Then you should have no objections to coming with us." The largest of the intruders grabbed Vladimir's arm.

"But I'm a loyal comrade…" said Vladimir weakly, allowing himself to be led away.

"Shut up!"

Suddenly Vladimir was gone.

Lisya stood, shocked, staring at the door which had just slammed. Other ashen faces peered fearfully from barely-opened doors, then quietly dissolved into the darkness.

All the next day, everyone stayed in their rooms. At last, Lisya emerged and accosted Sergei on his way to the bathroom.

"Do something!" she demanded.

"What can I do? If he was arrested, he must be guilty. There's no smoke without fire." And he dodged into the bathroom and locked the door.

Vassily was less abrupt. While he, too, assumed Vladimir was guilty, he assured her that Vladimir would only be sentenced to hard labor. "Convict labor," he explained patiently, "makes a useful contribution to The Plan. It can often replace expensive machinery which must be bought with hard currency."

Lisya slammed the door in his face.

For hours, she paced restlessly in Vladimir's empty little room. Finally, toward morning, she returned to her own.

"I have to find him," she announced quietly.

Evgenia nodded and left the room, returning eventually with a bundle. In it was a loaf of homemade bread, a jar of jam, a pair of hand-knitted socks from Katya, a change of underwear, and a picture drawn by Nadya of two bears holding hands. One of them was very large and wore huge medals on his chest; the small one had corkscrew curls and a big bow on her head.

After Lisya had wrapped herself in her warmest clothing, Evgenia embraced her firmly and handed her the bundle. Outside, a bitingly cold wind blew snow around her as she slowly made her way to 2 Dzerzhinsky Square. At last, ahead of her loomed a huge frighteningly dreary building – the Lubyanka, prison of no return.

As she approached the grey forbidding entrance, she took her place at the end of a long line of women. For hours, they all stood quietly in the freezing snow, as the line moved slowly into the menacing gates.

Finally, it was her turn. Trembling inwardly, she walked up to the snarling grill just inside the door. To her inquiries about Vladimir, a cold voice replied mechanically, "We receive information, we don't give it." Whoever was in the cage, however, did agree to forward the package. Stunned, Lisya returned home. After several hours next to the stove, she stopped shivering.

A few days later, she tried again. This time, she resolved not to be intimidated by the grill. Vladimir, after all, was one of the Old Bolsheviks. He had been around a long time, and was well known in Leningrad for the decent way he treated his subordinates. Sooner or later, she was bound to run into someone at the Lubyanka who owed him.

And so, several times a week, Lisya made her lonely pilgrimage to the most dreaded place in the city. Sometimes, the woman ahead or behind her was willing to converse in brief whispers. And occasionally, the voice behind the grill held a hint of warmth and gave her a crumb or two of what she wanted to know. From the women outside, she surmised that most of these latest arrests were somehow connected to the army. And from the barely perceptible nods and shrugs and murmurs which sometimes emanated from the window grill, she was able to piece together that Vladimir was alive and reasonably well in the Lubyanka, and that he had probably been sentenced to several years of hard labor in Siberia.

Which, she knew, was tantamount to a death sentence. *No, no*, she despaired, *I have already lost too many.* Suddenly the thought of never again seeing Vladimir, of not even being able to say goodbye, of him going off to die without any comfort – suddenly Lisya could not bear it. She knew she could do nothing to change his fate. But she had to see him again – just once.

Sergei nearly collapsed with fear when she asked him to help. After shouting that she was insane, he ran into the bathroom and threw up.

Vassily was more civilized. He warned her that such action would seriously endanger her life. He sternly admonished her to stay away from the Lubyanka; her visits there had already compromised the family's safety.

Lisya, however, had long since decided that if Vladimir's arrest hadn't already jeopardized the family, her visits to the Lubyanka weren't likely to make their situation any worse. Her own welfare, however, was another matter – but that was her business.

Over the months, she had noticed certain patterns at the Lubyanka. She had spotted several guards whom she knew had reason to be well-disposed toward Vladimir, picked out which of them seemed easiest to get around, and noted when they were on duty. And she knew that activity at the Lubyanka, as elsewhere, slowed down and grew more lax during holidays.

After careful planning, she selected what she hoped was the most propitious day. She dressed carefully in the stylish suit Tatiana had brought her from Paris so many years before. Striking a pose before the cracked mirror in her room, she noted with satisfaction that though the outmoded ensemble fit more snugly now, she still cut a noticeably elegant figure. Holding out her hands, she eyed them critically. Clean fingernails, no callouses – good! – the hands of a lady. No jewelry, no nail polish – better yet, a politically correct lady.

This time, Evgenia gave her no bundle. Instead, she solemnly made the sign of the cross and embraced her – then let her go with an approving smile. And for the last time, Lisya took the grim path to the Lubyanka.

As she neared the familiar gate, she saw the usual group of women straggling patiently before it. Lisya thought of Kschessinskaya, and marched boldly to the head of the line. Imperiously, she handed the official looking, elaborately worded document – to which she had forged Sergei's signature – through the grill. To her relief, the guard on duty was who she had expected, as was his superior – to whom he handed the paper. Both of them looked uncertainly at it and conversed nervously for several minutes, glancing often at the elegant and confident lady who had presented them with this unexpected problem. Lisya graced them with what she hoped was a regal, yet sufficiently friendly, smile. Finally, they shrugged, opened the door next to the grill, and let her in. A faint aroma of liquor briefly enveloped her as she passed by them.

A third guard lead her quickly through a labyrinth of dismal corridors. Strange muffled sounds occasionally provided grim counterpoint to the clomp of his boots and the clicking of her high heels. Lisya tried not to imagine the why of what she was hearing.

Finally, the guard wordlessly motioned her into a small bare room and slammed the door behind her. It echoed ominously as she sat down on one of the two wooden chairs. Leaning her elbows on the table, she looked at the door and waited, firmly ignoring the clamoring voices inside which screamed that she should be terrified.

After what seemed forever, she heard more clomping boots in the corridor, then fumbling at the door, which creaked reluctantly open and slammed shut again. Suddenly, standing before her, astonishment all over his haggard face, was Vladimir.

After a long moment of shocked silence, he held out trembling hands which she grasped tightly in her own. They sat down, the table between them, his hands gradually steadier in her firm grasp. Vladimir's huge frame was gaunt, and there were dark circles under his eyes. His thick hair was closely cropped.

"Ah well," he shrugged, brushing his hand quickly over the stubble on his

381

head, "it's starting to grow back again. By the time I get out of here, it should be long enough to keep my head warm."

"And when will that be?" Lisya tried to keep the quaver out of her voice.

"Soon, I imagine. They've already sentenced me."

"But you're innocent!"

"That's what I said when they told me. 'Shut up!' they yelled back. 'Of course you're not guilty! Would they have only given you 10 years if you were?'"

"But how," Lisya shook her head uncomprehendingly, "can they sentence you for nothing?'

"I confessed."

"But why?"

Vladimir look away. "The interrogators – they don't let up until you confess – to anything." Then, seeing the shocked look on her face, "No, no – not that way. Mostly, they just don't let you sleep. You'd be surprised how persuasive that is, after a while. And my cell has been boiling hot. Though I'm not sure that's on purpose."

He managed a weak grin, which Lisya tried to return.

"But I haven't informed on anyone. And I won't!" Vladimir's tired eyes suddenly looked worried. "Lisya, do you know who most of the prisoners in here are? Army officers! The top ranks! Commissars like me, and Generals all over the place! Even Marshals and Admirals! And from prisoners transferred in from other places, it sounds like this is happening all over the country."

Vladimir got up and began pacing the tiny room.

"Lisya, I've kept track! At least half our officer corps is being wiped out. And it's the most experienced that are being hardest hit. My God! What will we do if Hitler invades us, too?!"

Abruptly, he sat down again, his weakened body not able to sustain his tirade.

"That's why I won't inform," he said quietly. "I wish others had done the same."

"Someone informed on you?" Lisya asked incredulously. "But who?"

"Someone I had every right to trust." Vladimir looked down sadly, and was silent.

"I spend a lot of time thinking," he began again, reflectively. "What else is there to do? I've thought a lot about the Revolution, about how we took this train called Russia by storm, even built some new cars and a locomotive, and began to drive it from Station Promise to Station Hope – oh, so confidently!" Vladimir's face darkened. "But Lisya… I think the train is moving somewhere else… not where we want it to go – and it can't be stopped – and no one can get off!"

Vladimir got up again, paced a few rounds, remembered how weak he was, and sat down again.

"Yes, I confessed." Agony deepened the lines etched on his face. "Because I am guilty."

Lisya tried to protest.

"No, no," he waved her unfinished words aside. "Not of being a Trotskyite Fascist Wrecker – whatever that is. But I *am* an enemy of the people." He held up clenched hands and looked loathingly at them. "Their blood is all over my hands! I'm completely drenched in blood! All of us in here are!"

And he buried his face in his hands and began to sob noiselessly.

Finally, when his remorse abated, Lisya took his hand again and pressed it gently in her own. "I have known you all your life, my dearest brother, and I know that – whatever you've done – you did it because you believed it necessary."

"But you don't know –"

"Volodya, listen – after all our poor bleeding Motherland has been through, who among us has *not* shed blood. But what choice did we have? What choice have we ever had! Clean hands are a luxury few Russians can afford."

"Lisya…" Vladimir hesitated. "Do you think that I will ever be – can ever be… forgiven?"

"I don't know, Volodya. But *I* forgive you. And you can forgive yourself."

He put his other hand on top of hers as weariness suddenly engulfed him. "I'm so very tired," he sighed. "I've given all I had."

Lisya stroked his cheek gently.

The sound of approaching boots startled them.

"You shouldn't have come here, Lisya." Vladimir stood up suddenly. "It's much too dangerous."

Lisya stood up and threw her arms around him, trying to shield him from what was beyond the door. Vladimir wrapped his arms tightly about her, all trembling gone.

"You shouldn't have come," he repeated, "but I'm so grateful you did."

As the rusty door creaked open, they looked deeply into each other's eyes.

"I love you, Volodya," said Lisya. "I always have."

"I know," he smiled back. "Thank you… I'm not easy to love."

He kissed her hand – and then disappeared into the darkness of the Lubyanka.

Ж   Ж   Ж

Sergei was furious.

"How could you do this to me!" he roared. "How could you risk the family for that Trotskyite traitor!"

"Vladimir is part of this family, too!" Lisya yelled back.

"Not to me, he isn't!"

"Is that why you betrayed him?"

Anguished guilt passed fleetingly across his face. Lisya knew she had guessed right. Sergei retreated abruptly into his room and slammed the door.

Vassily was less direct.

"You took a terrible risk, you know," he said, trying to control his voice. "I'm surprised they let you out again. And I doubt we've heard the last of this."

And with that, Lisya could not argue. It did not seem possisble that she could get away with such a blatant act of insubordination. *Only let the punishment fall on me,* she prayed fervently, *not on my family.*

And, eventually, it did. One morning, when she arrived at the Conservatory, she was abruptly informed that her lessons had been cancelled – permanently. She walked slowly home, a dull ache growing inside, grey dread dragging her down.

A few days later, during rehearsal at the Maryinsky, she was told to leave – and not come back. Her cheeks burned, as she packed up her violin and left the chair she had occupied for so many years. Threading her way out of the familiar clutter of music stands and instruments, only Olga dared meet her eyes with a quick look of compassion.

Slowly, Lisya climbed out of the orchestra pit and walked up the aisle of the beautiful theatre where she had spent so much of her life. At the door, she took a last look at the boxes and stalls, the ornate ceiling and the elegant chandeliers, and finally the stage itself. For just a moment, she heard the applause and the bravo's as Chaliapin sang and Nijinsky leaped and Kschessinskaya bowed regally. And then, with a shock, she realized that she had never before seen the Maryinsky from this angle.

Tears welled up in her eyes, as she felt something in her soul crack.

Ж   Ж   Ж

For weeks, Lisya stayed in her room, seeing no one but Evgenia. Olga moved into Vladimir's empty room. Several times after, she knocked on Lisya's door, all to no avail. Even Katya and Nadya were not admitted. Sergei, of course, did not want to see her, nor did Vassily or Alexei try to approach her.

In the room itself was dismal silence, broken by day only by the clicking of Babushka's knitting needles. By night, Vassily and Ludmilla argued on one side, Alexei and Katya on the other. Sergei, meanwhile, roared up and down the hall in the throes of increasingly hysterical fear.

As if from a great distance, Lisya realized that all this dissension centered around her. But somehow it didn't seem to matter, as she gazed dully at the piano and violin gathering dust in the corner.

Then, late one night, there was another loud knock on the apartment door. Sergei began to scream – and then to gasp horribly. By the time Vassily and Alexei got to him, he was dead. His lifeless eyes stared up at them in stark terror

When they opened the door, no one was there.

Ж   Ж   Ж

The new apartment, Lisya decided reluctantly, was not all that bad. The rooms were bigger, and they had their own kitchen. The bathroom they shared with people down the hall, but its plumbing was newer and clogged up less often.

Vassily had used his rapid promotion in the Party to find himself and Ludmilla their own apartment. He had also used his influence to find better living quarters for his younger brother's family – which Katya insisted included Lisya and Evgenia. Olga, meanwhile, stayed at the old apartment, joined by her mother and niece from the country. The librarian who had befriended Evgenia also moved in with her husband, daughter and son-in-law.

Lisa now shared a room with Nadya. Evgenia had insisted on that. At first, Lisya had protested, not wanting to inflict her depression on her beloved grandchild. By the end of the first month in the new room, however, it was apparent that the little girl had problems of her own. She, too, was unusually morose and silent.

Finally, one night, Lisya's fitful sleep was interrupted by loud miserable snuffling. Slowly, the pathetic sobbing cut through the grey barricade which had surrounded her since leaving the Maryinsky. Half-awake, she stumbled out of bed to Nadya's small cot and gently wrapped her arms around the weeping child.

"Oh, Grandmere," wailed Nadya forlornly, "I miss Grandfather so much!"

Lisya knew that she did not mean Sergei. Though a proud and doting grand-

385

parent, Sergei, the father of boys, had never quite known what to do with a girl. It was Vladimir who had told her stories and made her toys, whose big kind hands had often wiped away her tears, and whose lap she had always ended up on after supper.

"I know, I know," murmured Lisya into the child's tangled curls, "I miss him, too."

And together they cried, until Nadya fell asleep on her shoulder.

The next morning, it was Lisya who took Nadya to school. Walking home along the Neva, she thought about how upsetting the last year had been for her granddaughter. Wrenched from the cherished center of a warm affectionate family, she had been left stranded by terrified wounded strangers. As Lisya pondered how to help, a tiny ray of light penetrated the gloom which had enveloped her for months.

A few mornings later, she opened the small trunk she kept under her bed, and took out her saffron velvet dress. Carefully she unfolded it and ran her hand lovingly over its now faded softness. Wisps of nostalgia flitted over her as she remembered the first – and last – time she had worn it.

Slowly, she refolded the elegant old dress, and put it in a covered shopping basket. Resolutely closing the door behind her, she left the apartment and walked to the Haymarket.

Hours later, she returned. Nadya was already home from school, sitting at the kitchen table helping Evgenia peel potatoes. Both of them looked at Lisya with surprise, first at the smile on her face, then at the basket she placed in front of Nadya. It began to wriggle mysteriously, a tiny black paw darting tentatively out. After much scrabbling and thumping, the lid came ajar, and a small furry head with impudently pointed ears peered triumphantly out.

Nadya's face lit up as the kitten jumped out and began to sniff out her new home. Eventually convinced she had nothing to fear, she eagerly lapped up a saucer of milk. Then she became playful – grabbing at Evgenia's knitting needles and chewing on the big floppy bow attempting to restrain Nadya's curls. Each of the kitten's antics elicited peals of ringing laughter from the little girl. Which was, Lisya decided, the most beautiful music she had ever heard.

Little by little, they all began to heal – and started to become a family again. There were, of course, certain topics which could never be discussed; often it was awkward trying to maneuver around the painful memories which loomed so large. But what had happened was so searingly hurtful, so inextricably enmeshed in so much that mattered so deeply, the very thought of trying to sort it all out was overwhelming. And so, by tacit agreement, no one ever mentioned Vladimir or Sergei. The strain was especially hard on Katya and Alexei, whose marriage was now marred by abrupt bouts of angry silence. Gradually, however, other things began filling the void, and the uncomfortable distance erupted less frequently.

Katya, at long last, triumphantly finished her doctorate – and to her great joy, found an important job at the Hermitage. Alexei was promoted at *Leningradskaya Pravda*; he, too, enjoyed his work. And Lisya finally got her grand piano.

Madame had been mortally ill for some time. But she had continued giving lessons almost until the end. The day before she died, she summoned Lisya to her studio.

"Take care of my piano," she said, pressing Lisya's hand with her sensitive fingers. "But take it home with you, where you can play it for your family – and yourself."

Madame smiled, at peace. The two women said goodbye, knowing that what had connected them would go on.

Katya borrowed one of the Hermitage trucks – and some of its custodians. Somehow they maneuvered the huge piano out of the Conservatory and into the fortunately large kitchen of the apartment, where one of Lisya's former colleagues volunteered to tune it.

Finally, with no little trepidation, Lisya sat down to play. For a moment her fingers froze, but then, seeing the expectant faces of her family, she searched tentatively for chords which felt familiar. Slowly the tension in her fingers eased as the joy of making music once again began to flow, and she found herself playing the Rachmaninov prelude which had been Alexander Pavlovich's favorite. And when, at the end, the family applauded, it seemed that somehow he, too, was smiling and clapping.

A few weeks later, she was invited to join the newly organized Radio Orchestra. Nervously she dusted off her violin case and went to the first rehearsal. She returned home that afternoon feeling years younger. It wasn't the Maryinsky – but it was music. It would do.

Best of all, Katya became pregnant again. This time, there was no doubt, no anxiety. Her pregnancy was healthy, labor brief, the birth uncomplicated. And when a cheerful chubby baby boy burst happily into the world, his family received him with boundless joy. Husky little Sasha greeted them exuberantly, with an already formidable set of lungs; his robust temperament soon spread like a buoyant sunbeam through all of them. Smiles and laughter began to fill their home, and hearts began to mend.

Several months after Sasha was born, Lisya found a letter with her name on it in their mailbox. It had no stamp and was not signed.

"I write this to fulfill a promise to a truly noble soul. I was in the camps with your sainted brother, Vladimir. In the midst of unbearable degradation and suffering, he was a beacon of light, giving hope and comfort to all around him. I would not have survived but for him. And many others will say the same. He told us often of your brave visit to him in prison. He said it was what gave him courage to go on. And he asked us to give you a message, should any of us ever be released. He said to tell you that there, in the camps, he finally found what he had been searching for all his life.

When he died, his spirit ascended peacefully, and there was no fear in his eyes. Those of us who were with him will never again fear death.

Thank you, dear lady, for loving your brother. Through him, it touched us all. May the Source of love send peace to all who mourn, and comfort to all who are bereaved."

Amen.

Part V

Leningrad, 1941

Chapter 20: INVASION

A shining blue sky greeted Katya as she left the apartment. A quiet smile welled up and spread slowly across the strong contours of her face. She stood for a long moment, looking up at the welcome sight of the sun in a clear sky, and decided to walk.

It had been a cold and windy Spring, with snow even on May Day. The parade past the Winter Palace had slogged by in wet boots and soaking coats. Fog had brooded in from the Baltic throughout June, until finally thunderstorms broke out. And now, at last, the sun was shining on the day of the summer solstice.

She turned a corner and began to walk along the river. The Neva, too, had turned from grey to sparkling blue. The sound of the water imperturbably flowing around everything in its path reminded her of a song she had learned from her grandmother. Silently, she began to hum along.

As she started across the Palace Bridge, the Hermitage appeared before her. She stopped – as she always did – and let its architectural magnificence resonate. Of all the buildings on the Neva Embankment, the soaring song of the Hermitage was most inspiring.

Eagerly she crossed the bridge and entered the side door. Inside, too, the beauty of the great museum reverberated. Each of the huge rooms had its own song, as did all of the artistic treasures which filled them. To wander through the galleries and gaze at these singing jewels made Katya feel in tune with herself, and part of something even bigger than the museum.

Resisting the temptation to linger, she strode purposefully through the echoing halls toward her new office. A Russian Culture Department had just been established, and she was one of its curators. Packing cases filled with thousands of Russian art treasures now jammed the storage area and blocked emergency exits. With an exasperated sigh, she remembered that the galleries for these new exhibits were still waiting to have the walls painted. The scaffolding had been up since the beginning of May, and the Construction Trust kept promising to send painters at the "earliest possible moment." Orbeli had somehow extracted a firm date; the work was supposed to start on Monday.

Iosif Orbeli was Director of the Hermitage. An energetic man with the beard of an Old Testament prophet, his dedication to the great museum was absolute. Katya did not doubt that Orbeli had said no to Stalin himself to save most of its priceless collection from being sold abroad.

Katya herself had started at the Hermitage right after getting her doctorate at the University. Her advisor, a friend of Orbeli, had recommended her highly; Vassily, now a prominent member of the Leningrad Party, had vouched for her political loyalty. Sometimes she wondered if her encounter with Orbeli about the missing paintings had influenced the decision to hire her. Neither of them, of course, ever mentioned that unfortunate incident – and no other paintings had disappeared since. In any case, it was clear that he liked her lyrical approach to Art History and genuinely appreciated her passion for Russian art. Almost immediately, he put her to work developing the Russian Culture Department. Ever since, she had immersed herself in the rich earth tones of Mother Russia, each artifact stirring a rich chorus of booming bass, soaring tenor, and melancholy contralto.

When younger, Katya had fancied herself an artist. But by the time she graduated from the University, she realized that she would never be able to create the kind of art she envisioned. So she decided, instead, to study the art of those who could. Far better to surround herself with the work of great artists than with her own mediocre creations. Though unable to match her own work with her artistic vision, she was able to recognize when it was done by others. And eventually she realized that what mattered was that *someone* had done it – and that she could give this great art the respect and protection such beauty deserved.

She had never regretted her decision. The Hermitage was where she belonged.

The shortest route to her office was through the gallery devoted to artifacts from the Mongol Era of Tamerlane. Usually Katya detoured around this oddly silent room; it was the only part of the Hermitage that did not sing. But the 500th anniversary of that period's greatest poet, Alisher Navoi, was approaching and the museum was gathering material for a celebration. An expedition had even been sent to Samarkand to examine the mausoleum where Tamerlane lay buried. Just last week, the archaeologists had carefully lifted the great green slab of his sarcophagus.

As Katya cut quickly through the Mongol exhibit, she thought about the article Alexei was writing for *Leningradskaya Pravda*. "Popular legend, persisting to this day, holds that under this stone lies the source of terrible war." He had smiled while reading this part of it to her. That war could be unleashed by moving an ancient stone was, of course, absurd. Yet something cold galloped through the pit of her stomach – just as it had, the other night, when she had noticed the concern in Alexei's unsmiling eyes.

Ж Ж Ж

Katya left the Hermitage early that afternoon. Orbeli had convinced her that the painters would, indeed, show up on Monday and that soon she would be able to set up the new exhibits. Walking along the Neva to the Nevsky Prospekt, she saw groups of students spilling across the Palace Bridge from the University Embankment. Today was the last day of examinations; boys in pressed blue suits and girls in white voile dresses were already beginning their celebration. The singing and dancing, promenades and rendez-vous' would go on and on, for this was the longest of the White Nights – when darkness never came at all.

Remembering that it was on such a night, years ago, that she and Alexei had first declared their love, Katya smiled. How wonderfully uncomplicated it had all seemed then!

Katya turned onto the Nevsky Prospekt and strolled down the great boulevard so beloved by Russian poets. Snatches of their lyrical accolades skipped through her mind as she passed yellow daffodils and pink cherry blossoms on sale at kiosks. Near the Gostiny Dvor, she slowed down to look in the windows of some of its shops.

Catching sight of her own reflection, Katya paused. Large brown eyes, slightly slanted with high-arched eyebrows, looked squarely and unflinchingly out over high cheekbones and a strong chin. Thick black hair, tied loosely at the nape of the neck, flowed down the long torso of a slender shapely body. Firmly re-fastening her insistently straight hair, she continued her unassumingly graceful stride and turned at the Griboyedov Canal.

Tomorrow was Sasha's first birthday and Katya was on her way to buy him a present. As she thought of her son, her face lit up, bright as the surrounding sky. She shifted the shopping bag she was carrying to her other hand; inside were cigarettes and scented soap she would trade for a wooden sled.

A babble of haggling became a roar as she turned into Haymarket Square. Just as she hoped, the fair weather had attracted a crowd of peasants with winter crafts to barter. At many of the stalls lining the market, there were beautiful little sleds to choose from. After careful scrutiny, she selected a bright red one trimmed with charmingly painted dancing bears. Handing her bag of tobacco and soap to the bear-like old man who had made it, she hoisted the sled over her shoulder.

She walked quickly now, partly because the sled was heavy, partly because the Haymarket always made her uncomfortable. As a student, she had accompanied Alexei on pilgrimage to places nearby where Dostoyevsky had lived and written, trying to imagine the underworld in which his novels were set. The Party said that now, of course, the new Soviet state made thieves and prostitutes unnecessary; the Haymarket had accordingly been renamed "Peace Square." But no one ever called it that. And some of the women, especially, who sauntered among the stalls did not look like proper proletarians to Katya.

She stepped onto the crowded tramcar and made a small space for herself under one of the overhead railings. As the dark noise of the Haymarket receded, the sunny little song that was Sasha danced in her ears. She knew he would be delighted with the sled. He wouldn't, of course, be able to slide on it for a while; but until it snowed, he would use it for his own games in his own way.

How like his father Sasha was! Katya smiled, as the image of her son grew effortlessly into that of her husband. Both were so exuberant, so wholehearted in their laughter and tears. Sometimes, in fact, it was difficult to tell them apart. Both father and son expected unconditional adoration from the women of their household. And usually got it. Occasionally, Katya worried that they were spoiling Sasha – and maybe Alexei, too. But such doubts were always overwhelmed by their irresistible boyish charm.

Even after years of marriage, Katya felt pleasantly disturbed thinking about Alexei. How sensitively his fingers caressed a pen, how engagingly his hands gestured as he recited his poems, how endearingly his eyes filled with tears when she sang to him. Ah, how beautiful he was – and how zestfully he embraced life! Every event was high drama, every new idea enthusiastically explored. Whenever he walked into a room, it felt warm and crowded.

Tomorrow was Sunday, and they were all going to the family *dacha* to celebrate Sasha's birthday. A wave of darkness suddenly swept through her as she remembered that Vassily would be there too. Being with him always reminded her of what *had* to be forgotten. Alexei, too, was tense around Vassily; both brothers tried too hard to pretend that things were as they used to be, before their father died. Back then, the brothers had been at ease, not needing to detour around emotional minefields. Back then, she and Alexei had told each other everything.

Back then, she had not feared his anger when painful memories surfaced. Katya sighed, thinking how drunk Alexei would undoubtedly be by afternoon.

But, as Evgenia always reminded her on these occasions, she was fortunate that vodka merely turned her man into a bad poet spouting maudlin verse. And Alexei was usually careful not to get *really* drunk around Sasha and Nadya. Sometimes, watching him play with the children, Katya thought he seemed more like their playmate than their parent. Nadya, especially, was delighted by attention from her father.

Nadya. Vague regret welled up as she thought about her daughter. Nadya – not quite a child anymore, and growing up so fast! *And I still don't know her.*

There had never been time. Always she had been so busy, studying and working and being a loyal Comrade. And Alexei and Sasha took so much energy! There never seemed to be anything left over for her daughter. Not that Nadya had been neglected – between them, her mother and grandmother had seen to that – but sometimes Katya wished that Nadya needed her, too.

She got off the tramcar, walked the few remaining blocks to their building, climbed the stairs and slipped quietly into the small entry hall of their apartment. Going directly through the kitchen to the room her mother shared with Nadya, she hid the sled under Lisya's bed. Their cat, Koshka, was curled up on top; she yawned, rearranged her tail around her paws, and then went back to sleep. Sasha would not dare look there.

On the other side of the kitchen was the room Katya and Alexei shared with the baby. Evgenia slept in the kitchen near the stove. All the rooms had high ceilings and were filled with books, toys, art objects, musical instruments, desks, trunks, and a few odds and ends of furniture.

Yes, it was crowded, thought Katya as she made herself a cup of tea, but they were fortunate to have three whole rooms to themselves. And it was better to be away from that other place, where her family had been torn apart.

Ж   Ж   Ж

Katya knew something was wrong the moment Alexei walked in the door. He wasn't smiling – rare for him, especially before a holiday. And he was late. Evgenia and Sasha had long since returned from the park; Lisya had already picked up Nadya from the Pioneer Palace on her way home from rehearsal. Dinner was waiting, and they sat down around the big kitchen table as soon as Alexei arrived.

"Orbeli said the painters are coming on Monday," said Katya, passing the bread. "For sure, this time!"

"Let's hope he's right – this time," said Lisya, taking a piece of bread.

"But they will come," said Evgenia, passing the cucumbers, "eventually."

"Perhaps an editorial in *Leningradskaya Pravda*," Lisya smiled at Alexei, "might prod them a bit."

Alexei, however, was uncharacteristically preoccupied.

"My father has more important things to write about," sniffed Nadya.

"Like what?" Alexei grinned at his daughter, suddenly himself again.

"Like the new tiger at the zoo," Nadya grinned back. "They're probably going to name him something stupid."

"Like Comrade Stripes?" suggested Alexei, striking a pompous pose.

"How about Comrade Growl?" giggled Nadya.

"Maybe we should ask Comrade Koshka." Alexei pointed toward the cat, who was carefully trying to retrieve a piece of jam-covered bread dropped by Sasha.

Everyone laughed as Koshka darted between the baby's sticky fingers and ran off triumphantly with her prize.

For dessert, to celebrate Midsummer, Evgenia had baked *pryaniki*, cleverly molded into wonderfully whimsical bears and gorgeous birds decorated with frosted plumage.

"What time will we leave for the dacha tomorrow?" asked Nadya eagerly, helping herself to one of the gingerbread birds.

"As soon as everyone's up," said Evgenia, giving her a pointed look.

"I can't help it if Grandmere sleeps too long," giggled Nadya.

"You'll just have to wake me up on time," laughed Lisya, who then excused herself and went to their room.

"And Sasha, you must wake *me!*" Nadya playfully grabbed one of her brother's little feet.

"Sasha is always the first one up," said Katya, looking fondly at the baby in her lap.

"Like a little rooster." Nadya gently squeezed his foot.

Sasha leaned back against his mother, his attention focused on the gingerbread bear he was munching. Koshka hovered close by, just out of reach.

When the *pryaniki* were almost gone, Lisya entered regally from the bedroom. She bowed graciously as the family applauded. Then she sat down at the huge grand piano which dominated the living room half of the kitchen. Her long black concert gown fell in graceful folds, decorated only by a string of deep amber beads; her hair was combed up in a knot, fastened with a gold brooch. This was her performing costume, and she had worn it ever since Katya could remember.

"Tonight I shall play Tchaikovsky," she said, in the elegant voice which always went with the outfit. And soon she was absorbed in the joy of playing his exquisite music on her magnificent piano. How wonderful to have an instrument so worthy of great music!

"Encore! Encore!" shouted the family, none of them begrudging the space taken up by the piano.

Lisya complied with Tchaikovsky's sparkling *Troika*.

"Bravo!" The family applauded enthusiastically. "Bravo!"

Lisya sank into an elegant bow.

Alexei gallantly presented her with a flower snatched from the bouquet in the center of the table.

Sasha bounced and gurgled enthusiastically on Katya's lap, as Lisya swept off to change her costume.

"Tell us a story, Babushka," begged Nadya.

"Yes, yes," Katya joined in, "about Baba Yaga."

"Baba Baba," echoed Sasha, slipping off Katya's lap and onto Evgenia's. The old woman waited until Lisya, more plainly clad now, returned and sat down.

"In a certain kingdom, in a certain land, namely, in the land where we are living, there lived a witch..." And images of huts on chicken legs and flying mortars-with-pestles filled the room. By the time Evgenia reached her customary epilogue, Nadya was leaning sleepily against Lisya, and Sasha was sound asleep.

Lisya led Nadya to bed. Evgenia tucked Sasha into her own bed and gave Katya a meaningful look. *She noticed, too,* thought Katya without surprise, as she and Alexei went into their room alone.

As soon as the door closed, Alexei began pacing restlessly in front of the window, agitation crackling through his curly blond hair. His light blue eyes were worried; his mouth was bare of its usual charming smile.

Katya sat on the bed and waited for him to speak.

"Damn it, Katya," he finally burst out, "What if they're right!?!"

"About what?"

"That the Nazis might attack us."

"But hasn't the Party assured us that the Pact with Hitler will prevent invasion?"

"How can we trust Hitler? Last year – Denmark, Norway, France! Yugoslavia and Greece just this spring! He's conquered all of Europe! Rommel's moving in North Africa, and England can't hold out much longer. What then? How do we know he'll stop?"

"But Comrade Stalin –"

"Vassily says Comrade Stalin won't listen to anyone who disagrees with him. And Comrade Stalin has decreed that the Germans will not attack – not this year, anyway. Never-mind that our border guards have been reporting German troop build-ups and illegal overflights of their planes. The Kremlin insists that these are rumors circulated by the English, and that anyone caught in a 'provocative act' against the Germans will be shot for treason."

"Does Vassily think there's anything to the rumors?"

"I'm not sure. Anyone of his standing in the Party has to say it's all war-mongering nonsense. But..."

"But... ?"

"Vassily stopped by the office today and we walked home together. That's why I was late. He'd just come from a Party meeting at Smolny."

"What did he say?"

"They were all warned not to get too far away, that there may be something coming up tonight. He tried to act like it was nothing, but I know him, Katya! He's really worried! He can't say about what – but what else could it be? Whenever the rumors about the Germans come up, he always changes the subject – but he never denies them."

"But Alexei, even if the Germans do attack, surely the Red Army won't let them stay on our soil."

"Yes, yes, I know. 'War will be fought on alien territory with a minimum of bloodshed.' So says the Party. But Vassily says that as far as he knows, there's no strategic plan for the military in case of invasion. It's all very well to order carrying the fight to the enemy's territory, but how does one do that without 'provoking' war with the Germans? And how do you minimize bloodshed in an army led by inexperienced, untrained officers?"

At that, Katya winced; Alexei turned abruptly to the window and looked out over the city. A long painful silence stretched out, as that which could not be said hung heavily between them.

If only we could talk about it, Katya thought, desperately wishing that she could somehow get past his anger and her own fear.

Instead, she carefully pushed back the dark churning memories threatening to break loose.

"Katya, Katya," Alexei finally said softly, "This beautiful city of ours is so vulnerable. I know, I know, we have the Baltic republics now, and the Finnish territory, as buffers. We aren't so close to the border as we were. But still..."

Katya walked over to the window and stood next to Alexei, her head almost level with his, her dark straight hair in vivid contrast to the golden blond of his thick curls. He put his arm around her and said quietly, "What will happen to us if the Germans come?"

"We will fight," she replied, leaning close.

Ж   Ж   Ж

Katya was walking with Alexei along the Neva in the magical luminosity of the Midsummer White Night, singing a duet of unearthly beauty. Each note was a giant golden tear hovering gently in the air above them. Alexei lifted her to his shoulder so that she could catch the glistening spheres. The translucent globes slowly wafted into her hands and nestled up against her body, and she floated, with him, suffused by their light.

Suddenly the luminous bubbles began to shatter, one by one, drenching her with their tears. Alexei disappeared and she crashed to the ground, crying desperately.

She struggled awake. It was her mother, knocking on the door. "Alexei! Katya! I'm sorry to wake you, but Vassily is on the phone. He says it's urgent."

Katya was suddenly wide awake as Alexei got out of bed and went to the phone in the entry hall. When he came back, his face was grim. "I'll be at *Leningradskaya Pravda*, rounding up the rest of the staff," he said as he hurriedly got dressed. "I'll call as soon as I know anything." He embraced her, and then left quickly.

The next few hours felt like many more. Nadya and Sasha were still asleep, but Evgenia and Lisya had lived through too much to go back to sleep after such a phone call. Evgenia made tea, and the three women sat silently around the table, waiting.

Katya fidgeted nervously, looking across at her mother, who was trying to appear calm. Not quite as tall as she herself was and somewhat heavier, Lisya was still shapely and carried herself with just a hint of imperiousness. Her dark brown hair was usually swept up in a well-disciplined knot, with streaks of grey arching up like silver wings. This morning, however, the wings were hidden by thick tresses hanging heavily around her face.

Katya looked anxiously into her mother's deep-set eyes, searching for the translucent blue which sometimes glowed there. Now, however, the usually reassuring eyes were clouded with anger, their wrinkled corners drooping with decades of loss. Irritably, Katya wished her mother would comb her hair; she needed to see those wrinkles flying bravely up to meet the silver wings.

Next to Lisya sat Evgenia. Shorter than both her daughter and granddaughter, Evgenia's body was solid and cylindrical – rather like a tree trunk – and her strong capable hands were red and calloused. Remarkably clear blue eyes gazed sadly but unflinchingly out of an intricate network of deep wrinkles. Wisps of snowy hair quietly resisted the firmly tied scarf on her head. Katya smiled at the slightly drooping nose and wiry hooked eyebrows, suddenly soothed by how much her grandmother resembled an old, very wise owl.

Finally the telephone rang. "Katya," said Alexei's impersonal telephone voice, "It's happened. Keep everyone at home and listen to the radio for the announcement. I can't say more. I'll be home when I can… and Katya" – the voice was Alexei's own now – "I'm sorry about Sasha's birthday."

Katya slowly hung up the phone, walked to the radio and turned it on. "Alexei said there would be an announcement," she said quietly. Evgenia got out her knitting, Lisya began to darn socks. Katya went back into her room and paced back and forth in front of the window, occasionally stopping to look out at the city.

Just as the streets began to stir, Sasha woke up. A little surprised to find himself in Evgenia's bed, he half-crawled, half-toddled into his parents' room.

"Mama?"

Katya turned and saw her son standing on uncertain legs, clutching the door and looking for another mooring to aid his upright progress into the room. Finding none, he plopped down on his well-padded little behind and started crawling toward his mother.

Katya laughed, walked to the door, scooped him up and hugged him. Sasha was big for his age, and had a voice to match. Just like his great-great-grandfather Mikhail, Evgenia often said proudly. *And just like him, too,* said her eyes.

Katya sighed. Sometimes it was so hard to remember that they had to forget.

Sasha began to wiggle. Smiling, she bestowed noisy smacking kisses on his tiny nose and plump cheeks and carried him into the kitchen. Nadya was sitting at the table now, too, sulking sleepily that there would be no outing in the country.

Katya sat down next to her, Sasha on her lap.

The baby started wiggling again, then slid off his mother's lap. Carefully holding onto the table, he wobbled over to his sister's chair and smiled up at her expectantly.

"Go away, Sasha," she grumbled, her pouting face framed by unruly red curls. "I don't feel like playing."

Undeterred, he tried to climb into her lap.

"Go away!"

Sasha dropped to all fours, and crawled under the table after Koshka.

The cat, however, was not in a playful mood, either. She quietly hid under Evgenia's chair.

Sasha sat under the table for awhile, looking around at everyone's feet, then scooted over and started tickling Nadya's toes.

"Stop it!" Nadya got up and went to the other side of the table.

Gurgling gleefully, Sasha scrambled after her and resumed his tickling.

"Stop it! I mean it, Sasha! Mother, make him stop!"

Sighing, Katya fetched the wooden sled from under Lisya's bed, and put it next to the table.

Sasha crawled out to have a look, and sat down to contemplate the strange new object. Suddenly his face brightened. Pulling himself up to the table, he grabbed the wooden spoon on top, then plopped back down next to the sled. Energetically he began beating on it, thoroughly delighted with his new toy.

"Sasha! It's not a drum!" Nadya finally exclaimed irritably. "Oh, all right. Here, I'll show you what it's for."

Putting him on the sled, she pulled him around the table. Sasha was even more delighted.

Finally, he rolled off and tried to push Nadya onto the sled.

"Sasha, I'm too big for this sled," she explained amiably, finally awake. "And you're too little to pull me. But I have a better idea."

Dragging Koshka out from under Evgenia's chair, Nadya put the cat on the sled and started pulling it around the table.

Sasha laughed uproariously and wanted to give the cat a ride, too. When he tried, Koshka immediately jumped off.

Sasha burst into tears.

"Don't cry, Sasha," said Nadya, putting her arm around him. "I have an even better idea."

Nadya retrieved Koshka, this time from under Lisya's chair, and stood the cat on her hind paws on the sled. Sasha beamed, his tears instantly forgotten. He crawled back to the sled and started pulling it, squealing ecstatically. Nadya hopped behind, crouching over and holding Koshka upright, laughing almost as hard as Sasha.

Koshka looked beseechingly at Lisya, who finally rescued the cat when the sled hit one of the legs of her piano.

"All right, children, that's enough. I think Koshka's tired," she said firmly. "Let's save the sled for winter."

Koshka scuttled gratefully under Lisya's chair.

As the children were calming down, the radio announcer interrupted the music which had been playing all morning.

"Comrade Molotov," he said solemnly, "has an important message for the Soviet people."

Katya looked at the clock; it was exactly noon.

"Men and women, citizens of the Soviet Union, the Soviet Government and Comrade Stalin have instructed me to make the following announcement: At 4 AM, without declaration of war, German troops attacked our country in many places and bombed Zhitomir, Kiev, Sevastopol, Kaunas and other cities. This attack has been made despite the non-aggression pact between the Soviet Union and Germany, a pact whose terms we have scrupulously observed."

Molotov spoke flatly in his usual unemotional way. Only an occasional tremor revealed his apprehension at what was commencing.

"The government calls upon you, men and women of the Soviet Union, to rally around the glorious Bolshevik Party, around the Soviet Government and our great leader, Comrade Stalin. Our cause is just. The enemy will be crushed. Victory will be ours."

Katya turned off the radio. There was a loud silence.

Evgenia put her knitting basket under her chair and crossed herself slowly, compassionate sadness in the wise old eyes that had already seen too much suffering.

Lisya stared angrily off into nowhere, remembering the past, which seemed to be repeating itself.

Nadya picked up Koshka, and buried her face in the cat's soft black fur.

Sasha was perplexed that he was, for once, not the center of attention. Crawling over to the piano, he hoisted himself up to a standing position next to the piano stool.

"Mama!" he called, as he let go of the stool and lurched unsteadily across the great void between it and the table. Pausing occasionally to wobble, he marched proudly into his mother's arms.

"Oh, Sasha!" Katya held him as tightly as she could.

Ж Ж Ж

After Sasha fell asleep, the women got busy.

While Katya took stock of the family resources, Evgenia and Nadya went shopping for food. Several hours later they returned with two huge sacks filled with everything from flour to caviar.

"We bought whatever was left," shrugged Evgenia, in response to Katya's questioning gaze.

While they were unloading the food, Lisya returned from her errands. She was dressed in her woman-of-the-world suit – complete with dashing chapeau – which she always wore when transacting serious business. She had gone to the bank, withdrawing everything from the joint savings account she had with Evgenia, and then bought as much vodka and as many cigarette packs as she could carry.

Nadya stared at all the cartons and bottles on the table. Only her father smoked, and vodka was for special occasions.

"In times of war," said Lisya matter-of-factly, "this will buy more than rubles."

After everything had been discreetly put away, Evgenia opened the trunk in the corner near her bed. Lifting out a small bundle, she closed the lid. Wrapped in the russet and gold wool shawl was the *Virgin of Vladimir*. Reverently, Evgenia kissed the icon and leaned it against the wall on top of her trunk. On one side she put a candle, on the other a few fresh flowers. Tying the shawl around her head, she lit the candle, and knelt before her improvised altar. Crossing herself, she began to pray, eyes closed and lips moving soundlessly.

For awhile, the others sat in silence. Then Lisya put Nadya to bed.

From their room soon came the dark rich tones of her violin, playing a sad sobbing song Katya hadn't heard since her own childhood. Evgenia began to rock back and forth with the music, her prayer seeming to merge with the song.

Katya sat listening, absorbed in its tragic beauty. Finally, she took Sasha into their room, and gently lay the drowsing baby in his little bed. Softly she began to sing in her deep full voice. Long after he was asleep, the music echoed sorrow-fully through the night.

Ж   Ж   Ж

Katya was still asleep in the rocking chair next to Sasha's bed when Alexei came home. She opened her eyes and saw her husband hurriedly packing a small duffle bag.

"Where are you going?" she asked, in alarm.

"To the Front," he replied, trying to sound calm.

"But why? You're not in the army."

"They need correspondents," said Alexei, pulling his bag shut tightly. "I volunteered. I'm flying to Riga tonight, and from there will try to get as close to Kaunas as I can."

"That might be a problem?"

"It will if even half the rumors are true. I've been at Smolny with Vassily. There's talk that Kaunas is being abandoned without even a battle!"

"Alexei, that's impossible!"

"That's what I thought. But it seems the Red Army is retreating on all fronts. Whole divisions have apparently been lost. Individual units are resisting, but rifles and hand grenades are no match for German tanks and planes."

"What about our planes?"

"Still on the ground – what's left of them. Most never even got the tarpaulins off before they were blown to bits. They say the Air Commander of the Baltic District has already been ordered to Moscow to be shot – if someone can find a bullet. Seems we're running out of ammunition again." Alexei sat down abruptly on the bed and buried his face in his hands. "This isn't supposed to be happening. It can't happen. Not again... It can't!"

Katya got out of her chair, sat down beside him, and put her arm around his shoulders.

"Vassily says back then... when we were still in the other apartment... when father was still with us, and others, too... Back then, half our officers were... eliminated... and maybe the new ones don't know much about fighting a war... not much training..."

Once again, the darkness came between them. Katya said nothing, but Alexei felt her arm stiffen. Realizing that he had trespassed onto a forbidden memory, he was suddenly silent.

Finally, he began to mumble quietly into his hands. "At Smolny tonight...

404

it's so strange… it's like all this might not really be war… but of course it is… we all know that… but all those troops retreating… and no one telling them what to do…"

He stood up and faced her. He suddenly looked years older than he had in the morning, and there was something in his eyes she had never seen before.

"That's why I have to go," he said resolutely. "I *have* to know what's going on. I have to know if *someone* is in charge."

He picked up his bag and kissed her quickly. Stopping by Sasha's bed, he tenderly patted the sleeping child's cheek.

"Happy Birthday," he said sadly, and was gone.

Chapter 21: MOBILIZATION

The phone rang early again the next morning. This time it was Orbeli from the Hermitage. "Come to the museum now," he said urgently. "We have work to do."

Katya dressed hurriedly, and grabbed half a loaf of bread on her way out the door. Seeing a tramcar approaching, she ran for the stop at the corner, and climbed on just as it was pulling away.

She jumped off near the service entrance to the Hermitage. Nodding to the security guard, she walked quickly to Orbeli's office. Most of her colleagues were already there, still out of breath.

The meeting was brief and to-the-point. "German bombers have already attacked a dozen cities. At any moment they might appear over Leningrad. We must begin evacuation procedures at once." Orbeli spoke rapidly but calmly. "All the paintings of Leonardo da Vinci, Raphael, Rembrandt and Rubens have already been taken from the walls. We will begin packing them now. We will continue with the rest of the collection until all our treasures are safe."

He then gave detailed instructions to each department. Orbeli was ready; he had started preparing for this moment two years ago.

The next nine days passed in a blur of frantic activity. Like everyone else at the Hermitage, from Orbeli on down, Katya virtually lived at the museum. Speckled with cotton wisps from packing stuffs, they all lifted and carried and packed an unending parade of masterpieces by Titian, Van Dyck, Velasquez, El Greco into strong wooden packing crates. They cradled the massive canvases in tons of wood shavings and cotton wadding, and then carefully stacked the enormous boxes in the great Hermitage Hall of Twenty Columns.

No one slept for days, but Katya did not complain. The Hermitage was worth it. And now there was no time to worry about Alexei. She threw herself into the monumental task with grateful relief.

Somehow they got it done in time for the first train, which was to transport the Hermitage collection beyond the Urals, deep into the Interior. All through that white night, an endless column of trucks drove up beside the museum, each driven by a soldier who helped load the heavy crates. When Katya's assigned truck was as full as it could bear, she hopped in the cab next to the driver. Motors echoing in the deserted streets, the continuous cavalcade drove watchfully down the Nevsky Prospekt to the October railroad freight station.

After hours more of straining and loading, the train was finally ready. Slowly, it moved carefully out of the station. First, a pilot locomotive chugged ahead to clear the tracks. Then came the long train itself: two powerful locomotives, an armored car for the most valued objects, four Pullmans for other special treasures, a flatcar with an anti-aircraft battery, twenty-two freight cars filled with canvases and statues, two passenger cars – one for museum workers and another for the military guard – and finally, at the end, another flatcar with another anti-aircraft battery.

Katya stood at the end of the platform, watching the train leave. As it slowly disappeared down the track, the muted music of its muffled treasure faded. She looked at Orbeli, standing near a lamp post. He was holding his hat over his heart, tears running down his cheeks.

They waited until the last car was out of sight. Finally Orbeli turned and ordered his exhausted staff home for a few hours of sleep. "But be back early tomorrow. We still have two more trains to load."

Ж   Ж   Ж

Katya slept the dreamless sleep of utter exhaustion. She awoke, partially refreshed, to the sight of Alexei sitting dispiritedly in the chair beside Sasha's bed. His face was grey with fatigue.

She sat up slowly, stretching the sleep out of her aching limbs, then walked over to the chair and knelt at his side.

"Alexei?" Alarmed, Katya took his hand. "Alexei, what is it?"

Finally he looked at her, eyes filled with disillusion. "It's even worse than I feared," he said slowly.

The darkness in his eyes frightened her. She put her arms around him, trying to dispel it.

"I talked to some survivors of the Taurage border guards." Alexei spoke with quiet bitterness. Taurage was a town on the Tilsit-Riga Highway, where it crossed the Ura River and the Soviet-German border.

"You'd think such an important border crossing would be fully garrisoned and adequately armed, wouldn't you? But no – there weren't even any regular

408

Red Army units – just some special police troops. Before the attack, they could hear the German tanks across the river, but their orders were to just sit and wait. When the Nazis finally attacked, all they had to fire back with were pistols and machine guns."

"Twelve hours later," he continued with grim sarcasm, "what was left of the border guards got their new orders: Set up roadblocks, halt the spread of panic, and liquidate the Nazi 'intruders.' Intruders!" Alexei stood up angrily and walked to the window.

"But where was the Red Army all this time?" asked Katya, not wanting to believe what he was saying.

"Falling apart," replied Alexei tersely. "An officer from the 125th Division told me they had no tanks, hardly any anti-aircraft guns, and were almost out of hand grenades. What else, they retreated – and not in good order. And his unit wasn't the only one. Some never even made it to the rear."

"But Alexei, I don't understand –"

"At the time of the German attack, most of our troops were dispersed all over the Baltic area. Out of the whole Eleventh Army, only a handful of divisions were anywhere near the border, and most of them had only one regiment in line. The rest were in barracks 25 miles away, with half their officers on leave!"

"But how –?"

"Because Comrade Stalin specifically refused all requests by the Commanding General to concentrate his forces on the border – despite extensive intelligence about German troops massing at the border." Alexei ran his fingers through his disheveled hair. "All those new fortifications on the Baltic perimeter? Only about half were ever completed, and even many of those just had a few 'show' guns to satisfy inspectors from Moscow. The new airfields? Not ready either, and several of the old ones were being repaired."

As his anger grew, Alexei began to pace. "Our tanks are old and need repair, our planes are outdated and unserviceable. Our guns have no mechanized transport and haven't the power to match German artillery and tanks. There's a shortage of shells, ammunition and spare parts. No wonder we're retreating!"

Gesturing angrily, Alexei's voice grew louder. So, too, did the dark fear growing inside Katya. She motioned desperately at Sasha's bed, where the baby – a remarkably sound sleeper – was still asleep. Alexei paused, then began speaking more softly.

"Before the attack, some officers – acting on their own initiative – took precautionary steps. And of course brought down Moscow's wrath. Special investigating committees appeared at their headquarters and accused them of exaggerating the war threat and creating 'dangerous tensions.'"

Alexei threw up his arms. "How can soldiers do their job if they're more concerned about protecting themselves from their own government than from the enemy!"

Dark panic overwhelmed Katya as Alexei's voice rose to a shout. Sasha's startled wail suddenly interrupted his tirade. The force of his anger abruptly collapsed as he picked up his son. Sasha's cries echoed the fear inside Katya and she watched, paralyzed, as Alexei tried to soothe the baby. When Sasha finally subsided, Alexei sat down, rocking him in his lap. Sasha soon fell asleep.

Alexei looked at Katya, his shoulders sagging under the weight of what could not be said. *If only we could talk about it*, he thought, desperately wishing that he could somehow get past his anger and her fear. *Maybe if we could understand what happened, it wouldn't hurt so much.*

But soon, Alexei, too, was asleep. Weak with relief that once again the darkness had been held at bay, Katya gently covered father and son with a blanket, and tiptoed out of the room.

Ж   Ж   Ж

The city of Leningrad prepared for war.

The regular army mobilized; thousands more volunteered. Trucks full of troops singing the *Internationale* drove through the streets. Soldiers paraded to patriotic songs down the Nevsky Prospekt. After the parade, their women marched silently to the factories.

All essential industry was ordered onto eleven hour shifts. Within weeks, factories were turning out artillery, mortars, tanks, armored cars, and flame-throwers. Toy factories made grenades, musical instrument shops made anti-tank mines, distilleries made Molotov cocktails.

Air-raid patrols were quickly organized. By nightfall of the first day, thousands had been assigned to posts. Special fire fighting units were stationed in factories, offices, stores and apartment houses. Round the clock watches were posted on the roofs of most buildings; anything burnable was removed from attics. The fire department built concrete reservoirs and installed new water hydrants. Volunteers dug air raid shelters in all the city parks.

Meanwhile, the city was disguised from the expected German bombers. Camouflage nets were strung over headquarters at Smolny. The all too visible golden dome of St. Isaac's Cathedral was dimmed with dark grey paint. Engi-

410

neers put up rigging from which a long grey painted canvas case was dropped over the gleaming spire of the Petropavlovsk fortress. The Admiralty tower was scaled by amateur mountain climbers, who splashed its gilded surface with dirty grey paint. Backdrops from Leningrad's theatres were hung on the outside of office buildings. Brigades of citizens painted trees on apartment buildings, and doors and windows on streets. Set designers at the Maryinsky made decoy guns and tanks out of papier-mache.

Sand-laden trolleys rolled in from the country. Women unloaded them, shoveling the sand into bags made out of old clothes. The whimsical gaiety of the giant patchwork barricades contrasted oddly with the city's increasingly grey purposefulness. Follow up squads eventually removed this bright and easily targeted incongruity with buckets of drab paint.

Lisya attended Air Raid Patrol school, where she learned fire fighting techniques. She took charge of their apartment building, organized its ARP watch, and saw to it that all its inhabitants were equipped with gas masks. By day, she sewed camouflage nets and painted fake tanks. By night she sat on the roof with sand pails, water buckets, shovels and axes.

Like everyone else, Lisya slept little, her energy fueled by grim anger. What had happened before was happening again – this time to her daughter. Despite all the promises, all the hard work, all the sacrifices, they had been invaded. Determinedly, she tried to keep at bay memories of those already lost, tried not to worry about losing still more. Shuddering, she remembered all the turmoil the last war had caused. Must they endure all that again?! Must her grandchildren's world be torn to pieces, too?! No! It must not be. She would fight however she could.

Evgenia, too, watched the past replaying, but she had seen too much of life to be angry. Instead, she sewed endless piles of sandbags, enlisting Nadya and her friends in the project. Collecting old clothes and carrying the finished bags down to the women loading them with sand, the children were too busy to be afraid. And everyday, on her way to get bread, Evgenia walked past the great equestrian statue of Peter the Great; seeing her sandbags in the steadily mounting pile rising round the Bronze Horseman was reassuring.

Then, suddenly, the bronze horses guarding the Anichkov Bridge were gone. Katya told her later that they had been removed during the night, and buried in a place of safety. But the next morning, the last of the horses – still waiting its turn – was standing in the middle of the Nevsky. It was an evil omen – even the

411

horses were running away from the Germans! Evgenia made the sign of the cross as she hurriedly walked by the fleeing horse.

Ж   Ж   Ж

"We ask you to mobilize, from those physically able, 75 citizens. All must be provided with shovels, picks, crowbars, saws, axes. Each must carry five days' food supplies, a cup, spoon and pot, a change of underwear and clothing, and money."

Katya stared at the bulletin board outside her office at the Hermitage. Announcements of art lectures and archaeological finds were what she was used to seeing there. And then, alongside the hastily printed flyers enlisting civilian volunteers, a different kind of notice began to appear. An archaeologist, killed on duty with the Red Army, was the first Hermitage casualty. The day after it was posted, Katya went out to dig fortifications on the Luga Line.

The Luga Line was almost 200 miles long. Thousands of Leningraders – mostly women – were digging its trenches, mine fields, gun emplacements, dugouts and tank traps. 60 miles south of Leningrad, it was the last line of defense before the city itself.

The construction site was teeming with purposeful but disorganized activity. Wondering where to go, Katya finally approached one of the army sappers who appeared to be directing the work.

"I'm here to help dig," she said hesitantly, feeling out of place.

"Well," he said, eyeing her clean clothes and smooth hands, "I guess we can use all the help we can get."

Katya flushed, then put pick and shovel firmly on her shoulder. "Where should I go?"

"Over there," replied the sapper, pointing to one of the nearby trenches. "Good luck."

Squaring her shoulders, Katya walked to the trench and climbed down beside several other women.

They nodded and made room for her, but did not stop digging.

Katya took the unfamiliar tools off her shoulder and energetically threw herself into the unfamiliar task. For what seemed like a very long time, she jabbed ineffectually at the unyielding earth. Eventually, stopping in frustration, she watched what the other women were doing and tried to copy their movements.

"Here," the woman next to her finally said, "Hold them like this."

412

It was impossible to guess how old the woman was, but her eyes reminded Katya of Evgenia's.

After a few hours, Katya had improved her digging to the point where she was beginning to feel useful. The July sun was blazing in the sky, and she began to sweat. Gusts of wind blew whorls of dirt back into her face and all over her dripping body. Dust mingled with perspiration, producing a grimy coat which clung tenaciously; salty gritty beads rolled into her eyes.

"This will keep the sweat out of your eyes," said the women, pointing to the kerchief on her own head.

Katya stopped digging, looked up at her, then nodded. Taking the kerchief from around her own neck, she pulled it tightly around her head , tucked all her hair in, and fastened the scarf at the nape of her neck.

The woman nodded, then resumed digging.

So did Katya. And as the sun began its slow descent, the clinking of tools and movements of her body, in counterpoint to those of the other women, eventually fell into a rhythm which was somehow soothing. She could feel the woman next to her moving in harmony. And despite her now aching muscles, Katya felt calmer than she had since that terrible day when war had been declared.

And so her first day on the Luga Line passed. Hours after she thought she could dig no more, the women around her suddenly stopped working, climbed out of the trench, and headed for a haystack in the nearby field. Katya went with them and sank to the ground, too weary to even care how dirty she was. She fell instantly asleep.

She awoke a few hours later, looking up into the strong, weathered face of the woman with eyes like Evgenia's.

"Here," she said, offering a rusty cup.

Katya sat up slowly, gratefully accepting the tea. As she rummaged in her knapsack for bread to eat with it, she noticed that her hands were covered with blisters. Standing up, every muscle in her body screamed with pain.

That morning was unending torture. Her sore hands frequently lost their grip on the shovel, dumping heavy loads of dirt on her feet. By noon, her feet were bruised and her hands bleeding.

"This will help," said the woman, as they sat by the trench eating a hurried lunch. And she helped Katya tear her underskirt into strips and bind up her hands with them.

The afternoon passed more quickly. Katya's aching body grew numb and her mind dissolved into the repetition of the unending toil. After a lean supper, she sat quietly, listening idly to the half-hearted banter of her weary digging comrades.

"Where are the digging machines?" she asked, during a lull in the limping conversation.

"I saw a few steam shovels and cranes near Kingisepp," shrugged a young woman. "On loan, I heard, from the Leningrad Subway construction crew."

"But where are *our* digging machines?" persisted Katya.

The other women just laughed and pointed to themselves. Then they all collapsed into sleep.

The next day the attacks started. As German planes flew low over the trenches, bombing and strafing, Katya stood upright, blinking uncomprehendingly at the planes overhead.

"Watch out!" shouted the woman, pulling her down and crouching next to her. "Put your shovel over your head – like this."

Terrified, Katya did as she was told.

All that day, she almost vomited with fear – the whine of bombs, the thud of explosions, the screams of the wounded, all invaded her gut and churned terrifyingly inside.

But still she kept digging. One day she dodged too slowly, and a ricocheting bullet ripped her forehead as it sped by. Blood spilling down her cheek, she felt a cold clammy moment of panic – and then nothing at all.

When she came to, the woman with Evgenia's eyes was wiping the blood off her face. She ripped off the hem of Katya's dress and bound up her wound. Then she went back to work. Katya soon did, too. And the rhythmic chant of the digging went on, punctuated by the savage burst of shells and the intermittent drone of German planes.

And then, one day, as they were digging, digging, digging, a whole squadron of German planes flew over. One of the planes came straight at their trench and let fly a burst of shells. Katya dived down and, a few seconds later, felt someone fall on top of her. Terrified, she remained motionless.

When she tried to get up, she noticed that whoever was lying on her felt strangely inert. Slowly she extricated herself. Blood was oozing quietly from a dozen holes in the body which had shielded her own. Reluctantly she reached out and gently turned it over. The woman – and Evgenia's eyes – stared lifelessly up at her.

They buried her in a nearby field, under one of the few trees left standing.

They dug her grave to the same silent chant with which they had labored together on the Luga Line.

I didn't even know her name, thought Katya numbly, as she shoveled dirt hastily over the body. Reaching deep into her childhood, she put down her shovel and crossed herself slowly.

"*Gospodi pomilui*," she said quietly, "Lord, have mercy."

Ж   Ж   Ж

Body aching and bruised, hands raw and bleeding, Katya stumbled along with the disorderly throng retreating toward Leningrad. Soldiers were falling back from the Front, lashed by the force of the Nazi blitzkrieg. Refugees clogged the highway, carting hurriedly assembled possessions and driving frightened bleating livestock. Dozens of mongrel dogs ran alongside the mob, howling and barking. Katya was so weary she barely noticed that her clothes were in rags and that she herself was filthy beyond recognition.

She had eaten the last of her food on the Luga Line. As she plodded hungrily toward Leningrad, her head wound throbbed. German planes strafed the retreating column, periodically forcing her to dive into the ditch along the road. Utterly fatigued, she tried not to give in to her tired body. All day and all night, she dragged herself slowly on, resolutely shutting out the memory of the hasty funeral beside the Luga Line.

Finally reaching the city, she slowly made her way home. As she stumbled into the kitchen, there was Evgenia, still reassuringly alive. Katya felt strong arms wrap firmly around her, and she began to tremble violently. Great gut-wrenching sobs welled up, as she grieved for the nameless woman at the Luga Line – and her own future.

Ж   Ж   Ж

Alexei crumpled up the paper he had been laboring on for the past hour; only with difficulty did he restrain himself from throwing it at the wall.

Ever since his return from the Baltic Front, he had been in turmoil. Glancing at the other writers whose desks crowded the office at *Leningradskaya Pravda*, he wondered if any of them were having so much trouble writing the patriotic columns which now exclusively filled the paper.

Alexei rubbed his eyes and stared out the window.

The problem was not patriotism. No, that he could do – even if it meant withholding certain unpleasant truths, or even doing a whitewash job in the interests of public morale. Though he had always tried to stay faithful to his conscience, sometimes compromise seemed unavoidable. On such occasions, he had usually been able to justify it as forwarding the cause in which he truly believed.

Sometimes, though... Guilt swept suddenly through him, its heaviness weighing painfully. Desperately, he tried to push away the ugly darkness that jeered up at him from his idle pen.

But even then – during those terrible days when his family had been so deeply and irrevocably wounded – even then he had believed that *THEY* – The Party, The Kremlin, Comrade Stalin – knew what they were doing, that it was somehow necessary for the defense of the nation, that those in charge really *were* in charge. But now...

Sighing, Alexei smoothed out the crumpled paper and picked up his pen. Angry doodles darted out as he remembered the morning after his return from the Front. He had started writing an article about what he had found – and immediately ran into a wall. The officers he had talked to had done so off the record. If he reported what they had told him... well, who knew what might happen. Reluctantly he decided to write only about what he himself had witnessed.

The dilemma grew as reports of still worse disasters rolled in. The Navy, too, was retreating – first from Libau to Riga, then to Tallinn, and finally back to Kronstadt, naval bastion of Leningrad. Survivors told hair-raising tales of their harrowing two hundred mile odyssey through heavily mined waters and German occupied coasts. The Baltic Fleet had limped back to Kronstadt with heavy losses and shocking casualties.

At *Lengradskaya Pravda*, he had run into another wall. "We can't print this," said his editor. "If people know how bad things are, the city will panic." and with that Alexei could not disagree, especially with his own unresolved disillusionment whirring noisily inside.

Alexei looked at the paper in front of him. The angry doodles sprawled all over the page. Resolutely he turned it over and began writing in small, tightly spaced letters.

It was a terrible piece, he knew, soft-pedaling the disaster, exaggerating what few bright spots of hope could be found. As he read it over, he thought of all the ugly rumors sweeping the city. In the absence of reliable information, what else could one expect? Maybe public morale might be less undermined by the truth, after all.

Alexei's sigh turned into a quiet grunt of disgust as he crumpled up the paper again and threw it into the wastebasket. Then he stood up and tried not to stomp out of the office. Walking home in a dark mood, he brooded over the fact that he was the only member of his family not doing anything useful for the war effort.

He opened the door of the apartment house and bounded up the stairs, two at a time. Surely Katya would be home today. Only for five days, that was what she had assured him when she had left for the Luga Line. She was already two days overdue. If only he had tried harder to talk her out of going!

Eagerly he burst in the door. And there, sitting quietly at the kitchen table, Evgenia gently sponging an ugly gash on her forehead, was Katya. He barely recognized her.

Relief was soon followed by anger. After being assured that Katya's wound was not as bad as it looked, Alexei retreated to their bedroom. That his beautiful wife should be so bruised and battered while he sat at a desk writing stupid lies! How ashamed he was!

And how confused and guilty he felt about what had happened back then, when his father died. He knew that somehow Sergei had betrayed Vladimir. But as to how and what had occurred – about that he dared not think. He also knew that what had happened to Vladimir – and Sergei – had happened to many other families. But no one, of course, dared speak of it.

If only he could tell Katya about the doubts lurking in the corners of his mind. If only somehow he could say he was sorry – for exactly what, he was not sure. If only he could tear down the barrier between them, and go back to the days when they had told each other everything! But somehow, whenever he tried, his anger overwhelmed him.

And Katya, he thought, would probably not understand his disillusionment. Working amid the beauty of the Hermitage surely insulated her from such things. She understood even less about what had happened than he did. So who could she blame, if not Sergei? But that Vladimir had perished because of her *husband's* father – that was a connection neither he nor Katya dared make. And so they dodged the painful memories which rose between them, hoping that somehow they could find each other in between.

Somehow he had to make sense of all this. Somehow he had to fix things. Somehow he had to make it right. And not just for himself and Katya.

The next morning, Alexei joined the People's Volunteers.

The People's Volunteer Corps was a civilian army helping the Red Army defend fortifications. Because Alexei was a Party member, he was enrolled in a short training course hastily set up for officers. His unit was quartered in the

417

Pavlovsky Barracks, once home to the Tsar's Life Guards, where they slept on iron cots lining its corridors; they drilled on the Champ de Mars, ancient parade ground of the Tsar's troops.

At the end of the month, the Volunteer officers were assembled. Tomorrow, it was announced, they would go to the Front. Tonight they should go home to their families. One of the leaders made a short speech.

"Comrades," he said, "many of us here are fathers. Each of us must face the future. Our sons and daughters will someday ask, 'What did you do to beat the enemy?' What our answer shall be soon will be clear."

Ж   Ж   Ж

Triumphantly Evgenia set the *paskha* in the center of the kitchen table. Food rationing had started at the beginning of July, but she had somehow managed to scrounge enough ingredients for the traditional dish.

It was Nadya's birthday – and the first time since Midsummer's Eve that the family had properly shared a meal together. Next to the decorated pyramid of cheesecake, Evgenia placed a tall mushroom-shaped loaf of bread. The family aaahhh-ed appreciatively as she lifted the frosted crown off the *kulich*, horizontally sliced off a piece for everyone, and then carefully replaced its cover of round golden crust.

"But Babushka," piped up Nadya, "why are we having *paskha* in the middle of summer?"

"Because," replied Evgenia slowly, "we are celebrating Easter early this year."

Lisya looked at Evgenia, wondering. "*Paskha* is too good to eat only once a year," she added quickly. "Isn't your birthday as good a reason to celebrate as the coming of Spring?" She gave Nadya an affectionate squeeze and a quick kiss on top of her head.

After dinner, Alexei recited some of his latest poems – the ones he had planned to read at Sasha's birthday party. Sasha, meanwhile, was happily squeezing *paskha* through his fingers, giggling delightedly at the squiggles that plopped on his plate. Koshka waited under his chair for the globs that missed.

When Alexei had finished, Lisya played patriotic music the whole family joined in singing. Sasha waved his mangled piece of *kulich* in time to the music. Then a toast to victory. Then another to the Motherland.

After the children had been put to bed, Alexei and the three women sat around the table munching the remains of the *kulich*. Lisya asked about the Hermitage, and Katya described the progress made in evacuating the rest of its collection. By extraordinary effort, a second train had been dispatched three weeks after the first.

"Orbeli thinks one more will do it," she said. "We still have wood for crates, but no more packing materials. Many of the pieces left are so old and fragile – I'm not sure how we'll manage."

"At the Library yesterday," said Evgenia, "I heard they sent the Pushkin collection to a safer place." Once a week, without fail, Evgenia went to the Leningrad Public Library. "They've closed the main reading room, but the smaller one on the first floor is still open. God be praised for that."

"The Philharmonic has been evacuated, too," added Lisya. "And so have the Opera and Ballet, and the Conservatory, and many of the theatre companies."

"And most of the animals at the Zoo were sent out last week," said Alexei.

There was a long silence.

Finally, Alexei cleared his throat. "Katya, I think you and the children should leave, too. Vassily said you could all go with the Kirov workers being sent East next week. Or maybe you could ask Orbeli to send you with the next Hermitage train."

"Will you go with us, Alexei?" asked Katya.

"No. I can't. Not now." Then he added softly. "We've been ordered to the Front. Tomorrow."

More silence.

"I can't leave until the evacuation of the Hermitage is finished," Katya finally said, struggling to keep her voice steady. "With so many in the Army and doing defense work, Orbeli is short-handed as it is." Then she added with a rush, "And I won't go anywhere without you!"

Silence, again.

Alexei looked appealingly at Lisya. She met his eyes, and shook her head. "I will not leave my city. No. Never again. And it would be shameful for someone my age to hide in the rear while my children were fighting and risking their lives. No," she shook her head again, "my place is here."

Finally they all looked at Evgenia.

Evgenia stared at her hands a long time, and then said slowly, "I will go wherever my family is." She paused and stared at her hands again. "'When the invaders come, hide in the forest.' That's what *my* babushka used to say. But I don't think that will help – not now, not anymore."

Then Evgenia stood up. With great dignity, she crossed herself and solemnly blessed her family.

"*Gospodi pomilui*," she said fervently. "Lord, have mercy."

Even Alexei bowed his head.

Ж   Ж   Ж

Katya and Alexei lay side by side, bodies comfortably fitting together, quietly savoring the warmth of the bond between them.

"How wonderful it is to be with you like this," murmured Alexei, gently squeezing her hand. "It's as if we've been together always."

"We have – almost," smiled Katya, leaning closer. "I can't imagine my life without you."

"Remember the time we put a mouse in your mother's bed?"

"She was so angry!" giggled Katya. "And tried so hard to pretend that she wasn't."

"'Get that disgusting creature out of her!'" mimicked Alexei. "She didn't usually yell that loud."

"When I saw how upset she was, I ran next door and borrowed the neighbors' cat."

Alexei and Katya both laughed, remembering.

"And remember how hard you tried to teach me to sing?" Alexei chuckled.

"You were impossible!" Katya shook her head. "I never could understand why you couldn't do something so easy."

"But at least I knew I sounded awful," grinned Alexei. "My father didn't realize he was tone deaf, and your Uncle Vladimir used to get just as impatient with him…

Alexei and Katya were abruptly silent, trying not to remember.

"Remember when we discovered we were best friends?" said Katya, after awhile.

"When Dmitri – disappeared." Alexei nodded.

"Mother wouldn't – couldn't – talk about it. And I needed to – desperately. If you hadn't been there, I don't know what I would have done!"

"I missed him, too." Alexei pressed her hand sympathetically. "More than anyone, he encouraged me as a writer."

"I felt like I was losing my father all over again…"

Katya and Alexei were once again silent, trying not to remember.

"What if we'd met after we'd already grown up?" Alexei finally broke the silence. "Would we still love each other so much?"

"Probably," replied Katya, "but we wouldn't know each other so well."

"I'm glad I knew you as a little girl. It makes it easier to understand the woman you are now."

"Sometimes I don't think I'll ever understand *you*," sighed Katya. "It was easier when you were a boy."

"Katya, I don't want to leave you!"

"Yes, I know."

"But I have to do this!"

"Yes, I know."

"Forgive me…"

"Shhhh…" whispered Katya, kissing him gently.

At that moment, looking into each other's eyes, they saw only love and trust. There was no room for fear.

Ж   Ж   Ж

It had been weeks since Alexei had gone to the Front. Nervously, Katya waited and watched. And then, one night, he limped wearily into the kitchen.

"The Luga Line has fallen," he announced hoarsely. Then he went into the bedroom and fell immediately asleep.

When he finally awoke, Katya was sitting on the edge of the bed, looking at him with quiet anxiety. He sat up slowly, and sipped the tea she offered.

"We were outnumbered and outgunned, Katya. Terribly, horribly outgunned. We yelled 'Hurrah!' and attacked. The Germans started to run. Then their planes and tanks hit us. We had nothing to hit back with." He shrugged wearily.

"When we marched off to the Front," he went on, his voice grim, "we had only hand grenades and Molotov cocktails. There weren't even enough rifles to go around. A lot of men carried nothing but picks and shovels and axes and hunting knives. Some had guns they'd used back in 1918 against the White Army… And some went to fight with only their bare hands." Alexei's shoulders slumped with fatigue; even the tight whorls of his hair drooped in lank coils around his haggard face.

"Ah, Katya," he continued, with an ironic smile, "you should have seen us. A motley-clad troop of untrained boys and middle-aged men, shovels on our shoulders, marching out to meet the invincible German Wehrmacht! None of us knew what to do, but still we marched off behind an out-of-tune band, waving homemade red banners."

The boyish tilt of Alexei's arrow straight nose protruded incongruously from his unshaven face. "They took us to the Luga Line in boxcars... Utter confusion! German planes attacking, peasant villages burning, roads jammed with refugees – women with babies and old men with canes, bellowing cattle and wildly fluttering chickens... Somehow we groped through all that smoke and chaos to the trenches."

He paused and drank some more tea. "In battle we were ludicrous. Those lucky enough to have guns were firing wildly – standing up like on a rifle range. Some were so terrified they forgot to fire at all. The casualties were horrendous... Whole units wiped out... and the screams! We couldn't even find some of our men... what was left of them."

Alexei walked to the window and stood for awhile looking out. "I was terrified, too, Katya. Especially when they started in with the heavy artillery. It was like a volcano erupting." He shuddered. "I wanted to throw away my rifle and run."

"But I didn't," he continued, wonderingly. "And neither did my comrades. Katya, half the people out there defending the Luga Line were People's Volunteers like us. And in spite of everything, we held the Line for over a month. With our picks and shovels, we slowed them down – and even stopped them for awhile. We stood up to Hitler's finest Panzer Divisions!"

Alexei turned and faced Katya. His new beard, she noticed, was darker than his hair – and already starting to coil. "Hitler thought he would be celebrating victory in the Winter Palace by now – but we spoiled his plans. *WE* did. Not the Kremlin, not Comrade Stalin. No. It was us, the People of Leningrad." A note of pride rang in his voice as he continued with growing conviction.

"Hitler understands nothing about our people. He thinks we will give up like the French, or be ground up like the Poles. But he is wrong. We will outlast – and bury – him. We always do. Katya, Katya – it was a mess out there, but so much courage, so much heart, so much strength of will! If untrained volunteers can fight like that with empty hands and no one to command, think what our armies will do when Headquarters gets organized and gives us weapons!"

"How close are the Germans now?" asked Katya, relieved to see a spark of her husband's old fire.

"They'll soon be at the city gates. We must prepare to fight them there, and on every streetcorner – if it comes to that. Every step we take back must cost them so much that eventually they will have to retreat."

"Like Napoleon?"

"Like Napoleon," repeated Alexei firmly.

Then he kissed her – as he had in the days of their youthful idealism.

Ж   Ж   Ж

The next day Alexei went to Smolny. An emergency meeting of the Leningrad Communist Party had been called by its Boss, Andrei Zhdanov.

Zhdanov gave a rousing speech. "The enemy wants to destroy our homes, wash our streets in blood, enslave the free sons of the Motherland. It shall not be!"

The entire Party rose and swore a solemn oath to die before yielding the city of Lenin. Then they sang the *Internationale.*

All Party members were put on 24-hour duty. Plans were drafted for the defense of the city, block by block, house by house. Workers' battalions of women, teenagers, and men too old for the army were organized to defend each sector, each one armed with rifles, shotguns, pistols, Molotov cocktails, daggers, sabers, pikes – whatever was available. In every neighborhood, street barricades and anti-tank traps were set up. In every park and open square, machine gun posts were built to mow down German parachutists; heavy stakes were stuck into the ground to impale German planes attempting to land. Fire fighting and first aid units of the Air Raid Patrol were brought to full strength, and more air-raid shelters were constructed.

Party leaders also met with the staff of *Leningradskaya Pravda.* It was time, they said, to stop the rumors. Zhdanov wanted all prepared for what was coming. The people needed to know what was happening. With enormous relief, Alexei began doing the articles he had been trying to write since his return from the Baltic Front. His pen soon sprouted wings.

At the next Party meeting, members showed up at Smolny red eyed and gaunt, all carrying side arms. Zhdanov, pistols in holster and pointer in hand, showed them on a large map exactly where the Germans were breaking through.

"The enemy is at the gates," he said solemnly. "It is a question of life or death. Either we will be destroyed – or we gather all the strength we have, hit back twice as hard, and dig Fascism a grave in front of Leningrad."

It was a short meeting. "No backward step!" ordered Zhdanov. All over Leningrad, gigantic posters appeared on city walls. "The Enemy is at the Gates!"

The sewer department laid out underground supply lines through its conduits. Manholes and sewer openings were equipped for firing at tanks. Hundreds of thousands of schoolchildren, old men, and women of all ages worked day and night building hundreds of miles of anti-tank barriers and digging thousands of miles of trenches. Guns, grenades and Molotov cocktails were stacked on streetcar platforms. Improvised anti-tank guns were mounted on trucks and buses. Old flintlocks and muzzle-loaders were taken down from museum walls; even long-bladed hunting knives were distributed.

As the city desperately prepared for savage guerrilla warfare, Lisya organized her neighborhood's defense. She directed the building of barricades and supervised the digging of anti-tank ditches. She taught the older children how to throw Molotov cocktails, and drilled their mothers on defensive kitchen knife tactics. And as she sharpened her own knives, she recalled the desperate years of the Civil War. This time, she thought grimly, it would not be so hard; killing Germans would be easier than fighting other Russians.

Evgenia, meanwhile, expanded her sandbag operation, and added to it the production of Molotov cocktails. Nadya and her friends collected empty bottles and old socks, cut up for fuses. The young people also trooped about with pails of whitewash, painting over street signs and blanking out house numbers. If the Nazis broke in, they would get lost in the maze of nameless avenues and numberless buildings.

Everyday there were more notices on the Hermitage bulletin boards. "To the trenches!" Katya went – and spent long hours digging. By now, her hands were calloused and she knew how to use her shovel.

The Germans moved inexorably closer. First the surrounding villages went up in flames, then the nearby *dacha*s. Propaganda leaflets began to rain down: "If you think Leningrad can be defended, you are wrong. If you oppose German troops, you will perish in the wreckage of Leningrad under a hurricane of Germans bombs and shells. We will level Leningrad to the earth and destroy Kronstadt to the waterline. Beat the Jews. Beat the Commissars. Wait for the full moon. Bayonets in the earth! Surrender!"

Then the Germans were in the suburbs. What was left of the Baltic Fleet began a ceaseless cannonade. The nose was deafening. It bothered Katya even more than the endless digging. Long military columns passed constantly by her trenches. Some rode in mud-covered vehicles, some in dusty carts pulled by tired horses. Most walked, slowly and with exhausted steps, their dogged resignation providing grisly counterpoint to the salvos of the battleships.

And so the people of Leningrad transformed their city. Barricades obstructed its broad boulevards. Lawns and flowerbeds were crisscrossed with trenches. Anti-aircraft and anti-tank batteries filled its spacious squares. Its monuments were covered and its colorful buildings muted.

Grey and grim, Peter's city was now a fortress.

Chapter 22: SIEGE

It was an astonishingly beautiful day, with a clear crisp blue sky stretching over-head. As though to compensate for the drabness of the fortified city, the leaves were already turning deep russet and glowing amber.

Katya had left the Hermitage early, and was going home for a rare evening with her family. Between digging trenches and evacuating the rest of the muse-um, she'd hardly seen them for weeks. Tonight, however, was Alexei's birthday, and everyone was taking a few hours off to celebrate.

Under the trees were carpets of mushrooms. An ill omen, Evgenia said. Many mushrooms, many deaths. Katya shuddered, and noticed that rubbish was begin-ning to collect in the gutters. The main avenues had always been washed down just after dawn and swept each night, but there was no time for that now.

Dinner that night was not lavish, but in the martial spirit of the times, Evge-nia had baked some Suvorov biscuits. The family sat quietly around the table for a while, drinking tea and savoring the rare lack of activity. Even Sasha, curled up in his father's lap munching one of the small jam-filled cookies, was still. Nadya leaned against Lisya; Koshka, after licking off the plate under Nadya's chair, jumped onto her lap and began giving herself a bath. Katya, her arm linked with Evgenia's, sat gazing out the window at the waning twilight. When at last it dis-appeared, she rose and carefully drew the black-out curtains.

Katya sang one of Alexei's favorite songs – a poignant love ballad from Ev-genia's village. Nadya recited one of his favorite poems by Pushkin. Then Lisya played sad Gypsy music on her violin until Sasha was snoring quietly in Alexei's lap; even Nadya was too tired to beg Evgenia for a story.

After the children were in bed, Alexei and the women sat around the samo-var – silently struggling with what was never far from their minds. This time, it was Lisya who broached the difficult subject.

"Mother," she said, as she refilled the old woman's tea cup, "I've been think-ing. Perhaps some of us should reconsider leaving." She put a sugar cube on the saucer. "I think you should take the children and go on the next train." She handed her the tea.

"Vassily and his family left yesterday," agreed Alexei. "I think you should, too. I would feel safer with the children out of the city."

Evgenia sipped her tea thoughtfully. "I heard that some of those evacuation trains got caught in a bottleneck just out of town," she said softly. "And people were stuck there for days with all their food eaten up."

"And I heard," said Katya angrily, "that some of the trains were bombed."

Alexei reached out and squeezed her hand.

"Last week on the Nevsky," Katya continued in a tight voice, "they were loading children onto evacuation buses. They all carried bundles and wore little knapsacks. The children were crying and the parents looked so worried... Horrible military music was blaring from loudspeakers... all out of tune... I know how close the Germans are... but I don't think I could bear to say goodbye to Sasha like that." She covered her face with her hands.

Alexei put his arm around her. Lisya patted Evgenia on the shoulder. And once again, their dilemma washed over them.

Finally the phone rang. Alexei went to the hall to answer.

He returned, his face white with shock. "That was *Leningradskaya Pravda*," he said shakily. "The Germans have captured the station at Mga. There will be no more trains out of Leningrad."

The family sat, stunned, their faces a kaleidoscope of despair and relief, fear and anger.

Finally, Lisya stood up and went into her room, then returned bearing one of the hoarded vodka bottles. With a defiant flourish she filled everyone's glass and proposed a furious toast: "To the downfall of that Archviper, Hitler! May he rot in his own carrion for all eternity!"

They all drained their glasses and threw them at the stove.

Ж   Ж   Ж

Early in September, the bombs finally came. Almost every night, the sirens sounded and the planes droned. High explosive bombs rained on the city, smashing buildings into bits of brick and clouds of plaster. The air grew almost too thick to breathe. Even worse were the incendiary bombs, igniting devastating fires all over. Many people died in the yellow dust and black smoke and roaring explosions.

Katya was on Air Raid Patrol, guarding the roof of the Hermitage. Standing watch next to the huge skylight over the main picture gallery, she could see incendiary bombs showering down around the Petropavlovsk Fortress, rolling down its thick walls like rivers of fire. Suddenly there was a thunderous explosion – a thousand flaming serpents hissed around the roller coaster at the nearby amusement park. Katya was busy all night, extinguishing fiery sparks and bits of blazing paint pelting the Hermitage roof.

At dawn she sat, covered with soot, staring gloomily at the charred framework and twisted girders over in the park. She remembered when Alexei had taken Nadya on that roller coaster. The girl had screamed and squealed and clung to her father; he had roared and hurrahed every time they charged down the track. At the end of the ride, father and daughter had jumped happily off the car and walked arm-in-arm toward her, their windblown curls framing faces shining with exhilaration.

That same day they had taken Sasha to the Zoo. He had clapped his chubby little hands for the bears, screeched back at the monkeys, and pointed excitedly at the big koshka's. And he had been absolutely fascinated by Nikha the Elephant. Staring with wonder at her huge ears and clever trunk, he had squealed in protest when his parents finally carried him home.

Katya's smiling memory was suddenly replaced by a flood of angry horror. The Germans had bombed the Zoo two nights ago. Nikha – who had stubbornly refused to be evacuated – had been mortally wounded. The elephant's death throes went on for hours, her terrifying cries joined by howling dogs at the Pavlov Institute.

Lisya, too, spent many nights protecting the rooftops. On one of her few evenings off, she went to the Musical Comedy Theatre with Olga. Between the first and second acts, the sirens sounded. The performance went on, the boisterous chatter of anti-aircraft guns in the background. As they later walked out of the theatre, Lisya noticed a strange reddish light reflected on the square. Turning the corner, she saw a mountain of smoke pouring up toward the sky. Shot through with long tongues of reddish flame, it reached thousands of feet over the city. She hurried home, where she joined Evgenia and the children in the bomb shelter.

The sirens were busy that night, as alarm followed alarm. The sound of planes and anti-aircraft guns was only partly muted in the depths of the shelter. Sasha slept fitfully in Evgenia's arms; Nadya leaned close to Lisya, clutching Koshka tightly. The girl's eyes were large with fear; the cat trembled and tried to burrow deeper into her arms.

When at last the all-clear sounded, Evgenia went up to the roof of their apartment building. A greasy blood-red cloud of smoke was gradually covering the whole city. Across the Neva to the Southeast, she saw a huge tower of flaming smoke blazing apocalyptically. She thought for a moment, trying to locate the source of the fire. A horrible suspicion gripped her, propelling her down the stairs and out into the street. Walking rapidly in the direction of the holocaust, she joined streams of people carting sand and carrying water, all hurrying toward the blaze. With every step her apprehension grew, and when she finally reached the scores of fire trucks battling the gigantic flames, she saw her worst fears in the roaring inferno.

"The Badayev warehouse!" she screamed into the hellishly bright night. "Oh God, no!"

The smell of burning meat filled the air. Choking on the acrid stench of carbonized sugar, Evgenia lined up in a bucket brigade. All night she worked, the heavy scent of burning oil and flour taunting her like a demon. And when at last she gazed at the smoking ruins of Leningrad's main food warehouse, she crossed herself slowly.

"*Gospodi pomilui*," she said softly. "Lord, have mercy."

Ж   Ж   Ж

Alexei was standing on the back of a small truck, hastily outfitted with makeshift armor plating and an old machine gun. Next to him was the chairman of the Izhorsk factory Party committee.

The Izhorsk industrial complex was one of the largest in the whole country. Its steel mills, tank plants and artillery factories were vitally important to the war effort. It was on the edge of the city and directly in the path of the rapidly approaching German Wehrmacht. Alexei had been sent to organize a workers' battalion.

"We don't need anyone drooling in terror," said the Chairman bluntly when the workers had gathered. "Let the real Izhorites take their guns and – forward march! There's no time to waste. If we do not halt them, the Germans will advance to the gates of the city."

Alexei looked at the crowd, many of them elderly workers, trembling with fatigue from long shifts in the factory and even longer hours digging trenches and building barricades.

"Before dawn," said the Chairman, "we'll be on the firing line."

A few hours later, the battalion was lined up in the dark streets outside the factory. Most of them were armed with drill hall rifles; some had grenades and pistols.They still wore their factory overalls.

Out of the factory they marched, past the stadium just outside the city, and on toward Kolpino – where many of them lived. On a tall column behind them, the statue of a heroic factory worker – gun in hand – waved them on.

At dawn, they reached hastily constructed fortifications along the Izhora River. Alexei's unit positioned themselves in the trenches, flanked by a few more of the armor-plated trucks with machine guns. Altogether, there were only a few thousand of them defending the barricades. Beyond this line, the highway led straight to the southeast gates of Leningrad.

The fighting was fierce, but the Germans did not break through. Somehow the vastly out-numbered and out-gunned band of volunteers held the line. But though they stood firm, the Germans were now close enough to bring the factory under point-blank artillery fire. During the constant bombardment, hundreds of workers were killed and wounded. Production continued with difficulty. During lulls in fighting, battalion members divided their time between Plant and Front. By day they made tanks and ammunition, and at night went back to the trenches. Meanwhile, several of the production lines were laboriously disassembled and flown out of Leningrad.

Throughout it all, Alexei exhorted and worked and fought alongside his rag-tag troops like one possessed. Everything he believed in, all that he valued, the meaning of his entire life seemed to be on this line. If they could hold out here, then at least someone, somewhere, was in charge. If he and his valiant little battalion could resist the Germans, then all the sacrifices and compromises would be vindicated. And maybe, somehow, they could all be forgiven.

Not one step backward. Yes. It was time to stop retreating – and not just from the Nazis.

Ж   Ж   Ж

As the autumn equinox approached, tension in the city mounted. The Germans were so close that troops took streetcars to the Front, now only ten miles from Palace Square. Everyone capable of holding a gun was moving toward sectors of the city already under fire.

By night the city was silent. Every window was dark. Leningrad was in hiding, its shape so changed that sometimes people could hardly tell where they were. The shadows were deep, black and menacing. The weather was surly. Off

431

in the distance, burning buildings glowed faintly and mortar blasts broke the silence.

The situation was desperate. What was left of the Red Army was a decimal of its battle strength. To command these exhausted troops, Moscow sent the toughest troubleshooter in the Red Army, Marshal Georgi Zhukov. And from the moment he landed in Leningrad, Zhukov made it absolutely clear that someone was now very definitely in charge.

Heads rolled rapidly, as he shook up headquarters. He threatened commander after commander with the firing squad. And meant it. And he insisted on one thing: Attack! Attack! Attack! It made no difference how weak the unit. It made no difference if they had no weapons or bullets. It made no difference if they had been retreating for weeks. Attack! Those were orders.

Attack or be shot – a simple equation.

And they obeyed. Every commander went to the head of his unit and marched into battle. Officers told their men: "If you retreat, I kill you. If I retreat, you kill me. Leningrad will *not* surrender."

Attack – or die. The people of Leningrad took up the grim slogan. Attack – or die. Death to cowards. Death to panic-mongers. Death to rumor-spreaders. Discipline. Courage. Firmness.

And then a new rumor swept Leningrad: If the enemy breaks into the city, he will die in its ruins. All the buildings will be blown up and everyone will march out to do final combat with the Nazis. There will be no victory parade past the Winter Palace; Hitler will not review his troops in Palace Square. If need be, everyone – and everything – will go down in flames in one last desperate battle.

The People's Volunteers, the workers' battalions, and the remains of the Red Army fought with desperate fierceness which kept the German army – vastly superior in everything but determination – out of Leningrad long after it should reasonably have fallen.

And then, at last, the Germans halted. First, driblets of astonishing intelligence reports, too fraught with possibility and hope to be believed. And then a steady stream which still seemed too good to be true… Motorized infantry moving from Leningrad… Regrouping of troops away from Leningrad… Germans loading tanks on railroad flatcars… Germans building permanent trenches and dugouts… chopping down trees for command posts and heated quarters… Installing stoves… moving in beds, furniture.

News of the Germans digging in flew about Leningrad. Lisya heard it on the streets, where she guarded the barricades. Katya heard it on the roofs, where she liquidated fire bombs. Evgenia heard it in the bomb shelters, where she rallied the spirits of frightened children.

And very early one smoky, foggy morning, Alexei knew it was true. Asleep in a dugout, he was awakened by one of the men in his battalion.

"Comrade," the man said urgently, "come quickly to the command post."

Alexei threw on his greatcoat, groggily aware of the smell of wet leaves in the air. As he climbed out of the dugout and began running, the sun broke fitfully through the clouds. At the command post, he found a crowd gathered around a telescope. Anxiously, he waited his turn at the eyepiece. And finally, there they were: German soldiers, hard at work with shovels and hammers, building dugouts and permanent trenches.

It was true. There could be no doubt. The offensive was over. The Germans were digging in for the winter.

Alexei walked away from the group crowding around the telescope to what was left of a nearby tree. He fell down next to it, and buried his face in the earth.

Later, relieved of his position by a Red Army officer, he rode the tramcar home. Katya was waiting for him at the door. With a sob of relief, she threw her arms around him.

"Katya, Katya…" Murmuring her name over and over, Alexei clung to her, letting her soft warmth ease the cold fatigue of the past months. Leaning wearily against each other, they stood together, too tired to move, tears streaming silently down their exhausted faces.

After everyone else had gone to bed for their first real sleep in weeks, Evgenia sat alone in the kitchen. Finally, she knelt before the icon enshrined on her trunk in the corner. Crossing herself slowly, she implored the Virgin to protect the city. For now, she knew, the *real* struggle was commencing.

Ж   Ж   Ж

Katya shook her head at the thick callouses lining her palms. No more trenches to dig. What a relief! Maybe now her hands could get back to normal. And her life.

For awhile – a very short while – life did seem almost normal. The bombs continued to fall. Factories still worked round-the-clock. But her work at the Hermitage resumed some semblance of what it had been before the invasion.

After the evacuations, there was, of course, much less art to watch over. But with so many at the Front, there were also fewer of them to take care of it. And

433

all the manuscripts and documents for the Russian Art Exhibit were still piled on her desk, waiting to be studied and catalogued.

In the evenings, when she was not on ARP duty, she was with her family again. She cherished these times. They all did.

"Does the Hermitage feel different with so much of the art gone?" asked Lisya, as usual darning the family socks. Alexei was helping Nadya with her homework. Evgenia was knitting.

"In some ways, yes," replied Katya, lightly kissing Sasha, asleep on her lap. "So many of my favorite paintings are gone, and I miss them. But the Hermitage itself is still the Hermitage – only now the empty spaces make it seem bigger."

"So it still feels like home?"

"Oh yes! Nothing could ever change that. It's why I must stay and protect it."

"You are fortunate to have such a place," sighed Lisya.

"You must miss it very much," said Katya tentatively. "The Maryinsky, I mean."

"I spent some of my best times there," Lisya replied quietly.

"I remember how much I liked going to the opera with Papa, and how proud I was that my mother was making the music."

"I had the best seat in the house." Lisya smiled "And I made good use of it."

"I remember the ballets, too – especially when Aunt Tanya danced –" Katya hesitated.

Lisya was silent.

"I am fortunate to have had a place where I belonged," she finally said. "And that it gave me so many wonderful memories."

"Do you ever feel angry?" Katya again hesitated. "About having to leave the Maryinsky, I mean."

"I have never regretted what I did," said Lisya carefully. "I knew there would be consequences, and I chose to do it anyway. So – angry? Not anymore. But sad, yes, that all I have are my memories."

"I don't think I could bear to lose the Hermitage."

"Yes, you could. But I hope you never have to find out."

"I'm not as strong as you think I am."

"You're stronger than *you* think you are," insisted Lisya.

"How can you be so sure?"

"Because you *have* to be." Lisya's eyes clouded for a moment, then brightened. "And because you are your mother's daughter."

"And so are you," added Evgenia, looking at Lisya across the table, her knitting needles click-clicking in comforting rhythm.

Katya smiled, and hugged Sasha closer.

Then one night, Alexei came home with a determined look on his face. He went immediately into their room. Katya followed.

He was packing again. She sat down on the bed and waited. At last, Alexei paused. Slowly he turned and lowered himself onto the edge of the chair by Sasha's bed, where he perched uneasily opposite her. He looked at his hands – hands meant to hold a pen, not a gun – and then finally spoke.

"I joined the Red Army today," he said quietly. "Tomorrow I leave for the Moscow Front."

Katya stared at him with dismay. Against the heavy silence, he raised his eyes to meet her wounded but steady gaze.

"All the German troops withdrawn from around Leningrad are heading for Moscow. Hitler is massing his forces for a knockout blow there. Where else can a loyal Soviet citizen be now, and still call himself a man?!"

Katya lowered her eyes.

"If the Germans take Moscow," Alexei pleaded, "they'll come back here, in even greater force. How could we possibly hold out against such odds!"

Katya looked up at him again, her eyes filled with tears.

Alexei's gaze faltered. He stood up and walked to the window. "When I was fighting with the Izhorsk battalion," he mused softly, "suddenly everything was so clear – like a great shining sword cutting through the darkness…"

"Katya, Katya," he was suddenly kneeling before her, "I don't want to leave you, but I have to! Please understand! I *must* do this. Not just for the Party, but for myself… and for my father… and for *him* – for *all* of them."

Katya looked quickly away. Gently, Alexei turned her chin back to face him. Warily she met his steady gaze, and then sighed sadly. Slowly, she reached out and began stroking his hair. He rested his head in her lap and then, taking her other hand in his, tenderly kissed it.

When the tension had passed, Alexei sat up and reached in his pocket. "I should have given you this at our wedding, but back then such things seemed too bourgeois." In his open palm was a wide gold band, embossed with two hands intertwined.

"It's beautiful!" exclaimed Katya.

"Promise me you'll wear it always," said Alexei, as he put it on her finger. "And I promise I'll come home."

"I'll wait for you, Alexei," said Katya, caressing the clasped hands on the ring. "No matter how long it takes."

Their kiss was long and sweet, full of gentle memories.

Then Alexei began to touch her, lightly caressing the curve of her thigh, the length of her leg, the arch of her foot. Sitting beside her on the bed, he lovingly traced the outline of her arms and shoulders, and let his fingers run down the sweep of her back. Unbraiding her long thick hair, he gently stroked it, then tenderly kissed her.

"My beautiful, wonderful Katya," he murmured softly, "Let me take you with me, let me remember all of you."

Leaning back on the bed, Katya looked up at Alexei. His vivid eyes were smiling, and his thick curls swirled appealingly around his dear familiar face. Gently she ran her finger down his nose and traced the curve of his lips. In the light of the single candle by their bed, he looked remarkably like the boy she had grown up with.

Alexei the man bent down and kissed her, the lingering brush of his lips on hers growing more insistent. Surrounded by fears of tomorrow, Katya clung to him, returning his fervent kisses and wrapping her quivering body around his. The passion between them ignited, burning and blazing and exploding, until a blinding moment of fusion eclipsed all dread of parting.

Ж Ж Ж

Katya huddled in a dark trench, hiding under a giant shovel. A dead body – the woman from the Luga Line – fell next to her. But when she turned the corpse over, it was Alexei's face staring up at her.

Just then the telephone rang. Katya struggled into a half-awake stupor and stumbled to the phone. *Who could be calling me here?* she wondered confusedly. She picked up the receiver with trembling hands.

"Until the end of the war," said a crisp, impersonal voice, "the telephone is being disconnected."

Katya sank to the floor. When she finally picked up the dangling receiver, it was dead.

Till the end of the war. Who knew when that might be?

Evgenia, too, wondered and worried as, each day, she checked her diminishing food hoard. Then food rations were reduced. Except for the Army, everyone received one-third loaf of bread a day. Each month, they were also supposed to get one pound of meat, a pound and a half of cereal, and three-quarters pound of butter. Distribution of the non-bread items usually fell below schedule. To get anything at all, Evgenia often had to stand in line for hours. More than once, not to lose her place, she stayed there even when the air-raid alarm sounded.

As time went on, bread was often the only food issued. And the bread itself became ever more ingeniously – and unappetizingly – contrived. Tons of malt appropriated from closed breweries, along with oats requisitioned from cavalry warehouses, were mixed with the flour. Salvaged grain from barges sunk in Lake Ladoga – all sprouting and moldy – was also added. A formula for edible pine sawdust was worked out by scientists at one of the Institutes; that, too, went into the bread. Even cottonseed cake destined for ships' furnaces ended up there; high temperature treatment supposedly removed the poisons.

Evgenia knew – as did everyone else – that her family could not survive on what eventually amounted to a pound of food a week. Periodically she went to the countryside, trading cigarettes for cabbages. Sometimes she dug up a few potatoes or beets from gardens of burned out *dacha*s. And occasionally she even ventured to the Haymarket to barter vodka for sausages – whose content she carefully avoided wondering about. Even so, everyone was hungry all the time.

Winter came early that year. The first snow fell on October 14th. The thermometer began to drop; within a month, it was 20 below and still falling. Central heating systems, damaged and lacking fuel, ceased to function. Everyone lived in several layers of clothing, by night wrapped in blankets, huddled around small stoves.

Electricity, too, was carefully rationed and – except where absolutely essential – all but disappeared. Then the kerosene was used up. As the days grew shorter and darker, the nights were illumined – if at all – by a few candles. And then, one morning, when Lisya turned on the water in the kitchen sink – there was nothing. The pipes had frozen.

She collapsed on a chair and burst into tears. Finally, her sobs subsiding, she blew her nose. Without a word, she picked up the large bucket under the sink and walked out the door. Much later she returned, the bucket filled with water. She set it on the stove and sat down, breathing hard. She looked at her hands and sighed heavily.

To fuel the stove, Katya chopped firewood with squads of other young women. The work had much in common with digging trenches, and she was grateful for her callouses. En route one day to the chopping site, she saw an old man lying on the sidewalk, face down. Alarmed, she stooped down and gently turned him over.

"Don't bother," he protested feebly.

Katya tried unsuccessfully to help the man to his feet. Then she found a policeman. He was very thin and also looked hungry. He returned with her to the old man. But first aid was no longer necessary. He was dead.

It was not until a few weeks later that the experience penetrated. Once again on her way to chop firewood, Katya was waiting for the tramcar which would take her to the city limits. After a long time in the freezing cold, she noticed an eerie silence echoing in the streets. She began walking slowly along the tracks. After several blocks she turned a corner and, through snow which had begun falling, saw a large immobile object. Hurrying, she approached and made out the shape of a tramcar. It was dark and empty. She stopped for a moment in confusion, then continued along the track until she reached another deserted streetcar. Alarmed, she half ran to the corner where another tram-line intersected. Up and down the long broad boulevard, she saw dotted against the snow the black hulks of silent streetcars.

They're dead, she thought, panic rising within her. And she remembered the old man dying on the street. *He died of hunger*, she remembered, *and so did the tramcars.* She stumbled to the nearest one and, trembling, sat down on its steps. As she gazed dumbly at the big iron corpses scattered along the track, a mounting horror of what awaited the city seized her.

"No," she whispered to herself. "*NO!*" she stood up and screamed. And she began to run, away from the desolate vehicles, away from the dead bodies, faster and faster, until she finally collapsed inside her own door.

It snowed all night. The next day German leaflets rained down on the city: "Lie down in your coffins and prepare for death."

Ж   Ж   Ж

Precisely as scheduled, the meeting started at 2 PM. Long before the war, Orbeli had planned this celebration of the 800th anniversary of Azerbaijan's national poet. Bombs or not, he had insisted that everyone attend. Katya was sitting in the third row of chairs, lined up for the occasion in a big gallery relatively unscathed by bombing. Except for the strange assortment of clothes in which they were all bundled, the ceremony was a welcome page from before the war. It ended all too soon, a few minutes before the customary afternoon air raid alert.

Later, walking home from the Hermitage, Katya passed an artist painting at the Anichkov Bridge. He wore an old fur cloak, felt boots and overshoes wrapped in rags. She stopped and looked long at what he was doing.

"These days, one must paint more and talk less," he said after awhile.

"But how can anyone create beauty," she replied despondently, "in the midst of all this?"

"One must reach deeper into the soul." He painted on in silence.

"Do you like this?" he finally asked her, stepping back from his little painting.

Katya studied it carefully. The bridge, the sky, people walking on the Prospekt – it was a familiar scene, yet somehow terrifyingly different. It reminded her of how eerie the stranded streetcars had seemed that day on the snowy boulevard. The painting sang a terrible song, but was strangely beautiful. Down in the corner, he signed it 'Andrei R'.

"It's all strange – all alarming," he said, turning to look directly at her. "But the sky is still there, as always."

She saw him again, after that. Every week or so, he would quietly appear near the Anichkov Bridge. Always he wore the same old fur cloak. Always he painted very slowly on a painfully small canvas with a carefully measured palette. And always what he painted was infused with a tragic beauty which somehow comforted Katya.

Without realizing it, she began to look for him by the bridge.

Ж   Ж   Ж

"I want to tell you about a young girl in a factory who decided she must celebrate the glorious valor of our Red Army and Peoples' Volunteers," the math teacher said as she presented a problem. "So what do you think she did? No, she didn't go to the movies. She decided to increase her output. The first day she exceeded her norm by 15%, the second day by 20%…"

The students scribbled industriously and then raised their hands enthusiastically. "In one week," Nadya answered approvingly , "the girl exceeded her production norm by 184%."

Suddenly there was a deafening explosion.

Nadya dived under her desk. And waited, hoping the terror in the pit of her stomach wouldn't make her sick – like the boy under the desk next to hers.

And then she heard what sounded like a mountain of ice collapsing.

Nadya pulled up her knees and ducked her head, wrapping her arms protectively around her body. The boy started retching again.

439

When, finally, all was quiet, Nadya opened her eyes and cautiously looked around.

All over the floor were layers of broken glass. Reflected in the light of the shattered windows, the shards glinted like icicles.

The boy had stopped vomiting and was crying quietly. Nadya put her arm around him – to steady herself as much as to calm him – and waited for their teacher to declare all-clear.

But today there was no reassuring voice. Puzzled, Nadya slowly extricated herself from the glass fragments covering her desk and looked toward the blackboard. That, too, had shattered, and slumped beneath it was the inert body of the teacher.

Nadya stifled a cry of alarm, and carefully waded through the slippery glass. By the time she reached what had been the chalkboard, her ankles were cut and bleeding. So was the teacher – from several dagger-like pieces of slate, which had pierced her body. A pile of glass shards covered her legs.

"Is she… ?" asked a classmate, whose hands were bleeding.

"Yes," whispered Nadya, "I think so."

"We should go down to the bomb shelter."

"Yes," agreed Nadya, trying not to look at the teacher. "Over there, in the back – the glass doesn't seem so deep."

As the students slowly filed out, holding hands to keep from slipping on the sharp clinking fragments, Nadya noticed the teacher's coat, hanging from the rack still standing in the midst of the rubble.

The coat was old and threadbare, only a shadow of its former elegance. But the teacher had worn it proudly before the War. Since then, she had carefully hung it on the rack every morning, a symbol of her determination to keep her class going, regardless of the chaos outside.

Remembering, Nadya smiled sadly, then took the coat off its hanger and gently covered the teacher's body. And then slid over the chinking spars to follow her classmates down to the bomb shelter.

At school the following day, classes were held in the air raid shelter. The temperature was below zero and the only light was from a kerosene lamp. When the kerosene ran out, they returned to the classrooms. Teachers and students together cleared away the broken glass, bricked up the smashed walls, and put plywood in most of the windows.

As the temperature dropped, Nadya and her classmates huddled around a little pot-bellied stove, scarves wrapped around hands, faces hidden in coat collars.

Ink froze in the ink pots. The stove often smoked, and occasionally the smell of burning felt warned that someone's boots had gotten too close to it. Finally the fuel ran out; sharp icy drafts started blowing down the pipe.

The next day, several minutes after the bell rang, the principal walked in. "There will be no classes today," he announced "We must all go tear down a house to get more wood." Nadya trooped out into the piercing wind and helped with the demolition.

When the blizzards started, walking to school took longer. Nadya got up earlier to get there on time. But rarely did she miss a day. Neither did her teachers. Periodically, though, one of them would simply go home and never return. No one talked about it, but everyone knew why.

Lisya, too, refused to give in to the bombs and blizzards. After most of the faculty at the Conservatory had been evacuated to Tashkent, she was asked to resume giving piano lessons to the students who remained.

Walking back through a door which had been slammed in her face years ago was not easy. But despite the circumstances, she was glad to return to the place that had nurtured her music. What was left of the faculty tried to act as though she had never been cast out. Not that anyone had forgotten. The war, however, was allowed to get in the way of awkward memories as much as possible.

She also continued to play violin in the Leningrad Radio Orchestra. The group performed for troops at the Front – often under fire – and broadcast concerts. From loudspeakers set up in streets and shortwave radios in flats, the music provided blessed relief from gnawing hunger and relentless cold.

One morning, Lisya was rehearsing Tchaikovsky's Fifth Symphony with the orchestra. Four bombs dropped right next to the rehearsal hall. Several people were wounded, including some musicians arriving late. But they stayed the rehearsal and played the broadcast concert that evening, despite their bandages. At the performance, the warning siren went off again just as the orchestra started the third movement of the Symphony. In the middle of the Finale, the whole building shook. A bomb landed just outside, but the orchestra played on.

The music throbbed with Tchaikovsky's pulsating rhythms; the last chords hung triumphantly around the musicians. Outside, bombs were still falling, but no one in the orchestra moved. Reluctantly, Lisya put away her violin and slowly left the hall. Walking home, she was not cold. And when she went to bed that night, she was not hungry.

Evgenia went for sustenance to the Leningrad Public Library. It never closed.

Hundreds of people sat there in fur hats and overcoats, huddled over books, reading by the light of small oil lamps.

And as often as she could, she went to the little church nearby. The wildness of the diminutive forest surrounding it reminded her of home; the dark gold beauty of its small, crowded sanctuary caressed her hunger and put the pangs to sleep. Lighting candles before her favorite icons, she lined up to kiss the *Madonna of Unexpected Happiness* and the *Resurrection of the Perished*.

"If our Mother Church is dear to us," intoned the priest, "do we not hold equally dear our Motherland! We must defend the sacred borders of our homeland against the German barbarians. God will grant us victory."

Evgenia went down on her knees and bowed her head to the ground. Singing and bowing and making the sign of the cross, she gave herself up to the incense and the chanting, feeling at one with those around her.

"*Gospodi pomilui*," she prayed, "And may the Virgin protect *Rodina*."

Ж   Ж   Ж

Evgenia was kneeling in her icon corner, as she often did, these days, when no one was home. Her praying, she knew, made her family uncomfortable.

One day, however, Nadya came home from school early, and found her great-grandmother deep in prayer. Sitting down at the kitchen table, she waited, not sure what to say or do.

Evgenia crossed herself, kissed the icon, then set it on the table in front of Nadya. "Your great-great-grandfather painted this and gave it to me on the day I married his son – who was your great-grandfather."

"Grandmere says he was a priest and a very good man," replied Nadya, "but very stubborn."

"So was she," smiled Evgenia. "I think that's why they argued so much."

"What did they argue about?"

"Mostly about what to believe in," replied Evgenia, pleased at Nadya's questions. "But eventually they understood that his church and her music were just different parts of the same thing."

"Do you believe in this – picture?" asked Nadya, tentatively.

"I believe in what it represents," said Evgenia, thoughtfully, "and in what – and who – I remember whenever I look at it."

"Does it make you think of Great-Grandfather Ivan?"

"Oh, yes." Evgenia smiled, remembering. "We loved each other very much."

"Why didn't he come to Leningrad with you?"

"Because he gave his life to defend what he believed in."

"Like my father is doing?"

"Well," Evgenia hesitated, "Well, yes. Yes, he is."

"Is he going to die, too?" Nadya's gaze was apprehensive but unflinching.

"I don't know," replied Evgenia, hesitating again, "But I hope not."

"When you kneel in front of the picture of this Woman," Nadya continued uncertainly, "Do you ask Her to take care of my father?"

"Yes, I do. Always."

"Would it help if I did, too?"

"Only if you believe in what She represents."

Nadya looked at the icon. "I think She looks like you, Babushka," she said finally. "And I believe in you."

"There are grandmothers all over Russia who pray as I do," said Evgenia, putting her arm around Nadya. "The Woman in the icon unites us all into one voice."

"That everyone can hear?"

"That everyone *will* hear. Someday."

Ж   Ж   Ж

It was Evgenia's birthday. In honor of the occasion, everyone had a sugar cube with their tea. Nadya had just returned from the roof, after checking that the buckets were filled with sand and water.

Lisya turned on the radio as Nadya sat down next to her. The girl was thin and pale, and rarely smiled anymore. Sasha sat listlessly in his mother's lap, his rosy chubbiness gone, dark circles under his eyes. Koshka curled up on the bed nearest the stove, waiting for Nadya to join her. She was no longer the fat sleek cat she had been before the War.

Dmitri Shostakovich was speaking on the radio. "Just an hour ago," he said, "I completed the second movement of my new symphony." It was his Seventh Symphony, and he had been working on it since July. "Despite the dangers threatening Leningrad, I have been able to work quickly. The life of our city is going on, even though all of us now carry military burdens. Our art is threatened with great danger. Let us defend our music. Let us work with honesty and self-sacrifice that no one may destroy it."

Lisya nodded emphatically. Then she turned off the radio and removed the tin can from over the candle. Supper – what there was of it – had been cooked on this make-shift stove to save fuel for the cold night ahead. Lisya passed the candle to Evgenia for her nightly reading of Tolstoy's *War and Peace*. In the chapter that night, Pierre had just joined the Freemasons and was enthusiastically explaining his new creed to a skeptical Prince Andrei.

Evgenia read with ease, greeting the words as old friends. "... 'We must live, we must love, we must believe that we are not only living today on this clod of earth, but have lived and will live forever there in everything.'"

After Evgenia finished reading, there was silence, as each contemplated Tolstoy's words.

"I wish *I* could believe that," said Lisya, after awhile.

"But surely," argued Katya, "the Party is leading us to the day when real Communism will be possible. And then this 'invisible dominion of goodness and truth' Pierre talks about will be on earth."

"Maybe," replied Lisya skeptically. "Actually, something like Freemasonry and Marxism aren't entirely incompatible. Or at least, they wouldn't have to be."

"Well," conceded Katya, "I suppose all that about – what is it again?" She reached for the book and paged quickly until she found the passage. "Ah yes, here it is. 'If I see clearly the ladder that rises up from vegetable to man, why should I suppose that ladder breaks off with me and does not go further.' I suppose that could be another way of explaining the dialectic of the class struggle. And certainly the emphasis on equality and brotherhood is similar."

"The main problem with Marxism," Lisya objected, "is that it's too small-minded and mundane. It doesn't soar! It doesn't transcend! It puts all its faith in *men*. I have seen too much of life to believe that the world could go on for long if it were left only up to them – especially the lumpish masses Party rhetoric so loves to exalt!"

"But what else is there?" asked Katya.

"There is God," Evgenia said quietly.

"But Marx said religion is the opiate of the people," protested Katya.

"And so it often is," agreed Lisya, "but organized religion and believing in God aren't always the same thing. The Party was right to attack the Church. Before the Revolution, it was a corrupt tool of tsarist oppression."

"But not anymore," interjected Evgenia firmly. "Suffering has purified the Church. The hypocrites have been weeded out."

"Babushka..." Katya hesitated. "When you go to church... what is it like?"

"It feels…" pondered Evgenia, "like I am – in Tolstoy's words – 'part of a vast, unseen chain.'"

"Yes," agreed Lisya, tapping the book. "'Part of a vast, harmonious whole.' That's how I feel when I'm making music."

Evgenia smiled and nodded. "The church rituals are the same now as when I was a girl," she said, looking at Nadya. "When I hear the same prayers and chant the same songs, now as then," she waved at her book, "I know that 'I always have been and always shall be!'"

"Is that why you had Nadya and Sasha baptized?" asked Katya.

"Old women must preserve the wisdom of their past by passing it on to their future," Evgenia shrugged. "Why else does God allow us to live so long?"

"So… then…" Katya hesitated again. "You really do believe in… God?"

"I know that God is," replied Evgenia carefully, "but it's the Virgin, the Mother of God, I believe in. God is forever flying about the universe seeking Truth. The Virgin plants her feet in *Rodina*. She's closer to the earth and what's real."

The candle flickered out.

"And She is not afraid of Death," Evgenia added, reaching out to her daughter and granddaughter, firmly clasping their hands.

445

Chapter 23: FAMINE

The sleds began appearing after the tramcars stopped. Small sleds, children's sleds, painted bright red and yellow, they were soon everywhere. The squeaking of their runners sounded louder than the shelling. In the cold dark silence it deafened the ears.

Lisya was pulling Sasha's little sled behind her. Though the bucket sitting on top was empty, she walked slowly. Ahead was a sled with a bundle of wood, across the street another with a chest of drawers to be broken up for kindling. Both were drawn by tired grey shadows still recognizable as women. Two other women passed, pulling a third who was pregnant, hurrying to the hospital. Lisya caught a glimpse of the skeletal face on the sled, and shook her head sadly.

At the corner, she waited while a sled carrying a coffin crossed her path. She could tell by the way it slid from side to side that it was empty. Last week a sliding coffin had struck her ankle. She was still limping a little and gave this one plenty of room. Down the street she overtook a sled bearing a corpse wrapped in an old curtain. She passed carefully to avoid entangling its whitish-yellow hair in the runners of her sled.

Lisya was making her daily trek for water. Only when it snowed was she spared this ordeal. Then she simply melted the freshly fallen snow from the courtyard. Once it had frozen, however, no one had the strength to chip it away. And better not to know the unpleasant surprises which lurked beneath.

Halfway to the river, she stopped to rest in a tramcar frozen in the ice. Gratefully she sat down inside, out of the piercing blasts of cold. How silent it was – only the wind whining along with the squeaking sleds. Except for a daily afternoon shelling, even the bombing had almost stopped. No need to waste ammunition where famine was waging so efficient a battle.

There's no more music in Leningrad, she thought dully, too exhausted to shed the tears in her soul. Even the Radio Orchestra was no more. She remembered the weekly memos: "The First Violin is dying, the Oboe died on the way to rehearsal, the French Horn is near death…" There were not enough of them left to

447

make music together. The empty chairs and gaping silences at the last rehearsal had been too painful.

Reluctantly, Lisya stood up. *I must not sit too long,* she reminded herself, *or I'll end up like those other passengers back there.* In the rear seats were three frozen corpses.

As she climbed down from the streetcar, she was glad to see no one coming in her direction. It was terrible to meet people you knew on the streets. Exchanging news consisted of who had been wounded, who had starved, who was dead. Even worse was to notice how ghastly they looked, and to see in their eyes the reflection of your own hunger. Some were pale white, some earthen grey; some were swollen, some skeletal. Lisya hadn't looked in a mirror for weeks, and didn't intend to.

She walked on, past doorways where people were sitting on icy steps, heads in their hands. They had been there – unmoving – for days. And on a bench near the Embankment, she saw a couple huddled together, resting, it seemed, from a long walk. They had been there yesterday. The snow had drifted around them overnight.

As she approached the big granite steps leading down to the Neva, she joined hundreds of women, pails in hand, moving toward holes broken in the ice. Steam rose from each opening and frosted the trees which lined the river. The steps were sheathed in frozen water from spilled buckets; Lisya clutched the railing and descended slowly. As she reached the bottom, the woman ahead of her slipped and fell. She struggled to rise and then became still. Lisya and two women passing by finally got her back on her feet. She opened her shriveled lips, muttered a few garbled words and fell again, dead.

"Well," one of the other women shrugged, "we tried." And they all walked on around the dead woman to the water holes.

Lisya made her way carefully, winding around dozens of corpses half covered with ice and snow. Periodically the frozen little mounds disappeared, only to rise again. Probably, thought Lisya, that accounted for the sweet stench of the water she drew from the river. No matter how long it boiled, she could never get the taste out. Even in the strongest tea, that distinctively ghoulish flavor was there – faintly sweet, faintly moldy, tainted with death.

Breathing hard, Lisya carried her full bucket up the treacherous icy slope the steps had become. Stopping at the top to catch her breath, she was again struck by how the smell of the city had changed. No more gasoline or tobacco. No more horses, dogs or cats. Even the smell of people had vanished. Now the city smelled of raw snow and wet stone. And above all, the bitter odor of turpentine. Trucks, bound to and from the cemeteries, were drenched with it. The harsh smell lingered in the frosty air like the very scent of death.

Lisya put the bucket of water on Sasha's sled and began pulling it slowly home. The runners squeaked as she trudged on. After what seemed a very long time, she stopped to rest in front of one of the kiosks scattered around the city. Handwritten notices on bits of yellow, white, and blue paper were posted: "Will buy or exchange valuables for records of Vertinsky and Leschenko;" "For Sale: Complete works of Leonid Andreyev, Edgar Poe, Knut Hamsun;" "Will remove corpses – for bread;" "Lost: little girl, seven years old, in red dress and fur hood. Anyone who has seen or met her…"

Lisya shuddered and noticed that daylight was fading. Darkness fell at 3 PM in Leningrad now. The sparkling white nights of summer had turned into the long dark days of winter. She quickened her pace and hurried home. The squeaking of the little sled echoed in the empty street.

Ж Ж Ж

The lead editorial in *Leningradskaya Pravda* announced the bad news: "We must reduce rations in order to hold out until the enemy is pushed back, until the blockade is broken. Difficult? Yes. But there is no choice. And this everyone must understand…"

Lisya discovered that the first week was the worst. She suffered terrible pangs the first day. And the second. But gradually the pain faded into quiet despondency, a gloom that had no end, a weakness that advanced with frightening rapidity. What she had done yesterday, she could not do today. She found herself surrounded by obstacles too difficult to overcome. The stairs were too steep to climb, the shelf too high to reach, the toilet too dirty to clean. At a distance, she saw her body changing – her legs wasting to toothpicks, her arms vanishing, her breasts turning into empty bags. Her skirt slipped from her hips. Strange bones appeared. Sometimes there was loud ringing in her ears.

Hunger did strange things to the mind, too. One of the few remaining Second Violins became obsessed with the notion that Hitler was besieging Leningrad just to kill him. He began to babble apologetically and constantly begged his colleagues not to blame him for the blockade. "I would kill myself if it would lift the siege," he repeated to everyone he saw, "but I am a Christian and it is not possible."

Hunger also gave birth to new kinds of crime – violent robbery of bread and

449

ration cards, food scams to bilk the rationing system. The new thieves were usually ordinary citizens driven to desperation. Professional criminals meanwhile became bolder, as the police department – like everyone else – grew weaker. Skeletal squads worked eighteen to twenty hour shifts daily. Justice was swift; people were shot for stealing a loaf of bread.

Those who clung desperately to their basic decency were surprised by outbursts of uncharacteristic behavior. Such as on the day Katya dragged herself to the Hermitage. Orbeli had planned another festival, this time celebrating the 500th anniversary of Alisher Navoi, the great poet of Samarkand. Katya was exhausted, but she didn't want to disappoint Orbeli. As she slowly moved toward the staff entrance, she remembered that he had been preparing for this event on the day before the Germans invaded.

After greeting Orbeli at the door, she made her way to what had once been the State Council Hall of the tsars. Entering the great room with high ceilings and long windows, she had difficulty recognizing the other bundled figures. It was cold, very cold, and their faces were ravaged by hunger and thin as hawks.

Orbeli opened the meeting, energetic as always, though his long beard was now heavily streaked with grey. Suddenly there was a tremendous explosion.

"Don't be alarmed," he said, with no change of voice. "Shall we move the meeting to the shelter?"

No one rose.

"Very well," he continued, "the meeting will go on."

Katya left the Hermitage that day uplifted by Orbeli's dedication and courage. As she slowly crossed Palace Square, her mood was shattered by the shrieks of an angry mob. A crowd of women spilled into the Square, dragging a frightened white-faced young man. From one of those on the edge, Katya learned that he was a German flyer whose plane had been rammed by a Soviet fighter pilot. Short of ammunition like everyone else, the diminishing Leningrad air squadrons had began ramming Nazi planes as a last resort.

The young man at the center of the mob had parachuted into the hands of women whose fury temporarily overcame the lethargy of their hunger. They were screaming incoherently, beating him with their fists and whatever else happened to be in their hands. To her horror, Katya suddenly found herself yelling and pushing through the screaming women. Rage such as she had never known flooded her. Her hands clutched the air, yearning to choke the life out of the wretched German swine, to beat him to the bloody pulp he deserved, to tear his miserable limbs from his despicable body.

Fortunately for the pilot, the women were too exhausted to sustain their attack. Eventually he was taken, bleeding and terrified, to a hospital.

Katya walked, trembling, to the Palace Bridge. Halfway across, she stopped and stared into the Neva. *At least I didn't actually hit him,* she thought. *But only because I couldn't get close enough.* Shame overwhelmed her as bitter tears froze on her cheeks.

Evgenia, too, had her moments of shame. One day, she was standing in an enormous line waiting for bread rations. The queue did not disperse even when air raid sirens sounded.

"I've waited since four o'clock this morning," the woman ahead of her said. "I've not eaten all day."

"I can't go home yet," the woman behind her said. "My children are starving."

Shells fell all around them. Bodies were blasted to bits. Evgenia and the other surviving women quietly picked their way over the human wreckage and reformed the queue. It was not until she had brought the bread safely home that she, too, wept tears of shame.

For Lisya the problem manifested itself differently. She became obsessed with animals. And as the nonhuman population of Leningrad sharply diminished, her obsession grew.

First to go were the crows; they flew off to the German lines. Next were the gulls and pigeons; they were hunted and eaten. Then the sparrows and starlings vanished. They died of cold and hunger, just as the people did. Some said they had seen the small birds drop like stones while flying over the Neva, frozen to death in flight.

The cages of rabbits and guinea pigs at the university and hospitals were soon empty. Eventually, the pet population thinned out, too. Dogs became so rare Lisya noticed – and remembered – whenever she saw one. Dinka, the watchdog at Radio Headquarters, was frequently on her mind. And one day she encountered a very thin man carrying an even thinner dog. Lisya stared at the poor beast so fixedly that both the animal and its owner recoiled. After they had passed, she thought of the terror in their eyes and felt ashamed that she felt no shame.

But worst of all was being at home with Koshka. The cat was always nearest the stove; her constant presence tormented Lisya. Koshka was thinner than before the war, but she was still in better shape than anyone else in the family. She was a good mouser and had, at first, provided well for herself – and, Lisya suspected, occasionally for the rest of them. The first time Koshka brought home a

451

rat, Lisya had felt sick.. Evgenia, however, had patted the cat approvingly – and then whisked away the rat. Lisya couldn't eat her soup that night.

It had been a long time since Koshka had brought anything home. The mice had disappeared, and people said the rats had abandoned the city and deserted to the German lines. Koshka, however, still had enough meat on her bones to make Lisya salivate. Resolutely, she struggled to push what followed out of her mind. She herself had given the cat to Nadya when just a kitten. Since then, Nadya and Koshka had been inseparable. Lisya loved Nadya more than anyone, and was deeply ashamed of the base thoughts she harbored for her granddaughter's beloved companion.

But one day, the demon got loose. Coming home from the river, she noticed that a horse had fallen on the ice. Next morning, only half the horse was there – and not for long. The dam burst. Thoughts of the not yet emaciated feline body never left her mind. Fantasies of succulent cat stew haunted her dreams. In Koshka's presence she was overwhelmed by rage.

Gone was the elegant musician. Gone was the loving mother. Gone was the woman Nadya called Grandmere. All that remained was a hungry girl named Lisya.

Her obsession suddenly took a practical turn: How? She remembered that the Bass Viol had eaten his dog last month. The porter had butchered it in return for one leg and the intestines. But, Lisya calculated, there wasn't that much of Koshka to go around. The last of the Violas had taken her dog to a toxicologist to be put to sleep. Unfortunately, the man was so weak he bungled the injection. Lisya decided that wouldn't do, either. Koshka must not suffer needlessly. And then she heard that the Tuba had strangled his cat.

She waited until a rare day when no one was home. Koshka was asleep under the stove. Lisya sat down on Evgenia's bed and gently lifted the cat onto her lap. As she slowly stroked the soft fur, she remembered how on cold mornings, after Nadya left for school, Koshka would jump onto her bed and nestle up against her back. The cat began to purr. A large tear rolled quietly down Lisya's cheek, as she realized that she loved Koshka almost as much as Nadya did.

Then the rage of hunger – not just her own, but that of her family as well – swept through her again. Stealthily she put her hands around the small furry neck. The cat's green-gold eyes looked up at her, trust turning to fear as Lisya began to squeeze. She closed her eyes and pressed harder. Beads of sweat broke out on her forehead, despite the frigid temperature. Koshka began to struggle. Lisya held on, increasing the pressure of her fingers. The cat raked her claws across her hands and arms; pain and blood mingled with rising nausea. Feeling Koshka's life throbbing through her vise-like grip, her hands began to shake. Koshka let out a mournful cry of terror. Lisya's strong well-trained fingers suddenly refused to obey her. Her muscles turned to water and the cat sprang out of her lap, looking frantically for a place to hide.

Lisya fell back on Evgenia's bed, trying not to faint. And she remembered rumors that the Tuba, after eating his cat, had tried to hang himself. The rope, they said, had not held. Falling to the floor, he had broken his leg and frozen to death.

To Lisya, at that moment, the fate of the Tuba seemed just. She rolled over on the bed and vomited into the chamber pot underneath.

Ж   Ж   Ж

New Year's Eve was cold and dark that year. The family sat silently around the table, trying not to think about the delicious feast of the year before. Tonight there was only the usual watery soup and the daily bread ration, such as it was. Everyone ate slowly, trying to make the scanty fare last as long as possible.

After supper, Katya brought in the New Year's "tree." It was a fir branch stuck in an old milk bottle, decorated with little toys from past holidays and a candle cut into four pieces. Lisya put some tinsel in her hair and announced that she was Snegurochka, the Snow Maiden. The children managed a wan smile when she gave them the few pieces of candy she had been saving for the occasion. Evgenia then pretended to be Father Frost, and gave them each a "cookie" which smelled of cod liver oil. Even Sasha giggled a little at her long pointed nose.

After that, they simply sat quietly around the stove, waiting for midnight. Except to chop wood, stand in line for bread, and get water from the river, they rarely left the apartment these days. Only Nadya, who continued to go to school, had even the remains of a normal life. All the children were given a meal at school. Part of the food came from the Army, who got extra rations, and some came from the teachers, who did not. Even so, Nadya started staying home when the weather was especially bad. She no longer had strength to battle the blizzards.

In normal times, New Year's was for visiting friends, giving gifts and sharing food. Now, however, there was nothing to share. And who knew in what state one might find one's friends. Katya remembered the last time she had gone to the neighbors down the hall. She had knocked repeatedly, then finally opened the unlocked door. They were all sitting around the stove, but no one answered her greeting. Approaching them, she noticed that the fire in the stove had long since gone out. She saw their staring eyes and quickly left the room, closing the door behind her. There was nothing she could do.

At midnight they turned on the radio. The Spassky chimes in the Moscow Kremlin played the *Internationale*. Lisya brought out a small bottle – the last of the wine – and they toasted the new year. Outside, navy guns on the Neva answered the German New Year's shelling with a special salvo.

Nadya lit the candles on the makeshift tree. Sasha's eyes, too, lit up for just a moment. There was silence, as each contemplated the tree and its candles. Would light ever be reborn in Leningrad? Or were they doomed to go on in darkness, until…

The candles flickered out. Sasha began to wail. The freezing blackness closed in.

Ж   Ж   Ж

Ever since her traumatic encounter with Lisya, Koshka had been a different cat. Most of the time, she hid in the farthest corner under Nadya's bed. At bedtime, Nadya would entice her out with scraps from her lunch at school. Wrapped in the girl's arms, the cat would lie trembling, eyes wide with fear, until Nadya fell asleep. Then she would dive under the bed and cower in her corner.

Periodically she would creep over to the door, prowling back and forth in front of it. If anyone approached, she would arch her back, hissing and baring her fangs, her twitching, bristling tail punctuating a whining growl. In vain, Nadya would explain to her, over and over, why it was no longer safe for a cat to go out.

One day, Lisya got home with water later than usual. She opened the door to Koshka's pacing. The cat froze, staring at her. Letting out a terrified shriek, she tore out the door between Lisya and the water bucket.

"Koshka, come back!" screamed Nadya, and ran out after her. For hours she searched in and out of the building, looking in all the cat's favorite haunts, calling her name again and again. Koshka, however, would not be found. Finally, Evgenia took Nadya firmly by the hand and put her to bed. Nadya slept alone that night for the first time in years, tears drenching her pillow.

Every night for weeks, Nadya searched and called and cried herself to sleep. The girl's forlorn sobs cut Lisya to the quick. Her remorse almost smothered her hunger.

But soon, another unfolding tragedy filled the void left by Koshka's disappearance.

It was pitch black. The stove had gone out hours ago. Katya shivered and drew Sasha closer. The baby stirred, then whimpered and made a coughing noise. As his little body stiffened, Katya felt something wet and sticky on her hand.

"Sasha has always had such a strong stomach," said Katya, after lighting a candle. "He's hardly ever vomited before."

"But he's just a baby," said Evgenia, wiping Sasha's face. "His little stomach isn't used to all the rough stuff they've been putting in the bread."

Katya sat on the rocking chair by the stove, trying to soothe the baby. He fretted uncomfortably in her lap, sometimes clutching his stomach and crying.

"We'll feed him only the real food, from what I've been saving," said Evgenia, trying to sound confident. "I'm sure he'll feel better then."

"And I'll boil the water longer," added Lisya, awakened by Sasha's cries. "That should help, too."

Katya nodded, somewhat relieved. Eventually Sasha fell asleep on her lap.

The next day, after school, Nadya brought home a small box of real tea.

"Look, Sasha," she said, playing peek-a-boo with the box. "It's from my history teacher."

Sasha smiled weakly and grabbed listlessly at her hair.

After the water had boiled twice as long as usual, Lisya added the tea. After it had steeped, Katya gave Sasha small spoonfuls.

Gradually, as the vomiting subsided, Sasha fussed less and smiled more. The hovering women breathed a cautious sigh of relief. Katya felt the vise around her heart loosen a bit.

But then, eventually, there was no more "real" food in Evgenia's hoard. And there was nothing left at school for which Nadya could trade her lunch. And so, like the rest of them, Sasha had to eat bread containing things no human stomach was ever intended to digest.

Sasha started to vomit again. And, soon, had bouts of diarrhea in between. Despite the cold, the stench was formidable.

"We'll need more water to clean up with," said Evgenia, remembering her hygiene campaigns in Derevnia.

"I'm already making two trips to the river," worried Lisya. "I don't think I can manage more and still get home before dark."

"I'll go with you," said Katya quickly. "With both of us pulling the sled, we can fill more than one pail."

After that, water was always boiling on the stove. And, for awhile, Katya was able to bathe Sasha often enough to keep his flowing body fluids from searing his tender flesh.

"We're almost out of fuel," said Lisya one day, trying to sound matter-of-fact. "By tomorrow, there will be nothing left to keep the stove going."

"But by the time we get back with the water," protested Katya, on the verge of tears, "it's too dark to go chop wood."

"I'll go chop wood," volunteered Nadya.

"No!" responded all three women immediately.

"You MUST keep going to school!" exclaimed Katya, more vehemently than she usually spoke to Nadya.

"But why?" Nadya was startled.

"Because you're our link to the world," said Lisya, putting her arm around Nadya. "And to the life we had before."

"But we must have wood!" Nadya began to cry.

"And we do," said Evgenia quietly. "All around us."

The next day she resolutely took axe in hand and started on the furniture.

And so the water boiled on. But Sasha's body continued to dehydrate. And when Katya bathed his pathetically thin little buttocks, he began to scream in pain.

"Maybe this will help," said Evgenia as she gently applied some salve to the boils and sores. But, like their food, the makeshift remedy lacked too many essential ingredients to be effective.

All of them took turns trying to soothe Sasha, but nothing eased his pain. Eventually his screams subsided into quiet sobs, and then became barely audible whimpers.

Each scream had been a knife twisting in Katya's heart. *But this is worse*, she thought, as Sasha lay silently on her lap, looking up at her in dull agony. *Oh, so much worse*. Knowing there was nothing she could do, Katya sat by the stove, holding him and rocking, watching the life flow out of her little boy. And feeling her heart being drained along with it.

Day by day, the furniture disappeared. When the axe first hit the kitchen table, Evgenia winced; but it kept the stove going for a long time. Finally there was only Katya's rocking chair and Lisya's grand piano.

Lovingly, Lisya ran her hand over the smooth wood of this, her greatest treasure. She opened the keyboard, closed for months, and tried to play. Her cold stiff fingers would not move. *The music has gone from my soul*, she thought sadly. Slowly she leaned over the piano and shed tears of silent sorrow.

After a while, she straightened up and looked at Katya, rocking Sasha by the stove. With a deep sigh, she picked up the axe and raised it above the piano. Closing her eyes, she let it fall. Hideously jarring discord assaulted her as she sank unconscious to the floor.

By the time she came to, Evgenia was feeding one of the piano's legs to the stove. Lisya turned over to avoid the sight of the wounded instrument, leaning like a crippled animal. She closed her eyes and went to sleep. When she finally awoke, Evgenia had finished dismembering the piano. Its innards lay in the corner, covered by a blanket.

And then one day, Sasha simply ceased to be. He died quietly, almost imperceptibly, in his mother's lap. Katya stopped rocking and stared at him.

Evgenia put her hand on Katya's shoulder.

Katya looked slowly up at her. "No!" she screamed, a wild look in her eyes. Still holding Sasha's body she stood up and suddenly bolted out of the apartment, down into the street. She ran and ran, until finally she reached the hospital.

Breathing hard, she entered the reception room and sat down to wait, still clutching Sasha's body and making little crooning, comforting noises to it.

Finally, an emaciated nurse approached her.

"Please help my little Sasha," pleaded Katya. "Please."

The nurse looked at him, then at Katya. "I'm sorry," she murmured sadly. "So sorry."

"But there must be something you can do!" Katya said desperately.

"So sorry," the nurse repeated even more sadly. She patted Katya's arm sympathetically, and then moved on to the others in the waiting room. Many of them were dead, too.

Katya sat among the corpses, too exhausted to do anything else.

Finally Evgenia came to find her.

"Come with me, Katya," she said gently, sitting down beside her.

"No, Babuska, I can't," Katya answered politely. "No, I have to wait here for someone to help Sasha."

"Come with me, Katya." Evgenia put her arm around her granddaughter. "I will help Sasha."

Still clutching Sasha's body, Katya allowed herself to be led through the corpse-lined corridors of the hospital, out into the corpse-strewn streets. A heavy sledge, heaped high with bodies, passed by. They were thin, blue and terrifying, skeletons with skin stretched tight and splotched with lilac-colored death marks. Next door to their apartment building, a truck had stopped. A pile of corpses under the staircase was being loaded.

Back in the apartment, Katya sat down again in the rocking chair by the stove, still clutching Sasha's cold little body. She began to rock, and then to sing. First lullabies and silly tunes to amuse a child. Then laments and all the old songs from Evgenia's village. All night she rocked and sang, the others silently keeping watch with her, the dark melancholy of her grief embracing them in deep sorrow.

Finally, in the murky dawn, she stopped. Evgenia reached out and clasped her hand.

"He's gone, Katya," she said, gently.

Katya nodded mutely. Slowly she reached down and closed her baby's eyes. Then she carried him into the other room and made a little bed for him. Before she drew the covers up over his head, she kissed him tenderly. Returning to the other room, she collapsed on the mattress...

When she finally awoke, Lisya was feeding the arms of the rocking chair to the stove. Katya looked away. Evgenia handed her some watery soup. She ate it silently, trying to focus on something which would not trigger the avalanche of grief threatening to break loose. Her eyes fell on the little sled by the door. A flood of sunlight momentarily warmed her, as she remembered the day she had bought it for Sasha. Carefully she edged around the yawning pit of what had followed, and neatly jumped across the precipice of his death to the practical problem of his burial.

First, she got a coffin from the Hermitage. It was made from a packing crate intended for the last shipment of art, caught when the Germans closed the ring. Katya gently laid Sasha in the coffin and carefully tucked his blankets around him. Evgenia helped her carry it down to the street. It was a very small coffin and fitted neatly on the little sled.

Katya and Evgenia set out for the cemetery, pulling the sled behind them. The squeaking of its runners broke the silence of the cold morning. They stopped every block to rest.

They fell in with other sleds, most of them bearing corpses. Some in coffins, others covered with rugs or swaddled in sheets like mummies. A few were wrapped in paper, tied with string. Most were pulled by pairs of women, gaunt shadows plodding forward soundlessly.

Slowly the funeral cortege made its way to the Piskarevsky Cemetery on the edge of the city. Profound silence accompanied the procession. As they got closer to the cemetery, the trickle of sleds became a small but still silent stream.

Off in the distance, steam shovels were at work. New fortifications, Katya thought. Coming out of town, they passed small houses with dead gardens and orchards. And then, on both sides of the road, a formless heap which grew higher and thicker as they approached the cemetery's entrance. As the passage between grew narrower, what at first appeared to be cords of wood turned out to be enormous piles of dead bodies.

Katya tried to blur the scene. She tried not to see the small bodies tangled in that unending mountain of unburied flesh. She tried not to see the chunks of flesh cut away from arms and thighs of corpses. She tried not to see that next to the stacks were randomly strewn bodies, fallen in the act of trying to bury their dead. She tried – and failed. And would have fallen with them, had not Evgenia kept her marching stolidly on.

On through the avenue of death they went, until they found a little clearing under a small tree. They stopped, untied the pick and shovel fastened on the coffin, and began digging. The ground, however, was frozen solid. The tools clinked as though striking metal. They beat on the earth's door for a long time. It would not open. Finally they sank to the snow, and leaned against each other.

A loud explosion from the direction of the steam shovels startled them. Puzzled, Katya stood up and walked slowly through the tombstones to a small hill overlooking the rest of the cemetery. Below, she could see a huge trench being dynamited by army sappers and excavated by steam shovels. Nearby she saw more of the macabre stacks lining the road.

She looked at the useless pick still clutched in her hand, then at the huge steam shovels. Wiping away a few tears threatening to become a flood, she walked resolutely back to where Evgenia waited. Without a word, she put the small coffin back on the little sled and began to pull it toward the trench. Evgenia followed silently.

They passed a small squad of Red Army men throwing corpses into the trench. The bodies were frozen and rang like metal horseshoes when they landed. Katya and Evgenia found a place where the ground was still open and empty. Gently, they lowered Sasha's coffin into the trench and covered it with clods of frozen dirt. Then they stood looking at the little mound until they heard the burial squad approaching.

"*Gospodi pomilui,*" murmured Katya, remembering another hasty funeral along the Luga Line. "Lord, have mercy."

"He's with God now," said Evgenia, crossing herself. "The Virgin will protect him."

Neither of them dared look back. Out of the valley of the shadow of death, back through the maze of frozen corpses, into the city of the dying, Evgenia led. Katya stumbled behind, staring at the empty little sled, its dancing bears moving in a taunting pavanne.

When, at last, they returned home, Katya felt a terrible pain inside, about to dissolve her. Evgenia grasped her shoulders and looked long and deep into her eyes.

"No, Katya," she said firmly, "Not yet. We can't afford the luxury of tears now."

And looking back into Evgenia's compassionate eyes, Katya knew she was right. As Evgenia wrapped her arms around her, Katya felt the old woman's strength flow through her.

Ж   Ж   Ж

Nadya was at school. Katya and Lisya were getting water. Evgenia was home alone, worrying.

It was all gone. Despite her careful management. She had bargained shrewdly with the cigarettes and vodka. She had spun out the food hoard an incredibly long time. She had improvised imaginatively with unorthodox food sources. She had even converted Alexei's briefcase to meat jelly and scraped the paste off the wallpaper to make dough. But it was still all gone.

Except for two mattresses huddled by the stove, the room was empty. Her trunk had long since gone for fuel, and all her clothes were on her back. Only the icon and her books were left, wrapped in the old flowered shawl. Slowly she unwrapped the little bundle and carefully spread the last of her possessions in front of her. After gazing at them thoughtfully, she re-wrapped the icon and a volume of Pushkin in the shawl, and put it under her pillow. The other books – mostly by Pushkin and Tolstoy – she picked up, one by one, and lovingly paged through them.

She had read them so many times, she could almost have recited them with her eyes closed. Not that she had ever tried. The real magic was not just in the words, beautiful as they were, but in the act of being able to read them. For Evgenia, the wonder of those mysterious marks creating whole new worlds inside her head had never dimmed. Slowly she bowed over each book and respectfully

460

kissed its cover, as if saluting a venerated elder. Then she wrapped them carefully in an old pillowcase and went down into the wind-swept streets.

She walked along the Neva, across the Palace Bridge, down the Nevsky Prospekt to her favorite shop. As she entered the secondhand bookstore, she noted that business had been brisk since her last visit, months ago. Old books were stacked everywhere; it was hard to get through the aisles. Such an abundance of riches made her hungry in a way that not even food, these days, did. Resolutely she maneuvered through the stacks to the proprietor's desk.

As he watched her emerge from the maze, the book trader knew by the carefully cradled bundle that she, too, had come to sell. His heart ached dully as she reverently laid her books in front of him. A glance at the inexpensive bindings and rough paper and cheap print was enough for him to know that, even in the best of times, editions such as these had little resale value. But he, too, loved books and could recognize the love that had been lavished on these over the years. So he picked them up gently and nodded appreciatively. He gave her more than he should have for them, and regretted volubly that he could not pay her what they were worth. Which was at least partly true. She smiled proudly, and he was glad that he could ease what he knew was an anguished parting.

From the bookshop, Evgenia walked reluctantly to the Haymarket. Everything was for sale there now, and the traders who had suddenly appeared that winter frightened her. They were like characters in the Dostoyevsky books she had borrowed – once – from Alexei. They stood like rocks over their wares, and were obscenely fat among the thin shadows who drifted by.

Evgenia looked longingly at the hardtack and linseed oil and bacon fat priced beyond her means. She almost bought a packet of tooth powder for pudding, then remembered she had no flour or starch left to mix with it. She ended up with a few large bars of library paste and a big glass of "Badayev earth" – plain dirt dug from the cellars of the burned warehouse, into which tons of molten sugar had poured.

That night at supper, Evgenia gave her share of "custard," made from Badayev earth mixed with library paste, to Katya. She gave her bread to Nadya, who was less emaciated than the rest of them – thanks to the school lunches. The students often ate at the teachers' expense. Which, Evgenia reflected matter-of-factly, was how it should be. And from that moment, she ate no more.

At first, it didn't seem to make much difference. Her lean old body, accustomed to hard times and religious fasting, did not seem to need as much as the others. Hunger was an old acquaintance, with whom she had long since reached

461

an understanding. Gradually, however, her strength began to ebb. Lisya assumed the task of getting the bread rations, and Evgenia stopped going out. All day, she lay quietly near the stove, praying silently.

"You must eat, Babushka!" insisted Katya, thrusting her bread ration at the old woman.

"No, Katya." Evgenia shook her head. "That is for you and Nadya."

"But you'll die!" Katya's voice was desperate.

"At my age, there are worse things."

"But we can't lose you, too!"

"Listen to me, Katya." Evgenia took her granddaughter's hand and held it firmly. "As we have lived, so we must die."

"You mean like Grandfather and Papa did?"

"Yes. And like your Uncle Vladimir –" Evgenia paused, as Katya winced and looked way.

Katya was quiet, but did not let go of her grandmother's hand.

"The women in our family have a tradition, too," Evgenia began again. "No Babushka ever eats at the expense of her grandchildren. When there isn't enough, we give what we have to our daughters."

"But we need you!"

"But it's my time, Katya!" insisted Evgenia, with more force than she had mustered for days. "Let me go."

Finally Katya nodded. She held Evgenia's hand all night. But she did not – could not – allow herself to cry.

On the first of the month, Evgenia mustered her remaining strength for one last errand. Ration cards were reissued monthly; everyone had to appear in person to get a new one. Those of dead family members were supposed to be turned in immediately. Failure to do so was, like everything else, punishable by firing squad. In the circumstances, the threat was meaningless; ration cards of the dead ended up a bonus to the living. And so, that morning, Evgenia walked – straight and tall – to the station where the cards were issued. With her family, she waited patiently in line until they were all re-certified.

Returning home, she knelt and unwrapped the small bundle beside her pillow. She put the shawl on her head, kissed the icon, and made the sign of the cross. She prayed silently for a long time. Then, just before nightfall, she called her family to her.

She picked up the volume of Pushkin, bound in red leather, and handed it to

Nadya. "This is the first book I ever owned," she said with a smile. "When you want a story, read it and think of me."

To Katya she gave the icon. "For when it is time to grieve." She looked deeply into her granddaughter's eyes. "I hope you, too, will find the Virgin."

She gave them both her blessing. Katya kissed her hand; Nadya was crying.

"You don't have to weep for me." Evgenia patted Nadya's cheek. "I'm going home – to the Volga."

Then she turned to Katya. "Which way is Stalingrad?"

Katya pointed to the opposite wall.

"Please God," Evgenia prayed, making a small cross in that direction, "Watch over Alexei. And help his soul find peace."

Finally, she took off her shawl. "And now, Lisya," she said, wrapping it around her daughter, "Now *you* must be the Babushka."

Ж Ж Ж

Evgenia died quietly that night. They found her in the morning, cold as granite, a faint smile on her face and no fear in her eyes. They carried her into the other room, covered her with a blanket, and closed the door.

Now they were weaker than ever. Losing Sasha had cut out their heart. Evgenia's passing had taken the family's soul. The hunger of their bodies seemed all the worse.

Nadya continued to go to school. Lisya took over, permanently, Evgenia's job of getting bread. Katya went to the river to get water, closing her ears to the squeaking of the little sled bumping along behind her. The rest of the time they lay listlessly around the stove, covered with blankets.

And then, near the end of the month, there was nothing left to burn. Vaguely, Lisya formed the thought that, since she was now head of the family, she should do something. But the idea could not get past the paralysis of will which had afflicted her since Evgenia's death. They went to bed that evening huddled together next to a cold stove.

When the central heating had failed, months ago, thousands of little wood-burning stoves had been hastily installed all over the city. Makeshift and cranky, poorly attended by the dying and dead, hundreds of fires resulted. Walking back from the river earlier that day, Katya had passed one of these burning buildings. No one was making any effort to extinguish it. Everyone knew that the fire hydrants were frozen, that there was no fuel for the fire trucks, and that most of the fire fighters were too weak to answer a call even if anyone bothered to put one in.

Lisya was roused from fitful sleep by awareness that something was wrong. Her nose caught the scent of smoke, her eyes focused on flickering light from outside.

Fire!

"Katya! Nadya! Wake up!"

"Grandmere?" asked Nadya sleepily, as Katya sat up on her other side.

"Put whatever we have into whatever we can carry," directed Lisya. "And hurry!"

She went out in the hall and quickly climbed the stairs down which smoke was billowing. Three flights up were flames. Coughing and choking, she knocked hastily on those doors behind which she had last seen living faces, and then hurriedly returned to her family.

They were ready. There wasn't much left to pack. Each of them shouldered a bundle, then hesitated, looking at the closed door of the room where Evgenia's frozen body lay. Without a word, Lisya picked up her violin and led her daughter and granddaughter out of the place that was no longer home.

They stood in the street and watched it burn. The heat of the fire melted the ice, attracting a crowd of people patiently filling their pails with the water. The upper storeys were blazing, and reddish shadows played on the snow. With the other survivors, they warmed themselves near the burning building.

Finally, golden flames began licking the windows of their apartment, casting a strange light on the darkness below. Lisya watched, transfixed. Bathed in the amber glow, the flickering face of a woman seemed to gaze out from the heart of the fire. Like an ancient icon, it smiled compassionately. A familiar voice seemed to be singing – one that had been silent too long. And then, for just an instant, the faint echo of bells joined the chanting. The flaming river blazed up once more and then flowed gratefully into the Earth.

Chapter 24: SPRING

Lisya awoke suddenly.

"Fire!" she thought with alarm, feeling the warm light on her cheek. Opening her eyes, she saw instead the sun streaming in through a dirty window. Breathing out in relief, she looked slowly around the still unfamiliar room. It was filled with cots and couches, office desks and wooden packing boxes, stacks of newspapers and a few dozen people, pecking at typewriters or sleeping where they had collapsed. At opposite ends were two small stoves for cooking meals and heating water.

After the fire, Lisya had moved into Radio House. It was very crowded – and blessedly busy. At night there were always long discussions around one of the little stoves; people talked endlessly about the books they would write, the music they would make, the plays they would stage. Lisya said little, but listening by the flickering light, the aching void left by her lost family was more bearable.

For the first time, she was living apart from Katya and Nadya. She missed them sorely. And about Sasha and Evgenia, she dared not think. Instead, she threw herself into the collective effort to keep the radio going. It was the city's pulse, its ticking metronome sounding in loudspeakers set up in streets and apartments and offices. For many, it was a lifeline. Maintaining it, in turn, sustained those who lived at Radio House.

And then, on an especially cold day, the power failed. People from all over Leningrad appeared, asking when the station would be back on the air.

"Look here," said an old man tottering in, cane in each hand, "If something is needed, if it is a matter of courage – or even if it is a matter of cutting the ration. But let the radio speak! Without that, life is too terrible – like lying in the grave."

Lisya nodded, and offered him some tea. He accepted gratefully, but refused to leave until broadcasting resumed.

As he finally waved goodbye, the metronome once again ticking, Lisya felt a surge of hope. Maybe Spring would return, after all.

Ж Ж Ж

Katya sat huddled at a makeshift plank table, bundled in heavy clothes, trying to write by the light of a flickering candle stub, pausing often to warm the near-freezing ink with her breath. Behind her, Nadya lay despondently on a small cot. After the fire, they had moved to Bomb Shelter No.3 of the Hermitage. In the subterranean chambers of the great museum, they joined two thousand people, working and studying, living and dying under low ceilings and amidst row after row of cots.

A splotch of ink dropped on the paper Katya had been laboring over for the past two hours. Trying to blot it up with cold hands, she accidentally smeared it with her cut-off mitten. Irritably she threw down her pen. If only her mother were here! She would know what to do – especially about Nadya.

Katya had moved several of the books and notebooks from her office down to the shelter. But it was difficult to concentrate. She was acutely aware of Nadya's presence, and could feel the girl's eyes staring at her back. Finally she turned to meet them.

"Would you like to see what I'm doing here?" she asked, clearing her throat uncomfortably.

Nadya hesitated, then sat up slowly.

"I'm writing about some Russian artists who called themselves 'The Wanderers'."

"Why?"

"Well, so when people come to see their paintings, they will know who they were."

"No – I mean why did they call themselves Wanderers?"

"Because they traveled around Russia and made paintings of all the suffering they saw," replied Katya, pleased at Nadya's interest. "Before the Revolution, I mean."

"Was one of them a big picture of some men pulling a barge up the Volga?" asked Nadya, after an awkward pause.

"Why – yes," answered Katya, surprised. "How did you know?"

"Babushka brought me to see it."

"Oh." Katya looked away, not knowing what to do with the pain that flashed through her.

Nadya lay back down on her cot. Katya turned back to her desk, pretending to concentrate on the paper. The words blurred and seemed to run off in different directions.

They were all on the minimum ration of 125 grams of bread a day. To this was added a modest glob of jelly, made out of the museum's large supply of paste and the linseed oil intended for painting the galleries of the Russian Art exhibit. Katya remembered the bureaucratic wrangles which had so concerned her before the invasion, and wondered ironically how many lives would be saved because the painters had been delayed.

Despite painful rheumatism, Orbeli made a daily inspection tour of the Hermitage. Soon after she had taken up residence, Katya walked with him through all the mostly empty halls. The windows were broken, some covered with plywood; the walls were coated with ice. Mirrors reflected Orbeli's stooped figure, clad in peasant jacket and fur hat. Catching a glimpse of her own reflection, Katya did not recognize herself.

With most of the art gone or packed away, Katya was more conscious of the building itself. Though wounded and in massive disarray, the beauty of the Hermitage shone undiminished, its nobility enhanced by all the suffering. Katya was comforted by its familiarity and heartened by its enduring grandeur.

One evening, the chief architect invited Katya and some other colleagues to his corner in Bomb Shelter No. 3, where he had arranged an exhibit of sketches he had made of the Hermitage that winter. Katya and the other guests crowded around the bed and table on which the drawings were laid, and examined them by the light of three altar candles.

"Here is the domed roof of Bomb Shelter No.2 under the Hall of Twenty Columns," the architect pointed out. "And here is the frozen Neva seen from one of the windows – broken, of course."

"This one looks like Bomb Shelter No.5 under the Egyptian Hall," said Katya, indicating one of the other small drawings.

"Yes, it is," said the architect, pleased that she had identified it.

"And here is a smashed interior wall near my office upstairs. I recognize what's left of it." Katya frowned.

"You're wondering why I would want to draw all this destruction?"

"Well – not exactly. To transform such scenes into something of beauty – which you have done here – that is important for artists to do. But…"

"But shouldn't we also provide visions of hope?" The architect completed her thought. "Yes, of course. And that is why I'm now drafting plans for an Arch of Triumph. It will welcome our troops when they liberate Leningrad!"

Admiring his spirit, Katya returned to her desk and tried to concentrate on her own work. Sometimes she was almost able to lose herself in the candle-lit words of books and papers. Page by page, she kept the giant tear at bay. Doggedly she told herself that working was important. But what had so absorbed her a year ago, now no longer seemed a sufficient reason for being. Her depression deepened.

Some weeks after the architect's exhibit, as Katya slept fitfully in her small corner of the bomb shelter, she heard muffled sobs from the next cot. She tried to block out the sound, as she had on so many nights before. Tonight, however, it would not leave her be. The desperate sobbing drilled away at her head, slowly seeped in, and started echoing inside. Finally, Katya got up and sat down awkwardly on the edge of Nadya's cot. Hesitantly, she reached out and tentatively stroked the girl's tousled hair. Nadya's heaving shoulders paused uncertainly. Suddenly she sat up and fell into her mother's arms. Gently rocking her, Katya felt the sobs eventually subside. And as she dried Nadya's tears, she knew that her daughter – at last – needed her.

Ж Ж Ж

"Tell me more about your father," asked Nadya, as they lay in darkness on their cots.

"I was younger than you when he went away," began Katya. "But I remember him very clearly."

"What was he like?"

"Well – in most ways, he wasn't much like *your* father."

"No one is like *my* father," said Nadya, a smile in her voice.

"Yes, I know." Katya smiled, too. "My father was much more dignified, and very serious. Grandmere always called him Alexander Pavlovich."

"No, really?!" Nadya giggled – just a little. "I can't imagine you calling Dad 'Alexei Sergevich.'"

"Neither can I." Katya – almost – giggled, too. "But sometimes, around me, Papa forgot to be serious. He used to make up silly stories and we would laugh and laugh about nothing at all."

"He sounds nice."

"He was," Katya smiled again, remembering. "I'm sorry you never met him. But you should be proud to be his granddaughter. He was a very dedicated doctor, and he helped many people."

"When he went away," said Nadya, hesitating, "Did you miss him a lot?"

"Yes, of course," replied Katya, also hesitating. "I didn't understand why he had to go off to war."

"And why did her?" asked Nadya, after a long pause.

"Mother said it was to do his duty as a doctor."

Neither of them spoke for awhile.

"Did Dad go to do his duty as a writer?" asked Nadya finally.

"No," said Katya quietly. "He went to do his duty as a man."

"Aren't there other ways for men to do their duty?"

"Yes, of course." Katya's voice was tinged with anger. "But not in Russia. War always seems to get in the way."

More silence, to which both of them had, by now, become accustomed.

"How did you feel when he didn't come back?" asked Nadya, just before she fell asleep.

"I was sad," replied Katya "But not as sad as Grandmere was."

Touching the gold band Alexei had given her, she felt the embossed hands reassuringly clasped. But the ring itself no longer fit, and was disturbingly loose on her finger.

Ж   Ж   Ж

Slowly, slowly, the nights grew shorter. As the sun hesitantly began to penetrate the gloom, Katya started to lose her dread of leaving the dark womb of the Hermitage. And as the sun gained courage, so did she. And when, at last, it became warmer outside than down in the bowels of the Hermitage, she emerged to take a walk.

From force of habit, she took her customary route to the breadline. At a frequently crossed intersection, she looked up at a familiar building. Suddenly, a winter memory flashed before her. Shuddering, Katya remembered a young woman's body falling from an upper window. The corpse had sprawled on the sidewalk for several days until it had finally disappeared.

Green buds were on the trees, she reminded herself quickly. She looked down to watch the snow thankfully running off in rivulets from the path she had trod for months. And there, right under her feet, was a woman's hand, reaching up from beneath the dirty ice.

The whole city was choked with filth. Lunchrooms and cafeterias were so dirty they defied imagination; dishes and tableware had not been washed for months. People were even dirtier. There had been no running water – no baths, showers or laundries – in the city since the end of December. Worst of all were the mountains of corpses everywhere.

Cleaning up started on International Women's Day. Thousands of women, spades and shovels in hand, tackled the filthy streets. Katya was among them. The City Council ordered all able-bodied Leningraders into the streets. Posters went up and radios blared the appeal. Hundreds of thousands of old men, women and children, all weak and feeble, answered the call and removed tons of unimaginably awful garbage. By the end of the month, Katya had her calluses back.

Meanwhile, most of Leningrad had been inoculated against typhus, typhoid and plague. Food dispensaries were cleaned up and public baths opened. Hundreds of disinfecting stations and several quarantine units were set up. The few outbreaks of contagious disease were isolated and contained. No major epidemics swept Leningrad that spring.

Scurvy, however, was universal. A science professor at the University devised a process for extracting Vitamin C from pine needles, which Nadya and her classmates went out to the forests to gather. Buckets of the strange tasting brew were distributed to all schools and offices and factories. Citizens were urged to drink as much of it as they could stand.

As the ice thawed and some semblance of health returned, so did other things. After the broadcast one evening at Radio House, a group formed around a poet just returned from Moscow on one of the infrequent transport planes which dodged Nazi fire. Lisya listened eagerly to his news and stories from the outside world. He even told a joke. A bad one, about Hitler.

After the punch line, there was silence. Then the face of the woman sitting across from Lisya began to quiver awkwardly. The old man next to her emitted a few strange-sounding rumbles. Lisya herself felt the corners of her mouth begin to twitch into an unaccustomed shape. After a moment of alarm, she relaxed just long enough for a small smile to escape. As she looked around at the other thawing faces, she realized with a shock how long it had been since she had seen anyone smile.

For Katya, the thaw started when the tramcars did. Walking down the Nevsky, she heard the sound of streetcar bells. At first she thought her ears were ringing. But as the clatter of the car over the rails grew louder, something she had not felt all these long cold months started to flutter feebly. She looked up and saw a moving tramcar off in the distance. She stopped and stared at the sparks bursting out at the crossings. As the streetcar approached, the fluttering inside grew stronger. Nearer and nearer, the tramcar came like a triumphal chariot. People were running after it, cheering. All around her, tears streamed down faces. As the procession passed, Katya recognized the feeling stirring within. Cautiously she saluted hope, a once familiar friend, and allowed a tiny drop of the giant tear to carefully descend.

Ж   Ж   Ж

There were no parades, no demonstrations, no bands. Instead, a May Day proclamation announced extra rations – meat, cereal, dried peas, herring, sugar, even vodka and beer – brought in across the Lake Ladoga ice road, just before it melted. Best of all, it was a beautiful sunny day, with a hint of summer in the air. Women in army overcoats and workers' boots carried little bunches of marigolds and violets and dandelions, letting the healing sun strike deep into their thin bodies and wasted arms.

The Germans, however, decided to celebrate May Day properly. The shelling was exceptionally heavy, and there were many casualties.

The next day, Lisya took Katya and Nadya to the Summer Gardens. The City Council had divided the park into vegetable plots, offered to anyone willing to tend them.

"We're really going to have a garden?!" Nadya was delighted to be outside.

"And we're going to make it grow!" Katya was relieved to see Nadya smiling.

"Grandmere, I didn't know you were a gardener!" chirped Nadya, enthusiastically. "How did you learn how to do this?"

"Babushka taught her," answered Katya, "when they lived in Derevnia."

Lisya smiled at Katya's unintentional irony. She had never told her how much she had hated gardening as a girl. But now, from far back in her mind, she heard Evgenia – and Old Ekaterina – telling her exactly what to do. And then heard herself repeating to Katya and Nadya what had somehow lodged in her memory.

After so much death and destruction, all three of them welcomed the chance to make something grow. To Lisya's relief, Katya made the cucumbers her specialty. Nadya became guardian of the carrots. Lisya herself even began to take pride in her cabbages. And she was surprised at the comfort she derived from work she had forsworn decades ago. Digging into the earth, her hands did not recoil from the warm mud; the fat wriggling worms and shiny burrowing bugs no longer repulsed her.

Mother, daughter and grandmother met among the vegetables whenever they could. And sometimes, in their little garden, they felt almost like a family again.

Leaning against the tree at the edge of their garden, Lisya watched Nadya finish weeding the carrots. *How much she reminds me of Tatiana! Even with all those wild curls.* She smiled, letting Tatiana's memory warm her. Only with Nadya could she allow herself to do so.

"You are so like her!" said Lisya, when Nadya sat down next to her.

"Your sister?"

"She was my best friend, too."

"She went away a long time ago, didn't she?"

"Before the last war – long before you were born."

"Mother told me she was a dancer at the Maryinsky – back when you played in the orchestra there."

"Those were very happy times," sighed Lisya.

"Do you still miss her? Even after all this time?"

"When someone you love goes away, it never stops hurting." Lisya put her arm around Nadya. "But it doesn't hurt so much when I'm with you."

"Because I'm like her?"

"Yes, and because I can talk to you like I did to her."

"Mother said maybe she's still alive – in America."

"I hope so."

"I wonder if she has a granddaughter, too?"

"I know she had a daughter – before we lost contact."

"So maybe I have an American cousin?" Nadya was excited.

"I hope so."

"Maybe someday I can meet her!"

"How do you know it's a 'her'?" smiled Lisya.

"Because I just do." Nadya's laugh was a shimmering cascade of sunlight – so like Tatiana's.

"Maybe someday you'll be able to find her."

"I'll try, Grandmere," promised Nadya. "I'll try."

A few days later, Lisya was leaning against the same tree, watching Katya finish weeding the cucumbers. *How much she reminds me of Alexander Pavlovich! And of myself, before the war.*

"Sometimes you are so like him," said Lisya, when Katya sat down next to her.

"You mean Papa?"

"You have his eyes." Lisya allowed the memory of Alexander Pavlovich to warm her. "And his determination."

"It must have been hard for you back then – when we lost him."

"Yes, it was," sighed Lisya. "It felt like my whole life had been ripped apart."

"How did you bear it?" Katya's voice was unsteady.

"I had you."

"I don't think I could standing losing Alexei." Nervously twisting her wedding ring, Katya noticed that it no longer turned on her finger quite so loosely.

"You'd survive," said Lisya gently, "because you have Nadya."

Neither of them dared think of Sasha.

"Why do men think they must be heroes?" Katya's voice had an angry edge.

"I don't think your father was trying to be a hero," replied Lisya, remembering when she herself had asked the same question. "I think he was just trying to be true to his principles."

"Doing his duty?"

"Yes, something like that."

"That's what I told Nadya, when she asked about *her* father." Katya hesitated. "But I don't think I believe it myself."

"I don't think Alexei is trying to be a hero," said Lisya, treading very carefully. "I think he's seeking forgiveness."

"For what?!" snapped Katya, and turned away.

Lisya waited for Katya to break the silence.

"Is that what – Dmitri – was looking for?" This time it was Katya treading carefully.

"Maybe," said Lisya, "Or perhaps he just had to end his pain."

"Why did he hurt so much?"

"I was never really sure." Lisya shook her head sadly. "Which is why I could never talk to you about it."

"I had a hard time dealing with his disappearance. In some ways, even more than when we lost Papa."

"I'm sorry. But I didn't know how to explain to you what I didn't understand myself."

"Talking to Alexei about it helped a lot.

"Is that when the two of you became such good friends?"

"Yes. It was." Katya smiled, gently caressing the clasped hands on her ring. "We could always tell each other everything. Until –"

Katya again looked away, and was silent.

"Whatever it is that Alexei is searching for," said Lisya finally, putting her arm around her daughter, "he is trying to be true to himself."

"But what if he never comes back?!"

"I pray that he will," replied Lisya evenly, "And even more, I pray that he will find what he is looking for."

Ж   Ж   Ж

Spring also meant the Nazis were on the move. Soviet armies fell back toward the Volga. Once more the German Wehrmacht was on the offensive, and again the Red Army was retreating. There were ominous signs of a new thrust at Leningrad.

Lisya and Katya and Nadya cultivated their garden, as did many other Leningraders that summer. As the Nazis gathered force, the cabbages burgeoned and spread throughout the city, winding about the palaces and cathedrals and monuments. Amid frequent and prolonged shelling, the cabbages marched across the Champs de Mars and through parks of venerable old trees which – even during the worst of the freezing dark winter – no one had chopped down. Cabbages even manned the front lines, tended by soldiers among the trenches. Soon, every dug-out had pickled and stored barrels of them.

If it came to that, they would be ready next winter.

Ж   Ж   Ж

Lisya read the announcement about the new orchestra on the evening broadcast. On the designated day, she arrived early with her violin. So did about thirty other musicians – less than she had hoped, more than she had expected. The first rehearsal was short.

At the next rehearsal, the director proposed that they perform Shostakovich's new symphony – dedicated, as promised, to Leningrad. Lisya was enthusiastic, as were the others. But the score called for a very large orchestra; where would they find enough musicians?

The director appealed to the Party, and to the Leningrad military command. Enough army musicians were given temporary leave to fill out the orchestra.

After several weeks of rehearsal, Shostakovich's *Leningrad Symphony* premiered in the city which had inspired it. From the first quiet downbeat, through the four long agonized movements, until the exhausted triumph of the final chords, audience and orchestra were as one. It was as if the performers were reading in the dark pages of the music a living chronicle of themselves and those listening.

As Lisya played, the events of the last year passed before her. Poignantly nostalgic tones reminding her of gentler days gave way to the relentlessly martial cadence of invasion. Grotesque cascades of bombs and obscene blasts of sirens descended upon the raging discord of battle, until the will of Leningrad rose up to push it back. Off in the distance the war machine marched on, in counterpoint to the long bleak winter of famine. The low, slow notes plunged into anguished grief and sorrow too deep for tears. But under all the pain and agony and despair, a granite-like strength throbbed stubbornly.

The final movement of the Symphony foretold fighting and dying and suffering and overcoming, again and again and again. As Lisya's violin groaned and sobbed, she knew the battle would rage on. But her people would endure, as they had so many times before. Through determined sacrifice and dogged heroism, they would outlast the Germans, no matter how long it took. Someday, she knew, her city would rise again from the ashes and the rubble and the death. And she vowed that she would be there to witness it.

Chapter 25:   LETTERS

"The Post Office is bursting," said the leader of the Youth Brigade. "Mail hasn't been delivered for months. Who will volunteer?"

Nadya immediately raised her hand.

She soon discovered that delivering letters was not an easy job. Many of the addresses no longer existed. Worse yet, neither did most of the addressees. Still, she trudged patiently among the rubble to those buildings relatively intact, carrying a large mail sack filled with envelopes that looked almost as exhausted as Leningrad itself.

At the end of her first day, she climbed the stairs of an apparently deserted building and knocked on the door of an apartment. It opened slowly into a room full of people sitting motionless around their kitchen table. Nervously, Nadya held out a letter to the person nearest the door. The old woman – who rather resembled Evgenia – stared through her with blank eyes. Slowly, Nadya edged the letter under one of the wrinkled hands resting stiffly on the table and backed out of the door. Then she bolted down the steps into the street and ran back to the Post Office. It was closed. Taking off the mail pouch, she sat down in front of the locked entrance, tears rolling down her cheeks.

The next day, however, she returned to the Post Office. Eventually, she discovered several letters for her family. There was one for Alexei from Vassily, who had evacuated to Cheliabinsk with the Kirov Plant, and one for Lisya from her friend, Olga the cellist, who had left Leningrad via the Lake Ladoga ice road. And Katya finally heard from Alexei, though by the time his letters from Moscow reached her they were months out of date.

All the letters were worn and ragged. On Sunday, Nadya brought them to the vegetable garden for her mother and grandmother to read aloud. With difficulty, Lisya kept her voice steady as she read the first one. It was for Evgenia – from Derevnia, her village on the Volga. Nadya had never actually been there, but Evgenia had told her so much about it that she felt as if she knew everyone there.

Usually it was Elena who wrote with news of the collective farm where they all lived; this time, however, the letter was from Vasilisa, Elena's daughter.

Dear Aunt Evgenia,

Tomorrow Father is going to Kuibyshev to find more gas for our tractor. I'll send this letter with him and hope that it finds its way to Leningrad. Mother has been worrying and wanting to write, but she's so busy with the clinic and school and the war I said I'd do it for her.

Most of the men have gone to the Front. Since my brothers are driving tanks instead of tractors, Mother and I and the rest of the women are doing the farming. The children help, too, but we try not to take them away from school unless we have to.

When the men went off to fight, they took all the trucks and tractors and horses with them. But we're luckier than most. We still have a few skinny nags and an old tractor Father refitted with a gas generator. So we didn't have to pull all the plows ourselves. Last harvest, people from the towns helped. But Father is worried that this time it won't be enough unless we get more gas for our tractor.

Since the Germans took the Ukraine, all the farms here in the Volga country have to grow more food. We planted our fallow fields this year with sugar beets and sunflowers, and hope these new crops will be good ones.

We work from sun-up to sun-down, and sometimes through the night. But we do not complain. We know that someone must feed our soldiers and the workers who make their weapons.

Mother sends you her love. And also to Lisya and Katya and the children. We think of you often – especially on Sunday when we sing in the circle of oak trees near the river. Don't worry, Mother won't let the Germans chop them down! And neither will I.

Your loving niece,
Vasilisa

Dear Alexei,

Here we are, at last, in Cheliabinsk. I'm sorry I couldn't write sooner, so you'd know where we are and that we're safe, but there hasn't been time for anything.

As you know, my section of the Kirov Plant just barely made it out before the Germans cut the railway lines. I wish we could have said more than a hurried goodbye, but loading the diesel works was a big job and left no time for that. It took us, I don't know how many, days and nights – but I'm glad now we didn't stop to rest.

We rode in boxcars behind the machines – very crowded, no amenities, not much food – though at first we were too exhausted to notice. You can't imagine the heat and the stench – and we were delayed a lot at railroad junctions. Factories from all over Belorussia, Central and Eastern Ukraine were being evacuated, too, so there were bottlenecks which took days to unjam.

Most of us made it here alive. We were fortunate to be routed to the Urals rather than Siberia. We were also fortunate to be merged with the Cheliabinsk Tractor Plant, rather than dumped in the middle of nowhere in Kazakhstan. The Kharkov Diesel Works has joined us, too, and together we're all making tanks. Around here, they call us "Tankograd."

But first we had to build something to put the machines in. People here turned out with shovels and pickaxes to help. All day and night, women and old men and even children hacked at the earth, laying the foundations. Blizzards raged as the walls went up, but before the roof was on, the machines were back in operation.

We all put in 15-hour days now, and walk several miles to and from work. Building supplies were used up on the factories, so living quarters nearer the Plant aren't likely for awhile. Housing in general is terribly overcrowded, and sometimes there isn't really enough to eat. But none of us are starving, and there's not much grumbling. We all know how urgently our work is needed. And now we know who the Enemy is.

At first, dear brother, I felt terribly guilty not staying with you at the Front. But the longer I'm here, the greater my conviction that this is where I can best fight the Germans – and perhaps, too, the ghosts who haunt my dreams. And believe me, we are fighting quite a battle here! What with the labor shortage, about half as many of us are doing twice as much work. And since we lost most of our coal when the Germans overran the Donbas, several new mines are being sunk here in the Urals. Likewise, new molybdenum and manganese mines in Kazakhstan. We're also converting some of our blast and open hearth furnaces to replace the high grade steel lost with the Ukraine. Given the climate and terrain, these projects would have seemed impossible in peacetime. But now we have no choice. We must do the impossible.

We know there isn't enough of anything at the Front right now, especially weapons and ammunition. For a while, I'm afraid, things will probably get worse before they get better. But everyday I see and hear of countless instances of self-sacrifice, of people going beyond the limit again and again, so that our troops can get what they need to drive out the Germans. How different it all is from the last war! This time, we won't fall apart.

Alexei, I'm so proud of our People! And so proud to be one of them! Somehow we have transplanted our factories thousands of miles, and gotten them going again in just months. Surely this is proof that our System works! And surely all that we've had to do in building it is now being justified. Despite constant fatigue, I feel alive as never before, as though a great weight has been lifted. Someday, when this is over, we will drink toasts to these days – and talk all night about things too long unsaid.

Meanwhile, dear little brother, tell your comrades to have faith. We will not fail you!
>   Yours,
>   Vassily

Dear Lisya,

Finally we are in Gorky. I'm writing to let you know that most of us made it here. And also to let you know what we had to go through, in case you are considering leaving Leningrad over the ice road. A *Pravda* correspondent I met on the train is returning to Zhikharevo tomorrow, and promised to give this letter to one of the Ladoga truck drivers. I hope it reaches you.

The morning we left, we went early to the evacuation center – though not early enough to get a seat in one of the heated buses. We ended up in a truck with a canvas top and an open end. But it could have been worse. Many of the trucks were completely open to the wind; I even saw people clinging to the outside of gasoline tank trucks.

The radiator of our truck needed water. The Griboyedev Canal was frozen solid, so we had to detour to the Fontanka. The convoy moved slowly, though, so we caught up outside the city. The road to the lake was very narrow, with hardly room to pass. Some of the trucks got off the ruts and landed upside down in ditches. And there were a few traffic tie-ups before we reached Borisova Griva.

At the railroad station, it was like a giant conveyor belt – hundreds of trucks unloading thousands of boxes of food, and then turning around to go back across Lake Ladoga. We waited a few hours at Borisova Griva until the traffic untangled.

On the frozen lake we joined endless columns of trucks. The road is wide enough to pass, so everyone goes full speed. On either side are high snow walls thrown up by snow scrapers. Traffic officers camouflaged in white stand at each kilometer, shielded from the wind by half shelters of ice blocks, some with fires inside. At greater intervals are repair shops and white camouflaged anti-aircraft posts. And here and there, half covered with ice and snow, lie the carcasses of burned trucks, unable to dodge the Nazi strafing and shelling.

Sometimes our truck had to detour around cracks in the ice. And all the way across, the north wind blew relentlessly – the driver said it was 40 below. We were lucky not to stall and freeze to death.

By the time we reached the opposite shore, it was dark and the truck's radiator was steaming. No one seemed to know where to go, where the train was, or when it would leave. So we spent the night in the truck. By morning my poor niece – already weak with dysentery – could scarcely move, and Mother's feet were so swollen she could hardly walk, but somehow we found the train. It was very crowded, so we had to sit on our suitcases.

The train moved slowly and stopped occasionally. Each time, someone would knock on the door with a hammer: "Any dead? Throw them out here!" But at some of the stations there was food – real soup and cereal! We overate, at first, and our poor shrunken stomachs rebelled.

After four days on the train, Mother finally collapsed. I couldn't get her to a hospital in time, but we got off at Cherepovets to give her a decent burial. Alas, it was impossible, so I just had to leave her on a pile of corpses at the cemetery gates.

It wasn't easy to get us back on a train, but a soldier on a hospital train finally took pity and let us on. The train eventually took us to Gorky.

When you left, during the last war, was it so difficult? I remember how hard it was to stay, but I understand now why you decided not to leave this time. I still mourn Mother and wonder if I did right to move her, weak as she was. But for Marina, I think, it was best. As for me, I feel rather like a deserter. I pray that this war will soon be over, so that we may all come home.

Give my love to your family. I still regard them as part of my own, and think often of all we have been through together. And thank you for keeping watch over my cello.

> Your friend,
> Olga

Dearest Katya,

I greet you from the Moscow Front. I've scarcely had time to sleep, let alone write letters. Today – in honor of the Revolution – we have a few hours off. Also because the Germans have slowed down – temporarily. Losses have been heavy on both sides, but for the past week, they've made little progress. The prisoners we've captured blame it on the rain and the mud, but we have to put up with the bad weather, too.

Our Army is putting up a stubborn defense against the Nazis, fighting to the last man. I've seen soldiers – and even Volunteer Battalions – attacking German tanks with nothing but hand grenades and Molotov cocktails.

This morning we were in Red Square. Guns were booming and fighter planes patrolling overhead. "Comrades of the Red Army and Navy, workers and partisans!" Comrade Stalin exhorted us. "We are celebrating the Anniversary of our revolution in very hard conditions. The enemy is at the gates of Moscow and Leningrad."

"But Russia has survived worse than this. And this time, the whole world is looking to us to destroy the German robber hordes! The enslaved peoples of Europe are looking upon us as their liberators. We must be worthy of this great mission! The war we are waging is a war of liberation, a just war. May we be inspired by our heroic ancestors – and be blest by great Lenin's victorious banner!"

"Death to the German invaders!" shouted Comrade Stalin. "Long live our glorious country, its freedom and independence! Onward to victory!"

I yelled until I was hoarse.

Comrade Stalin is right; this *is* a war of liberation – but not just from the Germans. And whatever the sacrifice, we *must* win.

It has been a long time, my dearest, since I've slept more than an hour. The pen is falling from my fingers. My love to Grandmere and Babushka. Kiss the children. I embrace you in my dreams.

Wait for me. Please
   All my love,
   Alexei

My darling Katya,

As I sit here tonight in the trenches, waiting to welcome the New year, I think about what a dark year this has been for our Motherland. The Baltic Republics – gone! The Ukraine – gone! The Donbas and the Crimea – gone! Kharkov and Kiev – gone! But if we can just hold on, I know that victory will be ours – someday.

Because despite everything, we are learning from our mistakes. Our officers are coming up the hard way; the incompetent and inept don't last. All that's holding us back now is the shortage of weapons. But until we get what we need, we must fight on with little more than raw courage.

As we recapture areas occupied by the Germans, we are seeing very clearly what they have in mind for our people. Everywhere they are robbing and looting and raping and killing – wanton destruction and brutality beyond belief! The swine have insulted our people and defiled our land! I am filled with such anger and hatred I am sometimes overwhelmed.

At such moments, I think of you. You are my anchor, my link to sanity in the midst of all this madness.

Wait for me, dearest Katya. Please.

Your loving husband,

Alexei

Ж   Ж   Ж

Every night, just before she lay down on her narrow cot in the deep caverns of the Hermitage, Katya reread Alexei's letters. Sometimes she was able to conjure up memories of happier times – before he had left, before the war, before the angry silence she dared not name. Then dreams of Alexei's arms around her would sometimes give her a few hours of blissful sleep. Usually, though, worry and anger churned in anguished turmoil which tore at her heart. She knew she could not allow herself to think about why she was so angry; but at night, she was often visited by fearful nightmares.

Finally, more than a year after his departure for the Front, Katya received another letter from Alexei.

Dearest Katya,

I write you from Stalingrad, on the eve of what we hope is the beginning of the end of this horrible war. General von Paulus has been given an ultimatum – surrender or annihilation. We are waiting for his answer. No one expects him to surrender, so we are preparing our last attack on the encircled Germans. It will be the first step toward Berlin.

It's ironic to think of the Germans under siege, freezing and eating their horses. I think of Leningrad and feel no pity.

It's been a long, agonizingly hard battle. When I transferred to this Front last July, the main fighting was inside the Don Bend. Despite stubborn – often ferocious – resistance, we were slowly pushed back across the Don to Stalingrad.

I was assigned to General Chuikov's command. He is tough, courageous, a fine officer. He has a good sense of humor and a loud laugh. His teeth are all crowned in gold and when he smiles they glitter.

The Germans were advancing on Stalingrad from all directions. We had no tanks and no aircraft; one of our major ammunition dumps was blown up by a German bomber. Supplies were short, and reinforcements blocked except from across the bombarded river.

"We shall either hold the city," announced General Chuikov, "or die here." And he meant it. Fighting was bloody, often hand-to-hand. Mamai Hill and the Central Railway Station changed hands I don't know how many times. General Rodimtsev's 13th Division was bled white, having stood firm to the last. Likewise, the 1st Battalion of Colonel Yelin's regiment. And countless others, buried beneath the rubble of what was once Stalingrad.

The Germans crashed ahead. Whole columns of tanks and motorized infantry broke into the center of the city. Convinced that the fate of Stalingrad was sealed, drunken Nazis jumped off trucks, playing mouth organs, bellowing and dancing on the pavements. But we clung to a few strips of the city, our backs against the Volga, and fought on.

Fierce fighting raged over every inch of territory, every heap of rubble. The Germans, supported by aircraft and tanks, usually attacked during the day. The night, however, was ours. And Chuikov, observing that the Germans weren't good at precision bombing, ordered close combat. The no-man's land never exceeded the distance of a hand grenade's throw, which kept our front lines more or less immune from air attack.

We knew the Germans were preparing an all-out offensive. I heard German soldiers shouting from their trenches: "*Russki*, you'll soon be blowing bubbles in the Volga." For a few days there was a relative lull, and then all hell broke loose.

They bombed and stormed our troops without a moment's respite. German guns and mortars rained shells and bombs on us from morning till night. We could barely see through all the smoke and soot; separate shots and explosions became an unending, deafening roar. Our dug-outs were shaking and crumbling like so many houses of cards. Anything made of glass shattered into a thousand pieces.

Our losses were very heavy. In just two days' fighting, Zholudev and Gorishnyi lost most of their troops. And Zholudev's men, in particular, were really tough – all of them young and tall and strong, with knives and daggers stuck in their belts. They went in for bayonet charges, and would throw dead Nazis over their shoulders like sacks of straw. "We shall never surrender!" they cried as they were encircled. And they didn't.

But we knew a counter-offensive was coming. Comrade Stalin's speech at the 25th Anniversary of the Revolution had promised that soon there would be a "holiday in our streets." A few weeks later, we heard the sound of distant gunfire. We knew what it meant! Our joy – and relief – was indescribable! A few days later, we learned that Russian troops from the northwest and south had closed the ring around the Germans in Stalingrad.

The ferocious fighting continues – hand-to-hand, house-to-house. Only now *we* are on the offensive. It has made all the difference, even though just as many die. Our men are fueled by intense hatred of the Germans; they now face situations which would have thrown them into retreat a year ago. And for the first time, the Germans are showing signs of confusion. Many beyond the encirclement are retreating in disorder, abandoning enormous masses of equipment. They make an easy target for our aircraft. The prisoners we've captured sing a different tune, too. They are disillusioned, have lost their self-assurance, are stunned – unable to understand what the devil is happening. Now they know they're not invulnerable. And now we know it, too!

Our generals have offered the starving Germans in Stalingrad a chance to surrender on far more generous and humane terms than if the shoe were on the other foot. We are all waiting. Since presenting the ultimatum, there has been a truce of sorts. No guns have been fired on either side. I've even seen a few Russians venture across no-man's land, urging the German soldiers to lay down their arms. Everyone on both sides, however, seems to think that Hitler will not hear of surrender. Alas, probably true.

Last week, on New Year's Eve, I thought about how far we've come in a year – and what a price we've had to pay. There are many reasons for the turn-around, not least of which is that we are finally getting enough equipment. And all of it is Soviet made.

Despite the freezing cold and all the other difficulties, despite even all the death and suffering, I am proud to be here. We all are. It's as though our whole generation has resolved to sacrifice itself. So that our People may survive? In expiation of our fathers' crimes? I don't know, but sitting here, waiting for the fighting to begin again, I feel strangely cleansed and at peace with myself.

It's all right now, Katya. Really, it is. What happened back then, what came between us – between everyone – is being wiped clean – here at Stalingrad, back in Leningrad, all over the Motherland. So remember those we had to forget, and forgive them all.

And forgive me! But wait for me, dearest Katya. Please wait for me.

Your devoted husband,

Alexei

485

The radio had just broadcast the final report of the Stalingrad command: "The troops of the Don Front at 4 PM on February 2, 1943, completed the destruction of the encircled group of enemy forces in Stalingrad. 22 divisions have been destroyed or taken prisoner. Military operations in the city and area of Stalingrad have ceased."

No one cheered. But for the first time since the war began, everyone knew that victory would come – someday.

But there were no more letters from Alexei.

Chapter 26: ENDURANCE

It was almost 11 PM. Fierce fighting had been raging for days, ever since the counterattack. Everyone was waiting anxiously. And then, finally, came the long expected news.

"The blockade has been broken!" declared the radio jubilantly.

At Radio House, everyone cheered.

Lisya threw her arms around the man standing next to her. The woman on the other side kissed both her cheeks. Someone turned on music – joyous, victorious, triumphant music. And dozens of writers and poets lined up at the microphone to read speeches and poems they had written long ago for such a day.

Lisya could not hear most of what they said over the blaring music, but she did not care. No one did. Relief was all over all their faces. To express it after so much anguished waiting was enough. The words themselves did not matter. The radio stayed on the air until everyone who wanted to speak had their chance.

Around 3 AM, a lone bottle of champagne miraculously appeared and was passed around. As Lisya swallowed her allotted mouthful, she remembered other occasions on which she had so celebrated. Faces from her past appeared in her mind's eye. All were welcomed in the joy of the moment.

At the Hermitage, meanwhile, Katya and Nadya climbed out of their subterranean shelter and ventured into Palace Square.

"Mother, look! It must be true!" exclaimed Nadya. "The blockade is broken!"

Katya threw her arms around her daughter, and did not let go.

All around them, people were waving flags and kissing each other. Soldiers started dancing across the Square. Others took hold and followed; soon a long line was snaking around the monument in the center.

Nadya grabbed her mother's hand and pulled her into the singing crowd. As they danced through the streets, Katya remembered other occasions on which she had so celebrated. Resolutely she pushed the memories aside. But she held on to her daughter's hand, and did not let anyone wrench them apart.

A few weeks later, a special ceremony was held at the mangled Finland Station. At 10:09 AM, a locomotive pulling two passenger carriages and a string of freight cars chuffed into the station. It had come from the new line connecting Leningrad with the "mainland." On a platform decorated with red flags, a band struck up and the crowd cheered. The Mayor spoke and so did the Party Secretary. Just before noon, the train dispatcher shouted: "Train No. 719, Leningrad-Volkhovstroi, is ready to depart!"

And so it did, by an indirect and roundabout way, over temporary bridges and running a murderous corridor of Nazi artillery fire. For though the Germans had been pushed back, they still sat on Leningrad's doorstep. A hole had been punched in the ring, but the city knew its tenuous connection with the rest of Russia could be broken at any moment.

Despite the victory at Stalingrad, most of the western territory was still occupied by the Germans. Allied operations were moving ahead in Africa, but there was still no second front in Europe. Supplies from the United States were, as yet, only a trickle. The tide was slowly turning against Hitler, but this was barely evident to besieged Leningrad. And the Germans, to compensate for being driven back a few miles, shelled the city more savagely than ever.

After the first joy of piercing the blockade, the people of Leningrad once again settled down to wait.

Ж   Ж   Ж

Shortly after the blockade was broken, Katya reclaimed her old office at the Hermitage. She soon began spending as much time there as the renewed shelling would allow.

One morning, emerging from Bomb Shelter No.3, she found an official-looking envelope on her desk. Without picking it up, she noted that it was from the government. She had seen such envelopes before. They appeared frequently these days; what was inside always ended up clutched tearfully in despairing hands.

Katya sat down slowly and stared at the envelope for a long time.

Finally, she grabbed it and ripped it open. With trembling hands, she unfolded the letter. The words "hero" and "sacrifice" and "for the Motherland" leaped out, blurred by her tears.

Resolutely, she wiped them away. No. It was not possible. There had been a mistake. Someday Alexei would come home. She would wait for him. Just as he had begged her to, just as she had promised. And as long as she waited, he would still live.

Katya looked at the wedding band Alexei had given her on their last night together. The golden hands were still firmly united. Covering the ring protectively, she pressed it to her heart.

Then she hastily stuffed the letter back into its envelope and buried it in a back corner of the bottom drawer of her desk.

After that, she came to her office less willingly. Each day, she added to the huge stack of paper building on the desk and the pile of books in front of the drawer. But each day, the avalanche of unshed tears became harder to keep at bay, the unspoken fear more difficult to dodge, the unacknowledged anger more arduous to repress. Fortunately, her work at the Hermitage took a turn that helped.

When the Germans had encircled Leningrad, they had also occupied the beautiful summer palaces surrounding the city. Turned into People's Museums long before, these relics of tsarist times had become a proud part of Leningrad's heritage. The Germans had gone out of their way to defile them.

One evening, when the shelling was especially heavy, the architects of the Hermitage called a meeting. Some of them had recently returned from reconnaissance missions to the palaces. Accompanied by partisan scouts and small Red Army squads, they had gotten close enough to survey the damage.

"I have just come from Peterhof," the leading architect announced, his voice trembling with barely controlled rage. "The Nazis have burned the great Rastrelli Palace and destroyed the park. The canal has been stripped of all its statues and the fountains broken up and buried as garbage!"

Katya and the others listened in shocked silence.

"And Samson…" the architect's voice broke, "great, golden Samson, the center of the grand cascade… Do you know what those German swine did to him? They cut him up in pieces and sent them as scrap to Germany!"

A murmur of indignation swept the assembled group.

"I was at Pushkin yesterday," one of the other architects said. "The facade of the Catherine Palace is still intact, but inside it's a ruin." His voice was quiet, but – like so many others in the city – his face had two hard little lines on each side of his mouth. "They turned part of the Palace into a barracks," the lines beside his mouth deepened, "and they violated one of the oldest linden trees outside with four big hooks. There were bodies hanging from them."

"At Pavlovsk," added another of the architects, "they cut down all the trees in the park." He burst into tears and could not continue.

At Gatchina, it was the same story – buildings and grounds purposely destroyed, at great cost and effort. "Wasn't it enough to have looted all the Palace's art treasures?" shouted the last of the reconnoitering architects. "Wasn't it enough to have turned it into a brothel?"

"They did the same thing at Tolstoy's house at Yasnaya Polyana," one of the curators chimed in, indignantly. "In the room where *War and Peace* was written, they had drunken orgies. They even defiled Tolstoy's grave!"

"And at Tchaikovsky's house," yelled one of the historians wrathfully, "they used the floor as a latrine!"

The discussion continued, growing louder and angrier with each new disclosure of German atrocities against Russian Art. Katya had never seen her usually sedate, scholarly colleagues so agitated. They were enraged almost to the point of hysteria.

"The Germans should be locked up in a giant cesspool for life," shouted a gentle janitor.

"May the blood-sucking Nazis feed only on stinking carrion and the dung of diseased pigs!" yelled a once portly Oriental Studies expert, a notorious gourmand.

A prim, elderly librarian screamed an oath she would never have allowed in the books in her keeping.

"People who deliberately destroy works of art have no right to own any," shouted Katya. "They cannot have any real love for art!" Loud applause, followed by a unanimous resolution to demand compensation in kind from German art galleries after the war.

"But first," the chief architect reminded them, "we must have some place to put what we get back. Which brings us to the purpose of this meeting. We must begin rebuilding now. From the archives of the Hermitage, we must draw up exact blueprints of these destroyed monuments. When the fighting stops, we will rebuild them exactly as they were."

A great cheer went up. Katya was swept into the excited discussion of who would do what and how. With desperate relief, she released the anger festering within, turning it loose on the Germans.

Never had she known such rage. As she worked on plans to rebuild what the Nazis had destroyed, the invasion theme from Shostakovich's Symphony hammered incessantly inside, keeping her anger white-hot. She pictured hordes of ant-like Huns swarming over the Samson fountain, packs of mangey Aryan curs urinating on Tchaikovsky's music, gangs of swinish Teutons rooting and fornicating in Tolstoy's study. She imagined herself stomping on the loathsome insects, taking a lash to the wretched dogs, castrating the disgusting pigs as they squealed in terror.

The righteousness of her wrath drove her on – toward the hope of building anew over the rubble of destruction and defilement, away from the yawning abyss of grief too searing and sorrow too heavy to bear.

And – almost – it kept Alexei's image at bay.

Ж   Ж   Ж

Katya looked at the blueprints with interest. Several of the city architects were showing their work at the Hermitage. Throughout the blockade, they had been drafting plans for the Leningrad of the future – not just for its reconstruction, but for a veritable Renaissance of the city. The city they envisioned was to combine the old grandeur of Imperial Petersburg with the new greatness of Soviet Leningrad. One of the projects was austerely classical in line, another emphasized trees and open spaces, still another showed long rows of huge buildings and giant statues of workers. All exuded unquestioned faith that a stronger, more beautiful Leningrad would emerge from the ashes of war.

Other artists, too, were busy, creating their own documentary of the war – and of what they hoped would come after. Impromptu exhibitions popped up in odd corners of the Hermitage, one of them arranged by Katya for Andrei R. After the Spring thaw, he had returned to his customary spot by the Anichkov bridge. Katya always stopped to study his work. They rarely exchanged more than a few words, but his presence had a strangely soothing effect on her.

Andrei R's exhibit had several poignant little paintings of desolate streets buried in snowdrifts and breadlines of gaunt, hungry women. Most powerful, however, were his portraits.

"The human material, these days, is so striking," he said, shrugging his shoulders, "the result is bound to be good."

Looking around the improvised gallery at faces of people eagerly viewing his work, Katya saw what he meant.

"Take our soldiers," Andrei R continued. "Usually quite an ordinary face, nothing at all heroic about the shape of the nose – but have a look at him, and he's a lion!"

"And the civilians," he went on, "some of their faces are even more wonder-

491

ful. Suffering has honed them to their true spiritual essence. Just watch people passing on the streets. Many of them are living icons."

Katya nodded as Evgenia's image rose in her mind.

After that, Andrei R was a familiar face at the Hermitage. Regularly – though not often – he showed up to sketch the people there. On most of his visits, he usually ended up drawing Katya. He said little, as did she, but she found herself looking forward to his infrequent visits.

One day she broke the silence, and asked him what he would do with all his sketches.

"Use them for a War Memorial," he answered quietly.

Noting her surprise, he elaborated in a rare moment of verboseness. "No, no, not the usual steely-eyed hero on the prancing steed. We have enough bronze horsemen charging around the city – and, I would imagine, the rest of the world. Such monuments make war seem only a glorious game. We, here in Leningrad, know better."

He paused, drawing in silence for awhile.

"My monument," he continued, "will not glorify war. It will be a tribute to the endurance of Leningrad. Not just the soldiers, but the people. Especially the women. They're the real heroes."

Katya nodded, and waited for him to go on.

"Women have no illusions about war. They know, right from the start, what it costs. Yet they do what they have to, suffering in silence, and somehow endure – more often than not, alone. And that," he concluded, finishing his speech and his sketch, "is real heroism. That is why life goes on. And that is what my War Memorial will say."

Katya thought of Evgenia, and allowed tears to trickle silently down her cheek.

Ж   Ж   Ж

All the Hermitage workers were lined up in the throne room of the Winter Palace. His awesome beard now completely grey, Orbeli presented the medals. They were inscribed "For the Defense of Leningrad" and were being given to everyone who had survived the Siege. As Orbeli solemnly pinned her medal on and kissed both her cheeks, Katya remembered how proud she had been when Nadya received hers at Komsomol Headquarters. Lisya, too, had gotten one at Radio House a few days earlier.

The Hermitage workers were visibly moved. "This little metal disk," said one of the curators quietly, "joins each of us to all of Leningrad." The rest of them nodded silently.

To mark the occasion, Katya decided to go to the Nevsky Prospekt, the one place in Leningrad with some appearance of normality. Her footsteps echoed as she walked through Palace Square. But as she turned onto the Nevsky, the scene changed. The great avenue was alive. There were crowds on both sides of the street and a great deal of traffic. There was no shelling that morning; everyone was enjoying the absence of noise, and gambling that the first shell of the next barrage would not land on them.

About half the people were soldiers. There were also many young women, some in uniform. And of course the ubiquitous old women. But despite the crowds and activity, the Nevsky was not noisy. People moved quietly, their faces solemn and their eyes strained There was no laughter. Still, compared to the rest of Leningrad, the Nevsky seemed almost festive.

One of the soldiers passing by suddenly wore Alexei's face. Katya reached out – and just as suddenly the face was that of a stranger. Abruptly, she turned at the corner and, walking toward the Anichkov Bridge, found herself at her favorite bookshop. She had not been there since before the Siege.

It was now crowded with towering stacks of books. There were several sets of Gorky and Chekhov, Dostoyevsky and Tolstoy, Pushkin and Turgenev, some first editions and autographed. There were rare little volumes of poetry, historical works, recently published prose, foreign books, even Shakespeare in Russian! Katya was almost overwhelmed by the literary riches which surrounded her. It was rather like being turned loose in a fully-stocked food store in the midst of the famine.

The euphoria passed, leaving her with a sobering realization. All of these books were second-hand. And their owners had not parted with them willingly. She picked up a worn volume of Pushkin's *Eugene Onegin* and wondered how many times its former owner had read the lyrical verses, perhaps aloud to his family – and, closing the book gently after each reading, had run his hand reverently over the cover. Suddenly the image of Evgenia's strong work-roughened hands caressing one of her beloved books, just so, flooded Katya's memory with a painfully beautiful light.

Carefully, she began sorting through the stacks of books. All afternoon she searched, until finally she found what she was looking for in a back corner of the shop: a cheaply printed, poorly bound copy of Tolstoy's *War and Peace*, worn by numerous loving readings and reverent caresses. She pressed the book to her heart, and felt warmed as she had not since her grandmother's death.

Slowly she walked up to the counter to pay for the book. The proprietor looked at it and then at her face, and charged her much less than he had paid for it. And when she left, there was a smile in his eyes for having helped a beloved book find its way home.

Every night, for the rest of the blockade, Katya read from Evgenia's book – sometimes aloud to Nadya, more often just to herself. And she remembered what Evgenia had said in those long discussions during the dark famine winter. Much of what had puzzled her then, especially about Evgenia's religious beliefs, came back to her now, clothed in the understanding of suffering and loss. It gave her strength to endure.

And endurance was what was needed as the blockade ground on and on, interminably, well into its third year. To the People of Leningrad, living on little more than nerves and raw courage for too long, it seemed their city had been under siege forever. Surviving each day took a supreme act of will.

To Katya, the siege seemed more interminable than even Tolstoy's voluminous epic. She measured the months by how many times she read *War and Peace*. It seemed to her that Napoleon had already retreated from Russia several times by the time the final counter-attack against the Germans at last began.

Chapter 27: LIBERATION

No one slept in Smolny that night, nor at Blagodatny Lane where the 42nd Army had its headquarters, nor in the mangled outskirts stretching from shell-torn Sheremetyev Park to Pulkovo and Srednyaya Rogatka. There, first divisions at forward positions waited to attack.

Leningrad awoke next morning to a thunderous artillery barrage; chandeliers swayed and plaster cracked. But everyone knew what has happening. For three years, the city had awaited this day. The shaking earth and roaring heavens were welcomed with grim joy.

Charging after the fierce barrage of artillery and bombers, Russian tanks and troops attacked across German minefields. Fighting was ferocious; the enemy yielded ground reluctantly.

Hospital staff did not eat or sleep for days, as the wounded flowed in – most of them unconscious. One soldier's foot had been blown off. Sticking his bleeding stump into an empty shell case, he had continued to fight with blood pouring over the sides. Only when he finally lost consciousness did he allow them to take him to the hospital.

After days of cruelly bloody frontal attack, the Russians captured Ligovo and Finskoya Koirovo. After that, envelopment tactics speeded the counter-offensive. Soon Pushkin was liberated. But not many prisoners were taken.

By the second week, the Germans were retreating in disorder. Their lines fell so quickly, Russian troops had difficulty keeping up. Pavlovsk, Mga, Novgorod, and Luga were retaken. After a month, the Russian offensive had cleared the entire Leningrad province of Germans – except for thousands of Nazi corpses.

On a cold night at January's end, 1944, the city of Leningrad accepted the salute of 324 cannon. Over the tall sword-point of the Admiralty, over the great dome of St. Isaac's, over the broad expanse of Palace Square, over broken buildings at Pulkovo and battered machine shops of the Kirov works and scarred battleships in the Neva, roared a shower of golden arrows and a flaming stream of red, white and blue rockets. The siege of Leningrad was finally ended.

A surreal stillness abruptly descended. Outside the city stretched a strange white lunar landscape, occasionally pierced by fantastically shaped brick fragments and abandoned siege guns. Here and there a leg or head protruded from the snow. A lonely tree stood watch nearby, raising bare shattered arms helplessly into the winter sky.

In Leningrad itself, wonderful silence reigned. As Lisya walked slowly down the Nevsky, luxuriating in the safe stillness of the short sunlight, she remembered something her mother had said during those first harrowing months of the blockade. "Soon death will be more afraid of us, than we of death."

Evgenia had been right, as she had about so many things.

Ж   Ж   Ж

For Katya the silence was excruciating.

When the hideous discord had finally ceased, the stillness was – at first – balm to her wounded, exhausted ears. After a while, however, she began to feel strangely uncomfortable. Day by day, her discomfort grew, until she finally recognized it as emptiness.

Before the war, a continuous symphony had filled her. Each activity was a different instrument in the orchestra of her life, each person had their own leitmotiv, each event had its own song. During the war, however, the music had gradually changed to noise. And then the noise had stopped. Now there was only silence.

Desperately she tried to fill the void with her work. But even the most beautiful works of art failed to stimulate anything inside her. Mutely, dead canvases mocked her and corpse-like statues leered at her. They looked no different than the rubble outside.

Finally, one day in her office, she gave in. She closed the book she had futilely been trying to read, and laid down her pen. She leaned back in her chair and listened to the silence.

She sat motionless until the sun had almost set. There was a soft knock on the door. Andrei R walked quietly in, acknowledging her silence with a look of compassion. Without a word, he laid a large drawing on her desk. Then he turned and left the room as noiselessly as he had entered. A random image of Alexei making a typically explosive entrance flitted momentarily across Katya's mind. Like Andrei R, it went as quickly and quietly as it had come.

Slowly she picked up the drawing and looked at it. A detailed sketch of a group sculpture – a trio of Leningraders mourning their dead – it was obviously

496

intended as a war memorial. Lighting a candle, she studied the drawing, focusing on the figure of a young mother – hungry, but still beautiful – holding the emaciated body of her dead child. The baby was not yet two years old, about the age Sasha had been when… Katya jumped out of her chair and began pacing around the small cage of her office.

The candle was burning low when she sat down and looked again at the drawing. Its strong lines pulled her eyes to the face of the mourning mother, indelibly engraved with a look of unutterable sadness. Somehow, Andrei R had captured the poignant tragedy of children sacrificed to war. Somehow he had gathered the collective agony of their mothers. Somehow, he had put it all on that face. And that face was hers…

"Oh, Sasha!" His memory – at last unlocked – flooded her heart. The tears which had hovered so long finally burst…

It was not until dawn that the tears were spent. Slowly lifting her head in the dim grey light, she lit another candle and picked up Andrei's drawing again, this time focusing on the second couple in the group. Another woman – prematurely old – was kneeling, the head of a dead soldier in her lap. On the woman's face was grief – and – Katya looked closer – something that looked remarkably like anger.

Why does that woman look so familiar? Katya stood up and looked out the window.

Remember those we had to forget – the words jumped, unbidden, before her eyes. Alexei had written that in his last letter, the one from Stalingrad, the one that had dared speak of what had never been acknowledged.

Remember those we had to forget… And, at last, their images rose before her. Hearty, blustering Sergei – Alexei's father. Huge, gentle Vladimir – who had been as a father to her. How she had loved him! How much they all had! And how hard it had been to blot out his memory all these years! Fearful pain tore at her as she remembered the betrayal which had ripped their family apart.

But who had betrayed whom? Had Sergei betrayed Vladimir by denouncing him? Or had Vladimir betrayed them all by becoming an Enemy of the People? As inconceivable as that seemed, the alternative was even worse. For if Vladimir was innocent, then the Party – and maybe even Comrade Stalin… No, that was unthinkable. How could a loyal comrade believe that and still keep faith with the new order! How could any patriotic citizen doubt the veracity of those who protected the Motherland against all its enemies! And how could even the most loving marriage survive all that murky doubt and angry blaming!

What came between us is being wiped clean. Alexei had written that, too, from Stalingrad. But no, no – the price was too great. Sons should not have to atone for their fathers' sins.

Katya sat down, exhausted. Breaking into a sweat, she began to tremble.

Then, from deep within, she heard a trusted voice. Wordlessly it told her what to do. Turning to her desk, she shoved away the barricade of books, and pulled open the bottom drawer. Pushing aside the letter in the official envelope, she found the icon Evgenia had given her.

Putting it on top of the desk, Katya looked at the *Virgin of Vladimir*. She knew, of course, that the legendary icon bore the stamp of Andrei Rublev, most famous of all icon painters. But other than as an art treasure, she had never really seen it before.

The copy she beheld was a rather primitive one, but it reproduced faithfully the spirit of the original. Dark and brooding, the icon exuded a quiet strength. The infant held in the Virgin's arms was a strange mixture of man and child.

As the Virgin's wise, mysterious eyes looked deep into her soul, Katya felt profoundly still. This was the silence – not of emptiness – but of peace. She closed her eyes, and let the sweet calm of forgiveness flow through her.

"Yes, my dear Alexei," she sighed, "I will wait for you." The letter in the bottom drawer would remain there. Until he came home…

The sun was bright, illuminating her office, when Katya looked at the third pair in Andrei's drawing. The living half was a person of indeterminate age and gender. The dying partner, however, was unmistakably female and very ancient. Her face was deeply furrowed and bespoke centuries of suffering. Her eyes were open, fixed on something beyond the gaze of her deeply grieving mourner.

Katya followed the old woman's eyes – back to the figure of the grief-stricken mother. Looking deeper, she noticed that even in her agony, the younger woman's body had a surprisingly determined stance. With a stubbornness almost approaching defiance, it seemed to say, "This, too, can be borne. We will endure!"

Katya placed the icon beside Andrei R's drawing, and gazed once more into the calming eyes of the Virgin. *She looks at me like Babushka did.* Katya looked again at the old woman in the sketch, studying her intently. She, too, resembled her grandmother! And from deep within, Evgenia's prayers, chanted softly before the *Virgin of Vladimir*, welled up in Katya's soul. They wound around the icon by Andrei Rublev and the drawing by Andrei R, entwining them inextricably.

Evgenia's spirit would always be with her, rooted in the Motherland's abiding strength, illumined by *Rodina*'s weathered beauty. And she, herself, would endure.

Ж   Ж   Ж

For Lisya, too, the silence was difficult.

Like Katya, she had at first welcomed it. For the first few days after the guns finally stopped, she simply sat in the sun, drinking in the silence like a plant after a long drought. Eventually, however, uncomfortable rumblings – deep, deep down – began stirring within.

She went hunting for a new home for her family. Housing, of course, was even scarcer now than before the war; the best she could do was one room in a communal apartment. They would share a kitchen with two other families and a bathroom with several more. But the others were women who had also suffered through the siege. And the apartment would not seem crowded after the bomb shelters.

Lisya spent several days scavenging for furnishings and materials with which to make repairs. As soon as it was livable, she moved in. And for awhile, she was alone. The rumbling within grew louder.

During the day, she was flooded with memories of the village on the Volga. She remembered the strong sense of rootedness which had made her feel safe, and the stubborn ignorance that had driven her away. She heard her grandfather chanting the Orthodox liturgy and saw her father celebrating the traditional mass, and felt once more the need to connect to something larger than herself. In her music, she had often made that connection. Even so, said the strange noise inside, something was still missing.

By night, the rumbling turned into pain. Restlessly, she paced the room, then sat shivering by her candle, terrified of the desolate dreams sleep brought.

Then the ghosts broke out of her dreams, swirling around just out of reach. Desperately she tried to grasp the elusive images. The silent shadows smiled sadly and then – at dawn – left her.

Haggard and disheveled, she sat down on the floor before a box which held her few remaining possessions. At the bottom was a package carefully wrapped in old newspaper. Hesitantly she picked it up, tentatively holding it in her hands. Then, very slowly, she opened the small bundle. In it was the shawl her mother had always worn to church – the one she had given her the night she died.

For a long time, she stared at the faded flowers in the worn russet wool. Then she buried her face in it and cried like a lost child. When, finally, she looked up, the tiny pane of glass in the boarded up window was turning grey. Stiffly, she got to her feet and lit the candle on the table. As she stared into it, a dim memory played around the edges of the small circle of light. Concentrating, she remembered a night during the famine winter. They were all there, talking about Tolstoy and God... and the Virgin. Her mother was speaking, but – what had she said? She strained, listening hard to a memory she knew she must not lose. "And She is not afraid of Death." As she finally heard the words, she felt Evgenia take her hand.

Lisya slowly draped the shawl around her shoulders. Then she stood up quickly and left the room. Down the stairs and out into the street, past buildings she had never noticed before, through alleys she never knew existed, her feet finally brought her to a wild little forest, tucked away in a corner of the city. She hesitated only a moment before she opened the gate. Approaching the small church, she could see its onion-shaped domes gleaming through the trees. She climbed the steps, opened the door and went in.

The years fell away. She was a child again. There was her father saying mass, there was her grandfather chanting Vespers in his deep, booming voice. The candles were lit and the incense thick. Worshipers were bowing, crossing themselves, kissing icons. An overwhelming sense of Home swept through her; healing tears poured down her cheeks.

As the chanting continued, she began to hear it all with new ears. She could feel her father smiling, as the barrier between them finally dissolved. She gave herself up to the music. It reverberated off the walls of the church, enveloping her with echoes of all those loved and gone away, weaving a mysterious thread connecting her to all of the Motherland. *I feel like I am part of a vast, harmonious whole.* As she remembered Tolstoy's words, she looked around. The church was suffused with a deep amber glow, which gently filled the void in her soul.

Next to the altar were several icons of the Virgin. She walked slowly to the largest one and stared at it. Then she knelt and touched her forehead to the ground. In that moment, fragments of herself, too long separate, came together at last. The bonding resounded like a mighty chord resolved. She was no longer alone. She was Home. She had found *Rodina.*

Ж   Ж   Ж

Lisya stayed in the church long after the mass was over. She left only when the Deacon came to lock up. She walked home slowly, stopping often to look at the full moon. She did not return to her room until it had set.

Carefully, she lit the candle and looked again in the box. Hidden away in a corner, she found a tiny pouch of red silk. In it was the cross her father had placed around her neck at her baptism – and a small icon of the Virgin from her mother. Gently she held them in her hand, feeling their familiar warmth. Reverently, she hung them once more around her neck.

Then, rummaging in Nadya's box, she found a mirror. Resolutely, she looked at herself for the first time since the famine winter. At first she did not recognize the face reflected back. It was hers, and yet not. She stared in disbelief at the broad furrows ploughed across her forehead, the long valleys carved down the sides of her mouth, the deep crevasses radiating out from her eyes. Yet the strangeness was familiar. She had seen it before.

Slowly she lifted the shawl to her head; the soft fringe fell around her shoulders like a mantle. She looked again in the mirror. This time she recognized the face looking back. She smiled.

"Now *I* am the Babushka."

Ж   Ж   Ж

Lisya walked along the Neva embankment, a spring in her step almost resembling her old briskness. Like the city itself, she was tired but full of enthusiasm. Party Secretary Zhdanov had summed up this new spirit at the recent plenary session of the Leningrad Party, the first held since before the war.

"Our task," he said in a two hour speech, "is not just reconstruction, but to create an even better city."

Even though the war itself was far from over, Leningrad was already rebuilding. The shattered Maryinsky Theatre was rising again, and the restoration of Palace Square was underway. Soon the bronze horses would be back on the Anichkov Bridge. Best of all, the Bronze Horseman was emerging from his sandbags.

In the spirit of the times, the family was planning its first real celebration since the beginning of the war. Tonight was Midsummer, and each of them had special surprises. Lisya smiled as she thought of the gift she was carrying in her small basket.

That morning after Matins, as she was leaving church, a small scrawny cat had peeked cautiously around a tombstone. As Lisya walked toward it, the cat ran away, flushing out – in the process – several other hidden felines. Walking around the small cemetery, Lisya saw enough to surmise that here was a veritable cat sanctuary.

501

A wild hope surged through her.

"Koshka!" she called softly. "Koshka! Koshka!" she shouted, as she wound through the little paths of the cemetery.

Silence. She sat down on a grave marker and put her head on her arms.

Finally she stood up and walked out of the churchyard back to her room. On the small table in the middle was the basket she used to carry bread rations. In it was a piece left over from yesterday. She picked up the basket and hurried back to the church.

Softly she prowled the cemetery, and carefully picked out the prettiest gravestone. She sat down beside it, opened the basket, left a scrap of bread in it, and waited quietly. Eventually she heard bushes rustling, and felt several pairs of eyes watching. A hungry-looking kitten surreptitiously crept out of the shrubbery toward the bread in the basket. Lisya pretended not to notice as the little creature ravenously gobbled up the small crust. Slowly she held out her hand with another piece. The cat backed off, but did not retreat into the bushes. Lisya placed the bread in the basket and withdrew her hand. Again the kitten advanced and devoured the scrap of food. Several times, they repeated this ritual.

And then she held out the bread in her hand. The kitten hesitated, waiting for her to drop it in the basket. Finally, pretending not to move at all, the cat crept very slowly to her hand, sniffed it carefully, and ate the bread out of it. By the end of the day, the kitten had climbed into the basket, given herself a bath, and curled up for a long nap. Lisya carefully fastened the lid on the basket, held it reassuringly on her warm lap for awhile, and then stood up. Before she left the churchyard, she put a donation in the collection box.

Ж   Ж   Ж

Nadya and Katya arrived together, talking and laughing companionably. Lisya greeted them warmly, suddenly struck by how much both had changed since before the war. Her daughter had aged prematurely. *She looks more like me now than I do.* And her granddaughter was no longer a child. She had grown up into a beautiful young women – *like her mother used to be.*

The women embraced affectionately and sat down around the small table. Katya reached into her shopping bag and triumphantly pulled out a can of Spam. Not to be outdone, Nadya took three Hershey bars out of her pocket.

"I got these at Komsomol Headquarters. They're from the Americans. When we passed them out to the Young Pioneers, I kept a few for us."

"A toast to the Second Front!" said Lisya, setting her prize on the table with a flourish. Flanked by the Spam and Hershey bars, the small bottle of French champagne looked elegantly incongruous. "And to our Glorious Allies," she laughed, as the cork bounced off the ceiling, "who finally invaded Normandy!"

They sipped the champagne slowly and ate small bites of Spam and chocolate, mmm-ing appreciatively and smacking their lips with exaggerated gusto. Amid the giggles, a loud meow sounded. The smell of Spam had awakened the kitten.

Lisya pulled the basket out from under her bed and put it gently in Nadya's lap. Then she sat back to watch as her granddaughter lifted the lid with eager hands. The kitten stood up, stretched, and licked Nadya's fingers. She gently stroked the small animal with her other hand. Then she smiled, like the little girl she had been before the war.

After the kitten had finished the piece of Spam Nadya gave her, she began to explore the room. The three women watched, enchanted by her baby antics. Though pitifully skinny, the cat was a pretty little creature. Most of her fur was dark, the same color Koshka's had been. There was, however, a large white patch on her chest, and the tip of her tail was white.

"When we've fattened her up," said Lisya, as the little cat climbed on the table and sniffed her way across, "she'll be beautiful." After completing her inspection, the kitten jumped on Nadya's bed and curled up for another nap.

Nadya cleared her throat, and then pulled a piece of paper out of her pocket.

"I wrote this in school last week," she said nervously.

It was a poem about Evgenia – and magical horses and bears and firebirds, and the other wonderful creatures from the stories she had told. As Nadya read, her self-consciousness dissolved. Her unruly curls danced exuberantly around her expressive face, and her body began to sway gracefully, her slender limbs enthusiastically punctuating the rhythm of the words.

How like Alexei she is! A tear trickled slowly down Katya's cheek.

And how like Tatiana… Lisya, too, was moved.

And then Katya proposed another toast.

"To a man we all loved – and who will *never* be forgotten."

Lisya smiled, tears in her eyes.

"To Vladimir!"

Out of its prison at last, Vladimir's memory filled the room.

Suddenly a shout from the street drew them to the window. Looking down, they saw a makeshift cart with an old piano in it. Katya stuck her head out and hailed the small group pulling it. They waved back and stopped in front of the door to the apartment building.

"My gift to the family," Katya said proudly.

"Wherever did you find it?" asked Nadya excitedly.

"In the crypts of the Hermitage. Orbeli said we could have it if I promised it would be played." She looked at Lisya, who was staring at the piano.

Workers from the Hermitage had pulled it all the way from the museum in the only vehicle they could lay hands on. En route the odd little procession had picked up some naval cadets, who were now struggling to unload the piano. After a great deal of straining and groaning and good-natured advice from the crowd which gathered, the piano finally appeared in the kitchen of the communal apartment. There it stayed.

The other occupants came out to inspect the new acquisition. Lisya's friend, Olga the cellist, lived with her niece in the smallest room of the apartment. Vera, who worked at the Leningrad Public Library, shared the other room with her pregnant daughter.

Lisya sat down at the piano; everyone in the apartment and from the street crowded around. She ran her fingers over the keys in glistening arpeggios; her hands struck dark, rich chords. After several minutes, she stopped in satisfaction. The battered old upright was out of tune, and she was out of practice – but both could be fixed. In celebration, she played Tchaikovsky's rollicking "Troika." It was not her best performance, but it was certainly her most enthusiastic audience. When she finished, they all cheered and whistled.

Vodka bottles appeared from nowhere, and endless toasts were proposed and drunk: to the piano, to Tchaikovsky, to Our Beloved Motherland, to our Glorious Troops, to the Second Front, to our slow but still glorious Allies, even – as the kitten poked her head curiously into the room – to the new cat. In the ensuing uproar, she dived under Nadya's bed.

Everyone laughed. And then someone proposed a toast to more music. Lisya obliged with some lively folk-tunes. The naval cadets began dancing energetically; Olga brought out a balalaika and began to play along. And so, through the long White Night, the festivities continued.

How much they had all changed since that fateful Midsummer's Eve three years ago! How different things were since that long white night when the war had invaded their lives! Strains of bittersweet nostalgia wove poignantly among the notes of the long overdue celebration. What a long road they had all traveled since then! And how many had fallen along the way!

As dawn approached, Lisya began to play old songs of river and forest and steppe, those their grandmothers had brought from their villages. The group quieted. Someone asked Katya to sing.

She hesitated, and then stood up uncertainly. Lisya played the introduction to one of Evgenia's favorite songs. Katya opened her mouth, took a deep breath – and remembered the last time she had sung. Tears stung her eyes, as she felt Sasha's lifeless little body in her arms. The notes stuck in her throat.

Then Nadya stood up beside her and began to sing, her voice now full and mature, like her body. And as Katya heard herself in her daughter, her heart began to release the music it had held captive. She put her arm around Nadya and softly joined in. Gradually her voice grew stronger and began to weave dark, vibrant harmonies around Nadya's clear, bright melody.

> The Volga flows,
> Rodina grows,
> Giving life to the Motherland.
> Mother Russia suffers,
> But her children will endure.
> The Volga flows,
> Rodina grows,
> Giving strength to the Motherland.

As she sang, Katya noticed someone standing at the door – someone familiar and yet not, someone with a face like that often glimpsed on passing strangers – and yet not. Katya shut her eyes, as she always did, to the bittersweet memory.

This time, when she opened her eyes, he was still there. But his uniform was worn and faded, his hair more grey than blond, his face thin and unshaven, and his eyes much too old for the image she carried in her heart and still saw everywhere.

As everyone joined the last chorus, the familiar stranger slowly limped through the crowded room. Katya shut her eyes again, but again when she opened them, he was still there.

After all that had happened… Was it possible… Could it be…

As the song ended, Katya knew it was.

"Alexei!" she cried, as his arms were suddenly around her.

Looking in his eyes, she found no trace of the boy she had known. That Alexei lay beneath the rubble of Stalingrad – just as the girl she had been was buried with Sasha. But in his sorrow – a reflection of her own – the woman she was now recognized the man he had become. And knew that the strength of their love had allowed the miracle of his return.

Nadya was staring, stunned by the unbelievable apparition embracing her mother. Katya, one arm locked around Alexei, wrapped the other around Nadya. Alexei kissed his wife and daughter, and held on to them with the tenacity of one who had walked hundreds of miles through hell to find them.

Over Alexei's shoulder, Katya saw her mother, relief and joy glowing from the face which now looked so much like Babushka's. Then Lisya's arms enfolded all three of them.

As word of who Alexei was – and where he had been – swept the room, people began murmuring excitedly. Soon they were cheering the miracle of his resurrection. If he could return from the grave of Stalingrad, there was hope for all those that they had lost.

Finally, Lisya once more sat down at the piano, and repeated the song with which Alexei had reappeared. On the last chorus, everyone again joined in. And as they sang, they opened themselves to its healing beauty. The music resonated with new life, reassuring them that what was most essential would never be lost. Out of great suffering had come great strength. They had been plunged to the depths, but they had transcended, emerging as big inside as the Motherland's limitless horizons.

They would sing on, affirming *Rodina*'s priceless gift of sorrow and hope. And Mother Russia would endure.

EPILOGUE

Katherine wrapped her wet hair in a towel and gratefully stretched out on the bed. After a few weeks in Derevnia, the hotel room which had seemed rather shabby a month ago now looked positively opulent. While in the country, however, she had not really missed the relative comfort she was now luxuriating in. For from the moment she had stepped off the train at the little village south of Kazan, she had been surrounded by a small host of generous, affectionate relatives who led her from one house to another in a feast which never ended.

The chairman of the *kolkhoz* was married to a cousin named Elena. A few years younger than Nadya, she took Katherine to a picturesque little grove by the Volga, where she answered many questions about their mutual ancestors.

Walking back to Derevnia, they stopped in a circle of tall, strong oak trees. Under a leafy canopy protectively overhead was a sturdy bell-tower, its lone bell crowned by a graceful onion dome.

"I was married here," said Elena quietly. "And it was here that we said good-by to my mother before we buried her over there." She pointed to the nearby cemetery.

Katherine leaned against one of the straight, solid trunks and gazed up at the lofty swaying branches. From her pocket, she slowly withdrew a small box containing the small wooden cross she had found in Babushka Tatiana's trunk. Carefully she slipped her hand through the slim gold chain on which it hung and raised her palm up to the waving leaves above. The wind sighed in gentle blessing as she slowly placed the cross around her neck.

The entire village saw her off at the railroad station, amidst a barrage of hearty Russian hugs and a deluge of lugubrious Russian tears. It took all of the long train ride back to Leningrad to recover from the huge hangover which resulted from the marathon celebration in her honor.

There had been a lot of that in Leningrad, too. Eventually, however, it had settled down to all night conversations and endless cups of tea. Nadya's family had welcomed her as one of their own, and would willingly have made room for

509

her in their crowded apartment. Katherine, however, insisted on keeping her room at the hotel.

Everything here was so *intense!* And the people were so *real!* It exhausted her. People not only shared their memories, but took her to where they had happened. In those places, she could still feel the blood and tears, the suffering and sorrow.

With Nadya herself, Katherine developed a deep and satisfying friendship. After little more than a month, she felt as though they had known each other all their lives – which, in a sense, they had. The resemblance each had noticed to her own grandmother was more than physical.

"Your Babushka must have been terribly homesick," said Nadya, one day.

"Yes, she was," agreed Katherine, "though she never talked about Russia with anyone but me."

"My Babushka missed yours very much, too, but she only talked about her with me."

"You're *so* like her," nodded Katherine, "I can see why."

"And you're so like *her* – it's almost like she's here again."

"I missed her terribly, when she died – the way she missed Russia, I think. But now I understand why she was always so sad. Why she left, why she never returned – she could never talk about that – not even to me."

"Losing what is really important sometimes leaves a wound too big for words."

"Yes, I understand that now, too." said Katherine, squeezing Nadya's hand. "But how will I ever explain all this to people back home?!"

Nadya's daughter, Tatiana, retired from the corps de ballet of the Kirov Opera, was now teaching at the State Ballet School. Tatiana the Younger took Katherine to the Maryinsky. Sitting near what had once been the Imperial Box, she eagerly watched the dress rehearsal of *Swan Lake*, imagining that Babushka Tatiana was one of the swans gliding gracefully *en pointe* across the stage. Down in the orchestra pit, she saw a young woman among the First Violins, her enthusiasm apparent even under the frown of earnest concentration. Katherine smiled. It was all just as her grandmother had described it.

After the rehearsal, she sat with Tatiana, reluctant to leave. "Babushka loved it here." Katherine's voice echoed in the empty theatre. "To her, it was a magical place."

"It still is," said Tatiana reverently.

"I'm glad I came back."

"I think she is, too."

Katherine looked down at the deserted orchestra pit. "Did your Great-Grand-mother Lisya ever return?"

"Only once. And not, of course, down there," Tatiana replied, gesturing toward the semi-circle of chairs and music stands, "but to see me dance. It was my debut with the corps de ballet, and she sat in this very box."

Katherine slowly ran her hand over the railing.

"It was *Swan Lake*, I remember." Tatiana smiled. "She gave me flowers afterward – and then grumbled about how I should change the ending."

"It must have been quite an occasion – for both of you!"

"Mother said she cried during the whole performance… A week later, she died."

Listening to the silent ghosts, Katherine wished that she could have returned sooner.

Katya, too, was gone.

"Mother died a few years after Tatiana's little Zhenya was born," explained Nadya, as they sat one night at her kitchen table.

"And your father?" asked Katherine.

"He never fully recovered from Stalingrad," frowned Nadya. "It's a miracle any of them survived. My father often said that knowing Mother was waiting for him gave him strength to crawl out from under all the carnage. And with so many wounds, it's even more miraculous that he somehow got back home."

"And how were things between your parents after the War?"

"Good enough for them to have some years of happiness," smiled Nadya, "with the cloud of Uncle Vladimir's death gone."

"And between you and your father?"

"No one but Mother expected him to return. So for me, it was truly a miracle," replied Nadya, tears in her eyes. "He was never again the Dad I adored before the War – he was in too much pain from his war wounds. But the *father* he became was able to help me understand why the Stalin Purges were so traumatic for all of us. And thanks to him, I was able to appreciate the full significance of the Great War's sacrifice."

"When did he finally die?"

"Shortly after Stalin did. Though – again – no one expected him to survive that long. Except probably Mother." Nadya smiled, shaking her head. "After his funeral, she gave me this."

Nadya held out her hand, displaying the gold ring Katherine had often admired. Its symbolism now clear, the unusual design of two hands clasping seemed even more beautiful.

"I've worn it ever since." Nadya caressed the ring, as she had seen her mother do countless times.

"And did she continue her work at the Hermitage?" asked Katherine, warmed by the loving gesture.

"Almost until the end," replied Nadya, remembering. "She seemed in good health – then one day, she came home from the Hermitage and just stopped eating. A few days later, she called us all to her bedside. I was holding her hand and crying – then suddenly there was this radiant smile – she looked like she did before the war... So beautiful... So happy... And then she died..."

It was not until a few days before her departure that she finally accepted Nadya's often repeated invitation to go to church.

Religion had always been a problem in Katherine's home. In the small town where she had grown up, there was no Russian Orthodox church. The nearest one was several hours away, and getting there required the cooperation of Katherine's father. Of Russian Jewish descent he was less than sympathetic to the creed which had so rigorously persecuted his own ancestors, nor did he approve of his mother-in-law's wish to pass on her Orthodox faith to his daughter. But since there was no synagogue in town, either, he would occasionally drive to the city and expose Katherine to her Jewish roots. Babushka Tatiana, of course, always rode along, and politely insisted that Katherine go to church with her afterward. As the tension escalated, the frequency of these religious forays decreased, leaving Katherine with confused memories laced with tacit conflict.

From time to time, Katherine's mother had attempted to mediate the always unacknowledged dispute by taking her to one of the American churches. That was even worse. Scrubbed and brushed, Katherine would glumly endure the meaningless rituals and empty words, wondering why so many grown-ups willingly attended something they didn't seem to understand either. On the rare occasions Babushka went along, she always came home grumbling about what paltry spiritual fare American churches provided.

Eventually Babushka resigned herself, and did most of her praying in her icon corner, making do with small, badly reproduced paper icons carefully enshrined in incongruously ornate frames. The image of her devout grandmother on her knees before that pathetically ugly altar pained Katherine deeply.

Which was why she knew she had to go to church with Nadya. Even so, she put it off until the last possible moment.

Katherine was surprised that the church was so close. She had passed it several times without noticing the onion domes hiding modestly inside a small thicket of evergreens. Just before entering the unassuming front door, Nadya took a worn shawl from her ubiquitous shopping bag. Carefully draping it over head and shoulders, she pinned it under her chin with a large golden brooch shaped like a flaming sun.

Katherine followed Nadya inside and was amazed. In stark contrast to its drab exterior, every inch of the church's interior gleamed softly. On the walls were golden-hued icons, gazing compassionately out of sad gentle eyes. The thick warm scent of incense and burning candles filled the air, and the amber tones of a small but perfectly-pitched choir echoed sonorously off the walls. Katherine was transfixed; never had she experienced such concentrated, all encompassing beauty as that which now so completely and benevolently surrounded her.

The church was filled with people bowing and kneeling and crossing themselves, intent on the reverently intoned words of the resplendently bedecked priest and the answering chant of the deep booming bass. Here were people who not only understood – but *believed!* How Babushka must have missed all this! Katherine was suddenly overwhelmed by the sorrow of her grandmother's exile. No wonder she had suffered so!

Then she looked at Nadya, praying fervently beside her. In the shimmering light, shadows played across her face, accentuating the lines which traversed it. Honed to its essence by suffering, crisscrossed with joy and overlaid by endurance, it glowed with an earthy beauty which radiated from deep within. It was Babushka's face – as it should have been, as it would have been had she not been cut off from *Rodina*, as it was for just an instant at the moment she died.

Gospodi pomilui. Katherine repeated the words she had heard so often from her grandmother's icon corner. Crossing herself, she knew that Babushka's soul had at last found its way home.

Ж   Ж   Ж

For the last time, Katherine walked to the open window and looked out at the War Memorial across the street. The statues had become friends – especially those inside the Ring. Each morning, they reminded her why she was here; each night, their mournful song lulled her to sleep.

With each passing day, she had found herself increasingly drawn to the statue in the center, which somehow she had barely noticed that first day. It was the dying old woman, who seemed to be both chief mourner – and principal focus of

513

those grieving. The ancient eyes were full of compassion and strangely comforting, reaching deep into places she had never known. When she looked into those eyes, she could feel her grandmother's shattered past healing.

Last night, there had been a farewell feast in Katherine's honor. All of Nadya's family and friends were there. Tearfully, Katherine had hugged and kissed them all. Some of them she knew she would never see again.

Nadya had given her, as parting gift, a treasured family icon. "Our great-great-grandfather painted it for our great-grandparents' wedding day," she had said, smiling. "It belongs in *your* icon corner now."

Katherine had recognized it immediately. The *Virgin of Vladimir* had been the focus of Babushka's icon corner. So this was why Babushka had left the crude icon in her trunk! So this was what she had seen when she knelt before that shabby copy every night! No wonder she had longed so for this familiar rendition of it, the one she had grown up saying her prayers to at home by the Volga. Examining the old icon closely, Katherine saw that though it was a rather unsophisticated facsimile, it glowed with the same grounded Light she had witnessed in the church.

After a breakfast she barely touched, Katherine went across the street to say goodbye to the War Memorial. Walking down into the Ring, she reverently laid a small bouquet among the flowers around the base of the statues. Looking up at the perpetually grieving women and the dead they mourned, she recognized them all – and marveled that anything so permeated with tragedy could be so beautiful. She wept, the tears flowing unhindered and unashamed, and when she was through, felt cleansed.

In the amazingly short – and yet terribly long – time she had been pressed to the hardy bosom of Mother Russia, Katherine had found what she sought. She had returned to the Motherland, whose limitless horizons demanded people just as big. She had discovered *Rodina*, whose profound soul had transcended suffering over and over and over again. And she had learned of brave men who knew how to die – and strong women who knew how to endure.

They had shown her how beautiful Humanity could be. They had made her proud to be one of them. They had given her hope.

She would never forget. And she, too, would endure.

Footnote

Had this book been a work of nonfiction, the reader would have been blinded by a blizzard of footnotes. Fortunately, fiction does not demand such detailed attribution. I am, however, indebted to numerous authors, artists and performers, without whose work I could never have written this novel. To all of them, I am enormously indebted for information, insight, and the wealth of detail without which no historical novel can be authentic.

As much as possible, I have endeavored to stay faithful to history. Characters with surnames were real people who really did and said what I have them doing and saying. Those without surnames are characters of my own creation, though I sometimes put words in their mouths and grafted behavior onto them that real people actually said or did in similar context.

(Note to the uninitiated: Russian names need not be confusing if you understand what a patronymic is. All Russians have first and last names, and in the middle a patronymic – their father's first name plus *ovich* or *evich* for men, *ovna* or *evna* for women. Thus Vladimir, son of Ivan, becomes Vladimir Ivanovich; Elisaveta, daughter of Ivan, becomes Elisaveta Ivanovna. Addressing someone by first name and patronymic is formal and respectful, the equivalent of calling them Mr. or Ms.; e.g., in the former Soviet Union, one would have properly addressed Mr. Khrushchev as Nikita Sergevich. There are also a host of nicknames in Russian. As elsewhere, they denote familiarity, affection, and/or inferior status.)

All the major events to which my characters react really happened. I made up none of the wars, revolutions, plagues, famines, assassinations, purges, etc. The literary, artistic, religious and revolutionary movements also occurred more or less as described; so did several of the performances – though I took many creative liberties with most of them. I also took a few minor liberties with the chronology of certain events, simply because it made a better story that way.

Most of what my fictional characters did, of course, is a product of my own imagination. I tried, however, to have them behave in ways consistent with how people in that time and place and situation would have been likely to act. I also

517

tried to explain the complex events and developments through which they lived from *their* perspective rather than from the one most familiar to Americans.

In writing this novel, my intention was to tell a very important story the way it really was. Though I sometimes modified the facts, I never consciously distorted the truth. As a trained historian, I know better than most that good fiction is often more truthful than what passes for objective history.

Should any Russians chance to read this book, I hope they will forgive my presumption in daring to write about their tragic past so intimately. I did so in hopes of broadening and deepening my own country's understanding of theirs. If I have read the Russian soul at all correctly, I think that they will not begrudge my sharing their suffering and strength. In any case, I am profoundly grateful for all I have learned in telling their inspiring story.

Printed in the United Kingdom
by Lightning Source UK Ltd.
122718UK00001B/113/A

9 781412 078764